BETWEEN
the
DARKNESS & DUST
BOOK TWO OF FATE'S CRUCIBLE

By T.B. Schmid & R.Wade Hodges

Cover art by Todd Schmid

Acknowledgements

First and foremost: Thanks to everyone who took the time to read our work and offer us their comments, criticisms, encouragement and support. We can't emphasize enough how much we appreciate everything you give back to us. We're not an Empire without you.

The Lions

For my family, especially my parents. To my mother, whose creativity and compassion were robbed from this world far too soon; and to my father, whose quiet strength, integrity and love have long been my keel. And my sincere gratitude to Wade for his technical prowess, constant humor and overall creative genius. If not for him, I would not have had the courage to begin.

T.B. Schmid

To CJ: Promise we'll be together - at least until Book 3. To Tess: You're still my favorite daughter out of all my daughters, even the imaginary ones. To Geri and Jess: Thanks for taking the time to read along. To Theresa, Winston & Leesa: For occasionally allowing me to win at Descent. Last, but not least, thanks to Tim: Somehow we keep getting better with age.

rwh

Last but certainly not least, we would like to thank our Beta Readers for their time, patience and suggestions. You are all fantastic.

Tim and Wade

The Known Lands of Ruine

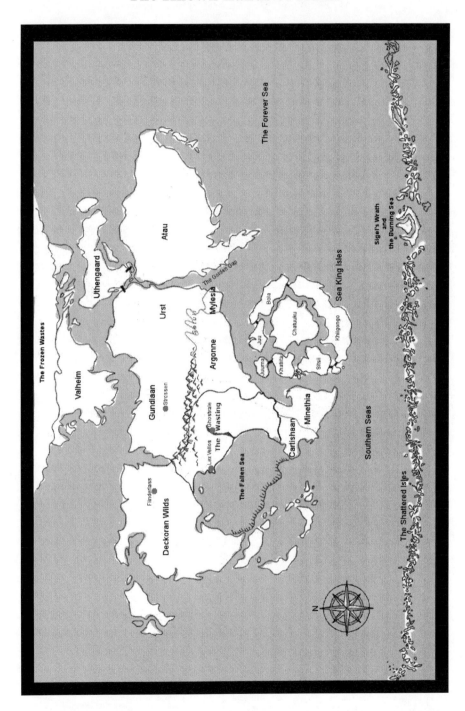

Newly Discovered Lands
beyond the Burning Sea

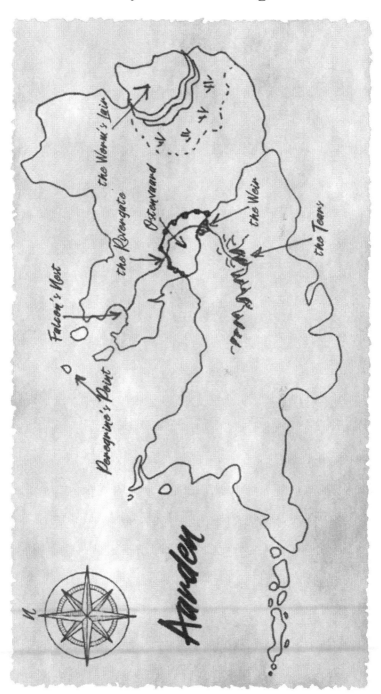

Understanding the Between

An excerpt from the journals of Merekith Nerah, formerly of the Order of Veda, written prior to the fall of Ehronhaal:

The prevalent theory I've read in older texts is that the Between is a wall separating our world from the Dark, the formless nothingness from which most believe Maughrin was birthed - and, perhaps, to where our souls return.

My travels outside of Talmoreth, however, have given rise to a different view: perhaps the Between is more akin to the surface of a lake, a permeable barrier that can both suspend some things while allowing others to pass through. As a lake can hold feathers and leaves afloat, the Between can support our thoughts and dreams, allowing us to skate across the surface like small insects. Making contact via Twineroot Seeds (and possibly other means, but more on that later) lends credence to this theory.

It is the extrapolation of this comparison which disturbs me most, however. I have come to believe that the use (or outright breach in extreme cases) of the Between is a dangerous proposition, since the ripples of such an action must spread, signs that could be read on either side of that surface, in our realm above... or in the Dark beneath.

Water can reflect our images depending on how we look upon it, or allow us to see through it. Are we similarly looked upon by whatever may exist on the other side? I shudder thinking of the secrets I have helped bury, glimpses of what may lay beyond the fragile skin of the Between.

Thankfully, the Young Gods are here to protect us.

Prologue: The Counter's Tale

One barrel of water, half full. A full butt contains one hundred and fifty gallons, or three hundred graff. We have about one hundred and fifty graff left. One hundred and fifty daily rations for a crew of six - seven if you counted the monkey, which I won't. However, these traitorous pukes have made it a pet, so it will get its daily, rest assured.

So one graff per day for each hand is seven gone every day. If we don't see any rain, our half barrel will last us only twenty days...

He squinted up at the flat slab of gray sky overhead. No more water in those clouds than he had in his pisser, but at least they would have some relief from the Bitch Twins today. The crew had done their best to create shade by rigging several canopies from sailcloth, but the worn fabric was only partially successful. And no matter how creative they were, they never seemed to be able to block the reflection from the water's surface. It was enough to get out of the suns' direct path, but not enough to ease their hot, scratching caress on his cracked and blistered skin. Today, at least, the cloud cover would spare them that torture.

Twenty days of water left if it doesn't rain... or someone doesn't die.

He smirked, wondering who might go first. Not him. *No bloody way.* He had a duty now, a mission, and a means to perform it. Not that fucking monkey, surely - somehow it was holding up better than any of them, even better than Biiko, that bloody Unbound freak, though he'll likely outlast them all just out of sheer stubbornness. A gruesome vision rose in his mind: the mute warrior's grim face bent over his body with a long curved knife. Past Biiko he could see Snitch, absurdly holding eating utensils and licking his monkey lips. A sharp cramp twisted his gut, so he forced his thoughts back to his counting.

So how long? How long have we been drifting? How long to get back?

He thought back to the *Peregrine's* outgoing voyage. They had taken nearly fourteen months to reach Aarden, but that had included a couple of weeks while Captain Vaelysia searched the coastlines of the

Shattered Isles. The trip probably would have taken longer but for the fierce storms that had blown them so far south, but it was hard to say by just how much. Estimating was his business though, so he reasoned that they would not have gained more than a week, perhaps as many as ten days. It was close enough to offset the delay in the Shattered Isles though, meaning he could assume roughly the same amount of time to sail from Aarden back to Niyah.

So, on the return trip, we were ten months, three days out when she went down. They say the gods are dead, but never have I seen the seas rage so, like Shan himself come back to punish us for our audacity.

The weather up to that point had been unusually favorable - unnatural, if you asked him. Any seasoned sailor knew that good seas were a roll of the bones: the longer you pressed your luck, the more likely you were to run out of it. And the storm that had broken the *Peregrine's* back had been the foulest weather he'd ever sailed in, their luck paid back in full, all of it bad.

The next couple of days after the wreck were a blur. They'd just floated there for at least a day after rescuing Mister Scow and that treacherous brat, Halliard. He glanced at the boy now, careful not to let his gaze linger. He couldn't keep the sneer from his face, though, so he ducked his head.

Ungrateful little bastard! After everything I did to keep us alive!

He was the highest ranked surviving officer, and had rightly taken command of the emergency launch. As Captain, it was he, Lankham Voth, who had roused them from their despair, and assigned them duties so that they had purpose. And how had they repaid him? By mocking him, resisting his orders at every turn, and eventually doing the unthinkable: leading a mutiny against him!

They've betrayed the Corps, the Chancellor and the Kings, and they think they can get away with it, because no one is watching! The impudent little puke is keeping his own log book, and likely believes his story will be the only one that Fleet Command hears if we make it back.

Voth smiled to himself. *We shall see about that.*

From the day he had assumed command, until the day they had betrayed him and tied him to the mast like livestock, he had dutifully kept his own log. No pretty pictures or fanciful tales, just facts and figures. The cycle of the watch, the roll call, the weather log, stores, bearings, maintenance, and any unusual activity, what the Corps called "Noteworthy Events". Everything logged exactly according to Protocol, and something he had quite looked forward to showing to Fleet Command upon their return.

They had taken it from him, though, and now he was forced to keep track of things entirely in his head. But if there was one single thing about him even his harshest critics must acknowledge, it was that he was brilliant at logistics. Yes, it was more difficult to remember things these days, but he compensated by repeating them to himself over and over, making use of the one resource he seemed to have in limitless supply: time.

He had another reason for wanting to commit everything to memory as well: he had discovered a chance to get the truth to Fleet Command well ahead of the mutineers, regardless of whether they ever made landfall or not. It had renewed his sense of purpose, but even so, it was difficult to focus on one thing for very long.

Where was I? Day five - no, six...

On day six, Acting Captain Fjord, Wiliamund Azimuth, and the ship's boy Braeghan (the Corps did not bother to record boy's surnames, and therefore he would not be bothered with learning them) were rescued, and almost immediately afterwards the ridgeback had attacked. Braeghan was killed, as were Pelor and the apprentice cooper, Jode. Sometime later that night, Fjord committed suicide by tying himself to an anchor and jumping overboard.

What could have possessed the man to do such a thing? Voth could not imagine. Fjord had been a capable officer; disciplined, just, and always practical. The head wound he had sustained had clearly addled his wits, but enough for the man to want to drown himself?

Except that something else likely got him before he drowned, so it did. Likely the same black bitch that did for the boy and the oarsman, Pelor. Too bad she didn't swallow that fucking Mylesian whore instead.

Lankham Voth suppressed a shiver. That had been a bizarre and terrifying ordeal, and he did not like to think about it. Fortunately, the wind had picked up considerably and on day seven they were able to get the boat moving again. By the time the Releasing Ceremony for the three dead crewmen was completed on the afternoon of the eighth day, they were pulling at least twelve knots and putting vital distance between themselves and the sight of the wreck.

That was the day he had found the seeds.

While preparing for the Ceremony, he had been going through Captain Fjord's meager belongings and had come across a small, well-made pouch. At first he'd thought it was empty, but decades of working as a Provisions Officer had taught him never to discard any type of container before thoroughly inspecting it - especially if it was some type of pouch or purse someone could conceal on their person, where most people kept the things they held dear. Like secrets. Voth had come across many a juicy secret in his time, from rare coins to notes from lovers and even, once, a spy's list of signal codes.

Fjord's pouch contained none of these things - or perhaps all three. When Voth opened the purse and shook it carefully over his palm, three small seeds tumbled out. He recognized them immediately as twineroot seeds. Although he had never used them, he'd inventoried either the seeds or the trees that spawned them several times over his career. Their distinctive white and blue shell and the soft luminescence they emitted when viewed at night made them easy to mark.

He hadn't the faintest idea what to do with them at that moment, and did not want to appear uninformed to either his first officer or the rest of the crew by asking them, so he stuffed them back in the pouch and stuffed the pouch into his pocket. Looking back on it now, he considered that to have been a very prudent and captain-like decision, because on the eighth day, he saw his first sign of the troubles to come.

It began when the Unbound stunned them all, not only by actually speaking aloud, but in what he had said: "The dead still have something left to give." As if they were supposed to eat their dead! And then, to his disgust, that fool Rantham had started in with his preposterous tale of cannibalism. Even though the topic had not been discussed openly since, he often imagined the others whispering about it as things continued to deteriorate.

Still, as shocking as Biiko's outburst had been, the real surprise had been Voth's first inkling that Mordan Scow was beginning to harbor seditious thoughts. Captains must be vigilant to that sort of thing, and he had once again shown his qualifications by instinctively recognizing the trap he was being led into. He resolved then and there to befriend Pelor's brother, Sherpel Icefist, in the hopes of shoring up his position. He spent the next two weeks taking the surly Valheim under his wing, keeping his counsel as Scow pulled further and further away. During that time, he had also been thinking very carefully about the twineroot seeds, keeping the matter entirely to himself until he realized that they presented an opportunity: by confiding in Icefist, he would test the man's shrewdness and loyalty. That was on the fifteenth day after the destruction of the *Peregrine*. The brute did not afford him much in the way of insight, but he was a useful sounding board, and he agreed with Voth's assumption that Captain Vaelysia must have parceled out some of her Fleet-issued twineroot so that Fjord could communicate their progress and location to Fleet Command, particularly if they ran into trouble. As a lower-deck officer, Voth had never been trained in their use, but he decided that if Fjord could do it, so could he. Indeed, it was his duty as Captain. Besides, things were becoming increasingly tenuous on the launch, and he was eager to get his side of the story to his superiors in advance, in the event more drastic measures had to be taken.

So with Icefist keeping watch, he swallowed one of the seeds in the predawn darkness of day sixteen. He had no idea what to expect, and was wholly unprepared for the experience.

The effects began almost immediately: at first, his vision sharpened to a strength and clarity he had not possessed since he was a cadet. He marveled at the level of detail he could see in the objects around him - the grain of the wooden deck, the weave of the sails... but then he began to see better than that. He looked at the back of his hand and saw thousands of tiny holes in his skin, wondering if he was hallucinating: if his skin were so porous, why was his blood not seeping through?

Soon after, his head swam with drowsiness. He tried to warn his second mate to make sure no one disturbed him, words slurring, then barely made it into his hammock, feeling like the hundreds of drunken Seekers he had watched perform this same comedy over the course of his long career. From there, things only got stranger.

He fell asleep immediately, except that he was aware that he was sleeping. Even now he could still remember how his body had felt warm and soft, his muscles completely relaxed. The usual aches and pains that troubled his bones every day had subsided to a distant throb, more like a swollen foot than the typical grinding coldness. Other than this very basic self-awareness, though, he did not have any other coherent thoughts for what seemed like a very long time - until he began to dream.

It started more as a sensation than a series of images or the kind of disjointed memory of a typical dream. The soft warmth began to feel like the wrapping embrace of his hammock, or of a cloak or blanket that had been drawn around him. Someone or something pulled on it, lifting him up. But it was not the lurching, jolting motion you might expect from someone heaving a body. Instead it was smooth and effortless, as if he were floating upwards.

He opened his eyes, but all he saw at first was a pale blue glow. The floating embrace of the blanket grew stronger, pulling at him, dragging him upward, and then suddenly he broke free of some great weight or tether, like a sail torn from its mast by a powerful gale.

Shapes coalesced from the blue incandescence: a wide, flat expanse filled the area below him, although he could not have said if he were standing up or laying flat, or even rolled over on his belly. Below it - no, beneath it, he thought as he realized it was the sea - were shadows of various shapes and sizes, some small and bunched together in large groups, while others - some much larger than the launch - swam independently. He saw one or two massive shapes that drew him towards them with a malevolent strength that froze his blood, but fortunately the wind driving him was stronger still, carrying him over and past them. There was a voice woven into that wind, chanting in a strange, haunting cadence. It was just a murmur, as of voices from a nearby room, but he sensed an inexorable power in it. He could not understand the words, but he knew instinctively that they were meant for him.

Darker shapes appeared in front of him; still far away but drawing closer on a line he thought of as the horizon. Huge pillars, rising from the flat plane of the sea and thrusting upwards. Gleaming columns of stone, sheer cliffs, towering walls bristling with the battlements and gates and slender spires of the Sea Kings' island fortress, all etched in different hues of that same twilight color. Beyond them was land - *land!* - and upon its blue-green brilliance were countless tiny structures rising in graceful terraces. One tower shown forth with particular brightness, and it was from there that the song came.

Although he was not sure of the turret or the campus that surrounded it, he did recognize the sprawling cluster of opulence nearby as Khatiita's Palace of the Suns, whose halls he had never been deemed worthy enough to visit.

A portico stuck out from one side near the top, rising up before him as if he had picked it up in the palm of his hand, until he could see a figure sprawled upon a couch below him. It was a man, with long dark hair swept back in a tight knot to reveal a face Voth found both beautiful and mildly familiar: he had seen it at the Ministry or perhaps somewhere around the Sea Kings' court, though he could not recall his name. The man's eyes were closed, but his mouth was partially open, and from it rose a thin, serpentine stream of glowing blue smoke, like the mist of someone's breath on a cold day; but thicker, more substantial. Rather than disperse, the smoke snaked around the sleeping figure, rolling down the sides of the divan and across the portico floor, pulsing faintly with the alternating rhythm of the chant.

Voth stared at the sleeper's lips, sure that the song was coming from them, though they remained still. He tried to reach out and shake the man's shoulder, but nothing happened - he felt his arm and hand extending before him, but he did not see any physical representation of his limb. When he looked down at where his body should be, there was only the pulsing blue smoke.

Speak, Sender. What message do you bring?

This thought occurred to him in his own internal voice, but it felt strange, as if it had been pulled from him.

Just then the chant's cadence changed subtly, and the wind that had carried him here died. In its place rose an irresistible force, a current whose wellspring seemed to come from somewhere deep inside. Images and impressions flooded his mind; fragmented recollections of things that had happened to him, and things he had feared might happen to him. It was as if the sleeper had commanded his mind to dream. The images came rapidly in the first few seconds, racing through his mind of their own volition: landfall on Aarden; his final inventory in Thunder Bay, on the day before the *Peregrine* set out on her maiden voyage; erecting the pole at the center of their encampment, which some melodramatic fool had named "Falcon's Roost"; a young cabin boy he had raped during his time aboard the *Cloudsprint*; a beggar's store of supplies laid out before him on the deck of the emergency launch: one sack of moldy hardtack, three jars of pickled herring, and half a dozen overly-ripe jenga melons…

At that moment, Voth remembered regaining some control over his errant thoughts. The familiar act of counting anchored them, grounding his mind in the well-trodden pathways of his logistical prowess. He concentrated on that image, forcing himself to count them again, to walk that path he had spent his entire career following.

One sack of hardtack, three jars of pickled herring, but now only five overly-ripe jenga melons and young Braeghan's head - No!

One sack of moldy hardtack, three jars of herring, six jenga melons for six of us, no seven if you count the monkey. The melons are nearly spent so we will need to eat those first. Three days' worth...

The chanting began to fade, and the pulling sensation returned, only now it was pulling him back, dragging him away. It was weak, but he sensed that would change quickly. With sudden urgency bordering on panic, he forced his thoughts to obey him.

Three jars of pickled herring, six jenga melons constitutes our remaining stores aboard the SKS Peregrine's emergency launch... the Peregrine's lost, and we are somewhere north and east of the Burning...

" - Sea!" The link broke and Voth came awake with a start.

"See what, Cap'n?" grumbled a rough voice. He was back on the launch with Sherpel Icefist standing nearby, looking at him suspiciously.

Voth had not the strength or wits to answer. He promptly fell into a heavy, dreamless slumber, not stirring until Icefist shook him awake for the morning meal.

He kept the experience to himself over the next few days while he considered all of the implications. To the man's credit, Icefist only asked him what happened once, shortly after waking him. Voth had been curt, telling him only that he had succeeded in notifying Fleet of their whereabouts, adding in a rare flash of inspiration that Protocol forbade him from discussing the details of his report. Icefist had not bothered to hide his disdain, but - more importantly - neither had he broached the subject again or breathed a word of it to the others so far as Voth could tell.

That was one decision Voth had not needed to consider for long: he had resolved immediately not to tell the others. At the very least he wanted to learn how to use the seeds better, to control his message and provide more useful information. He could easily imagine Halliard or the Mylesian bitch twisting things around and making it look like he was incompetent - or worse, they might realize their careers were at stake and try wresting the seeds from him so that they could deliver their own message. He was confident Icefist could handle the two of them, but if the Unbound chose a side - and the dead gods knew he appeared to be watching over Halliard - he would be doomed.

Time had proven him right again. Voth glanced down at the tether around his raw ankle, his face twisting in a sour scowl. He had felt so good about letting Fleet or the Ministry know about the *Peregrine*, and that there were Seekers in need of rescue! He had even given their approximate location, which he thought was rather astounding considering the circumstances.

Further proof that my instincts were true; that I deserve to be a captain.

But he was too new to command; he hadn't learned to fully trust those instincts yet. As a result, he had deliberated too long before trying to send again, wanting first to learn how to deliver a more coherent message; one that not only gave their geographic position, but more importantly, solidified his political one. There were two more seeds, so only two attempts to get it right. He had no idea if each sending would be the same, or wildly different the way actual dreams could be. He was comforted by how his mind had organized around his memory of taking inventory, though, and eventually he decided that this was the most rational way to approach the process. He would lay out the message as if it were a list of ship's provisions, then review it over and over again until he could recite it in his dreams.

While he was planning his next move, the factional divides among the crew deepened. On the nineteenth day he had promoted Icefist to Second Mate, thinking to give Scow a clear warning that his disloyalty would have consequences if it continued. He realized now that he had overestimated the old crab; the fool had been too dense to appreciate Voth's subtlety. He should have just promoted Icefist directly to First Mate, clapped Scow in irons for sedition, and that would have been the end of it.

They were becalmed for almost a week, during which time he rehearsed his message over and over. Then, just as the wind came up and they were at last making headway again, the kettle finally boiled over. He never had an opportunity to try it before the treacherous pukes mutinied, murdered Icefist, and tied him up like he was a common criminal. Him! Captain Lankham Voth! Scow's death was unfortunate, but had the stubborn old bastard stayed true to the Corps, things would have turned out differently.

If he was very careful, he would have an opportunity sometime tonight, while most of them slept. The remaining seeds were still in his pocket, so assuming they removed his gag before then, he should be able to take one once everyone bedded down for the night. The most important part of his message was ready: his name and rank, their location, his best approximation of the date, the *Peregrine's* fate, and the list of mutinous crew members - oh yes, he would be sure to remember that little detail.

He had organized this information by priority, in case he lost the link again. After the crews' names, the content became a bit more muddled. Initially he had planned to provide a chronological list of noteworthy events to provide some account of their discovery and exploration of Aarden. He knew from limited briefings by Captain Vaelysia that this had been the *Peregrine's* principal mission, and he wanted to be sure to attach his name to the historic discovery when it was relayed to Fleet, and ultimately to the High Chancellor himself.

He knew that there was much more to Aarden than he'd been told - something had happened during the exploration of the interior that Captain Vaelysia and the other survivors were keeping from the rest of the crew. Something big, and it was ludicrous that Halliard and gods knew who else were better informed than he was. He resented the fact that he had been left out of the Captain's circle of trust, and vowed not to forget this when he finally went before Fleet Command and the Chancellor. But it wouldn't stop there, would it? Something like this would have to be brought before the Kings as well. A tiny shiver of anticipation shook his bony shoulders. He had already amended his mental list to specifically call attention to Halliard and his journal, being careful to refer to him as the leader of the mutiny. He could not abide the treacherous little brat being pardoned as some kind of hero, and he would not accept that this was something much bigger than any concerns Fleet might have had for Seeker Protocol.

By the time the moon rose that night, Voth had managed to compartmentalize his misgivings to keep his message pure and professional.

Not long now. The rest of the crew were dispersing, and he was soon left alone at the base of the mainmast. Even Rantham was absent - no doubt being lowered over the side by the Unbound so that he could move his bowels.

They should have removed his gag by now and brought him something to eat. He rolled his head slowly from side to side, trying to relieve the pain in his neck and shoulders. All he succeeded in doing, though, was to tighten the gag, which had already made the sides of his mouth and cheeks raw.

"Careful now, Lanky," came a soft, deadly whisper from over his shoulder. "I might slip and cut something vital."

The Mylesian whore materialized beside him like some sea-born wraith. He would have pissed himself had he been passing more than a hand's count of drops every day, dry as he was.

Dreysha's hair brushed his neck and the side of his face. "Mmmm," she whispered, sniffing at his neck, "is that a pig I smell?"

She crept around him, moving silently on all fours like some kind of prowling beast. She paused to inhale again. "Or rat, maybe..."

He caught the glint of metal out of the corner of his eye, then felt the cold press of bare steel just below his jaw. He closed his eyes and whimpered, but could anyone blame him?

She leaned in close and breathed in his ear. "Lucky for you, I have my orders, you dry old cock. For now." Then the knife slipped beneath the makeshift gag and cut it away. He kept his eyes squeezed shut for several moments, certain that she was going to do something horrible to him, but eventually he could not bear it any longer. When he opened them, she was gone. He heard the soft rasp of the cloth as it parted and settled to his shoulders, but of her he hadn't heard a whisper as she left his side.

On the deck next to him was a bowl containing his meager rations, and next to it the battered tin cup they used to dispense the water. He took them up with trembling hands and ate, rehearsing his message all the while, concentrating fiercely on the portion that told of the mutiny. By the time he swallowed the Twineroot seed, it had moved to first on his mental inventory.

This sending was much different from his last. His preparation, combined with a mind that had spent decades keeping track of things, lent itself well to the process, and he was able to communicate a fairly clear, structured message to whomever was at the other end, at least at the outset. He worked through his 'inventory' methodically, starting with the mutiny and making sure to name each traitor, even Scow. Next he gave their approximate location and heading, and finally a list of their supplies (he had not planned to do this, but could not help himself), and finally his four Noteworthy Events from what little he did know about their discoveries on Aarden. For a novice, he did remarkably well to get as far as he did while still maintaining control of the send. But he was no Master, and besides, there were other powers at work in The Between.

Voth's third Noteworthy Event focused on a name he'd overheard during a heated discussion between Captain Vaelysia and her first mate. They referred to an exiled god named "Ossien", of which he knew little and cared even less. But from what little he'd heard of that argument, it seemed to be a name that might capture the attention of his superiors as well. It did, but they were not the only ones.

***

Keranos Lugger sprawled, insensate, on a balcony clinging to the topmost floor of the tallest tower in the Ministry's Khatiita campus. As The Counter's send faded, that one name hung in his mind like the last discordant note from a broken lute string. He passed from the fugue of Interpreting into a deep, exhausted slumber, but the note wormed its way into his dreams.

He was reading an old book, but there were no words on the pages. As he trailed his finger across the blank parchment, he heard old Amiel's voice in his head:

"In your casual arrogance you call this place The Garden, but never forget that its roots touch the Between, which, despite our efforts, remains largely undefined." The old man's voice whispered and scratched like dry leaves, while a sense of dread crept into Keri's heart. "And while few actually agree on more than a handful of its traits, there is one characteristic most believe is true…"

The note started to tear, the sound growing ragged and distorted beneath Amiel's voice.

"It is a vast, taught drum, a spider's web, a still pool…"

The tearing sound grew in pitch and intensity. Keri tried to cover his ears, but his arms would not respond.

"Time and physical distance are meaningless: cast a stone here, and the ripples will be felt even at its farthest shores…"

On one of those distant shores, two eyes shone silver-white, like tiny moons in the darkness of the ruined city. Eyes that had long lay closed in a city long since abandoned: her time had come.

The sound became a scream, ripping its way from Keri's own throat…

- 1 -

Emeranth Awakens

I am needed.

She sat upright, her eyes wide, gasping for breath before she realized she did not have to. Her lungs rattled and bubbled as the air tried to displace what was already inside.

She had been submerged. In fact, part of her still was: from her chest down, she was immersed in something thicker than water, a viscous liquid that had the smell and feel of oil. The air was thick with the strong smells of copper and stone. Her mouth was overfull and her stomach heaved as her body reflexively expelled what it could, vomiting and coughing until her throat scratched and burned from the effort.

The thick, cold sludge was gone, but even so, something else remained. Something that gave strength to her limbs once more.

There were spots dancing in her vision, the only indication in the total darkness that her eyes still worked.

It required a supreme effort just to move. Everything felt heavy and sodden and her muscles ached in protest, but she forced herself to stand and shuffle forward.

There had been a disturbance, like a stone skipped across the surface of the water, spreading ripples outward each time it touched down. Something had called out to her, as clear as if it had been standing there in the room.

She was alone now, and could not recall who, or from where the challenge had come, just that it was a clarion call to action. A call she could not deny.

Her desire to discover the truth of it drove her legs forward. Two steps more and the slime began to thin. Two more beyond that, she found stairs and began to climb. The sound of her armored boots scraping against the stone steps rattled around in the hard corners of the chamber and echoed back to her, unhindered by the dark. Strength returned to her limbs as she moved, the weakness quickly fading as her focus sharpened on the task ahead.

What happened to the others?

Reflexively, her left hand strayed to the pommel of the longsword sheathed at her side, and she was assured by its presence. Her right hand tightened around the...

She paused.

There was nothing in her right hand. The spear must be somewhere else. Could someone have taken it? She would most certainly not lose it, but details seemed elusive to her at the moment... perhaps they would become more clear as she moved forward, so she shrugged it off and continued to climb.

Her eyes had begun to adjust, allowing her to discern subtle changes in the darkness. Ahead and above her, it softened, and shapes began to have harder edges, suggesting there was a source of light, spurring her onward. At the top of the steps, the corridor split out to her right and left. She turned right, following the breeze that kissed her cheek.

Her right hand suffered the emptiness of the absent spear, so she trailed her aching fingertips along the familiar glossy black jhetstone walls of the passageway until it ended. She walked out under the full and naked night sky, hundreds of stars shining down to bear witness to her return. She drank in the sight. They were beautiful, wonderful...

Different.

The time of year was wrong. The stars were not how she remembered them.

That wasn't the only problem. The buildings were wrong.

Not the wrong buildings, but they don't look the same. They had been ravaged by the elements: worn, broken and ruined. She spun in a slow circle, dragging her gaze across the shattered landscape. This was no day or two of decay. It was years - decades possibly - worth of damage and neglect.

How long have I been sleeping?

Her feet moved her forward from the doorway to the street, which was covered with a thick layer of sand and dust in the places it was not missing altogether. Her thoughts strayed to the Temple.

Yes! The Temple...

It rose up in her mind, a memory that refused to be forgotten. Perhaps in its presence, she would recall more answers. It seemed the best choice in the absence of any other options.

She instinctively looked for well-known shops or buildings, but the street was now devoid of superficial reminders. Only broken husks remained, hollow shells of the civilization that had once thrived here. Fortunately, a half-collapsed cupola was unique enough for her to gain her bearings. She held onto that sliver of recognition and let it guide her.

Lex Vellos is shattered, she thought. Whatever remained here was a mere echo of its previous grandeur.

Lex Vellos… the name had come to her naturally as she walked. Other things came back to her as well: visions of tall spires, proud statues, teeming markets and pennants of bright colors snapping in the wind. These memories had only been a few steps away; certainly there were more to discover.

Yes, it seemed that moving forward was the best option.

With her direction determined and a destination set, she moved with purpose through the carcass of the great city. Along the way she found herself searching in vain for any scrap of the familiar, but time was a greedy vulture and had apparently picked the city's bones clean.

There were no plants. Whatever disaster had befallen the city had stripped the green from it, save for a few spiny bushes with sparse, shriveled leaves. There were no bodies, at least none she could see out in the open. There were also no tracks in the thick sand, nothing to even suggest recent traffic. A lone dog's skull in the corner of a doorway and a lean rat darting away from it were the only signs of life at all.

What of the lands beyond the city? Of Cartishaan itself?

Cartishaan… another name in a jumble of names in her head. What did she know of it?

For a fleeting moment, memories of the lush green just beyond the city's walls took hold of her mind. She thought of the farms and orchards, the rolling hills to the north, the verdant grasslands to the south. How far did this devastation reach? Did any of that still remain?

Despite her distraction, some instinctual memory remained, even if she hadn't been fully aware of it. Though in a fallen state, she still found the hulking Temple a few blocks away. She fought the urge to run the last few hundred feet, trying to keep her numerous fears and fading hope in check. She stopped short at a corner that opened up into the expansive courtyard leading to the Temple's main steps.

How long had it been since she'd marched across that courtyard, head held high, wrapped in her bold cape, leading the procession? She could not recall, even as she remembered the feeling of it. Her hand strayed to her neck, expecting...

Nothing. Whatever had been there was gone, lost, just as her city now was.

She felt the anxiety, the tension around her chest, but she realized she was not breathing heavily, nor was her heart jackhammering as it normally might. Instead, they remained still, as silent as the stars above her. If there was a part of her that should be concerned by these things, it also remained quiet.

Laughter, bright and quick, drifted into the night sky. She peered around the corner and saw a fire with eight strangers gathered around it. They were soldiers by their attire, long leather armored jackets and short blades, bundles of short bows and arrows within reach. Spears were set around their perimeter, driven into the ground near where they sat or stood. A couple of them were watching outward while the rest talked to each other across the warm flicker of the firelight.

It was the banner that vexed her. A black standard had been tied to another spear, emblazoned with a golden lion holding a sword, the blade shaped as a lightning bolt. She knew of no such standard. It represented none of the High Houses or their followers.

Was this some huunan upstart? Seeking to claim what rightfully belonged to the Arys? She felt her jaw clench. Her hand strayed once again to her sword.

No.

She stayed her hand. All of this was terribly wrong. She leaned back into the shadows, trying to figure out what could have done this to the city, and what could have possibly happened to her. The ruin of Lex Vellos was certainly beyond the power of these eight soldiers. She felt it was best to wait and try to make some sense of things...

"I say flatten it all!" One of them was yelling in her direction, though not at her. She stood at the edge of the campfire's light, with her breeches undone, urinating freely into the darkness, yelling loud enough so that her friends could hear her.

"It's old and creepy and we should bury it rather than try to dig it up! Piss on it all!" she roared with delight, rocking her hips back and forth to accentuate her point. Her companions laughed along with her.

They had no right to say such things. Her blood should have been boiling, her skin flushed with hot rage. Instead, she only felt cold, focused anger.

Insolent dogs.

She strode around the corner with purpose, her eyes fixed on the cur who dared to defile her city. The darkness of night afforded her some cover, but her armored boots striking the uncovered paving stones betrayed her advance.

"What in the rutting Dark...?" The boastful woman stumbled towards her friends and the fire, trying to drag her breeches back up and clumsily claw for her sword at the same time.

"Arms!" cried the only other one standing, pointing the business end of his spear and shifting his feet into a position that showed some measure of training. The others scrambled for bows and blades while she closed the gap.

"Identify yourself!" she snapped.

"You first!" the vandal cried, having finally fixed her pants before drawing her short blade and moving next to the spearman.

"You have been warned," she growled, stepping into the circle of light thrown out by the fire. She saw the surprise in the soldiers' eyes and she could practically taste their fear.

"Loose!" one of them cried, his bowstring twanging almost simultaneously. A short flurry of arrows streaked towards her. Two of them missed outright, one ricocheted off of her armored breastplate and the final one somehow managed to find an unguarded space in her throat, just under her left ear.

Without breaking stride, she reached up and snapped the arrowhead off where it stuck out from the back of her neck before flicking it away. She pulled the shaft back out the way it had come, even as she ripped her sword free with her other hand. The arxhemical runes etched in the bluesteel blade blazed to life.

It hurts!

So far this was the most surprising turn. It was not the wound from the arrow, but the sword that caused her pain. She likened it to pulling a hot iron from a fire, so she got rid of it, throwing it with a snarl and a snap of her arm. It was an ungainly attack, but the blade still struck true, knocking one of the bowmen back from the impact, the large blade stuck halfway through his torso. It probably would have cut him in two if his spine hadn't gotten in the way.

She was now weaponless, but it mattered little. They were just common curs, little more than an annoyance.

Even though she was several heads taller, a spear was thrust in her face, which she deflected upward with one of her gauntleted forearms. The offending spearman took her boot to his chest. She heard his ribs crack as the force of the kick threw him several feet backwards through the fire. His body scattered the contents of the firepit, throwing ash and embers into the air. That was enough to set the horses into a panic.

One of the six remaining soldiers foolishly tried to control the beasts while the belligerent female dashed at her, sword upraised. She stepped into the swing, leaving her attacker critically open. Her hand was already on the soldier's throat, the other inside her reach at the elbow. As she lifted her into the air, the woman flailed at her exposed face and head with a remaining empty fist.

Pitiful.

She crushed her throat and threw her body at an advancing spearman. The corpse crashed against him and both fell clumsily to the dirt in a tangle. She plucked a nearby spear from the ground and drove it through both bodies, pinning them to the ground below, the live one struggling under the weight of his dead friend while his lifesblood quickly leaked out.

No matter how long it had been, she felt no less strong, swift or confident. In fact, she felt better than ever, powerful and energized. Whatever had happened to her had pushed her past the distracting limitations her body once had. She felt a sense of clarity about how best to kill these defilers as quickly and efficiently as possible - and she enjoyed it.

Another arrow buckled and splintered against her armor. The pieces flickered away. When she reflexively turned her head away from the shards, she felt a spear pierce her breastplate and the ribs beneath it. Another spear was incoming, but she avoided the thrust and caught the weapon in her hand, right below where the spearhead met the shaft. She stepped forward, pushing both of her attackers off balance, then snapped off the top of the weapon trapped in her hand. Using the spearhead as a makeshift dagger, she drove it into one of their chests. The other stood awestruck until her mailed fist caved the side of his head in.

The final bowman had turned to run. With a grunt, she pulled the intact spear from her chest, ignoring the lack of blood from her own wounds. She took a second to test its weight before cocking back her arm and throwing it in one fluid motion. It caught the fleeing man in the small of his back, punching through him cleanly as if he were a paper doll. The spear stuck into the ground a good ten feet ahead of him. He was too shocked to even cry out, but he fell face-forward, tripped up by confusion and his own feet.

She was impressed that he showed resolve the others had not, raising himself on shaky legs and stumbling slowly on, one hand clutched at the freely flowing wound in his gut. It had not been a killing shot, but would quickly be fatal, because even if the blood loss didn't kill him, the trail he left behind him was clear enough that she could follow it and finish him off with ease.

She let him stumble off, knowing that moment could wait.

The last of the soldiers stood transfixed. He was smaller than the others, both hands fearfully gripping the reins of the only horse he'd kept from running off. He had soiled himself, which was foul enough, but more distinctly, she realized she could smell his fear. Once she had caught the scent of it, it overwhelmed everything else, and it was so succulent it made her mouth water. A few short strides brought her close. She towered over him.

The horse panicked again, its reins slipping out of his trembling fingers. It sprinted away, leaving the man alone, too terrified to move.

"You... you can't..." he babbled.

She stared at him in contempt. *So pathetic.* How any of her brothers and sisters - to say nothing of the Arys - could stomach them was beyond her. His eyes fluttered and his gaze darted about wildly. She smiled coldly, pacing slowly around him, watching him shiver with fear, crossing his arms over his chest, as if somehow that might provide some measure of protection.

"We're... we're not alone..." He was trying to force out the words between gasping sobs. "More are coming... I don't know what you are... but... but they'll stop you."

In front of him once again, she stooped, bringing her face level with his, placing her hands on either side of his head. To someone looking on it might seem as if she were the adult, comforting a distraught child. She even used one of her thumbs to rub the tears flowing from his eyes.

"Wh... what... who... are you?"

Who was she? As before, the memory was sudden, but complete. She found her own name…

"I am Emeranth Kell," she said, her voice taking on a calmer tone, "and this is my home. You say others are coming, and I believe you. I could send you to warn them…"

On some level, this mention of release must have provided some measure of reassurance to him, because his eyes closed and his head nodded, a constant whimper of "please" on his trembling lips. Somewhere inside he still maintained a flicker of hope.

She snapped his neck with a sudden twist of her hands. It had happened too quickly for his face to register any sign of shock. He looked peaceful as she released the body, letting it slump roughly to the ground.

"…but why, when your corpse will suffice."

Standing up, she sniffed at the tears she had collected from him before slowly dragging her thumb across the surface of her tongue.

The sensation sent a shiver down her spine, a sweet rush of pleasure. It was almost as satisfying as a clean kill.

There was, unfortunately, no time to savor such things. If this one was correct, there would be others coming soon. She would need to prepare for their arrival. This was her city, after all. It was still her duty to defend it, and despite her new circumstances, somehow she knew that she was no stranger to duty.

She lingered on these revelations. Regardless of what had happened to her... whatever changes had reshaped the city around her... she still had a purpose, one strong enough to last even beyond death.

Under the silent night sky, Emeranth Kell suddenly remembered the familiar words that had given her the strength and skill to stand against the unremembered terrors of her past. More importantly, she knew they would help her endure whatever might come next. Recovering them made her smile, a vital piece of the mystery finally revealed. She spoke them aloud, a declaration to herself and the world.

"En'vaar et Laegis."

- 2 -

The Fracture

The Thundering Lance's standard was black, with a golden lion holding a sword shaped like a lightning bolt. Casselle Milner was not one of their ranks, but she rode underneath their banner.

The one hundred and sixteen soldiers of the Lance's company bracketed the contingent of fifty Laegis Templars of which Casselle was a member. The Templars had been given a place of honor in the procession, just behind the Field Command group of the Lance. Lord Richard Lockewood and his son, Commander Arren Lockewood, rode at the head of the column, with the Lance's company captains and other officers close by. Casselle watched this group shift position often, based on the whims of Lord Lockewood and whomever he chose to listen to as they moved on.

She was almost as tired of trying to keep up with the changes as she was the ride itself. Thankfully, today promised to be the last day of this leg of their journey, a much longer affair that had started shortly after General Raandol Vaughan assigned her to the Templars that were, for reasons she could not completely determine, put under the command of the Thundering Lance. The order came on the heels of her return to Strossen, during an inquiry questioning her role in the burning of Flinderlass, a town on the border of the Gundlaan frontier. The town had been overrun by a force of wolves, led by a powerful creature in the shape of a woman. Those wolves and that Wolfmother cost many of the villagers their lives, and if that were not enough, their town as well.

There was a moment during the inquiry that she thought the Templar leadership would dismiss her from the Laegis as well. After all, as a woman of no notable lineage, it was no secret that they held her in low regard. She was a blemish on the gilded facade of their egos, which they branded as "proud tradition." Instead, they threw her directly into her next assignment, a venture that Lord Lockewood had described as "saving the world." She had come to discover rather quickly that was shorthand for "do as you're told and ask few questions." It irritated her, but that was hardly a new experience.

The first week of their journey, they had ridden in formation through the forest and farmlands south of Strossen. The last couple of days, however, they had been threading along a series of narrow valleys and hand-hewn tunnels cut for travel between the lands of Gundlaan to the north and the desolation of the Wasting to the south. Three hundred years ago, the Wasting had been Cartishaan, largest of Niyah's territories, a verdant expanse of life and civilization. That changed when the floating home of the Young Gods, Ehronhaal, fell from the sky. Half of Cartishaan became a gaping hole, and the bulk of what remained had either burned immediately or slowly withered away, as if the land itself had simply died of grief at the Young Gods' passing.

Thankfully, Ganar's Bones, the massive wall of mountains that separated Gundlaan from Cartishaan, had spared the northern lands from any real damage. It was through those mountains, along a path appropriately named The Fracture, that the Thundering Lance traveled presently, and the Laegis with them. It was a slow, almost solemn procession, stopping only when necessary for short stretches of rest or to pass from one nearly navigable path to the next.

Casselle found that the Bones were named so for a reason. The tall cliffs of stone were mostly smooth and almost bleached of color, with pitted surfaces and knobby protrusions. At any given angle, it could have been mistaken for the skeletal remains of a beast so massive the entire army would have been less than fleas on its hide. It was morbidly fascinating for the first few hours, but relentlessly monotonous for the days that followed. On her own, Casselle could have easily lost herself in her thoughts for the whole trip, but the army around her had no shared love of silence.

Though they tried to keep their voices down, echoes bounced off the hard stone, making the collected riders sound easily two to three times their own size, a thunderhead of noise drifting along through the pass.

Full of thunder indeed, Casselle thought to herself as she looked behind her.

She hated the enormity of this affair. Aside from being noisy, they were also slow, magnified by the rough passage through the Fracture. Casselle and her squad had covered three times as much ground on their way to Flinderlass in the same amount of time. Then again, there had only been five of them traveling over easy roads for most of that journey.

Five...

Five had left together, but only three had returned alive. Of those three, only two remained in service, the final one having lost an arm and choosing to give up his commission in the Laegis. This was important to her because those five were no strangers to each other. Four of them had joined the Templars at the same time, were sorted together as initiates, none of them expected to succeed. But under the watchful eye of the Captain that believed in them, they trained together, helped one another, succeeded because of each other and graduated proudly as a united squad. They travelled together to Flinderlass in order to make a difference. They all volunteered to sacrifice themselves so that others might live. It was the kind of courage and camaraderie that are told of in fireside tales, but Casselle certainly didn't feel like a good tale was worth the loss of her friends.

Odegar... Raabel... Jaksen...

"I actually think this saddle is chafing my tender bits."

Casselle turned and smiled at Temos. She was grateful for him breaking her away from less cheerful thoughts. The two of them were all that remained of the group of friends thrown together by chance so long ago. Their squad had survived years of rigorous training through skill, determination and teamwork, knitting them together as an invincible force in the face of adversity.

The hopeful boasts that they would meet and conquer all challenges with equal success outside the walls of Strossen seemed almost childish now, a time forever distant to her present reality.

"I know we are bound for a forsaken wasteland," Temos continued, "but the thought of that seems much better to me than this festering stew of heat and horse sweat."

"I'm more concerned with the horseshit from up ahead," grumbled Greffin Ardell. He was one of the two Templar captains assigned to the Thundering Lance, answering directly to Commander Zanith Cohl, who rode with the Lockewoods at the front of the column.

It felt odd to transition from a small unit of Templars to one of this size. This was the largest group she'd been assigned to; fifty knights, an entire Fist of Laegis. The term came from the Young Gods themselves, and although the numbers assigned to the divisions had varied slightly over the years, based on the size of the Templar population itself, the names had remained constant.

The smallest unit was a Knuckle, or Knot, or most commonly called a squad. Two Knuckles made a Finger, five Fingers comprised a Fist. Currently a Knuckle was four Templar and a leader. Typically between the two Knuckles that comprised a Finger, one of the leaders would be a Captain, like Ardell, and the other leader would be a subordinate, like a Sergeant or a Veteran.

In this Fist, Captain Ardell commanded two Fingers of Shield Templars, close quarter heavily armored soldiers like Casselle and Temos, who were part of the Captain's individual Knuckle. Lennard Torks lead the second squad in their Finger and Sergeant Duran Holst and Jonn Kettel commanded the two Knuckles of the other Finger.

The remaining three Fingers that comprised the Fist of fifty Templar were directly lead by Captain Jaan Boen, who directly presided over a small cluster of Sergeants and Veterans that helped guide the smaller squads. Casselle had learned during her studies that this was an old tradition amongst the Laegis. All were expected not only to lead, but to fight alongside those they commanded.

Casselle assumed all soldiers worked in a similar fashion, but had heard there was a growing trend among newer mercenary groups, especially those that worked for profit, to have leaders that issued commands from behind, reaping the benefits of those that died while risking little. She wondered if the Lockewoods were like that.

She wanted to ask Captain Ardell about it, since he tended to give his opinion whenever he felt like it. In this regard he was much like their previous Captain, Odegar Taumber. Unlike Odegar, however, Casselle knew that Greffin tended to prefer the quickest path to making his point, which didn't leave much maneuvering for pleasantries. The Captain took a small drink from his waterskin, rinsed his mouth and spat onto the ground.

"Is there anything more you can tell us, Captain?" Finn Archer asked, saving Casselle the trouble. Despite his family's name, Finn was a horrible bowman. In fact, if not for his size and prodigious resiliency, he would probably have been a very average warrior at best. He appeared young, with an unruly tumble of blonde hair and a thin beard that threatened to thicken every day, but never succeeded. He reminded Casselle of Jaksen the most; fairly quiet, and mostly unassuming. But he was easily as large as Raabel had been. Casselle winced, realizing what she'd been doing and wondering how long she'd continue measuring up her new squadmates to her old ones.

Captain Ardell set a thumb to the side of his nose just beside his eyepatch and blew hard to clear the opposing nostril. There was a bit of a grumble from the other Templar and Finn wisely let the matter go without further inquiry. It was evident that the Captain was as equally in the dark as the rest of them.

Rounding out Casselle's squad of four was Jhet Anlase, a Shield Templar in name only, because he preferred the use of two shortened swords rather than the traditional longsword and shield. Temos had heard rumors that he was the best swordsman in the Fist, if not the entire Laegis, but for the moment those stories remained unconfirmed. Jhet certainly did not boast about himself, or talk much in general, perhaps because of the damage he hid behind the black scarf wrapped about his lower face. A small spike of melted skin where his left ear met his jaw was telling enough why he kept the wrap in place. His missing eyebrows and the tightly shaved black hair that clung to his scalp gave him a grim, unsettling appearance.

Jhet cast a glance backwards, to the next Knuckle of Laegis behind them. Casselle was still getting to know them all, trying to match names with faces, but one of them was easily identified and as obviously out of place as a three-legged Harox in a pig pit.

Vincen von Darren rode in the front of the second squad, just behind them. The smug self-assuredness she had become used to was gone for the moment. Instead, his face was red all over, flushed with anger and embarrassment.

"The problem is that your family may be rich, but they have not proven themselves as being durable enough to join a proper society of longstanding, established bloodlines," one of the other Templars was saying to him, a thin fellow with a big nose that remained slightly upturned at all times. Ingst Engmar the Seventh was the third son of Ingst Engmar the Sixth. He had a detailed story why his two older brothers did not inherit the name, but Casselle cared little for his account of it or even Temos's biting recap. The only thing that amused her even slightly about the fellow was that he was very good at aggravating Vincen by reminding him that back in Strossen, his family was far less important than it had been in Flinderlass.

"If your family had been a part of Southside, I mean a genuine part, not just a recent homeowner there, we would have been more than glad to point out that you should never send your first son into the Laegis," Ingst informed him. "I mean not unless you don't like him very much, or unless he has a younger brother that is much sharper at numbers, I would think. 'Send your name off to War, not your business,' my Father would often say."

"Never mind Ingst," instructed Passal Cooper, the sandy haired Templar on Vincen's other side. "He's stuffed with more bluster than sense. All the evidence you need that younger siblings feel like they have more to prove."

"You're one to talk about proving something," Ingst huffed. "Your family makes barrels."

"My family makes the finest barrels," Passal replied with a calm smile, "for the best wines and spirits... you know, like the ones your mother tends to find herself crawling into from the hours between one sunrise to the next."

"Hah! He's got you there, Seven!" burst out the Templar riding just behind Passal, a mountain of a man in a sleeveless armorjack. Gunnar Hawken was proudly Vanha and looked every bit as heroic as one might expect from the direct bloodline of the Young Gods. He had a chiseled face sporting a consistently fierce grin, and arms as large and hard as a gnarled oak. Casselle had seen him training and knew that, despite his size, he also had the grace of a wild cat. She had yet to see him angry, and thinking on it, she was grateful knowing that if she did, it would be pointed at their enemies.

"I still don't even understand how this happened," Vincen grumbled.

"As I hear it," Temos began smugly, "you were squired on the field of battle by a previous Templar who went quite mad. Then you insisted upon maintaining your commission when you returned to Strossen, which was clearly a request you didn't understand the scope of. Much to everyone's surprise, they actually let you keep it."

"I mean I don't understand how I got assigned to this! I haven't even been properly trained," Vincen bit back. This immediately unleashed a barrage of replies from those riding nearby. Ingst was trying to make a comment about house training dogs when Gunnar trampled over it by reminding Vincen that the pointy end of the sword goes towards the "other guy." Even Passal, who had leapt to his defense earlier - or perhaps had simply been motivated to vex Ingst - chided his squadmate about receiving more than he wished for. Vincen realized his mistake too late, and chose to remain quiet, wearing a face like he'd sipped curdled milk.

"Alright, settle down, children." The command came from Veteran Lennard Torks, the leader of Vincen's squad. He typically didn't talk much, but when he did it was almost always with a sly grin. His long chestnut hair was usually tied back at the base of his neck, but currently it was loose. As he tucked a stray strand behind one of his ears, Casselle had to admit that he was a handsome man, even though she didn't typically notice that sort of thing. To hear Temos tell it, though, many other women did.

Torks had been a longtime squadmate of Captain Ardell. The other leaders in the Finger, Durran and Jonn, shared the same distinction, but their squads trailed behind. At night, though, she'd seen the four of them exchanging words and sips from flasks while the rest of the Laegis went about their nightly duties.

She barely remembered the names in Holst's group, but at least they were Shield Templar, like she and Temos. Captain Boen's two Fingers of Lancer Templars and a single Finger of Archers were almost always only seen from a distance, given their different roles during a battle. Even though she didn't know them all personally, she felt closest to these fifty Laegis, a complete Fist of rigidly trained Templars reporting to Commander Zanith Cohl. How they had been loaned out to Richard Lockewood still confused her. Certainly this one self-proclaimed leader didn't have authority over the whole of the Laegis, regardless of which Young God he might have been related to.

Casselle was still stewing over the cool and casual confidence Lockewood had displayed when making the request. Historically the Laegis had served the Arys directly. His relation to them did not justify his right, much less his arrogance, to treat them like his property. She could tell she was going to have problems letting this go.

"You're anxious," Temos told her.

"I'm..." she struggled for better words, but had none. "Yes. I am."

"You're not alone," he replied, with a subdued smile. She found she had one to return, and was glad it did not feel forced, just weak. There was still much left ahead for them to face, most of it intentionally left unclear by their leadership, but she felt strength in her convictions and knew she was where she needed to be. For the moment, she let herself be at peace with that.

***

The Fracture ended abruptly, the jagged gap across the otherwise unbroken expanse of mountains stopping as cleanly and sharply as the Bones themselves did. There were no foothills there, just a flat open desert of featureless sand, endlessly deep and wide.

Casselle had expected it to be hotter. The worst part was the wind that rushed and snapped at her, making her wish she had something like Jhet Anlase's black scarf to keep blasts of blown sand from stinging her face.

She heard commands issued to the Thundering Lance. In short order they drew on cleverly constructed hoods secured to the soldiers' armorjacks, and fashioned with a loose mask that could be fastened to the inside, covering their noses and mouths. Casselle noticed the casual ease with which they performed the transformation, as if they had planned this long before even departing on this trip. She also noticed the looks of annoyance on the faces of the Laegis around her, who were as unprepared as she was. She wondered if any of them were harboring the same resentment she had for the Lockewoods that they had not bothered to inform the Templars to make similar preparations. Hearing Greffin chew on several colorful expletives without saying them outright was confirmation enough.

Captains Ardell and Boen instructed the Templars to do the best they could, and Casselle hastily improvised something as they stopped just outside the Fracture, preparing themselves for the first night in the Wasting. The tight formations they had hoped to avoid after leaving the confined path through the mountains turned out to be their best defense against the biting breezes, their clustered tents diffusing the constant abrasion to a much more tolerable level.

Even so, by the end of the camp's construction, Casselle felt like the sand had slipped through every crack and crevice of her wardrobe, if it hadn't created several others outright. She certainly wasn't the only one: at dinner that night, Temos complained about the fine layer of grit that covered everything, from the stew to the bread, to the lip of his own water flask.

"I feel like I'm eating more sand than stew," he groaned as he struggled to put his back to a wind that shifted direction every other minute.

"If you don't want it..." Gunnar Hawken began, having finished his own, plus the leftovers of some of his other squadmates.

"I never said that," Temos replied quickly, stuffing as much in his mouth as he could, looking slightly uncomfortable as he chewed. "It just shouldn't be this rutting... crunchy."

"It'll put hair on your chest, Pelt," Captain Ardell jested.

"I pray it doesn't. You could practically knit a sweater out of what's there already," Temos responded, not bothering to scrape the last bit of remains from the bowl.

"Hairy men stay warm at night," Ardell offered without any sort of accompanying explanation. He immediately went into snapping off orders about cleaning, maintaining gear and preparing for the following day's trip. Vincen von Darren, however, was called out for training.

"Milner, you're with me," Captain Ardell said, much to her surprise. Greffin had been training Vincen on tactics more than anything else during their trip. Whatever happened, he wanted the rank novice to have enough understanding to assist when necessary - or at least to get out of the way of other Templar. More than once during these lessons she'd smirked when the Captain had repeated the phrase: "If you do not move when this happens, we will walk over you. It will not be intentional, but it will hurt."

The fact that he had called her out to help could only mean one thing, which made her surprisingly happy. Some of the other Laegis gave each other sidelong glances before moving on to their duties. Casselle hastily cleaned her mess kit, stowed it, and reported to Captain Ardell. He was standing off to the side of the common circle they'd formed by ringing their tents around a central firepit.

Vincen was already there, being lectured by the Captain. Casselle knew those lectures. Along with Odegar, Greffin was a regular combat instructor for Laegis Initiates. Though they had never served directly alongside each other before this mission, the Captain had been one of her first combat instructors, and as much as she respected Odegar, Greffin was clearly the better fighter between them. She moved close, but not close enough to disturb the two of them. She didn't pay much attention to what was being said until Vincen spoke up in opposition.

"I still don't understand why I'm even here if all you're going to do is tell me how not to be in your way." Casselle looked up to see Greffin's one good eye narrow its focus on Vincen's face. She could tell it disturbed the younger man.

"It's the lesson you need to learn most. I was told by my Commander to take you in and train you," Greffin growled. "I suppose it's because someone has seen some worth in you. I sure don't see it, but it's not my job to question them. My job is to make you a functional part of this unit, either by making you a fighter, or making you aware of when you need to get out of our rutting way.

"Your job," Greffin continued, tapping Vincen on the chest, "is to shut your gods-damned mouth until I tell you otherwise." A wide eyed Vincen nodded mutely.

Lennard Torks showed up with two wooden practice blades, handing the first to Vincen and the second to Casselle. He gave her a smile and a knowing wink before moving away to check on other things. Casselle felt the weight of the sword, giving it a couple of light swings to get familiar with the balance.

"You were whining about not getting any training in Strossen before receiving your title," Captain Ardell told Vincen, who was eyeing Casselle warily. "So we're going to spend some time teaching you a few basics."

Vincen scowled. She knew he'd received instruction from a tutor, someone hired by his family. That was something he'd gone on about at length during her time in Flinderlass. What she didn't know was if he'd had any interest or aptitude in it. If so, and with a decent teacher, there was a chance he'd been given enough lessons to make him competent. Casselle imagined that it was probably nothing like the rigorous instructions the Laegis put their members through, but she was admittedly biased in her opinion. She'd never seen him in combat, so she tried to reserve her judgement.

It was the hardest thing she'd had to do since the trip began.

"Milner, Cadence Five if you would," Ardell told her. Casselle nodded and immediately began the motions of the Fifth Cadence Drill. It was mostly chopping, thrusting and footwork, but the important part of each drill was the timing, which is why they were called Cadences. The theory was that if all the Templars were taught according to a specific tempo, all of them would be more in tune with each other as a combined fighting unit. That tempo, at least for the drills, was also designed to push them physically, to improve strength and endurance through repetition.

"This is what you're going to be teaching me?" Vincen's words hung heavy in the air, clearly critical. Casselle smirked as she continued the Cadence, adjusting her balance and footing on the subtlety shifting ground.

"These are the basics," Ardell reiterated.

"I think I'm a bit beyond the basics by now," Vincen scoffed. Casselle remembered a similar scene from her first training sessions, and didn't have to see Ardell's face to imagine the look on it.

"So you think we should skip ahead a bit?" the Captain asked, almost innocently.

"What are we skipping, Captain?" came a voice from around the tent. Casselle continued her drill, even though she was curious about who'd spoken.

"Evening Commander Cohl," Greffin replied before acknowledging others that were out of Casselle's line of sight. "Lord Lockewood. Commander Lockewood."

"Pardon us, Captain. We were just out for a walk." Casselle immediately recognized the cool, deep voice of Richard Lockewood.

"No apologies necessary, sir. The men are making themselves useful. I was working on educating Master von Darren on our battlefield techniques," the Captain said. Casselle noted the slight. Greffin should have addressed Vincen as "Templar von Darren" but had chosen not to.

"Is he not familiar with the Akist?" Richard Lockewood asked.

No, Casselle thought. Vincen would not be familiar with the Akist, but she was surprised to discover Lord Lockewood knew what it was. Passed down and refined since the first ranks of the Templar organized themselves while in the service of the Young God, Obed, the Akist became the name of the rules and techniques the Templar had discovered and refined on the battlefield. In their forgotten language it simply meant "the Point," like the tip of the sword, but the concepts were far more complex than the simple name implied. Learning the Akist was the bulk of her studies for years and it was not talked about lightly, even amongst the Laegis themselves.

"He was not inducted in the traditional manner," Zan Cohl said.

"He's the one from Flinderlass, then?"

"Yes."

"HE is right here, you know," Vincen interjected, perhaps too sharply. Casselle wished she could see the look on their faces at that moment, but she was turned in the opposite direction, walking through the final steps of the Fifth Cadence. She did recognize the long silence that followed his outburst - long enough that she was able to make the final strokes with her practice sword, return it to her center and settle into a resting stance.

"Over here, Milner," Ardell ordered. Casselle rested the training blade against her shoulder and moved to stand next to Vincen, facing her Captain, Commander and the leaders of the Thundering Lance. This was the closest look she'd had at Zan Cohl. He seemed a bit too slight for his armor, almost delicate. His long blonde hair was pulled back on the top and bound behind his head, but ran loose from behind the ears and almost down to his shoulders. His beard was a shade darker, hugged his sharp face and was immaculately groomed.

"You and I share something in common, Templar von Darren," Richard Lockewood said. "I, too, was offered a battlefield commission into the Laegis, at a time when the practice was more common. Although my grandfather had insisted upon Laegis training, he also made it clear I was never made to enter the Templars."

According to the histories Odegar had mentioned to her when they had first met Vincen, that practice had fallen out of favor prior to the Ehronfall. That easily made Richard Lockewood three hundred or more years old and a Vanha, since only they could live so long. The oldest one she'd ever met was Odegar, and although he'd been over a hundred years old, he didn't look half as young as Richard. If Lockewood's blood was that pure, it could only mean he was a generation or two removed from the Young Gods themselves. She gave a passing consideration trying to figure out which one his grandfather might be…

"Who was your grandfather?" Vincen asked pointedly, as if his own heritage could possibly measure up to Lockewood's.

"His identity is irrelevant to the point I'm trying to make," Richard dismissed. "Just know that it's a great honor to be offered such a thing. One who accepts should be trying extra hard to prove themselves worthy of it."

"So I'm reminded," Vincen replied, "quite often."

"You seem to think your opinion in this matters somehow," Commander Cohl interjected sharply. The abruptness of it caught even Casselle off guard. "The only opinion we weighed was the one from Captain Renholf Krennel. He was a friend of mine, and an excellent Templar. His word alone is enough for us to give you every opportunity to prove that. Know that whatever merits he weighed to make that decision no longer matter here. Moving forward, the only thing that matters is your desire to succeed. If you fall short, understand that I will not assume that his assessment was incorrect, but rather that you lied to us about the commission."

"I... that is..." Casselle heard the fear in Vincen's voice. Even when they first met back in Flinderlass, Casselle had assumed the same thing. Vincen certainly did not seem like the kind of person that would garner the respect from a trained Templar. Then again, Renholf Krennel had been driven mad by the time they had arrived. It could well be that his judgement had been compromised.

Even still, she began to understand why Vincen was here. The reason the Laegis worked so well together was because of trust in each other. Even when you didn't like the Templar standing next to you, it was never in doubt that you could trust them. That's probably why Odegar was shocked, but had never spoken negatively of Renolf's choice. Had he been the one to recommend Vincen, would Casselle have had as much of a problem with it? She would need to give this more thought, and was mildly annoyed that it might make her enjoy what was about to happen slightly less than she might have hoped.

"Let's see if we can coax out a display of what Renholf might have seen in him," Richard suggested. Commander Cohl agreed and nodded to Captain Ardell.

"Milner, Darren," Ardell barked as he walked, pointing to the positions he wished for them to assume. Casselle did as she was told, moving to the place where she would face Vincen for sparring.

"This should be interesting," Richard was saying to his son, who merely nodded in response. Casselle watched Vincen settle into his position and look to Ardell for the next instruction.

"Get used to this Master von Darren. You'll probably be seeing a lot of this in the coming days. The goal is to get your opponent on the ground or to have them voluntarily take a knee," Captain Ardell instructed. "We'll begin on my mark."

Casselle immediately was in motion, before Vincen could even turn to face her. Unguarded and quickly unbalanced, he found himself on the ground. A few choice expletives streamed out as he tried to get himself standing again.

"She moved before I was ready! Before you said to... How is that fair?" Ardell and Cohl both smiled, both clearly recalling their own history with Akist training.

"Milner? Do you have anything to say to that?" Greffin asked innocently.

"Fairness and rules are for games, Captain. On the battlefield there is only victory or defeat," she said loudly and clearly, as she moved back to her starting position. She remembered it well from the first time she found herself on the ground. It always felt better saying it than hearing it.

"Well said, Templar," the Captain replied. Vincen clearly did not like that answer.

"Do it again," Ardell instructed.

Vincen charged. Casselle had already anticipated that, as he was clearly angry at being humiliated. She almost felt bad putting him on the ground so quickly a second time... almost. When the Captain called for a third round, Vincen had managed to regain most of his composure, enough so that he at least did not charge in blindly again. Although still angry, he tried to focus his efforts through his sword instead.

He was not without skill. It was clear after the first exchange or two that Vincen had listened to what he had been taught. The effectiveness of what they had taught him was certainly up for discussion, but there was strength behind his blows and determination in his eyes. Even so, his style was loose, and his motions had too much flourish in them. They were bold, but garish, clearly designed more for show than practical application. His wide swings were equal parts challenge and bluster. Against an untrained foe, he certainly would have posed a threat and looked good doing it. He might have even been a match for any casual duelist, something she expected he might have done with other idle rich young men. The confidence in his face indicated as much.

To Vincen's regret, however, Casselle was no idle young man. She watched him move and swing, avoiding many strikes, deflecting or blocking the rest. It took almost no time for the confidence to drain from his face. When he launched an exceptionally weak thrust that left him exposed, she took advantage, twisting into his center and using that momentum to throw him to the ground roughly.

"Alright, that's enough," Ardell instructed. "Return to position."

Casselle offered Vincen a hand, but he batted it away. She wasn't surprised, so she moved back to her position, turning just enough to also be facing the Captain. After some groans and muttering grumbles, Vincen returned to his feet and shuffled back to his mark.

"If you noticed," Richard was telling Arren, "she never really even used her sword for that. It was all about positioning, momentum and balance."

"Templar Milner, what does Master von Darren need to work on most?" Captain Ardell asked her.

"He needs to drill on fundamental footwork, Captain. It was too easy to unbalance him."

"Agreed," Ardell answered. Vincen shot her an ugly look. If it were possible, he might have broken his own jaw just by clenching it so tightly.

"Master von Darren, what does Templar Milner need to work on?" Ardell asked. Vincen turned to him, stupefied.

"I don't understand," he said.

"What did she do wrong?"

"Nothing, I guess. She won," Vincen replied, still confused.

"Very well, I'll do it myself," Ardell huffed. "Your throws could have been better, Milner. Cadence thirty-four by five."

"Yes, Captain," she said.

"What'd she do right?" Ardell asked Vincen.

"Everything?"

Ardell rolled his eyes at the reply. "Your timing is much improved. Not perfect, but definitely better than the last time I saw you."

"Thank you, Captain," Casselle replied.

"What'd he do right?" Greffin asked her. Vincen, clearly surprised to hear the question, looked at her as well.

"He got his emotions under control quickly, sir. In a frustrating situation, he looked for a better solution." She'd seen plenty of raw Initiates lose themselves to fits of rage under similar conditions. The fact that he was able to reign it in so quickly was good. He was clearly shocked to hear anything positive coming from her.

"Agreed. At least we have that to work with," said Greffin. He turned back to Commander Cohl and the Lockewoods. "Anything further from these two?"

"Not for the moment, Captain," said Cohl. With a nod, Ardell barked a dismissal to both of them. Vincen wandered away for a few steps before Gunnar Hawken stepped up beside him and encouraged him to follow. The two moved away from the firelight.

As they left, Casselle heard Gunnar telling Vincen that the Laegis were just as much about breaking down each other's bad habits as they were about building up the good ones. She wondered how long it would take for that lesson to sink in.

She moved a few steps away and began to do her five repetitions of Cadence thirty-four, as instructed. She could have done it later, but Commander Cohl and the Lockewoods had lingered, and were talking amongst themselves. She was not trying to eavesdrop, but they were not trying hard to conceal their conversation, either.

"As you can see, it's very effective, but the whole of it takes years to learn," Richard was telling his son.

"That's why you made changes," Arren Lockewood replied.

"Our soldiers are not Templar. I use them differently. I took what I needed and discarded the rest," Richard said.

"Is that why you need us along?" Cohl asked. "Because you need something from the parts you previously found irrelevant?"

"One of the reasons." Richard was wearing a knowing smile. It looked slightly out of place on him.

"There are others?"

"Is there ever only one reason for anything?"

Greffin huffed at Lockewood's reply. Like her, he had little tolerance for cryptic answers.

"I understand your desire for secrecy, but I would like to know what danger we're all marching towards before we blindly trip over it," Zan Cohl said.

"No danger yet," Richard replied calmly. "Let's focus on getting to the Ghostvale and then we'll discuss what comes next."

The Ghostvale? To most, the hidden valley of the Khaliil was spoken of like a legend, a place the Young Gods once dwelled when the world was new. The thought of seeing it in person seemed as unreal as seeing Ehronhaal amongst the clouds once again, or Maughrin…

Casselle almost lost her place in the Cadence.

She remembered the scroll from the ruins underneath Flinderlass, the absolute black that ended in a fearsome, gaping maw.

She hoped that her fear was misplaced. She'd had her fill of legends already.

- 3 -

Two Steps Back

Tarsus!

Triistan woke instantly, with none of the usual fog of sleep.

He felt... good. His skin was still scratched and raw from sunburn, his joints ached, the empty sockets in his gums were still sore, and there were at least a dozen other undefined sources of discomfort, but he'd grown used to that misery. The pain of Mordan Scow's loss was also still there. His murder at the hands of Sherpel Icefist had robbed Triistan of the closest thing he had to a father, but since presiding over The Mattock's Releasing Ceremony, he had gradually come to terms with it. He knew the daily reminders of his mentor's absence would continue to hurt, but he no longer felt like a rudderless skiff. And with last night's discovery of the Tarsus constellation, the bog of despair and self-pity he'd been wallowing in were yielding before the rising sense of hope and excitement at the prospect of finding their way home.

It has been thirty-one days since the SKS Peregrine *went down. We few are all that remain of the Seekers sent back to warn the mainland of our terrible discoveries on Aarden. And we few are all that remain to carry word of those we left behind, beyond the Burning Sea.*

It was a heavy responsibility, and yet today, for the first time, he felt strong enough to carry it.

The weather reflected his mood: the morning was warm and clear, the sky an endless stretch of brilliant blue. As they broke their fast on fish, hard tack and water, he tipped his head back to enjoy the warm caress of sun and wind; he knew that everything was about to change, and he wanted to savor this feeling as long as he could.

"If I were a god, I would create a way to stretch moments like this out indefinitely."

"You mean, eating stale bread and drinking rainwater that tastes like piss, while we're drifting lost at sea? You like this?" Wil whined.

Well, that didn't last long.

"Mung's got the right of it - you need to get out more, Triis."
Dreysha sat down across from him, her meager breakfast clumped in
a battered wooden bowl. "I can think of a few moments I'd rather let
run on forever, but they don't involve picking weevils from my teeth -
what teeth I have left, anyway." For emphasis, she spat one out onto
the deck, and then gave him a meaningful look. His ears grew warm
and he was thankful his sunburn hid the fact that he was blushing. He
knew she was chastising him for the night before. He was a fool: after
finally having the courage to kiss her, he'd become distracted as he
recognized the constellations overhead, then left her to consult their
charts without so much as a "by your leave".

He told himself he would get another chance, especially now that
he believed they could find their way home.

I will make the opportunity if I have to, he thought, recalling how
she had felt in his arms, relishing the memory and the sweet ache of
longing it aroused. *But not yet. There is still too much to be done.*

He considered the task ahead while Rantham, Dreysha and Wil
began discussing what meal they would choose for their first, once
they reached a safe harbor. They were still weeks away from any kind
of land, and all of that through open water where anything might
happen.

Weather was still their biggest threat, but food and water were no
guarantee either, and the closer they got to the southern shipping
lanes, the greater the possibility of encountering pirates. The brigands
called themselves "Kingsbane", men who had forsaken their
homelands and refused to acknowledge any of the regional powers.
Each ship was its own nation, each crewman a patriot, and the ruling
captains would only ever yield to superior steel or the unconquerable
sea. The one thing that united them was their hatred of the Sea Kings'
claims to sovereignty of Ruine's waterways, and while most of them
steered clear of the Fleet's fearsome war galleys, they hunted
merchant and fishing vessels in open defiance of the Isles' dominance.
Many a Seeker vessel had fallen prey to their sleek corsairs, which
was one of the primary reasons why the *Peregrine* had carried her
complement of Reavers.

He shrugged off his doubts. There was a better chance they
would be picked up by a "merchy" - a merchant vessel - or one of
their own patrols, and they had little choice in the matter, anyway.
There should also be Sea Kings ships actively searching for the

Peregrine. She was now several months overdue and according to Captain Vaelysia, her mission had been sanctioned by both the Kings' Council and the Ministry. He seized on the idea of a fleet of his own countrymen looking for them and wondered what more he could do to hasten their rescue.

As he sucked on a piece of stale biscuit, trying to soften it, he consulted his chart again.

"So just where in the rutting Dark are we now?" Rantham asked curtly.

Triistan forced himself to look the injured man in the eye rather than down at his now useless legs. Rantham sat upright, leaning forward. Biiko crouched next to him, changing the dressing on the knife wound in his back. They had long since run out of clean bandages, so the Unbound had taken to shredding sailcloth into strips, soaking them in sea water and then hanging them out in the hot sun in a crude attempt to sterilize them. Fortunately, whatever ointments and other exotic ingredients he carried in his apparently inexhaustible field kit seemed adept at preventing infection as well. Although wounded at the same time as Scow, none of them had expected Rantham to survive his injury. Initially, Triistan was certain that he would die and Scow would survive, but somehow Rantham had grown steadily stronger. He no longer slept as often, and his appetite seemed equal to any of theirs. He had changed, though. Before his injury, Rantham's personality had matched his physical swagger. But now he was sullen and combative. Not that Triistan could fault him for it, which was why he ignored Rantham's refusal to address him as "Captain". That, and the fact that he also found the notion absurd.

"Here, I can show you. Well... sort of." He moved closer and spread the chart out on the deck. He pointed to an imaginary position on the weathered planks, a few inches away from the bottom edge of the map's waxed parchment.

"We're actually not quite on the chart yet, but based on our reckoning last night, I'm sure we're not far, and we should be...", he moved his index finger back onto the bottom of the map, "somewhere around here within a few days - perhaps sooner if this wind holds up."

Wil drew closer, tilting his head almost comically, trying to read the map upside down. Triistan wondered if he knew how to read a chart, or if he had ever bothered to even look at one before now. Wil was the son of a Ministry official and from the stories he shared during their voyage, had led a rather lazy, privileged life. Although he should have had access to an excellent education, such trivial details as how to get from one location to another would have been someone else's problem.

"Then what?" he asked.

Triistan pursed his lips. It was the question he had been grappling with since fixing their position.

"If we hold east, it will take us back to our original launch point in Thunder Bay." He traced his finger along a gentle eastward curve, taking them through a gap in a series of barrier islands just south of the Bay. "It would probably be the quickest way to make landfall, but there's a greater risk of storms rolling in from the Forever Sea this time of year."

Dreysha crouched next to him and his pulse quickened as her shoulder brushed his. She spoke around a mouthful of biscuit, pointing at the chart with her punch dagger.

"Bad idea if you ask me. Why not keep north, towards the Haven?" She swept her dagger above the area marked 'Niht's Haven', the narrow sea that lay between the Sea-King Islcs and the mainland. It was renowned for its crystal-clear waters, gentle seas, and abundant fishing. Other than the Golden Gap, it was the most heavily-trafficked stretch of ocean on Ruine.

"Make for Sitsii. Longer route, but odds are we'll be picked up by a merchy long afore we'd reach Thunder Bay."

"Or worse," Rantham said darkly.

"Worse?" Wil squeaked. "What do you mean, 'worse'?"

Triistan frowned. "Kingsbane - the closer we are to known shipping routes, the greater the chance we'll be spotted by them as well."

"Aye," Rantham added. "They'll be prowling the southern edges like ridgebacks 'round a wreck."

Lankham Voth laughed from where he sat tethered to the base of the mainmast. "Nothing to fear, there. You treacherous bastards should feel right at home, then."

Drey shot him a venomous look. "Your tongue's looking awfully tasty, Lanky. I'd keep it hidden if I were you." Voth blanched and snapped his mouth shut.

Rantham, Wil and Drey began to argue about the risk of the Kingsbane compared to the volatile weather of the Forever Sea. Wil and Rantham were in favor of the eastern course, while Drey scoffed at their fears.

Triistan tried his best to ignore them, deliberating on the two routes and their respective dangers. Whether they were deserving of their notoriety or not, the Kingsbane presented another problem. If they captured him, they would find his journal, and he was afraid to contemplate what they would do with that information. At the very least, it would not reach his masters, and the consequences of that could be disastrous.

He knew what needed to be done, and the real reason he had been trying to stretch the morning out. His crew needed to know everything that was at stake here, and this decision would come much easier to them all once he had relieved himself of a burden he had already borne alone for too long.

He rolled the chart back up. The others grew quiet, turning expectant gazes toward him, and for a moment he balked. He was still getting used to being the focus of their attention, and he had to suppress the urge to scamper up into the crow's nest. He thought of what Mister Scow would have done in his place and the answer came quickly: "Tend to your ship 'fore you tend to yourself."

He pulled himself to his feet, noting the direction of the wind from the northwest. "Biiko, take the helm if you please. Swing two points a-port until she's in a beam reach. Drey, hard on the kicker straps when she gets to the leeward mark."

"Hard on the straps, aye, Captain. Just the way I like it," she grinned and moved to stand ready by the mainmast. Triistan was only partially successful in hiding his smirk.

Wil lurched to his feet. "What can I do, Tri- uh, Sir?" Snitch scampered down one of the ratlines, up Wil's pant leg and onto his shoulder, chattering away.

"Take in the nets, Wil. We're going to run her out today." The day before, they had woven two crude fishing nets by unraveling some spare cordage to create a finer mesh. They found odd items to use as weights, tying them to the nets so that they would submerge a few feet below the surface.

As the prow swung to port, the mainsail snapped full. Timbers creaked in protest, followed by the rapid staccato ticking noise as Dreysha turned the winch to tighten the boom vang. The launch surged forward beneath his feet and he heard the increased rush of water along her flanks. A thrill ran through him: he felt charged, like a storm cloud brought to life. Somewhere in the back of his mind he could hear Scow's rolling laughter.

He took a deep breath and drew forth his journal. He hated to leave the moment, but that sense of responsibility he'd felt on waking this morning had grown heavier. The crew needed to know Aarden's secrets, and he needed to face them.

Once he was convinced they were getting as much speed out of the launch as they could, Triistan gathered them around the helm. Will and Drey picked Rantham up and carried him over, then made him a comfortable place to sit. Biiko remained at the wheel.

"It's past time I told you all of the Aarden Expedition - what we found there and what we… what really happened to the men we lost." *Welms and Jaegus, Pendal, the Reaver Taelyia…*

He glanced up to find the others watching him expectantly. As his eyes found Biiko's, the Unbound gave him an almost imperceptible nod, as if to say "Go ahead, you're doing the right thing." Had he been waiting for this as well? Even after months traveling together, having the mysterious warrior shadowing him, protecting him, Triistan was still unnerved by the man's silent, subtle influence. He had learned much about Biiko's Unbound order, but it was still difficult to accept that his life had become wrapped up with one of Khagen's Sons.

He spoke haltingly at first, groping for a way to begin. He decided to try reading directly from his journal, but after the first few passages, he stopped. It felt too personal, too close to the original events - he could feel himself being drawn back there to relive those moments all over again. It had taken him weeks to gain control over these flashbacks and the emotional turmoil they caused, and he did not think he could continue a coherent narrative this way. So after the first few pages, he closed the book and started reciting the tale from memory.

He first described the formation of their company, listing off each member of the Expedition and commenting on why he felt each had been selected. He stumbled over the first few names of those they had lost, but it became easier as he went. After that he gave them a general accounting of their first days on the river and the amazing discoveries they made. He told them of the strangeness of the water, how it glowed when disturbed at night, and the dark shapes that moved beneath the surface. When he described their encounter with the graybole monkeys, they all groaned, recalling the pests that had also invaded the base camp. When he reached the point where they set up camp on that first night, he paused, knowing that once he told them of the Captain's revelation of their actual mission, there would be no turning back.

But that's the idea, isn't it? He pressed on.

"On that first night, the Captain showed us something that none of you were told about upon our return. We were sworn to secrecy, and it is one of the reasons why I have not spoken of these events until now. I'm sorry for that, but we had our orders." They continued to stare silently at him, and he coughed nervously.

"We'd made three or four leagues on that first day, and when we made camp at night, Mister Tarq drew forth a strange tube, like a map case, only it was made of bone. There were runes carved into it - some of them looked like a few we use in the Releasing Ceremony. Anyway, it acts as some kind of ward, as Mister Tarq cut his thumb and dribbled some blood onto it. There might have been a dull flash of bluish light, and then he seemed to think it was ok to open."

Rantham interjected. "The Whip had a fucking fire-tube? What was in it?"

"A what?"

Dreysha answered: "An immolation case - it's a scroll or map case inscribed with an arxhemical ward - if you open it without disarming the formula, it will explode, destroying the contents… and probably you," she added with a cruel smile.

"Oh. Yes, I suppose that's what it was. Anyway, inside was a chart. I had it with me before we - well, it doesn't matter, but it's lost now. I did sketch it in here somewhere, though." He rifled through several pages before locating it, then turned the book around to show them.

"Up until then, I'd never seen a chart like this before."

There was a mixture of gasps and muttering as they realized what it depicted: the Shattered Isles in a ragged necklace across the top, and the shapeless mass that could only be Aarden several leagues below. This was the first time they had heard that there was a map of the continent.

"Are you saying that they knew it was there?" Rantham asked. "That we intentionally sailed off course?"

"Perhaps. I have my suspicions, but I'll get to those. Suffice it to say I'm sure they knew it was out there, somewhere." In truth, they knew much more than that, but he was still getting comfortable with the idea of telling everything he had sworn to keep secret. He knew he would have to reveal it all eventually, but not yet.

"Too bad we don't know someone important we could ask." Rantham looked at Wil pointedly.

Mung winced. "I don't know what you're getting at, but Father never discussed work… at least not with me."

"What I'm getting at is the remarkable string of coincidences here. First, we receive orders at the last possible moment that we're to train a new Echoman, who just happens to be the son of Wiliamund Azimuth the Third, distinguished member of the Ministry's Board of Foreign Relations."

"Coincidence number two," he continued, ticking his points off on his fingers. "Our good Captain and her Whip are advised of the prospect of discovering a continent most don't know exist, and even given a map - origins unknown - to help them locate it."

"Three: while taking on water and stores in Thunder Bay, we're joined by a bloody Unbound. We all know that they don't take random cruises to see the world, and since we weren't supposed to be making port in any other harbors, it seems clear he wasn't just looking for a ride - oh and I suppose it bears mentioning that both the Captain and the Whip have had their heads so far up his arse you'd think he was shitting gold - no offense meant," he added hastily in Biiko's direction.

The color drained from Wil's face. "If you're suggesting that I was some part of a - of a conspiracy -"

"That's exactly what I'm suggesting, Mung. The Ministry knew precisely where this place was, and what's more, they knew *what* it was, and they deliberately didn't tell us about it because -"

Triistan cleared his throat and held up his hands. "Please, let me work through the story in order, and I promise your questions will be answered in good time. I will come back to who knew what, exactly, and then you can judge for yourself, Rantham."

Rantham made a disgusted sound, so Triistan pushed on. He picked up his story where they'd found their supply boat ransacked the following day and suspected the troop of graybole monkeys. He told them of the chilling roar they had heard several times, though he didn't tell them what it was right away.

Retelling the tale from memory was better than reading from his journal, though he still felt as if he was skirting a bog, treading cautiously along a treacherous shore that pulled and sucked at his every step. For the moment he was keeping the experience and emotions at arm's length, but there was no telling when he might fall into the murky water. He looked for more solid, stable footing in parts of the tale the others had already been told; the parts the survivors had agreed to share when they returned from the expedition. Judging from their expressions, his companions were being drawn in as well; he even caught Voth, with all his talk of disrespect and mutiny, listening with rapt attention.

Triistan spent time describing the Reavers and how they interacted during those first few days, particularly his early observations of the relationship between Captain Vaelysia and Commander Tchicatta. He remembered being surprised at how much respect and leeway she had afforded him. Most of the *Peregrine's* crew had known little of their grim escort or his men, and Triistan felt a strong need to tell their story. Most people considered Reavers as something less than citizens, barely above the level of slaves or pit-fighters. Safely out of earshot, they referred to them as "scrubs", criminals who'd had their memories erased through reformative scrubbing, then given a chance at redemption through military service for the Corps. But Triistan had come to know them, and if the Firstblade and his comrades were any indication, the Reavers were badly misunderstood. He wanted to share this with his fellow survivors, perhaps as a way for him to acknowledge the sacrifices they had made.

Eventually, he came to his entry describing the approach to Rivergate. The mental footing grew more perilous.

He turned his journal around so that they could see his illustration of Ahbaingeata. The remaining five dugouts they had built to travel upriver were in the foreground, drawn up on a grassy shore and laden with supplies. Leading away towards the center of the rendering, the banks of the river were roughly sketched, thick with overhanging foliage that seemed to stretch out over the water to either side, like grasping hands waiting for the boats to dare their passage. The river itself ran true until it reached the foot of a massive stone structure, a barbican stretching from one end of the narrow river canyon to the other, towering well above the forest canopy. The rolling, indistinct mass of shadows and half-sketched trees that depicted the jungle ran hard up against the wall, stretching random tendrils up its sides, but unable to reach the crenellated battlements far above.

The river ran from a huge arch in the wall's midpoint, where its surface bubbled and frothed over and around the wreckage of a pair of twisted, shattered gates. They dwarfed their surroundings, suggesting that they had not been built by men. That portion of the illustration was drawn with considerable detail, and Triistan remembered how it had pulled at the expedition's collective focus, like the inexorable current approaching a waterfall. They had grown quiet and subdued, each wondering not only who had built them, but what could have caused so much damage to such an immense structure. He knew now, of course, but he wasn't ready to tell his fellow survivors just yet. As his old teacher, Doyen Rathmiin, used to say, "If you tell me the end first, boy, there's no point in saying anything else."

He told them of the attack of the kongamatu swarm and their first two losses, Welms and Jaegus, carefully avoiding the grisly details as he tried to block out the memory of their dismemberment. He was only partially successful.

He moved abruptly to the party's flight into Ahbaingeata, describing how they were forced below by the arrival of the apex jharrl and its pack mates. Trying to maintain his forward progress, he began describing in detail the incredible scale and complexity of the Rivergate.

For help, he turned to the illustration he'd made for the Expedition. This was good, solid ground, and he felt a surge of pride as he looked at it. The cut-away view was one of his best, showing the structure in profile, with most of the outer wall removed, allowing him to depict what was inside. He showed them the huge wall, the valley floor on both sides, the great hall they had discovered at the end of the tunnel with its magnificent waterfalls and statues, the mountain of rubble and a long, sloping ravine on the far side of the collapse.

"What in the Endless Dark is that thing?" Wil asked, pointing to Triistan's rough outline of the desiccated armaduura shell. The question triggered a memory so strong it was as if it were happening all over again:

Wrael was standing at the edge of the thing's severed tail, looking back down the hole they had just emerged from, and favoring Triistan with a rare grin. "Well, Titch, looks like you were right. But I still feel like shit."

He glanced down at the drawing, smiling faintly. "That was the back door."

He guided them through the rest of the rendering, pointing out the significant elevation change from the floor of the river valley they had followed in from the coast, up to the highlands on the south-east side of the wall. A cliff separated the two, close to two hundred and fifty feet high, and the wall had covered the cliff face and risen another three hundred feet beyond that. Because of its size, it had hidden the dramatic elevation change from the expedition's vantage point on the lowland side. The tunnel had stretched well past the wall itself, bending gradually upwards until it joined the great chamber where the carcass of a gigantic creature called an armaduura had lain amidst the rubble of a massive cave-in, providing a conduit for the river they had named the Glowater. By the time they emerged from the husk's ravaged tail, they had climbed nearly six hundred feet in all.

"And this...?" Wil swept a finger across the top of the drawing, where Triistan had sketched a series of vague shapes: rectangles and columns, arches, stairs, trees, pyramids and spires. They stretched from the wall over to the armaduura's damaged tail where it protruded from a lake or large pool.

"That is Ostenvaard, Stronghold of the Forgotten."

There was a clamor of excited questions, mostly from Wil and Rantham, but he raised his hands again. "Please, I'll explain everything in time. But you have to give me a chance to tell it in the proper order. Please, be patient. I just… just give me time."

Triistan pointed back to the base of the wall, where he had drawn the mouth of Ahbaingeata and the pile of debris blocking it.

"As I said, we were driven through here, over the top of a massive pile of debris that had built up over the years, caught up by the twisted remains of the portcullis. It was a close thing, caught between the devil seam and the deep Dark. Nobody knew if or when the kongamatu would return, or the size and strength of the pack following our scent..."

Captain Vaelysia's voice echoed in his mind: *"This expedition will continue upriver. There is far too much at stake here, and I'll not have it said that the crew of the SKS Peregrine couldn't stomach a bit of danger for the sake of making history. Make no mistake: we WILL go through that tunnel, lads..."*

The gaping black maw of Ahbaingeata yawned in Triistan's mind's eye. He thought he caught a whiff of the wet, mildewy air emanating from below, laced with a hint of something else. He shuddered involuntarily, and with alarming abruptness and force, he was suddenly back there, picking his way down the side of the debris pile, the others in a sinuous line out in front of him and behind him.

He could feel Biiko's implacable presence at his back, and knew that Jaspins, Taeylia and Creugar formed the rear van.

A massive, vaulted chamber rose all around them, lit faintly by the ghostly luminescence of the river gurgling below. When the Captain commanded them to light their torches, the flickering orange glow reached the barrel-vaulted ceilings, revealing the murder holes that peppered it, as well as the telltale signs of struggle. He saw the slagged and blackened stone, whole sections of wall and timbers pulled down, revealing the chambers and passages that had given defenders access to their breastworks. And within their crouching shadows, he saw the malevolent glitter of thousands of tiny eyes...

"Triis? Are you alright?"

Drey's voice pulled him back. "Sorry, just lost myself in the memory is all." He cleared his throat self-consciously. "Ah... sorry, where was I?"

"You were describing Rivergate and the tunnel beneath the wall. Then you sort of blanked out, mumbling something about 'eyes'. Was there something in the tunnel?"

He nodded. "Nests... we found the kongamatu nests. There was rubble - great piles of it where sections of the tunnel had collapsed. Stone and timbers - but on such a scale you can't... you just can't imagine it. Some of the piles blocked the tunnel and had to be scaled. As we picked our way up one of these, gods, the stench..."

Something long and serpentine, with dozens of spidery legs, skittered across Triistan's hand. He pulled it back and shook it in revulsion. Glancing down, he nearly lost his footing as he saw dozens more like it crawling through the wreckage...

He shook his head to rid himself of the vision. "Above the pile we could see into the chambers beyond, which the Oathguard - sorry, the original occupants - must have used to access their defenses - murder holes, arrow slits... the tunnel was riddled with them.

"But what I had first taken to be treasure of some kind were actually eyes reflecting our torches - hundreds of nesting kongamatu, right above our heads. They seemed to be asleep, but their eyelids somehow reflected the light. Probably some kind of trick to ward off predators."

He drew a deep, unsteady breath. "Anyway, we had to crawl, single file, directly beneath the opening in the ceiling. Most of us had crossed through and started down the other side... we thought we were safe. The 'matu hadn't so much as flapped a wing."

"But they weren't alone." He swallowed and turned the pages of his journal to his study of one of the kongamatu, reversing it so that they could see.

"You probably recognize this - they could be cousins to the birds that nest along the southern cliffs of Sitsii and Khigongo, though they're larger and fiercer than the matu we know. The nesting matu looked different - softer, somehow, and smaller, with swollen abdomens in most cases. But as I was crossing beneath the nest, something else attacked us. Something... I don't know, unnatural..."

"Unnatural?" Wil echoed.

"Yes, like... like it didn't belong on Ruine... or more like it had been cobbled together from parts of other creatures and grown to monstrous size. Part insect, part lizard... with a tail like the manticore's stinger. It was deadly fast, and nearly took my leg off." For emphasis, he lifted up his grimy trouser leg to show them the scar that spiraled around his calf.

He then told them of their ensuing battle with more of the creatures, which they had taken to calling 'nest guardians'. He described the way the Reavers had fought, their incredible courage and coordination. He recounted how Taelyia had been killed, impaled on one of the things' tail-spikes and smashed to bits, and how he had asked for her sword afterwards to honor her. That was the moment he had started to change inside. He remembered feeling guilty and selfish watching others putting themselves in harm's way to protect the rest of the party.

"She shouldn't just be forgotten," he told them at the time. But there was something else as well: a strong sense of familiarity when he'd picked up Taelyia's sword, an overwhelming feeling that it was right. As if he'd held the weapon before, or one like it, which was ridiculous. He'd never wielded a sword in his life.

He shook himself and straightened. He needed a break. By now it was late afternoon, and the first of Ruine's twin suns was hovering above a dark line of clouds creeping up from the horizon. He hoped they would be able to take another reading of the stars before the clouds reached them, but the Long Evening was still a full watch away.

He gave out some perfunctory orders and told them he would continue after dinner, then retrieved the azimuth and climbed quickly up to the crow's nest. Dreysha followed him up not long after, once she had finished making the adjustments he'd requested. She left Wil to prepare their supper. It was one of the few jobs they had entrusted to him, and although the grimace of disgust never quite left his face, he was surprisingly good at it.

"You okay?"

"What do you mean?" He tried to duck the question. "With what?"

"You know with what - you look like a vosk has your balls in its teeth trying to tell that story. Is this about breaking your promise?"

He shook his head and turned the azimuth over in his hands, avoiding her gaze. "No, it isn't that - not anymore."

Dreysha just looked at him expectantly, until he was forced to continue. "Honestly, I think I'm a bit relieved at not having to carry all of this around inside any longer, and I think it's important that we all know the truth."

"Then what is it? What's bothering you?"

He lifted his head and looked her in the eye. "I'm afraid, Drey."

"Of what?"

"It's hard to… to go back there, to relive those moments. That's why I stopped reading from the journal and just told the story as I remembered it. There's just something about reading my entries directly - I don't know, it's like I am there all over again. I thought if I just recited the story from memory, skimmed over parts, it would be better. It was, at first, but I can't… I can't..."

As he trailed off, she reached up a hand to touch his cheek. "Triis… it's over, it's just a story now, just memories. Maybe you -"

"No, that's what you don't understand. It isn't over - and it's not 'just memories', not for me. It's real, like I'm there. I've been fighting it since we returned from the expedition. Writing and drawing in my journal helped - a lot, actually. Over time, I gained control over it, locked it away. But now I'm opening that lock again and I don't know what will happen."

His voice dropped to a whisper and he took her hand in his. "It wasn't just what we saw. There are parts I didn't record in the journal, even though the Captain commanded me to include everything. We - I… did things… terrible things, Drey. We had to for survival, and for mercy's sake, but-"

She cut him off, her voice tight, impassioned. "Listen to me, Triistan. I don't give a titch monkey's balls what you did. We've all done things we're ashamed of, believe me, I've written that tale more than I'd care to admit. But sometimes that is what life requires of us to

- 50 -

survive." She placed both of her hands on his face now, pulling him closer. "Whatever you did, I'm sure you had a good reason, and I for one am grateful for it, because you're here, with me now. That's what we do, what we are. We survive, Triis." She paused.

"Want to know what I think?"

He gave her a faint smile. "No, but I'm sure you're going to tell me anyway."

"I think you have to face this. When you've run as hard and as far as you can, but the dogs are still at your heels, the only option left is to turn and fight them. Maybe you have to go through it, share it with someone else so that you're not carrying the burden by yourself."

He studied her face, chewing on the inside of his cheek while he considered her words. "I don't know… I've been carrying it around for so long, alone… "

She stepped closer, pressing her body against him and lifting her face to his. "You're not alone, Triistan Halliard. Not anymore."

She rose up on her toes and he bent to kiss her, hard. She responded eagerly, hungrily, moaning low in the back of her throat. He worried that she would feel his arousal, until she reached down and squeezed him and then he didn't care about anything but her touch, her mouth, her body -

"Ahoy the crow's nest!" called an overly-cheerful voice from below.

They pulled apart, panting heavily.

"Mung!" Dreysha made his name sound like a curse. "I'm going to gut that annoying little bastard and feed his insides to his bloody monkey!" Triistan couldn't help grinning.

"Is there something important you require, Mister Azimuth?" he called down.

"Aye, sir! Just thought you might like to know that supper is ready!"

Dreysha's eyes met his, her lips curling suggestively. "I'm tired of fish. I've something else in mind for supper… "

She unlaced the front of his breeches, and the cool touch of her hand made him gasp, half from pleasure and half from panic.

"But we'll be seen," he protested weakly. Dreysha smirked and slowly leaned out over the side, her hands never leaving him.

"Coming in just a moment… "

She had been absolutely right: there were much better moments to let stretch on forever.

- 4 -

The Ghostvale

"This is the one we captured, Commander."

The prisoner was draped from head to knee in loose sand-colored cloth. At first it looked to be a simple hooded cloak, but what could easily be mistaken for folds, turned out to be more complex layers which allowed for a great range of motion without betraying that coverage. Just understanding this brilliant, versatile concealment explained much about how they had remained undetected up until now.

Casselle had been standing bored in Lord Richard Lockewood's command tent for some time when the Thundering Lance sentries abruptly brought the stranger to him. She noticed that the captive's hands were loosely bound before her.

"I wasn't captured, I came of my own accord," the woman corrected.

Both Lockewoods were there, as were Casselle's Captain and Commander. The other few were people she had only just become acquainted with.

"I believe her," spoke up the smiling black-haired soldier seated at a nearby table, her long legs propped up on its edge. Commander Arren Lockewood had previously introduced her as Indalia Nox, the Lance's Scoutmaster. Nox carved off a slice of apple with a wicked looking knife. She had an array of them on her belt and she struck Casselle as someone who would welcome others to assume many other blades were concealed elsewhere on her person.

Arren dismissed the guards, who left the way they came, glaring at the prisoner with distrust before disappearing out the front and into the night.

"My company has taken to calling you 'Sand Ghosts'," Richard said.

"They wouldn't be the first."

"After kidnapping nearly a dozen of my sentries without a trace, I was beginning to wonder if the name was more accurate than I cared to admit." Richard put down the paper he had been reviewing. He looked the cloaked woman over as he stood up from the table.

"Your people are alive. They will be returned to you once you leave," she offered without prompt.

"You mean, if I leave," Richard said.

"If you do not leave, they will die, as will you," she replied calmly. Her accent was odd. Casselle thought it felt old, in a way she couldn't quite understand.

"I'm not here to die, or to leave. I wish to talk to the Khaliil," Richard replied. "I wish to enter the Ghostvale to speak with them."

"The Vale is dead. If you wish to speak to ghosts, you may save me the effort and cut your own throat," she answered. Next to Casselle, she heard Greffin Ardell "hrumph" in response. She was not entirely sure why the two of them were there, but Templar Commander Cohl made it clear that one of the Lockewoods had insisted on them representing the Laegis for strategic discussions. Casselle wasn't sure if she had been requested specifically, but she wasn't going to argue with her Captain.

Before the cloaked stranger had been brought before them, there had been a lot of discussion about what might happen when they reached Ghostvale. There had been an equal amount of speculation that it might never happen, given their lack of luck over the last week. If the prisoner before them spoke truly, it might now no longer even be an option.

"You seem very determined to guard something you insist no longer exists." The man speaking had been introduced as Theander Kross, one of the Order of Veda. Known to most people as the Ashen, the Order was a group of scholars famously known to practice the magic of the Young Gods. Like the Laegis, Richard had also recruited a small group of Ashen to accompany the Lance on this excursion. Theander was their leader, a physically imposing figure easily as tall as Richard - certainly not the appearance one would expect of an academic. The one thing that did seem to fit was his somber colored coat; with its deep hood, it looked more like a priest's garments than a simple travelling outfit.

"The Khaliil remember. We preserve the remains. You are not welcome there."

"The Khaliil survive better than you would have us believe," contradicted Richard. "You have artists in Minethia, merchants in Strossen, explorers aboard Seeker vessels… they must come from somewhere."

"Small tribes wander the Wasting, the rest…"

"The rest wander to find a new home," Richard finished. The woman's eyes narrowed under her hood. "I've heard that line from many Khaliil before you and though you may convince others, I know better. Before you try to pull another lie from underneath that fabulous jiisahn of yours, consider this: I know you will never willingly acknowledge this or agree to take me to see the Vale without consulting the Voice of One first."

The cloaked lady did not move, but Casselle saw a flash of recognition in her eyes.

"Tell them the Gods are dead, but their blood is not. They should know better than most. Then give them this." Richard took something from around his neck and handed it to her. She reached up with a single hand to receive it, the bonds that had tied her wrists together moments ago now missing.

"I promise nothing," came the reply, while the item and her hand vanished from sight. Giving another look around the room, her eyes lit on Greffin and Casselle.

"Het Laegis, yiin?" she asked, her odd accent sounding more at ease with the ancient words.

Casselle nodded in affirmation. Without bothering to see if there was more to discuss, the cloaked lady turned and walked to the door. Arren Lockewood looked as if he might try to stop her, but his father laid a restraining hand on his arm. She was gone before anyone could say anything more.

"What was that she asked you?" Arren addressed Casselle.

"She was asking if we were Laegis," Greffin replied.

"You have your own language?"

"It doesn't belong to them exclusively, but like them, it's from long ago, a relic of the past," Richard answered. "If you like, I can teach it to you someday."

Arrogant bastard, Casselle thought. If anyone in the room was a relic, it was Richard, caught up in some crusade he'd invented for himself before the Ehronfall, or even the Godswar itself.

"Is that why we were called here?" Greffin asked bluntly, pointing after the Sand Ghost.

"That was merely a fortunate coincidence," Richard replied, "but now we can confidently prepare for what is to come next."

"The Ghostvale?" Theander asked.

"Yes. They will be back and will invite a small number of us to follow them there. You're all here because I want you to be part of that group."

"You seem pretty sure of yourself that they won't say no. Or they won't drag us halfway to nowhere and just try to kill us all," Nox commented, seeming very much amused by herself.

"They're reclusive, but not bloodthirsty." Richard poured himself a cup of water from a pitcher on the same table Nox's boots happened to be resting on.

"Just the six of us?" Theander asked.

"Not quite. Arren already knows he'll stay here with the Lance," Richard said while his son nodded reflexively in agreement. "Indalia and you and I will be escorted by Captain Ardell's squad. I've already confirmed this with Commander Cohl."

"I'd like to bring Master Oolen with me," the arxhemist said.

"No. We're only going to get away with bringing as many as this because they are Laegis," Richard said. "The Khaliil will respect their unit cohesion." At that moment Casselle did not feel comfortable being a small cog in Lord Lockewood's larger scheme, the purpose of which still remained unclear. Theander took it slightly better, nodding in assent.

"When we get there, we may be asked to split up. Politely accept whatever they request. Be on your best behavior. Know that the Khaliil are not our enemies. They are not necessarily our friends yet, but they are most certainly not our adversaries," Richard stressed. "Hopefully by the time we leave, if they are not yet allies, at least we will have made good strides towards that goal."

"Allies for your master plan?" Theander asked, with a healthy amount of skepticism in his voice. Richard replied with a cold stare.

"The Young Gods are dead. The Children of Tarsus must grow up: they can afford to be childish no longer. The Elder Circles that govern the cities and towns of our civilizations were local authorities, but the Gods held the final word in things. In their absence, they are a stopgap measure at best. They are already being tested to their limits."

Casselle didn't like Richard's condescension, but she had seen the unrest firsthand. As much as she hated to admit it, he wasn't entirely wrong.

"You may think I like meddling with such things, but I only do so because to do nothing invites further disaster."

"If the H'Kaan were ready to catch us unprepared, don't you think they would have done so by now?" Nox asked.

"You're asking me to understand the mind of a demon? Aren't I busy enough trying to keep civilization from collapsing while simultaneously making provisions to thwart Maughrin's return? That is enough to keep me busy without adding idle conjecture," Richard replied. "For now, we concentrate on the matter at hand. I intend to be prepared, even if I have to drag along the rest of the world behind me."

***

The missing sentries showed up the following morning, followed by two cloaked Khaliil. The freed captives appeared fine, but acted disoriented, as if just having awoken from a deep sleep. They were taken away for care while the Khaliil were taken to Richard Lockewood's tent.

Casselle's squad was already preparing for the journey ahead by the time Commander Cohl showed up, followed by Sergeant Duran Holst, Lennard Torks and Jonn Kettel. Holst would command the remaining three squads of the Shield Templar's in Ardell's absence, helped by Torks and Kettel.

"I'm here to tell you everything you already know, Captain, as is my job," Zan Cohl said. Just behind them, Captain Ardell's team was securing the equipment they would take with them. Casselle assisted each one, tightening a loose strap here or a stray cord there.

"Get on with it, then," Greffin said as Casselle fell into rank behind him alongside Temos Pelt, Finn Archer and Jhet Anlase.

"I place you under the command of Richard Lockewood. You will do as he instructs as long as it is in accordance with, and does not betray the rules and ethics of the Laegis Templars. Upon your return, you will resume the standard chain of command and deliver a report of your activities to the ranking Laegis officer," Commander Cohl instructed.

"You planning on going somewhere?" Greffin asked.

"Do you understand your orders as I have explained them, Captain?" Cohl asked, not bothering to answer the jibe. Much to his credit, Captain Ardell pulled to attention and saluted with his fist clenched tightly against his chest.

"Understood and acknowledged, Commander. En'vaar et Laegis."

"To the bitter end, Captain," Cohl replied with a smile. "Be safe out there."

"Aye," Ardell answered his superior officer. Turning to Holst and his Veterans he added: "You old horses think you can keep the wagon moving with just three wheels?"

Kettel and Holst nodded. Torks told the Captain to bring back something pretty from the Ghostvale.

"I'm sure I can find a lovely lady or two worthy of such an exotic gift," Torks added with a smile and a wink.

"You should ask us to bring back perfume," Temos said, "at least that will cover up the smell of your patronizing horse shit."

Torks looked like he took a slap to the face as his friends broke out laughing. Even Captain Ardell, who was thought to have a mostly permanent scowl, managed to crack a slight smile.

"You'd best get moving," Commander Cohl said.

"Aye," Greffin acknowledged, "best we do."

"It's not just me, is it?" Temos asked Casselle in a whisper. She gave him a reassuring pat on the back.

"Not just you," she affirmed as they walked out of the Templar section of camp on their way to Lord Lockewood's tent.

"Even if I didn't come from a family with four sisters I'd like to think I'd agree with you," Finn chimed in. Jhet said nothing, but was nodding in agreement. He tended to talk less than she did, which she had previously thought was impossible. It was something she found herself respecting him greatly for.

It would have been impossible to miss Lockewood's tent, even if they hadn't previously been there. Almost every soldier kept glancing in that direction, hoping to catch sight of one of the "Sand Ghosts" they'd been talking about for the past week. Casselle thought them to be a slightly gossipy, disorganized bunch, but she could not argue with one thing: they were prepared.

Whereas the Templars had tried to improvise improvements to their own uniforms in an effort to stave off the harsh conditions of the Wasting, every member of the Thundering Lance had been provided properly tailored dustcoats made of thin, lightly colored cloth to keep them cool under the sun. Each coat had attachable hoods and veils designed to help keep out the sand and dust. She considered this detail to planning as she thought of the trip ahead. Perhaps it had only been one of Lockewood's quartermasters that had thought of this, but she would not be surprised if it came from the man himself. She did not like to admit it, but he did always seem to be one step ahead. His soldiers may have appreciated it, but it made her worry.

His plans, frankly all plans, are based on assumptions. Some assumptions bred by observation and study, others by intuition. Regardless, assumptions were never conclusive until they happened or not. Certainly he couldn't be so arrogant as to never expect his well laid plans to fail.

She shifted uncomfortably under the weight of her own concerns and the actual armor resting on her shoulders. The Templar were taught to endure, but her leather armorjack was hot and stifling under the naked suns above. While she understood that patience and endurance were virtues, she also knew she would feel much better about them if virtues could at least keep the sand out of her teeth.

Casselle saw the cloaked Khaliil standing alongside the Lockewoods. Indalia Nox and Theander Cross were nearby, as well as a large contingent of Lance guardsmen that didn't bother hiding their resentment; the Khaliil may have returned their captive comrades, but it was clear the injury to the Lance's pride was festering.

"Captain Greffin Ardell, reporting as assigned," the Templar Captain said as he brought his squad to a halt just in front of the tent.

"This is too many." It was the same woman from yesterday, Casselle noted.

"There are only three of us. Officially the Laegis are not part of my army," Richard said. The woman looked to her companion and then the two of them leaned close, exchanging words.

"Do you serve this one?" the other Ghost asked, pointing to Richard. Her voice was husky and her accent heavy.

"We serve the High Houses," Greffin replied, "or what's left of their memory. We've been asked to help him. As long as that means we do what's best for all, that's what we'll do." Casselle thought that sounded like an accurate, if slightly truncated explanation of their duties. The Young Gods had been tasked to defend all of Ruine against the Demon Dragon Maughrin and her endless spawn, the H'Kaan. The Young Gods were powerful, but they were not abundant. The Laegis Templars became the army they needed. They were supposed to defend everyone against greater evils.

After the Godswar, the Templar remained. Though depleted, they did what they could to help. With no real sighting of the H'Kaan since the Ehronfall, "help" was usually limited to keeping order in cities and patrolling roads for brigands. Though she didn't agree with

Richard Lockewood, she was hoping that his offer to "save the world" wasn't just hollow rhetoric for consolidating his own power. She believed in the Laegis. She didn't want to believe they could stand for something less.

The two Sand Ghosts conferred in their own language.

"They may come," one finally snapped.

"Then we are ready to go," Richard said.

***

The suns were halfway to the top of the sky before the group stopped for the first time. The Khaliil, still mostly an enigma wrapped in their elaborate outfits, had called the stop, much to the squad's relief. The Laegis huddled a few feet away from the others and Casselle accepted the waterskin that Temos passed around.

"I don't understand how he doesn't look winded at all."

Temos was talking about Lockewood, who looked just as fresh and rested as when they left the camp earlier in the morning. Out of all of them, he was wearing the most, carrying the most and certainly talking the most to his companions.

"He's Vanha," Finn grunted, accepting the waterskin.

"That only means he's part God," Temos said, "and even they could bleed. I assumed that meant they would sweat as well."

"Odegar would sweat," Casselle said.

"Kross is Vanha, too," Greffin added. "He sweats plenty." The Captain swished some water around in his mouth before spitting it out.

"Don't waste it," Temos moaned. Greffin shot him an angry look.

"Sir," Temos added quickly. "Don't waste it, sir."

"Better," Ardell grumbled.

"How far do you think we are from camp?" Finn Archer asked. Jhet held up three fingers.

"Three leagues?" Jhet held his hand flat before tilting it back and forth slightly.

"Three leagues give or take," Finn confirmed.

"Certainly long enough to be out of sight of the camp," Temos said. He leaned in and dropped his voice to a whisper. "Do you think they tried to follow us?"

"I don't see how that's possible," Finn replied. "It's empty and open. Where would you hide?" Jhet chuckled at that answer.

"What?"

Jhet nodded his head towards the Khaliil. Finn turned to look, as did the others.

There were now six of them. Four more had just appeared from nowhere.

"How? Where?"

"They're Ghosts, Templar Archer. What'd you expect?" Greffin replied calmly, watching as Richard and his companions noticed the same thing. They appeared as unfazed as Captain Ardell, continuing their own conversation as the Khaliil talked among themselves.

"We must be close, then," Temos said.

"I don't think we are," Greffin said. "I don't think they'd let us get close enough that we could stumble upon it so easily, less than half a day's march from our camp."

Jhet nodded and Casselle was inclined to agree with them. The four new arrivals moved towards an unremarkable sand dune a few hundred feet away.

When she watched the dune collapse, she almost wasn't surprised: it was the kind of thing she had begun to expect from the Khaliil. She was shocked, however, when they drove back three sleds, each of them drawn by horse sized lizards.

They were not tall, but they moved quickly, long tails slithering in concert with short legs making wide strides. They seemed to glide almost effortlessly across the sand, drawing just short of the group. They were colored dull brown and yellow, with pale red accents around the eyes and lines or spots down the spine.

"They're vosks," Temos said in awe.

"I thought vosks were from Valheim? From the North?" replied Finn.

"So did I, but they're certainly a type of vosk... I mean based on drawings I've seen."

Casselle took Temos' word for it. He was a trapper's son. He was the one fascinated by animals. If he said they were vosks, she was inclined to believe him.

"I've never heard of anyone taming vosks," Ardell said.

"Maybe the ones from Valheim are angry and untamable because it's so rutting cold all the time," Temos offered. The discussion was cut off by Richard Lockewood, who was waving the Templars to join them at the sleds.

Ardell led the walk over, his one good eye squinting suspiciously at the large reptiles. They appeared patient, even relaxed despite their bondage, only occasionally shifting their long-toed feet in the sand. Casselle had heard vosks were bristling with poisonous fangs and deadly claws, but these looked little different in appearance from the thin green skinks she'd seen occasionally around her home, albeit much larger.

"We will take these from here," explained the female Khaliil that had left camp with them that morning. Aside from slight variations in height, their obscuring garments made them almost indistinguishable from one another. There was no way that could be a coincidence. Casselle recognized her by her accent, but was trying to pin down other differences, like her wide bright blue eyes that looked out from between the layers of beige cloth around her head. "Three per sled. It will be cramped."

The bundles on the sleds were unloaded, leaving space for Richard's entourage and the Templars to fit in their stead, but it was crowded nonetheless. Finn was the largest, and was paired with Jhet on a sled by themselves. Casselle shared the narrow space behind Greffin and Temos, one of the Khaliil taking a place behind them. The sleds were built to carry supplies comfortably, not people, especially not the number of people they'd brought with them.

Somehow they managed to get everyone seated, and the sleds got underway, the three drivers calling to the vosks while they lightly snapped the reins. After pushing the handles of the sled until it got up to speed, the Khaliil stood on the runners, behind the living cargo seated awkwardly before them.

They left three of the Sand Ghosts behind, almost immediately lost to sight as the sleds dipped down a long slope. At first, she thought it was part of the gradual rise and fall of the desert, but rocky ledges began to take shape beside them, indicating they were dipping into a deeper ravine. It was hard to see around Temos and Greffin, and the further they went, the harder it became to see anything as the walls reached up and over them, closing on top of them and strangling out most of the daylight.

Mercifully, it was cooler here and the sting of the suns and sand was totally absent. The sled rocked and jostled as the vosk pulled it ever forward. She should be nervous, terrified of what might happen were the sled to turn over, but she felt completely at ease listening to the echoing refrain of the sleds shifting and sliding on the ground beneath them.

It didn't last forever, though. Soon enough there was light, and shortly after that, the sleds were on the surface again, skating across the sands at a brisk pace. The terrain was slightly different here. Instead of the flat plains of sand they had encountered at the Fracture's end, there were rocky hills and columns of sand-bleached stone. The columns did not tower over them, but they were still tall enough to cast deep shadows on the ground.

The vosks moved on, effortlessly carrying them further from the relative safety of the camp, into the hidden depths of the Wasting.

***

The second time they stopped was during the Long Evening, when Ruine's first sun had already dipped beneath the horizon, but before the dull red second sun retreated as well. The Khaliil circled the sleds and while two of them dug out a small fire pit for use, the third set up one of the collapsible domes that the Khaliil had engineered from the same cloth as their travelling clothes, making them look like sand dunes when complete. One of these could have been set up mere feet from the camp and it would have probably gone undetected. Even now that she knew what to look for, it was still nearly invisible.

The vosks slipped inside and Casselle caught a glimpse of the interior as she brushed the sand from her clothing. The lizards appeared quite at home coiled and stacked on top of each other, quietly resting before the next day's run. Once a flap on the dome was secured, they disappeared altogether.

Each Laegis carried their own provisions, enough for a day, and although the vosks had done most of the work, Casselle was hungry. She worked through the jerked beef and trail bread they'd been given by the Lance's Cookmaster. Finn was happy to finish up Jhet's leftovers, of which there were plenty. The man seemed to subsist mostly on blade oil, as Temos was fond of saying, watching as he inspected his swords while the rest of them ate. She suspected he might be embarrassed to reveal his scars in front of others, but kept quiet about it. If it was something he didn't want to speak about, she didn't feel it was her place to say something either.

The Khaliil sat close together, sharing bits of dried fruit and nuts and consuming some unknown mix of food wrapped in a thin, flat bread. More interesting than any of that, however, was that this was the first time since she had met them that they had unwrapped their faces. The two men each had the sides of their head shaved, hair pulled back into a braided knot for one, a ponytail for the other, the color of each an unnatural gem tone. One was garnet colored, the other more like citrine; neither was overly bright, but both were wondrous.

The female Khaliil was even more striking. Like her male companions, the sides of her head were also clean-shaven, but her hair was a bright aquamarine, distinct strands of blue and green woven together from the top of her scalp to the back, where it ended in a short cascade that barely reached past the base of her skull.

Each of them was tattooed to a different degree. Tiny symbols and characters encircled the neck of the woman, hidden where her cloak still rested around her shoulders, but visible on at least one of her hands back up past the forearm. The red-haired man had ink over half of his face and the yellow haired man had been tattooed over every inch of visible skin, and probably all the parts unseen too, Casselle assumed.

After the initial shock, she found it more fitting than odd, and by the look of things, the amount of tattoos was related to their age, the woman being the youngest among them.

"Come, friends," Richard said aloud, breaking the silence of the Long Evening, "this trip should be about fellowship, let us sit together around the fire." He motioned to both the Templars and the Khaliil. They hesitated, but when Captain Ardell moved to find a space around the fire pit, the other Templars followed his lead. The Khaliil had a small discussion amongst themselves, then repositioned themselves next to Nox and Kross, completing the circle.

"Much better," Richard admitted. He turned to his companions.

"Perhaps we should take a moment to introduce ourselves in order to get to know each other better," he prompted.

"I am Theander Kross, a Master in the Order of Veda, of Talmoreth. I lead a small number of my fellow arxhemists that have been sent to aid and advise Lord Lockewood. Thank you for being our hosts in this inhospitable land." His words sounded sincere, but with his bald head exposed and his subtly golden eyes almost totally hidden by a thick and furrowed brow, he looked more severe and imposing than ever.

"Indalia Nox, Scoutmaster of the Thundering Lance's 1st Company." A black headband kept her raven hair back out of her eyes, which were wide, bright and constantly in motion, searching for details in everything. She had a graceful ease in her speech and motions that radiated confidence in herself and her abilities.

"Captain Greffin Ardell of the Laegis Templars," the Captain began, going on to introduce each member of the squad himself. Casselle, Jhet and Finn merely nodded as their names were spoken, but Temos felt it necessary to add a "hello there," as Greffin finished with him. There was a bit of tension in the air as they waited for the Khaliil to speak.

"I am Lorelen'nevrevan-lus Kha-nesre," spoke the woman with the aquamarine hair.

"Keles'thesreltan," said the man with the yellow braid.

"Nevet'chorither-ne," the red-haired man said, finishing the introductions.

"I've always been fascinated by the Khaliil and their names, perhaps you'd like to explain to our friends what they mean?" Richard inquired politely.

"No," Lorelen replied coldly. Richard, for the first time since Casselle had met him, looked shocked. It was an odd look for him.

"We know enough about you, Lord of the Locke Woods. We do not wish to be friends with you, to share with you or to have fellowship with you," she continued. When Keles reached over to put his hand on her shoulder, she brushed it off and gave him a burning look.

"Look, I'm not sure what you think you know, but we are guests..." Richard started.

"No," Lorelen interrupted sharply. "You are not guests. You have been allowed entrance to the Ghostvale out of respect for your ancestors, but you are most certainly not welcome there."

"Well, at least she's direct," Nox chuckled as Richard's face hardened. Casselle could tell he did not appreciate voices of dissent.

"We shall see when we get there," Richard said.

"Indeed we shall," Lorelen said before stalking away from the fire pit.

"Pardon us," Nevet said, before he and Keles moved away to join Lorelen. Richard watched, his jaw working the whole time. After a few moments of silence, he tersely recommended that they all get some rest for the coming day.

"This is going to be a much longer trip than I expected," Temos said in a quiet aside as the Templars also retreated to bunk down for the night.

"What do you think that was about anyway?" Finn asked. "They know about him? What did that mean?"

"Best not to worry about it," Captain Ardell said.

"But if they don't want him there and we're supposed to be helping him, couldn't that put us in a situation we don't want to be in? Like surrounded by hundreds of unfriendly Khaliil warriors?" Temos asked.

"They're going through a lot of trouble for this," Greffin said. "I think we'll be ok."

"But what if...?" Temos started, but Casselle put a hand on his arm. When their eyes met, she shook her head.

"Alright," he said, settling down like the others.

Greffin assigned watches for the night, which passed without incident, but as Casselle was awakened for her shift, which would take them into the morning, she noticed the Khaliil had done the same. She shared the early morning hours trying to avoid eye contact with Lorelen, who was also waiting for the twin suns to rise.

When morning finally came, they ate a quick breakfast and then the journey by sled continued, though the general mood seemed far more somber. When the vosks pulled to a stop leagues later, as the suns reached their zenith, it was clear the passengers had long since exhausted their patience for the ride.

"I feel like all the teeth have rattled right out of my head," Temos said, trying to work some circulation back into his lower legs.

"Are we actually there?" Finn asked, massaging a kink out of one of his large shoulders.

"We're there," Nox said. "Though I could understand why you wouldn't see it. Very clever."

Casselle tracked where Nox was looking at a random rock outcropping, part of a small jagged ridge that ran away from them into the distance. The three Khaliil moved towards the rock, and as they did, the rock seemed to fracture into discrete pieces.

More of the framed structures, Casselle noticed. Whereas the dome they used on the journey was the color of sand, this cloth was treated with some sort of plaster to make it look harder and painted expertly to resemble sand-bleached stone. The frames had been positioned to create a seamless barrier in front of a passage cut into the rock. Out of the rock came a number of new Khaliil, cloaked but not hooded, brightly colored hair bound or braided behind them, arms and faces marked with varying degrees of tattooed script and images.

The vosks were led away in one direction by some, sleds in another, while Lorelen motioned the group forward.

Keles and Nevet flanked either side of the entrance as Lorelen moved through the open portal into a darkened passage beyond. Captain Ardell took Jhet with him and followed directly after, signaling Casselle and the others to pull up the rear. The Captain had not bothered to check with Richard but treated him as they might any other person they would escort. Lord Lockewood appeared slightly annoyed in general, but he had been that way since last night's fireside snubbing, as far as she could tell.

He marched in after Greffin, trailed by Indalia Nox and Theander Kross. Casselle, Temos and Finn followed, leaving the hot mid-day suns behind them as they entered the cool darkness inside the rock.

There was no real time required for adjusting their eyes: although the passage appeared dark, small holes in the ceiling streamed in plenty of daylight. The stone corridor itself was cleanly hewn and sloped downward slightly for about a hundred feet before flattening out and widening into a larger room, dominated by four columns and a large, metal circle on the ground.

Lorelen motioned for them to stand in the middle, then she nodded to another Khaliil who had materialized from the shadows along the wall.

Ghosts indeed, Casselle thought as the second Khaliil acknowledged them and worked a couple levers set into the wall.

"Watch your footing," Lorelen said as the platform shuddered and shook before starting to move. Casselle stood stunned as the ground beneath them slowly descended, accompanied by the sound of chains and gears. She immediately thought of a well, and the platform as a giant bucket without sides, being lowered to something below. She heard the sound of rushing water and assumed they might be headed towards it, but she found instead it was running freely down the chains anchored against the four pillars extending down as far as the platform travelled.

It wasn't a quick trip, but they seemed to cover a significant depth, perhaps another fifty to sixty feet straight down before the platform shuddered and stopped. There was light ahead, an opening some twenty feet away. Beyond it was open sky. Lorelen moved the group forward.

The tunnel ended before a balcony that curved out and back twice, a set of lazy arches set sideways. Two Khaliil guards stood there with short spears and long knives, where a delicate railing prevented one from stepping out into open space.

The guards spoke tersely with their guide, who responded in kind, words Casselle couldn't understand. The guards stepped aside and motioned for them to move to the right side of the balcony.

"Move all the way to the front," Lorelen advised as she allowed them to file on first. Finn was the last of them, and Lorelen stepped onto the balcony after him. She helped the guards place an additional railing that closed off the balcony at their rear, but Casselle was distracted by something far more amazing.

Beyond the balcony, as far as she could see, was a long, deep valley, a verdant expanse between two canyon walls. She couldn't guess how deep or wide it was, but it felt larger than Strossen ever had. Stone pillars jutted up from the ground and water cascaded from a break somewhere below the balcony, disgorging a raging fall into a churning lake far below, obscured by heavy spray.

Light streamed in from above, breaking into a shower of colors on the mists below and dancing across the petals of wildly hued flowers that grew in the cracks and crevices of the valley walls.

She reflexively grabbed the railing as she felt the balcony shudder under her feet. She turned to watch as it slowly slid away from the edge of the cliff, where a second removable railing had been set, much like the one that blocked off the back of the balcony. As with the lift, the motion was mostly smooth, but they did not descend straight down: instead they moved at a slight angle, arches on the sides of the moving platform reaching up to grip at a thick cord above them, which Casselle had mistaken for a simple thick vine upon first glance. It was not rope or leather, but some sort of metal strands tightly twisted around each other. She could not imagine how such a thing could be accomplished on such a large scale. She caught Theander staring at it as well, similarly impressed.

A flight of small, colored birds flitted by, so close you could almost reach over the rail to touch them. In fact, the whole valley teamed with life: lizards nesting on shallow ledges, monkeys in treetops far below and glimpses of other beasts partially obscured by plants or shadows. It was a stark contrast to the barren, blasted terrain they had been surrounded by since leaving the Fracture.

Ahead of them, a platform grew larger as they approached. It was actually a series of buildings set on long poles anchored into rock pillars and ledges below them and supported by ropes strung from the sides of the valley. The architecture was open and light, all arches and thin walls. The basket appeared to be headed for a docking position similar to the one they had left.

As they crawled closer, Casselle noticed a great number of Khaliil on the arriving platform, most of them dressed similarly to the guards they had met at the top of the descent. Something felt wrong. There were too many guards here. But there was also nowhere to flee. Trying to leave the balcony was a suicidal drop several hundred feet down to the valley floor.

Captain Ardell tensed beside her. Though it looked as if his hand was casually resting on his belt, she saw him flex it several times, as if he might need to draw steel at any second. Temos and Finn were oblivious, but Jhet Anlase seemed aware of the tension. He kept his body relaxed, but his eyes were sizing up those ahead. It did not seem as if any of the guards on the platform were preparing to attack, but as the moving balcony drew to a stop, one of the Khaliil stepped forward.

"Richard Obed'enla of House Lockewood, you are being placed under arrest on the authority of the Voice of One for crimes against the High Houses."

"It's true then," Richard replied, dryly. "The Khaliil do remember."

- 5 -

Visitors

Triistan found it difficult to keep the ridiculous grin off of his face as he ate his supper.

His moment in the crow's nest with Dreysha had not lasted forever, unfortunately. In fact, it was over too soon, much to his chagrin. While he'd heard plenty of tales from his mates about docksies and the tricks of their trade, he had never had the pleasure of a personal experience. He was dumbfounded.

Immediately afterwards, he tried to apologize, feeling horribly embarrassed, but she would have none of it.

"Oh, stop your blubbering, Triis. From what I've seen, it's pretty common on the first go-round, especially with that... technique." She had then pulled close, dark eyes glinting from beneath half-closed lids. "But to be honest," she stretched up to whisper in his ear, her breath hot, "I think I could break an Unbound's will if I really tried."

Then she had kissed him lightly on the cheek and swung her leg over the side of the nest. "Let's go. I'm still hungry," she grinned.

"What? Wait! Shouldn't we... I mean, don't you want me to..." he trailed off miserably. Dreysha laughed.

"What, repay me in kind? Of course, but that will take time - you've a lot to learn and I don't yield so easily." She glanced down at the deck. "Besides, I'm certainly not going to hang my ass over the side while Mung and Voth watch. Don't worry, Twitchy Titch, I will come to collect your debt." With that, she swung her other leg over and slid down one of the ratlines to land with cats' feet on the main deck.

That had been the moment he realized - or at least, finally admitted to himself - that he was utterly in love with her. He could not wait to get her alone again. He wanted to do the same thing to her and wondered what it would be like, his mind wandering down --

"Halliard!"

He looked up to find everyone staring at him. Triistan made an effort not to glance at Dreysha, though he could see her smirking from the corner of his eye.

"Yes?"

"I asked if you'll be continuing your tale now," Rantham repeated.

"Uh, yes - yes as soon as we're done eating." *Damn.* It would be hours before he would get an opportunity to even speak privately again, let alone touch her. He grew anxious, worried that she might change her mind, or think he was ignoring her, or that he hadn't liked it -

OK, there is no WAY she could think you didn't like it. This is absurd, get ahold of yourself. He needed to finish his story of the Aarden Expedition before he would have any hope of another private moment with Dreysha, and even as that thought took shape, he realized how petty and selfish he was being. Besides the daunting task of just simply surviving long enough to be rescued, he carried on his person and in his head information that could quite possibly change the world - or at least forewarn that violent change was coming.

He sobered somewhat at those thoughts, and though the ache in his loins did not subside, the one in his chest did.

When you've run as hard and as far as you can, but the dogs are still at your heels... Whatever else may come of his encounter with Drey, he was going to take her advice and stop running from his memories. It would mean reliving everything that had happened, but if she was right, and the only way to leave it behind for good was to go all the way through, it was worth the pain.

He took his time finishing his meal while he composed his thoughts. The Crone succumbed to the veil of clouds he'd noted earlier, causing the wind to shift and swirl, plucking at the sails and their clothing with phantom fingers. The temperature dropped and the shadows cast by the rigging grew sharper where they crawled across the deck. He brushed his hands off on the legs of his threadbare breeches and stood.

"Alright, dogs, let's see what you're made of," he muttered under his breath, steeling himself to leave the shoreline and plunge straight into the bog he'd been trying to avoid for so long.

"So then, we left off at the battle with the nest guardians, yes?"

"Aye." Dreysha nodded towards his leg. "You were nearly skewered by one of those things' tails, so they patched you up right before the rest of them attacked. Fortunately they didn't hit anything vital."

He coughed and jumped straight into the narrative, hoping no one could see him blushing. "As soon as we'd slain the last of them, we set off again as quickly as possible. We had no idea how many more of those things might be out there, but we did know what would happen to us if the kongamatu swarm returned. The only way out was to go further in."

Creugar, Jaspins, grab her gear. Miikha, you'll take her place in the rearguard. Let's go.

He could hear the Firstblade's command clearly, could still see the pained stoicism with which Taelyia's comrades had stripped her mangled remains of pack and weapons and dumped what was left of her unceremoniously into the river.

He talked of their flight into the great hall, taking some deliberate pleasure in detailing the hall's magnificence. It was impossible not to feel that same overwhelming awe as he described the enormous statues, very similar to the huge one in the bay; the incandescent water cascading from wide scuppers carved in the likeness of the High Houses' sigils; and, of course, the wall of rubble and the great beast buried within.

He pointed to his rough outline of the creature in the cut-away diagram he had shown them earlier.

"It was called an 'armaduura', or armored giant. We found living ones later, but this was the first time any of us had ever seen such a monstrous, amazing creature." He described the scene effortlessly; even were his mind not already given to memorization, the image was so incredible that it had been indelibly seared into the memory of every member of the expedition.

Water trickled through the collapse in a thousand places, coating everything in the soft, blue-green glow. Only the thing's head, a foreleg, and part of its immense shell were exposed, but it was more than enough to convey its overwhelming size. The head was gigantic, with a broad, triangular cap of thick bone or cartilage, a prominent brow, and four curved horns emanating from either side, each twice as long as their tallest man. Its neck was twisted, so that the head lay partially on its side, propped up on a large broken slab as if it had fallen asleep there. The lowest side of its skull was submerged, the water glowing brightly around it - the telltale sign that had eventually led them to their way out...

Triistan launched into the return of the swarm, recounting their battle with the kongamatu in painstaking detail, including the loss of Pendal and the heroics of the others. When he described their escape through the armaduura carcass, Voth snorted in disbelief and muttered something about "self-indulgent fantasy".

But Triistan never heard him. By the time he brought them all through the massive husk, and climbed up the inside of its tail, he was no longer just telling a story: he could feel the spray of the water as it found its way past them, and see the glittering prisms all around as sunlight - golden, glorious, sunlight - rode the cascade down from somewhere above. When the expedition climbed up onto the atoll surrounding the armaduura's ragged tail, Triistan was there again, crying and dancing, singing and hugging right along with them.

***

It was close to moonrise later that same night, and Triistan was scrawling feverishly in his journal, intent on carrying out the Captain's orders and recording every scrap of detail surrounding their journey through Ahbaingeata. After swimming the short distance from the atoll to shore, the Aarden Expedition had set up a temporary camp adjacent to some kind of guard barracks. A tall, stone drum tower rose up from the tangled vegetation that grew around, over and into the barracks. After searching the base of the tower, they discovered that the only access was through a large door in the rear wall. It took them most of the day to clear the dense undergrowth and force the door open, but eventually they were able to get topside for a good look at the exotic landscape around them. The vantage point had helped Triistan confirm his assumptions of Ahbaingeata's design, in particular the use of the river passage and reservoir as a form of defense, and he had felt intensely proud of how accurate his diagram was.

He was sitting outside on the ground, leaning against the barracks wall, in order to take advantage of the light from the watchfire burning just a few paces away. Taelyia's kilij lay nearby in its scabbard. Biiko had just finished changing the dressing on his wounded leg and had gone back inside, where most of the crew was already asleep. Other than the sentry posted at the top of the tower, only Captain Vaelysia and Jaspins remained awake, here on the ground with him. They had been pacing impatiently around the perimeter of the camp since the end of the Long Evening, waiting for Commander Tchicatta. He had left to scout the ruined city shortly after mid-day, taking Miikha, Myles and Wrael with him. They were supposed to return by nightfall, but as of yet there had been no sign of them.

Occasionally, either the Captain or the Reaver lieutenant would stop and listen, as if they'd heard something, but with the jungle's infiltration into the city, its nocturnal denizens had moved in as well. Given the cacophony of cries, hoots, whistles, screams, grunts and snarls coming from the ruins, Triistan wondered whether they would have heard the Commander coming even if he'd ridden up on horseback.

Just before midnight, a drenching rain began suddenly, as it often did in the jungle. Triistan welcomed it at first, seeking relief from the oppressive humidity, even though he knew from experience that unless it were a major storm moving through, it would only grow muggier. Still, the first light shower felt cool on his skin. Even better, the din seemed to be subsiding as well, suppressed by the soft hiss of the rain. He closed his journal and lifted his face to it, enjoying the peaceful hush as it descended around them. Before long, the hiss grew to a roar and drove the three of them back into the barracks for cover. Their fire sputtered out soon after, and the night closed in.

Biiko joined them as they stood huddled together in the doorway, listening to the downpour as it hammered away across the uneven floor of the plaza. There were channels cut through the flagstones, bisecting the area in a wide grid pattern, which acted as gutters to help carry the water away. Earlier in the day he had noticed a drain with a twisted tangle of vines as thick as his waist growing from it. A heavy iron grate was barely visible at its center, and he wondered if the sewer system was completely choked with vegetation.

He soon had his answer as the plaza began to flood, and was thankful for the shelter the guardhouse provided. He wondered if the scouting party was tucked away in some similar place.

"Should I fetch a tor-" he began, but Jaspins placed her hand over his mouth. She pointed back out into the darkness.

"Storm and sea..." the Captain whispered beside him.

The impact of the heavy rain caused the surface of the reservoir to glow with the same ghostly luminescence they had observed in the tunnel, wherever the water was disturbed by a swift current or as it brushed past some obstacle. The light rose a short distance above the lake, creating a faint, blue-green fog as it lit the falling rain, though not strong enough to illuminate the surrounding ruins.

It was eerily beautiful, but it was not what Jaspins was pointing at. Triistan inhaled sharply.

Much closer to them, perhaps twenty or thirty paces off to their left, a pair of large, almond-shaped eyes shown from the darkness. They glowed a deeper, richer blue than the water, and were at least as large as Triistan's hand, widely spaced, and floating three or four feet off the ground. They disappeared for a moment, then reappeared again, narrowing to a pair of inverted crescents. Triistan heard a low rumbling noise which he first took to be distant thunder. It made the hairs on his neck and arms stand up, and he took an inadvertent step back.

The eyes rose higher into the air. When they reached a height of seven or eight feet, the rumbling noise ended abruptly in a low huff, the eyes winked out, and the rain and the night returned.

Triistan realized he had been holding his breath. He exhaled and glanced at the others questioningly, but they were still staring into the darkness, immobile, listening. He was struck by how quiet it had become. What he had at first took to be a reaction to the deluge now seemed much more ominous: the nocturnal chorus of birds, beasts and insects had ceased completely, as if the jungle were still waiting to exhale, and the only sounds came from the sleeping men behind them and the wet rush of the rain.

They stood this way for several more long moments, until finally the downpour began to let up. A few intrepid insects or frogs (he could never tell which) started up nearby, but what they'd come to know as the 'normal' sounds of the night did not resume for hours, and when they finally did, the calls seemed subdued, or perhaps came from a greater distance away, as if the animals were giving them a wider berth. Although the rain did not stop completely, it did subside to a misty drizzle, and eventually they were able to restart their fire. The Captain ordered them to stoke it much higher, before she and Lieutenant Jaspins resumed their vigil.

The rest of the night passed uneventfully. Their visitor did not return, but neither did the Firstblade or his scouts.

* * *

The following morning, Captain Vaelysia organized two search parties of three men each. She took personal command of one and assigned Jaspins to the second, leaving the rest behind to watch over the wounded. Biiko remained behind with Triistan, who was under orders to complete his record of their passage through the Rivergate and then to begin mapping Ostenvaard as soon as he could.

"And by mapping, I mean strictly from what you can see from the watch tower, Mister Halliard. No one will leave this encampment until we return; we've no idea what's out there and I'm not losing any more men, is that clear?"

"Aye, sir."

He was careful not to sigh aloud with relief. His leg hurt so badly it was difficult just to stand there. He had asked Biiko to apply more of the numbing paste, but the Unbound had refused. As best as Triistan could discern from the man's gestures, it slowed the actual healing, and would be used only in an emergency or other extreme situation. When Triistan had replied with, "This feels pretty extreme to me," Biiko had given him a look that clearly said, "I will be the judge of that" and walked away.

Before she left, the Captain set Creugar in charge of strengthening their position by clearing away more of the vegetation in the immediate area, to improve sight lines and make it more difficult to approach the camp under cover. Before getting started, they searched the area where they thought their visitor must have been the night before, expecting to find some tree or other structure the creature could have scaled, but they found nothing nearby except vines and low rubble. Perhaps the combination of the rain and darkness had created the illusion that the beast was much closer than it had actually been, since there were some low buildings and taller vegetation another hundred paces or so north of them, but Triistan didn't think so. Given the size and spacing of the eyes, he thought it much more likely that the thing was just plain *big*. He shivered and hoped it was also strictly nocturnal.

And a plant-eater, too, just for good measure.

Unable to help with the clearing, he found a comfortable spot out of the way and set to carrying out his orders.

Ten and Two, Vehnya, 256, The Ninth day of the expedition, thirty-second since Landfall - Mid Morning...

It was hard to believe they had been on Aarden an entire month already. He gave a brief recounting of the night's eerie visitation before continuing:

Last night's encounter was unnerving, like having been visited by a ghost. Still, the wildlife here continues to intrigue me. I have the sense that it is becoming increasingly hostile and strange the further from the coast we venture. For instance, the nest guardians were like nothing any of us have ever seen... or perhaps that isn't entirely accurate. They do share some characteristics with several creatures we are familiar with, but in a combination and scale that is not found on Niyah, at least to my knowledge. In the case of the guardians, it was as though they had been forged from a nightmare, blending parts of separate beasts together the way a dream sometimes confuses different elements of one's memories of people and places. I will attempt to sketch one here...

As Triistan drew, the others worked to improve their encampment. Under Creugar's direction, they cleared out a large area around the guardhouse and built a crude palisade by piling rubble in a large arc, then burying long poles cut from trees so that they protruded outward. These he sharpened himself before they were placed, needing only three or four cuts from his great axe to create a suitably deadly deterrent.

As they were placing one of these stakes, Biiko approached Creugar, holding a long, straight shaft of criedewood. It looked close to twelve feet long, and had something metal and sharp affixed to its end. Looking more closely, Triistan realized it was the blade of a poniard; the hilt had been slipped inside the hollow center of the criedewood shaft up to the crossguard, and twine or perhaps a length of vine had been used to lash it in place. The cord was wound several times around the crossguard and extended close to a foot down the length of the pole. He had made a very long spear.

"What you have for Creugar, eh Blackblades? That is an impressive pole, my friend!" he chuckled. "Are you going hunting or whoring?" Biiko did not seem amused, which made the big Reaver laugh even harder. Eventually though, in the face of the Unbound's implacable silence, his laughter subsided and he raised his hands in mock surrender.

"Ah, very well. Peace, my friend." He took the spear and inspected the blade at the end, frowning and nodding his head as he did so. Then, with surprising quickness, he tossed the spear up, caught it deftly just forward of its midpoint, and hurled it at the wooden door of a collapsed building adjacent to the guardhouse. The spear punched clear through the door and disappeared inside. Creugar winced comically, and Triistan swore he saw the faintest hint of a smile on Biiko's lips. The two of them retrieved the spear, and as they exited the building, the Reaver was nodding and grinning.

"Very clever, my friend, and a much better use of those wee carving knives our Seeker friends wear." The blade affixed to the end of the spear was a standard, Seeker-issued dagger that most of the crew carried with them; good for sticking a man in the back or cutting a line loose, but virtually useless against the wild creatures they had seen so far.

Creugar's eyes swept the surrounding ruins as he spoke those same thoughts aloud. "We are going to be needing every man, I am thinking, and none of them will be wanting to get close to the beasties that might be looking to have us for supper." His gaze landed on Triistan and flicked over to Taelyia's sword, lying in its scabbard beside him. Although they had been able to adjust it to fit him, the thing was damned uncomfortable to wear, so he'd gotten into the habit of carrying it around rather than wearing it. Creugar pursed his lips.

"Better start getting used to wearing that knitting needle, monkey-boy. Don't belong on the ground, ya? Soon as that leg of yours will bear it, I would be practicing if I was you." Triistan felt his ears grow hot with shame, but the big Reaver had made his point and didn't belabor it. Instead he grinned at Biiko.

"Lucky for me, I am not you. And lucky for you, it seems that we have our own Master-at-Arms now, so you will be taking advantage of him soon I am thinking." He clapped the Unbound on the shoulder and returned to work.

Shortly after lunch, Jaspins returned to the camp, with Izenya and Chelson in tow. She and the Captain had agreed to check back around mid-day, whether they'd had any luck or not. By the look on her face, it was obvious they hadn't. A cold knot of dread tightened in his gut. Losing Commander Tchicatta and the archer, Miikha, as well as Myles and Wrael, would be devastating. It was hard to imagine what could be responsible for such a formidable group simply vanishing, and his thoughts inadvertently drifted back to those eyes...

"How's that leg feeling?" Jaspins crouched next to him, reaching out a hand to feel his forehead. Her touch was so cool he flinched in surprise. She frowned.

He hated that look. It was the same dubious expression he had seen countless times before from healers as they tended to patients whose condition had somehow caught them by surprise.

"Fine right now, I guess. Hurts like the Dark when I try to stand on it."

"And the rest of you?"

"The rest of me?"

"Aye, the rest of you." She removed her hand from his forehead and laid the back of it against his cheek. The frown deepened ever so slightly. "How is your appetite?"

He shrugged. "I'm not hungry, if that's what you mean."

"When was the last time you had anything to eat?"

It was his turn to frown as he tried to recall. "Last night I think?"

"You think? You can't remember?" There was the slightest inflection on the word "you". This was not going well. By now, everyone in the Expedition knew about his gifted memory.

She slid off his boot and rolled up his pants leg. He half-expected there to be signs of festering, but other than the angry red burn marks from where his wound had been cauterized, there was no seepage or abnormal discoloration. Jaspins bent close and sniffed at it carefully, then sat back on her haunches.

"Well, the wound looks good, but you have a low fever, Corpsman. I don't like the fact that you're not hungry, and I think we both know it's unusual for you to have trouble remembering something. Is anything else bothering you? Pain? Lightheadedness?"

Triistan shook his head. "I feel a little sluggish, but other than my leg, everything else feels normal."

"Well, something's going on, but I'll be damned if I can tell what. Try to eat something, and drink as much water as you can. Let me know if you begin to feel worse." She moved away and asked Biiko to assist her with Mister Tarq, who was lying on a makeshift cot inside the barracks. After receiving an ugly wound to his forehead and face that destroyed his left eye, the First Mate had fallen unconscious during their flight through the armaduura and had remained that way throughout the night.

Captain Vaelysia strode into camp a few moments later, followed by Anthon and Jaegus the Younger. She scanned the camp quickly, her eyes coming to rest on the new defensive works.

"Very good, Mister Creugar, I see you've made solid progress. Has Lieutenant Jaspins returned?"

"Aye, Cap, our boys been working hard..." he grunted as he lifted another one of the long stakes into position, the muscles in his shoulders and arms standing out like so many boulders. He gestured with his chin towards the guardhouse. "Jaspy's in havin' a look at the Whip."

"Excellent. Gather the men." Without another word of explanation, she crossed the camp and entered the guardhouse. Triistan caught Creugar's eye.

"Do you think she found them? She doesn't look very pleased… ". Creugar lifted a large chunk of stone and set it on the end of the stake to hold it in position until more rubble could be piled up around its base. Then he stood and wiped his brow, where sweat ran freely from his big bald head.

"Creugar will tell you something about the Commander, Triistan." He hailed from Chatuuku, and his heavy accent made Triistan's name sound like "tree-stone". "Do you know what we Reavers call him? That is, what we call him when he can hear us?" The big man grinned, his teeth flashing bright against the contrasting dark brown of his skin. Triistan shook his head.

"No? We call him The Grey Vosk. Grey, because he is so old," he laughed.

Triistan smiled. "...and Vosk?"

"Ah, now I tell you something else you did not know, even as smart as you are. What is the one creature in all of Niyah that will hunt the jharrl?"

Triistan couldn't help but smile wider as he gave the obvious answer, "I'm guessing… the vosk?"

Creugar's eyes grew big in mock surprise. "You are toying with poor Creugar, monkey-boy! You already knew this tale. Perhaps you can now tell him why the vosk can hunt the jharrl. Is he bigger?"

"No."

"Stronger?"

Not likely, he thought, though he had no way of truly knowing, so he simply shook his head. The truth was, he was tired and wished Creugar would just get to the point.

"You are not so dumb as a monkey, monkey-boy. No, the jharrl is much bigger and stronger… but the vosk is smarter," he drew this last word out for emphasis. "He is a cunning, patient hunter, and he will isolate the weakest members of the big jharrl's pack. When he find one, he drop down on them from the trees. With one bite," he brought his two hands together in a thunderous clap that made Triistan jump, "he snap the jharrl's neck."

He lowered his voice and made a show of looking around, as if the Firstblade might be stalking them right now. "But it is not the strike that make him so dangerous. It is the thinking and patience that precedes it. And this be why we call the Firstblade the Grey Vosk, because as sharp as his teeth are, this," he tapped the side of his forehead with a thick forefinger, "is his deadliest weapon. So, I am not worried about the Commander, little Triistan. Someday we all must fall, but my heart tells me that I will fall first.

"So," he hefted another stake onto his shoulder, "if I am still here, then he must be too."

Triistan started to say that he hoped he wasn't around to see either of them fall, then thought better of it and mumbled, "Thanks, I hope you're right."

Creugar gathered the rest of the men, so while he waited, Triistan returned to his sketch of the nest guardian. He was having a difficult time working out the details of the tail - specifically the barbed spike at its tip - which he found intensely frustrating. The thing had nearly taken his leg off and he ought to be able to remember every single detail of it. He closed his eyes tightly and pinched the bridge of his nose; it was starting to give him a headache.

A moment later there was a sudden chorus of glad shouts as the Captain appeared, followed closely by Biiko and the reason for the commotion, First Mate Tarq. Jaspins came last, fidgeting with something small and metallic-looking in her hands. The Whip was leaning on Biiko for support, and the left side of his head was heavily bandaged, but the fact that he was awake and on his feet had caused the men to break out in spontaneous cheers and applause. The big Khaliil was one of the most loved, respected, and feared officers in the Seeker Corps. His recovery was a major boost to their morale.

He gave them a lopsided smile and lifted his arm in acknowledgement, before sitting down heavily on the remains of what might once have been a raised planter made of stone. Its surface was badly damaged; scarred and pitted like the walls inside the tunnel, as if it had been partially melted. Captain Vaelysia held her hands up for quiet.

"We believe we've found Commander Tchicatta's trail. There is an elaborate sewer system beneath us, with tunnels many times the height of a man. It appears they were also used as a means for defenders to move rapidly throughout the city, as there are ladders and access hatches leading to the surface, at least in the small area we explored. Much of it is impassable - completely overrun with vegetation - but some of it has been.... "

There was a general murmur of excitement, drowning out her last word so that Triistan couldn't hear it. He wanted to stand; the rest of the party had naturally crowded together around her, and he wanted to see her expression, as well as what Lieutenant Jaspins had been carrying. He pushed his way up, using the wall behind him for support, but a wave of dizziness stopped him when he was halfway there. He waited for a few moments, bent over, his hands resting on his knees.

"So where is the Firstblade?" blurted Thinman.

"Aye, and why's he down in the sewers?" someone else said, but Triistan couldn't tell who. The dizziness faded, and he was able to stand just as Creugar raised his voice enough to be heard over the tumult.

"How do you know they went down there, Captain?"

She looked at Lieutenant Jaspins, who held up the object Triistan had seen earlier. His heart sank. It was the battered tin cup the Firstblade typically kept in his field kit - the one he used every night and every morning, the one every man who had ever campaigned with him would instantly recognize as his. It was as much a part of him as the axe and sword dangling from his belt, and it had been said that he would sooner ride to war without one of his blades than forget that cup.

Several others groaned as well, but Creugar stepped forward and held out a massive paw. Jaspins handed the cup to him. "Where did you find it?"

"Sitting on the edge of a low wall surrounding a wishing pool. There was a broken statue of The Bard in its center, but otherwise it was nondescript and we would have passed it by unnoticed if not for that cup."

Creugar nodded, as if he had expected her response. "And in the pool...?"

"In the pool we found one of the hatches I mentioned. The mud and other debris around it had been swept aside, and although it was still wet from the previous night's rain, there was no standing water. We found the hatch at the base of the pool's wall, on the opposite side from the cup. It looked to have been forced open at some point, but it was bolted when we found it - from the inside."

The big Reaver laughed and pointed at Triistan. "You see, Monkey-man? The Gray Vosk has left us a sign. He has gone below, down into the belly of the beast."

Jaspins nodded her agreement. "Creug is right - there's no way the Commander leaves that cup there accidentally. But why re-secure the hatch after they went through? And where are they now?" She turned back to Captain Vaelysia. "Did you make your way below as well?"

"Aye, we were loath to force the hatch again, not wanting to attract any attention to ourselves, but the trail was already cold enough. We broke it open and found an access shaft below, with sturdy iron rungs anchored on three sides, leading all the way down to the floor of the tunnel - which was so far below we could not see it at first. I counted thirty rungs to the bottom, with each rung set perhaps a yard apart."

Triistan forgot about his sore leg and headache, intent on her description. Nearly a hundred feet down! The engineering and scale of this place was stunning.

"We had not brought torches, but there was a little light from the water running down a wide channel in the center, and here and there seeping through the blocks that comprised the tunnel's walls - a good thing, since daylight only reached the area immediately below the access shaft. The tunnel led both ways, but he had scratched an arrow pointing in one direction - we knew it was him because he also left his mark.

There was a draft coming from that way as well, so we followed the passage until it emptied into a much larger one - a great avenue perhaps twenty feet across, with another channel cut into its center where the water ran. Its ceiling was close to thirty feet high, and our passageway intersected at something close to its midsection. Whoever once manned this city could have easily moved an army through there.

"We could see three other passages similar to our own, but all of them - and much of the main tunnel leading off in one direction - were overgrown and inaccessible. But away to our right, it was passable; the growth was quite a bit thinner in fact. There was also a rough path leading from our tunnel out into the main passage, so we followed it for a bit. The vegetation kept thinning as we went, until it died away completely - it was like emerging from a jungle into an open clearing, except that the clearing was underground and made of stone. There were more side-tunnels connecting, and we turned back after the second such intersection. We searched them as carefully as we could, but found no sign to tell us where they might have gone."

"Or been taken to," Triistan blurted out. All eyes turned towards him, some of them hostile. He knew that fear prevented them from wanting to acknowledge the implications.

"Taken, what the bloody Dark you mean, taken, Titch?" growled Izenya. "You heard Jaspins and the Cap'n: the Commander left his cup there on purpose, to tell us where he went!"

Triistan's headache had him feeling foul-tempered, so he couldn't keep the acid tone from his response. "And then locked the hatch behind him so that we couldn't follow? And if he left his cup as a sign -"

"...then he would have left more than just the one below, so that we would know which tunnel he'd taken," Jaspins finished for him in a much calmer voice. She was looking at him closely, but he just nodded curtly.

"I agree," said Captain Vaelysia. "It would have been easy enough to mark the walls again. And I can think of no reason why he would bolt the hatch shut behind him, especially considering he had no idea what might be down there, and whether they would need to make a quick exit."

Creugar's grin had faded and he looked troubled. "There are few things in this world that could take the Commander alive if he did not want it so. What could have done this thing?"

"Not what - who," Jaspins answered. Captain Vaelysia raised an eyebrow and looked at the Reaver lieutenant, but not before darting a glance at First Mate Tarq.

"What makes you say that?"

Jaspins met the Captain's gaze unflinchingly. "You said you found no further sign of them, therefore no sign of a struggle, either. If it were an animal, the Commander would have fought back. If they had journeyed further into the tunnel system - willingly - he would have left you a sign." She nodded her head in Triistan's direction. "And he would have had no reason to re-bolt the hatch. The only plausible explanation is that they were taken unawares and captured somehow, then led away. What is it that you're not telling us, Captain?"

She blurted out that last question so quickly on the heels of her response that it caught most of them by surprise. The captain just smiled, though.

"Commander Tchicatta chose his Second well, Lieutenant. I admire your... directness." She turned to face the rest of them. "Lieutenant Jaspins' deductions are probably correct. We also know that someone has kept areas of the sewer system cleared for access, and that someone probably bolted the hatch shut afterwards. They appear to be using the network of tunnels as some sort of defense.

"As for what we're not telling you, you will recall the chart we are in possession of, and the Ministry's desire to locate Aarden. We've all heard the legends, but few know the full story, and we don't have time to tell it to you now. Suffice it to say that someone built this fortress, and they have been lost to Niyah and the rest of Ruine for nearly three centuries.

"We believe that they are still here, that they have taken the Firstblade...

"And we're going to find them and take him back."

- 6 -

Contact

It took the Expedition the better part of an hour to prepare to go after Commander Tchicatta and the rest of the scouting party. Lieutenant Jaspins had insisted that everyone be armed with spears like the one Biiko had fashioned from lashing a dagger to a criedewood pole. Triistan and Mister Tarq, neither of whom were in good shape to travel let alone fight if it came to it, argued that they should be left behind so as not to slow the group down. Ultimately, however, it was Jaspins' pragmatism that decided them: they could not spare any additional men to look after the wounded Seekers. So they made Triistan a better crutch and set off into the ruined city of Ostenvaard.

They had made their encampment on the southeastern edge of the city, so the vast bulk of the sprawling fortress lay to the west and north. As they crossed the wide plaza surrounding the reservoir where the armaduura was submerged, Triistan tried to forget the pain in his leg by imagining what the city had looked like when it had been inhabited.

The plaza seemed to have once been an area for public gatherings, with a number of pools, seating areas, and raised gardens on the north and south shores of the man-made lake, as well as a large, open amphitheater covering most of the western bank. He wondered what else lay beneath the water, since the great chamber below actually rose up from the center of the reservoir; its architects would have had to plan for a flood if they ever shut the River Gates, so presumably the area surrounding it must have been kept relatively open. Perhaps it had once been a grand bazaar of some kind, easily moved if necessary.

He pictured what it must have been like strolling along up here, looking down at streets and alleys made from multitudes of brightly-colored silk tents, pavilions, banners and awnings. Perhaps there were even more of the glassy black statues like the watchful sentries inside the great hall. He peered into the water, but like the Glowater that fed into it, the lake was so dark as to be nearly black unless it was disturbed by something. Its depths were impenetrable, its secrets safely kept.

It was hot, the air heavy and still. Spectral clouds of mist rose from the surrounding vegetation and anywhere water had pooled in the plaza, to be impaled by giant golden spears wherever the suns found their way through the thick canopy. The calls of birds and insects seemed muffled and sluggish. By the time they reached the amphitheater at the far end, Triistan was drenched with sweat and his tunic clung to him uncomfortably. His leg was on fire, the makeshift crutch was digging cruelly into his armpit, his head was pounding, and if he wasn't feeling miserable enough, his stomach had turned sour on him. But the weight of Taelyia's sword and scabbard thumping against his hip goaded him as he lurched along, determined to fulfill his promise to himself and not be a burden to the rest of the party. He ground his teeth against the pain and the taste of bile and limped on.

They passed the amphitheater and slipped gratefully into the shade of other buildings. These were a mixture of cut stone and heavy, reddish-hued timbers, their steeply-peaked roofs capped with clay tiles. A wide avenue led away from the plaza, but they ignored it and followed the line of several structures that faced the amphitheater and reservoir, until they came to a narrow alley between two buildings. The Captain led them down the alleyway without hesitation.

Delicate arches spanned the space high above them, and Triistan realized they were footbridges linking the large patios nestled amongst the rooftops. Dozens of thin rusted chains hung from beneath the bridges, some still holding onto their original purpose: wide, shallow copper bowls that probably once served as hanging gardens. Now those that still hung by their chains were floating pans of choking weeds and serpentine vines that crawled up and over the bridges above. One of the pans swung noticeably, and something dark with too many legs skittered out of it, up the vines, to disappear over the side of the footbridge above. Triistan thought it might have been an enormous spider, but it had moved so quickly it was hard to say. He remarked on it, but no one else appeared to have seen it.

Captain Vaelysia led them quickly down the alleyway, past several wide doorways to either side, and finally out into a large courtyard ringed by more of the same types of buildings. Rather than arching foot bridges, though, here there were large balconies hanging from multiple floors on many of the buildings' facades. The Reavers eyed them suspiciously as they slowly fanned out into the square. There were three more alleys leading out of the courtyard, one of which was much wider and looked like a main thoroughfare.

"That connects to the main avenue we bypassed in the plaza," the Captain said. "And this," she continued, "is our pool and hatchway."

At the center of the courtyard was a low wall, about waist-high, with a marble cap and decorative designs along its face made from inlays of small glass beads. A badly-worn statue of Flynn the Bard, god of music and storytelling, graced the center of the dry pool.

They crossed the courtyard, following Captain Vaelysia to where the hatchway yawned darkly in the bottom of the pool. The trap door itself lay in two pieces off to one side. Triistan wondered how it could have been crafted so as not to allow the water to drain from the pool, but he could not hold onto the thought. Instead he found himself wishing the pool was full so that he could climb in.

"Mister Brehnl, Anthon, the torches if you please." The two men lowered their packs to the ground and fished out three torches apiece, distributing these amongst the rest of the Seeker crew. First Mate Tarq took one, but Biiko, the Captain, and the Reavers remained unencumbered, ready for a fight. When they had them all lit, the men replaced their packs, and signaled they were ready to go.

"Lieutenant, take Izenya and Creugar with you first. When we know it's clear, the rest of us will follow."

Lieutenant Jaspins was already at the hatchway, her kilij in hand, legs dangling over the edge. She nodded briskly in response and began her descent. Izenya went next, followed by Creugar. As the giant Reaver's shoulders passed through the opening with ease, Triistan was struck by how large it was. He was used to the tight hatchways aboard most sailing vessels, where someone with shoulders like Creugar would have to pass one arm through, followed by their head and then the trailing shoulder. However, they could have fit two men of Creugar's considerable build through this opening with minimal effort.

After a few tense moments, Izenya gave the 'all clear' signal by waving his torch slowly back and forth. Biiko went next, so that he could guide Triistan down the thirty rungs to the bottom. The Unbound descended slowly, bracketing Triistan as he hopped from one rung to the next on his good leg, using his arms to lower himself.

He made it to the bottom without incident, but the exertion was the last straw for his disgruntled stomach; he dropped to his knees and vomited at the base of the wall. The strain of heaving made his head hurt even worse, so badly that for a few moments he thought he was seeing spots.

"Easy, Triis. Here, let me have a look at you." Jaspins took his arm and helped him back to his feet. Frowning, she brushed something off his chin. "Seeker, bring your torch closer, please."

Izenya complied, lifting the brand higher as he approached.

"Splinter me bullocks what the fuck are those things?" exclaimed the bosun's mate. He was a burly, thuggish looking brute with a square nose and half an ear missing, and an attitude to match. He was a good, reliable sailor though - someone Scow had told Triistan to stay near "if things got dirty".

"Blackblades and them Reavers will take good care of you all," the Mattock had told him, "but I never seen a mate as tough in a tight scrape as Izzy."

Just now, Izenya was also seeing spots - a dozen or so small, slimy black beetles scurrying across the face of the wall where Triistan had just been leaning. He held the torch closer for a better look, and they all disappeared in a matter of seconds, finding various cracks and holes in the wall's mortar joints. Triistan shuddered at the thought of those things crawling on him. All he wanted to do was sit down and rest, but suddenly every surface seemed to pulse and shift as if it were covered with the things.

"The light, Seeker," Jaspins said impatiently. She leaned in close, examining Triistan's face. He was conscious of the others watching them as she felt his brow and then pulled down on one of his lower eyelids. Her own eyes were narrowed, her expression a mixture of concern and puzzlement. She shook her head as she drew back.

"I don't like it. Vomiting, eyes are bloodshot, and your fever is worse. You need rest and clean water, neither of which I can give to you now -"

Her eyes dropped to his chest and her frown deepened. Triistan looked down and recoiled; one of the beetles was stuck to his tunic. Before he could brush it off, though, Jaspins caught his wrist. The strength of her grip surprised him.

"Wait!" With her other hand, she plucked it from his shirt and held it up to the torch. This one wasn't moving - it was curled into a tiny black ball, less than the size of a pea. She pinched it between her thumb and forefinger, and the insect opened reflexively, revealing six small legs and a tapered body covered by a soft, segmented shell. It did not appear to be alive, but she gave it a final squeeze and slipped it into a small pouch that hung from her belt. She met his eyes again.

"How do you feel now?"

His throat burned, and there was a foul taste in his mouth, but he was determined not to be a burden to the rest of the group. "I'm fine," he answered hoarsely.

"Well, you look like mung. Let me know if you feel any worse. Hopefully we'll find some sign of the Commander and get an idea of what we're up against, then maybe find a place where you can get some rest."

The others descended rapidly, and soon they were setting off again, leaving the bright shaft of daylight filtering down from the access hatch and plunging into the eerie blue-green glow of the tunnel. Fortunately for Triistan, their pace was slowed by caution and the walls of strange vegetation that crowded in on them from both sides, giving him a chance to catch his breath. It did nothing for the pain in his leg, and his stomach still hurt, but at least his headache receded some when he didn't have to strain as much. It was considerably cooler down here as well, although he hadn't stopped sweating yet.

As Captain Vaelysia had described, the tunnel they were in soon intersected with a much larger one. The ceiling flew away above them, almost beyond the reach of their torches. In the dancing shadows he could just make out a series of vaulted arches that reminded him very much of Ahbaingeata, though this place looked to be in much better condition.

The floor of the larger tunnel was some six feet below them, and perhaps twenty-five or thirty across. A wide channel ran down its center. As they made their way down another series of iron rungs anchored in the wall, Triistan's stomach began to cramp up badly. When he reached the bottom, he stayed bent over, his hands on his knees, waiting for it to pass while the others filed by towards the channel. Many of them looked at him strangely as they passed, and all of them gave him a wide berth. It made him feel even worse, though he understood their fear that whatever was afflicting him might be contagious.

When the cramp eased, he straightened slowly. He cast a last, longing glance back the way they'd come, then started after the others.

He thought briefly that it must have gotten cloudy above, since he could no longer see the shaft of light from the trap door.

The dense tangle of strange-looking roots and vines that hedged them on either side was definitely much thinner to their right, whereas to their left it rose in a great, looming wall that nearly reached the ceiling. Strangely, it appeared to have been hacked and burned back, though higher up, it actually curved somewhat overhead, as plants from behind struggled to climb over the stunted growth facing them. It was as if a great wave of vegetation had come rushing down the tunnel and been frozen in time the instant before it collapsed.

The channel in the center of the floor was broad but relatively shallow - maybe five or six feet deep - with a wide stream of luminescent water running down its center. Normally, he would have mulled over the design for some time, his mind expanding out into an imagined labyrinth of connecting tunnels and drains, but he was distracted by another rising wave of nausea. He ran to the stream, fell to his knees, and retched again. There wasn't as much this time, though he did nearly choke on a couple of hard pieces of something.

Did I have some of those pondflower seeds Thinman had been eating for breakfast? He couldn't remember.

Biiko helped him back to his feet. Standing on shaky legs, he realized that everyone was staring at him again. Worse, as he approached, a few of the Seekers took a step back, some making odd warding motions they had learned or created during their time in the Corps. Jaegus the Younger was holding a charm to his lips - a braided lock of the Captain's golden hair threaded through a ridgeback tooth - and whispering to it. Creugar's face was a blank mask, but even he avoided looking Triistan in the eye.

Only Jaspins came forward, muttering something about a "bunch of superstitious goat-shaggers". She handed him a wineskin and told him to sip slowly from it as they walked, then helped him sling it around his neck so that he could manage it while using his crutch.

He nearly choked on the first swallow; he'd been expecting water but it was some kind of spiced rum. The warmth from the alcohol soothed his sore throat though, so he took another long pull, until Jaspins laid a hand on his arm.

"Whoa, slow down, Seeker," she laughed. "That's for medicinal purposes."

He was so thirsty, though, so he took one more pull before lowering the skin and replacing the stopper. He could feel the rum's warm glow spreading through his belly, momentarily easing the discomfort.

"Thank you, Lieutenant," he said with a weak smile. "I feel better already."

They fell into line again, following the rough trail as it hugged the edge of the channel. It wasn't long before they left the clutching growth and came to the clearing Captain Vaelysia had described. She stopped and waited for all of them to file out from the path. Triistan could see a stone bridge spanning the channel not far ahead.

"Just past that bridge we'll come to our first intersection," she told them. "Now that we have torches and men, I want to conduct a thorough search of each juncture to see if we can find some sign of which direction they may have gone. We'll work in teams of two: one tracking with a torch and a spotter. Spotters keep your backs to the light and your eyes on the connecting tunnels. Questions?"

Under normal circumstances, someone would have responded with a crude joke, but these men and women were as far from normal as they had ever been. A few muttered 'Aye, sir', but most just glanced and nodded at each other, confirming their pick for partners. No one looked at Triistan, but he told himself that was because they all knew Biiko would be his spotter, anyways.

"Alright, then, let's move."

About fifty feet past the bridge, they entered the intersection of another tunnel nearly as large, running off in both directions and virtually clear of undergrowth. Its floor was at the same level, but its ceiling was lower, and the channel that bisected it was nearly dry. Triistan thought he caught a musky scent from the passage on their side of the channel, and Izenya confirmed it.

"Smells like an old docksy I used to know," he growled.

"Smells like every docksy you used to know, Iz," Anthon whispered, his eyes and teeth gleaming in the torchlight.

"Fuck you, Anth."

"Not after seeing where you've stroked your oar, thank you."

"Alright," cut in Mister Tarq. "Stow it you two. I'm surprised either of you still has a cock considering where you've shipped your oars. Take the passage on the far side of the channel and keep your echoes out. Thinman and Jaegus, go with them."

'Keeping your echoes out' was a phrase the Whip had coined himself, referring to a ship with her echomen deployed, searching for a hidden coast line in bad weather. As bad as Triistan felt, it was good to hear him starting to sound like himself and exerting his authority again.

He took another swig of rum while Brehnl took two more torches from his pack and lit them. He handed one to Triistan and another to the First Mate, then each pair began slowly moving through the huge space looking for clues; Mister Tarq and the Captain, Brehnl and Chelson, Anthon and Izenya, Thinman and Jaegus the Younger, and finally Triistan and Biiko. Creugar and Lieutenant Jaspins each took up posts on opposite sides of the intersection, keeping watch over everyone.

Triistan scanned the uneven stone floor, slowly waving his torch back and forth as he limped his way towards the adjoining tunnel. He didn't get far before he dropped to one knee, feigning a closer inspection while trying to spell his dizziness. The floor was littered with bits of debris and muck - detritus left behind from when the sewer channel in the center of the tunnel overflowed, he supposed - all over a thin layer of caked dirt, mud or mold, it was difficult to say which. He started out looking for the most obvious things, like boot prints or maybe some dropped or discarded item they would recognize, since the floor was such a mess it was hard to imagine what it should have looked like. The entire surface was covered in random, swirling marks and there were no clear 'trails' that he could see. Then something occurred to him. He picked up his crutch and struggled over to the bridge as quickly as he could. It was an arched span, and at its peak over the center of the channel it was some fifteen feet high, giving him a much broader view over the area.

"Damn, not enough light to see it all," he muttered to himself. No matter, if what he thought he was seeing was correct, he should be able to tell by looking at the adjoining tunnels. He limped his way back to the intersection and began to move into the side tunnel. Biiko had watched him mount the bridge without moving, but now, as Triistan entered the darker passage, the warrior hefted his makeshift spear and moved ahead.

He caught another whiff of the musky odor, which seemed to be much stronger here. He inhaled deeply, trying to identify the stench, but instantly regretted it as his stomach twisted and contracted in protest. He took another quick swig from the wineskin, then bent and swept his torch back and forth, only a foot above the floor.

There.

Just a few feet in from the intersection, the swirling pattern stopped. The floor was still covered with filth, but its color and texture was more uniform, with no discernible patterns.

"Shove a mast up me arse..." he whispered, echoing a phrase he'd heard Scow say a thousand times. Someone had swept the whole area, trying to cover up any tracks.

"Captain -" he began aloud, but Biiko suddenly grabbed his arm and dragged him towards the main tunnel.

"Move, now," was all he said. Triistan dropped his crutch and tried to pick it up, but the Unbound propelled him forward, handling him as easily as if he were a child. As he looked back over Biiko's shoulder, he gasped. Two glowing blue eyes shown from the dark tunnel like giant twin sapphires.

He was transfixed, watching as the orbs floated towards them. Their owner remained hidden down the dark passage, but there was no question they were drawing closer.

A low rumble rolled from the shadows, so low it felt as if his bones and teeth were vibrating. If he had not heard it before, or if he had not been watching those eyes approaching, he might have assumed that some distant part of the tunnel had collapsed. But it was the same noise he had heard the previous night in camp, and as the creature drifted into the light, there was no question that it was a growl.

It materialized from the shadows, like smoke coalescing into some corporeal form. Its head came first; broad and definitely feline, but huge, many times larger than any of the great cats he was familiar with, and unquestionably related to the greatest.

"A bloody fucking jharrl," someone said.

"A Monarch, actually," Triistan whispered in awe. He had seen illustrations of them once - a highly detailed study in an old tome he'd come across in Doyen Rathmiin's library. But they were thought to have been extinct.

It was beautiful despite the obvious danger it posed: large ears pricked forward, alert; a wide, prominent brow that furrowed in the center and sheltered its striking blue eyes; a broad snout flanked by long, glossy black whiskers that wrinkled as it tested the air; and a powerful-looking lower jaw tipped with a long flowing 'beard' of silver fur. Two curved, bone-white blades bracketed the jaw - the trademark tusks that distinguished the jharrl from the other great cats. Over all was a fine, silky black fur shot with jagged silver stripes, and here and there edged with a deep jade that gave it a vague brindle pattern.

The massive head swung back and forth. Unlike a standard jharrl, this beast had a mane of much thicker fur that extended from just behind its ears, down its neck and onto its chest; more like a wolf's than a lion's, though, since it was the same color as the rest of the beast's hair.

It checked around both corners as it entered the intersection, wide black paws falling soundlessly on the stone floor. Even beneath its fur, he could see muscles coiling and stretching as it moved. But what truly stunned him was the thing's size. Its head was lowered somewhat, yet still at a level with his own, and its powerful shoulders and broad back were another foot or two above that - and would be higher still if the creature were not crouching as it prowled towards them.

There was another commotion from the opposite side of the main tunnel. Izenya and Anthon burst from the opening, shouting a warning but stopping in mid-stride as they saw the beast on Triistan's side.

"Talk to me Mister d'Gara," the Captain said as Izenya cursed again.

"Aye sir. We've got another one of these hairy nightmares comin' from our tunnel. Think it's time we cut and run, sir."

An earsplitting roar exploded from further down the main passage. Triistan's mind went blank with terror. If Biiko had not had an arm wrapped around his chest, he would have collapsed to the floor and covered his ears. He was dimly aware that some of the others had done just that. Jaspins and Creugar were shouting something, trying to get them back on their feet. For a few moments, though, it was as if they were all underwater. Movement seemed slow, and sound was muffled. He saw the Captain whirl to meet this new threat, and Izenya and First Mate Tarq moved to stand shoulder to shoulder with her, brandishing their spears. Brehnl collided with Triistan as he and Chelson dropped their spears and ran past, back towards the bridge. He thought he heard Lieutenant Jaspins calling for them to fall back to her, but it was difficult to think clearly.

In the main tunnel, in the opposite direction from where they had entered, something huge and misshapen was moving towards them.

The two monarch jharrls closing from the side-tunnels answered their leader's call. Those who managed to keep their wits began to form up into an arc, spears out, slowly falling back into a tighter group.

"Hold your ground!" the Captain roared over her shoulder. "Gods DAMMIT hold your ground!! Any man runs and you'd better run all the way back to Niyah because I WILL find you and I WILL feed you your own worthless bollocks!!"

The *Peregrine's* Captain had never lacked for leadership, and even the most panic-stricken men were brought up short in their flight. They remembered themselves, and remembered all those moments at sea when it looked like things were lost, but for the relentless will of their Captain. The group came together, with the front line slowly contracting, and those in the rear who had broken picked up their weapons and moved forward to take up positions on either flank.

The first two jharrls stayed close to the walls and did not attack. They seemed to be waiting for whatever was approaching down the tunnel, which by now Triistan assumed would be the very thing they had originally fled from on the other side of the Rivergate: the Apex. Somehow it and its pack had found them here.

It was close enough now that the light from the stream and the water seeping through the walls began to give it definition. It was clearly larger than the other two. It moved with sinuous grace, its stride unhurried, but not hesitant, either. It was the measured, confident stride of a top predator approaching its kill.

Or a king.

It did not pause as it entered the intersection and drew into the combined light of their torches, revealing its full majesty to the astonished gasps and shouts of the party. It was half again as large as the other two, with more silver hair visible on its forehead and muzzle. Its 'beard' was longer too, more white than silver. The jagged stripes in its fur were more defined, but no green was visible, and they appeared to taper off at its massive chest and shoulders; the rest of its powerful body was cloaked entirely in sable. A thick tail twitched and waved slowly behind it, like a long banner in a faint breeze. It was magnificent and beautiful and terrifying - and it was not alone: a god walked with it.

Triistan squeezed his eyes shut and rubbed them. Though his head was still pounding and his stomach felt as if it would betray him again at any moment, he had forgotten his misery in the intensity of the past few moments. As he opened them again to watch the impossibly tall warrior stride into the light, one hand resting casually on the apex jharrl's shoulder, he thought that whatever poison was sickening him had reached his mind. Surely he had gone mad. This was either a god or one of the statues they had seen come to life.

The figure was over twice his own height - well over thirteen feet tall - with broad shoulders encased in elaborate black pauldrons, a broad chest, narrow waist, and legs like ship's masts. Its body was wrapped in a strange-looking armor that seemed to blend and shift as the figure moved, obscuring its form by blending in almost perfectly with the stone blocks of the tunnel behind it. He could not tell the material, either; it was clearly not metal armor, as it did not reflect any of the light from their torches. He felt slightly dizzy when he tried to focus on it and had to glance away.

The creature bore a man's head, with a severe, ageless face and close-cropped, silver hair. In his left hand he carried a giant trident, the three-pronged fork made of the same bone-like material they had seen on the statue in the bay, set at the end of a long, ebony staff with intricately-wrought silver hand guards at the middle and end of the pole. A cloak of some kind hung to about mid-thigh, fastened to his left shoulder by a gleaming black brooch and covering most of the arm that carried his trident.

Captain Vaelysia swore viciously under her breath, then called out in a clear voice: "We have no quarrel with you - release our friends and we will leave your city in peace!"

The warrior did not show any sign that he had understood her. Instead, he raised his harpoon high, then looked at each jharrl and gave a command word in a language Triistan did not recognize. The great cats bounded towards both flanks, snarling and snapping their huge jaws. The expedition reacted by lifting their spears and backing closer to one another.

The jharrls did not press their attack, however. They lunged and feinted, snapping at the makeshift spears, but appeared more to be harassing the party, herding them together. Triistan was wondering why when suddenly Creugar called out.

"Behind us!"

They whirled back in the direction they had come from and several of the men cried out in alarm. Standing atop the bridge and at either end were three more giants, but these did not look like men so much as man-shaped bits of the jungle that had suddenly shot up out of the floor. One of them bent down at the foot of the bridge and reached out a gnarled arm draped in moss and vines to take hold of something just below it.

"Down," he heard Biiko say as the Unbound put a hand on his shoulder and pushed him forcefully in that direction. At the same time, the giant warrior with the trident barked another command, and Triistan turned just in time to see his arm drop. There was a heavy clunk from the direction of the bridge, followed by a whirring noise and the loud rattle of chains above them. He looked up and cried out, thinking that the entire ceiling was collapsing. Biiko kicked the back of his knee, dropping him to the ground just as a huge net landed on the entire Expedition. They all collapsed beneath its weight, even Creugar. Triistan fell awkwardly, pressed downward on his side by falling bodies and the incredible weight of the net. Panicking, he reached out and grabbed hold of it with his free hand, trying to create space to get up, then cried out and let go when something bit into his flesh. Many of the others were doing the same thing, and he realized the net's strands were made of chains, with additional links woven into it. These were broken and twisted, their ends sticking out and creating cruel metal thorns. Anything caught inside would tear itself to pieces if it struggled.

They cursed and shouted, some struggling to get their knees under them, trying to lift the net together. Triistan saw many hands and some faces slick with blood from numerous small cuts. Thinman suddenly fell across his legs and lay motionless. There was a nasty gash across his forehead, but he was still breathing. He heard a grunt from another man trying to rise beside him, twisted to see that it was Anthon just as he collapsed as well, bleeding from a wound behind his ear.

He twisted still further - Thinman and Anthon's bodies had created a small space between him and the biting chains - and found himself staring into the most terrifying face he had ever seen. It belonged to one of the jungle things he had seen by the bridge, and it was looming over him, a fearsome apparition of gnarled roots and vines that formed a mask of sorts, though the only recognizable facial feature was a pair of empty, dark sockets that might have been the thing's eyes.

It was holding a long, slender tube that made an odd whooshing noise.

Something bit him sharply in the side of his neck, just below his ear, and the world went black.

- 7 -

The Grand Index

"I'm not fond of waiting, but I won't argue that the amenities are nice," Temos said. He orbited the platter of fresh fruits and cheeses that had been brought earlier with their breakfast, while burning off some of the nervous energy walking around their temporary lodgings.

Casselle was with Greffin Ardell, standing on a balcony that looked out into the Ghostvale. This place seemed leagues away from where they had arrested Richard Lockewood. The valley was wider here and packed from wall to wall with walkways, homes and open promenades busy with commerce. The softly glowing lanterns that provided light after the suns had crossed over the valley's open roof dimmed with the rising of a new day. Everywhere she looked, she was impressed with the level of detail and ingenuity that went into not only the architecture, but the mechanics by which it could remain perched on rock columns and suspended over the valley floor, which was still wild and lush with life.

On a roof ledge, just above her and out of reach, a small furry creature skittered along the edge. It looked to be a rodent of some type, smaller than a rabbit, but with triangular ears that looked just a bit large for its head. It leapt out into the open air, arms outstretched and long flat tail stiff behind it. A thin furry membrane was stretched between its forepaws and legs, which kept it from plummeting sharply. Casselle watched it glide downward at an angle until it landed deftly on a rooftop below them and then scurried out of sight. Just beyond, a small flight of birds with bright red and blue plumage glided past, banking sharply away from a gentle cascade of water pouring out of a breach in the cliffside closest to them.

"It's beautiful," she whispered softly.

"We're lucky to have laid eyes on it," Greffin said, "let's hope it's not the last thing we see."

"You don't think they'll keep us here, do you, Captain?" Finn was propped in the doorway just behind them. Temos and Jhet were at the table, one sharpening his swords, the other blunting his appetite.

"I try to only deal with what's in front of us," Greffin replied, "but part of my job is to expect the worst and help prepare you lot for it."

"What's the worst look like from that balcony?" Temos asked.

"A quick shove over the railing and a sharp drop to the bottom," Greffin replied dryly. Before he could elaborate, Jhet was on his feet, blade in hand just before a rap was heard at the door. The Captain nodded towards it and Jhet smoothly spun the blade in a circle that ended with it being sheathed at his side, a step before he was at the handle.

It was Lorelen, the guide that had led them from the Thundering Lance's camp and through the Wasting. It was jarring not to see her covered in the complex sand colored garment that had previously been draped around her at all times on their journey to the Ghostvale. She now wore something not unlike the guards of the Vale: a sleeveless leather vest, knee-length pants and soft soled boots. Unlike the more heavily armed guards, Lorelen wore only a long-bladed knife hanging from the back of her belt.

"Good day," she began, without stepping inside. "I have been asked to bring you before the Voice of One."

"Alright then," Greffin said. "You lead, we'll follow." Lorelen nodded and walked off slowly, motioning for them to follow. Jhet closed the door behind them, but trailed a few steps after the others, taking the opportunity to get a good look around as he moved.

Casselle had observed that he was a canny tactician in the short time that she'd known him and assumed his delay was to assess places to retreat, positions of advantage and natural chokepoints. The rest of them were simply trying to keep up with the seemingly unending array of amazing features locked inside the Ghostvale. Another ride in the moving balcony, which Lorelen called a 'cable-cart', gave them a good look over several suspended gardens and clustered homes. Children ran in packs, playing some sort of game that involved dashing between platforms on smaller versions of the cable-cart or swinging on suspended lines, shimmying up ropes, or sliding down poles, all the while calling to each other and tossing a leather ball between them. Concerned parents called out in cautious refrains, more times than not buried underneath bright laughter and cries of encouragement.

She saw Khaliil men and women filling water buckets from large tubes that didn't appear to be connected to a nearby well or reservoir. One larger garden actually had what looked to be pipes made of dark clay suspended over the soil, fine drops of water leaking from the bottom, like tiny rain showers.

The cart moved past all these, climbing slightly, which amazed Casselle even more. She understood how something could slide down the line, but sliding *up* still fascinated her. They climbed towards the top of a thick tower of dark rock that almost filled the valley, but touched neither side. Many suspended bridges and covered walkways, some even made of stone, closed the gap between the dark shard and the valley walls where other buildings were set in amongst the ledges.

The stone looked to be dull red, like rusted metal instead of rock. The formation tapered downward, becoming almost a point as it dipped below the surface of the rushing water on the valley floor. It was an impossible looking feature, like a flint spear point stuck defiantly into the widest point of the river.

When Temos commented how out of place it looked, the most they could get from Lorelen was that it was "of the Old Gods."

As they came closer, Casselle could see it was an enormous chunk of ore: cut, hammered and chipped away at. It was most certainly hewn rather than worn by the elements, though they had seen fit to wear away at some of the sharper edges. All along the surface, clusters of shiny black bubbles dotted the object, like the night itself had been trapped inside and slowly simmered to the surface.

Large holes were carved out in the face of it, the openings sculpted into a style that she had seen influence a hundred doors, windows and rooflines all along the way here. At a dozen feet out, she could see where the object had been cut, smoothed and polished at each of the openings, leaving them a shiny black-silver. The platform they were arriving at cut through the entire stone, some hundreds of feet deep. The darkness might have been overwhelming but for the same colored lanterns that dotted the houses of the vale, reflections of the light caught here and there, glowing shards that seemed trapped just below the smooth black surface.

There was plenty of the rust colored patches as well, large swaths of marbled color that seemed purposeful in places and purposefully random in others. The Laegis arriving at the platform were quiet as the cable-cart pulled to a stop, just as awestruck as Casselle.

"Follow me, please," Lorelen said as the rails of the cart were pulled aside to allow them access to the interior. Casselle fell in step behind Greffin quite naturally, with the others following behind. The only one that seemed altogether unimpressed was Jhet Anlase. Casselle wondered if he would reflect upon it later and appreciate the beauty of it all.

Lorelen led them up a broad set of steps that spiraled around on themselves more than once. They emptied into a room and turned a corner, following a curved corridor until they came to a set of doors on their left, while the hall continued to run past them and out of sight. Lorelen knocked on the doors, which promptly folded inside, allowing them to enter. Two guards were there, heavily armed and armored compared to those they had seen previously, but neither wearing the heavy plate the Laegis would have worn under similar circumstances. Another set of double doors faced them on the opposite side. After they filed into the antechamber and the set behind them closed with a dull crash, the doors ahead swung wide, admitting them to another room. It could be best described as a study, though on a grand scale, with walls twenty feet high, lined with bookshelves along the whole outer circumference of the room.

There were only two lights here, suspended from the ceiling, one burning a warm, bright yellow, the other a more subdued red-orange, like Ruine's own twin suns. They cast their rich light upon the shelves and spines of books from the top of the room to the bottom. From where she stood, they all appeared in excellent shape, well-tended, unlike some of the volumes she'd seen at Strossen's University.

There were four large desks inside, each elevated on a platform a few feet from the ground. The desks were circular, which Casselle surmised was to allow several volumes of books to be opened beside each other, though there were plenty of closed books stacked on them as well.

There were five Khaliil inside, two of them seated at the desks, three standing in the middle, one heads taller than the others. As the Laegis entered, the two shorter Khaliil on the floor moved over to occupy the empty desks, while one motioned for the Templars to come closer. Wrapped in a rich robe of varied colors, she was a head taller than even Finn, the largest of the attending Templar. If the tattoos on her arms and neck were any indicator, she would be roughly Lorelen's age, but the hair that had not been shaved was a natural soft white, and her face bore many lines. She moved with a grace and ease that made her age difficult to gauge, however.

"Deuth paas, hospis verendiis," she began, in a rich calm voice that set Casselle's nerves at ease.

"Pardon, but we don't speak much of that these days," Greffin said politely. "Aside from a few 'march left's' and 'stand straight's', we're not fluent in the old language anymore."

"It saddens me to hear that," she replied, her expressive golden eyes lending authenticity to her regret. "I am Taleera'nilonqua-ne Kha-lu Apa'asheil. It would please me to have you call me Taleera."

"Thank you, Taleera. I am Captain Greffin Ardell, and these are the Templar assigned to me directly, a small squad of a larger unit waiting with the Thundering Lance," the Captain said before introducing them one at a time. The Khaliil at the tables were busy writing, looking up and down, undoubtedly recording this encounter as it occurred. Lorelen had moved to the side of the doors that had closed behind them, standing next to two more of the heavily armed guards.

"It is a pleasure to meet you all," Taleera said. "I apologize that it must be under these circumstances."

"What circumstances might those be?"

"We have called you here to pass judgement on Richard Lockewood," Taleera said kindly.

"Judgement?" the Captain asked.

"On the crimes he committed against the High Houses," Taleera said. "We cannot decide if he is lucky for having you along or it was a cleverly calculated move. Without you here, we would have just detained him indefinitely."

"I still don't understand," Greffin said.

"This is an Elder Council?" Temos tried to confirm.

"Of a sorts," Taleera replied. "For the Khaliil we serve that function."

"What do you mean 'for the Khaliil?'" said Temos.

"When we discuss internal affairs, for those of the Ghostvale we act as arbiters much in the way that your Elder Councils do. We also serve another purpose for the Arys, just as you do."

"Not do... did. The Young Gods are dead," Finn said, sounding as if he was barely keeping up with the conversation.

"Yet you serve them still, do you not?"

"The Laegis acted on behalf of the High Houses directly, yes. In their absence, we try to keep to the spirit of that service and protect what they no longer can," Greffin said. Taleera nodded.

"The Khaliil were never pressed into that service directly, but the Young Gods dwelled here first amongst us before any others and shared with us the secrets that had been left to them by Tarsus. We dwelled as one and lived as one..."

"...and spoke as one," Casselle ventured, catching a nod from Taleera in reply.

"Yes. We are the Voice of One, speaking with knowledge the way no other Elder Council ever could," she explained. "Because the Khaliil do not simply remember the Arys, we *are* their memory."

She lifted her arms, slowly turning to indicate the shelves around them and the books lining those shelves.

"Histories?" Temos questioned.

"Transcriptions of a living narrative," Taleera corrected. "Each of us is a witness and a scribe: the written account of what we see and how we affect the world around us." She turned her head to the side, indicating fresh marks on her neck.

"Last night we captured Richard Lockewood. Once his fate is determined, this too will be recorded on those that have played a part in this historic event."

"And for some reason we are to determine that?" Greffin asked.

"The Voice of One speaks with knowledge, but not authority. The Khaliil remember, Captain Ardell, on behalf of the Young Gods, carrying on our sacred mission even after they have left us. It is the honor of the Laegis to bear the responsibility to act in their stead," Taleera explained.

"You don't feel you have the right to judge him," Casselle surmised. "His crime was against the Gods. The Laegis are the ones that mete out that justice."

"Exactly," Taleera said.

"What precisely did he do?" Temos asked.

"He murdered his grandfather, Obed the Guardian. Then he gave those remains to others, which we know were at least used to mount a final assault against Ehronhaal, and..." Taleera paused for a moment.

"...may well have been the first link in a chain of events leading to the destruction of our world as we know it."

***

"He broke the rutting world!" Temos screamed.

- 103 -

"And what about the destruction of the world as we know it?" Finn asked of no one in particular. "As in what he already did or is this something new?"

"I knew he was a pile of Harox mung, but I just thought it was because he was an entitled rich bastard," Temos fumed. "I mean, I hated the von Darren kid, too, but he didn't kill a god and cause the sky to literally fall on our heads!"

"I think she means Maughrin," Casselle told Finn. "Without the Young Gods..."

Finn nodded, not necessarily in agreement, but at least in acknowledgement.

Jhet was completely calm, which she found mildly disturbing. Captain Ardell, at least, appeared deeply shaken by the news. Casselle was unsuccessfully trying to wrap her head around the entire thing. Thankfully Taleera had given them some time and space to process what they had just learned. They were a floor or so under the study, in a comfortably furnished room with refreshments that only Temos had eaten from, in between fits of choicely worded insults and wild speculation.

"Do you have a plan?" Casselle asked Captain Ardell.

"No," he said calmly. "I have no idea what to do. They seem intent on making us judge him guilty or not."

"I'd say guilty," Temos snapped. "We've been travelling in the remains of his decision for the last few days. I'd say that's a pretty clear choice"

"Would they be lying?" Finn asked. "Could they lie? They say the Khaliil remember, but do they lie? I've never met one before now."

"They're pretty much like the rest of us," Ardell replied. "Some have better manners than others, but the few I've known well haven't been prone to deceit. Then again, the ones I've met have been Laegis... so..." He let the statement hang, instead reaching for a cup of water.

"What happens next?" Finn asked.

"Whatever happens, we're bound to have some uncomfortable conversations once we ride back to camp," Temos said. "Hi, Commander Lockewood. We had to pass judgement on your father for killing our Gods and most everyone in Cartishaan about three hundred years ago. Sorry we're later than we expected to be."

"We don't know he did it," Finn said.

"We don't know that he didn't either," Temos shot back. Finn looked discouraged.

It had been a good while since they'd been given an opportunity to think about things, but Casselle sensed they were just as confused as when they had first walked in here. As an awkward silence settled over the room, there was a knock at the door before it cracked open. It was Taleera, with Lorelen just behind her. Theander Kross was there as well, his hood drawn low, but the lower half of his face clearly expressed his displeasure.

"I am sorry to disturb, but I thought I might see how you were doing. I know this is an uncommonly heavy task, but I may be able to offer some assistance," Taleera said. "I am taking Master Kross to view evidence of the crimes. I would like to offer this to one of you as well."

"Not all of us?" the Captain asked.

"Where we are to take you is a sacred place to the Khaliil," Taleera said. "Were it not for the magnitude of the crimes we have asked you to judge, then we would not even have considered revealing it to you." The Captain nodded in understanding.

"Milner, go with them," Greffin said. Temos and Finn looked up, but Jhet merely nodded his head slightly in agreement.

"Why...?"

"Why you? Because I think you're the calmest head amongst us. Don't argue, just go. That's an order from your commanding officer." Although Ardell didn't appear fully convinced of his own decision, his tone made it clear that he did not want to debate the issue.

"Yes, Captain," she replied formally, if reluctantly. Taleera smiled and motioned for Casselle to join them in the hall. She fell in next to Theander and Lorelen finished the procession. Casselle looked over at the arxhemist, but he seemed preoccupied with the walk rather than who shared it with him.

The Templar tried to keep track of their route, but it quickly devolved into a series of left and right turns that eventually confounded her sense of direction. They might have even crossed one of the enclosed bridges from the rust colored spear point over to one of the sides of the valley, since the rock in the corridor around them changed drastically, but no comment of it was made. The only thing that interrupted their progress was another set of double doors like the ones they had passed through to meet Taleera for the first time.

She paused before the guards opened the doors.

"I am extending a great deal of trust to the two of you. Trust that the Voice of One did not unanimously agree should be offered."

"But now we are here," Theander said.

"Here we are, yes." Her expressive golden eyes were distant, as if she might say something further, but after a moment she merely motioned for the sentries to allow them entrance. Two sets of guards and two sets of doors later, they were inside.

The Council room had been exceptionally tall and round. This room was half as high, but there was no discernible end to it. Columns and arches seemed to arrange the space into orderly sections, but Casselle couldn't see any walls save the one the door was anchored to. Bookshelves upon bookshelves were the predominant feature, arranged in orderly rows. As they descended a few steps, she could see where sections had been cleared for different sorts of furniture. In a section to the left, there was a long table with chairs neatly arranged around it, but a bit further down to the right was a desk like the one she'd seen in the Council room, a circular countertop with a chair in the middle.

As they walked through, Casselle saw different Khaliil here and there, looking through the stacks, reading in chairs or performing more exhaustive research. Some of the alcoves had privacy curtains blocking her view of what might be happening inside. It was mostly quiet, but there were hushed whispers that drifted around corners and crept between the shelves.

Casselle's eyes couldn't help but wander. There was so much here to take in, and that was not even counting the titles of the endless leather-bound tomes that filled almost every empty space.

If there was no book, there was always another item: some vase, a helmet, an intricate sculpture cut from some rare stone. She was staring at such a thing when she almost bumped into someone, another visitor that had cut across their own path.

"Pardon me," she stammered, feeling embarrassed that she hadn't noticed the person before nearly colliding with them.

His face was slender, no wisp of a beard on his smooth cheeks, which at first made her think he was young, but his hair was silver, and the lines on his face deep. Moreover, his eyes told the tale of many years - experience and patience colored a startling deep gold. His smile was kind and forgiving, and he nodded in acceptance of her apology.

As he moved away, she saw Theander Kross regard him as well, a word forming on his lips as the man in the darkly colored jiisahn carried his bundle forward.

"Unbound."

Casselle glanced at the arxhemist, wanting to ask the most obvious question, but halted as Kross continued to scrutinize the stranger. She looked back and watched him part a thick curtain a few feet away.

Here was a place different than the rest of the library, something that appeared more like a shrine, candles arranged in neat rows, framing and cradling an array of miscellaneous items: a sword, a pair of sandals, even a fishing rod...

"Keep moving, please," Taleera urged them, breaking away Casselle's attention just as the curtain fell back into place.

Theander had already fallen back into step beyond her, and the Templar hastened a few feet to follow suit. She left that question unanswered behind her, but there were plenty more ahead to take its place.

Her eyes lingered on the sight of a woman in a type of chair that allowed her to lean forward comfortably, leaving her back raised and exposed to another Khaliil, who was adding fresh ink to it. There was already a large array of work there, a tree with outstretched limbs, though that was clearly composed of smaller words, pictures and symbols. The artist was adding a fresh branch to the existing work.

"The body-scribe is denoting that she has completed the study of another of her family's volumes," Taleera explained, answering the question that Casselle had been afraid to ask. They continued walking. "The history of each family is inscribed in these books. A young Khaliil's duty is to study that history, keeping alive the lessons their ancestors have passed on to them. Some of the first art scribed onto each of them are the names of the volumes they have studied, honoring the sacrifices of those that have come before. How they choose to display it is between themselves and the body-scribes, but it is a reminder that we are all part of the unbroken narrative of a story started long before us."

"Your names... they reference this as well," Theander observed in a quietly respectful tone.

"Very perceptive, Master Kross. Our family name and the volume number of our ancestral records are indeed part of our individual names. If there is a significant event that we played a part in, it is also possible that we will carry an additional reference to the Khaliil Grand Index, the volumes that are written to reflect our people as a whole, a process that collects and condenses many separate perspectives into a single narrative. The Asheil, our librarians, compile this information and provide working drafts. The Evinal, what you might call an auditor, debate and correct these accounts for the final works. The Asheil and Evinal work together to maintain the integrity of our history. The leaders of those groups sit on and act as living reference for the Voice of One."

"You're one of them," Casselle said. "When you introduced yourself..."

"Yes, Templar. Apa'asheil means 'Great Librarian'," Taleera confirmed. "I lead the librarians and speak on behalf of the Voice."

"You claim to be living references, but books are books. Are we to assume the writers of these books to be honest?" Theander asked.

"An odd claim to be leveled by a man who is, himself, a product of intense study. Are the texts of Talmoreth assumed to be similarly biased?" Taleera asked.

"Arxhemestry is often called magic by others, suggesting it works beyond our understanding. In truth, it is a language of math, carefully formulated. It may work on a level many do not comprehend, but it does not have an agenda, it works or fails based on very rigid rules," Theander replied. "Arxhemestry itself has no motive. But someone's account of events, their observations, these can most certainly be recorded to serve a specific intent."

"And you work through this how? To provide your students with the best truth you can?"

"We present evidence, formulate different opinions and try to settle disagreements with healthy, honest debate backed by verifiable evidence whenever possible."

"Our methods are not so different. Different observers may take away different experiences from the same event; some details are emphasized, some missed altogether. In relating our stories, we move from simply observing to relying on our thoughts, perceptions and references to communicate to others. The Grand Index is what we choose to be definitive, even though there is a chance it will not always be without error. To minimize this, even conflicting sources are referenced and notes are made by the Evinal when there is significant cause for doubt. No system is perfect, but ours is very thorough, and we invest our very lives to make it so."

"Invest your lives?" Casselle asked. Taleera nodded and pulled them to a stop outside one of the alcoves closed off by curtains.

"What you are about to see has not been witnessed by anyone outside the Khaliil before. I ask you to remain quiet and be respectful."

They both nodded, Theander adding a polite "I will". Taleera pulled back one of the heavy curtains just enough to allow them to slip inside. The lighting was dim, but there were enough of the ever-present lamps to maintain a warm glow inside the alcove. In the center of the room was a raised bed, roughly waist high for the attendants surrounding it. At the foot of the bed, a small metal pot filled with sand held a small fan of slowly burning incense sticks. An elderly Khaliil rested lay on the bed, one eye an unfocused milky white, the other reading the face of the young woman who was wiping their brow with a cool cloth. Two others fretted over a large, leather bound tome, carefully coating exposed blank pages with a blue-tinted paint or paste of some kind. It looked as if several had been prepared before this, thin wooden markers resting between the leaves to keep them separated. A bald Khaliil with a comforting smile was talking in hushed tones to the patient.

The recipient of all this care appeared to be listening, alternately nodding in agreement or speaking in their own whispery replies. The bald attendant, apparently satisfied with the answers, motioned for the book-keepers to come closer. They lifted the book and moved to the side of the bed, holding it open between them.

The patient reached forward with a hand knotted by age, spreading their fingers as best they could. With gentle patience, the bald attendant guided the old one's palm to rest against one of the prepared pages. Taking the patient's free hand in his own, the attendant began a low, throaty noise, a deep humming sound. The book holders chanted in a mid-ranged tone, and the woman comforting the bed-ridden Khaliil added a slightly higher tone of her own. Taleera finally joined in, her eyes open, hands clasped together. Casselle could not help but notice there was a trickle of moisture running down the Great Librarian's cheek. Their combined voice was not loud, but it was rich and moving. Casselle felt it surround her, dance across her skin and eventually settle into her bones.

The dying Khaliil, for that is what Casselle now understood them to be, began a chant of their own, in a voice straining and wavering, yet still clear. They spoke in words that she could understand, but from Theander's wide-eyed reaction, she wondered if they were arxhemic in nature. Were the Khaliil arxhemists as well?

As the chanting continued, the Khaliil in the room shifted their tone to accompany the patient. It was beautiful, and despite Theander's earlier protest, whatever the ultimate purpose of the ceremony was, it certainly seemed magical to Casselle.

A blessing perhaps? As she tried to determine the nature of it, she picked up another smell beyond the pleasantly sweet incense: a sharper, less pleasant scent. She saw the strained look on the patient's face, trying hard to keep their voice steady while clearly in pain. The Khaliil with the cloth wiped sweat from the patient's brow, her voice never wavering, her face full of compassion and concern. Hers was not the only one. Master Kross looked particularly upset, his body language and face tense and concerned. It looked as if he was struggling mightily to keep himself quiet.

When Casselle saw the soft glow underneath the scribed tattoos on one of the patient's exposed arms, she understood. Whatever this ritual was, it was killing them. She had seen the same expression on Odegar's face in Flinderlass when he used arxhemestry to save Jaksen's life at the cost of his own. She found her hand at her neck, resting over the place her mother's ring hung on the leather cord underneath her clothing.

The chanting continued. Even as the words, images and symbols that had been inked onto the patient over the course of a lifetime began to glow and burn slowly, they continued to speak the words guiding the arxhemestry destroying their body from within. It became hard for Casselle to watch, but the patient's face was resolute, even as the last of the script on their neck and face burned fiercely for just an instant before fading into dim embers below the skin.

The harmony stopped, but the vibrations lingered in the air for a moment, like memories of a quickly fading dream.

The patient's hand fell away, hundreds of tiny burns still smoldering slightly. The Khaliil holding the book drew back. The woman beside the patient, tears on her cheeks, tenderly shut their eyes. The bald Khaliil whispered more words over the body and then turned towards those holding the book. They used tiny brushes on the pages, knocking away some blue ashen debris. They held the book up enough for them all to see that the formerly blank pages were now filled with words, images and symbols.

"She gave us her story," Taleera said, "and it will be shared. The Khaliil remember."

Then the others in the room looked up at Taleera and intoned in unison.

"We remember."

***

Casselle stood by uncomfortably. Theander Kross was reading from a book that the Great Librarian of the Khaliil had pulled for him. He had read several, in fact, for some time after Taleera had moved them from the curtained alcove to another area of the great library. Taleera had invited them to read the passages in the books marked for them, but the writing was beyond the Templar's comprehension. Theander, though, was fascinated and quickly immersed in reading the marked sections.

They had been offered food and drink, but both had declined. She was beginning to regret that decision now - not that she was overly hungry, but whittling away at one of the exotic fruits from the Vale at least seemed like something to do.

"The process," began Theander abruptly, "it's not just the words. There's something more here."

Taleera had been reading a seemingly random book from a shelf, but nodded in agreement.

"Part of the teller is bound into the story," she said. "As you read their account, you can feel as they did. The body-scribes chronicle the events, but after we are given the gift of any Khaliil's story, those events are given weight and feeling by the giver. That is why you can read multiple accounts which may have similar facts, but feel different responses. One may witness a death and feel satisfied if justice has been served, or mortified if it was unjust, or devastated if it is a loved one."

"It was fascinating to feel these things, but it made some of them quite difficult to read," said Theander. "It is both amazing and frightening."

"But some conclusions are inescapable," Taleera replied.

"Yes. Regardless of what they felt, these Khaliil witnessed the death of Obed at the hands of Richard, his grandson," Theander said.

"And that is what the Laegis must judge."

"I understand now," Theander said. "Obed was slain in cold blood, far from the battlefields of the Godswar. By most accounts he was always more concerned with the threat of the H'Kaan and stayed out of the conflict as much as he could. At the time, Richard was more concerned with bringing the war to a swift close, regardless of the cost. He mentioned the act, but I assumed the circumstances were different... that it was not simply murder. We only spoke of it twice and that is..."

Theander paused a moment to consider his next words.

"That is one of the few regrets he has ever expressed to me. As long as I have known him, he is not a man who lingers on regret."

"But it caused the Ehronfall somehow," Casselle said, "and it killed the Young Gods."

"Many were already dead by that point," Theander replied, "and Richard's gamble was no wilder than some of the other desperate plans hatched in those final days, but you are correct. What happened was a direct result of his actions. Rash, perhaps. Foolish for certain... but no less devastating."

Casselle furrowed her brow.

"We have these... stories..." she said. "We can believe them?"

Taleera did not answer, she simply looked to Theander Kross.

"I believe them," he said. "I do not want to believe them, but I feel the truth in them. The stories are consistent. Having witnessed the ceremony first hand, I'm inclined to believe no one would want to undergo that simply to perpetuate a fraud, and it becomes much less probable when you think of that being the same motivation of multiple people."

"We learn to witness," said Taleera, "but we are not dispassionate. We teach that our feelings are an honest part of what we share, and it is part of why we capture them in our histories. We are not here to pass judgement on what our people think, we are simply tasked to remember it."

"But even that must have a purpose," Theander insisted. "Simple memory is not enough. Certainly there was a purpose for all this when it was designed?"

"That is not important now," Casselle said. "We have been asked to judge this man. What if we cannot decide?"

"If you cannot decide, it may be taken by the Voice of One that you have either misrepresented yourselves as Laegis or chosen to abandon the ideals they are supposed to uphold. Neither will be looked upon favorably," Taleera said bluntly.

"What is the punishment?" Casselle asked.

"Death, I would presume," Theander said grimly.

"It is whatever the judge decides it to be," Taleera replied.

"So we could decide he is guilty, but allow him to go free?"

"I do not think the Voice of One would consider that fair. They are likely to, as I said before, declare that you have abandoned the ideals of the Laegis, because they pledge that when the Gods themselves cannot reply..." Taleera prompted.

"We are the fist of righteous fury," Casselle finished, her heart heavier for saying so.

"I know you are under a great deal of pressure, you and your squad, but I urge you to speak to Lord Lockewood," Theander told Casselle before turning to Taleera to add, "and I encourage you to allow it. There are other things at play here."

"We did not expect you to make a blind decision," Taleera replied. "That is why we eventually decided to give you this opportunity to review all the available testimony."

"Okay," Casselle said. "Let me speak with the others. I'm sure my Captain will want to speak with Lord Lockewood afterwards."

Taleera nodded in agreement and then moved out into the path between the sectioned bookshelves. Casselle moved to follow, but Master Kross caught her by the arm.

"You must be careful. The lives of every living thing on Ruine may be at risk if Richard Lockewood does not leave here."

- 8 -

The Verdict

"I am most assuredly guilty, and in front of the Voice of One, you must judge me as such."

Richard Lockewood stood with his hands clasped behind his back, staring out of the tiny, ornately barred window of his cell, which looked more like a converted guest room rather than a secure place to keep a prisoner. Casselle and Captain Ardell were there with Richard, but only as visitors. Though the distinction between them was paper thin, since Casselle currently felt like the whole of the Ghostvale was a beautiful cage with no easy means of escape.

It had only been a short while since she'd witnessed the sacred ceremony with Taleera and Master Kross in secretive chambers called the Grand Index. Taleera had granted Casselle permission to summarize her experience for the other Templar, as long as she left out several specific details. Unable to reveal the magic behind the Index, she settled on the simple facts that the Khaliil library was large, extensive and that several accounts from different sources had accurately confirmed what they had been told earlier.

Captain Ardell demanded immediately to be taken to Lord Lockewood in order to confirm the story with him, as well as to hear what he might offer in his defense. The Khaliil did not keep them waiting. Along the way Casselle had wondered if Master Kross would keep his word about the Index, but standing in front of a calm, almost arrogant Richard Lockewood, she was more concerned with whether or not they would ever be able to leave the Ghostvale. Lifelong imprisonment would certainly keep the secrets of the Khaliil safe.

"Didn't you know this would happen? Why did you come here?" Greffin asked.

"It was a calculated risk. The Ghostvale has many secrets, and the Khaliil are the key to unlock that treasure trove of knowledge. If I could gain their support, it could only be a benefit to realizing the most important of my goals," Richard said.

"To save the world?" Casselle asked.

"I'm glad you remember."

"Master Kross insisted that we talk to you," Greffin growled. "He cautioned that we could... that everyone everywhere would suffer, if you do not leave here. Is that part of all this? You want to explain what that means, now that you've put us in this Gods-damned position?" His anger was more tempered than it had been this morning, but clearly was not gone.

"Theander's warning is a bit dramatic, but do not discount it. We are all in danger, Captain. With the Arys gone, we are the only thing that has a hope of beating back the Darkness under our feet."

"Never mind the Gods you apparently helped kill, but what specifically do you mean? I'm tired of the vague references to evil and darkness and destruction."

"Maughrin, Captain. I'm referring to the Demon Dragon Herself. She destroyed the Old Gods and when she returns, she will certainly destroy us."

"Maughrin's a myth. By all accounts, she's been dead and gone since long before the Godswar," Greffin responded. "The H'Kaan were real enough once, though now they're all but extinct. You're swinging at shadows."

Casselle felt a pang of doubt at that. She'd seen the Wolfmother. She'd been touched by Death. The place on her arm where he gripped her seemed to react with hot pins and needles of pain for a fleeting second as she thought about it. That was real, and the thought of Maughrin's return seemed all too plausible.

"The H'Kaan survive," Richard said. "They have retreated to build their strength for Her return, but they are real. As real as the chains that bind their Mother, which are weakening every day. We must act before they break. Even now they strain against Her might."

"You paint a pretty picture with your colorful phrases. I suppose you have some kind of proof of all this?"

"Can you offer me proof that the suns will rise tomorrow? Some things you must take on faith. Such as the ludicrous assertion that the Gods actually cared for us," said Richard.

Captain Ardell's anger started to boil over. Casselle saw his fists clench and moved to stand between them.

"Are you saying they didn't?" she asked.

"Some did more than others, to be certain. The common story is that the Godswar started because the Auruim sought to punish you, the Children of Tarsus, for daring to challenge their authority and that the Dauthir would not allow you to suffer their wrath."

"That's not true?" Casselle asked.

"True enough. There were growing rifts between the two factions from everything I understand and the war itself was never so narrowly defined. Not all the Arys, Auruim and Dauthir alike, were motivated solely out of their love or hate of your kind. Like most deeply divisive things, the reasons were longstanding and varied. The Godswar may have had a single starting point, but it had no one cause, and regardless of what started it, the conflict quickly became about power and control.

"I'm sure you have heard the dramatic stories of the High Houses divided and in constant strife, but the truth is that not all of the Arys were so thoroughly consumed by the war. Obed the Guardian, for instance, worried more about what he couldn't see than what was going on around him. This is how I first met him at Senhaal, when I was assigned to train with the Laegis Templars he commanded there. I was much younger then than my son Arren is now. My father had me stay with my grandfather in order to keep me far from the conflict.

"I quickly discovered how differently even we Vanha are from the Arys themselves. Obed did not believe in shows of familial warmth and I soon came to realize that he must have hated himself greatly for succumbing to any desires of the flesh, much more that the target of his affection had been a common woman, a powerless huunan.

"I came to know him as a solemn giant, quietly brooding inside of his tower, staring into the black, open maw of a cave just at the edge of sight from us. I suspected it to be the final refuge of the H'Kaan, though my suspicions were never validated. Regardless, days upon days he would stare into that darkness, cold and vigilant, even as more and more reports came in about the escalating Godswar.

"I thought I would see some reaction from him when the news came in that his son... my father... had fallen under the sword. I was allowed to deliver the news myself, and I hoped to finally see him shaken enough to speak for peace, or enraged enough to seek vengeance." Richard stared down at his own hands for a moment as he clenched them tightly.

"Instead, he called the war folly and he named them all fools, and in retrospect, I suppose he was at least partially correct. But at that moment, his words filled me with white-hot rage. I was not the only one who felt that way, mind you. Several other Vanha assigned to Senhaal had lost parents and siblings, friends and lovers. So many of us felt angry, but helpless. The Laegis there were bound by oath and tradition, and although feeling betrayed, they felt unable to act and unsure what to do even if they'd had the chance. Those conflicting emotions bound many of us together.

"These were our thoughts and feelings, you see, when we received a most unlikely visitor. Another Arys, Theckan, arrived suddenly to pay Obed a visit."

"For what purpose? To barter for reinforcements?" Ardell asked.

"Of a sort," Richard replied. "He sought me out, having known my father, hoping that I could soften an approach to my grandfather. He needed a key that could unlock something that might, as he said: 'Change the entire course of the war and bring it to a swift end.' When I pressed him on what this miracle might be, he told me that it best remained a secret."

"And you believed him?"

"Even now, much older and wiser that I am, I am not certain that I could have refused the Rogue. Of all the Gods, he had a way of making even the sourest of lies sound like the sweetest truths."

"So you introduced him," Casselle said.

"They were not strangers, but I did announce him." Richard paused for a moment, his face growing slightly dark.

"He did not even let Theckan speak before thundering out his refusal. No! He would not help Theckan or the Arys or even the Dauthir for that matter. His post was Senhaal, and his mission was larger than any of them, he said, before commanding the Rogue to leave.

"I begged my grandfather to reconsider, if not for me than for the memory of his son. I told him it would be a mistake to at least not listen to Theckan.

"Obed looked down at me with cold contempt. He said the only mistake he'd ever made was getting in bed with a huuan. He told me that such weakness was a curse, the only curse that had the audacity to renew itself with each passing generation."

Casselle had not known Lord Lockewood for long, but he had seemed to have had a good rein on his emotions, until this moment. The rage that he had spoken of earlier remained, perhaps diminished in size by the years, but no less hot.

"So you killed him," Casselle said.

"I attacked him," Richard said. "It was foolhardy, as I was so clearly beneath his skill. He toyed with me, telling me he would let me live, but not without teaching me a lesson in respect. In short order, he'd crushed one of my legs and nearly cost me an arm.

"But you survived," she observed.

"Yes. Just when I thought he'd changed his mind and did intend to kill me after all, Theckan stabbed him in the back. When he turned to face his fellow Arys, thinking me no longer a threat, I summoned what remained of my strength and stabbed him from behind, driving a spear through the rents in his armor Theckan had left. My weapon struck true, killing him instantly."

Casselle and Greffin remained quiet. Richard cleared his throat, and his emotions, before continuing.

"You see now why I never claimed my actions were justified. It was an act of desperate cowardice and petty anger. This is why I told you that you must judge me guilty, because it is entirely accurate," Richard confessed.

"But why didn't they arrest you then and there?" Greffin asked.

"I don't think anyone had the heart for it. I was near death for a long time. Theckan stabilized me before leaving, but I was unconscious for weeks and bedridden for months afterwards. I learned that most of those assigned to Senhaal had left with the Rogue. The few that remained either deserted their posts to return to their families or lingered out of some sense of respect in order to maintain the tower. A few I talked to thought the war would be over soon and one of the Arys would take Obed's position. The others simply had no place left to go." Richard wrung his hands together for a moment.

"Nevertheless, in the days of my recovery, I realized why my grandfather was so obsessed. When I was finally well enough to move, I took my exercise to climb the tower and sit in his chair. I sat in that place and stared into that same darkness that had captured his attention since my arrival. I came to many realizations upon those walks, but the most powerful truth I found sitting in that chair...

"... because I knew something was staring back."

Casselle felt a chill crawl up her spine. Greffin had not stopped staring at Richard, his one eye narrowed.

"Knew it? Or saw it?"

"I knew it. You cannot mistake such a thing."

"It sounds like guilt," Casselle said.

"Or anger, or despair, or even just fear of what would become of us... I felt all of those things. But this was different," he said coldly. "She was there. Something changed in those days. I've yet to discover the truth of it, but I am not alone. There are others that sense it, too. Maughrin still waits. She will return."

"Unlike my grandfather, I would not sit idly by," Richard continued, his voice more energized. "I thought to reach out to Theckan, but he had disappeared, so I contacted the Stormfather instead. I needed the Godswar to be done, in order for us to focus on a greater danger. It mattered little to me which side won, so I offered up Senhaal's secrets to Shan. They provided him a means to slip into Ehronhaal with the rest of the Dauthir, to catch the Auruim unawares and hopefully force an end to the fighting.

"But Thunor would not stand down, regardless of the odds, least of all to his 'little brother.'" Richard glanced sidelong at the two Templar. "For an immortal, I never expected him to have so little patience."

"How do you know that?" Greffin pressed.

"The results speak for themselves," Richard said. Casselle could not deny that. The Wasting and what was left of Cartishaan had become their dying testimony.

"So if you hadn't..." Greffin growled.

"'What if' is a game for cowards and fools, Captain Ardell. I heard that once from another Templar. You'd be wise to heed those words. We survivors must go forward fully aware that we live in a world where the Gods cannot help us any longer. Someone must stand against the Living Darkness, and it must be us. I will bear the responsibility, but I need an army.

"I need soldiers like you at my side," Richard continued, "and you need weapons that can actually finish the job that Tarsus failed to do. I know of a few, but the Khaliil can help us find many. They claim to be the Memory of the Gods, and they can give us the best indication of where to look."

"That's why you risked coming here?" Casselle asked.

"Yes, but it is only one of several contingencies I have in play. The Khaliil would be fine additions to allies I've already made amongst the Ashen, the Laegis, the Sea Kings and even the rogues of Mylesia," Richard said. "The world may hate me for what I have set in motion, but even if I do not drive the blade home, I will orchestrate the final demise of that Demon. I have killed a God, after all. How many do you know that can claim such a thing?"

"None that would sound so proud to admit it, I should think," she replied.

"It is not a boast, it's a fact. Until you can find someone more qualified, I shall continue to command as best I see fit."

***

"That's what he said?" Temos asked. "What an insufferable jackass!"

"Yes, I know I set the house on fire, which is why I'm the best one to add more fuel to it," he added in his best Richard Lockewood impression.

"The Godswar was already in motion," Captain Ardell said, "We can blame him for the murder of Obed and the decision he made to let Shan storm Ehronhaal, but he didn't start that fire."

"He confessed, though. How do we not judge him guilty? Is there any reason we shouldn't?" Finn Archer sounded remarkably meek considering his commanding physical presence.

"He and the Ashen both claim we'll die when Maughrin returns, unless we follow his plans to uncover powerful weapons to fight the dragon," Casselle said. She was uncomfortable thinking of all this. She'd been trained to be a soldier, not a judge. There was no Cadence for speaking to an Elder Circle.

"As much as I hate to admit it, but after everything we've seen, I'm inclined to agree. It may not be Maughrin, but there is something going on," Temos said to Casselle, who nodded in reply.

"Our opinions on the subject notwithstanding, we wouldn't be here if the High Command didn't think there was merit to Lockewood's agenda," Ardell said.

"I suppose I should feel better that General Vaughn and Command know more about this than they bothered to tell us, but wouldn't it have been nice if they'd at least warned us unlucky bastards swinging the swords? I certainly don't want to kill any of Richard's 'mystery allies' by accident," Temos quipped.

"Not our call," Greffin reminded him.

"No of course," Temos replied with a wan smile. "That'd make too much sense."

"So what do we do about this problem here?" Finn asked, trying to bring them back around to more immediate concerns.

- 120 -

Casselle caught Jhet's eye as the quiet, cloaked swordsman inspected the edge he'd been applying to his knife. He looked at her and shrugged as if he'd been the one Finn had asked directly. The unspoken exchange between them lingered for a moment before he leaned over the whetstone again, working on the edge's opposite side.

"I don't even begin to know," Temos said. "I've managed to exhaust all of my witty replies."

"The Voice of One said we must judge?" Greffin asked, less of a question and more of a confirmation.

Casselle nodded.

"And they said if we didn't give him an appropriate punishment, we forfeit our protection here?" Casselle nodded a second time.

"So the only question is, once we say he's guilty, because even he says he is... what do we do?"

"Do we know for sure they want him dead?" Temos asked.

Casselle shook her head.

"Even so," she confirmed, "we just can't be lenient on him. I think they would be fine with us saying he should die, but I feel they wouldn't settle for him peeling potatoes."

"What if he's wrong?" Finn asked.

"Meaning?" Greffin challenged.

"What if there is no Maughrin, not like the stories say, but we let him get all these weapons anyways?"

"You mean what if he stockpiles an armory of incredibly powerful and dangerous weapons and keeps them all to himself?" Temos clarified. "I'm sure only the best things will happen. Certainly that decision, in no way, would come back to haunt us later." Finn scowled at the obvious sarcasm.

"I don't think we're ranked high enough for this," Greffin confessed. "I joined the Laegis because I like to hit things and help people. Seemed the best fit. Never expected to be the one having to make these kinds of decisions."

"But we should," Casselle offered.

"If we are to forge a better tomorrow," said Temos, "than it should be for the people who need it the most, those that don't have the money or power to stand up against people like Lockewood."

"I didn't ask for my family to be important," Finn said, somewhat ashamed.

"Being fortunate ain't no crime," Captain Ardell said, "but being Laegis means you put others before you. We turn this over to anyone else, they're bound to think of themselves first. People with means tend to put their own interests in front of everything else."

"My father says those that don't have only want to take from those that do," Finn said.

"I've never known my father to put the death of some rich bastard over the desire to put food on the table," Temos said, before quietly adding, "maybe after dinner, though..."

"But for this here, shouldn't we think of ourselves?" Finn countered. "If we don't get those weapons, and the Dragon comes, what if we can't stop it?"

"What if she comes, we have the weapons and we can't stop her anyway?" Temos countered. Finn looked confused.

"Don't matter none," Greffin said, trying to refocus them. "We have to decide what to do with him and we all should agree upon it. That's the best we can do to be fair. The High Marshall will have to thank us or punish us later."

"Agreed," Casselle said. Jhet and Temos nodded. Finn was hesitant at first, but he eventually nodded, albeit less enthusiastically.

"So who's got a good idea?" Greffin asked.

There were several exchanged looks, but no words.

"I'm fairly certain we don't have enough time or ale to come up with a good idea, so perhaps we settle for something slightly less good?" said Temos after a long silence.

"I might have something," Casselle said.

***

"Speak then, Templar Casselle Milner. What is your suggestion for the punishment of Richard Lockewood, found guilty by confession and testimony for the death of Obed, Auruim of the High Houses, one of the mighty Arys?" Taleera asked. She was missing the kind smile that she had worn when they first stood before her in this room, surrounded by books and judged by the four other Asheil, the Auditors of the Khaliil Grand Index. There were a few others here as well, members of the Ghostvale's other elders, though not members of the Voice of One, as well as a token number of armed guards to stand around Richard while he was being judged.

They had already settled the matter of his guilt rather quickly. Even though they had the passages Theander Kross had read earlier in the library, it was mostly irrelevant since Richard chose to confess. Casselle was prepared for something much longer but was only required to add her own agreement to the Voice of One's decision on behalf of the Laegis in attendance. Richard Lockewood was most certainly guilty of murdering a God.

Now the Council waited for her to speak, to present the suggestion for punishment that her group had agreed upon. It was not a unanimous decision and not without a healthy amount of skepticism, but they agreed it was at least something when the rest of them had come up with nothing. There were some discussions on wording and details, but most of it remained as Casselle had proposed it.

"Lord Lockewood came to the Ghostvale to seek the aid of the Khaliil," Casselle began, her voice quiet and nervous, but gaining some volume and confidence as she proceeded. "He came seeking knowledge of weapons lost to time or the Ehronfall, a means to defend all of us from Maughrin. We think he should get this information and continue with his mission, but recognize he must be held accountable for his actions.

"So we propose two things: First off, Richard will accept the commission he was offered long ago and become a Laegis Templar, forsaking lands and family as required by our order and subject to our rules and discipline. The Laegis will then formally request, as he was planning to, for your help in finding weapons that we will take into our custody. We will swear to only use these weapons for defense against the Demon Dragon, should she arise. In her absence, they will remain safely locked in our vaults." Casselle finished and remained quiet, though her own heart beat madly in her ears and her own breath seemed thunderously loud in the silence that followed.

She watched the curious look on Taleera's face before the Great Auditor turned to speak to her peers. No longer the focus of scrutiny, Casselle looked over to Captain Ardell and her squad. Greffin was nodding in approval and Temos flashed her a quick thumbs up. Finn was watching the Voice of One quietly debate, while Jhet seemed more interested in Richard's reaction.

Lord Lockewood was scowling slightly. Casselle couldn't tell if he was annoyed with the request, disappointed with the scope of it, or merely put out by the proceedings in general. Her interactions with him suggested that he had a well constructed manner about him, a suit of expectations on the *way* he should be rather than who he might be underneath.

Casselle didn't have any more time to ponder the question as Taleera returned to stand before the others, addressing the rest of the room.

"The Council does not find this punishment suitable, though we acknowledge your attempt to balance a difficult situation," Taleera said. Casselle felt her heart grow heavy. "For the boldness of this crime, and most serious repercussions of the events that followed, we expect a physical sacrifice: blood for blood."

There was an excited murmur that rattled around the room as Taleera continued.

"As the accounts of the event detail..."

"My arm," Richard interjected.

"We have not..."

"But that's where you are going, isn't it?" Richard asked forcefully. "Obed nearly took my arm and my leg in our fight, but they were saved by healers skilled in arxhemestry. You're going to propose that one or the other be taken, in accordance with the old laws of the Arys, yes? Then I propose my arm. I suppose you could ask for both, but it doesn't seem quite like you all to suggest that. I already knew that if you had planned to kill me outright, you wouldn't have bothered to drag the Laegis into this.

"So let's skip to the point: My arm if I get to choose, my leg if I don't or both if that is what, indeed, you judge is best," Richard sounded more annoyed than angry at this point.

So he didn't expect to die? Casselle thought. Maybe all he expected was a better proposal from the Templars. Unfortunately, she knew they were just soldiers, not skilled in law like judges or politicians. Even still, she regretted being the one that had come up with an idea so uniformly disregarded and felt foolish now having suggested it. If it was any consolation, at least she wasn't the only one who felt frustrated by all of this, if Taleera's furrowed brow and the continued whispers around the room were any indication.

"You speak out of turn," Taleera scolded. "You are not the authority here."

"Perhaps I should be, since I am the only one preparing for the inevitable."

"Your hubris is not the best measure of your competency, nor are you the only option for salvation. Just because we haven't shared our preparations with you does not mean we have none."

"Go then and hide beneath your books. Your memories have little bite and the faith you invest in them will not protect you from what comes next.

"I realize now that killing my own grandfather was the best thing I could have done. It taught me that you cannot wait idle by, ruminating on the past, while the future rushes headlong to meet you. So take my arm, my leg or even my life if you choose, but do so quickly so that I can move onto more pressing business," Richard growled.

With a glance, Casselle confirmed that she was not the only one stunned by his defiance of the Khaliil's Voice of One. When the whispers had stopped, it felt as if a cold wind had dropped the temperature in the room. Though there was no expectation of violence, time seemed distorted, like those seconds stretched thinly before the beginning of a battle.

"Richard Lockewood, for your role in the death of Obed the Guardian and the High Houses of the Arys, you shall pay a blood price as punishment. Furthermore, your petition for assistance from the Khaliil is denied and any attempt to return to the Ghostvale will see your life made forfeit," Taleera said sternly. "Take his arm and toss him out of our home."

As the guards removed Richard from the room, it exploded in noise. Many assembled either jeering at Richard or attempting to catch the attention of the Voice with their cries for more severe punishment. The Laegis were mostly stunned, save for Greffin, who had regained his familiar scowl. Richard hadn't tried to protest or reply, but allowed himself to be quietly escorted from the room by the guards. His face was calm, if not altogether serene, a mask that no longer betrayed any emotion. It made Casselle wonder if this was all a performance on a level she couldn't yet comprehend.

She walked away from the middle of the room, anxious to rejoin her squad, but found a surly looking Lorelen in her path. The Khaliil guide motioned for her to follow. Casselle caught Captain Ardell's eye and his nod of confirmation. They walked only a short distance to where Taleera stood huddled with the other Asheil that formed the Voice of One. There were some sharp angry words in their language she did not understand before Taleera invited them into the circle.

"Templar Casselle Milner, thank you for your squad's participation in our proceedings," she began. Casselle wanted to apologize for her naive suggestion and her own ignorance, but her tongue was heavy with embarrassment, so she opted to simply nod in agreement.

"There are always so many expectations in situations like this, emotions and logic tied together and rarely satisfied, even once a solution has been reached," the tall woman said, making Lorelen huff slightly in response. From her statement the other day, Casselle was certain that she would have only been satisfied with Richard's immediate death as the solution.

"Lorelen and her team will return you to your company," Taleera continued. "Please do not mistake our haste to remove Richard Lockewood as a criticism against you and your squad. You have been patient and accommodating. You have represented the legacy of your order well here in the Vale."

"Do you believe what he said? That Maughrin is real and is coming for us?" Casselle asked. Taleera exchanged a few sidelong glances with the other members of the Voice before answering.

"The Khaliil remember," Taleera said. "Maughrin is indeed real. Our first histories have accounts from the Young Gods themselves, they have witnessed her, they helped bind her..."

"But now that they are dead, those bonds might be weakened," Casselle deduced. Taleera gave a measured nod of her head in agreement.

"We know this to be the case."

"Then is his plan to secure proper weapons not a sound one?" she asked.

"We cannot entrust such power to him..."

"Or even to us?" she interrupted. "The Laegis?"

"Your leaders work all too willingly with him. We fear they bend too easily to his desire," Taleera said.

"That may be," Casselle replied hotly, "but not all of us have a safe hole to hide in. The rest of us will have to fight her if we hope to survive."

"Lord Lockewood presents himself as your last and only hope - do not be so easily swayed. His plans and contingencies are not the only ones in play," Taleera coldly replied.

"You're saying there are others? Who?"

Taleera opened her mouth to reply.

"Apa'Asheil," a member of the Voice of One began, his subsequent words indecipherable, but the meaning clear. Taleera nodded and turned back to address Casselle.

"Lorelen will return you to your lodging now. Luck be with you, Templar."

As she rejoined her squad, Greffin read the anger left on her face and told the others to get a good final look around.

"I doubt we'll be coming back here anytime soon, if ever," the Captain said.

***

They had spent one final night in the Ghostvale, savoring the food and watching the daily life of the Vale unfold around them, but there were no further visits from Taleera or Lorelen or any of the others that had been so friendly to them during their short stay.

In the morning, they were escorted out the same way that they had arrived, less a few dozen armed guards. At the top of the Vale, where the hidden tunnels deposited them back into the vast emptiness of the Wasting, Lorelen, Nevet and Keles all stood waiting with their vosk-driven sleds. Some cushions had been provided for the trip back, but given the rough journey they had experienced on the way in, Casselle expected they would provide marginal relief at best.

Richard appeared no less confident, even with one less arm, Casselle noted. Theander Kross remained outraged that the Khaliil had used arxhemestry to remove it, his scowl not able to be hidden, even underneath the dark hood of his Order. Indalia Nox seemed a bit more amused, but held her tongue; jokes made at Richard's expense would certainly not be tolerated.

They had not taken his sword arm, Casselle noticed, nor did he once mourn the loss of it, even on the long trip back to the Thundering Lance. Most notably, he did not speak to the Laegis, either, save a few terse exchanges with Captain Ardell to confirm that his squad was ready to travel each day.

That set the tone for the entire trip, an exceptionally quiet affair, save for Indalia Nox, who eventually tried to maintain a lengthy discussion with Theander Kross about the beautiful sights she'd seen touring the Vale.

"Makes it sound like she'd been on some sort of pleasure trip," Temos commented, clearly annoyed. It was virtually the only scathing comment he said that entire day, which was unusual.

That night at dinner, Richard did not repeat his offer to dine in fellowship, preferring to keep quiet company with his advisors. Greffin did not bother to assign a watch for the evening, but Casselle had trouble sleeping. She wasn't the only one, either, and found herself with Jhet, quietly watching the stars long into the night.

They'd be back at the camp the following day, if the trip to the Ghostvale was any indication. Things seemed so vastly different now, she thought as she looked at the stars dance and twinkle above her. She couldn't help but worry that her failed attempt in front of the Voice of One would give Lord Lockewood more reason to put her and her fellow Templars in unreasonable danger. If what she witnessed during that judgement held true, then he was far more volatile than he had ever let on before, though it may be that he only ever felt relaxed when he had an entire army at his back. Neither option put her mind at ease.

The morning was chilly and quiet. As the suns rose in the sky, the cold vanished, but the silence did not. Only the uneven slicing sound of ski against sand and the whistle of wind against her cheek provided her the reassurance that she had not turned suddenly deaf.

"Look there!"

Temos' voice broke the stillness. He'd been the first to see the black plumes of smoke on the horizon, thin reeds from the camp's cooking fires. The Khaliil had brought them back much closer than she had expected. They were still a way off, but as the sleds pulled to a stop, Casselle surmised that this would be as far as they would be carried.

As they stood up, stretching stiff legs and massaging sore muscles, the Khaliil helped them retrieve the packs that had been lashed to the sleds.

Lorelen held out Casselle's pack to her, and the Templar just now realized that she'd been ashamed to even look her guide in the eye the entire trip back. She expected to take the bag back easily, but the Sand Ghost still had a tight grip on it. Surprised, Casselle finally met the gaze of the cloaked Khaliil.

"You should all check your belongings to make sure they are intact before we leave." Lorelen's voice was insistent. There was something in her eyes. Something more than simple concern. The others began to do quick checks of their bags, but Lorelen did not turn her gaze from Casselle, nor did she release her pack until a few tense seconds had ticked by.

Confused, Casselle opened her pack. The spare clothes were where she had packed them, as were her travel necessities. Just before she was about to dismiss Lorelen's caution, she saw a small leather-bound book, wrapped about with a cord, tucked at the bottom of the bag. It was not one of hers. She was about to say something when

Lorelen silenced her with a subtle shake of her head. The Khaliil's eyes clearly tracked over to Richard Lockewood before she let go of the bag.

"Thank you for your hospitality," Casselle said meekly. She felt worse for not being able to say more.

"It is a comfortable hole to hide in," said Lorelen quietly, "but we have not forgotten you."

"It has been said that the Khaliil remember."

"And I have heard that there are many tools," Lorelen said, casting one quick glance at Casselle's pack before looking up at her, "but the Laegis are the hand that guides them."

"You have my word on it," Casselle said firmly.

Lorelen nodded and whistled sharply to her fellow Ghosts. The sound caught the attention of the vosks as well, who shuffled in their harnesses, eager to get back to the journey.

Richard and his advisors had already struck off for camp as the Khaliil pulled away, moving in a different direction than the way they'd come. Casselle watched them leave, clutching her pack as the other Templar slung theirs and set off after Richard.

She fell in behind them, casting a final glance over her shoulder before the sleds dipped out of sight, disappearing under the bright light of the twin suns above.

- 9 -

Gut Check

Triistan's recollection of what happened next was a shifting, nightmarish tapestry. Some of the memories were his own, but these were incomplete and distorted by whatever had made him so sick; the rest merely bits he and his companions had pieced together later to fill in the gaps.

He had blacked out almost immediately after being struck in the neck by a poison-tipped dart, then regained groggy consciousness only a few moments later, soon enough that he was able to watch their captors remove the barbed steel net. He remembered trying to get up as the weight of the chain lessoned, only to discover that he could not move. He could not even blink or slide his eyes from side to side.

He could hear, though. Someone was speaking in sharp, brief sentences, although he couldn't make out the words. There were other noises too, and his mind reeled from one to the next like a sailor after too much drink: the sound of movement all around him, the shuffle and scrape of booted feet, the rattle of chains, splashes, a whispering, cracking noise like trees moving in the wind. These thoughts scattered like crows when he heard a sonorous, rhythmic sound that made him afraid without knowing why. It was something primitive, something he felt sure he should recognize and avoid at all costs, but then his mind lurched on, running headlong into the belated realization that he had no idea if his comrades were still alive, or even nearby for that matter. There were no sounds of struggle, no voices raised in protest - not even a muttered curse or groan. Were they all dead? Was he? Had they somehow escaped and left him?

He was helpless to do anything but lay there and await his fate, partially turned on his side, his neck twisted so that his face stared up at the ceiling. He watched the steel net rising above him with a kind of dazed trepidation that felt strangely like vertigo, like he and the floor beneath him were falling, until the net eventually disappeared into the crisscrossed shadows of the vaulted eaves. And then those same shadows bled down around the edge of his vision, where they pooled and crept inward as he slipped under again...

***

Sometime later - how long he had no way of knowing - he slowly regained consciousness. His head throbbed, there was a horrible taste in his mouth, and his body ached so badly that he decided he would be better off going back to sleep - until with a jolt he remembered being paralyzed with his eyes open and right now he could not see a thing. He panicked, thinking he'd been struck blind, before he realized that his eyelids were closed. He forced them open with considerable effort but could not keep them that way for more than a second or two. It was long enough to make out dim shapes and objects around him, however, so at least he hadn't lost his eyesight.

His panic receded and he became aware of other sounds and sensations. He was draped face-down over something that swayed beneath him. His cheek was pressed against a coarse blanket, surprisingly warm. Again he heard that strange, deep rhythmic noise and beneath that, another sound: the steady rumble of a heartbeat. His blood went cold when he caught the familiar musky odor he had first smelled coming down the intersecting tunnel, just before they were attacked.

He was lying across the back of one of the monarch jharrls.

He tried to move, but leather thongs bit into his wrists and ankles. He struggled weakly for a few moments: though his muscles were beginning to respond, they were still heavy and sluggish, the way his boots felt slogging through thick mud. He could turn his head just enough to see that the material he had taken to be a coarse blanket was actually the jharrl's fur. It scraped roughly against his cheek, even though the coat was thick and the hairs long.

He forced his eyes open again and got his head around far enough to see that someone else was slung next to him, facing the opposite direction. Only their lower legs were visible, but just beyond the swell of their calves, he could see the flaxen hair, back and shoulders of the Captain: she appeared to be bound facing the same way he was, with someone between them.

Captain! he tried to whisper, but it came out in a dry, slurred croak. His tongue was thick and clumsy and the inside of his mouth sticky, as though it were full of cobwebs. He worked up what saliva he could and tried again.

"Cap!" He was able to form the simpler word this time, but his voice was so weak he could barely hear himself. At least he wasn't alone.

Small consolation. His pounding headache threatened to match the drum beat of the jharrl's heart, and the alternating crawl of heat and chill across his flesh made him ache all over. Worse, there was now a pain in his stomach as well; a subtle burning sensation just below his bottom rib.

At least there was no nausea at the moment: no need to provoke the massive beast he was strapped to by puking all over its flank.

The raw power and heady smell of the jharrl evoked an instinctual fear that warred with his innate sense of curiosity and the honest amazement he felt at being so close to such a magnificent creature. He must be just behind the thing's shoulders: he could feel its muscles bunching and releasing, alternately up by Triistan's chest or down by his knees. It created an odd rocking motion that reminded him of one of his rig-tits, making it almost impossible to concentrate on anything for very long. Despite his aches and pains and despite the fear and awe, he grew drowsy. He listened to the great pumping bellows of the beast's lungs for awhile longer before slipping below the dark waters of unconsciousness once again.

***

He drifted in and out of awareness while his captors took him deeper into the labyrinth of tunnels, vaguely cognizant of random drafts of air and changes in sound, sometimes close and flat, other times expansive and full of echoes. He heard the roar of at least two waterfalls, and they passed close enough to one to feel the spray, but he couldn't even muster the strength to shiver.

He knew he should be trying to keep track of his surroundings, but it soon became impossible to care about anything but his growing illness. The subtle burn in his stomach intensified, the fire gradually spreading across his entire abdomen, and his nausea returned. Lying trussed on his stomach was not helping, and if they didn't stop soon, he was going to be tethered to a wet and very unhappy jharrl. Just then a painful cramp rolled through his bowels and he moaned aloud.

"Halliard!" the Captain whispered hoarsely. "Are you alright?"

"I... don'think'so..." he muttered. "Somthin... wrong... wrong withmy -" Another wave of pain and nausea rose up and he retched violently, horrified as a gout of bright red blood splattered on the ground below him.

Oh gods, that can't be good.

He heaved for several more minutes, though he did not bring up much more. When the convulsions finally subsided, he realized that the jharrl had stopped. Someone grabbed a handful of his hair and lifted his head. He found himself looking into the face of another giant warrior like the one that strode alongside the jharrls, feeling like a child staring up at the face of a very large and unhappy adult.

This one appeared older, though. His shock of white hair was also cropped short, but was much thinner, and the skin around his pale blue eyes - so pale as to be nearly white - had gathered in heavy folds. An ugly scar ran diagonally across his face, from the bottom of his right eye, across his lips and over the sharp square edge of his lantern jaw.

The giant said something, sounding blunt and angry. Triistan caught a questioning tone, but he could not understand the words.

"I d'know," he mumbled, not knowing or caring if the giant understood him. "Stomach... pain..." he trailed off in an agonized moan.

The giant sniffed at his face, before letting Triistan's head drop. He growled something in his strange tongue, and a moment later Triistan felt someone examining his wounded leg, pulling off the bandages. The hands were rough, mercilessly squeezing and probing at the wound. The giant blurted something else out, and then another voice answered sharply. A third joined the conversation, sounding a lot like Biiko, but again it was all in the alien tongue of these strange, godlike warriors.

"Stand fast, Mister Halliard," the Captain said. "I believe you've just met their healer. Besides, you do not have my leave to die." He would have smiled if he had been more lucid, but her words were just noises without meaning - familiar sounds, to be sure, but more like the notes of some old tune he was trying to recall. He was dimly aware that they had started to move again, but the pain in his stomach had reached an angry pitch, leaving no room for other considerations.

He had no idea how long it took them to reach their destination. By the time they finally stopped, it had felt like hours and hours of relentless, burning pain, punctuated by bouts of vomiting. He had never seen so much of his own blood. As someone unbound him and lifted him from the jharrl's back, he passed out again, his last conscious thought that if he was going to die he wished it would come quickly to spare him this misery.

The cruel giant with the scar across his face had other ideas.

***

As Triistan described his capture and worsening condition to the other survivors on board the emergency launch, his voice finally gave way in a dry croak. Like a shipwrecked survivor, he crawled from the dark sea of his past onto the warm, dry sand of the here and now.

He had been speaking steadily for nearly four hours, though if anyone had asked him how much time had passed, he would not have been able to say. The memories were all-consuming.

"Here, it's about bloody time you took a breath."

Dreysha handed him a dented metal cup filled with water. He reached out to take it but froze as an image of Commander Tchicatta's battered field cup took its place. A feeling of loss washed over him, tightening his chest and throat, making his eyes burn. He forced out a dry cough to hide a sob, then took the cup from Dreysha. He drained it slowly, letting the sorrow pass, giving his mind time to reorient itself to his present setting. He was shaken by how real the memories had felt, as if he had really been back there - back *then* - again.

"Thank you." His companions waited quietly while he drained the tin cup. The tiny band of survivors were perhaps all that remained of the hundreds who had first boarded the *Peregrine*, full of swagger and the almost endless possibilities that christened the start of every voyage.

Drink up ye glory now, boys, he heard Scow growl in his head. *For it, like rum, will turn to piss soon enough.*

They stared at him with a mixture of incredulity, expectancy, and something else - a touch of dread, perhaps? They knew the Aarden Expedition had encountered danger and tragedy, but perhaps now they were only just beginning to realize its scope. Captain Vaelysia had commanded the survivors to tell no one of their experience, so while there had been wild speculation, this was the first time Dreysha, Mung, Voth and Rantham were hearing the full story. The implications must be stunning. It was remarkable that none of them had interrupted him as he told his tale. Or perhaps they had; at the moment he wasn't sure if he would remember it either way.

"You must have questions." He stood to stretch and get his bearings, surprised that night had not only fallen, but that the waning moon had dipped her lower half into the ocean. He wondered about skipping through time, as a flat stone across the surface of a pond.

Eventually the stone sinks, though, born down by its own weight and form.

"Please..." *Please what? Forgive us?*

He was exhausted. "I'm tired. I need to sleep, and will tell you the rest tomorrow."

He retreated to his bedroll, grateful that no one protested. He could hear them talking in low voices, a murmur that ran counter to the pulsating whisper of the sea sliding by the hull. He first wondered what they might be saying about him or his story, then found that he did not care, and moments later he fell into a deep, dreamless sleep. He woke once, when he felt Dreysha lie down behind him and wrap her arms around him, pressing herself against his back. Or perhaps he had dreamt after all, for when he woke the next morning, his back was cold and he was alone.

***

While he slept, the weather had taken a strange turn for this region of the world. The clouds hung low and flat, an oppressive gray slab of stone. The light was dead, rendering everything in drab, washed out tones. A cool breeze blew truculently across the sea, raising small, choppy waves that mimicked the gooseflesh on his arms and made him wish he had something else to wear other than the tattered and stained rags that hung much too loosely from his sharp hips and shoulders. He studied the horizon for a few moments, until he was satisfied that the unusual weather did not have the look or feel of an approaching storm.

He noted the angle of the sails, the tension on the lines, and the pitch of the deck beneath his feet. He knew instinctively that the launch was trimmed just right and couldn't stifle a smile: they had become a crew that would have made The Mattock proud - or at least less inclined to tirades laden with imaginative curses.

He found Dreysha at the wheel. She favored him with a flashing grin that chased away the chill wind.

"Good Morning, Captain Titch, Sir," she taunted. "Did you sleep well?"

"Well enough, I guess." He winced, hearing the inane response echo back in his head. As usual when he was in her company, he suddenly couldn't think of anything remotely intelligent to say. Fortunately, Wil approached just then, carrying a bucket with the morning's catch: a couple of brilliant silver maren, foot-long fish that were often seen leaping from the crest pushed by a larger ship's prow.

They had long, fine tail- and dorsal-fins that came in a variety of brilliant blues and greens and trailed behind them like horse manes.

"Can't recall the last time I've seen maren, can you?"

"Unhappily, I can. We were two days out from Sitsii and I was leaning over the rail to get a better look at the - ah, the... the line in the water where it changes color, where the waters of the Haven end and it gets really deep, what was that called again?"

Dreysha and Triistan exchanged a look. "The Deepline?"

"Yes! Yes, the Deepline, of course. Makes perfect sense. Anyway, I, ah, I leaned a bit too far and -"

"- and you fell overboard, yes, Mung, we all ken that day as well," Dreysha said. "I think Rantham won the bloody pool too - I'd had you going by the boards much sooner, and by someone else's hand." His eyes grew wide.

"You... you placed bets that I would fall overboard?" She shrugged nonchalantly, but Triistan recognized the cruel glint in her eye.

"No, I wagered you would be thrown overboard... but you do have a way of surprising us, Mung."

"Anyway," Triistan interjected, "I would think this is a hopeful sign that we're getting closer, at least to some sort of land. As far as I know they're a shallow-water fish."

"Aye if you say so, Tit- sorry, Captain," Dreysha answered mischievously. "What say we get'em in a shallow pan, have a bit of breakfast and the rest of that story, sir?"

Annoyed and amused at the same time, all he could do was smile and shake his head. "Come on, Wil." He threw a companionable arm over his friend's shoulders, adding under his breath, "let's go before we're filleted ourselves by that tongue of hers."

He asked Biiko to relieve Dreysha at the helm, since the Unbound already knew the full tale. As they set about preparing breakfast, Rantham wasted no time opening the round of questions that Triistan had managed to avoid the night before.

"So who - or what - the Dark were these giants, Halliard? And why didn't any of you tell us you found other people there?"

Why, indeed. I was just following the Captain's orders, that's why. But that was too easy, and he knew Rantham would never settle for that answer, anyway. Besides, he owed them all the whole truth, at least as he knew it. He had put this off long enough.

"It's… complicated, but the short story is that we were operating under orders directly from the High Chancellor himself."

The others murmured in surprise.

"What orders?"

"Aye, and who's 'we', Triis?" Dreysha added. She was leaning forward, her eyes bright with eager curiosity.

Next to her, Wil was scratching his head and mumbling something to himself. Triistan opened his mouth to answer, when Voth barked out a harsh laugh, reminding them that he was still there, hobbled to the base of the mainmast.

"Now y'can add treason to your list of transgressions, boy!" he cackled, but his laugh quickly devolved into a wet, racking cough. Triistan did his best to ignore the bitter ship's Provisioner, though it was difficult as Voth spat a great gob of mucus out onto the deck. "Uh, oh, looks like I've made a mess o'the Captain's ship, and such a fine Seeker vessel she is, too, all twen-"

Dreysha had moved around behind him and deftly slipped a strip of sailcloth over his mouth as a gag. She tied it cruelly, the rag pulling both of Voth's cheeks back and separating his teeth, so that his normally-gaunt face looked like a grinning corpse.

"You'll clean that deck with a holystone before you have another bite to eat, Lanky, and thank me for not making you use your tongue."

Voth glared up at her from beneath the few remaining strands of greasy grey hair that clung tenaciously to his bulbous, mottled skull. But he remained silent and did not try to remove the gag, even though his hands had been untied so that he could feed himself. She winked at him, snatched his bowl away and replaced it with the promised stone.

Triistan stared thoughtfully at their prisoner. By the man's comment, it was clear that he had been privy to the Captain's orders as well, which Triistan found disturbing - not because of any deepening of the mysterious conspiracy between the Ministry and the *Peregrine's* officers, but because part of him had to respect Voth for keeping that counsel to himself. It gave him a fragment of common ground with the old man that made his skin crawl.

"So, you were saying, Triis, about the High Chancellor…" Dreysha prompted.

He brought his focus back to the conversation. "Aye. I'll answer your second question first: by 'we' I mean that the entire crew was operating under the Ministry's orders, at least technically speaking.

Command just didn't see fit to share the mission - the real mission - with us. At least not all of us.

"You'll recall the fragment of chart Mister Tarq showed to the members of the Expedition - the one in the Immolation Case showing Aarden's location?" They nodded. He wished he'd still had it, but the case and its contents - and a great deal more - had been lost in their flight from Aarden's interior.

"I learned that the Ministry has had that map in its possession for nearly fifteen years - ever since the crew of the *SKS Osprey* found it in the ruins of a strange shipwreck while exploring the western end of the Shattered Isles."

"So how did the Captain get hold of it?" Rantham asked, his tone dubious. "And why now, so long after they found it?"

"On the *Osprey's* return voyage, she was capsized in a storm and sunk, sending all hands into the Dark. All but one: a young officer who washed ashore on an atoll along with several pieces of flotsam and the *Osprey* captain's sea-chest. The map was inside it. The officer survived for several days before a merchy limped in to refit after being savaged by the same storm."

Here he stopped and smiled thinly. "Three guesses who the officer was."

Rantham snorted. "I always wondered why people called me The Rogue, when her luck is legendary. I heard that story before. Most would be spurned and labeled Darkspawn, like they were cursed. But somehow it made our good Captain a bloody hero. It's no secret that the Old Blood runs in her veins, and I can't help wondering if that brings with it some bit of blessing. The gods might be gone, but sometimes you can still see their shadows."

Shades would be more accurate, Triistan thought with a chill.

"Or it might be she's just better than the lot'o you boys," Dreysha goaded. "I heard the same tale, though never a word about this bloody treasure map, nor a whisper that we was on a mission for it. Thought we were mapping the 'Isles and that was that."

Triistan sensed some subtle note of falsity in her tone, but maybe that was just because she had already read much of his journal and was trying to cover that up from the others. *It bears watching, anyway*, he thought, and continued his tale.

He had skirted this issue initially, still partially clinging to his oath of secrecy, but he knew he could not avoid it any longer.

"I had asked you to be patient when the question was raised yesterday, but our original mission was mapping the Shattered Isles - mapping and looking for the remains of that wreck. According to Captain Vaelysia's report, it was a craft like none she had seen before or has seen since, its timbers hewn from a wood she did not recognize at the time, and its scale larger than anything we have put to sea, including the *Peregrine*." He paused, letting that sink in. The Sea King Isles were the foremost sailors and shipbuilders in all of Ruine. For one of their own prodigies to state such things was tantamount to saying she had seen a boat made of steel.

"The Ministry had some idea of what this chart portrayed, and they wanted to discover it - or rediscover it I should probably say - before anyone else did. The chart was incomplete, though, so they had hoped to find additional clues that might have washed ashore since."

"That explains why the Cap kept rowing ashore and insisting we survey every rock, ridge and wrinkle of coastline."

Triistan nodded. "But thanks to the way the Isles migrate, whatever bite those clues had drifted into is nowhere near where the Captain found them originally. Our survey mission gave them the perfect cover to search for the wreck, as well as get us to the launching point."

"Launching point?" Rantham echoed. Triistan nodded vigorously. Even after everything he had been through, the audacity of their original mission still awed and excited him if he allowed himself to forget about the consequences.

"Aye, our launching point. You've all served aboard her long enough to know that the *Peregrine* is much more than your line-built Seeker ship. It is no coincidence that she was the first bluewater built in the fleet. She was - and I mean this literally - *built* for this mission. Her reinforced hull and extra storage capacity - gods, just her sheer size - were designed and built with the intent to sail beyond the edge of our known world, and bring back the ultimate prize: a whole continent the rest of the world has forgotten for at least three hundred years."

The wind gusted, scraping the tops of the waves and showering them with cold spray. Triistan shivered, but not just from the cold and damp.

"So," Drey responded, "the Cap found a scrap of chart on some remote island, brought it back to the Ministry, and not only convinced them to build the most modern ship in the entire world - sorry, the second most modern ship in the world - but to give her the command as well? I'd always thought the Ministers favored young boys, but she must have sucked and fucked her way through the entire House to pull that off."

Wil bristled at that. "The House is a place of honor and I am sure she earned that commission. Why there isn't a single soul who's ever served under her -"

"Or over or behind her either, I'd wager" Dreysha smirked, unable to help herself.

"That's enough, Drey," Triistan said. His tone was subdued, but there was no mistaking the warning it contained. She looked at him angrily and he braced himself for a stinging retort, but then suddenly the look was gone, replaced by cool nonchalance, like a hood being drawn over the head of a falcon.

She raised her hands in a gesture of surrender. "Fine, just havin' a bit of fun is all. My point was that it seems highly unlikely that the Ministry would authorize such a… noble endeavor as this based on a faded bit o' parchment with some uneven shapes scrawled upon it. I'm not saying the Cap isn't as fine an officer as ever sailed, but for the *Peregrine* to be her first command…?"

Triistan shrugged. "There was something else on the chart I haven't told you about - words and symbols in one of the Old Tongues - Theranghel, to be specific."

"The Templar's cant?"

"You know it?" Triistan asked in surprise. He'd learned a smattering of the ancient language during his time with Doyen Rathmiin, but it was not exactly common knowledge.

She shrugged. "I've heard the name kicked around some. Not my first fishing trip, Sir," she added with a wink.

He thought he heard that hint of falsity again, but didn't want to push it further in front of everyone else.

"Aye, the same," he continued. "The Ministry's Lore Wardens translated it, and while the Captain never told me everything it said, whatever it was must have convinced the Chancellor and the Ministers of its authenticity.

"And on top of that, it wasn't her first commission, Drey. A year after her return, they began construction on the *Peregrine*. Five years in dry-dock, and another three in the harbor. During that time, they began grooming her for command - though, knowing Captain Vaelysia I have to think Fleet already had their eye on her. She was made First Mate aboard another ship - the *Shrike*, I think - where she met The Whip, who was her Second at the time. When the *Shrike's* captain was killed in an engagement with three Kingsbane, she assumed command, sank one of the attacking ships by ramming it, then outran the other two. She received her sash as soon as they returned to Chatuuku. The *Peregrine* was ready for sea trials within the year, and the Captain given her command."

"A fine story, but still seems a bit too coincidental if you ask me," said Rantham.

"I confirmed it with Mister Scow, and for me, that's as solid as the deck beneath my boots." As it was for the rest of them, even the embittered Rantham. There was a moment of quiet reflection, brought on as much by one of Scow's favorite euphemisms as by the tale they were trying to digest.

Dreysha broke the silence. "Hard to argue with the Mattock, I'll give you that. But what about the storms?"

"Storms?"

"The storms that blew us gods-know-how-many leagues off course. We just *happened* to be blown to Aarden?"

Triistan smiled again. "Not exactly. Who was it that first spotted land?"

"So what?" Rantham asked. "You claim she was working for the Ministry and trying to find this place, but she found it *after* we were blown off course - it doesn't change Drey's point that in all the wide world, how strange that we should end up at the place she had been searching for from the beginning!"

"Exactly," said Triistan, still smiling, like a teacher who knew his student was standing on the threshold of understanding but refusing to step across. "There was nearly a week between those storms, when we all thought we were beyond the reach of our charts, lost at sea. While all the while the Captain and First Mate were plotting our course. They steered us through the second storm as well..."

"...and it was the bloody Cap who first spotted land..." Dreysha filled in as the pieces finally came together for her.

Triistan nodded. "Because she already knew where to look."

"So, Captain Vaelysia found the chart, brought it to the Ministry, they translated it and decided to build the most advanced sailing vessel the world has seen since the Young Gods nearly destroyed it, and then, over a decade after the Cap's discovery, they finally decide they're ready to start searching. They handpick the cr- "

Dreysha stopped mid-word and glared at Wil.

"You."

He had been sitting very quietly through all of the discussion, appearing very small, and as Dreysha turned her attention to him, he winced visibly. Triistan could see the corner of his torn shirt trembling. What was she after…?

"Rantham was right after all."

Then it hit him. *Of course.* Wil had been added to the crew as their fourth echoman, courtesy of a last-minute communiqué from Seeker Command. As soon as she laid eyes on him, the Captain had deduced he was no sailor and requested a replacement. Her request had been denied, with only a vague statement about him 'having the best pair of ears on Niyah'. He had proven to be a serviceable echoman, but Triistan wondered if the Captain had suspected to who those ears (and tongue) actually belonged. Wil's father, Triistan had learned sometime later, was a Minister. He had forgotten this point, but now he realized why Wil had taken offense at her comment about the Ministry and young boys. It struck awfully close to home.

"Looks like Snitch and Snatch didn't catch all of the rats, did they, Mung?" Dreysha growled. Wil squeaked in fright, and Triistan had to clamp his teeth together to keep from laughing. Whatever his purpose for joining them had been originally, and despite his many shortcomings, he had proven himself a dedicated member of the crew and a good friend. And he had been a decent echoman as well. Triistan was curious about his motives, but not threatened by them.

"Time to come clean, Wil," he prodded gently. "Why were you assigned to the *Peregrine*?"

For a man who had perfected the art of looking awkward and embarrassed, Wil could not have looked more uncomfortable if his pants had suddenly dropped around his ankles.

Then he sighed and sat down in a heap. "Very well, then, I don't suppose it matters much anymore.

"'When charting the far horizons, there must always be an Azimuth'," Wil said in a mocking tone. "That's what Father said. He's very big on furthering the family name… even if it's right over the edge of the world." He kept his head down.

"I mean this should be a historic occasion - the *Peregrine*, the Corps' finest vessel, setting off for lands unknown is a story-worthy tale in and of itself, but it's also a way for we Islanders to continue our natural ascension in filling the vacancy left behind by the…

previous administration, shall we say. That was the talk around the house, when it had been decided that I would be thrust into this venture. For a while I was swept up in the majesty of it, being part of something that was as big as the tales told of the times before the Godswar. As I came to find, however, it was a tale constructed only to hide the real goal…"

"Which was…?" Rantham said in frustration. "Speak plainly, Mung."

Wil finally lifted his head. A faint, almost apologetic smile flitted across his face. "For that answer, I think I will defer to our good Captain. I was never actually told the full mission, but have heard and seen enough now that I believe I finally understand their… ambitions." These last few words fell out surprisingly bitter.

"I know you all, at times, have cursed me for being a lackwit and a coward… and I have never argued against the idea that I lack much of the vital aggressiveness and courage that a true Seeker should bear, but I count myself fortunate that I'm not so blind to the truth as my Father, who was caught up in the pageantry of it all.

"Ever a man with a nose for opportunity, here was a chance for the family name to be counted among what would surely someday be a ship's manifest of Heroes and People of Significance, about whom stories would be written and songs would be sung! Even if I failed to distinguish myself sufficiently to actually be mentioned in the song, Father would at least be able to raise a goblet when it was sung and say, 'Harken, for my son, my namesake, Wiliamund the Younger, was aboard that glorious ship!'

"For him, the opportunity was a way to tether his accomplishments to my own. Even better (if you asked him, I am quite sure he would tell you, as he told everyone else) since I had not yet lived up to my, ah… potential, he saw the dual benefit of forcing me into my manhood.

"'Either the Seekers will make a man of ye,' he said, 'or they'll make of ye their woman.' Father did love to butcher the High Speech at every inappropriate moment." As he finished, Snitch scampered across the deck and clambered up onto Wil's shoulder, wrapping his arms and tail around the young man's neck like a protective mother.

Dreysha actually managed to look somewhat abashed. "Seems I owe you an apology, Mung. I'd figured you for an agent of the Chancellor."

Mung snickered. "Oh, no, the High Chancellor is a bit above the Azimuth circle of influence, I assure you. Still... as dedicated a Minister as father is, I don't think he would have been able to assign me to the *Peregrine* on his own. I doubt very much it came from the Chancellor himself, but Father had help, I am quite sure of it, and I suspect his parting gift of twineroot seeds had more to do with spying than sentimentality. 'You can use these to keep in touch with us, let us know how you're doing' he said as he pressed the small pouch into my hand, but he passed them to me as you would a conspiratorial note. He even looked around as if he suspected someone might pop up out of one of the flower pots, I mean...

"What? Do I have something in my teeth?"

Triistan's jaw had dropped open - a look mirrored on Dreysha's and Rantham's faces as well. "You have twineroot seeds?" he sputtered. "Do you have them still?"

"Oh. Those." He dropped his head and sighed. "Alas, no. They were... taken."

"Taken? Taken by whom?"

"Oh, this is not going to go over very well." He took a deep breath and started speaking very rapidly, the words tumbling over each other so quickly it took Triistan a few moments to catch up and grasp what he was trying to say.

"I thought that perhaps some kind of contact with Command might help him... I don't know... reconnect in some way. And I have to say I was eager to get rid of them, especially if someone else could put them to good use. I did receive some training before I left, but it's one thing to talk about it and pretend you were Sending - quite another to actually Send, I can assure you. I had used one the night we set sail from Aarden and found the experience altogether horrifying and distasteful - like someone else was inside my head dreaming. No, that's not right. It was actually knowing that I was dreaming and having some level of control that made it feel like I was in someone else's head... of course, control is a highly relative term, isn't it? I mean I thought I was doing well until suddenly certain, ah, private images began to surface and, well, let's just say I have no desire to experience it again, and besides, I'm certain I loused it up anyway. The gods only know what the poor bastard at the other end was able to make out from my nonsense. Anyway, the point is that I thought if he had a chance to do his captainly duty and alert Fleet Command of our predicament - in effect to rescue us - it would bring him back from.... from wherever it was he'd gotten run off to… up here, I mean," he finished, tapping the side of his head.

Dreysha made a painful expression, pinching the bridge of her nose.

"By the Storm Lord's salt-stained scrotum, you gave the bloody things to Fjord?!"

Wil squeezed his eyes and mouth shut tight and nodded, clearly waiting to be struck - or worse. Triistan had to admit that he could have strangled his friend right there. Just one seed could have saved them - they could have sent a message to Fleet Command weeks earlier, and there would have been ships already out looking for them. They might already be back home by now. Instead, he'd given them to Captain Fjord, who had been mentally incapacitated by a bad blow to his head when the *Peregrine* sank.

"When did you give them to Captain Fjord, and what did he do with them?" he asked despondently, already knowing the answer.

"Well, as I said, it was after… "

"After? After what, Wil?"

He looked like he was going to be sick. "After I realized he wasn't… you know, right… in the head." There was a collective groan. "As I said, I thought it might help him."

"Oh, fuck-all!" Rantham spat. "I don't suppose anyone found them in his belongings before the crazy old bastard's Releasing Ceremony and has them tucked away for safekeeping?"

They all looked at one another, but Triistan thought he already knew the answer to that question, too; it seemed preposterous that if anyone had found the seeds they would have kept them to themselves.

"I wonder if that's what made him go mad," Dreysha said thoughtfully.

Triistan recalled the glimpse he'd had of Captain Fjord as he had made his way to the fore, just before tying himself to an anchor and leaping overboard. Fjord had been moving woodenly, in some sort of trance, and now Triistan wondered the same thing; had he ingested one of the seeds and that had triggered the Captain's bizarre behavior?

"I've never seen them used - do they do that - have that effect I mean?" he asked her. Some vague intuition was scratching at the back of his mind.

Dreysha seemed about to say something, then closed her mouth and simply shook her head, shrugging. Rantham spoke up, though.

"Not that I've heard of, unless you take too many or unless maybe you're already touched - which Fjord was, of course. Maybe having his watch-bell already rung did him in, or maybe it had nothing to do with it at all. I've served on two other vessels with a Sender on board, and normally all you do is eat the seed, slip into a weird sort of trance-sleep, and pass your messages down the line - which is no easy task, I hear. As Mung's already said, it's not a sure thing you'll get it right, as dreams have a way of twisting themselves."

"So who gets this... dream message?" Triistan asked distractedly. He was trying to corner a hazy memory of Dreysha. She'd been asleep beside him and woke with a start, claiming to have had a dream about Biiko. Shortly into their conversation, he'd discovered where she had previously folded a corner of a page in his journal and deduced she must have stolen and read it. Hurt and angry, he'd stalked off. Since then, however, they had made amends and talked at length about her dream. She revealed things about Biiko she claimed she'd dreamt, but the information was too specific, too real -

"Did you hear me, sir?"

Triistan shook his head sharply and focused his attention back on Rantham. "I'm sorry, could you repeat that?"

"I said, whoever has the matching seed will receive the message. They grow in pairs on the plant; one is picked and sent with the messenger, and its twin is left on the vine. When the 'messenger seed' is ingested, its sibling will blossom. Whoever has the plant knows their partner has used it."

"Then what, they eat the matching seed and experience the person's dreams?"

"No, from what I hear that is very dangerous - I don't know why, I just know that it is something that should not be done," answered Rantham. "Whomever tends the plant harvests the blossoming seed once its flower has fully opened, then steeps the petals in a kind of special tea made for this purpose. It is complicated, time-consuming, and even then the message may be misinterpreted."

They fell into a despondent silence that stretched on for several long moments. Triistan stole a discreet glance at Dreysha, but she seemed to be pointedly studying the horizon. His thoughts went from trying to remember who had searched Captain Fjord's belongings, to imagining what it would have been like if he had found them. Frustration and despair welled up within him and he wanted to cry.

You can't change the direction of the wind lad, he heard Scow's voice say, *but you can change the angle of your sails.*

He took a deep breath and blew it out slowly, trying to loosen the knot of frustration and despair in his chest. He needed to keep the others moving forward, get them to see the bigger picture and not place the blame on Wil. The last thing they needed was to return to the fractured, divisive atmosphere that had killed Scow and Pelor and maimed Rantham. He would not allow that to happen.

"Okay, well there's a chance that Captain Fjord was able to get some kind of coherent message through -"

Rantham snorted, but he ignored it and pressed on: "... and even if he didn't, at least they should have an idea of when we set sail from your attempt, Wil - which means they'll know when we're overdue." He forced a smile that felt like a ghoulish leer and clapped Wil on the back.

"Who knows; whomever you sent your 'private' thoughts to might have been impressed enough to commandeer their own boat to come and find you."

"Oh gods, no" Wil answered pitifully. "It would probably be Father." There was a moment of silence while they all pictured the same outrageous image. Then a sly smile twisted Dreysha's lips and Rantham actually burst out laughing. The release of tension was infectious, and Triistan found himself chuckling as well. Even Wil grinned sheepishly.

Finally, Dreysha brought them back to their original discussion. "So, let's say we accept your premise that our mission all along has been to search for Aarden, then why all of the secrecy? We all know we'll be trumpeting our discovery from every tower and hilltop in Ruine; so why not beat their chests about it when the *Peregrine* launched?

"What, exactly, were we looking for, Triis?"

A shadow crept across Triistan's heart, stealing the light from his smile. He glanced at Wil, saw the haunted look mirrored in his eyes; saw that he had probably guessed the truth.

And now we're come to it at last.

He pulled his journal out from its familiar spot, tucked into his sash at the small of his back. He drew it forth from its protective pouch and ran his cracked hands across the worn and stained cover, noting how closely his badly-weathered skin resembled the leather shell of the book. He did not open it, though. He didn't need to. Everything it contained was inside him as well.

He glanced over towards Biiko, perhaps the only other person still alive who knew the complete truth. The Unbound met his gaze with his peculiar golden eyes and nodded slowly. *This is your Path,* Triistan heard him say, as clearly as if he had been standing next to him, though the warrior was ten paces away and his lips had not moved.

Triistan drew a deep breath and began the rest of his tale.

- 10 -

A Children's Book

"It's a children's book," Casselle said, utterly crestfallen.

"Are you sure?" Temos asked.

Casselle handed the small, leather bound volume over to her friend, watching as he flipped through it. The opening pages showed Tarsus lifting the second sun into the sky, a burning sphere on the tip of his sword. It was a brightly colored picture followed by many other brightly colored pictures on the thick pages that followed. All the gods of the High Houses were there: Thunor descending on a writhing, dark mass of H'Kaan, his black wings spread wide; the Stormfather standing on a roughhewn rock as waves crashed around him, clouds above crackling with lightning; and even the frost cloaked Fjorvin the Reaper flanked by large white wolves.

"I don't recognize this one," Temos said, pausing on a page of a foreboding figure draped in black, books stacked to his sides and an obsidian tower framed behind him. "Probably don't want to, either. I can't see what's under that hood and nothing about it makes me want to."

"There are many I don't recognize," Casselle said, reaching over to flip to the back half of the book. The page settled on a large, muscular man who looked like a great statue made flesh, thickly chiseled arms and legs. "Who is this, for instance? I have no idea."

"And this was all there was?" Temos asked. "No hidden message or secret note?"

"I found this tucked into the spine of the book." Casselle held up a small metal sewing needle, curiously missing the hole needed to thread it. "There's a place you can slip it into the spine for safe-keeping."

"They're all about tattoos in the Vale. Maybe it has something to do with that?" Temos suggested. Casselle shrugged.

"I thought it was a way to find weapons. Lorelen said we were the hand to guide the tools."

"Maybe the book is the tool?" Temos guessed aloud. "Like it's filled with powerful arxhemical spells or formulas or whatever it is they call them?" He closed the book to look at the cover once again, hefting it in his hand. "It's kind of heavy. Maybe we throw it at evil?"

Casselle gave him a sideways stare.

"Yes, it's a terrible idea, but you've been thinking about it longer than I have. Give me a moment." He opened the book back up to a random page.

"The writing might be a clue... you know... if we could read it," Temos grumbled, running his fingers over the thick, bold text that accompanied the pictures. It was most likely written in Theranghel, the old language of the Vanha, which still seemed very much alive in the Ghostvale and had been a native tongue to the original Templar, but was now mostly dead save a few formal commands for parade and battle formations.

"Theander Kross knows it," Casselle said, remembering how the arxhemist easily read the books in the Khaliil Library.

"Yes, well, considering he's great pals with Lord Lockewood, who must have kept all of his good humor in the arm he lost, perhaps we should consider other options. We're not too popular on that side of the camp at the moment," Temos replied.

It had been several days since their return from the Ghostvale and many things had changed. Although Commander Cohl was still welcome to attend Lord Lockewood's advisory meetings, very little news trickled down to the rest of the Fist. Captain Ardell finally confirmed at dinner just moments ago that Richard had confessed to being "very disappointed" in the performance of the squad that had accompanied him to the Vale and wanted them kept at a comfortable distance from him. This explained why Greffin's two fingers of Shield Templars had been reassigned to the rear section of the Thundering Lance's procession, far removed from the position of honor they'd been given upon their departure from Strossen.

"Don't you worry. That man's opinions don't make our swords any less sharp," Greffin told Casselle after breaking the news to the rest of them. The Captain quelled the grumbles of his squad by taking the responsibility himself, and they all respected or feared him too much to contradict him. But the next day, Casselle was getting sidelong glances and Temos had ferreted out that many were blaming her for the slight despite the Captain's statement. Jhet was an unlikely source and it certainly would not be the Captain, leaving only Finn, who had developed an unsurprising aversion to looking Casselle or Temos in the eye right around the same time.

More than anything else, Casselle replayed it all in her head nightly, thinking of what she might have been able to say in front of the Voice of One that would have given them the best possible outcome. Not only could she not fix what had happened, she could not stop blaming herself either. On the night they had returned, she had at least hoped the book Lorelen had given her would be enough of a distraction.

After two days of marching, Cadences and fruitless searching through the book herself, she finally had confided in Temos that night after dinner. She didn't have to worry about the rest of the squad, because during their free time, Finn and Jhet chose to spend it elsewhere. Greffin might have chosen to stay with them - at least, Casselle hoped he would have - but being further away from the command group meant he spent more time walking over there and back.

"You've seen the cape, haven't you?" Temos asked, trying to distract her. Casselle nodded.

Richard had started wearing a short cape draped over the spot where his left arm had been. It covered the bare spot almost as if he had just been hiding it under there rather than missing it altogether. Having the arm removed had not otherwise slowed him down or made him seem any less imposing. In fact, with the cape, she thought he looked more regal than ever.

"Yeah, well, if having it lopped off was supposed to remind him not to be so much of a rutting bastard, I'd say it's not done a very good job of it," Temos said, going through the pages one at a time. "Are we sure she didn't give this to you as some sort of cruel prank?"

Casselle shook her head. Lorelen's words and actions seemed sincere. She was certain the book had a special significance, even if they couldn't figure it out at the moment.

"Yeah, well, keep it close then. If it's important, best we keep it within reach... our reach that is," he said with a smirk, "not Righteous Richard Righthand's."

She chuckled to herself as Temos returned the book to her, flipping through the pages once more. As she closed the cover, she knew there was a secret to be found there. She was convinced it was more important to solve that mystery than anything else, but as she wound the leather cord around it she knew her own self-doubt would linger on in the back of her mind.

"Oh! The Captain says we're three days out of our destination, and finally hinted at where we were heading," Temos said. "Lex Vellos, the great city of Cartishaan, or you know, former city. But it's where the Laegis had its largest presence!"

Temos was very excited, and even Casselle couldn't help but smile at his enthusiasm. Lex Vellos was to Old Cartishaan what Strossen is to Gundlaan. In reading Laegis histories she knew that it had been one of the largest of the cities before the Ehronfall, perhaps the largest city ever.

"I wonder if we shall stumble across the ruins of some old Templar barracks or uncover some lost tome from their library," he conjectured.

"Assuming we are allowed inside the ruins at all," Casselle answered, her melancholy having returned.

"Whether we are allowed or not, I suspect we shall explore them nonetheless," Temos said confidently, one eyebrow cocked. "Are we not the intrepid adventurers that braved the caverns under Flinderlass?"

"By intrepid do you mean cold and wet?" Casselle asked, finding a bit of mirth after all.

"Cold and bold, wet but ready!"

"That sounds horrible," Casselle laughed.

"Horribly exciting!" Temos proclaimed.

***

By the time they arrived days later, it didn't appear there was much left to explore. From this distance, Lex Vellos looked like the remains of an enormous animal, its bones picked clean and bleached by the heat of the two suns.

Temos stood up in his saddle, straining as best he could to see the whole of it. It was hard to determine how large it would have been in comparison to Strossen, the largest city she'd ever seen, since the borders had collapsed, been buried by sand, or both. In addition, the edge of the city furthest from them ended abruptly, claimed by the Fallen Sea.

It looked like the world had broken in half, which was not far from the truth. When Ehronhaal fell, it cracked the world. A large portion of Cartishaan and the Southern Sea collapsed more than a thousand feet down, forming the Fallen Sea at the bottom. Although the Sea Kings had since mapped the border where the Southern Sea spilled into it, Casselle couldn't see anything beyond where Lex Vellos had been claimed by that catastrophe save empty space.

"A city on the edge of a perilous cliff, filled with unknown danger," Temos mused as he sat back down. "I suppose that's something we haven't seen yet."

The Thundering Lance had been called to a stop as the city came into view. Word had come back that they were waiting for the advance scouts to return. They'd been dispatched the same night Casselle had revealed the book to Temos, but a short time after the official orders had circulated, the whispers had started: the scouts weren't just late, they were missing and presumed dead.

Casselle and Temos had just heard the news when they watched one of the Lance's squads of skirmishers break away from the main group and angle for the ruins, where they began a measured patrol along the edge of the city. The Laegis dismounted and stretched their legs, eager to explore, but grateful for the pause after the long morning ride. Several of them were discussing whether or not they should break out their heavier armor, the reinforced plates that were usually packed away during long travels, which could be worn over their normal armorjacks for additional protection when needed.

Listening to them, she realized that she felt alert and wary, but not nervous, not like when they had travelled to Flinderlass. The Wasting had been nothing but empty, with the sole exception being the Khaliil. She didn't expect what remained of Lex Vellos would be any different. Though it should have concerned her that the scouts were missing, it didn't.

Maybe it was because she'd found some inner calm once again after her experience at the Ghostvale. She had worried greatly about what the other Templar had thought of her after they had been moved to the back of the procession, but that was beginning to fade. Just because she had found acceptance with her last squad, there was no guarantee this one would be as tightly bound.

She thought of Jaksen, Raabel and Odegar, and as her hand strayed over the place where her mother's ring hung under her armorjack, she thought of her family as well. After she'd allowed herself a moment, she took a deep breath and exhaled slowly, reminding herself that she wasn't here for acceptance, but to do what she could to make a difference. Even though she'd been relegated to the back, it was better than not being here at all.

"Looks like we're posting up here," Temos said, dragging Casselle's attention back to the present. The Lance was setting up camp as they had so many other nights before. It was certainly too early in the day for it, but she assumed Lockewood chose this position in order to keep their distance from the ruined city. As tents went up and stakes were driven down, her thoughts were echoed by the other Templars who didn't understand why they had set up so far away either.

Once finished, the individual squads under Captain Ardell's command were instructed by his sergeant, Duran Holst, to work on Cadences and equipment maintenance. He deflected any questions directed at him.

"Questions are for the Captain," he said, rubbing a hand across his bald head and wiping the sweat on the leg of his pants. Holst was half as chatty as Greffin, and twice as surly.

"Don't take it the wrong way, kids. The Sergeant hasn't always been this way," said Lennard Torks, one of the Veterans in the Laegis and a former member of Greffin's old squad, like Duran. "When they make you Sergeant, they shove a stick up your ass... comes with the job."

Holst didn't try to stifle the chuckles, but he did slap Torks on the back of the head when his old squadmate lined up for practice.

Casselle was surprised to find Vincen von Darren had lined up across from her for Akist training. He must have found out from someone else during the trip that doing so was a tacit request for assistance and feedback. He still couldn't lock eyes with her for long, or anyone else for that matter, but he seemed sincere. She nodded and when Holst assigned them Cadence Five for ten repetitions, she did her best to set her pace slow enough for him to follow.

It also meant that they finished well after the others. Vincen was red and exhausted halfway through and by the time they were done, he looked spent and pale. The Long Evening had finally begun by then, but Casselle made sure he took a break for water while giving him terse pointers on stance and execution.

"Thank you," he said politely. It appeared that Greffin's speech and his embarrassment in front of Commander Cohl and Lord Lockewood before their trip to the Ghostvale had the intended effect. Vincen was trying to improve. There was an awkward pause, but if he had more to say, he swallowed it instead, moving away to where his squad was setting up for the night.

"That must be the most surprising thing I've seen in a long time," Temos commented quietly after drawing close, "and we've seen hollow metal men and a Wolfmother."

And as the mark on her arm suddenly grew cold, she recalled that she'd also seen Death, but she didn't mention that aloud.

***

Long after dinner, Captain Ardell returned to the squads under his command, two Fingers of the Laegis Fist attached to the Thundering Lance. He was cursing under his breath, hands tightly balled. His approach put him closest to Temos and Casselle, the bulk of the other Templars just beyond them.

"What's the news, Captain?" Temos asked. Casselle looked up from her brightly colored children's book, closing it gently around a finger to hold her place. She had been hoping that staring at the symbols might reveal some sort of pattern that she could figure out. She had only just reached the conclusion she might find easier meaning in attempting to read the stars or the campfire in front of them.

"Our Commander will be taking Captain Boen and his three Fingers along with Lockewood and the bulk of his Lancers into the city tomorrow," Greffin growled. Casselle knew this meant her actions had continued to punish the rest of the Shield Templars in Captain Ardell's two Fingers.

"Then all is well? They found the missing scouts?" Temos asked.

"What was left of 'em," Ardell said as he marched past them.

Temos and Casselle exchanged worried looks.

"Ah!" she hissed as her finger slid against one of the paper's edges, leaving her with a shallow but painful cut.

"You alright?" Temos asked.

Casselle nodded and stuck the finger in her mouth. She looked down to lament the drop of blood that had stained the edge of the page.

"I guess that means we're supposed to stay here at camp, then," Temos said, already moving on to voice his opinions. "Doesn't Lockewood know that with a missing arm, he's going to need the whole Fist to help out?" Giggling at his own joke, Temos looked back to Casselle for her approval.

She was preoccupied with something slightly more interesting. The drop of blood had disappeared. More correctly, it had been absorbed into the book until it had vanished altogether. Pulling her finger out of her mouth, she moved it back over to the open page and squeezed her finger until another drop swelled up in the cut and then fell to the paper.

The picture was of Ogund, the God of Making, his hammer raised, poised to bring it down on a black anvil. The red drop fell just to the side of his stern face, almost making it look as if he had been sweating blood while working.

"What are you..." Temos was just as shocked as he joined her in watching the drop of blood slowly shrink until it was a small red stain on the page and then disappear altogether.

"Okay, that's a bit creepy," he said. Casselle tried to squeeze out another drop, but the shallow cut had almost completely closed.

She set the book in her lap, freeing up her hands and rolling up one of her sleeves. She drew her knife, and despite Temos' protests, she cut a thin line on the top of her arm. She put the knife down and wiped up the blood with two fingers, smearing it down the length of the page, bloodying Ogund and his forge.

Temos was hovering over her shoulder, just as distracted as she was as the blood slowly vanished a third time, every bit of it absorbed by the page.

"It's warm along the spine," she said. For some reason, she thought of Odegar's last moments, as he lay outside the gates of Flinderlass, his body hot from the arxhemestry he'd used to save Jaksen, the magic that had also burned him up from the inside.

She flipped through the pages wildly, looking for some other sign. Something was happening and she was determined to find out what it was.

"There!" Temos said excitedly. Casselle had missed it, but the trapper's son had keen eyes and when she flipped back a few pages, she saw it, too.

An angry woman, heavily armored, lifted her weapons to the sky, crossed above her head. One was a sword that appeared burning with blue flames, the other a bright spear, both etched with bright blue runes and symbols.

Casselle remembered this page, but the subtly flickering blue flames had not been here before. The blue symbols on the weapons had not been here either and around the bold black text that accompanied every picture were now lines and lines of blue text filling the sides and spaces.

Then it flickered once and faded altogether.

Temos sat down next to Casselle and the two of them remained silent for a long time, listening to the campfire ahead of them crack and pop.

"I don't think that's just a children's book," Casselle finally confessed.

"I'm glad you say so," Temos replied, "I was beginning to think I'd been reading books all wrong."

***

The Thundering Lance was off at dawn, riding in formation towards the ruins of Lex Vellos. Commander Zan Cohl led two Fingers of Templar Lancers and one more finger of Archers alongside them, thirty highly trained Templar in lockstep with Richard Lockewood's soldiers.

Casselle watched Captain Greffin Ardell scowl and grumble, all the while absently kicking at the side of a low, flat rock that lay half buried in the sand next to him.

"Any orders, sir?" she asked.

"Hm? Oh... no. None really, Milner. Just make sure no one runs off with the rutting tents," he responded. He stomped off, passing by the bulk of the Shield Templars, who were casually finishing off their breakfasts. Since they had been informed the night before that they would not be riding into Lex Vellos, they had adopted a more casual attitude. Ardell didn't even bother to scold any of them.

Sergeant Holst had given them some small things to do to keep busy, but pretty much left them to their own devices. Given the restless energy of the camp and the fact that they'd been kept from the exploration, most of the Templar decided to work on Cadences or just spar with each other. Vincen sought out Casselle again and while the two of them practiced Akist stances and footwork, Temos found himself the recipient of a rather odd request.

"You want to practice against the best warrior in the Fist?" Gunnar Hawken asked a surprised Temos.

"Well, seeing as she's busy," Temos said, hooking a thumb at Casselle, "I suppose I could give you a few pointers." Gunnar laughed warmly and the two of them stepped away from the tents and other Templar.

"Why me?" Temos asked. Casselle paid attention to the answer. It had only been a short while, but perhaps opinions were beginning to shift.

"I'm not used to fighting people so much smaller than me. It takes different tactics, you know, so I thought I'd practice while I had the chance." Gunnar had a warm, friendly smile and if Temos' face was any indication, he, too, was having problems determining if the big man was making a joke about it.

"I know the air up there is thin, so I'll try not to wear you out," Temos replied. The big Templar chuckled and set aside his preferred weapon, a massive steel warclub about half as tall as the man himself, which made it almost as tall as Temos. Gunnar was what Casselle had pictured all Vanha as before meeting some of them in person. The stories her mother read her made them all seem like giants. Odegar seemed larger than life, but was roughly the height of her father, only a head taller than Casselle. Gunnar wasn't just tall, he was heroically large, with arms thicker than Casselle's legs and stood at least a head and a half taller above everyone else.

Temos made a couple of test swipes with his wooden practice blade before he squared off with Gunnar. The larger Templar had kept his sleeveless armorjack, but had picked up a quarterstaff wrapped thick at one end with canvas. It had a passing similarity to his warclub, but was clearly lighter and quicker in his hands. Temos tapped his helmet and then pointed at Gunnar's bald head. The Vanha Templar chuckled slightly and then nodded no. It occurred to Casselle at that moment that she'd never actually seen Gunnar wearing heavy armor beyond his sleeveless armorjack, and never any headgear. She tried to conceal a smirk as she politely corrected Vincen's posture coming out of a turn.

"Suit yourself," Temos said before indicating he was ready to begin.

Gunnar nodded in agreement and the two of them began to circle each other. Gunnar had the longer reach and poked out a couple of times, but Temos tried to keep himself at the edge of Gunnar's range while using his shield to deflect the makeshift club. The larger Templar was fast, though, faster than Casselle expected him to be. Temos was no stranger to fighting larger opponents, however. One of his primary sparring partners for the long years of Akist training had been Raabel Schuute, the tall muscular son of one of Strossen's constables. Much of their training had been designed to cover disadvantageous situations like this. Against people without Laegis training, Temos most certainly would have already used this to his advantage.

But Gunnar had also been trained by the Laegis, and had plenty of combat experience, so Temos spent most of his time on the defensive. Tense minutes crawled by.

"I don't think I would have this much trouble with other tiny people," Gunnar grunted after trying to bat away Temos' shield. Casselle could tell he was trying to be complimentary, but she also noticed that Temos wasn't talking. Given his normal demeanor, most would assume that would mean he was frustrated. She remembered Raabel commenting on it years ago, like it was just happening again: "No words left for me, Rabbit?"

That came just before Temos toppled Raabel for the first, but certainly not last, time.

Gunnar thrust out again, reaching just enough to make it look like he was overextended. Temos tucked in, moving with his sword to the side, his shield poised to deflect the strike. Gunnar wasn't overextended, though; he was just where he needed to be in order to kick at Temos' open side. It was a move most Templars performed with their shields in order to tip their opponent's balance, but Gunnar's size and strength were more than sufficient. But it was also based on the assumption that the attacker was charging directly forward, attempting to score a hit on the body. Temos, however, had left his sword behind him as he put both hands behind his own shield and veered directly into the Vanha's right leg, just below the knee.

Both of them became a blur as an unbalanced Gunnar was overturned, nearly smashing Temos in the head with his kick. The leg scraped the smaller man's helmet and sent him off balance as well, but not to the same degree.

Gunnar was face down in the sand after a hard fall, but rolled over laughing.

"I will now accept your surrender," Temos said proudly. Several of the other Templar broke into laughter. Casselle smiled, knowing that such a trick would never work a second time. She and Vincen had stopped altogether, merely watching the aftermath.

"Well played, mighty Templar!" Gunnar said, smiling as he picked himself up off the ground. "Perhaps a second turn?"

"I feel I've already proved my point," Temos said, offering a hand out to his fellow Laegis to help him stand. It was a very odd scene. "No need to drive it home further."

There were several groans of disappointment from those watching that were hoping for more. Gunnar, now on his feet, shook his head.

"Calm down. He's just trying to save me from further embarrassment," the large man said. "I, for one, am grateful."

He waved them off good-naturedly, and they broke into smaller groups to spar on their own or attend to camp chores.

"Sorry about the knee," Temos said.

"It does smart," Gunnar confessed, "but it was a lesson worth learning. I think I get too confident because of my size and heritage sometimes."

"I'm sure if you were poking me with that giant metal wall-breaker, things might have gone differently as well," Temos said, indicating Gunnar's warclub.

"Ha! Well, yes, perhaps. But then it is a special weapon, crafted of the finest bluesteel and handed down through our family for several generations. I imagine anyone that could wield it would have a distinct advantage in a fight against someone without a similar weapon."

"Gods and heroes with their mighty weapons," Vincen von Darren said, sounding surprisingly wistful. "Mother used to tell me stories of them when I was a child."

"I think most parents did," agreed Casselle.

"It's not so different for those of us related to them," Gunnar confessed with a grin. "My father would point out pictures hung on the walls of our home. He was always so proud of where we had come from. I can almost see them now."

"I wonder if any of them are like the ones in Casselle's book?" Temos mused aloud. Casselle's heart sank and her eyes grew wide. What the rutting Dark was he doing?

"What book is that?" Gunnar asked.

"Some book she found at the bottom of a shelf in the back of a bookstore in Strossen, years ago when we were training, got it for just a couple coppers. Beautiful pictures but can't read a word," Temos said. "She's carried it with her everywhere since then. Good luck charm or some such. You want to see it?"

"Temos..." Casselle began.

"Only if you don't mind?" The large Templar directed the question at her directly.

- 160 -

"No..." she said, still not sure what Temos was attempting to do, but deciding to trust him nonetheless.

"You carry books with you?" Vincen asked. It didn't sound like a criticism, more like a surprise.

"Just a few," Casselle said, surprised at her sudden embarrassment. She dug around in her pack, pulling it from between the few others she'd brought with her. She handed it over to Gunnar, staring at Temos sharply once the Vanha's eyes were on the book.

"That's a well made book," Vincen said. "Don't know if the merchant knew what he had, but it's clearly worth more than a few coppers. Good buy, Milner." Casselle didn't know how to take Vincen's unexpected praise.

"HA!" Gunnar said. "It's a children's book!"

"That's what I told her," Temos said. "Good pictures though."

"It's written in the old words," Gunnar said.

"Oh? You can read them?" Temos asked, sounding a bit more surprised than he ever did.

That was his play, Casselle thought, *to see if Gunnar could translate it.* Aside from Richard, he might have been the most pureblood Vanha in the camp.

"Most of it is just simple rhymes," he said. "Like this one here:
Flynn the Bard
His harp weaves music
Into pictures of light."

"That doesn't rhyme at all," Vincen said, wrinkling his nose. More like the Vincen they'd met back in Flinderlass.

"Lost in the translation," Gunnar grinned, flipping through the pages. "Quite a lot in here, I wonder if... Ah! Here it is."

"What's that?" Temos asked.

"Virilus and Der'krulsuus, the Dark Crusher," Gunnar said, turning the book to show an armored man with a fabulous beard brandishing a warclub identical to the one just a few feet from them. "That's my great grandfather.
"Strong Virilus
Crushing the Dark
Suns shine."

"Yes, that poetry is horrible," Vincen frowned.

"Your club is called Dark Crusher?" Temos asked.

"H'Kaan are creatures of the Dark. It crushes them," Gunnar said plainly.

"Fair enough," Temos said.

"Thank you for letting me look." The Vanha handed the book back to Casselle. "It was good to see that."

Casselle tucked it into a large pouch at the back of her belt. At least one mystery was solved. The book was written in an older language, but one that could be deciphered. Even though the clear text was of no real use to them, in time she'd be able to translate the hidden writing... if they had that kind of time left. Casselle wanted to know what it meant, but Lorelen had given it to her in secret. Clearly the Khaliil didn't want just anyone to have it or they would have given it to Lockewood.

"I've always wondered," Temos said, "when I heard these stories of the Gods and their great weapons, like Thunor's big sword or Shan's knives or even the Dark Crusher over there... how'd they never get lost? I mean I lose my shield like every other week and it's easy to replace. I imagine if you lose something like your club on a crowded field, it's a bit harder to replace."

"Ha! I'd be skinned alive by the ghost of my great grandfather if I ever lost 'kruls," Gunnar laughed. "Thankfully there are ways to find it."

"Ways?" Vincen asked.

"Magic," Gunnar winked.

"Arxhemestry," Temos clarified.

"Takes all the wonder out of it when you say it that way," Gunnar said, "but yes. When each weapon was crafted, it was given a hidden name, one that we can use to find it with the right tools."

"Like some sort of dowsing device?" Temos asked.

"Something like that." Gunnar smiled. "Don't want to give away too much, though. Family secrets and all. Let's just assure you that I'll make sure it stays in good hands."

"That's reassuring," Temos said.

Casselle was already thinking of what this might mean for the book. Could it be that those were the true names, a way to find them? Was the book such a tool?

"I've heard that there are many tools," Lorelen had said. She hadn't been talking about the weapons they could find. She was talking about the book itself. It was exactly what Richard had been looking for, a way to track down all the weapons he would need to take on a resurgence of the H'Kaan, or possibly even Maughrin herself.

Someone called for Gunnar to spar. The big Templar thanked Temos for the "lesson" and went off to trade blows with someone else ready to test the battle-hardened Vanha. Casselle let Vincen go as well, urging him to continue practicing the Cadence they had been working on.

Temos led her away from the others.

"What they must think of our little conferences," Temos mused.

"The book..." Casselle started, waiting to see if Temos was thinking the same thing she was.

"I think it's more than just the book," Temos said. "When my father and I would go out for weeks to check our traps, we had lots of familiar landmarks, but occasionally when the weather was bad or the night sky was overcast, he would use a lodestone to check our direction. Those things aren't perfect, but it was a good way to gauge if we were going in roughly the right direction."

"The needle," Casselle said, already jumping to his next thought.

Around the corner of a tent, out of everyone's immediate line of sight, she pulled out the book and removed the large needle from where it was tucked into the spine.

"Start with the club," Temos said. Casselle flipped through the pages until they found Gunnar's great grandfather. She flattened the page as best she could and set the needle on top of it.

They both stared at it for a moment, waiting for it to react.

"Wait!" Temos said, picking up the needle and using it to prick the end of his thumb. Making sure the bead of red blood was on the needle, he set it back onto the page where it was quickly absorbed.

The needle snapped to the center of the picture, spinning in a mad circle for just a second before stopping altogether. Temos took a step or two back, peeking around the side of the tent to confirm what he already expected.

"It's pointing straight at it," he said. The needle went idle, rolling off-center as the force that had been directing it was spent.

"Do the other picture," Temos insisted. "The scary lady from the other night."

Casselle flipped to find her picture while Temos coaxed another small drop of blood from the pinprick on his thumb.

The experience was the same. Once the blood had soaked in, the needle locked into the center of the page and spun quickly a few times before stopping.

"It's pointed at Lex Vellos," Casselle said.

"It must be the one Lockewood already knows about," Temos reasoned.

"Or it was a gamble that it remained here."

"So what do we do now?" Temos asked. "Now that we know the truth?"

Casselle returned his puzzled look with one of her own.

"I honestly have no idea."

- 11 -

Danor

Triistan could no longer recall who, but someone had once told him that Aarden meant "Land of Secrets" in one of the old tongues. Since his time exploring the dark interior of that strange country, he had been keeping many of those secrets, and had since discovered that such things were like wild creatures caught in a snare; they scratched and clawed and bit at themselves and their bonds until the snare, or death, set them free. Late on the morning of the thirty-second day since the SKS *Peregrine's* destruction, Triistan finally succumbed to their will - to Aarden's will.

He opened the weathered, cracked skin of his Oath and allowed his fellow survivors to read the pages within, telling them everything, and sparing himself nothing.

He dove headlong into his tale where he had left off: his feverish journey through the sewers of Ostenvaard, strapped to the back of a jharrl, while some terrible illness gnawed away at his insides and caused him to vomit blood several times along the way. By the time they reached their destination, his world had been reduced to the thick, rough fur rubbing his cheek raw, the sting of bile in his throat, the fire in his belly, and the insane hope that the jharrl would eat him and end his misery.

Time passed. How much, he could not have said, though he learned later that it took them more than half a day to reach their destination. He was dimly aware of changing sounds, lighting, and occasionally the slope of their path. Twice he heard the roar of falling water, once passing close enough to feel its spray. He remembered the great beasts growing agitated then, and the soothing, singsong words of their captors to pacify them.

Eventually, rough hands dragged him from the back of the jharrl and laid him on a hard bed. Unfamiliar voices spoke heatedly for a few moments in a language he could not comprehend, until one said something that sounded like a command. The conversation ceased abruptly. A moment later, he sensed someone looming over him.

Triistan forced his eyes open and gurgled a weak cry. The same terrifying face with the scar scowled down at him, absently rubbing their broad chin as if deep in thought. Triistan tried to lift his head to locate his friends, but the giant placed a heavy hand on his chest, pinning him effortlessly, as if he were a small child.

"No. Lie still," the giant told him gruffly, catching Triistan by surprise. He opened his mouth to speak, just as a second voice broke in angrily. The giant actually rolled his eyes - the expression would have been comical under different circumstances - before standing and turning away. Triistan tried to lift himself up on one elbow to look, but a wave of pain and nausea gripped his insides, making his head swim. He collapsed back on the bed with a loud groan.

There was another brief argument, followed by the sound of heavy boots clumping away, and finally the crash of a door slamming shut.

"Fuundaris idiomata," the giant growled from nearby. It did not sound like a compliment. "What do they call you, boy?"

Through the red haze of his pain, Triistan almost answered "Titch". But instead, he managed to whisper his true name through clenched teeth.

"Halliard," the giant grunted. "One of Shan's children then. I thought as much from the sun-copper hair and skin. You're a long way from home, boy." He dragged something heavy across the floor and Triistan squeezed his eyes shut, thinking the screech of scraping wood would surely split his head open. The giant said something else, but he missed it.

Another wave of pain rolled through him, and this time his stomach turned over. A slick, cold sweat broke out on his back and scalp.

"What's wrrrrrrong with me."

Another grunt. "What's wrong is that you are dying, boy. You are being eaten from the inside. Judging from the amount of blood you left out there, I would have blamed Theckan for dumping you at my door, had I not seen The Rogue die with my own two eyes."

Triistan's head swam with confusion. What did the dead God of Good Fortune have to do with him? What's more, how could anyone consider this lucky?

He squeezed his eyes shut against another cramp, trying to will away the rising nausea that came with it. From nearby came the discordant sounds of jars and something metal clashing together.

"Where are those fuundaris crystals?" the giant growled under his breath, then appeared to read Triistan's thoughts. "I imagine you are, at this precise moment, trying to work out just how anyone could possibly think of you as... no, those won't do at all - too large for the likes of you, but I know there were fragments around here somewhere... ah! Found you, you little pecturos. Exfanos pii nundiis. Yes, these should do perfectly, and end your suffering, Salt-spawn."

A large hand clamped around his lower jaw and squeezed just above his teeth with thumb and forefinger, forcing his mouth open. Two small, rough objects dropped into his mouth, and then the giant relaxed his stone-handed grip. "Do not try and chew those unless you would like to add broken teeth to your list of woes. Swallow them whole, Salty."

But for all his suffering, Triistan discovered that he did not actually want to die - certainly not from poisoning, which he was suddenly convinced this strange thing was offering. As soon as the giant relaxed its grip enough, Triistan turned his head and spat the objects out. They had felt like sharp stones, and left an odd sensation behind - not a taste, but more like a warm vibration, as if he had just been humming.

His captor was not amused. The stony grip returned, forcing his head back to face the giant. Though his features were in shadow, Triistan could clearly see his sharp blue eyes, as if they glowed just enough to be visible even in the dark.

"Now mind me, and mind me very well, Triistan Halliard." He pronounced it 'Hul-yarrd', with a slight roll of the 'r' that struck Triistan as vaguely familiar. "You have been stung by a Nagayuun - what you and your salt-spawned friends call 'nest guardians'. You have treated the wound, but not the blood. As a result, you have a few of the creature's younglings feasting on your insides. The blood you are puking is from the hole they have gnawed in your stomach."

He paused, letting the words sink in.

"I see I now have your full attention. Good."

Still keeping his grip on Triistan's face, he scooped up something off the bed and held it up where Triistan could see it. "Fortunately - in a manner of speaking - it's not your guts they're after, not really. It's this." Between his oversized thumb and forefinger was a semitransparent, bluish crystal. It looked like a sapphire, but one that had just been mined, still dull, with very few facets visible and no shine to speak of. Triistan recognized it immediately.

"Xhemium?" he gasped. Though the giant's mouth did not move, the corners of his eyes seemed to wrinkle, which Triistan supposed was the closest he came to an actual smile.

"Perhaps you are not as dumb as you look, Salty."

"But… so much… where did you find so much?"

The giant frowned. "I like not the implications of your question, boy, but there will be time enough for interrogations after. First, you will eat this, and give the nagayuun what they seek. From the look of you, they have already absorbed much of your own stores. And then…

"Well, we will ford that river when we reach its bank."

Triistan did not like the sound of that, but what choice did he have? As if in answer, another bolt of fire lanced his mid-section, and this time the wave of nausea that followed would not be denied. Fortunately, the giant realized what was happening, because he released Triistan's face and helped him lean over the side of the bed. He wasn't fast enough to slide the wide brass bowl into position, however, and muttered another curse in that strange other language as Triistan vomited onto the floor. There wasn't much, but what did come up was alarmingly red. Dark spots crowded the edge of his vision. If the giant had not been supporting him, he would have toppled over the side of the bed and onto the floor.

"I should make you clean that up when we're through, if you live that long," he heard in between heaves. Fortunately, the spasms did not last long, and when they passed, he was rolled onto his back. Once again he felt the strong grip on his jaw, but this time he did not resist; when the crystals were dropped into his mouth, he choked them down. The giant lifted his head and put a cup of water to his lips, which helped, but still they felt too large, like chunks of meat or bread he had not taken the time to chew. He wondered how long he would be able to keep them down.

"Just long enough, I should think," the giant responded, again as if he could read Triistan's thoughts.

But before he could process that idea, another searing wave of pain enveloped his abdomen. This one was different though, and far, far worse than anything he had felt before. He screamed and contracted his body, but it was no use. It was as if someone had shoved a hot spear into his belly and was twisting it. Unimaginably, it got worse, and he actually felt something moving inside him.

Looking back on it, he supposed he went mad for a time. He remembered trying to claw at his stomach, thinking that he had to get whatever it was that was inside him out, no matter how. The giant grabbed his arms, capturing both of Triistan's wrists in one huge hand. When he opened his mouth to scream again, he felt something like a rough wad of leather shoved between his teeth.

"Bite down on this, boy! It'll all be over soon, for better or worse." Triistan bit down convulsively as the pain intensified. He thrashed back and forth so violently that he must have surprised his minder, as for a moment he actually freed one hand.

The giant swore viciously and pinned both of Triistan's arms across his chest, using his considerable weight advantage to keep them there for the next few moments. Whatever was inside him must now be clawing its way out, tearing through his stomach. Some macabre instinct made him lift his head to try and see, but the giant's massive bulk blocked his view. He kicked, bucked and thrashed his head from side to side, while rage and terror tore at what was left of his sanity.

Unable to stand it any longer, Triistan spat the wad of leather from his mouth. "OH GODS MAKE IT STOP!!! PLEEEASE!!"

In a sudden, swift motion, Triistan found himself lifted from the bed, spun around, and then crushed against the giant's chest in a bear hug. He was facing away in the opposite direction, and felt the thing's massive fist thrust just above the spot in his belly where he was sure a full-sized nest guardian must be erupting from within. The giant jerked its arms, driving its fist up under his rib cage once, twice - and on the third such blow, Triistan felt the air driven from his lungs, followed close behind by the contents of his stomach. He felt the hard passing of the crystals he had consumed earlier, as well as something else - smaller and smoother, but definitely solid. The black and red spots threatened his vision again as he struggled to breathe, but his captor did not release his grip for several more agonizing moments.

When the giant finally let go, Triistan collapsed to the ground on his hands and knees, alternately gasping and retching. He was helpless to do anything else for the next several minutes, but eventually the spasms subsided. He remained on all fours, panting in great, ragged breaths, then lowered his head slowly to the ground to take the strain off his trembling arms. The cool touch of the stone floor on his forehead was the most pleasant, comforting sensation he had ever felt. He focused only on that, willing it to become his entire existence.

Eventually, the shuffle and scrape of someone moving about nearby intruded on his sanctuary, and he was forced to remember his situation. He pushed himself back up to a kneeling position and opened his eyes. His throat constricted again at the sight of the gruesome mess on the floor before him, but it was just a reflex; there was no nausea this time, and the pain in his belly had receded to a low ache. Grateful for the respite, he steeled himself and looked more closely at the former contents of his stomach.

The two xhemium crystals - now a dark, slimy reddish color - were there amongst the small pool of bile and blood, but they weren't the only objects: two elongated shapes, each about half the size of his little finger, were crawling their way through the slime towards the crystals. They looked like the things he'd seen after getting sick in the sewers; like small grubs, except that one end - which he took to be the front based on the direction they were moving - was shaped like a spade. From this 'head', their bodies tapered back to a thin tail that whipped clumsily back and forth in the spew. What had the giant called them? Naguyen or something - baby nest guardians. And they had been inside him… eating him alive.

A wave of horrified exhaustion swept over him and he fell sideways, out cold long before his shoulder and head struck the stone floor.

***

Triistan learned later that he slept for the rest of that day, through the night, and did not stir again until Ruine's twin suns had reached their mid-day zenith. When he did wake, he found himself staring into Biiko's remarkable golden eyes. His heart leapt, and seized by the thought that everything had been some terrible dream, he tried to sit up, convinced he would find himself in a camp alongside the Glowater, or at worst back by the guardhouse on the outskirts of the city.

But his hopes vanished when a massive hand reached across him from the other side of the bed and pushed him back down. Once again he found himself staring up at the craggy, scarred face of his giant captor.

"Welcome back, Salty. I hope you prove to be a better conversationalist than the Patroniis." Triistan looked back at Biiko, fearing the Unbound had been an illusion. He was still there however, and for answer only shrugged, his expression as impassive as ever. Over the past few weeks, though, Triistan had made significant strides reading subtle clues in the warrior's demeanor, and although the man's dark lips were pressed into a thin, straight line, Triistan felt sure he looked... happy. He tried to clear his throat, aware for the first time how sore and dry it was.

"Water," he managed to choke out in a cracked whisper. The giant produced a tall silver cup and a large pitcher. As he poured, Triistan caught a glimpse of clear, amber-colored liquid, and wondered if it was ale. If it was water, it did not look very clean, but he no longer feared poison - whatever the giant had done to him, it had clearly been to help, and at this point all he really cared about was something wet to drink.

Not trusting his trembling limbs, he took the cup with both hands and raised it to his lips. It tasted slightly bitter, but not unpleasantly so, and as soon as it slid down his throat, most of the soreness there evaporated. He drained the cup greedily, then held it out for more. A warmth spread from his stomach, as though he had just drank a cup of wine, and although at first he had not been aware of it, he realized now that there was still a sharp, insistent stab of pain from his gut as well.

He put one hand to his stomach. "Are they still there? I feel - I can still feel something. Pain... not nearly as bad, but it's there..."

The giant shook his broad head, his scowl twisting sardonically. "If they were, you'd be dead, and that would make your friend and I dead as well since we're talking to one another. Well, more likely you'd call it staring at each other, but you get the idea." Then, in a slightly softer voice - not quite sympathetic, but something close to it, perhaps:

"They're gone, boy. You're going to be sore for a few days, but your guts will stitch themselves back up just so long as you can listen as well as you puke: mind me and mind what you eat for a while, and you'll live. I cannot answer for Bryn or Tau, but the nagayuun won't kill you."

Triistan closed his eyes, relieved. "Thank you... "

He opened them again, realizing he did not know the giant's name, let alone who Bryn and Tau were.

"Danor," the giant said, eyes twinkling beneath stark white eyebrows as he deftly poured more of the amber liquid into Triistan's cup.

Triistan studied him more closely as he sipped the drink. He certainly looked like a man - a very large man, to be sure, but a man nonetheless. His hair was a close-cropped shock of silver-white that was matched by his bristly eyebrows, all of which, like his brilliant blue eyes, stood in sharp contrast to the deeply tanned skin of his face. He had a presence to him that was palpable; Triistan could feel it on his own skin like the warm glow of a nearby fire.

Unlike the godlike warrior who had first appeared in the tunnel walking next to the monarch jharrl, Danor wore no armor that he could see. Indeed his clothing was fairly simple - dark, loose fitting trousers and a beige, sleeveless tunic. His shoulders and arms were strong and well-toned, bare of any ornament save one; a tattoo on the inside of his left forearm comprised of a series of glyphs or characters Triistan did not recognize. He wondered if it was the same tongue the giant had been speaking in earlier.

He almost laughed. Freed of the fear and discomfort of his illness, his mind had caught up with his situation, and - as usual - was now racing off in every conceivable direction.

Focus, Triis. He was grateful for the soothing sensation of the drink, but he had so many questions and was afraid whatever healing attributes it had might also make him drowsy or, worse, befuddled. He turned to Biiko first.

"Are you - are the others - I mean… where is everyone? Are they ok?" One corner of the Unbound's mouth ticked upwards in what Triistan had learned was what passed for a smile. He nodded, once.

"All of them?" Another nod. He sighed and closed his eyes again, momentarily caught off guard by the enormity of his sense of relief. He was beginning to realize that he had come to care a great deal about each member of the expedition, feeling for the first time in his young life that he was part of something bigger than himself.

When he thought he could trust his voice again, he turned back to his minder. "With all due respect… um… sir… who… what… are you?"

A brief look of pain flitted across Danor's craggy face and he grunted. "You've some skill as a surgeon, boy, to cut me so quick. That is a tale for another to tell though, and a long one besides. He is… away just now, though he's overdue and I expect will be back any day now."

He stood, and it took Triistan's eyes a few seconds to refocus on him. A great, soft weight seemed to be settling over all of his limbs. He blinked, his eyelids heavy. When the giant spoke again, his voice seemed muffled, as if he were on the other side of a door.

"For now, you have my name, and that will have to do. As for what… "

Danor broke off, frowning slightly. Triistan's vision swam out of focus. He screwed his eyes shut, but when he tried to open them again, they refused. Danor continued, sounding even further away.

"I know what we were, once. But what we are now? Only the Lord Marshall can say."

Lord Marshall. The title reverberated through Triistan's mind, and a memory from his time as Doyen Rathmiin's apprentice echoed back. It was of an old, heavy tome he had found by accident, full of beautifully-wrought illustrations and a story that had captured his young imagination. An inscription on the last page floated up to him even as he sank into sleep.

"Where this wind ends, our Oath begins. Remember us."

He dreamt. Vivid dreams of giant, crystal-eyed warriors sailing great, beautiful ships for a faraway land, where they would devote their long lives to a cause the world would forget. Captain Vaelysia spoke to him from atop a high tower.

"This," she said, "is Ostenvaard, City of the Faithful and once home to the Laegis Centuriis… The Thousand."

When he woke the next morning, the answer to his question was perched on his own lips.

"Oathguard."

- 12 -

Lex Vellos

The Long Evening hadn't quite started when the first horse galloped through camp, riderless and frothing at the mouth, mad with fear. Before anyone could even think of reining it in, it had run out the other side before collapsing to the sand, dead from exhaustion and a dozen or more cuts along its flanks.

Not long after, wagons of wounded soldiers, members of Lockewood's Thundering Lance, rumbled back into camp. Those who weren't lost in shock whispered worrisome stories of ghosts and shadows.

"The exploration of Lex Vellos has proved to be more complicated than expected."

That was the rather poorly summarized account given to Captain Ardell and those under his command much later that night. Although Commander Cohl did not speak with the bulk of the Templars, Greffin relayed the message to them directly. It was not a message that was entirely unexpected, either.

"Some say they are an armed force, some report monsters," Greffin told his Templars. "Commander Cohl couldn't tell me more because reports are not consistent. When the Lance arrived yesterday, it was dispersed into smaller groups to start mapping the city, looking for key structures. Not all of the groups were attacked, but many were ambushed."

"Who could be living out here?" someone asked. *Marn was his name perhaps?* Casselle was still not familiar with all of them, but tried hard to keep names associated with faces.

"Don't forget the Khaliil live out here," someone else spoke up.

"Sand Ghosts in the ruins? Are you-"

"Quiet!" barked Duran Holst, Greffin's sergeant.

"We don't know who they are," Captain Ardell continued. "None of the engagements resulted in capturing a prisoner. If I'm to understand correctly, they actually took some of ours."

There were several wide-eyed stares until a general uproar of defiance broke the relative silence.

"Shut it!" Greffin shouted, quieting the uproar. "We're going to have our chance to meet them soon enough, but we go in there not knowing what to expect. Anger and vengeance are justified, but you can't count on them to carry the day. We need to know what we're fighting and work together to beat it. We're not common tin-plated thugs that jump at shadows."

"En'vaar et Laegis!" someone in the back said proudly. There was a chorus of gauntlets striking leather as those assembled put their clenched fists over their hearts.

"En'vaar et Laegis!" they all replied. Greffin nodded in approval.

"Get a good night's sleep and we'll show them what that means in the morning," the Captain said.

If the Captain had given the order, they would have marched out that night. Instead, they made do with the small chores necessary for tomorrow's departure. All the buckles and straps and plates of armor were oiled and polished. Equipment bags were checked and secured. Edges were sharpened, grips re-wrapped and quivers filled. Casselle and Temos watched several of the other Templars go through their Cadences, slowly, more as a means to focus their restless minds.

"Are we going to tell Captain Ardell what we found?" Temos asked quietly.

"I... I still don't know," Casselle confessed. A few moments passed while Temos stared into the fire, until Casselle asked him what he thought was best.

"I was rather hoping you didn't ask, because I'm just as stumped as you. The only thing I do feel is that sooner or later the truth will come out. Even if they never find out about that, they're going to want to know how you know where to look for these things."

"What if I don't look for them?" Casselle asked.

"Then why did you ask for it? If you thought it was better for us to have them, then your motivation is to collect them," Temos said.

"It was an observation born of frustration. I said that someone should have it. I didn't expect to actually be that someone," she confessed.

"It's more like a choice at this point. If you decide to do something, it's a responsibility. If you don't do anything..."

"A regret at best, a terrible mistake at worst," she admitted.

"Yes, but if the Dragon burns us all down, at least there won't be any historians to blame you for it," Temos teased.

"You're horrible," Casselle groaned. She took a deep breath, staring into the fire for a few minutes, before standing up and knocking the sand from her armorjack as best she could.

"I'm going to talk to the Captain."

Temos nodded. She had hoped to feel some sense of affirmation, but, despite his jokes, he appeared just as nervous as she did. There was a chance this could go horribly for her, and worse the longer she waited.

She made her way through the camp. It was unnervingly quiet. The day's encounters weighed heavily on those who knew they would be marching in at sunrise.

Captain Ardell's tent was the same size as the one she was forced to share with Jhet, Finn and Temos. Unlike her, Greffin only shared his tent with Sergeant Duran Holst, which left them enough room for a small round table. It was little more than a shield with legs, but it was a table nonetheless, a true luxury in this environment.

As she approached, she saw them sitting on the ground, across from each other at the table, splitting what passed for dinner as well as some dried fruit they must have brought with them from Strossen. Casselle hesitated, but Greffin saw her and waved her in.

"Templar," he acknowledged. "Something on your mind?"

She nodded, but the words seemed to stick in her throat.

"You're at liberty to speak, Milner," he said. Before she could think on it any longer, she pulled the small leather-bound book out and set it on the table between them. The brow over Greffin's one good eye arched upwards.

"Not much of a reader," he said. Duran reached over and flipped open the cover, letting the book fall open to a random page.

"It looks like… "

"It's not what it looks like. It's a tool. It's a way to find lost weapons and relics."

"Where did you get such a thing?" he asked, his eye narrowing.

"From the Khaliil, sir. They gave it to me just before they left."

"Why didn't you say something sooner?"

"Because I didn't know then. It looked as you see it. I thought it was a message at first, but I couldn't figure it out," Casselle said.

"Are you sure? You said it's a tool. How do you know?" the Sergeant asked. Casselle hesitated.

"Respectfully, sir, I can't tell you." This drew surprised looks from both men. Holst started to get red in the face and he was clearly about to give a well-worded angry rebuke, but Ardell reached out a hand to hold him back. Duran bit back his words, but was still visibly angry.

"Can't or won't?" Ardell asked calmly, studying her response.

"It was given to me under the intention that it would be used by the Laegis, not handed over to the Lockewoods."

Ardell nodded.

"I won't say that I disagree." He turned back to his meal and pulled a dried apple from the bowl on the table, taking his time to chew on it. Most of Holst's anger had disappeared, but the tips of his ears were still a bit red as he stared at Ardell.

"You should probably have someone look at that," Ardell admitted after a moment. "Someone who has knowledge of such things, someone who could verify your claims and tell us best how to use it."

Casselle's heart leapt to her throat: he was going to ask her to turn it over to Kross and his arxhemists.

"I'm thinking one of the Templar Librarians," Ardell finished, reaching for another apple slice.

"Sir, there aren't any Librarians here," Casselle said, somewhat confused.

"Better hang on to it until we return to Strossen, then," he said offhandedly.

"I... but what about..."

"Sergeant," Ardell prompted.

"Templar Milner! You have been given a direct order by your Captain!" Holst barked without hesitation. "When that happens you only need two words! Have you forgotten them or will I have to make you run sprints until you remember?!"

"No, sir!" she said, reflexively snapping to attention. Holst continued to stare her down while Captain Ardell regarded the book one last time.

"I don't see anything special about this book," he said, picking it up and handing it back to her. "Follow up with the Librarians unless you can show me something to back up what you claim."

"Yes, sir!" she replied, before taking the book from his outstretched hand.

"Dismissed," he said, before adding, "and make sure you get a good night's sleep."

"Yes, sir," she said. She paused for a moment, wanting to thank him, but Holst's steady glower made her think better of it.

***

The rising of the suns found them armored and marching in a slow procession towards Lex Vellos. The horses that had come back the previous day were reluctant to return and whatever had affected them disturbed the rest of the mounts as well. The fact that none of the horses would approach the ruins inspired little confidence in those with only two legs.

The Laegis Templars were no strangers to marching, though, and Casselle and Temos followed in step behind Jhet and Finn, all of whom were behind Captain Ardell. The other squads comprising the two Fingers under Ardell's command were arrayed beside and behind them.

The city drew closer, as did the yawning space beyond it. It was a deceptive threat, though, since the edge of the empty expanse could hide a drop as innocent as five feet, though Casselle knew it to be well over a thousand. The thought of walking the edge made her nervous, and she hoped she would not have any reason to witness it up close.

Lex Vellos was like a drowning man, struggling to keep afloat in an ocean of sand and debris. Buildings that weren't completely destroyed were tilted at odd angles, with most of them in advanced stages of decay. The Laegis pulled to a stop several hundred feet from the edge of the closest building as the orders were distributed to those in command.

The Thundering Lance had numbered one hundred fifteen members strong on its departure from Strossen, with eighty able-bodied fighters and the balance in support and command units. The Laegis had added a full fist of fifty men as well as a Commander. That count was already slimmer, just one day into the "exploration." The first squad of eight the Lance had sent to secure a foothold before their arrival had been slaughtered and the attacks yesterday had killed another six and wounded a half dozen more.

The Laegis had been deployed to assist Richard's men yesterday, and hadn't seen any of the fighting, the attackers mysteriously withdrawing before the more heavily trained Templars could arrive. Today it seemed that Richard intended to use that to his advantage, sending their full Fist in first.

Captain Ardell was still at peak scowl when he addressed the nineteen Templars under his command, two full Fingers when he was included in the count.

"The Lance will push into the center as a single force, securing an area in the middle of town, which has been their primary goal," Ardell explained. "Upon arrival, the Laegis are to split and begin sweeping the immediate surrounding area clear of hostiles. Groups too large to engage with single squads should be either pushed or lead to the center, where the Lance will be fortifying a position in order to cut them down."

The squadmates exchanged several looks. Even with a significant portion of the city collapsed into the Fallen Sea on the western edge, Lex Vellos was still huge, much too large for fifty Templars to canvas completely. Separated and diluted amongst the unfamiliar ruins of the city was either a vote of supreme confidence in the Laegis' abilities or a convenient way to get rid of them.

"Sir, that seems like a horrible idea," Temos volunteered. No one else echoed the sentiment, but several heads nodded in agreement.

"It was the decision reached between Commander Cohl and Commander Arren." Ardell ground the words out. "Don't want to hear nothing more about it."

There were nods from the assembled Templars, but it was clear few of them were happy about it. Their Captain's disposition hadn't helped any. Even Temos and several other talkative Laegis remained quiet during the march, which only heightened the unnatural calm of the barren land around them. It did not help anyone's mood that the wind lifting up over the edge of the collapse and through the hollow bones of the city sounded like the lingering lament of a people long since dead.

At the crumbling edge of the city, the Thundering Lance filed onto what remained of a large thoroughfare, flanked by fallen walls and short, empty boxes of buildings. Casselle couldn't help but feel watched from every shadowed interior or high roof they passed. What bothered her more, was that the mark on her arm had grown colder, a dull ache underneath her armor.

Under the hot suns and the mounting pressure, it was really no relief when nothing came for them; it only wound the collective knot in their guts around another turn or two. The only thing that followed them all the way into the square designated as the main staging ground was the heavy shuffle of their armored feet.

They filed into the empty space in front of one of the buildings that still stood proudly in height, if not appearance. It was the same sand bleached color as the rest of the ruins, but at one point in time it had most certainly been a Temple to one or all of the High Houses. A statue lay on its side near the steps, fractured and worn smooth by the harsh elements. If a twin had ever existed on the other side in years before, it had long since vanished.

Even the statues of the Gods forsake this place, Casselle thought to herself.

Arren Lockewood began issuing orders to his officers, who had their louder subordinates pushing people into action. Captain Boen, the leader of the two Fingers of Templar Lancers, began directing squads towards the areas he expected them to cover after conferring with Commander Cohl, who was now navigating the crowd to meet with Captain Ardell. The Shield Templars were used to working in smaller squads, unlike the large spear walls the Lancers were more familiar with.

"Ready to get moving, Captain?"

"Yes, sir," Greffin replied calmly. "My squads know their duty."

"I never questioned it. Just wanted to make sure they all knew not to take unnecessary risks." The Commander directed his next comment as much to the four squads as to their Captain, "Fight hard, but fight smart. Oh, and if something gets in your way... put it in the dirt."

"Yes, sir!" Captain Ardell replied emphatically.

"Yiin Su'ur!" replied the Shield Templars in unison. Casselle had been saying that on the parade ground for as long as she'd been addressed by officers during her time in the Laegis. She was told it was a formal way to say "Yes, Leader" but she had never questioned where it came from. Thinking back to the Ghostvale, and the book she now kept tucked in the pouch on the back of her belt, it didn't feel so foreign to her. It wasn't a completely dead language, perhaps just a heavy sleeper.

Commander Cohl smiled in approval of their commitment and watched as Captain Ardell picked out paths along the southern side of the square they were currently assembled in.

"Keep your ears open and loop back here often enough to know what's going on with the rest of us. Be bold, be strong and don't be stupid. If you think you've found something your squad can't handle, mark it and pick up reinforcements," Ardell instructed. The assembled Templars nodded, but remained quietly focused.

"By your leave, Commander," the Captain said. Zan Cohl nodded and took a step back. Duran Holst barked at each of the squads, dispatching them in turn. When he took his own knot in its assigned direction, it left Casselle alone with her unit. The Captain ordered them towards the path leading more west than south, which appeared to lead towards the edge where the city had collapsed into the sea.

Finn took a position up front with Casselle. Captain Ardell was in the middle and Jhet and Temos took the rear. Temos had his small bow at the ready, and Jhet hadn't even bothered to draw his weapons, though she could tell that he was as much on edge as the rest of them by the way he coiled and uncoiled his fists.

Past the first block of buildings or so, it didn't seem so bad. Casselle could still hear the clamor of the Thundering Lance behind them. The further they went, the more the city seemed to swallow that noise, until the only sound left was the shuffle of their own feet and the light rustling of their arms and armor.

The original buildings must have varied greatly in size and shape, because their hollow remains were as equally varied, save in color. Most of them had been stripped by sand and time over the course of years into the same bland beige. Aside from the shadows and the muted palette of their own gear, the world around them was maddeningly similar. Casselle thought it might make whatever they were looking for stand out more clearly, but every flicker of shadow seemed to hide some lurking menace. She quickly wore herself out trying to keep track of everything that turned out to be nothing at all.

Captain Ardell had them making cursory examinations of building interiors from the outside. If things didn't show signs of disturbance, they pushed on to the next one. Each structure seemed as uniformly unoccupied as the previous one. There were some remnants of furniture, but sand and dust had blown in unabated from outside, covering everything. Any trace of fabric was long gone, devoured by bugs perhaps, who had long since died or moved on.

Their trail lengthened behind them. Temos had been using one of his charcoal drawing sticks to mark the sides of buildings they had cleared. During a hasty retreat, the black marks on the light surfaces would be easy to spot.

"What do you think these places were?" Finn asked quietly.

"Shops, inns, pubs and homes," Greffin replied. It was clear that each of them was disturbed on a very fundamental level by the skeleton of civilization slowly decaying around them. Corners had lost their sharpness, doorframes sagged under the weight of ages and foundations crumbled, threatening to release walls from the burden of standing upright. These places once housed parents and children, thieves and constables, politicians and priests. Now they lost even the most rudimentary evidence of their existence.

"We helped cause this," Greffin said, drawing quizzical looks from Finn and Temos.

"I certainly don't remember dropping a city on anyone," Temos replied.

"The Laegis," the Captain explained. "We chose our sides and fought one another. The end of that conflict broke our world and our ranks. It's not something we should be proud of. It'd be easier to forget it, but we can't do that."

"If we... they... hadn't fought?" prompted Casselle.

"I think fighting was a forgone conclusion. In fact, everything I've read made it seem like standing against it would have been like trying to stop the tide with your outstretched arms," the Captain replied somberly.

"Do you think we'll suffer a similar fate against Maughrin?" Finn asked.

"Won't know until it happens," Greffin said. "The problem with every battle is that both sides expect to win."

"I'm of the firm opinion that the only thing we're truly exceptional at is being defiant, often times even against our own self-interest," Temos commented. Greffin grunted in approval.

"Mark there and break for water."

Temos drew a wide "X" on the side of the building indicated by his Captain and the squad moved to the shady side of the street, resting for a moment and sipping from their waterskins. After a short rest, Greffin ordered his squad back into action.

"Let's check in. We've been out long enough," he said. They reversed their course and began to follow Temos' markings back towards the camp. After a couple of blocks, they lost sight of the markings, as if they'd never existed to begin with.

"I know I kept up with them," Temos said. "Perhaps we took a wrong turn? I say that, knowing full well that I marked these all the same way, but I'm trying not to contemplate something more frightening."

Greffin had the squad stay together and check the possible turns in a logical order. After an exhaustive search, they found no markings.

"Something removed them," Finn said. "Who would do that?"

"Settle down. Let's not start jumping at shadows," Greffin cautioned, while calmly drawing his own blade.

"Still, I'm definitely unnerved, bordering on frightened," Temos said as he watched his squadmates follow their Captain's lead.

"Be ready, but keep your fear in check. Let's orient ourselves and make our way back to camp," Greffin said. "That building looks to have a good vantage over the others here. We'll get to the top and aim ourselves back to the square." He motioned to a taller building where a top floor stood exposed to the sky, the roof looking to have been collapsed by age.

They checked corners as they moved to the adjacent street, until they found themselves at the entrance of the building the Captain had singled out. They checked the interior, but much like the other buildings, it was vacant, an undisturbed covering of sand and dust blanketing the room. Stone steps could be seen in the far left corner, creeping upward into an unlit stairwell.

Greffin signaled to Jhet, who took point, leading with his swords, each shorter than the standard Laegis blade. The one in his right hand was gripped normally, the one in his left held the opposite way, with the blade resting up against his gauntleted forearm. Jhet moved with precision, and Casselle was surprised how quiet he was, even with the supplemental plated armor worn on top of their armorjacks.

Wordlessly, the swordsman slipped into the shadows and moved up the stairwell, disappearing from view. Casselle found herself counting her own breaths, trying to still her racing thoughts.

"Should we...?" Temos whispered before Greffin signaled him to be quiet. Another few tense moments crawled by before Greffin signaled the squad into formation towards the stairs. Finn took point, leading with his large shield. As they ascended, Casselle noticed there were breaches in the wall, brightening sections of the climb while leaving others obscured by darkness. As they reached the second floor, she thought she caught sight of something in the shadows. She turned to question the Captain, but he motioned for her to keep moving.

The stairs and surrounding walls ended on the third floor, a blinding reveal given the relative darkness of the stairwell. Jhet was there already, surveying the scene. From this height, they could see further, but the city was no less dense than it had been from the ground floor.

"There's the temple," Finn said, indicating the tallest building in view. It looked near enough from this vantage, but would still be obscured from the street until they got a bit closer. More importantly, they didn't see anything else around them, no enemy lurking below, just around the corner. The streets were empty. Weapons were sheathed and tense breaths released.

Temos shielded his eyes and looked to the sky to check the position of the suns.

"I think I can keep us on track as long as I can see the sky," he said. "Though I'd still like to know what happened to my marks."

"Let's worry about that once we've rallied back at the square," Greffin told him, giving him a reassuring pat on the shoulder. They took the stairwell to the bottom and filed back into the street. Temos waved them in the right direction and they began a careful procession back towards the square. All the buildings were unfamiliar, every step a possible new direction, guided only by the two suns above.

They had moved a few blocks from the building, keeping up a brisk pace, before Finn stopped short of the next turn.

"Wait," he hissed quietly. Jhet indicated the corner opposite them, drawing his blades with the barest of whispers.

The squad prepared themselves as Jhet peered around the corner.

One finger. One target.

Okay to proceed, he signaled.

"It's a girl," Finn said. As Casselle came around the building with her sword and shield at the ready, she saw a small child, certainly no older than eight or nine years, standing in the middle of the street just a few dozen paces from them. She wore a loose-fitting dress which appeared worn, but not old. It was dirty, though, just like she was, her hair a long, tangled mess that covered most of her face.

"What's she doing here?" Temos asked.

Before Greffin could reply, the child was off, running away down a side alley ahead of them.

"This is wrong, I don't think..." Casselle began. Then a shadow raced across the street. Like the light had been cut out of the very air itself, it moved like a cat, travelling in a springing stride that covered a wide swath of ground in just a couple of bounds.

"It's after that girl!" Finn said anxiously.

"Hold!" Greffin ordered. But when the small scream echoed around the corner, Finn Archer was off like a shot, sprinting after both of them.

"Gods damn it!" Ardell swore, urging his squad to follow. Casselle leaned into the run, knowing that she had the smallest stride. Jhet could have easily outpaced them, but the silent swordsman was keeping pace with his Captain, as they had been trained to do.

"Why?" Casselle asked, trying not to be distracted by the dark mark on her arm that throbbed and ached as they ran.

"His godsdamned sisters," Temos huffed. "It's all he talks about, making them proud. It's like a blind spot."

Finn took another corner at high speed, but the rest of the squad had closed some of the gap, coming around just after him.

It was a dead end, an alley cut off by a collapsed building ahead. The little girl was curled up, almost indistinguishable from the tumble of stones behind her. The shadow paced slowly in a menacing crouch. Twin barbed tails swayed back and forth. It was slightly larger than a wolf, hunched like a cat, but most resembled a lizard. But even the details of the creature were elusive, nothing was easy to make out. It was unnaturally black, and in the alley, it looked to Casselle as if the shadows were stretching out to meet it.

"Oh no." Her heart sank and the mark on her arm was so cold it burned.

"H'Kaan," growled the Captain just as Finn roared and rushed the thing, shield set before him, sword poised to strike. It looked like a desperate charge, but it was just the kind of thing the Laegis had trained for.

"Back him up!" Greffin ordered, moving side by side with Jhet. Temos dropped to one knee, nocking an arrow in his shortbow. Casselle drew into position beside him, ready to guard should the beast get by, at least until Temos could swap weapons.

The H'Kaan moved faster than any animal she'd ever seen, springing not at Finn, but at the wall to his left. It avoided the charge altogether, rebounding off the surface and throwing itself into the air towards Jhet and Greffin. The Captain reacted instinctively, pushing his subordinate aside as he brought his shield up. Jhet stumbled forward as the H'Kaan smashed into the raised shield.

It was heavy enough to throw Greffin off balance, sending them backwards to the ground. It was a hard landing, but he kept his shield between himself and the creature, who now lashed out with a flurry of wild attacks, trying to get around the barrier.

Temos put an arrow into it, then drew another. Casselle couldn't tell where it struck. Though it seemed to have the standard trappings of a wild beast, the very nature of the thing was constantly shifting, as if its inky black body was always undergoing slight alterations.

Casselle knew she didn't have time to dwell on such things as she moved to help her Captain, angling to the left as Jhet moved in from the right. Just as they arrived, swords already in motion, the H'Kaan leapt backwards, almost blindingly fast, but still not agile enough to escape both Templar attacking at once. Blood the color of ink splashed on the bright beige sand.

So, it can be hurt. That knowledge alone was enough.

It landed just in front of Finn, who had managed to turn himself around. As it hit the ground, he raked his sword across its back. Casselle wanted to say that the creature spun around, but it looked more like it simply flowed into a new position, facing Finn rather than being turned away from him. Trying to focus on it was difficult, almost painful, but she knew to avoid doing so could cost one of them their lives.

Another arrow found the thing's flank. As it reacted, another sword cut free a spray of black ink from the creature's side, splattering it against a nearby wall. As Casselle joined Jhet and Finn to hem in the beast, it turned in a tight circle, like it was winding up for another strike.

Instead, it leapt up, soaring over their heads to the wall of the nearest building. Then, before Temos could even knock an additional arrow, it slithered over the top of the building and out of sight, like an insect sliding away through a seam in the wall.

"Eyes!" Greffin commanded as he was getting to his feet. Temos offered him a hand up. Greffin signaled the squad close so they could help watch for the beast's return. Finn, however, was approaching the little girl, his arms wide to show he meant her no harm.

"Archer! Get back here! This is not secured," the Captain ordered.

"It's okay, sir, I got her," he said, as if he either misunderstood or was being willfully, but politely, insubordinate.

"Templar Archer, that's an order!"

"She's just a kid, sir," Finn said over his shoulder as the little girl tried to pull herself into a tighter ball. He stuck his sword into the ground next to him as he reached out an open hand.

Casselle saw the large eyes of the child from beneath the matted hair, staring up at the big, armored Templar. There was something wrong about them, like they were drained of color.

"It's okay," Finn said, in the most soothing voice he could find. His shield hand fumbled at the helmet on his head, as it came free he tried to reassure her. "Look, I'm just like you."

The little girl unclenched at those words, her body relaxing slightly. A small hand slowly reached out for his.

"Gods DAMN IT! Archer, do not!" Casselle had never heard such raw emotion from the Captain.

The little hand touched his palm, and Finn curled his fist around it gently.

"You're not like me."

The words came from the little girl, but they were not the voice of a small child. It was something older, something far more malevolent.

A barbed tongue shot out of her mouth straight for Finn's head. He jerked back, but the grotesque black tentacle was faster than him, raking the side of his face, and cutting deep grooves up along his cheek, jaw and ear. As Finn tumbled backwards, the arrow Temos had been holding caught the girl in the chest.

The squad moved in unison to surround and cover Finn as the girl scrambled up the collapsed building behind her. She moved almost as quickly as the H'Kaan had, but without the beast's fluid movements. Temos let another arrow fly, but it smashed against the rocks near her. With a sharp, bestial scream, the child bounded over the top of the pile and out of sight.

Finn was bordering on senseless as they closed around him. Casselle dropped to one knee, pulling her field kit from her belt. It wasn't much, but it had a bandage they could use to stop the bleeding on his face.

"She was just a girl," Finn muttered, his eyes unfocused and distant. He didn't even flinch as Casselle pushed the cloth against the bloody gashes and tried to clumsily tie it around his head.

"Milner, you need to get him on his feet," the Captain commanded, his voice cold and clear.

She understood his concern as she heard the second scream. It was just like the one the child made before vanishing over the rocks, but it had come from behind them.

Then another from the north... and two from the south...

Then so many filled the air that it seemed as if the city itself was screaming.

- 13 -

We Remember

"Oathguard."

The word came out in a hoarse whisper, but with the full weight and power of destiny behind it. Triistan felt gooseflesh rise along his neck and race down his spine. He sat up, wincing at a twinge in his gut. The pain was a minor distraction, though, as his thoughts chased themselves down this new path they had discovered.

He had first learned the story of The Oathguard from a book he'd found in his old mentor's library, purely by accident. At the time he'd thought it was just some old fable, heroes sacrificing to guard against a "great Darkness," which in his youthful naiveté he'd assumed had meant Maughrin. The brilliant illustrations and sense of tragic stoicism depicted in them had pulled at him. He wished that he made the effort to learn more about them, wondering how long ago that book had been written and when their journey was supposed to have occurred. From what little Captain Vaelysia had told him atop the watchtower, it was obvious now that Ostenvaard had been their ultimate destination.

Had the Captain told him that they actually built this incredible city? His memory of the past few days was still cloudy, but that felt right.

But why build such an elaborate fortress in a land most did not even know existed? And what happened to them? Until his conversation with the Captain, Triistan had never heard of the Oathguard other than in that book, and his old master, Doyen Rathmiin, had been studiously unresponsive to his questions. Why were they forgotten, despite the prophetic stanza scrawled on the book's last page?

"Where this wind ends, our Oath begins..." he whispered. He looked around quickly, but other than some furniture, the room was empty.

This was the first time he had paid any attention to his surroundings, and he was struck by how big everything seemed. The room's walls were made of huge blocks of laid stone, the joints tight and precise, their lines true. The ceiling overhead was supported by a widely-spaced grid of heavy wooden beams as thick as tree trunks. His bed was wide enough to sleep two comfortably and long enough for two more at their feet. It was set in one corner of the room, next to a long shelf full of various bowls, jars, flasks and other oddities he could not name. The shelf was actually the top of an exquisitely carved piece of furniture made of blonde-colored wood shot through with tiger-stripes of jade. Large cupboard doors hung on silver hinges along the base, and above the hutch were several more shelves, likewise full, and spotted here and there with dusty books that looked as large as Triistan's torso.

In the opposite corner was a heavy wooden door, which now stood half open, revealing a dim hallway beyond. His gaze was drawn past the doorway to the far wall of his room, which was covered from floor to ceiling with thick shelves containing still more tomes of various shapes and sizes. Brilliant yellow light streamed down cheerfully through a large opening in the ceiling at that end of the room, bathing the books in a warm glow. Triistan caught himself smirking at the obvious metaphor, then considered the implication of so much vivid light. There were a few fat candles burning on the table next to him, but the promising glow pouring in through that gap was daylight, he was sure of it. He must have been closer to the surface than he'd thought previously.

He suddenly craved the warm touch of that light, so he cast the covers back and swung his legs carefully over the side of the bed. Seated on the edge, his bare feet didn't reach the floor. Triistan had always been tall - he stood well over six feet when he remembered not to slouch - but here he felt like a small child, just as he had when Danor had restrained him. There was no question it was the scale of everything around him, but there was something else as well; a sense of quality and durability - of history - as if these things had existed for ages and would continue to do so long after he and his fragile flesh were gone. It reminded him of how he had viewed his parents when he was a young boy, believing that things would always be as they were: his mother, vibrant and beautiful and captivated by every little thing that he did or said. And his father: stern, proud, driven, but also devoted to his wife and son, at least in the early years. It was a sense of permanence that had been the core of his limited but joyful understanding of the world. He wondered why this place should evoke such feelings of nostalgia and whether it, too, would prove to be a lie.

He shook off the thought and turned his attention to inspecting himself. While he had slept, someone had removed his clothes. His right calf was wrapped in a clean, white bandage from just below his knee down to his ankle, but otherwise he felt whole and hale.

There was a stool pushed against the wall immediately next to the bed, upon which sat his clothes and journal, wrapped up tightly in the protective pouch he usually kept it in. His clothes were clean and neatly folded. As he shook out his trousers, he was pleasantly surprised to find that they had also been mended; the lower half of his right pant leg, which had been cut off to tend to his injured calf, had been replaced, the stitching along the seam neat and orderly. His sword - *Talyia's sword*, he reminded himself - was nowhere to be seen.

Moving slowly for fear of antagonizing his stomach, he slid his legs into the pants and stood up, groaning as he tried to straighten. He shuffled from one foot to the other, careful not to put too much weight on his right. The wound protested mildly, so he took a few more hesitant steps, keeping one hand on the bed for balance. Several more aches and pains made themselves known, but none of them serious, and the one he was most concerned with - the dull ache in his stomach - was but a feeble afterglow of the burning agony he had felt before.

All things considered, I feel good. Really good.

And hungry. That realization was a pleasant surprise, although immediately on its heels came the thought of his former 'guests', and the hunger pangs quickly soured.

The swath of sunlight extended out from the bookshelves for a couple yards, and as he approached, the floor grew warmer beneath his feet. As he stepped fully into the beam and its soft radiance washed over him, his skin broke out in gooseflesh. He closed his eyes and stood for a long moment, face uplifted and arms stretched wide, enjoying the sensation and grateful that he was alive to do so.

He opened his eyes and raised an arm to shield them from the glare, expecting to see blue sky through the opening somewhere above. To his surprise, the gap in the ceiling extended upwards in a sort of wide, flat chimney for only three or four yards, before the outside wall met a sloped ceiling that ran back towards the room, preventing him from seeing any further up the shaft. Both walls and ceiling of the chimney were lined with polished white marble tiles that reflected the light, carrying it down into this room from the surface somewhere above. His heart sank at the lack of view, so he let his imagination reach up the shaft and work out the details of this latest engineering trick. He was picturing what sort of elaborate drain system the builders must have fashioned to keep the rain out when the sound of approaching voices intruded on his reverie.

"... can't possibly expect us to wait here for another week," Captain Vaelysia was saying. "I mean no insult to your hospitality su'ul Danor, but we have to get word to my crew. They -"

She broke off as she strode through the open door and saw Triistan standing near the books. Danor came in just behind her, and there was another figure in the hallway, but he could not make out who it was behind the giant. He assumed it was Biiko, who never seemed to be very far away.

"Mister Halliard," the Captain said with genuine warmth. "It's good to see you on your feet again."

Triistan did his best to come to attention, feeling stiff and awkward. "Thank you, sir." She always made him feel nervous; he had to focus hard to keep from stammering.

"I owe master Danor everything, sir. He saved my life." She must already know this, but he could not think of anything else to say at the moment. To cover up his embarrassment, he turned to face the giant and bowed deeply.

"Master Danor, I owe you a great debt, sir. Thank you." He bowed again, feeling foolish but not knowing how else to show his respect and appreciation. When he straightened, Danor was regarding him as though the huge Oathguard had just swallowed a mouthful of curdled milk.

"I am no man's master, Salty. You would do well to remember that. Now, let's have a look at you." He shoved a large stool across the floor with one booted foot. "Have a seat, boy."

Chagrined, Triistan dropped onto the oversized stool, which was large enough to serve as a chair. As Danor crouched down next to him, he finally caught an unobstructed view of who had followed the Captain in.

"Commander!"

Firstblade Tchicatta stepped into the room. He did not grin as the Captain had, but he looked pleased nonetheless, the hint of a smile showing beneath his hawkish nose and short black beard.

"Topman. I concur with the Captain. Welcome back to the land of the living."

"The same to you, sir. We thought you were lost as well... or - well, I guess Creugar knew better, sir." Danor examined him as they spoke, muttering to himself in his own tongue as he poked and prodded.

The Firstblade folded his arms and leaned against the door jamb, looking mildly amused. "Did he now?"

Realizing he should probably not relate Creugar's story of their nickname for the Reaver commander, Triistan answered simply, "Aye, sir. He said you were very... ah... resourceful, and would probably outlive us all."

Tchicatta snorted.

"Let's hope not, or I'm not doing my job." He glanced at Danor's back. "How long before he can travel, su'ul?"

The giant shrugged. "A few days, if he listens well. But it matters not. There will be no traveling until Tau Xarius returns and decides what to do with you," he said with bored nonchalance, as if he were discussing the weather rather than suggesting they were prisoners being held against their will.

Captain Vaelysia shot Tchicatta a look before addressing Danor.

"Again, I say this with the utmost respect, su'ul: we must at least get word back to the rest of our crew. We are overdue, and we need to warn them. At least let us send runners. I cannot stand idle at the Lord Marshal's pleasure while my men are at risk. You have no right -"

Danor stood and turned to face her. His blue eyes flashed from beneath his white eyebrows. "We have every right, Captain. We have served beyond the edge of the world for more than three centuries so that your kind could survive and - perhaps - flourish if you managed not to destroy yourselves, as apparently we very nearly did. I suggest you tread carefully, because there are some among my companions who lack my patience, particularly with the so-called Children of Tarsus. You may be a descendant of the Vanha, but you are far from the spring; the river of your blood has been tainted by many lesser streams."

Captain Vaelysia stared balefully at the giant, but remained silent.

"Lastly, you do not await the Lord Marshal's pleasure, Captain. He is not off on a relaxing stroll through the fuundaris jungle. He may not even be alive, for all we know, but you will wait for him."

Triistan held his breath. He had never seen the Captain challenged openly before, and although Commander Tchicatta had remained where he was, leaning against the door, the tension was clear in his face and body. For the first time, Triistan noticed the familiar axe and kilij that typically hung from the Firstblade's belt were missing.

After a long moment, the Captain relented, and her voice softened.

"Where has he gone? Can we help look for him?"

Danor shook his head. "I have already said more than I should have. Bryn commands in the Lord Marshal's absence. You can ask him. He should be back this afternoon after cleaning up behind you and your crew. Likely you've left enough sign to lead the Exile's entire horde down here, so I would not expect him to be particularly pleased to hear your concerns. Temperance is not one of his virtues."

Captain Vaelysia and the Firstblade looked at each other, visibly startled.

"He is free?"

Danor studied them for a long moment before answering in a voice that seemed to carry the weight of the city above them. "Aye, He's free."

"Who?" Triistan blurted out. "Who is free?"

Captain Vaelysia opened her mouth to answer, but Danor held up a massive hand and cut her off. "We do not speak his name. Exi profundiis namonaas. Names have power. You of all people should know this, Captain."

Triistan had never been very good at knowing when to stop asking questions, and he was still trying to catch up to the other three occupants of the room, all of whom seemed to be leagues ahead of him.

"You said 'the Exile's horde' earlier - is it him? This 'Exile'? Is he one of you?"

Danor snorted and shook his head. "It seems the world has forgotten much since my brothers and sisters set sail for this place. Still your tongue, boy, before I regret saving it. I will say no more. You and your friends will remain here until the High Master returns this afternoon. Then, perhaps, your questions will be answered. You need to eat, and then rest. I will be back shortly." He strode from the room without another word.

Triistan looked from the Captain to Commander Tchicatta. "Sirs..? Who is he talking about? And who is the 'High Master'?"

The Captain sounded grateful for an easy question to answer. "Bryn Cazius Crixus, High Master of the Oathguard, second in command to the Lord Marshal."

Once again, Triistan felt the weight of her words. So it was true, then. They were the warriors he had first seen in that ancient book. Oathguard...

The captain crossed the room and began scanning the shelves near Triistan. "I wonder," she murmured to herself as she began running her fingers across the binders. Commander Tchicatta remained in the doorway.

"And the Lord Marshal is...?"

The Firstblade took this question. "Tau Regis Xarius the First, Lord Marshal of Ostenvaard."

"Is that who captured you, sir?" Triistan asked tentatively. He thought he probably had more questions than hairs on his head, but he did his best to restrain himself so as not to annoy either officer.

"Xarius? No, I have yet to meet him. We were taken by two sentries, in the same location you were captured. Whatever else they were - or are, I suppose - the Oathguard have mastered the art of concealment. It was as if the undergrowth came alive and attacked us."

Triistan remembered the shambling tree-things he had seen when he and the rest of the crew were ambushed. He said as much, and Commander Tchicatta nodded.

"Aye. They are actually costumes, ingeniously made. They don a harness woven from leather cords and straps - much like horse tack but there are no buckles or rings - then attach all manner of plant material to it by threading it through the harness. It distorts their shape and once they step into a patch of undergrowth, they effectively disappear."

Triistan couldn't help smiling in admiration. "Brilliant! You must have felt foolish when... I- I mean..."

Tchicatta just stared at him, his arms crossed, waiting for Triistan to rescue himself from whatever he had been about to say.

"I just meant that they must have... surprised you."

The Firstblade raised his eyebrows. Triistan cleared his throat nervously and decided to try a different tack.

"So... what happened? Was anyone hurt? Are Myles and the others here as well?"

Tchicatta's beard twitched in what might have been a smile as he finally relented. "Aye, Topman, they made fools of the four of us, you speak truly. Myles and Wrael are here, and Miikha as well, all whole and hale. They took us with such skill that no one had the chance to fight back. Myles and Wrael had our point, and just vanished. No sound of struggle, no cries. One moment they were there, twenty yards ahead of us, and the next... nothing."

He shrugged. "We barely had time to wonder what happened to them before the walls to either side just reached out and seized us, binding our limbs with a strength we could not match. Then they brought us here."

"Has anyone explained why? Where is 'here', anyway? Are we still beneath Ostenvaard? And who is the Exile? Are we in danger?" From Triistan's point of view, this was still restraint; there were ten times as many questions piling up inside his head. Nevertheless, the Commander was becoming annoyed. Or perhaps he was already irritated by the answers themselves.

"No one has explained why. Although it should be fairly obvious if you started asking yourself these questions. I've answered your next two already, and as for the last two..." Here he paused and looked at Captain Vaelysia, who was rifling through several rolled-up pieces of parchment that had been stacked at the end of one of the shelves. Without turning away from her task, she answered the Firstblade's unspoken question.

"Continue, Commander. I think it is time we told the crew everything, anyway. If He has indeed escaped..." She paused and looked at Tchicatta, but left the rest unspoken.

The Firstblade nodded. "Shall I fetch them now?"

"No, not yet. I would like to hear Mister Halliard's perspective on this first. Some of them will panic, and we'll waste most of our discussion trying to allay their fears. Find Tarq, though. He knows the tale better than I. And Jaspins, too - I want our own healer to get a look at Halliard."

"Aye, Sir." He disappeared down the hall.

Triistan felt a touch of nervous excitement. He liked the young Reaver lieutenant, Jaspins. What's more, he was intensely proud that he was being included in the Captain's inner circle. He wanted to tell her this, to thank her for trusting him, but he feared that would come across as childish, which was the very last thing he wanted to appear right now. Instead, he offered to help her.

"What are we looking for?" he asked after she accepted his offer.

She had finished searching through the pile of scrolls and had another heavy book open in front of her. After flipping rapidly through a couple of pages, she slid it back onto the shelf and pulled the next one down. Triistan caught a glimpse of the cover: it was a dull, weathered brown with faded gold lettering, but the characters were completely unfamiliar to him.

"Something I can bloody read would be nice, for starters. Most of these are in Theranghel, which of course makes perfect sense."

"It does?" None of this made any sense to him yet.

She looked up from her book. "I'm surprised at you, Mister Halliard. For such a learned boy, your knowledge of history appears to have suffered some neglect." Her grey eyes seemed darker, more intense, like storm clouds ready to spit their lightning at the sea. As usual, he tried to hold her gaze, but couldn't. However, something clicked in his brain and he remembered an old lesson.

"The Templar Script?" He winced, expecting her to laugh at his wrong answer. But she grinned instead.

"Theranghel - 'the second second tongue' they called it. Well done, lad. Perhaps I spoke too soon. But tell me why these books would be written in that ancient tongue."

Triistan thought hard, considering what he knew of the Templar order. Laegis Templar, they called themselves, clinging to proud traditions that had nearly been lost in the chaos and dust that was the wake of the Godswar. Now, what few of them were left tended to form loose advisory councils in the less-developed towns and smaller cities of Niyah. He had a vague notion there were a few territories in the north where they had re-organized in strength, but there were none among the ruling families on the Sea King Isles. In fact, he was not aware of even a Templar House anywhere in the island kingdom, although he supposed there must be at least one. They were generally well-regarded as knights and defenders of the common folk, but when the High Houses crumbled, they fell further than most, since it was said they were as close to the gods as men were allowed to come.

But try as he might, Triistan could not make the leap from the surviving remnants of the struggling Templar order to the giants they had encountered here on Aarden. Perhaps they had been an order of historians at one time.

When he relayed that thought to the Captain, this time she did laugh. "I should keep that suggestion in the privacy of your head, Mister Halliard. Our hosts would not take kindly to it."

She looked at the bookshelves behind her. The swath of sunlight seemed to have dimmed somewhat. "Although, it does have a sort of ironic truth to it now, sadly."

Triistan heard footsteps approaching down the hallway again.

The first one through the door was Tarq, the Ship's Whip. He looked much stronger than the last time Triistan had seen him. He still wore a bandage over one eye and a good portion of his head, but his back was straight and his grip strong as he took Triistan's hand.

"Well met, Halliard. You gave us quite a scare - no one wanted to be the one to have to tell The Mattock that we'd lost you." The big Khaliil grinned and winked, the elaborate tattoos on his face and scalp making his one eye look slightly wild.

The Firstblade came next, followed by his lieutenant, who greeted Triistan rather stiffly. She wasted no time in examining him, which included several very direct, personal questions. His face flushed and he started sweating when she asked him when he had moved his bowels last.

Biiko entered the room during this and stood quietly next to the door. He nodded as he made eye contact with Triistan, and the young man felt suddenly grateful that the Unbound was there. He was intimidated by the situation, surrounded as he was by most of the *Peregrine's* officers. But what bothered him most was the way Jaspins was treating him - cold, formal, almost as if she didn't know him. He had been excited to see her again, but he couldn't understand why she seemed angry with him.

He told her everything, though, giving as much detail as Danor had given him. No one seemed particularly surprised when he told them about the nagayuun spawn and how they had migrated to his stomach, so he assumed that they must have already known. They did question him carefully when he described Danor's process for removing the grubs, though.

"Are you sure it was xhemium?" Captain Vaelysia asked.

Triistan shrugged. "Aye, that's what he told me. I was surprised that he had so much of it - such a large piece I mean. He said he didn't like my question, but there would be time enough for that later."

"Then what?" This from First Mate Tarq.

"He made me eat two pieces, about this size." Triistan held up his hand, making a small circle with his thumb and forefinger. "He told me that he was 'giving the nagayuun what they seek'."

The Captain exchanged a look with her First Mate and shook her head. "Interesting. I guess you were wrong, Tarq."

"Perhaps, but they had the stink of the H'Kaan upon them. Once you have smelled it, even you would not forget it." He turned back to address Triistan. "What happened next?"

A rough voice answered from the doorway. "The spawn tore themselves from their nests in the lining of his gut and took the fuundaris bait, that's what."

Danor strode into the room, and the other occupants took a step back - all except for Biiko, who stood impassively where he was, arms crossed, and Triistan, who was seated and had nowhere to go. The giant carried a large bowl of green melons that had already been peeled, their flesh glistening wetly, making Triistan's mouth water. His stomach growled audibly as the healer approached.

"Pretty simple process, really. Like fishing."

"It certainly felt like I'd swallowed a hook."

Danor handed him the bowl of melons "These should go down much more easily. Eat your fill; they will help seal the wound in your stomach."

Triistan picked one up and took a bite. It was soft and succulent, like an overripe peach, about the size of his fist. The juice ran down his chin but he hardly noticed. It was delightfully sweet, and as soon as he swallowed he was reminded of the drink Danor had given him the day before; it gave off the same warmth in his gullet, like a swallow of wine. He was famished, so he wasted no time finishing that one off and starting on a second.

Satisfied his patient was following orders, Danor turned to face the others, fixing First Mate Tarq with an appraising eye.

"You have a long memory if you know the stench of the Endless Swarm, Tarq'nilonqua-hi," the giant said quietly.

Tarq shrugged his broad shoulders and nodded. "We are Khaliil, and we remember.

"My mother's mother fought side-by-side with the Dauthir and those Templar who had remained loyal to them along the Wide Steppes, beneath the shadow of Ganar's Bones. She was with them when they pushed through the passes to break the siege on

Deranthaal, Column of the Suns. When they sent her body home - what remained of it - her armor was soaked in their filth. Despite decades of flowers, incense and scented tapers placed in her tomb, you can still smell it if you get close."

"Then Tarq was right, su'ul?" the Captain asked. "The nest guardians - these nagayuun - are H'Kaan?"

But Danor ignored her. Instead, he made a fist and touched it to the center of his chest, making a slight bow as he did so in Tarq's direction.

"My blood for yours, Tarq'nilonqua-hi. You have our thanks."

Tarq returned the gesture, but his bow was much deeper than Danor's. "My bones for your blood, su'ul. The Laegis were ever friends to the Khaliil and Children alike."

Danor grunted. "Not all of us." Before the First Mate could respond, the giant addressed the group. "I've given you quite a bit more to talk about, I'm sure - much more than Bryn would approve of, but I'm a fuundaris doctor, not a politician. I will leave you to your own counsel now."

He strode from the room, as Triistan and the others stared at each other in dumb silence for several long moments. During that time, Triistan finally made the connection that Captain Vaelysia had been hinting at.

"Wait... the Oathguard are Templars?"

No one answered immediately. The Captain was still looking at the empty doorway Danor had just exited, her expression one of mild annoyance. Commander Tchicatta just shook his head and folded his arms. He did not speak a word, but his body language and face said "idiot child" plainly enough. Jaspins was re-wrapping the bandage around his leg, and Biiko simply returned his stare, looking vaguely amused. It was Tarq who finally answered him.

"Aye, lad. They were Templar - the best of the best, hand-picked to come here."

"But why? And why are they so... so... big? Is it the water here or something? If we drink it-"

"Peace, Mister Halliard!" Captain Vaelysia cut him off. "Eat your melons, and you shall hear the whole story. You must give the Whip a chance to speak, though, so still your endless questions!"

Triistan blushed again and sat back on the overlarge stool, feeling small in more ways than one. Just then, Jaspins stepped in front of him and placed both of her hands on either side of his face, tipping his head back.

"Open your mouth as wide as you can." Her hands were warm, her touch firm and confident. As Jaspins brought her face closer and peered down his throat, he abruptly forgot everything else. She studied him this way for a moment, and then her eyes flicked up to his and she winked, the ghost of a smile curling her lips, before stepping back and turning to face the captain. As she did so, the stiff dispassion she had been wearing when she had first entered the room descended over her face like a mask.

"Topman Halliard appears well, sir. I agree with su'ul Danor's prognosis and will follow up with him on dietary restrictions."

"Thank you, Lieutenant. Can he travel?"

The Reaver glanced over her shoulder and Triistan thought he heard a trace of warmth in her voice as she answered. "He is remarkably... resilient given what the su'ul tells us he's been through, sir, and he looks, ah, surprisingly hale.

"But until I know more about these nagayuun spawn, I must defer to Danor. If you'll excuse me, sir, I will go and speak with him now."

The Captain nodded, and Jaspins snapped to attention before Commander Tchicatta.

"Carry on, Lieutenant."

She bowed her head and without a backward glance - much to Triistan's disappointment - left the room. He caught Commander Tchicatta looking at him, his head tilted and one eyebrow raised, so he quickly selected another melon from the bowl on his lap and bit into it. He bit his thumb in the process and had to stifle a yelp of surprise and pain. The Firstblade continued to stare at him, but fortunately for Triistan, Tarq chose that moment to begin his tale.

"We are Khaliil, and we remember," the First Mate began in a strong, sonorous voice. He stood with his hands clasped loosely behind his back, his feet spread apart, as if he were beginning a speech of some kind. Triistan wondered if this was part of a ritual that the Khaliil orators practiced.

"I, Tarq'nilonqua-hi tell you this truth as it was told to me by Ma'lonquanani-xe, my mother, who learned it from her mother, Jon'quinani-xe, who they called Jon'qi the Untamed."

He relaxed and sat down on the edge of the bed, shrugging his broad shoulders nonchalantly. "Apologies for the formality, but it helps to recall the tale. At least I've spared you the full lineage preamble, and though my mother would not approve, I will give you the jib version rather than the mainsail.

"I shall assume you are at least familiar with the story of the Creation of Ruine and how Tarsus passed on his legacy to our gods, the Arys."

Triistan nodded.

"Good. And you know of The Divide?"

Triistan was eager to show off his education. "Aye, sir. The conflict between the Auruim and the Dauthir - what eventually led to the Godswar and Ehronfall."

"Good lad. The Mattock always said you were a quick study. Then you know that the Dauthir saw the huunan - your people - as their charge. It was the will of Tarsus, last of the Old Gods, that they should be guided and protected - raised, if you will, for they were in every sense His Children. While the Auruim took to the skies on their great wings and frowned down from their high places, the Dauthir went to live among you - among us, I should say. For the Khaliil, though different now, were once the Children of Tarsus as well."

This was something that Triistan had learned bits and pieces of from his old master, Doyen Rathmiin. The Khaliil lived in a deep, rich canyon that cut through the Wide Steppes in the southwest of Gundlaan. When Ehronhaal fell, its impact turned the Wide Steppes into a blasted, lifeless desert - now called 'The Wasting' - but the valley protected them from the worst of the destruction, and they had since rebuilt their city. It was now a place of legendary beauty and engineering which he longed to visit in person. Ironically, the Khaliil - one of the first tribes of Man to embrace the Young Gods - also became one of the first civilizations to embrace the idea that they were gone, and that those powers that they had once guarded jealously were now there for mankind to master. He knew these things from his limited conversation with the *Peregrine's* lookout, Longeye - she was Khaliil as well - but he had never heard the tale of their origin.

"It began as a friendly wager between two of the Dauthir: Ganar the Unbroken and Udgard, who we call The Planter. Ganar was God of the Mountains and keeper of the hard and precious stuff of which they are made. Udgard was a farmer and shepherd; it is because of his will and care that the soil yields its crops and the animals their meat. It was said that they had a long-running argument concerning the benefits of their respective domains, with much of the blow being over which was a better use of Ruine's land.

"Minet the Artist, whose creativity and playfulness was matched only by her beauty, descended from the Auruim's House of Knowledge as she often did to see what her Dauthirian brothers were about. Mind me, now: this was long before The Divide had taken hold of both factions, but in this tale you will still mark its earliest echoes.

"When Minet came upon Ganar and Udgard and heard their argument, she laughed at them and called them fools.

"'Why do you mock us, Minet?' they turned and asked of her. 'Come,' she laughed, 'and I will show you.' And she took them each by the arm and turned them so that they were looking at the beautiful, rolling Steppes and the deep gorge that plunged through them like a scar."

Tarq's good eye took on a far-away look, as if he could see the events he was describing.

"The three Young Gods strode arm in arm to the canyon's lip and gazed down into its cool shadows, where they beheld a mighty river issuing from one end and winding its way along the floor of the gorge like a great ribbon of blue glass. The center of the valley was dominated by a tower of star-forged metal, like a giant spearhead of ore, glittering darkly in the light of the twin suns. The sheer cliffs of the canyon walls were softened by lush hills; folds of verdant green that looked like slack sailcloth from where they stood. Several small camps dotted the hillsides on either bank - the first groups of Man coming together in our tiny tribes. The very first of my People.

"'The River cuts through your rocks, Ganar, working it the way a serrated rib shapes the clay on the potter's wheel. And it soaks your soils and gives life to your plants and beasts, Udgard.'

"The Dauthir looked and saw that this was so. Ganar's eyes reflected the greedy glitter of precious stones that winked out of the caves at the head of the valley, and Udgard's heart was gladdened by the orderly squares of chestnut-colored soil where the land had been tilled, which lay like tapestries upon the land along the river.

"'Here they can co-exist. Here the water links their divergent purposes' - and here, clever goddess that she was, Minet squeezed each of their arms with her own and favored them both with her breathtaking smile - 'the way I have joined with you.' This of course had their blood up, for ever has man been a slave to a woman's beauty, and the Young Gods were no exception. But Minet had other uses for their passion, and her hand was firmly on the wheel of their egos, if not on their tillers where they would have preferred - begging the Captain's pardon," he added with a sly grin. But Captain Vaelysia appeared not to have heard him. She was studying a map of some kind.

Tarq continued with a shrug. "Ganar, ever the bolder of the two," he winked again and Triistan couldn't help but grin and shake his head, "stepped forward and thumped his chest. 'I will teach the Children of Tarsus to shape the rock and draw forth its precious metals, so that they can raise their houses and build tools to better work your soils, Udgard!'

"Not willing to be outdone, Udgard responded by promising to teach Man how to use the beasts to move and erect the heavy stone, and to pull the tools that Ganar would make. Minet laughed, and it was like the sound of water running over chimes. 'Here is a picture waiting to be painted, brothers; a sculpture hidden inside a block of your precious jhetstone. Come, let us work together and reveal it to the world!' And with this, she released their arms and ran upon the wind, down into the valley that my people call 'Laha'na'li' - The Womb of the World."

"And so it was," the First Mate continued, "that three of the Young Gods did dwell among our people, and under their guidance did we flourish as no other civilization had at that time. The Columns were yet but a dream of the Dauthir - a dream whose first spark rose from the fire of Laha'na'li's torch - but at that time our land was the wonder of the world. More tribes joined ours, and many of the Young Gods visited to see what their siblings had wrought. Most moved on, but a few stayed on for many years after."

He frowned and shrugged. "The Khaliil enjoy long lives, but I do not pretend to know how immortality distorts things like time, so perhaps, for the Gods, a century spent in one place is of no consequence... in any event, although Minet did not deign to cavort with the Children, Ganar and Udgard had no such misgivings. Nor did some of their brethren. The point is that the first Vanha were born in Laha'na'li, and thus sprang the wellhead of godkin blood that flows through the Khaliil."

The First Mate paused, and Triistan seized the opportunity to ask another question.

"So did the Oathguard come from Laha'na'li? Were they from the first Vanha?"

"No - and yes," Tarq answered. "Though we were the first to live alongside the gods, we were not the only ones. Across Niyah, wherever mortals lived alongside the Dauthir - and even some Auruim, though they would not have admitted it, I think - Vanha were conceived from their union. Less in size and stature than their divine parents, but still mighty among their brethren, they naturally took on roles of authority and leadership among most burgeoning civilizations. They were ideal ambassadors between the gods and the Children of Tarsus, and out of this servitude a new order was formed: The Laegis Templars."

Triistan finally felt the pieces of this puzzle falling together.

"In those days, the Auruim were still... tolerant of Man, but not fond, and for their part they viewed the Templars as little more than shock troops to bolster their struggle against the H'Kaan. Even though She had been defeated and lay in captivity somewhere in the Deep Dark of the world, somehow Maughrin's spawn continued to ooze from the cracks and shadows of Ruine. In truth, most of the Auruim did not feel the Laegis would be able to stand against the H'Kaan, and thought a good bloodletting would prove to be an abject lesson for the upstart half-breeds...

"The Templars proved them wrong."

"For the Dauthir, who right from the start had thrown themselves wholeheartedly into raising the Children of Tarsus, the Laegis Templars would help defend and organize their fellow Man. Although in most cases they did not rule outright, they served as arbitrators, advisors, stewards and many more roles that supported the Elder Circles - the local governments that were being set up to mirror the High Houses of the Gods. The Laegis became the capstan that raised Man up from the chaotic mix of tribes and small villages, helping us unfurl the sails of our potential."

Tarq paused and held his hand out, gesturing at the bowl of melons on Triistan's lap. "I'd relieve you of one of those, Topman, if you've no objection. All of this talking's inflamed my eye and those have a wonderful way of putting the fire out."

"Yes, yes of course." Triistan held the bowl up. Looking at Tarq's long, heavily-muscled arm, completely covered in intricate tattoos, he wondered which of the gods had planted the First Mate's family tree. It was well-known among the crew that both Tarq and Captain Vaelysia were of Vanha descent - "of the old line" as the Seekers called it. They had a presence; a strength and grace to them that, along with their size (both were close to seven feet tall), made it obvious. Until now, Triistan had thought of them simply as Vanha and never really gave much thought to what extent they might be of the old line, until now.

What was it Danor had said to the Captain? "You are far from the spring; the river of your blood has been tainted by many lesser streams".

If the Captain and First Mate were several generations removed, then it suddenly made sense why Danor and his comrades were so imposing, and not just physically. It helped explain the sense of simmering energy that surrounded them, like the way the air aboard the *Peregrine* felt just before a big storm, when you could watch the sparks jump from grommet to cleat up in the cross-trees. If the Oathguard were indeed Templars, they must have been first or second generation, which would make them... well, Triistan could not say exactly how old, but it would make them very old indeed.

Tarq devoured half of the melon with one bite, then finished it with one more a moment later, drawing his arm across his face to wipe off the excess juice and emitting a satisfied sigh as he did so. Triistan bit down on his questions and tried to be patient while the Whip licked his fingers clean.

"Better," the First Mate said. "I was feeling rather piqued anyway - it must be getting nigh on near to supper now."

The light coming through the shaft above the bookshelves had dimmed considerably, taking on the gold-orange hue of early evening. He wondered when (or if) they would be allowed to see the High Master. Surely he must have returned by now.

Maybe that's why Tarq is stalling, he thought, *so that he doesn't have to tell the rest of his tale.*

"So..." Triistan prompted, "where did the Oathguard come from, and why are they here? You called them the 'best of the best' and said they were handpicked for this - " he gestured vaguely at the room around them. "But what is this place?"

The First Mate glanced at Captain Vaelysia again and she nodded without looking up from the map she was still studying. Commander Tchicatta stood nearby, leaning in the doorway, arms crossed and face unreadable. Biiko was there as well, still and solid as ever, but he struck Triistan at that moment as a bowstring at full draw. When Tarq turned back to face Triistan, his expression was grim.

"Plainly put, Mister Halliard: Ostenvaard is a prison. It was built by the Arys to hold one of their own, one of their most dangerous.

Triistan felt the bit of melon slip from his fingers.

"One of the Young Gods? Here?"

"Alive and well," Tarq confirmed before grimly adding:

"And free from his cage."

- 14 -

A Desperate Escape

Her legs ached. Her chest burned. The dark mark felt like an icy knife in Casselle's arm.

"There!" Temos directed the hasty retreat of the Templars towards an open archway further down the street.

The H'Kaan dogged their heels. She noticed that not all of them were the same as the first one they had encountered. They came in a variety of unique sizes and terrifying features. When any of them massed together, though, it looked as if a fragment of starless night sought to overtake them, the darkness broken only by reaching, clawed appendages.

They had appeared moments after the chorus of inhuman screams had echoed throughout the dead city of Lex Vellos. Like a murder of crows converging on a carrion corpse, the H'Kaan materialized from the shadows of doorways and windows, flowing out of slim alleyways and scurrying over rooftops, converging on Casselle's squad of Templars.

In the histories, the H'Kaan were often called the "endless spawn." That may have been an exaggeration, but there were certainly more than enough here to challenge any notion to stop and take count. Captain Ardell directed them to charge an emerging pair that threatened to block the squad's way out of the alley. The monsters reflexively moved away, giving the Laegis time to sprint past them.

Temos had been trying to navigate them back towards the main square, but because of Finn's wild chase after the mysterious child, his orientation had suffered. Now, in hasty retreat, he had almost no sense of bearing, in no small part due to the pack of H'Kaan bearing down upon them.

They took the corner and flew under an arch, down a small corridor and into a courtyard, probably at one time a showpiece for the house they stood in front of, a massive thing that took up the two sides adjacent to the entrance and one opposite it. What remained of a fountain, perhaps once majestic, now cracked and broken, sat in the middle of the otherwise empty space.

"Doors!" Ardell shouted, pointing. Most of the buildings they'd seen around town had none. This one had two double doors standing, the luster of metal still evident under layers of sand and dirt.

"I'll go," Temos said, peeling away from the others.

"Hold the entrance!" the Captain ordered. Against normal opponents it probably would have been a far more effective strategy, but the H'Kaan had little difficulty in running along the walls or ceiling just as easily as on the ground. Casselle had her doubts that it would work, but she did as her Captain told her, squaring up next to Finn, who took the center. There was just enough space for three of them, with shieldless Jhet remaining behind. She wondered why he didn't carry one for situations like this, but her concerns were forgotten as the H'Kaan rounded the corner, like someone had diverted a river of hot pitch into the opening; a frothing, undulating cascade of shadow.

The horde hit them like a stampede of wild horses. Casselle's body lit up with pain, and she was nearly thrown backwards by the force that buckled her legs and rattled her bones. Claws and barbs thrashed at the edges of her shield. Something scraped hard against her armored shins.

But she was alive, and now she would trust her training to carry her. As the pressure lessened slightly, she put her sword in motion, lifting her shield and stabbing deep into the creature attempting to bring down her defenses.

It cried in pain, an unnatural scream that raised the hackles on her neck. The black ink that passed for their blood sprayed the ground at her feet.

There was a blur overhead, one of them leaping over the backs of the others. With just a glance over her shoulder, she saw the blades in Jhet's hands move in lightning quick arcs, gutting the beast before it even landed. She refocused on the fight ahead of her, trusting him to cover their back.

The creatures were strong, but they were all fury, no tactics. They battered at the Templars' shields, but could not break through. A few more attempted going over, but Casselle heard Jhet dispatch them with quiet efficiency. She focused on keeping her feet, steadying her shield and cutting into anything that attempted to break through.

She wasn't sure how long they had been there, but her arms and legs were aching when Ardell gave them the ready to break the line. Years of training reinforced her resolve, silencing any irrational fears she might have had to withdraw from the safety of the shield wall. She pulled back several steps, lowering her own shield just enough to see over the top.

A pile of shadows lay at the mouth of the corridor, a testament to the Laegis's skill. For a moment, there were only the remains of the slain, the shadow that had clung so tenaciously to the skin of the H'Kaan now slithering free, like smoke from a smoldering corpse. The stillness was broken as fresh beasts scrambled over the top of the pile. Casselle's heart skipped a beat, waiting for a greater flood to follow these three, but it never came. One charged Casselle, a wide jaw filled with teeth flying at her, the most distinct feature of the smoky, black mass that scrambled across the ground. It was terrifying, a nightmare given form.

The creature cried in pain as an arrow sunk into its midsection, interrupting its charge. Yes, it was frightening, but that fear was blunted by the knowledge that it could be killed. Seizing the opportunity, she surged forward, striking the H'Kaan on the side of its head with her shield. It staggered and she struck down with her sword, cutting deeply at the base of its neck. It thrashed out with a claw, but she knocked it aside with her blade, shaving off a sliver of ebony flesh in the exchange.

It immediately began to favor the other front leg. A heavily barbed tail arced in from overhead as it attempted to skewer her like a scorpion might. She deflected it with her shield, but the blow was stronger than she expected, sending a needling shock along her left arm. Temos sent another arrow into the side of the beast, and as it recoiled, Casselle drove forward, chopping once again at its exposed neck.

It fell, thrashing on the ground until the last of its lifeblood slowed from a spray to a trickle. Jhet had helped Finn and Greffin finish off their respective foes and the Laegis collected themselves in the aftermath: bruised, bloody, but victorious. Temos had gone back to work on the door, his bow on the ground beside him. Casselle looked to retrieve his arrows, but the H'Kaan's dying throes had snapped them into pieces.

She studied the corpse more carefully now. The beast that had looked to be made of pure darkness when it was chasing them had changed after its death. It was more defined now; whatever power that seemed to blur the edges of it while alive and in motion had quickly vanished.

It was a brutal and ugly thing, even in death. It was covered by textured, leathery skin resembling snake scales, though it was no snake. This one had a jaw overlarge for its face and a mouth so stuffed with teeth there was no room for a tongue. Each leg ended with a random number of claws, all of them ruthlessly sharp. There was a second spined tail beside the one that had attacked her, but it was less developed. She looked at the others and noticed that no two of them were exactly the same, though they all had several aesthetic similarities.

"How's the door coming?" Captain Ardell asked.

"I can't get it open. Assuming I could even pick it open, I'd have to be able to find the lock first," Temos said. "There are a couple of windows up there that look breakable if we really wanted to get inside."

"I do," Greffin replied, "if only to confirm a clear route back." The windows on the ground floor were all barred and shuttered on the inside. It was certainly the most extravagant house they'd seen so far, if by no other measure than its ability to withstand entry.

Greffin looked over to Jhet, who was already moving to one of the inside corners of the courtyard. Though not quite as nimble as the H'Kaan, the silent Templar used the ledges and cracks of the building's surface to get up to a window on the second floor. It was locked, but a hard kick admitted him entrance. A few tense minutes later, they heard subtle clicks and a dull thud before the front door opened inward. Jhet was inside, motioning for them to enter. Once they passed through, he shut the doors behind them, and slid a heavy bolt into place.

It was dark, though not entirely without light. Dust hung in the air, its lazy dance given a spotlight by sunbeams that fell from windows above them, overlooking a balcony that could be reached by a set of curving stairs on the left. Unlike the other buildings they'd investigated, this one was not wholly empty. The light was enough to see that there were still some traces of history remaining. Furniture, mostly devoid of upholstery, lay scattered about in a disorganized fashion. Dust was thick everywhere, but the sand only lay in tiny piles a few places where cracks had finally yielded to let the outside in.

It gave Casselle the impression of luxury, even though there was nothing left to give direct evidence of the sort. Not leaving them time to dwell on it, Captain Ardell ordered them back up the stairs. The balcony emptied into another room, filled with windows against the back wall, and a door leading to a terrace.

"They haven't broken into any of this," Ardell mused as they forced the lock on those doors, granting them access to the outside on the back of the once opulent home. For a moment, Casselle wondered what kind of people had lived there. She recalled the home of Odegar's sister, back in Strossen, the closest comparison she dared draw. That serene place seemed a hundred years and a thousand miles away at this moment.

Such thoughts fled quickly as the squad reached the edge of the terrace, giving them a clear view of the city. They had been diverted much further west than any of them had anticipated, now just a few blocks from where Lex Vellos collapsed into the Fallen Sea.

Thankfully, they were also closer to the square and Temos was quick to point out the Temple. Unfortunately, they could also make out the near constant stream of black forms swarming towards it. They looked like roaches from this distance, a vast swarm skittering over the tops and sides of the buildings ahead of them.

"That is not good," Temos observed grimly.

"Where'd they all come from?" Finn asked.

"From some deep Dark pit somewhere in the city. Most likely underground," Captain Ardell answered. Casselle may have been the only one to notice the brow over the patch on his face twitch, the scars underneath remembering some unspoken origin.

"So what do we do?"

"We have to shut it down."

"I mean, even assuming we can find it, how would we do that?" Temos asked.

"I don't know," Greffin answered. "The only one we ever found was closed by a Templar Librarian who had a strong knowledge in arxhemestry. He burned it out, like cauterizing a wound."

"Too bad he's not here now," Finn said.

"Couldn't have come with us anyway. Closing that pit killed him, consumed him," Greffin said. Casselle knew what that meant: she'd held Odegar as it happened to him. She even thought she caught the Captain casting her a sympathetic look, but if so the moment was lost as Greffin pressed them on, asking Temos if he could keep them headed in the right direction now.

"I think so, sir."

"That'll have to do," the Captain said, urging them downstairs, so they could find a way out of the back of the house and onto the street. After a few minutes of stumbling around in the near dark, in a room underneath the terrace, Finn found a working door out into the open once again. Bracing themselves for an attack, they opened it cautiously, but the alleyway ahead of them appeared clear.

Captain Ardell motioned for them to move out in standard formation, with Finn and Casselle up front, Temos and Jhet behind him. They moved as quietly as possible, but knew that in a few blocks, the soft creak of leather and rattle of armor would be drowned out by the roar of battle and the screams of the wounded and dying. Temos quietly issued directions from the back rank, his eyes constantly moving between the sky, the path ahead of them and their own footsteps behind.

"Forward... left... second right..."

The buildings were nondescript, a blur of bleached beige and white with open doors and empty windows. Casselle didn't have a bearing to lose at that point, merely moving in step with her squad, all of them dependant on Temos' directions. Only twice did he call for them to slow down while he looked to the sky, trying to suss out the position of the suns behind a tall tower or a thick overhang.

They did not rest, though. This was no time for respite, no matter how brief, and soon the trapper's son had them moving again.

As they approached a fresh corner, something at the edge of her hearing caused her to hold out a hand. There was something ahead. Ardell signaled Jhet to the front, the swordsman slipping past them with a quiet grace no one in full armor should possess. He returned faster than expected, his eyes wide.

"Six or seven H'Kaan ahead," he rasped. Casselle felt for him, knowing he was straining to speak clearly against the pain and limitations caused by his old wounds. She soon understood why as he finished his report with the chilling addition: "...not alone."

Ardell narrowed his eye for a moment and then ordered them forward, his tone suggesting caution and alertness. Almost immediately Casselle saw why Jhet returned so quickly. Down the lane from them, a few H'Kaan were moving much slower than they should have been.

They were dragging bodies, one of which was wearing Laegis armor. Though the face was bloody, Casselle recognized Ingst Engmar, a Templar from Lennard Torks' squad. The other corpse was not a Templar, but did wear the black and gold tabard of Lockewood's Thundering Lance.

"I don't know why they want those bodies, and I don't care," Ardell growled. "Kill 'em."

The Templars immediately broke into a controlled run, falling into formation as they closed on the H'Kaan. They were about halfway to the creatures before they were noticed. Rather than drop the bodies to engage, the monsters tried to move faster, though even the extra effort wouldn't keep the squad from catching them.

As the Laegis closed, they noticed that the intersection was filled with more than just those scavengers. To their left, as the view opened, Casselle saw more Templars closing in, followed by a second, larger group of H'Kaan.

"It's Torks!" Temos exclaimed, pointing to the Veteran leading the remainder of his own squad. What could have been a rallying moment faded quickly though: Tork's knot appeared to have fared less well than their own. Gunnar Hawken was all but carrying a wounded Passal Cooper under his arm, his other hand gripping the massive, bloodied warclub of his family. Vincen von Darren looked panicked, but otherwise unharmed. Torks had lost his shield, and had a makeshift bandage wrapped around his left arm, but was pushing them forward.

"Captain!" Lennard hailed hastily. Ardell had already waved them closer, directing his squad to shore up the gaps in his Sergeants'.

"Anlase, Milner, those on the bodies. Archer, Pelt, you're with me," the Captain said, breaking his squad in two. Casselle didn't have a choice as Jhet took the lead, his stride quickening as he broke away from them, running full tilt towards the H'Kaan.

Ardell's group veered left, towards the much larger dark drift on the heels of Torks' squad.

"Shields flank Hawken!" he ordered. Gunnar's broad smile was the last thing Casselle saw before she focused on the enemies in front of her. One of the H'Kaan dropped his burden and bounded directly at Jhet, prompting the swordsman to pull short. As the creature leapt at him, he moved with a deftness she'd begun to appreciate, spinning out of the way as one of his well aimed blades opened up the monster's throat at the same time.

The remaining three H'Kaan dropped their burdens and sprang into action. Casselle shouted as she closed, making sure Jhet would not be set upon by all of them at once, though she was beginning to wonder if even those odds did not still favor the Templar.

She slid to a stop as one of the writhing beasts charged, cutting her shield down at an angle. Normally it was a move to strike a knee and throw an opponent off balance, but it caught the H'Kaan on the snout causing it to reel to the side. Her blade snaked out and cut deep into the creature's front left shoulder, crippling it almost instantly. She put her weight down on its neck as she stepped into the range of the next one, making sure her back leg was planted firmly on the ground.

It slammed into her, long arms attempting to get around her shield, claws scraping on metal. She repeated the same move she'd used previously, getting her shield high enough to stab into the thing's guts, four times before it weakened and fell over. Her breath came hot and fast as she looked up at the road: Gunnar was in the forefront, his bluesteel warclub making wide arcs in front of him, battering H'Kaan aside with ease. Any that tried to avoid the club by straying to the side met the steely resolve of Laegis shields and the swift rebuke of Templar blades.

Temos and Finn were on Gunnar's left side, keeping the H'Kaan from flanking him. Greffin and Vincen protected his right, the rookie Templar making a solid account of himself, even though most of his moves were wild and sloppy. If they survived, she'd have to help fix that. Lennard Torks was trying to fix up a bandage on Passal Cooper's head, huddled behind the wall of Laegis fending off the seething black mass of monsters just a few feet away.

Casselle knelt at Ingst Engmar's side, holding out hope that the Templar was not lost to them. But the pallor of his skin and his empty stare told her everything she needed to know even before she put her hand up to his face, hoping to feel his breath on her palm. His flesh was cold and she felt no trace of life in him.

She looked up at Jhet, kneeling beside Richard's fallen man. He met her eyes and shook his head. Why would the H'Kaan want the corpses? Did they eat the dead? Though they had flesh, the stories she heard never described them as animals in the conventional sense. They were always monsters with no natural appetites, merely an overriding desire to ruin and destroy.

Jhet reached over to touch her, returning her to the moment. All of her immediate fears suddenly felt distant, as if she'd thrown them over the edge of the city down into the Fallen Sea thousands of feet below.

Scrambling to her feet, she saw the approach of another cluster of H'Kaan from the direction they'd been dragging the bodies. This group, however, did not rush in a madcap pace. They moved slowly and deliberately, like a pack of well-trained hounds, at the heels of an armored figure easily as large as Gunnar Hawken, if not a few feet taller.

She was clad in armor, well worn, but finely crafted by the look of it. Her black hair was loose and unkempt, some of it hanging in front of her face. Her skin was the color of fresh ash, a white-gray shot through with a few blackened veins on her cheeks and forehead. Her eyes were darker than her hair, save the sparkling silver irises that flashed like the scales of a fish in a dark lake. She had a ragged sword in one hand, a crude thing of rough iron that she swung lazily in front of her with casual ease.

"Back up," Casselle said to Jhet. He nodded in response and they withdrew to join their fellow Laegis. The crowd they had been facing had thinned, several broken H'Kaan stacked up along the sides of the road where Gunnar's warclub had batted them aside. The survivors had stopped attacking and were backing out of reach of the Laegis, gaining a sudden restraint that Casselle found chilling.

Captain Ardell noted the change, and was taking a new assessment of the situation as Casselle and Jhet backed up against them.

"Dear Gods, what is that?" Vincen asked.

"She's Vanha," Gunnar said, before clarifying, "or at least she was Vanha. I don't think she is anymore."

Temos tapped Casselle on the arm to get her attention.

"Next time we leave Strossen, can we make a promise not to find ourselves boxed in by monsters lead by some terrifying monster woman? This is getting a bit too much for me," Temos said quietly.

"You were promised excitement, not variety," Casselle replied.

"How's Cooper?" Greffin asked as the Templar adopted a loose circle of defense. The armored woman drew to a stop, making a signal or two that the H'Kaan seemed to respond to. They fanned out, enclosing the Templars' circle inside a wider one of their own. At least it thinned them out. They looked slightly less ferocious when they were not clumped together, obscured in the clustering shadows that seemed to thicken the closer they stood to one another.

"I don't know if he's going to make it," Lennard replied. "He's bleeding right through the bandages, regardless of what I do."

"Just leave me," Passal groaned weakly.

"Stow that talk," Captain Ardell growled. "Hawken, do you think you can take her?"

"If not, it'll still be one hell of a distraction," Gunnar replied, a fierce smile on his face. The large Templar eschewed much of the heavy armor the rest of them wore. His shoulders and upper arms were exposed and scratched up, but did not appear to be seriously wounded. Was that because of his Vanha blood? The few other Vanha she knew wore armor, but none of them were as big as he was.

"Ok. Try to get her off balance when I say," Greffin instructed. "We're not trying to win, just disrupt them enough to keep moving. Temos, which way to the square?"

"To our left," Temos said. "It shouldn't be too much further if I'm right."

"What if you're wrong?" Vincen asked, his voice laced with desperation.

"Then we probably won't live long enough for you to complain about it." Temos' answer shut Vincen's mouth.

"Archer, give Torks your shield. You get to carry Cooper," Greffin instructed. "After Gunnar engages and I yell to break, we punch a hole and we don't stop running."

"What are you little birds squawking about?" asked the woman loudly, her accent odd, but her words clear. "Have you come to nest here?"

"Who might you be?" The Captain stalled while the others prepared.

"I am... no... I *was* Emeranth Kell," she said, her eyes somewhat distant before focusing on them again. "But you may call me Her Wrath, because I've come to pluck your feathers, little birds."

"'Her' Wrath? That sounds terrifying," Temos confessed to his squadmates. "If by 'Her' she means... No, I've changed my mind. I don't even want to begin to understand how that works."

"Vanha or not, it won't be working for long," Gunnar said, taking a step away from the circle and towards Emeranth. He spun his warclub deftly and eased himself into a ready position, his bronzed skin bright with sweat and stained with the black blood of the H'Kaan he'd killed.

"Get ready," Greffin said. Finn had already positioned Passal Cooper, lighter now that Lennard had removed the wounded Templar's heavy plate armor. The rest of them stood ready as well, trying not to betray their intent to run.

Gunnar edged forward, provoking literally no response from the woman. Even he must have sensed that something was wrong. Her casual ease with the situation set Casselle's nerves on edge.

The warclub flew forwards, a deliberate poke to gauge her speed and reflexes. She stepped back, not even bringing up her sword to help her. Gunnar followed his instincts and training, trying to press a perceived advantage. She was taller with a longer reach, but his club was longer than her sword and if she wanted to hurt him, she'd have to close in some, which might be difficult given that she had no shield.

Then the sword came up, almost casually. Casselle expected it to be easily batted aside by Gunnar's much heavier club, but it held firm, stopping his strike with resolute certainty. When she moved afterwards, Casselle felt a sinking feeling in her chest. Not only did she close in on Gunnar, she did it with a fearsome precision that Casselle had seen before.

She's using the Akist. She'd been trained as a Laegis Templar.

Gunnar was overbalanced. Having seen his fight with Temos, she knew it was one of the places he tended to be vulnerable and Emeranth was exploiting it. Once she shouldered open his defense and caused him to stumble, she used a half-sword grip to drive the point of her blade into his chest, most certainly aiming for his heart. Thankfully, his stumble and his armorjack must have deflected it just enough, though not sufficient to prevent a bloody stain from growing on the front of his armor.

He hit the ground and rolled back. Emeranth moved quickly to follow up. This was not going according to plan. Gunnar was up, but it was clear his left arm was injured.

"We need to go," Temos urged. Casselle knew he was right, but if Gunnar couldn't keep her occupied, their odds of escape decreased significantly.

"We should all rush her," Lennard growled. "Her or us."

Gunnar tried his best, but his warclub was much less effective without both his hands to control it. He caught a glancing strike off her arm, but she punished him for it with a heavy hit to the midsection. It did not break the armorjack, but the force of it would have certainly leveled anyone other than Gunnar.

Casselle looked to Greffin. She knew what had to be done, but knew he wouldn't order it. He was locked on Gunnar's fight, waiting... hoping for an opening that the group could exploit. Emeranth opened up a wicked cut on Gunnar's right arm, her blade inflicting more damage in one stroke than dozens of H'Kaan had failed to do.

"Break!" yelled Casselle, sounding the order that Greffin couldn't - or wouldn't. Conditioned by years of training, most of them began to move before they even realized it wasn't the Captain that had given the order.

As they charged to the left, Casselle broke away from them, moving forward, angling to come in on Emeranth's weaponless side, forcing her to turn away from the group if she didn't want to be flanked outright.

"Casselle!" Temos cried, finally realizing what had happened as they cut through the thin perimeter of H'Kaan Emeranth had established.

"Move!" Captain Ardell ordered, encouraging them on. Casselle had forced the play. If they didn't take advantage of it now, there wouldn't be a second chance. Even Gunnar moved, his strength diminished, but still able to bat aside a lunging monster with a swing of his club.

The gamble seemed to pay off. The H'Kaan didn't follow immediately, looking after the retreating Templar, but still restlessly remaining where Emeranth had deployed them.

The giantess turned to face Casselle, her eyes blazing hate, her teeth bared in a frightful scowl.

"You took my playthings away," she growled. "You think that we can't hunt them down? You think you can stop me?"

"Come find out," Casselle replied, trying to sound more defiant than terrified. Her only hope was that all those years of training against Jaksen and Raabel would pay off. Both of her former squadmates were taller than her, Raabel by at least a foot and a half. Emeranth was painfully larger than that, but the same principles applied... at least she hoped so.

Regardless, Emeranth was using the Akist, and that meant Casselle knew where to look for weakness. Gunnar pressed his attack, but Casselle held back, stepping close to where she suspected the edge of her adversary's range to be, knowing that her longer legs could close the gap faster than Casselle could retreat.

Past her opponent, down the lane, she saw her squad putting ground between them. Her distraction almost cost her dearly, her reflexes barely saving her as Emeranth's sword cut downward. Casselle didn't try to take the full blow, angling her shield so that it should have glanced aside.

Even though she didn't take the full brunt, it felt like her arm was going to shatter. Gritting her teeth, she tried to cut up into Emeranth's hand, but it was already gone. She backed away, her shield arm screaming in pain, her shoulder protesting as she tried to keep it up between them.

The second cut came quickly, and Casselle was not able to get her shield in position properly. It did stop the sword, but took the full weight of the blow, knocking her off her feet and to the side, like she'd seen Gunnar do to the H'Kaan. She hit the ground roughly, tumbling over herself.

The shield was in pieces and her arm wouldn't move. It was most likely broken. Her sword was a few feet away in the dust and she scrambled to her knees to retrieve it.

"You honestly thought you could stop me?" Emeranth taunted.

"No," Casselle said, her side burning, her vision blurred with pain. Her hand closed around the hilt of her blade and she lurched to her feet. It was foolish to try and block her. Even if the shield hadn't shattered, she wouldn't have been able to keep that up.

"You think you've sacrificed yourself so that others may live," Emeranth said, her words tinged with bitterness. "I know of such things. I remember... that feeling. It is a good feeling, to live your life in the service of something, to give yourself to a greater cause.

"Once I had a cause, I had a purpose... I made a sacrifice... and here I find myself, in the world that carried on without me, the death of my convictions standing as grave markers around me." She paced slowly around Casselle. "But She gave me a new purpose, a refreshed sense of hope... something new to defend. And from this nest, and others like it, Dark wings will lift us up to burn away the false promises of the past.

"You see... you think you have spared them, little girl," Emeranth explained calmly, "but the only one you have spared is yourself... spared from watching as I slaughter the rest of those that would invade our home."

"You've not killed me yet," Casselle replied. Her opponent paused for a moment, regarding her.

"You've got conviction, girl, even at the end. Let's see if that conviction will comfort you in the Dark."

Emeranth moved in.

There. That was the move Casselle was expecting. A proper strike on her exposed side. Reflex would have her flinch away, to retreat from the swing. Instead she met it, moving in, driving her sword into her opponent's wrist before the stroke could connect. Her adversary's own strength helped drive home the point of Casselle's blade, ripping through one side and out the other. Emeranth's sword flew wide from her disabled hand even as Casselle was knocked backwards from the force of her attack.

The giantess howled as Casselle hit the ground. The scream was taken up by the H'Kaan around her, an unnatural chorus echoing in the streets of the broken city.

As Casselle found the strength to rise once more, one of her ankles protested. She watched as Emeranth tried to dislodge the blade stuck in her wrist, finally twisting it free with a sickening rip. Her right hand came mostly free as well, hanging oddly, attached only by a small collection of skin and muscle. She tore the useless thing off, flinging it aside with casual disdain.

Then she moved with a speed Casselle didn't expect, and with her sprained ankle, couldn't avoid. The heel of Emeranth's boot smashed into Casselle's chest with all the force of a charging harox. For a moment, there wasn't any ground beneath her. Then she stopped, her back impacting against the side of a building, her head cracking against it a split-second later. Her body slumped down, but it didn't feel like hers anymore.

It was a great stone, weighing down the part of her that urged her to get up and keep fighting. It was pain and fire and cold, all the weakness she thought she had trained her body to be free of. Her armor pressed too hard against her chest. Her neck was wet, and something warm was running down into the back of her armor. Her mouth tasted of salt and copper.

The sky seemed darker as she tried to focus on Emeranth Kell. Her sparkling silver irises twinkled brightly as she leaned in close.

"You see," Emeranth sneered, holding the stub of her broken hand near Casselle's face. Writhing black feelers emerged from the ripped flesh, a few at first, then dozens more. They knit together, winding around each other, thickening and gaining definition. As another ragged breath fell from Casselle's lips, the mottled black flesh of the H'Kaan had already formed a grotesque parody of the hand she'd lost.

"Your sacrifice was in vain. Your conviction could not save you. But take heart... your friends will join you soon enough."

Casselle panicked as Emeranth reached forward with her wicked black hand, but she didn't have the strength to turn away. She felt the cold fingers touch her cheeks, two resting just above her eyes.

But it was too dark now; she could no longer see. But she could feel the fingers slowly draw her eyelids closed, almost gently.

...and then she felt nothing.

- 15 -

Judgment

As Triistan described First Mate Tarq's assertion that there was a living god running loose somewhere on Aarden, his fellow refugees stared at him in various stages of shock. Mung's mouth hung so far open it looked like his jaw had come unhinged; Rantham was shaking his head, a mixture of anger and disbelief vying for control of his features; and Voth - who had been watching them with contempt through most of Triistan's tale - now looked worried, eyes darting here and there as he muttered something to himself around the gag. A prayer, perhaps?

Now wouldn't that be ironic, Dreysha thought as she throttled an absurd urge to laugh.

She knew all of this already, of course. She had read Triistan's journal, and so had gained a more complete understanding of why her handler, d'Yano, had arranged for her to spy on the *Peregrine*. She recalled their conversation when he had given her this assignment, and how uncharacteristically subdued he had seemed at the time, even worried, particularly about 'the Client'.

"While the work appears to be... routine," he had told her haltingly, "they are unknown to me. Someone very influential - and very wealthy. And someone with sufficient resources and diplomatic talent to persuade the Mylesian Citizens Concern to offer me three times my normal rate and to insist that we work with the Client through anonymous channels. I ignored that requirement, of course, but although I was able to verify everything concerning the mapping mission, I came up empty with respect to our Benefactor. Somehow he has successfully eluded my own network of informants... and you know how difficult that should be."

The conversation had left Dreysha feeling uneasy, but not so much that she would have turned the job down. It had come at a critical time for her, when she had needed to disappear after taking down a high profile target - and really, what better way to disappear than a two-year sea voyage? What's more, d'Yano had offered her a substantial sum.

Though now, she thought with a gleam in her eye, *'substantial' would need to be renegotiated.*

There were really three layers of value to Aarden's discovery: on its surface, the fact that they found a mythical continent and all of the resources it contained would have justified her handler's original offer, even as generous as it had been. That Aarden contained ruins of great archeological and religious significance - like the colossal statue of an ancient Templar warrior she had witnessed with her own eyes - meant at least a sizable bonus. But the full truth - that these ruins were actually still inhabited by knights and gods from some fanciful old tale? She should be able to demand any sum she desired from any player or regional power anywhere on the face of Ruine. While she would never dare to cross d'Yano - the old spider had far too many strands to his web - this was one of the few times in her life she had actually given it serious consideration.

"But what... " Mung was stammering. "When - I mean, who... which one was it? Was it actually Oss-"

Triistan's hand shot up, but likely his gesture would have come too late to do any good. Fortunately, Dreysha was sitting next to Mung and clasped her hand over his mouth before he could finish. He looked at her with wide, fearful eyes, as if he expected her to break his neck, but she simply made a "shush" gesture with her other hand.

Triistan nodded gratefully. "Yes, Wil, your assumption is correct. The Exile survived Ehronfall and has since escaped."

"By the rutting Darkness, how? And where is He?"

"More importantly, why the fuck are you just telling us this now?" Rantham spat.

"We did what we had to do, Rantham. The panic that would have ensued there, not to mention if word got -"

"Fuck your panic, and your secrets!" Spittle flew from Rantham's lips. His face - already red and cracked from exposure - turned a deeper shade of scarlet.

"What about those we left behind?! Has anyone bothered to tell them that one of the fucking Arys is lurking in the jungle?" Dreysha was tempted to tell him to back off and calm down, but reconsidered. He did have a point.

"They all know what they face there now," Triistan answered, his voice rising. "The Captain will have told them, prepared them. The Oathguard that survived will aid them as well -"

"Aid them? Aid them how exactly? From what you've said there's barely a handful of them left, and in case I missed something, they're the ones that lost him in the first place!!"

"You don't know the whole story yet, Rantham. We had to choose betw-"

"That's the problem, SIR!" Rantham shot back, spitting out the last word with particular rancor. "You chose our fate for us! You lied to those crew members and sentenced them to death!"

"We did what we had to do!" Triistan snapped as he leapt to his feet. "It was the Captain's call, and she was operating - this entire bloody mission has been operating - under the direct orders of the Ministry and the King's Council!"

"So what, they ordered her to go find a supposedly dead god and then offer up half her crew as a sacrifice?! Why not send us all back aboard the *Peregrine*? That makes no bloody sense!"

This last exclamation hit home. Triistan just seemed to deflate as he collapsed back down, burying his face in his hands. He ran long fingers through the matted tangles of his hair.

"It was the only thing the Cap- that we - could think of to do. You saw what was left of us when we returned, the shape we were in. And there were some - the Captain and First Mate - who had to stay behind for other reasons, reasons that I'll get to. But no matter what happened, we also had to get the *Peregrine* out of there and get word of our discoveries back to the Ministry. All courses were bleak; all options evil. As I said, we did the best with what we had."

Rantham snorted in disgust, but his sudden rage appeared to be subsiding. "Much good that will do the mates we left behind... Sir."

Triistan winced visibly and lowered his head again. He was quiet for a long moment, hands clasped in front of him, elbows on his knees. The only sound was the slap and slither of water against the hull and the usual creaks and groans of the launch itself. Then Wil spoke up quietly.

"What about the seeds?"

"What?"

"The seeds - the Twineroot seeds," Wil said timidly.

Rantham snorted again. "A bit fucking late for that aren't you, Mung?"

But Dreysha understood his point. "Back off, Rantham. Mung's right, Triis, what about Twineroot? I thought it was standard practice for special missions to get them. Why didn't the Cap just use them to send back a warning and a call for help? I mean, then at least we could have fortified our position and we'd have had twice as many men to help search for the others."

"Twice as many to die, you mean," Rantham slipped in acidly.

Triistan was staring dumbly at Wil. "Why didn't she?" he repeated, his face clouding in thought. "There wasn't much discussion about the reasons we were doing what we were doing - the push was to get as many as possible out of Aarden and harm's way, and to ensure that the *Peregrine* didn't fall into the Exile's hands. It seemed like the obvious course of action at the time, but…" He trailed off, shaking his head.

"I… I don't know," was all he could say. "Perhaps she did… I guess I hadn't considered it before. But I don't think it would have mattered. Even if they alerted the Ministry, and so increased the likelihood that they already count us as overdue and have started searching for us, it wouldn't have changed our decision. We would not have stayed."

"Why not?" Wil countered.

Triistan looked at each of them as he sought for words to adequately describe the impossible choices they had faced.

"Because then we all would have been slaughtered." His words were like stones tumbling onto the deck at his feet. "No matter what else happened, we could not let Him capture the *Peregrine* and escape… but we couldn't just leave the others to face their fate alone… as I said, there were no good options."

He paused, holding his breath, waiting for the outbursts that must surely follow. But none came, to Dreysha's surprise. They all just stared ahead, lost perhaps in their own thoughts, imagining what terrible nightmares their comrades must be facing.

After several long moments of silence, Triistan took a deep breath and blew it out slowly. "Let me tell you the rest of the story, so that perhaps you can understand."

***

"Free?" was all Triistan could think to say in response to the First Mate's claim that Ostenvaard had been built to imprison a god, and that the god had escaped. He was struggling to process everything he had heard and experienced since waking from his illness.

"How?"

"That is the Question of the Ages, isn't it? Our... ah, hosts haven't been very forthcoming." Tarq swung his long legs up onto the bed and leaned back against the headboard. It was large enough that even he looked small.

"Which one was it? I mean... is it bad?"

Tarq's one exposed eyebrow shot up. "Are you asking if it's bad if an Arys all of the other gods saw fit to lock up for eternity has escaped? Because yes, I should think that would be pretty bad."

Triistan felt the tips of his ears growing warm. "I don't think it's as simple as that, Sir."

Captain Vaelysia spoke up from where she was still studying one of the rolled-up pieces of parchment she dug out from the wall of bookshelves.

"Oh? Please elaborate, Mister Halliard."

He had to fight the urge to duck his head and defer to them, especially now that the Captain had entered the conversation. It was strong, but the sense of conviction and purpose that had first begun to grow in the darkness of Ahbaingeata was stronger.

"Aye, sir. I was only thinking that, if the rest of the Young Gods destroyed themselves - and nearly all of us in the process - perhaps the Exile had only wanted to stop them."

Tarq chuckled, then threw his hands up in surrender as Triistan glared at him. "Peace, Halliard, I yield! Your theory is plausible, but, unfortunately for us, it could not be further from the truth."

Triistan balled his hands into fists. He wanted to challenge Tarq's presumption, but kept his composure and simply asked, "Why?"

The First mate's gaze hardened. "Because they feared him."

"Then why not just kill him?"

"Because you cannot 'just kill' one of the Arys." The deep, heavily accented voice startled Triistan. A shadow filled the doorway, dwarfing the Firstblade and Biiko, who were standing to either side, and for just an instant Triistan was overwhelmed by the irrational fear that Ossien had found them.

The shadow laughed, cruel and low, and then stepped into the room. Commander Tchicatta took a step backwards, but the newcomer's ice blue eyes were fixed squarely on Triistan.

"Guard your mind, child. I am not the One you fear, but His sworn enemy."

As the newcomer stepped into the light of the room, Triistan recognized him as the giant warrior leading the party that captured them in the sewers. It was the second time he had mistaken the Oathguard for a god.

He was even taller than Danor - at least twice Triistan's own height - with close-cropped, silver hair and jet-black eyebrows. His features were sharp and might have been considered handsome if not for the bitterness of his scowl. He was no longer wearing the strange armor Triistan had first seen him in, having traded it for a long surcoat made of black velvet and trimmed with a broad border of gold. The fabric looked old and worn, with several visible patches, but underneath was a shirt of beautiful silver chain mail that glittered as he moved in the candlelight. The giant's eyes skewered Triistan, pinning him where he cowered on his oversized stool.

"I am Bryn Cazius Crixus, High Master of the Oathguard. In the Lord Marshal's absence, I greet you and bid you welcome to Ostenvaard, City of The Thousand. Or 'Fortress of the Forgotten' as is our wont to say." He smiled at this, and Triistan thought his teeth looked overly sharp. *So this is how the rabbit feels when greeting the wolf.*

No, huunan, the rabbit would know enough to flee.

Triistan's mouth dropped open: the High Master's lips had not moved, but he had heard the giant's words clearly in his head. He was suddenly aware of a presence within his mind, sharing his thoughts, rifling through them as if they were so many sheaves of paper from his journal. It was like watching the pages being torn from their binding and scattered by a furious wind, until he became aware of a sudden, firm touch on his shoulder. It brought with it a calming sense of strength, and then he was alone again in his own mind.

Biiko stood beside him, one dark-skinned hand on his right shoulder. The Unbound was staring up at the High Master, golden irises flashing.

"His is a Binding Chain, under my protection. I will give my life to defend it." A rash of cold gooseflesh rippled down Triistan's spine as Biiko spoke. The Unbound's voice was deep and full of quiet power, like the roll of distant thunder.

Crixus frowned. "Does Khagan send errand boys to do his bidding now? The demon dragon's sleep is restless. We can feel it - she stalks the shadows of our dreams, always shifting, straining...

testing her bonds. You are a fool to bring one of the Chains here, of all places."

Biiko stood his ground, however, and left his hand on Triistan's shoulder. The High Master's lips twitched in a faint sneer and then he swept his gaze over the rest of the group.

"In your foolish arrogance, you have come where it is death to trespass. Our Oath is absolute, and if it were up to me, you would have been slain on sight. But not all feel this way, so we will hear your tale, and you will hear ours, in time. And then we shall judge.

"Come. I will take you to the Low Hall. It does not convey the proper eloquence for such... important guests as you," he glanced at Biiko pointedly, "but it is where we take our meals and our counsel these days."

He strode from the room, and the others shared a brief look before falling in behind him.

"I need to see to my men first," Captain Vaelysia said as they walked.

Without slowing, Crixus shot a look over one massive shoulder. "They will be brought there as well."

They passed by a branching corridor and the Captain stopped.

"I would prefer to see to that myself."

The High Master stopped as well, looking none too pleased.

"They are already on their way, Captain. Do not linger, or think to wander astray. Lax and Aja - two of the jharrls that greeted you in the jungle - patrol this section of the underkeep, and will kill anyone they find wandering alone outside of the suite we have provided you. They are not accustomed to your kind, and are as likely to mistake you for prey as they are to regard you as an intruder - though I should think either result would be the same." He spun on his heel and set off again.

The others waited, looking to their Captain expectantly. She muttered a low curse in disgust and gestured Triistan and Biiko to proceed.

Triistan hurried to catch up, his natural curiosity overcoming the fear and discomfort he felt when Crixus had invaded his thoughts.

"They are your pets then - the jharrls?" He had to lope at a near jog in order to keep up with the High Master's long strides, although there was an odd rhythm to the Oathguard's gait, almost a limp. The weathered hem of his surcoat was nearly long enough to brush the floor, but as they walked, Triistan glimpsed the man's boots; one looked to be armored, while the other was of some supple, dark gray leather.

"Not pets, no. Their sires were bred for war, but we lost most of those when... well, long ago. Several escaped into the jungle and joined the native monarch packs, a more intelligent species than those we brought with us. Over time we learned their habits and behaviors, and many of them, though now wild, remembered their old bonds to us. Since then, the threat of a common enemy has made us pack-mates again."

Triistan was fascinated, wondering what event Crixus had avoided mentioning. Probably the Exile's escape. As the High Master walked and the rest of them hustled to keep up, the long, wide corridor they were following from Triistan's room passed through a high arch into a slightly broader passage. Two massive doors were thrown wide, and a huge iron bar lay at the foot of one of them. He imagined it would have taken four or five of his comrades to lift that bar into place to secure the doors. Tarq gave it a sideways look as they passed through the archway.

"No wonder they wouldn't budge," he muttered.

They turned right and followed this new corridor past a handful of other archways opening onto similar passages - at least, he imagined they were similar, as the doors for most of these were shut and barred. For the few that were open, Triistan craned his head, but he did not see any jharrls, although he thought one might be close when they passed a dark opening on their right. Rather than a door, this one was barred by a heavy gate of black steel bars, beyond which he could see a set of broad stone steps descending into the shadows. A damp breeze drifted up out of the darkness: the hairs on the back of his neck stiffened when he recognized the musky scent it carried.

"Where does that lead?" he asked as they hurried by, nearly tripping on the High Master's heel as he searched for the incandescent blue eyes he felt sure were watching them.

"To Ahbaingeata - the River Gate. Or more appropriately, the defensive works above the tunnel you came through. That is Khazar you smell. He likes to hunt the nagayuun."

Triistan shivered, both at the memory of the parasites as well as the uncanny ease with which the High Master appeared to pluck his thoughts out of his own head almost as quickly as they occurred.

Eventually, Crixus led them through another double-doored opening on their left, from which Triistan could hear the subdued murmur of voices.

The Low Hall was actually a huge amphitheater, with semi-circular tiers that sloped away from them on three sides, down towards an open area dozens of feet below. The tiers appeared to have been made of the same gleaming jhetstone as the giant Oathguard statue in the bay, and each terraced row was punctuated by recessed seats every four feet or so. Huge braziers hung from the ceiling on long chains, ablaze with fire. Smoke rose from them in graceful curls towards the high ceiling, which was a sprawling dome formed by several teak-colored timbers arching overhead, each easily large enough to be the keel of a war galley. The space between these ribs was covered by layers of clapboard made from a lighter-colored wood, and from the way the shadows played on their surface, Triistan thought them to be bowed as well, creating vaults between each curved rafter. At the center of the dome where the ribs met was a wide circular opening in the ceiling, perhaps twice his own height across, and through here the smoke from the braziers below rose and disappeared. Triistan could just make out a heavy grate of thick bars covering the opening.

His gaze dropped to the far wall of the chamber, which was covered in what he first took to be elaborately carved columns intended to evoke gigantic trees. Before he had time to study them more, however, a chorus of glad shouts erupted from the seats below. The surviving members of the expedition were all there, rising in excitement as they realized their commanders and Triistan had entered. Creugar, defying his considerable bulk, was one of the first to his feet, striding directly up to Triistan with a wide, glowing grin that showed an impressive array of brilliant white teeth.

"Monkey-man! Creugar is glad to see you on your feet again! Now Wrael will have something else to make his 'I-just-drank-my-own-piss' face about when he pays off his foolish wager! And there, you see? The Commander is also whole and hale, just as Creugar said he would be." He leaned in and winked, lowering his voice conspiratorially. "I should have bet you as well I am thinking."

Several more from the party clapped him on the shoulder or shook his hand. Some even tousled his hair (those that could reach, of which there were few, given his height). They all seemed genuinely pleased to see him, and for the first time he did not feel like an outsider or nuisance. He was besieged by questions about his leg and stomach, what it felt like, what the parasites looked like, whether he thought they were all out, et cetera. It seemed that everyone had been briefed on his illness, and he had been the last to know what was really wrong. He was smiling at the irony and at the unexpectedly warm welcome of his shipmates just as Lieutenant Jaspins pushed her way through the men milling around him. His smile widened into a grin despite his best efforts to stifle it.

"What's so funny, Halliard?"

"Oh, um - nothing. I wasn't smiling at you - I mean, I was, but not at first when I first saw me - you, I mean. When I first saw you… " he trailed off awkwardly.

"I see." The hint of a smile flickered across her lips as she made a quick show of examining him. "How do you feel?"

"Fine, I guess. A little tired, and my stomach's a little sore - " he winced as someone clapped him on the back. It was the burly bosun's mate, Izenya d'Gara.

"Ya look a whale's cock better'n when I last saw ye, Halliard. Welcome back!"

"Thanks, Izzy," Triistan coughed.

Jaspins rolled her eyes as d'Gara moved away. "Well, you look a bit pale to me. Don't push it, and stay away from whatever it is they drink like ale. It isn't ale, nor rum, nor anything I've had before, but it is stronger than goat piss. It probably won't kill you, but you might wake up with the goat." She winked again, patted him on the arm and moved away. He imagined he could still feel the imprint of her touch for a long time after.

A loud crash interrupted the banter of the reunited expedition. Crixus had made his way out to the center of the amphitheater floor and now stood at its center, feet spread and arms clasped behind his back, but he did not make the noise. Rather, a towering pair of heavy doors centered in the rear wall had swung back, and through them and out of legend and myth strode the last vestiges of the Oathguard.

Even from Triistan's elevated vantage point, the figures entering the chamber below them were impressive. They were all of Crixus' height, give or take several inches, and of varying degrees of girth. They were dressed like the High Master, as if for court, and likewise Triistan could see that their garments, though once probably luxuriant, now looked worn and threadbare. They carried no weapons that he could see, but still they exuded a power and strength that was palpable, even from where Triistan and his comrades stood. Eight men and five women in total entered the room, each pausing in front of the High Master and bowing deeply before making their way to large seats that were carved at the base of each of the columns against the far wall. Several of the warriors ignored the expedition, but a few swept their penetrating gazes across the Seekers clustered above them. Triistan read everything from curiosity to outright hostility in those glares, but none of them appeared friendly.

When the procession appeared to end, two more figures strode into the room together - both adorned in heavy armor, except for their bare heads. Both were women, and from where he stood, he thought they could be twins. They were of the same height and build, with long blonde hair bound back in a series of braids that gave their sharp features a fierce, aquiline look. Both were garbed in the same strange-looking armor that Crixus had been wearing. Its color was difficult to name, as it appeared to shift and swirl as they moved. As he watched, Triistan realized that the armor was actually changing color to match the hues and shadow patterns nearby. Once the warriors stopped just inside the doors, it was hard to distinguish them from their surroundings until they moved again.

Each bore a long polearm with gleaming black staves capped by long silver blades. They bowed in unison before the High Marshall, then each took hold of one of the massive doors and swung them shut. With perfect timing, they spun smartly on their heels, spread their feet, slammed the butts of their polearms on the ground, and came to attention shoulder-to-shoulder in front of the doors. Triistan and his comrades stared in stunned silence.

"He does like his pomp," said a gruff voice from behind them. Danor made his way down the aisle. Unlike the other Oathguard, he was still dressed simply in dark, loose fitting trousers and a sleeveless tunic, although this one was a bright blue that matched his eyes. As he passed by Triistan, he winked. "Best take your seats; this may take awhile."

Rather than joining the other Oathguard, Danor walked down to the first row of seats on the lowest terrace. Triistan followed the healer, not knowing what else to do. As ever, Biiko followed him, and the rest of the Aarden Expedition's members filed in behind them. The low murmur of hushed conversation drifted up from the floor of the cavernous auditorium, as several of the Vanha talked to one another. The High Master remained standing in the center, watching them expectantly. The side of his face twitched as Danor stood next to Triistan.

"Paxus crient la a'samrih, brodiir?" the High Master called up to them.

"Someone should translate for our honored guests, don't you think, brodiir?"

Crixus stiffened. The other Oathguard had stopped talking and from the different expressions on their faces - some frowning or shaking their heads, but others wearing slight smiles - Triistan gathered that Danor was something of a pariah.

The High Master glared up at them for a moment, then forced a gracious smile. "As you will, su'ul. I submit to your superior sense of... hospitality." There was a ripple of quiet laughter from the other Oathguard, but Danor only grunted and sat down.

Triistan sat next to the healer on the lowest row, which was essentially a balcony perhaps a dozen feet or so above the floor - head-high for most of the Oathguard. A low wall topped by an ornate brass railing fronted the balcony. It had undoubtedly been constructed to accommodate the taller Vanha, for as soon as he sat down he was unable to see anything. Feeling foolish, he stood back up to take in the whole scene.

He was more or less at the center of the curved balcony, with an unobstructed view of the far wall and the assembled Oathguard. The tall columns he had first assumed were carven pillars were actually living tree trunks - or possibly unimaginably large roots. They rose up from semi-circular holes cut in the tiled floor, ran very near to straight up the rear wall, and disappeared through similar holes in the ceiling far above. The more he looked at them, the more convinced he became that they were roots, primarily because there were no branches, although there were plenty of smaller, vine-like trunks running alongside or crisscrossing over each column's surface. He learned later that he was looking at the tap roots of a massive citadel tree that grew in the center of Ostenvaard, high above them.

The base of each root-trunk was at least eight feet across, and had been carved out to create an elaborate... well, throne for lack of a better word, he thought, which made a sort of sense. The Vanha were the closest relatives to the Young Gods of the High Houses; if they were not nobility, who else could legitimately claim it?

There were twenty in total, all different, and all but one or two were stunning in their intricacy. The holes in the floor through which the roots grew left a gap of two feet or so around their perimeter; less than half the normal stride of one of these giants and not likely to cause them any discomfort, but still Triistan wondered how far down the holes went and what was below the floor. The familiar blue-green luminescence that seemed so prevalent in the water here flickered up through these gaps, and he had an idea that if he got close enough he would find water there. It was like Ostenvaard was a living thing and the luminescent water its lifeblood.

The High Master raised his arms and bowed to the seated Oathguard before him, then nodded to a tall, lithe woman seated to his far left. She was the last Vanha to enter other than the two sentries standing in front of the doors, and she bore a long ebony staff which she held upright with both hands before her. Its ends were adorned in elaborate, finely-wrought silver caps. The one at the staff's base was a swirling, scrolled pattern perhaps a foot or so long, while the top cap was twice that length and consisted of a series of faces carved in various expressions, all with their mouths open. She rose, keeping her grip on the staff, and Triistan saw that her hands and arms were covered by long, dark gray gloves. Her robe was of the same hue, with a deep cowl completely covering her head and face. She was the only Vanha whose features were thus concealed.

She spoke in the same archaic language that Danor and Crixus had used, and it sounded to Triistan as if she had asked the assembly a question. But rather than translate what she said, Danor seemed to be responding to Triistan's earlier thoughts instead.

"Brekha, Daughter of Veda. She wears the cowl to cover her scars. I saved her life, but not her sight, and she hates me for it."

The other Vanha responded to her in unison, "Yiin."

Danor leaned forward to rest his gnarled forearms on the railing. "She asks for permission to speak - redundant, since she holds the Speaking Staff, but we must follow ceremony - and they answer 'yiin', or 'yes'."

Brekha continued to address the crowd, her voice solemn and steady. While Triistan did not understand the words, her speech had the atonal rhythm of ritual.

"What happened to her?" Triistan whispered.

"She was careless and closed with one of the Worm's spawn."

"The Worm?"

The surly healer grunted. "'The Worm' is what we've taken to calling The Exile. Seems more appropriate, but we'll get to that." He jutted his square, whiskered chin towards Brekha again. "She states The Oath. Shall I translate it for you? Something tells me it has not been passed down through your history books."

"Yes, please."

"I am Brekha, Daughter of Veda the Arxhemist, of the Auruim House of Secrets."

"Truly?" Triistan whispered in wonder. "She is the direct descendant of the goddess Veda?" He was still trying to get his head around the concept that these were first generation Vanha.

But in answer, Danor only continued his translation:

"We are The Oathguard.

"We are the Living Wall; the First Line.

"I will hold that Line,

"To the last drop of my blood,

"The last dust from my bones,

"The final ash of my fire to ride upon the Wind.

"I, Brekha, Daughter of Veda, am the End of that Line,

"And I will hold my post until Ruine's Ending."

As she spoke each phrase, the other Vanha, led by Crixus, thumped their right fists against their chests in unison. But the effort seemed half-hearted and her voice lacked the emotion that Triistan thought must have once accompanied such a daunting and wholly selfless vow. Danor's voice was equally flat, with perhaps a hint of sadness or regret.

When she finished, the next Vanha stood and strode up to her on thick legs. He was a full head shorter than she, with a wide neck and powerful, hunched shoulders. A great mane of jet-black hair cascaded down his back, matched in color and nearly in length by the fiercely braided beard covering most of his face and broad chest. The beige colored sleeves of his tunic were rolled up almost to his elbows, showing burly forearms covered in yet more black hair ending at his wrists. His hands were huge, and as he reached for the Speaking Staff, he reminded Triistan of one of the great forest bears he had seen in the fighting pits, reaching out to maul some unlucky combatant. Brekha released the staff to him, nodded her head, and made her way back to her chair. She moved with grace and surety, even without the staff as an aid, making it difficult to believe she was blind.

The black bear spoke, and Danor interpreted.

"That is Kuthan Axus, Son of Jaleel, Lord of House Axus, and Fenness of the Dauthir, whom they called Fenness the Wild, of the

House of Wilds. I've always found it curious that our own beast master took on his father's house name, when his life's calling clearly comes from his mother." Kuthan repeated the same oath that Brekha had recited, and just as dispassionately. Danor did not bother to translate it.

And so it continued, as the remaining eleven Oathguard took the Speaking Staff and spoke the Oath. Danor supplanted each one with insightful, sometimes off-color comments.

There was Ariis, son of Udgard the Planter, who limped up to take the Staff with his left hand, for his right arm ended at the elbow: "Another beneficiary of the Worm's labors." Val, daughter of Shan, proud and beautiful, with long straight hair the same color as Triistan's sun-drenched copper, "and one mean bitch with that battle axe she usually has strapped to her back". Vendros, son of Ganar the Unbroken. That would have been Triistan's first guess; the man was huge, even for a Vanha. He towered above both Val and the High Master, and his arms and legs looked to have been carved from stone. Remembering Tarq's story about Udgard and Ganar and the creation of Laha'na'li, Triistan asked Danor if Val and Vendros had been playmates as children.

Danor gave him an appraising look. "Very perceptive of you, Salty. But they are much more than friends." He pointed back towards the floor of the Low Hall. As Vendros returned to his seat and passed by Val, she reached out and brushed her fingers along his arm. He took her hand in his and held it as he sat in his own chair, their arms outstretched between them.

Triistan was struck by how out of place this open sign of affection seemed in comparison to the overwhelming sense of fatalism that permeated the ceremony. He smiled.

After Vendros came Braxus, another son of Udgard.

"Now you know why they called him The Planter."

Then Eso, daughter of Estra of the House of Secrets, whose eyes were even bluer than Danor's, and who regarded Triistan with calm curiosity the entire time she recited her Oath.

"Careful Salty," Danor muttered in his rough bark voice. "If you think Crixus is good at plucking your thoughts from your head, Eso will pluck them, reshape them, and put them back, while you slap yourself on the back for being such a clever boy."

Triistan found that he could not look away from her, but he did manage to ask, "Can all of you do that?"

Danor chuckled. "No, it is a rare... gift."

Eso turned away as she finished her Oath, breaking eye contact with him, and Triistan felt a twinge of disappointment. He thought that her eyes - the same color as the aquamarine waters of Niht's Haven, he was sure of it - were perhaps the most beautiful things he had ever seen. He blinked and forced himself to remember what Danor had just said.

"It doesn't seem rare," the young man managed. "I mean... she is adept at it, as you say, and the High Master all but tore off the top of my head, or so it felt..." *And you keep finishing my thoughts as well*, he managed not to say aloud. Part of him did not want to insult the healer, who he was growing fond of, while the other part wanted to test Danor's own ability. So instead of asking him outright, he asked if there were any others besides those two.

His Vanha caretaker looked at him shrewdly, but did not let on if he had gleaned the rest of Triistan's thoughts. "They are the only two among us who possess the skill, though all of us have been trained to ward against it."

"What's it like - I mean, how does it work?"

Danor turned back to the ceremony; the next Oathguard was walking up to take the Speaking Staff. Like Val, she was tall and beautiful. But where Val was fair-skinned and lithe, this one was dark and sturdy, with broad shoulders and the confident stride of a warrior.

"Linessa, daughter of Obed, of the House of War. Not someone I would want to face on the field, and a shrewd tactician as well. It was her idea to weave the jungle into clothing that renders us nearly invisible. She is angry that the Lord Marshal did not take her with him, but she is too valuable to risk. We have all made our contributions, but she and Xarius are the principal reasons we have survived as long as we have."

"Where is the Lord Marshal, anyway?"

"The Lord Marshal's business is his own, and it will be his decision whether to share it with you." Triistan could hear the familiar exasperation creeping into the healer's voice.

But the young Seeker was undeterred. "Fine. So then will you answer my other question?"

"Perhaps - if I could remember which of your fuundaris centuriis questions it was that I haven't answered yet."

Triistan couldn't keep the smile off of his face. "How do Eso and High Master Crixus guess my thoughts? How does it work?"

To his surprise, rather than tossing another barb, Danor drew in a deep breath as he considered the question. Triistan began to suspect that, for all of his bluster, Danor was actually enjoying their conversation.

"I profess, Salty, that while I have some ideas, that is one of the great unsolved mysteries of our kind. It has something to do with the union between god and mortal - some kind of change that occurs in some of us. The ability... did not exist in the gods, so far as I know, and it is not very common in Vanha - fortunately, if you ask me."

Linessa finished her Oath and another woman approached to take the Staff. She was of medium height and build (for an Oathguard, Triistan reminded himself; she was at least an arm's length taller than him) and wore a tunic similar to the others - black, with gold border. But rather than a shirt of mail beneath, her arms and legs were wrapped snugly in dark, supple leather. Her knee-length boots of the same color hugged her calves tightly; Triistan thought they might have been wet, either with water or perhaps fresh mud. Draped over one shoulder was a long, multi-colored cloak that shimmered as she walked, its variegated blacks, browns and whites picking up the shifting light from the braziers in a dizzying display that was almost hypnotic. As she came closer Triistan even caught glimpses of jade, a deep russet, and here and there a blue the color of twilight. He let out a small gasp as he realized the cloak was made from thousands of feathers.

"That is Syr, daughter of Sylveth." There was an unfamiliar tone in the healer's voice which made Triistan turn his head. Danor was smiling. "Huntress, tracker, archer, scout and sentry. As swift and silent a killer as the falcons whose pinions make up yonder cloak. She is death's whisper... and my loving wife."

Triistan gawked. "Your wife?"

"Yes, my fuundaris wife. Why do you find that so hard to believe?"

"I... " but Triistan was at a complete loss for words. He thought it best if he changed the subject. "No reason, I... So what ideas do you have about how the High Master and Eso are able to understand others' thoughts?"

Danor snorted. "Clearly you require some aid in understanding your own, boy." But a sly glint in his eye took some of the sting out of his words, and as he continued, it was without hostility. He turned back to watch his wife hand the Speaking Staff off to the next Oathguard.

"In a moment. First, I think this one will interest you. That is Protaeus, the only known son of Cartis the Navigator. One of our brightest. A brilliant architect and engineer, and one of the original minds behind many of Ostenvaard's wonders."

That got Triistan's attention, momentarily distracting him from the topic of Eso and the High Master's "gift." As Danor provided his brief description of Protaeus, the young Seeker sat up to watch with interest, hoping he would get the chance to talk to the mind behind this incredible place. He still had so many questions, but "Will we be killed for trespassing?" never even occurred to him until later.

Protaeus was shorter than the others, with a wiry, athletic build. He walked quickly, head down, one hand behind his back and another scratching at the short dark beard that covered only his chin. It gave him a distracted air, and it was difficult to think of him in the same fierce context as the other Oathguard. Triistan thought he recognized a fellow intellectual.

"What do you know of the Between?" the abruptness of Danor's question caught him off guard.

"Little."

Danor stared at him with a blank expression, then pointed to himself. "This is my surprised face."

He shot a look over his shoulder at the rest of the Expedition members. "Are there still places of learning on Niyah? Schools? Libraries? Brothels or taverns, for fuundaris sake? Or do you all just sail around drawing pretty pictures of the coastline?"

Triistan found himself biting his cheek to keep from grinning.

"Perhaps later, if there is time," Danor finally added after no one responded to his jibe. "Let us first get through this minuerto. Next is Fyruun the Fair, son of Lyrin the Judicator. We call him 'Justice', but you would be unwise to assume he will afford you anything of the kind."

"Why is that?" Captain Vaelysia asked tensely from the row behind them.

"It was his mother's blood - spilt by huunan - that touched off the Godswar, or so Theckan has led us to believe. Fyruun did not take the news well, and is not likely to regard the Children of Tarsus with anything approaching fairness."

A handsome, broad-shouldered Vanha strode confidently up to take the Speaking Staff. He was clean-cut, with sharp features and sharper eyes - eyes that were presently scanning the Expedition even as he gave his oath. His gaze was coldly calculating, and made Triistan uneasy.

"That was over three hundred years ago!" the Captain protested in a harsh whisper. "You cannot possibly hold us responsible!"

"Rest assured that we can, Captain. Do you still not understand? Only the gods and the Oathguard may trespass on Aarden. All others are to be killed: that is the law."

"Your law," she hissed.

"And the only law that matters," came Danor's sharp rejoinder. But the Captain would not relent.

"Does it, still, su'ul? Ruine has changed. The gods you swore your Oath to are dead, wiped out. The only one left is the thing you've sworn your lives to imprison, yet He has escaped and you are the last of your kind, alone at the ass-end of the world. You need us."

Triistan winced at her boldness, but Danor did not seem to take offense.

"Indeed," the giant grunted. "But I am not the one who needs convincing, Captain. Like it or not, your fate - at least insofar as our say in it - will be decided here, in this chamber, today."

Below them on the floor of the auditorium, the last two Oathguard played out their roles in the ritual, while Triistan and his comrades watched in dread-filled silence.

***

Triistan paused in his narrative and rubbed his eyes. Gods, he was tired. His throat was dry and sore from talking for so long, and no matter how many times he did this, he was still surprised at the emotional toll that reliving those events took on him. He would not have been surprised to find Aarden's impenetrable coastline looming above the launch's mainmast, as if he had only just left.

But it was also cathartic to finally share these dreadful secrets with someone - anyone - so that he did not have to carry their weight alone anymore. He stretched and looked out across the endless black slab of the sea. There was still enough wind for them to sail by, but the air had grown heavy, so the water was calm. Above them stretched the deepening blue sky, where the first few stars were just now sparking to life. The moon, three-quarters to the full, hung like a misshapen pearl in the west, a forlorn grave stone to mark the passing of Ruine's twin suns.

"I'm sure we can all use a break, and I should plot our position while the skies are clear. Feels like we may be in for some dirty weather later tonight or tomorrow morning, so let's get the nets hauled in and everything lashed down." He started to make his way aft to where he kept the launch's azimuth, stepping over Voth's splayed legs as he did so. He made a mental note to bring the man his rations when he was finished taking his readings. It was probably time to remove his gag as well. Knowing Dreysha, she had probably tied it too tightly, and there was nothing to be gained by being cruel to the man.

Besides, he thought to himself, *other than his occasional outbursts, what harm could he do?*

- 16 -

Viviito Et Maugh

"Is this all there are then?" someone murmured from behind Triistan. He thought it might have been Wrael.

The thirteen Oathguard who had stood before High Master Crixus and restated their Oaths were now seated in their elaborately carved chairs on the opposite side of the chamber. The armored twins stood before a pair of huge entry doors, long blond hair done up in complex braids. Their black and silver polearms were crossed between them, and Triistan did not think they had moved at all since adopting this stance. If not for the uncovered alabaster beauty of their faces, they could have been smaller versions of the colossal statue that had first welcomed the *Peregrine* and her crew to Aarden.

Fifteen, plus Crixus and Danor and the Lord Marshal, Tau Something-or-other. And the monarch jharrls, don't forget those. He wondered if the Lord Marshal was reconnoitering alone or if he was leading a raiding party and how many more Oathguard would be with him. *Not to mention here in the city - there could be dozens that we haven't seen yet.*

For some reason he didn't think that was the case, though, perhaps because he would have expected most of them to be here for this… whatever it was. Trial? Public execution? Not that it mattered. The seventeen in this room looked to be more than enough to carry out whatever sentence they deemed appropriate for he and his fellow 'trespassers'.

Crixus approached the area where the members of the expedition were seated, long strides light with confidence and purpose. The High Master was enjoying this proceeding too much for Triistan's taste, and he reflected back on Danor's earlier remark about how he "loved his pomp".

Let's hope he loves justice and reason as well.

The giant stopped at a curved banister made of polished grey wood, adorned with silver and copper fittings. It was waist high for the Vanha - what would be chest-high for Triistan - and ringed the entire floor of the Low Hall, perhaps twenty feet inside the arc formed by the balcony and seats. There were periodic gaps in the railing, lined up roughly with three other sets of stairs like the curved one to his right.

"Deuth paas a-mani Ostenvaard, hospis verendiis," he said, spreading his arms wide. Without pausing to wait for Danor, he translated his own words: "Welcome to Ostenvaard, honored guests.

"You have been brought before a Cun've'dictuus - a Council of Witness - where you will be heard and your fate decided. Who among you will represent the whole?" He looked at each of them, but his eyes came to rest on Captain Vaelysia.

She shared a look with Tarq and Commander Tchicatta for a long moment, then shrugged and stood. They had little choice but to play along with whatever Crixus had in mind.

She squared her shoulders and bowed smartly. Then she lifted her chin and spoke in a clear, confident voice. "I am Vaelysia Be'landre, Captain of the SKS *Peregrine*." She returned the High Master's gaze without flinching. "And though I am far from the wellhead, I am told that the sire of my great-grandsire was Shan the Stormfather."

There were surprised murmurs from the rest of the crew behind her. The fact that the Old Blood ran through her veins was not a secret, but no one had ever heard her state her lineage before. The Oathguard seemed unimpressed, however: Crixus allowed a slight, crooked smile, and there were a few subtle nods, but for the most part her claim was met with an awkward, stony silence.

The High Master finally gestured to Triistan and the others.

"Do the rest of you, Seekers from Niyah and crew members of the SKS *Peregrine*, accept Vaelysia Be'landre as your champion, that her voice shall speak for yours, and her actions shall reflect your will?"

The expedition responded with a subdued chorus of "ayes".

Again that slightly crooked, knowing half-smile.

"So be it. Captain, you may descend to the floor. May you be found worthy of your ancestral claims, and the faith of your comrades." If he was being sarcastic, there was no sign of it in either his face or the tone of his voice. To his left, Triistan thought he could hear Danor's teeth grinding, but otherwise the healer remained silent.

Captain Vaelysia walked down the curved staircase, out onto the floor of the Low Hall. Her bearing was regal, confident, graceful -

much different than the rolling swagger she used on the pitching deck of her ship.

Triistan did not relate every detail of their "trial" to his fellow survivors - much of the questions asked in the first couple of hours or so had been difficult to make sense of because the members of the expedition had no context with which to assess them. He and his mates were confused and frightened, unable to comprehend why the Oathguard were so hostile and mistrusting, and their inquisitors made no attempt to explain themselves. Worse, for those first two hours the Vanha refused to communicate in Merchant's or any of the other common tongues, even though it became clear later that they all spoke several languages with perfect fluency. Danor translated for them, but it was hard to keep up with much of the back-and-forth.

Triistan watched them carefully, trying to read how they responded to the Captain's answers, hoping for signs of compassion and understanding, or at least patient interest and curiosity. Most of their expressions were guarded, and some were openly disdainful. Vendros, the mammoth son of Ganar the Unbroken, glared at them with what looked like open contempt, the long dark braids of his formidable mustache extending his frown until it just brushed the wide plane of his chest. In the seat to his right, his wife Val looked on with bright eyes, but otherwise her face might just as well have been carved from stone. Their eleven comrades bore similar countenances, and even Eso's piercing blue eyes seemed to have dimmed, as if veiled by clouds.

During this time, Captain Vaelysia was forced to stand at the center of the chamber's huge floor, while Crixus stalked around her, interpreting questions from the seated Vanha even as Danor translated for Triistan and the others. The questions came quickly, from every direction and without any apparent order based on seniority or other determining factor that Triistan could see. The High Master translated them almost as quickly as they were asked. When she answered, he would often pounce on her with a follow-up question and then interpret both for the gathered Vanha, while she maintained an attitude of relaxed attention, feet spread and hands clasped behind her back, as if she were a young Seeker cadet again. Whomever addressed her, she turned to face squarely, answering with perfect courtesy. If not for the seriousness of their situation, Triistan had no doubt that many of the crew would have relished the irony of seeing their captain 'dressed down' in such a fashion.

As the questions wore on, it appeared that the Oathguard regarded them as agents of their enemy, for reasons that the Seekers could not comprehend, and that this "Council of Witness" was just a formality. Based on how things were progressing, Triistan expected the entire ordeal to end in a summary execution.

Fortunately, Danor seemed to have already decided that they were not a threat, and as Captain Vaelysia's interrogation began its third hour, he intervened and recommended to High Master Crixus that they be given a brief respite "before someone defiles this great chamber of justice and truth". Unlike Crixus, Danor's sarcasm was unmistakable.

The High Master ignored it, though, and spoke directly to Vaelysia. "Do you require use of the privy, Captain?" She shrugged matter-of-factly.

"No, but I would be grateful for a brief rest and something to drink, Su'ul."

He grunted and dispatched one of the twin sentries to bring food and drink. She bowed, thanked him, and crossed the chamber floor to join her comrades. Triistan thought she looked tired, but was surprised she did not seem as confused or upset as he and his mates felt. He would have at least expected her to be angry or insulted, but her demeanor was calm.

"Well, how did I do?" she asked Danor.

The giant snorted. "Not bad for a treacherous, watered-down half-breed."

Several of the other Seekers voiced their outrage and fear in hissing whispers. Triistan joined the muffled outburst.

"Not bad? How can you say that? And Captain - with all due respect, sir - how can you be so- so… calm?" So far she had been almost absurdly respectful, practically submissive, and they wanted to see her at least put up some kind of fight for their lives. "They have no right to treat you this way! This whole thing is madness - we should be helping each other! How can they be such fools?"

Danor grunted. "The High Master is many things, Salties, but he's no fool. Nor are any of the rest of us - though that does not excuse us from having moments of foolishness. And neither is your Captain; she's played her part in this particular moment brilliantly."

Triistan just stared at him, dumbfounded. "She has?"

"You and your friends are still alive, aren't you?" Without waiting for Triistan's response, he leaned forward to speak to Captain

- 246 -

Vaelysia, lowering his voice. "Clever of you to let him continue translating, though don't think he doesn't realize you understand at least some of the language."

She shrugged. "Your tongue is the root of many languages I've heard across Ruine, so yes, much is familiar - but not enough to stake our lives on."

"Wise words, Captain. Have you marked them all yet?"

She looked back over her shoulder at the Oathguard, who were gathered in small groups having their own conversations.

"I think so. There are six others - besides Fyruun, of course. Kuthan, Ariis, Braxus, Linessa... Helix and Arthos?" These were the last two Oathguard to have entered the chamber before the sentries; dour, battle-scarred men with thick, unruly beards and shaggy manes of dark hair to match.

"There is an eighth," Danor answered. "Perhaps the most dangerous because of his gamesmanship."

Biiko, Commander Tchicatta, First Mate Tarq, and Triistan were close enough to overhear this conversation, but the rest of the crew were talking amongst themselves. Triistan looked at the Oathguard gathered across the room, trying to spot the reason the Captain had "marked" those particular names, but could see nothing that distinguished them from the other godkin. He shook his head in frustration. Clearly there was something larger going on here that he was just not grasping.

"What in the Dark are you two talking about?"

The Captain ignored him, frowning as she looked across the floor of the Low Hall. After a moment's reflection, she grinned back up at Danor.

"The engineer, Protaeus."

Danor gave her what passed for a smile for him - a slight narrowing of his eyes and pressing of his lips together - and sat back. "Well done. Now all you have to do is convince them. Don't waste your breath on Fyruun - frankly, I'm surprised he didn't kill you all before you reached Ahbaingeata. And Protaeus is too dangerous; be respectful, but don't engage him directly if you can help it."

The sentry returned with a large tray laden with bread, cheese, two large pitchers and several silver cups. She brought the tray over to the other Oathguard, who relieved her of all but one pitcher and one cup. These she carried across the wide floor of the Hall and handed to the Captain before returning to take up her post by the door, all without acknowledging Danor or the rest of the Expedition with either word or gesture - not even a nod when the Captain thanked her.

Captain Vaelysia poured herself a cup and drank it down greedily, then poured another before setting the pitcher aside. "I thought you said all I had to do was stall until the Lord Marshal returned?"

"That was before I realized Linessa's position. Arris and Kuthan were undecided - which I knew - but when their balls get squeezed they have a tendency to follow her lead. The best we can hope for now is a split and hope that the Lord Marshal returns in time - and that is a big IF, Captain."

Triistan finally realized they were discussing a vote on what to do with the Expedition members. "So what happens then?" he blurted out. "How do you settle a split? Surely not a holmgang?"

"A what?" asked the giant.

Captain Vaelysia glared at Triistan. "Mister Halliard is referring to our practice of trial by combat - known as holmgang - in cases where evidence and witnesses are in short supply."

Danor laughed. "Brutally simple, I'll give you that, but not very effective in meting out justice, unless you believe weakness automatically makes you wrong. You may have noticed that 'Divine Intervention' has been removed from the list of determining factors." He shook his head, still chuckling. "So much for the advances of your civilization."

Triistan forced himself not to duck his head in embarrassment, but couldn't keep all of the sulkiness out of his voice: "Fine, then how does a… a Cun've'dictuus settle a split in a civilized fashion?" Then a thought struck him and he stood up and began counting out all of the Vanha in the room again. Thirteen seated as "witnesses", plus the two sentries, plus Crixus and Danor -

"Seventeen, Salty," Danor finished for him. "But I can't vote."

"Why not?" Captain Vaelysia asked.

"I forfeited that right when I chose to sit here instead of on the Cun've'dictuus with the others."

"Why would you do that when you knew what was at stake?" Triistan sputtered. His insides tightened in anguish as he realized they would be missing a badly-needed ally. He was hurt as well; despite Danor's sharp tongue, Triistan had counted him as a friend, and could not understand why he would not speak on their behalf.

"Precisely because I do know what is at stake, Salty," the Vanha Templar growled. "If you'd been paying attention, you might recall that Brekha, Daughter of Veda, blames me for the loss of her eyesight. Presently she seems content to let things play out, and will likely cast her vote with Syr, who she greatly admires and respects - despite the fact that Syr is my wife I might add. If I were a participant in the Cun've'dictuus, however, Brekha would take up the opposing argument regardless of how she really felt, and she would be far more eloquent and persuasive for the other side than I would be for yours, potentially swinging another vote or two against you. You may have noticed that diplomacy is not one of my best traits," he added with a smirk.

As Triistan was digesting the complex politics, something else occurred to him. "Wait - if those are the eight arrayed against us, that means that the High Master does not want to see us killed..?"

Danor raised one bushy white eyebrow and settled back in his chair, smiling his not-smile. "Not yet, no. As I said, he is no fool. As your Captain will attest, one does not rise to leadership without being good at reading the weather, and I've a boil on my arse that tells me the same thing the ache in his leg is telling him: the sky's getting ready to open up and shit all over us. We've been complacent for decades, just waiting. Your arrival on Aarden was the wind shifting, and when that shitstorm hits, we're going to need every able body we can muster. I just hope Tau makes it back to us before the thunder falls."

The other Oathguard were returning to their seats. As Crixus started across the room towards Vaelysia, Danor nodded in his direction. "Looks like you're on again, Captain."

They settled back into their own seats, just as Triistan realized Danor hadn't told him how they would settle a tie vote. There was no time to ask now, though: the proceedings began in earnest as soon as Captain Vaelysia strode back onto the polished marble floor of the Low Hall.

The Cun've'dictuus took on a different atmosphere after the break. Rather than the assembled Oathguard riddling the Captain with question after question, there was considerably more discussion back and forth between the Vanha themselves, and so the two factions that had already been so obvious to Danor and the Captain started to materialize for Triistan and the others. They continued to speak entirely in Theranghel, the ancient tongue of the Laegis Templar, forcing Danor to translate, but gradually it became clear who favored immediate execution, and who called for temperance.

Eventually, Crixus called for a vote. While Triistan and his fellow Seekers held their collective breaths, the High Master posed the question to the assembly: "Viviito... et Maugh?"

"Live... or die?" Danor translated unnecessarily. To a man, the members of the Aarden Expedition silently came to their feet.

Each Oathguard also stood as they cast their vote, beginning with Brekha.

"Viviito," she said.

Kuthan stood, squaring his bulky shoulders. His huge hands were hidden in the thick tangles of his jet-black beard. When he spoke, even his voice sounded guttural and bear-like.

"Maugh."

Arris, son of Udgard the Planter, with his amputated arm: "Maugh."

Triistan felt his stomach tightening with dread.

But the rest of the Oathguard cast their votes just as Danor had foretold, and the decision was split. Crixus himself cast the last vote, and Triistan nearly sobbed out loud in relief as the High Master said "Live". Oddly, the assembled Oathguard accepted the split decision quietly, without a hint of protest or murmur of dissent as far as Triistan could tell. He supposed he should not be surprised considering that they had co-existed here for centuries; their capacity for mutual respect, acceptance and compromise must be nearly limitless.

High Master Crixus took up the Speaking Staff and held it up crosswise before him.

"The Cun've'dictuus is deadlocked. We will wait three full days for the Lord Marshal's party to return. In the meantime, the prisoners will remain in their suite where they will be kept under guard, as before. Kuthan, Syr, and Linessa, I would speak with you a moment please."

The other Oathguard filed out of the room, not giving the members of the Aarden Expedition so much as a second glance.

Danor stood and stretched. "Congratulations, Salties. You'll live at least another day, perhaps as many as three."

Triistan asked the question that they were all thinking at that moment: "Then what? What if they don't return?"

Danor grunted and motioned for them to start moving. He talked as they made their way up the aisle to the doors they had first entered through. "Then we have to decide whether to throw out our old protocols, disobey his orders and go looking for him."

"What about us? How is a split vote settled?"

"How is it settled? Conservatively, I'm afraid." But that was all he would say on the matter.

***

Several hours later, Triistan found himself sitting in the largest, most comfortable chair he had ever encountered, with a heavy tankard of watered-down sref - the very 'goat piss' Jaspins had warned him to stay away from - and a belly fit to bursting. A large fire crackled merrily not far beyond the reach of his crossed legs, which were propped up on a pillowed footstool.

Unfortunately the stool was a bit too tall for him, so that he had to lower his feet periodically whenever they began falling asleep. He was thinking about his journal: he knew he should be recording the day's events, but his mind seemed unwilling to focus. Under other circumstances, he should have been feeling satisfied and relaxed, even drowsy. But his insides were crawling with worry, and instead of feeling contented, he was anxious and afraid.

After Danor's ominous answer on how the Oathguard would settle a tie vote, the Vanha healer had promptly turned them over to one of the twin sentries - Rhea, he had named her - who they had found waiting for them outside of the Low Hall, in the wide passage that led back to their suite. Up close, Triistan found her striking, if aloof and wholly unapproachable; "like the snow-swept peaks of some distant mountain range, as forbidding as they are beautiful," he would finally write in his journal sometime later.

Rhea led them wordlessly back to their quarters after Danor bade them goodbye, saying that he had "work to do before dinner". The butt of her long poleaxe thumped in stony cadence while they marched along behind her in fearful, sullen silence. There had been several initial outbursts following Danor's non-answer, but when he ignored them, the Captain had abruptly put an end to their questions.

Their escort led them as far as the heavy double doors that marked the outer perimeter of their prison. There she stopped and told them that someone would make arrangements for dinner, then promptly swung the two doors shut in their faces. They heard her lift the thick timber that had been leaning against the wall on the other side of the doors and drop it into place with a solid thud. Already knowing what the result would be, several of the expedition members pounded, leaned or pushed on the doors anyway, cursing when they did not move.

For the next two hours they gathered in a large central common room. Its reflecting pool, columns, coffered ceiling and giant, opulent furniture made it the most luxurious of prisons, but a prison it was nonetheless. These niceties were lost on them as they debated their options, of which there seemed to be precious few.

Tensions were understandably high. No one planned to die without a fight, of course, but just how to go about winning their freedom when they were so obviously overmatched quickly turned the 'debate' into a shouting match. Curiously, the Captain and Firstblade did not try to quell the outbursts this time, but instead sat off to one side, quietly conversing with each other, while their crew took turns attempting to shout one another down.

At one point, Triistan saw the Captain summon Myles and Miikha over. After a brief discussion, Commander Tchicatta led the two men from the room, heading down the hallway that led to their sleeping quarters, not far past the study where Danor had treated him. He was about to ask the First Mate where they were going when Wrael and Brehnl got into a shoving match. It quickly escalated to an all-out brawl, and for the next several minutes there was pandemonium, until the Whip, Creugar and Lieutenant Jaspins waded into the fray and dragged the combatants aside. By the time order had been restored, the commander and the other two men had returned.

Not long after, Danor also returned to inform them that since Syr would not be joining him for dinner, "you salties will have to suffice, because I hate eating alone. I've enough for your officers and one or two crewmen; food is already being prepared for the rest of you and should be here shortly."

Captain Vaelysia pulled Triistan aside and asked him if he had his journal, and when he said "yes", she told him that he and Thinman would be joining the officers for supper. Now, looking across at where Thinman's huge bulk lay sprawled on a giant couch, snoring loudly, it was easy to see why the Captain had invited him: he ate and drank his fill without speaking a word save to acknowledge his appreciation for "such a kingly spread as this", then (after at least four helpings of everything) let out an outrageously loud belch to announce his surrender, finally stumbling over to the couch where he promptly passed out. No awkward questions or quarrelsome comments during the meal, and no witness to the more delicate conversation to follow, making him the perfect dinner guest.

Danor's home was just up a curved set of stairs not far from where they were being held. It was another suite, consisting of several lavishly furnished and decorated rooms that branched off from a large circular chamber, and dominated by the raised firepit before which Triistan now reclined.

An unexpected sight greeted them when they entered the apartment: a huge mass of fur and teeth growling that familiar low register that Triistan again felt vibrating in his molars.

Danor had entered first. He reached out his left hand and made some sort of rapid hand signal. The gesture was fluid and almost too quick to see, but it was obviously deliberate, and the effect was instantaneous: the jharrl stopped growling and lowered its broad muzzle to sniff Danor's hand.

"Easy, boyo. You'll have to save them for dessert." He flashed a rare grin and a wink at his guests, who had all frozen just outside the doorway. Seeing this, the healer nodded, his smile widening further. "You salties aren't as dumb as you look. One at a time, now, so I can introduce you."

Captain Vaelysia entered first. "This is Atuu, but we call him 'Tooth', for obvious reasons." The Captain approached slowly, with her hand outstretched, while Atuu regarded her with the same luminescent blue eyes as the other jharrls they'd seen. They held an unmistakable intelligence in them, and Triistan swore the beast was cocking one eyebrow speculatively. The fat stump of its broken right tooth stuck out from under long, grey whiskers, adding to the cockeyed expression, although its gleaming and intact twin - easily half a yard long - looked formidable enough to do the work of two, to say nothing of the scimitar-shaped tusks curving out from its lower jaw.

The jharrl did not deign to rise and greet them, nor did it lower its head or acknowledge the Captain as a dog might. It turned its head away as she drew close, as if bored with the whole ordeal now, although its long, dagger-shaped ears twitched and swiveled. As Captain Vaelysia withdrew, it swung its head right back to regard the next guest, First Mate Tarq. Triistan was behind the Whip and edged into the room for a better look.

Even though he had seen them before - had even been carried on the back of one - it was still hard not to be struck by the creature's size; even lying down, its eyes were nearly level with the Captain's. Its fur was silver-grey, with what once might have been black or dark blue stripes ranging through it, although it was clear now that Atuu was well past his prime: the stripes were so shot with grey and silver hair that they were little more than shadows. The bones of his hips and shoulders were visible, and there was a large, irregularly shaped patch of badly scarred skin along his right flank, as if he'd been burned long ago. Now that he was closer, Triistan saw that what he had thought was Atuu's raised eyebrow was actually another scar that arced above his right eye, then ran down across his muzzle until it disappeared in the grey spindles of his long whiskers, just above his broken tooth.

As the others were introduced, the monarch jharrl was equally dismissive, even summoning a wide and noisy yawn at Triistan's approach. For some reason that made Triistan smile and chuckle. Atuu's ears swiveled forward and the big cat cocked its head, regarding him with his speculative scar, those long gray whiskers drooping to either side like a disapproving frown. Triistan stifled his laugh and moved away, feeling as if he'd been scolded.

They were pleasantly surprised upon discovering that Danor had a passion for cooking, and that he was remarkably good at it. It seemed out of character for the irascible giant, whose rough mannerisms and sardonic observations seemed more appropriate for a military commander than a healer or master cook, but Thinman's pronouncement was not polite hyperbole: Danor laid out a table for them that would have been welcomed at any of the Sea Kings' royal banquets. Cooking and serving actually seemed to relax him: he was less surly and somewhat more open to their questions.

They learned much about the types of plants and animals that the Oathguard relied on for food. A great deal of what was set before them was vaguely familiar, either because it was similar to a common food back home or because they had experimented with it during their exploration of Aarden. Triistan noted (thankfully) that greybole monkey was not offered, and Danor laughed loudly when the young Seeker, remembering the troupe that had ransacked their supply boat after the expedition had killed one, described them to their host and asked if the Oathguard ever ate them.

"Only if you like being eaten by them in turn, lad. Clever little brokuuros, and as vengeful as a spurned wife. They multiply like the fuundaris H'Kaan - especially out near Haagen's Bay, where you're docked - though that isn't surprising anymore."

"Why is that?" Tarq asked after sipping from his tankard of sref. His tone was casual, but he'd looked directly at the Captain as he posed the question, his good eye glinting in the shifting fire- and candlelight. Danor had gone back into the kitchen.

"Just a theory of mine," the healer said as he came through the door with a huge serving tray holding a heavy block of whitish-yellow cheese. "But I'll be the first one to tell you that theories are like bungholes; everyone's got one and most of the time they're full of shit."

The First Mate chuckled along with the others gathered around the table, but he wasn't going to let his question go that easily.

"So humor us, Su'ul. Why do you think these monkeys multiply like the H'Kaan?"

Danor set the board and cheese down on the table, then lifted his mug of sref - a massive, silver thing that was more growler than tankard - and took a long pull from it. He swished some in his mouth as he looked at them thoughtfully, then swallowed and made a bitter face.

"Your lieutenant's right - tastes like goat piss. Too much water. But I'm supposed to watch you tonight, not kill you with real spirits, so goat piss it is." He wiped his mouth with the back of his huge hand and began slicing off large pieces of cheese for them.

"But I take your point, Salty. That's a long story, but aye it's the one you're all after, and it's as good a place to begin as any I suppose." He took another long pull of sref, ending with a throaty belch. "But not just yet, I think. Soon - but not yet. As you and your kin well know, Khaliil, stories have their own time and place, and anyway this one's not for the weak - or empty - stomach. So we'll fill our bellies and you'll fill my ears with news from home. For dessert, we'll sink our teeth into the Great Monkey Mystery and the tale of our missing prisoner as well. All of it. Perhaps Syr will be back with news of the Lord Marshal by then, and she can lend a hand in the telling."

So for the next two hours they feasted on one of the best meals Triistan could ever recall eating: warm bread slathered with a butter that tasted of spiced honey; several different kinds of mushrooms drenched in a light, delicious oil; greens of every description (including more than one that defied description), also drenched in the same oil; steamed crayfish, which were surprisingly sweet and grew to the size of lobsters on Aarden; grilled eel and trout; and a succulent, bloody meat that they recognized as soon as they tasted it.

"Kongabosk - 'King's Boar' we call it," Danor said around a mouthful of the stuff, bright red juice running down his chin.

"How in the dead g- how in the bloody Dark did you prepare all of this by yourself?" asked the Captain.

"Ha! Child's play, except for the boar. This is just a portion of the monster Kuthan brought in this morning. They've been roasting it all day in a smoke-pit, hoping to celebrate Tau's return some time tonight."

That caught their attention. "Did you hear from him?" Commander Tchicatta asked.

"No, but the jharrls are restless. Something's up topside," he gestured with his eyes and chin towards the ceiling while he sliced off more meat and passed it around the table. "That's why Crixy sent Syr and the others up to have a look. The cats have a bit of their own touch, especially when it comes to the Lord Marshal. Of course, they can also smell a fart in a cyclone so might be something else has their hackles up."

Triistan looked around for Atuu, but the old jharrl had disappeared not long after Danor had finished 'introducing' his guests, and they hadn't seen it since.

Their host would not elaborate further on the topic during dinner, instead steering the conversation back to Niyah. He was very interested in the state of mankind's remaining pockets of civilization, specifically which of those surrounding the great Dauthurian Columns had survived Ehronfall and what kind of condition they were in now. He was particularly impressed by how far Shanthaal had come.

"Shan's pride and joy, that one. Much of what it took to build this place was learned first from the Stormfather - how he raised and reshaped the sea floor in particular. Did you know that he deliberately set them in the shape of a storm? If you've ever looked at them on a map, you will see how they seem to swirl about the central isle, where he set his throne. Chatuuku you call it now you say. I think he would be pleased that it has done so well, the vainglorious bastard." He raised his huge mug in silent toast to the long-dead god of storms. Goat piss or not, he drained it clean.

The Captain nodded as she tore off a bloody slab of boar meat. She used a chunk of bread to sop up the juice on her plate, then wrapped the bread around the meat and wolfed it down.

"The Isles were fortunate that the mainland absorbed most of the impact of Ehronfall."

"Hmph," Danor grunted. "I'm not sure it would have mattered if Ehronhaal had landed in the sea next to you. I think even back then Shan did not fully trust his brother or the other Auruim, which helped explain why he put so much time and energy into those fuundaris sea walls. I imagine they still stand?"

Commander Tchicatta sat across from Triistan, nodding to himself, the firelight sparking a far-off gleam in his eye. Like the city above them now, the towering black sea-walls that linked each of the Sea-King Isles could only have been crafted by the gods. They were a source of great pride and confidence to those who fought beneath the Kings' banners, and the envy of every other military commander on the face of Ruine.

"Tall and true," answered Captain Vaelysia. "Though the barbican between Bola and Khiigongo is in disrepair. Bola's ruling family is rumored to be teetering on the edge of bankruptcy after pissing away most of that kingdom's royal coffers on failed social policies." This piqued Danor's interest and they spent the rest of dinner discussing the storm-ridden seas of the Sea Kings' internal politics. The island confederacy had done remarkably well, all things considered, but trying to get seven separate kingdoms to work together was bound to have its share of problems.

At Thinman's surrendering belch and subsequent toppling onto the couch, they all pushed themselves away from the table, thanking and complimenting their host. He nodded in acknowledgement, then walked over to a sideboard, opened a flat wooden box that gleamed a deep cherry in the dim light, and drew forth a curved smoking pipe with a stem nearly as long as Triistan's arm and a bowl the size of his fist. Held in the Oathguard's huge paw, however, it looked to be of normal size.

Danor packed the pipe's end from a weathered pouch lying next to the case, while walking slowly over to stand next to the fire. When he finally spoke, his voice had lost much of its hard edge.

"A parting gift from my father," he said, almost wistfully, before drawing a brand from the fire and using it to light the pipe.

Sensing that the opportunity had finally come, Captain Vaelysia spoke quietly.

"It is a fine piece, Su'ul." When he did not respond, she cleared her throat and spoke more firmly, with a formality Triistan had rarely heard her use:

"We are grateful that you have shared your home and your table with us, Danor of the Oathguard. You have treated our wounded and honored us with your hospitality. We are but beggars in these hallowed, historic halls, and have naught to repay you with but our own stories and knowledge, and the will to aid you however we can. It is clear that you and your brethren are in terrible danger, yet we would share that peril and stand beside you if you would allow it."

Danor chuckled quietly, a sound like boulders rubbing together. He did not answer right away, but instead drew on the pipe, the embers in the bowl flaring, casting his craggy features in their ruddy glow. Before him, the fire popped and hissed.

"... and I will hold my post until Ruine's ending," he finally muttered to himself. "Well, perhaps that time approaches. We are all so very tired... " he trailed off, lost in thought.

"Su'ul?" the Captain prompted quietly. Danor roused himself.

"Let it not be said that sailors only spit salt; that was well spoken, Captain, if naive." The sadness in his tone and face removed the sharpness from his words. He beckoned to them, pointing with the long, curved stem of his pipe to the comfortable-looking chairs set out along one side of the raised hearth.

"Come and join me and I will tell you why."

- 17 -

The Dark Son

"What do you know of The Divide - specifically, how it began?" Danor asked in his tumbled-boulder voice.

He stood by the fire in the center of his living quarters, one foot resting on the raised marble hearth that surrounded it, leaning on that knee, drawing thoughtfully from the end of his long pipe. Captain Vaelysia, Commander Tchicatta, First Mate Tarq, Lieutenant Jaspins and Triistan were seated in oversized leather chairs, arrayed in an arc facing him and the fire pit. Fortunately, their host had thought to add pillows to each chair so that they could lean back comfortably. Behind them, on a huge divan that made even his considerable bulk look small, Thinman snored peacefully.

"The rift between the gods? Some," answered the Captain. "Mister Tarq can tell you in detail, but the short version is that it began because the Dauthir lived side by side with man and the Auruim regarded us as little more than livestock."

"Hm," the Vanha grunted. "Or breeding stock. Though you would never hear them admit to it, I think." He pulled a long, sooty shaft of iron from a basket nearby and used it to poke at the fire, talking around the pipe stem clenched in his teeth. Sparks chased the smoke towards a grated hole in the ceiling; Triistan wondered briefly if during the day it let sunlight into the room like the shaft he had seen in his recovery cell.

"But that might be getting a little ahead of ourselves. No place to begin like the beginning, eh? And so we shall." Danor fixed each of them with his brilliant blue eyes to make sure he had their undivided attention. "Heed me well, Salties. Your lives and possibly the whole of Ruine may depend on it."

"Tarsus was the last of his kind, what you call the Old Gods. We know little of them save for him, and the mess left over from the battle against Maughrin. We don't know if he was the one to write the entirety of the Vertex, but he was the one to activate it. Some say the

Vertex was his greatest gift, a bit of Arxhemestry so powerful it had the power to turn the ashes of the old world into something new... others that it was his greatest mistake."

"How was it a mistake to rebuild what had been destroyed?" Triistan asked, forgetting himself and his place for a moment.

"Because you were part of the plan, Salties. The creation of the Children is just as much a part of that formula as the birds and the bees and the fuundaris trees." He set the poker down and drew on his pipe again, then blew the smoke towards the high, coffered ceiling. It smelled rich and so sweet he could taste it.

"But did you know that amongst all things new in the world, he made you first," he smiled his not-smile, "before the Arys?"

Triistan remembered looking at the others and seeing the surprise he felt reflected back in the faces of his comrades.

"No, I wouldn't think so. A rather embarrassing little tidbit for the gods, particularly the proud Auruim. Always wondered if that was where their hostility toward you began. You were His real children, a chance at a fresh start. While they were the afterthought, you see, his dying realization on how weak you would be at first. The threat of Maughrin and her spawn was not over, despite all His best efforts to kill her. So he took everything that was left of himself to create something strong to watch over you.

"Tarsus... and the other Old Gods as well, were more than the physical bodies they occupied. Their thoughts, beliefs, memories and emotions - their very essence - was released when the vessel that contained them was destroyed. As part of the Vertex, Tarsus took that energy and broke it apart, repurposed it, giving form to the Arys. So that they might protect you.

"Rather ironic, don't you think?" He hooked a chair with his foot and dragged it over near the hearth, where he sat down and propped his huge feet up on the stone.

"But so what?" the Captain asked. "What difference does it really make?"

"To you and I now, nothing, really. But to the Arys... well now, some saw it as a slight. How could mere mortals be first? And more to the point, did Tarsus really expect the gods to be wet nurses to you dirt covered savages? But it wasn't just when they were made that shoved sand up their arse, it was how."

"The Vertex?"

Danor shook his broad head. "No. I mean physiologically - that is, their physical make-up; what makes them different from you - and from us. For reasons only Tarsus knows, He made you - his 'new beginning' - from mortal flesh, even though he bestowed immortality on the Arys. But He changed something else in you which proved to be infinitely more important, which the Dauthir discovered in your very own valley of Laha'na'li." He jabbed the long stem of his pipe in Tarq's direction, eyes twinkling with amusement in the firelight. "The soil of your so-called 'Cradle of Ruine' was not the only thing to yield a crop when plowed."

Triistan and the others exchanged confused glances. "What are you saying, Su'ul?" Captain Vaelysia used the respectful term of address, but her voice had an unpleasant edge to it.

"I am saying that immortality has a price, Captain: the gods are barren. They cannot bear children - at least, they cannot conceive children with one another."

They stared back in stunned silence.

"Ah, so you didn't know that, either?" Danor chortled. "Well, I assure you it is true. Sex for them is - or was - for physical pleasure only, and who knows whether that was even true after so many hundreds of years. But while Tarsus made you individually mortal, he made your *species* immortal, or as close to it as you can get. What's more, the Dauthir experienced a level of ecstasy when lying with your kind that they had never felt with their own. Your mortality gives you an entirely different perspective... a higher level of sensation and emotion that you feel as love and passion. The gods' heightened empathy allowed them to share those sensations, and this, coupled with your... fragility, your vulnerability - proved to be an irresistible combination, first for the Dauthir but eventually for the Auruim as well, though they shunned the notion publicly. The Vanha were born of these couplings, as you know, and while we could not do so with your... tenacity, Tarsus' gift of renewal was passed along to us as well.

"But-" blurted Triistan. "But what about Eris and Taisha, both goddesses of love and lust?" He blushed and tried not to duck his head.

Danor chewed on the end of his pipe, nodding. "You're a shrewd one, boy. I could say that it wouldn't be the first bit of hypocrisy done by a god, but the truth is that the High Houses had not been formed yet. Or rather, they were still... under development, let's say."

"But how can that be so, Su'ul? Our doyen tell us that the Young Gods drew lots to determine what each would watch over, almost immediately after Tarsus' death," countered the Captain.

"It can be so because it was so, and your doyen are mistaken, Captain. The short-sightedness of the short-lived would be my guess. Looking back on history through a mortal spyglass tends to compress things, I think. It took time for the High Houses to coalesce, while they not only learned what this newly recreated world had to offer, but what its needs were and how their own powers could best... satisfy those needs." He grinned suggestively. "Eris and Taisha did not discover their particular talents until well after most of their siblings, so the House of Pleasures was formed last."

"You speak almost as if you were there, Su'ul," Commander Tchicatta said quietly.

"Nearly." Danor's expression darkened noticeably. "My father told me."

"Who was your father?"

"Who, indeed," he answered bitterly. "I am the son of Theckan, the one you call the Rogue."

He drained his mug, stood, and left to retrieve the pitcher of sref from the table. Triistan shot a confused look at his captain, who only gave a subtle shake of her head.

As Danor returned, he stopped by each of them and wordlessly gestured to refill their mugs. Both the Captain and the Firstblade politely declined. Triistan accepted, albeit there wasn't much to refill, since he had been sipping it very carefully. The giant set the pitcher down next to his mug and tapped the ashes out of his pipe on the hearth, then began repacking it with fresh leaves.

The Captain caught Triistan's eye, pointed to her own mug, and shook her head: no more. He nodded.

Danor finished lighting his pipe and settled back into his chair with a sigh. "That might just be the heart of the matter though, lad. Early on the Dauthir were discreet about their dalliances with mortals, and the Auruim seemed mildly amused, convinced that it was a passing fancy of their flightless siblings. It only fed their sense of superiority I think. They had not yet perceived the rapidly-multiplying Children as a threat, nor viewed the Dauthir's relationship with them with any hint of the jealousy it would provoke later.

"So, while that stew simmered, both factions lived in relative peace for a time. They worked on their wonders - the Auruim on their

- 262 -

fabled floating city of Ehronhaal and the Dauthir on their mighty Columns. During this time, the mortal population began to flourish. Your ancestors were timid at first, not quite sure what to do with the giants that lived around them in these fantastic structures. But in time, most of them got over it. They migrated closer, settling near the Columns, drawn by the promise of... of everything I suppose: knowledge, literature, art, science, medicine... not to mention the allure and protective embrace of these Young Gods. Once they lived together, a dramatic rise in the number of Vanha was not far behind."

Danor looked into the flames and drew on his pipe. Blue-gray smoke drifted across his craggy features, the hard edges of which were etched by the red-orange glow of the fire. It reminded Triistan of the view they'd had of Sigel's Wrath as the *Peregrine* sailed past the volcanic centerpiece of the Burning Sea, how many months or years ago he could not recall.

"Gods, what an Age for this world! There was a synergy between the three races where they fed off one another's strengths and filled in the voids of their weaknesses. Cities rose like young saplings - not just around the Columns but in every corner of Niyah and the surrounding isles. The Khaliil had Laha'na'li of course, but in the north Gundlaan saw the formation of The Three Citadels: Strossen, Naar Deran and Ostrell, while the south and west were dominated by Cartishaan - a vast empire that even Shanhaal had to acknowledge was its superior at that time."

"No more," grunted the Firstblade. "Ehronfall wiped out most of Cartishaan and now the Sea Kings make the same claim."

"Don't let the Gundlaanders hear you say that," Captain Vaelysia responded. "Ganar's Bones shielded them from the worst of Godsfall and the Three Citadels have recovered, although there's talk of civil unrest from up that way, if the merchy's are to be believed."

Danor, who had spent days discussing the post-Ehronfall state of affairs on Niyah with the Captain and First Mate while Triistan was healing, nodded in understanding.

"That may be so, but before The Divide became the Godswar, Cartishaan's rise was unrivaled by mortal standards. Enough even to attract the attention of the Auruim. Not all of them had shunned the Children, you see. Obed, whom your kind called the Guardian, had already pledged his eternal life to stand watch against Maughrin's return. He knew his task could not be accomplished from afar, so he embraced both Vanha and huunan alike in his efforts to build his fortress, Senhaal, the Unsleeping Vigil.

"Would that he had kept as careful a watch within his own ranks," he added ominously.

"Of Eris and Taisha you know, and the only other Auruim to mingle with mortals was Minet, who had moved on from stirring the progeny pot at Laha'na'li to sculpting the lands and waterways of her living tribute to Tarsus in what became - named by the Lords of Cartishaan, mind you - Minethia. I've been told that she enjoyed their attentions almost as much as she enjoyed pissing in the wine of her fellow Auruim about it."

Here the Vanha healer paused and drew on his pipe again, held it for a long moment, then blew the smoke towards the fire in a soft sigh. "Ironically, it was her goading that first drew the Worm out into the world."

"Talmoreth," Tarq rasped. The fire hissed and popped, sending a brief shower of sparks into the air.

Danor nodded. "Aye, the same. Personally, I've always thought the Argonnei had it right: 'Tsharthuuk' they named it. 'Torn Sky' for the way its jagged black spire marred their western horizon."

"A fitting name," Tarq responded. "It is like a great, skeletal talon clawing at the sky. 'Tis a wonder that boney spire withstood the Godsfall."

"Wonders and secrets were their meat and mead, Salty. The House of Secrets birthed those bones: Estra the Dreamer, Sylveth, Goddess of Puzzles, Trickery and Cunning... and The Worm."

"But I thought Talmoreth was well-respected?" interjected Triistan. "You make it sound like an evil place, but my old doyen used to make visits there to conduct research and share his own findings. He spoke very highly of both the students and instructors, especially the Rector - a man named Vaun, I think."

Danor rolled his massive shoulders in a shrug. "I cannot say what it is now, but despite its appearance and ill-sounding name, it was well-regarded then as well - at least for the first few hundred years. At the time, The Worm was a study in curiosity - as much of others trying to understand him as his own insatiable appetite for the deepest lore. Math and Arxhemestry were his passion at first, but he claimed Ruine had a natural power beyond our own, a wellspring that had fed Maughrin and empowered her with the strength to defeat the Old Gods. The other Arys were interested in his research, particularly his fellow Auruim, who were beginning to question the Dauthir-huunan 'alliance'. It had not yet been called a 'problem', but the resultant population explosion of both the Children and Vanha had gotten their attention. The fact is, the gods as a whole - Auruim included - wanted offspring for any number of reasons: legacy, species preservation, self-preservation, even some kind of fuundaris paternal or maternal instinct passed on to them from Tarsus for all I know. But while the Dauthir had no qualms about lying with 'lesser beings', most of the Auruim abhorred the idea.

"Enter our missing guest of honor. Clever god that he was, The Worm began to play on those prejudices. He suggested that the answer to the gods' infertility could be found in his research, particularly in this Ancient Power, although he was smart enough not to name names on the intriguing and highly controversial subject of his research -"

"The graybole monkeys!" Triistan cut in intuitively, and everyone but Danor looked at him as if he'd suddenly sprouted a second head. The big Vanha just nodded and smiled his crooked not-smile as Triistan sputtered to explain. "You didn't want to explain it at dinner, but you said that they multiplied rapidly, especially out near Haagen's Bay, that - that they multiplied -"

"That they multiplied like the H'Kaan, so I did, boy. So I did. Well done. The Endless Swarm: what better subject for reproductive experimentation than Maughrin's foul progeny? They've pretty much mastered the art, wouldn't you say? And it wasn't as if anyone would miss them."

"What of Obed?" asked the Firstblade. "The Guardian could not have abided this; you said yourself that he had pledged his eternal life to eradicating them and guarding against Maughrin's return."

"He would not have stood by idly had he known The Worm was actively breeding the fuundaris things, you're right about that. But our friend was not stupid. It was easy enough to send his minions - your kind flocked to Talmoreth in those days, eager for access to new lore with which to empower themselves - and beg Obed to capture a handful of the H'Kaan to help them learn more about their adversary."

"Still, someone must have known. Someone always talks," the Captain prompted.

"Yet the Worm was a master at distraction. He had a mastery of Arxhemestry that could barely be understood, much less replicated. He used that knowledge to churn out a steady stream of other things... helpful things. He showed us how to shape glass and metal as if it were clay, and mix different materials together to form new ones. His research made armor stronger, weapons sharper - your Patroniis' fine blacksteel blades are a refinement of the Old Gods' bluesteel, and were first forged in Tsharthuuk's belly, you know. He worked hard to make himself seem invaluable, and therefore, above suspicion, at least for a great while.

"So he used that time wisely to prepare. I don't believe anyone - neither Auruim nor Dauthir - had any inkling of the depth of his obsession with the Living Darkness, or how far he was prepared to go in his efforts to understand Her power. He had always been... amoral I guess is the right word in your tongue. When death has no hold over you, when there is no one to rule over you, no apex predator to cull your herd, there are no limits to what you think you can do, unless you set them yourself. Whether something was 'right' or 'wrong' was of no concern to him - that was the purview of Lyrin the Judicator, not his. His was the pursuit of knowledge, of understanding the how and why of things... no matter the cost to others, or even to himself."

Danor drew on the pipe again, setting the embers aglow, but then shook his head. "No, that isn't quite right. The Worm's passion wasn't the pursuit of knowledge, it was the mastery of that knowledge that he craved."

"What's the difference?" Triistan asked. Danor's blue eyes bored into him.

"The will to use it, Salty.

"You possess the knowledge of what it takes to kill someone, but your Reaver Commander and your Unbound bodyguard have mastered that particular skill. None of us will ever know if The Worm's original intentions were honorable or not, but it doesn't really matter: just as you cannot fully appreciate fire without getting burned, you can't understand Darkness by standing in the bright light of day.

"So he delved deeper, while his siblings were distracted with their own vainglorious pursuits. He began cross-breeding other species, and even when rumor reached the ears of the other Arys that he had begun using the Children in his experiments, they remained conveniently deaf and blind to it."

Something cold and wet began coiling around Triistan's insides as he listened to Danor's tale. "What about us? Why didn't mortals - or even Vanha for that matter - do something to stop it?" But even as the words left his lips, he knew how naive he sounded.

"Some tried, but early on they were thwarted by The Worm's cunning. He preyed on petty criminals, outlaws, whores, murderers... even peasants - the lowest rungs of your growing civilizations, the rungs no one else seemed to mind stepping on to climb up out of the filth. Remarkably, he had plenty of help from your own kind; his following had swelled, and, whether through his dark arts or for some other reason, there was a fervor in their devotion to him that burned much hotter than even the best relationships between gods and mortals elsewhere."

"Give me a madman over a zealot any day..." Captain Vaelysia growled in understanding.

"You can kill the madman," finished her First Mate, nodding.

Danor actually chuckled. "I think The Worm might agree with you there. Perhaps I'll suggest it to the Lord Marshal as our new mantra, for what are we - the legendary Oathguard - if not zealots?" He lifted his mug to the shifting shadows as if he were offering a toast, muttered something in his own tongue, and then drained the tankard down.

"Which brings us to... well, to us I suppose," he continued. "I mentioned how Obed had embraced huunan and Vanha alike in his efforts to build Senhaal and resist the return of the H'Kaan. That's putting it a bit too kindly I think, at least at the outset. Even then, the H'Kaan seemed to bleed from the cracks and caves of this world, as if Maughrin were Ruine and the crevices were her weeping wounds. In truth, Obed saw both of the lesser races as shock troops and laborers, tools to be used in his work. He was Auruim, remember, so that was to be expected. But both races surprised him, I think." He drew thoughtfully on his pipe again. Every once in awhile, through some trick of the light, if Danor's eyes were in shadow, Triistan thought he caught a flash of incandescent blue that reminded him of the way the jharrls' eyes glowed in the darkness.

"While elsewhere across Ruine these multi-racial communities grew like gardens - whole societies blooming like so many tropical flowers - Senhaal was at the farthest, sharpest edge of the world as we knew it, fighting a forgotten war.

"No, no garden could grow the likes of us," he said. "Senhaal was a fuundaris forge."

"The Laegis, you mean," prompted Captain Vaelysia.

Danor nodded slowly. "Yiin, Captain. I mean the mighty, fuundaris Laegis Templars." He stretched out a long leg and kicked a log that had fallen aside back into the flames. Other than the crossed straps of his sandals, his lower legs were bare, and Triistan saw that the skin along the back of his right calf, from his hamstring to his heel, was puckered and deformed. It looked like a burn scar and he wondered if it was the same fire that had scarred Atuu's flank.

"In their earliest days," Danor continued as he settled back in his chair, "the Laegis consisted of several dozen warriors - mostly Vanha but there were a handful of hardy huunan mixed in - who had organized themselves within Obed's larger army, mostly in the interest of self-preservation, I think. I'm not saying they were cowards or insubordinates - quite the opposite, actually. Their martial prowess spoke for itself on the battlefield, but it was their superior tactical abilities that drew them together at first. Once again, mortality has certain advantages, particularly when it comes to… conservation I guess you could call it. They looked for ways to reduce casualties, while Obed gave it no more thought than he would the gas that escaped his divine arse every now and then.

"So the Laegis organized themselves into concentrated fighting units of ten men each, led by one of their own in the field, but still mindful of Obed's overall command structure. This was relatively easy, since they were so few in number: there were ten men to a "finger" and five "fingers" made a "fist". When someone first named them "Laegis Templar", there were two fists - one hundred men. They bunked, ate, and trained together, developing tactics to coordinate their individual units - the 'Akist' they called it - and a series of signal flags to communicate with during battle so that the "fists" could support one another. In essence, they rebuilt Obed's army from the inside out."

"How did that go over with The Guardian?" mused Commander Tchicatta.

Danor shrugged. "It was impossible to ignore the results. Those hundred men were as effective as ten times their number of regulars. Whether or not he could be called a brilliant strategist, there was no doubt that Obed was a warrior, and the Laegis had earned his respect on the field. He gave them his full support and made them the vanguard of his army - the tip of the spear. Their ranks swelled from those first two fists to twenty in the first year; a hundred fists - five thousand fighters - by the end of the second year."

He sighed. "And then someone decided that they - we, I suppose I should say since I joined up as part of the 87th - needed to serve a higher purpose. We Vanha were full of nobility and purpose, you see - idealists if not quite zealots, not yet anyway. For one thing, we saw ourselves as living, breathing bridges - ambassadors not just between the Arys and the Children, but between Auruim and Dauthir as well. We knew firsthand how the Auruim viewed mortals, of course, but we also saw the early signs of strife between the gods that would eventually become The Divide. We were concerned even back then that their differences were an open wound that would fester if left unchecked."

"So we did what all good idealists do - zealots, if you prefer - and set out to fix it. The Templar movement you are most familiar with - where we became diplomats and the like, serving the Elder Councils primarily - began then. Our leadership had determined our best hope, our best use, lay in strengthening the foundation of each community. 'Be the mortar to their stones' they said."

"The Templar were heroes," Triistan said hurriedly. For some reason he felt compelled to sooth Danor's bitterness. "While their numbers are few, many still hold positions of respect and have done much to help rebuild -"

"To rebuild what they failed to protect - by the gods' moldering corpses what they helped destroy in the first place, Salty," Danor interrupted, blue eyes flashing in the shadow beneath his heavy brow. Seeing Triistan's abashed look, the giant relented, sighing. "My apologies, lad. I know you mean well, but now that we've cut the wound open, let me draw all of the poison out before you try to bandage it."

"In our travels we began to hear rumors of The Worm's... research. By then, Talmoreth was no longer a fresh cut in the sky, and the stories had not only persisted long enough but had also grown more commonplace. Enough that we felt we needed to act, if for no other reason than to prove to ourselves we were not puppets of the Arys, as many of our detractors claimed. So we sent a delegation to see for ourselves. They were turned away at the gates, by whatever watch-captain whose shift it was at the time - a deliberate snub, given the names and ranks of some of the Vanha who made up that delegation."

"When our requests to some of the Arys for assistance were ignored, a few of our more impatient brothers tried a more subtle approach. They staged a clandestine raid. Five made it inside. Two made it back out. Of those two, one never spoke another word until she took her own life, two years later. The other lost his right leg below the knee. These were the first loose stones of the avalanche to come."

"What did they find?" the Captain asked quietly. Danor's mouth twisted in contempt.

"Much and more. The stories we'd been hearing about abductions were true - several floors below the tower had been converted to holding pens. The first two were for all manner of animal species. The next floor below that was for the Children, scores of you, being kept in conditions that would have put a pig farmer to shame, although hygiene was the least of their concerns I think. The next floor down was actually two floors joined together, with the center cut out and a walkway encircling the entire inside circumference of the tower. Several more walkways hung from chains at the height of what would have been the floor of the upper room. Below these was a labyrinth of cells made of reinforced bluesteel bars, where The Worm kept his prized breeding stock: the H'Kaan - hundreds of the fuundaris things. Obed had granted him a dozen prisoners, and The Worm had put them to good use."

"For what?" Triistan asked. "The H'Kaan and Maughrin destroyed the Old Gods and nearly all of Ruine - why in the gods' names would he want to build an army of them?"

"Because he could?" Danor answered with a shrug of his massive shoulders. "To be fair, a few hundred H'Kaan is not an army - at least, not those initial spawn. Most of them were deformed, incomplete in some ways, sick or broken in others. The worst were those he had cross-bred."

The cold, wet thing in Triistan's gut began to squeeze. "Cross-bred?"

The Vanha fixed him with fierce blue eyes. They were definitely glowing.

"I warned you that this tale was not for weak stomachs, Salty. We are not talking about some ditchwater despot lording it over his subjects and torturing a few captives for sport. Understand something: Tarsus made these new gods and then died. There was no mentoring program, no doyen to walk them through the Twelve Disciplines. They were all different, with different strengths and weaknesses, all left to pick through the rubble of that old world in the hope of doing a better job with this re-made one.

"The Worm was better at putting the pieces back together than any of them. I remember overhearing a discussion between Obed and my father, when Theckan had decided to pay a visit to Senhaal. I spent as much time as I could hanging around the feasting hall, because I was curious about him. Theckan was griping about how pompous Thunor and some of the other Arys were becoming - how he resented the fact that they had begun asserting themselves as leaders over the others. 'Ossien understands so much more of the lore,' my father said. 'He knows it intuitively, as if he's always known it, but only forgotten bits and pieces. He has ideas none of them have ever thought of before...' When I think of how familiar Theckan seemed to be with The Worm... it still chills my blood, knowing that I should have been able to see what was coming..."

"Anyway - there are some who believe The Worm actually unraveled part of the Vertex, and it was that partial knowledge that first set him on the path of his descent. He was as driven as he was brilliant, and as I said earlier, no price was too heavy for any secret, especially when others had to pay it. You'll remember that he hid much of his work behind the guise of seeking a cure for the gods' inability to breed. It was less a disguise, however, than it was a clever emphasis on the aspects of his research that would appeal to the other Arys.

"He did indeed set out to discover why they could not procreate with themselves, but only as a means to gain further insight into why the H'Kaan could - and why they could do so with such amazing proficiency. Mortals, by comparison, were much slower, but still infinitely better at it than the gods.

"But why? He began to explore the basic structures of different species and what made them different, seeing in those variations clues to further understanding the Vertex. From there, it was a short step to what would happen if he combined the species - how would those basic structures complement each other? How would they change one another? Could he manipulate these combinations to create his own species and, by doing so, devise his own formula, one that might rival the Vertex itself?"

"Salt and stone," Tarq whispered and made a warding gesture many of the Seeker regulars used. Triistan took a large swallow of sref.

What in the dead gods' names have we gotten ourselves into?

"More like fur and flesh," Danor grunted. "The things they were subjected to, especially the women... " He drained his mug while the others waited in sickened silence, each struggling to rein in their imaginations; all of them failing.

"So, our dear Crixy can be forgiven for his... enthusiasm when it comes to our duties here, such as they are under the current circumstances. After what he'd seen..."

"The High Master was in the raid on Talmoreth?" Jaspins blurted in a startled voice.

"Yiin, though at the time he was only Captain Bryn Crixus. They fitted him with a nice bluesteel boot to match the stuff in his stiff spine, and less than a month later he was stumping his way into the Arys' council chambers at Deranthaal, Column of the Suns. That alone should tell you something about the High Master - a leg graft is a bit more complicated then stitching up a sword slash. The new limb is fused to whatever bone material is left, and it typically takes the patient four to six months of recovery before they are allowed to put any weight on it, and even then the pain is too much for many."

Triistan remembered the High Master's odd gait and what he had assumed was a different type of armored boot. It was remarkable that the Vanha second got around as well as he did, and the fact that he had been chosen to command such elite fighters suggested that he was able to do much more than just "get around".

"Rest and recovery were impossible for him, though," Danor was saying, "knowing what the captives - including now, his own men - were being forced to endure. Besides, here he was as proof - living, breathing, preaching proof - that one of the Arys was working in direct opposition to his siblings by actively breeding and seeking to create his own version of Maughrin's spawn. Worse, The Worm's followers were worshipping Her: Crixus and his team found a shrine to the Living Darkness and witnessed some kind of religious ceremony taking place there. Troubling, to say the least, and all of these things drove Crixus and the Templars to demand an audience with the Arys.

"What happened?" Triistan asked, unable to keep silent as Danor paused.

"They finally heard him."

"But did they believe him?"

"Not entirely, but enough to summon The Worm and present the charges to him, with the other Arys as witnesses. We were infuriated that they appeared to be taking everything so callously and wanted to launch an immediate attack on Talmoreth. A few of the gods - Obed and Shan most notably - seemed sympathetic to the idea, but other... factions were more convincing that day. In hindsight, that proved to be the wiser course of action, as I think the Godswar might have started much sooner had we marched on Tsharthuuk, and the outcome much different with The Worm still in the game."

"I'm not sure it could have been any worse than the destruction of half the world," quipped Tarq. Danor's blue eyes flashed.

"Fools much wiser than you thought the same," he said sharply. "But let me assure you that if The Worm had won the field, it would have been far, far worse. There would have been nothing to stop him and his followers from their ultimate goal: freeing Maughrin. Half the world is better than all of it."

There was a long pause while they considered this. Danor made a dismissive gesture.

"Anyway, the gods sent their summons, and remarkably, out of cunning, arrogance or insanity - likely all three, I think - he accepted their invitation. Oh ye long dead and rotting Gods, what a fuundaris scene."

"Word was spreading quickly of the High Master's daring mission and harrowing escape, easily setting alight the kindling that had already been laid by the longstanding stories of Talmoreth's dark secrets. By the time the Arys sent their summons, you could hear some version of the tale in every brothel, tavern and trade center within a hundred leagues of any of the Columns. Thousands flocked to Deranthaal to see the Dark Master of Tsharthuuk brought to heel. They lined the roads outside the city and mobbed the streets inside; from Dawn's Gate to the Grand Arena, people packed themselves in as many as eight or nine deep. Ironically, I think this was the first time that the Arys fully appreciated how many of our kind there were now, and likely it was their first introduction to the singular willpower of a mob. Some had come to see justice served, but all had come to see the spectacle, and The Worm did not disappoint them."

"He arrived with a retinue of one hundred of his followers and three teams of exotic-looking beasts pulling large wagons. Atop each cart was a cage covered in heavy black silk. Some thought they were loaded with gifts to appease the other gods; others a selection of prisoners The Worm intended to offer as a token of his good will.

Both were right, after a fashion, though none foresaw the full horrifying truth."

Danor drew deeply on his pipe again. "The Worm did not come with his tail tucked between his legs to kiss the hands or lick the boots of his fellow Arys. He did not come to bribe them with gifts or assuage them with symbolic gestures. He came to show them the wonders of his discoveries and the unlimited potential they promised.

"He came to brag."

The others listened intently, riveted. Triistan was imagining the scene: a line of ponderous carts groaning beneath the weight of their mysterious cargo while heavily muscled, scaled beasts with curved horns and matching tusks strained at their traces. They were flanked by long rows of robed acolytes, features hidden beneath dark hoods, ignoring the shouts and jeers of the crowd to either side. At the head of this procession, he could only see a tall shadow vaguely shaped like a man; try as he might, he could not picture Ossien in detail. Except for the eyes. Somehow, he knew that they were black, as deep and dark as black can be; two pools of liquid, starless, endless night.

He shivered despite the heat of the fire at his feet.

"He led his fuundaris parade into the center of the Grand Arena, which the Young Gods had prepared in haste once they learned of the multitudes arriving daily to see the spectacle, and where those same gods now stood, waiting on him, as if he were some honored diplomat or hero. Always the wily one, he had turned the tables on them yet again."

"Crixus was there with his own retinue of Templar notables, including Long Tau himself, Tau Regis Xarius the First, who was only a Master at that time, if memory serves." Danor paused and chuckled to himself, shaking his head. "I was there as well, though at that time I was still a Captain with the 87th and helping out with crowd control. Lousy fuundaris job, but great seats. To this day I don't think I've seen an attack of apoplexy quite like those two were having."

"Which gods were there?" Triistan asked.

"All of them, eventually. A few of the Auruim had also had the good sense to arrive late so that they could have their own grand entrance: watching Thunor and Obed descend on those great wings of theirs - the Conqueror's black as coal and the Guardian's silver-gray flecked with white - drew gasps and screams, and even some applause, from the crowd. Shan - never to be outdone, your

Stormfather - timed his appearance perfectly, just seconds after they'd landed, with a clap of thunder that shook the stones of the coliseum. I think they were enjoying themselves, while The Worm just watched, with that sly look on his face like he knows something you don't. Which, of course, he did."

"Shan and Thunor stepped forward to take control of things, while the other Arys formed a loose semicircle several yards behind them - except for Obed, who stood close by Thunor, with his gauntleted hands resting upon the crossguard of that massive sword of his. Thunor seemed a trifle bored, but you could tell that Shan's blood was up - the occasional vein of lightning that snaked across his skin was always a sure sign he was roused. But of all the Arys, I think only The Guardian saw The Worm as a true threat just then. It took only a few minutes before he had plenty of company, though.

"In the middle of their opening remarks, The Worm turned his back on the other gods - just completely dismissed them as if they weren't even there - and with one powerful beat of his own dark wings, landed atop the first of the three covered wagons. He tore off the silk cover and revealed what scribes later named his 'First Abomination'. There was a collective gasp from gods, men and Vanha alike. Never seen or felt anything like it before - several thousand people, utterly silent, completely stunned. Felt like someone had kicked me in the balls. And then the... the thing inside the cage gives this long, tortured howl of pain - pain and rage and what I have since decided was incredible sadness."

"What was it?" Captain Vaelysia asked.

"He called it the 'Worker'. It was a man of sorts - or had been I guess. It stood on two heavily-muscled legs and gripped the bluesteel bars of its cage with powerful-looking hands - four of them."

"Four?" several of them echoed at once.

"You heard me, Salties. Four. It had two normal-looking arms connected to broad shoulders, but beneath those, where your ribs would be, were two additional arms that were disproportionately long and covered with coarse gray hair or fur. The rest of the thing's body was covered in flesh and looked normal - filthy, but normal. It wore only a loincloth, so you could see it quite clearly and except for the arms, it was completely hairless.

"Strange, but the worst part wasn't the extra limbs. The thing that got me was that its face was unmistakably huunan... and completely insane. It threw itself at the bars, screaming and howling - no words,

- 275 -

just inarticulate screams and grunts, like a trapped animal. It was incredibly agile - leaping around like a fuundaris monkey - and I remember thinking how strong it seemed. The wagon was rocking back and forth, and each time it slammed itself against the cage I thought the bluesteel grates would buckle. After a few minutes it collapsed in exhaustion. Or despair, I suppose, for there was no mistaking the sound of its sobs afterwards."

"Did Oss- did The Worm explain himself or what it was?" Triistan asked.

Danor smirked. "Oh, he certainly did. As bold as a bull harox's balls, our friend. There was no apology, no equivocation. He was proud of the work he'd done and seemed oblivious to the horrified responses of the crowd. He told us he had learned how to 'modify the lower species, to improve their productivity and usefulness by identifying their core capabilities, extrapolating them, maximizing them, and reproducing them'. That's when he called the poor bastard in the cage 'The Worker' and said it represented one of three 'Primary Uses' for the huunan species as a whole."

"The bloody arrogance," Commander Tchicatta growled.

"What did the other Arys say when they heard this?" the Captain added.

"Nothing, at first - The Worm did not give them any opportunity. In some respects he was like an excited child showing his mother some exotic creature he'd caught. Once he started speaking, he couldn't seem to stop himself; it all came spilling out. The Arys, to their credit, were smart enough to keep their divine mouths shut and let him speak. Fortunately for us, I think, as he said more to condemn himself over the next several moments than Crixy ever could have proven. Wrapped in his own obsessive quest for knowledge and lore mastery, he was convinced that the other Arys would be pleased with what he had accomplished. Up until this point, he had completely dismissed the Children of Tarsus as cattle, the Vanha as half-breeds, and although he considered the Dauthir as lesser and somewhat embarrassing cousins, he fully expected all of the Arys to embrace him and his discoveries.

"So he revealed everything. He told us how, in order to understand why the Arys could not reproduce with their own kind, he had looked to the H'Kaan in his early experiments, and how that had led him into deeper studies of Maughrin and her powers. The longer he talked, the further our mouths hung open, I think; not just at his audacity and single-mindedness, but on the scope and breadth of his progress. As I said earlier, this research eventually led him to explore our fundamental structures - the individual blocks, keystones, and timbers that differentiate one species from another. He'd figured out how to break those pieces apart and recombine some of them, and he brought his Ternion to prove it."

"Ternion?"

Danor nodded slowly. "Worker, Warling, and Wonder. The trio of 'gifts' he brought for his fellow gods." The others all looked at one another, but Danor continued before anyone could voice a question.

"The second cage in The Worm's parodic parade contained a monstrosity we at first took to be some kind of bizarre military sculpture. It was man-shaped, though much larger, perhaps eleven or twelve feet tall. Initially I thought it was supposed to be a knight of some kind - perhaps a mockery of one of us, even - with piecemeal, oddly-shaped armor and oversized weapons; a double-bladed axe in one hand and a broadsword with a blade wide enough to use as a gangplank in the other.

"As I studied the thing more carefully, though, I saw that the piecemeal armor was so strangely shaped because it was sculpted to look like it was growing out of the body of the knight, rather than strapped to him... much like the hornshields on the armaduura or the spiked carapace of a giant buckler crab. It was roughly shaped and textured, like bone or ivory, rather than smooth and symmetrical like most man-made armor. The flesh was corpse-grey and looked fused and stitched wherever the armor protruded, so that it gave the overall impression that the knight's bones had been made to grow on the outside. It was an evil-looking monument; the kind of arcane monstrosity that fit perfectly with all of the whispered tales you could hear in every tavern within twenty leagues of Tsharthuuk.

"Just imagine our surprise when it moved."

That cold, clammy thing in Triistan's gut slithered up his spine.

"Whereas the four-armed Worker was clearly aware and distraught over its condition, the Warling was silent, moving with calm deliberateness. It brought its arms up in a sort of crossed salute and..." he paused and drew on his pipe again, shaking his head slowly. "I remember I had glanced away at the crowd so I wasn't watching closely at that point, and before that I'd been fixated on the strange 'armor' and hadn't noticed what was really wrong about the thing yet. Most of the people in the stands were too far away to see it in detail -

they were 'ooing' and 'ahhhing' at the sheer size and strangeness of it, but they couldn't make out at first what it really was either... until the young Templar next to me, Caxsil I think his name was, swore an oath most of my Veterans would have been embarrassed to use when he realized what he was actually looking at..."

He swept his gaze across all of them. "The weapons I had thought it was holding - the battleaxe and the sword - were part of the fuundaris thing's arms."

"Just below its elbows, its forearms were encased in steel and leather, and beyond that, where there should have been wrists and hands, the axe and broadsword just... just grew out of the thing's steel forearms. Thought I was going to puke right there. I don't know why it struck me as worse than the extra set of arms on the first one - The Worker - but it did. I just kept thinking that the Worm had made this thing, and no one knew at that time how many more there were, or what they were capable of."

"Was it Vanha?" asked Captain Vaelysia. Danor shrugged.

"Don't know. It was bigger than most men but not quite large enough to be one of the godkin. And it was so... so augmented by other things that it was impossible to tell. I couldn't even say if it was wearing a helmet or if some kind of... of shell was growing out of its neck and shoulders, or possibly even its skull. Afterward we discovered that the helmet and 'armor' on the thing were actually made of bone; somehow it had been made to grow through its skin and then shaped, twisted and hardened into some kind of protective carapace. Can't imagine what the Worm put that poor bastard through."

"What did the gods do?" Tarq asked.

"Oh, it got their attention - they seemed more curious than anything about The Worker, but this creation... this Warling as he named it... well that got the air humming."

"Humming?"

"When roused, the will of one of the Arys can be a physical thing - it's palpable, like the baking heat of direct sunlight or that charged feeling the air gets, just before a big storm. With so many of them in one place, you couldn't help but feel it, and when the Warling's true nature was revealed, I swear I could hear it, too. By the time he unveiled his third 'gift', you could see the sand jumping on the floor of the Grand Arena."

"What was the third gift?" Tarq prompted him.

"It looked like a gigantic bird of some kind, huddled on the floor of the cage with its wings folded before it, covering its lowered head. It shimmered in the suns' light, as if it were made of some precious metal, with a color somewhere between gold and bronze. The Worm said something - a name, I think, though we'll never know - and she stood."

"I can only imagine what kind of vile beast he saved for last," Jaspins whispered. Danor smiled his not-smile.

"I don't believe there was a single soul in that coliseum who wasn't thinking the same thing, girl. But that's the funny thing about worms; you never can tell their head from their ass, can you? So how do you know which way they're heading?" He looked at each of them in turn.

"The 'gift' he had saved for last was the most beautiful creature I have ever seen."

Even after so many years, even after he knew what it was and had personally suffered at the hands of its creator, Danor's voice still held a note of awe in it.

"She stood, and she spread her wings behind her - beautiful, gilded, shining things the envy of any of the Auruim except perhaps Minet - and I wanted to weep from the heat she stirred in my loins. I was so stunned I did not even realize that the cries of surprise and outrage I was hearing were coming from the Young Gods themselves."

"What? Why?" Triistan asked.

"He created his own kind," the Captain guessed, her lips pressed in a grim line.

"So we thought, yes," Danor nodded. "She was breathtaking: fifteen feet tall, completely nude, with almond-colored skin that glistened with oil or sweat, dark-brown hair spilling past her shoulders onto high, full breasts - every inch a goddess...

"And unmistakably pregnant."

When their reactions subsided, he continued. "The Worm claimed she was carrying his child, that he had broken the divine code. 'We do not need to cavort with beasts to ensure the continuation of our own bloodlines any longer!' he told them, his voice ringing with triumph. Had he stopped there, he might have prevailed. The other Arys were shocked and threatened, I think, but they also must have been drawn by his claims and the possibilities they promised.

"But as clever as he was, his pride and his... conviction betrayed him. He was so convinced in what he saw as self-evident truths that he could not conceive of anyone questioning him or his beliefs. So he did not stop; could not stop. When he finally began explaining to them that Tarsus and the Old Gods were wrong, that Maughrin's power was Ruine's power, and that keeping her imprisoned threatened the fundamental balance and structure of their existence... well, that was when they'd heard enough."

"What happened?" Triistan breathed.

"It was over almost before it began. The Worm was outnumbered, and the last thing he was expecting was a fight. Obed attacked first, moving so quickly it was as if he just appeared atop the last cage, that massive two-hander of his already in its downward arc. He sheared off half of one of the Worm's black wings, marking the first time the Arys had drawn blood from one of their own. The Guardian would have killed him outright if given the chance, but the others intervened, overpowering both. Obed was led away to master his temper, while The Worm was gagged and bound with chains and every ward his shocked siblings could devise. Thunor and Lyrin eventually carried him off, strung between them by his chains as they climbed skyward."

There was a moment of silence while they tried to process everything Danor had told them.

"Didn't they just kill him right there?" Captain Vaelysia finally asked. "That's what the histories show."

The Vanha healer let out a small, ironic laugh.

"Because that's what the Arys told them to say. But they did not kill him because of the one thing that they shared in common with you, Salty. They feared death."

"The Arys are immortal," Triistan quickly retorted.

"They were immortal," Commander Tchicatta corrected him.

"Not so much anymore," Danor confirmed. "As frightened as they were of The Worm, I think some of them feared Death even more. Part of me wonders if they were simply afraid to admit to one another that he might be right. That and there were other complications."

"Meaning?" Vaelysia prodded.

"You may have heard that killing a god is not so easy. As I've said, they are more than the physical bodies they occupy, and whatever they are is released when the flesh and blood vessel that contains them is destroyed. Where that essence goes depends on the god and what, if anything, it has done to prepare itself. In Tarsus' case, he gave himself over to Ruine, so that it might be restored after his war with Maughrin. No one had any grasp of the Worm's capabilities, but it wasn't hard to imagine after what they had seen him accomplish.

"Even if they had wanted to kill him, I don't think they would have. Much like they had convinced themselves that their 'Divide' would be repaired before it came to open war, I believe they thought the Worm would eventually come back around to his own sanity. Remember, they didn't have a history to guide them, and as we have established here, wisdom is not directly proportional to longevity."

"So they built this," he said, gesturing vaguely in the air above his head, "with the intent to imprison him here forever.

"In many ways, Ostenvaard is perhaps the greatest singular creation that the Arys have ever devised - at least together. Yes, some would argue that Ehronhaal - a floating fuundaris city for Dark's sake - was pretty impressive work. But at its core it was just another trophy, another exercise in self-indulgence. But this..." he glanced upwards with something that looked close to affection. "This took all of their considerable skills: Shan and Sigel raised Aarden from the very bones of Ruine at the bottom of the sea; Obed and Derant, inspired but not satisfied by their respective Columns, created Ahbaingeata and the fortress-city above it; Paola, Flynn, Minet, Wick and Estra worked to make it more than just a fortress, breathing life into it through pageantry, art, music, poetry, literature - a blend of culture the likes of which this world had not seen since the Old Gods ruled. Ganar the Unbroken carved its rugged coastline, shaping it so that there was only one way in -"

"Why?" Triistan interrupted.

"I thought that was clear, boy. For all of its trappings, Ostenvaard is a prison - or, more accurately I suppose, it's the keep around the true hold, but it's all meant to function together, one layer within the next. Only one way in - Haagen's Bay, where you landed - funnels any visitors or would-be Worm sympathizers directly into the rest of the defenses: the cliff, the river valley, Ahbaingeata, Ostenvaard - all of it makes us virtually impossible to attack with a large force."

"No, I mean, why did the Arys go to so much trouble? Why bring so much culture - art, music, and everything else you've said - to what amounts to a glorified dungeon?"

Danor smirked. "For the same reason they constructed The Sentinel - that giant statue you saw in the Bay. It was cast in the likeness of Vyus Haagen, First Lord Marshall of the Oathguard. They said it was to welcome and honor us - oh, but it must have twisted the ballsacks of some of the Auruim to admit to that minuerto! Put simply, it was for morale purposes, Salty. To shore up the final defensive ring."

"You." Although Triistan didn't intend it that way, he felt like he was passing judgement.

" 'L'Viviit Muurum' they called us...The Living Wall. We were the final piece of the Great Puzzle, a riddle of land, stone, steel, and flesh so complex that not even a god could solve it."

The others remained quiet; no one was willing to state the obvious. Danor shook his head and drained his mug, but this time he did not reach for the pitcher to refill it. His next words caught them by surprise.

"So they sent three."

- 18 -

A Walk with Death

Casselle felt like she was drowning. She gasped for air, struggling for a full breath that refused to come. There was no one to reach out for, no one to save her. She had been swallowed by darkness.

When the tiny flickering blue flame danced in front of her like a firefly, she couldn't tell if it was a dream, or if this was how death would claim her. As those thoughts weighed her down, the flame flitted away as quickly and mysteriously as it had appeared.

"Pardon me," said a voice. "I thought you were dead, but you're merely dying. I apologize if I've interrupted you."

Someone is there.

Instinct urged her to cry out for help. Her lips trembled. She wanted to say so much, but her voice would not cooperate. She was betrayed by her own broken body, which was giving up without her consent.

"N... n... n... no." It was her word, but it sounded so disconnected from the voice in her head. Someone crouched beside her. They smelled of old leaves and moss.

"Hold on a moment, you look familiar. Have we met before?" the voice asked her. It was old and gentle; something in it reminded her of her grandmother, a comforting memory from her past.

"N... n..." This time she couldn't even get the word out. She wanted to cough, but didn't have the strength for it. She heard the low, wet rattle of her breath as she attempted it.

"Oh, yes. You're really in no condition to answer me. You're in the middle of dying. I'm quite sorry. I didn't mean to disturb you. I can always come back later."

Later might be better, she thought. *Everything right now is pain and fatigue. Maybe after a quick rest...*

No!

She refused to rest. As badly as she wanted to, there was something she had left to do. Something that welled up from the bottom of her soul, filling her body with purpose.

"N..."

It felt as if she was trying to lift the world, the weight of it unbearable, torturous, but she fought past it and reached out with her good hand, grasping at the sound of the voice. When her fingers brushed against something, she gripped it with all her strength.

"Hm? What's this?" the voice sounded surprised, confused, but not angry. "Could it be you're not quite ready? That shouldn't be unexpected, I suppose. Are any of us ever really ready to surrender to..."

She found the strength to tighten her grip, sending sharp needles of agony across her back and chest.

"Yes, yes, apologies. This is an incredibly one sided conversation. I suppose I could fix that," the voice said. Then there was quiet, though she felt something shifting under her grip.

Red hot agony shot through her, as if her chest was being ripped apart. Her body trembled, shudders that replaced the screams she could not voice. Pain was the only thing left for her - pain, and darkness...

...until there was light. The flickering blue flame returned, fluttering like a moth in front of her. She felt fingers fumble at her lips, prying her mouth open. The fire was placed on her tongue, rough-skinned fingers pushing it back, forcing it down her throat. Every primitive impulse fired, her hand weakly pulling at whatever fabric she was gripping, her whole body struggling vainly against being choked out.

"I suppose I should warn you that you might experience some slight discomfort," the voice said.

Every measure of pain that Casselle had felt up to that point was nothing compared to what came next. She felt like she'd swallowed a burning coal that was cooking her from the inside while hot knives cut away her skin, inch by inch. It was as if every bone in her body had been cracked and pulled apart before being crudely set back into place. She lost all concept of time, aware of only the pain. She felt stretched thin, pulled in all directions at once to her breaking point.

And then, there was only stillness.

All was quiet save for the beating of her heart, a strong but quickened tempo. She was curled up on the ground, muscles sore and clenched tight, like after a night of fitful sleep. She slowly opened her eyes and uncurled her fists, looking at them for what felt like the first time ever, surprised that both appeared to be whole, even the hand at the end of the arm she knew Emeranth had shattered.

The remains of her breastplate sat just a few feet away, the front of it dented inwards at such an angle that she was certain her chest must have been broken as well. But as she breathed with casual ease, that injury appeared to be healed too. She was filled with a deep and abiding sense of calm.

"That worked out better than I expected," said the voice. Casselle found she had plenty of strength to sit up.

"It's you."

Crouched before her was the robed figure that had come for the Wolfmother, the one she thought of as the embodiment of Death. Back in Flinderlass, he had taken her by the arm, leaving a dark mark that had remained on her skin even after he had vanished shortly thereafter. He sat before her, his tattered black robes obscuring most of his form, save the thin fingers that delicately handled a tiny, flickering blue flame that slowly crawled over his hands like an insect.

"You're Veheg," she said, noticing for the first time ever that the mark on her arm, which normally responded by turning ice cold, now felt as if it were kissed by a warm ray of sunshine on a cool day.

"So I'm told," he replied as his fingers closed around the tiny flame before he tucked it away, somewhere inside the folds of his garment, like a street performer with a loose coin. "Now, on to the more relevant question. Have we met before?"

"You know me from Flinderlass," she said, awestruck, sitting in the presence of what she assumed to be a God. The few mentions Veheg ever garnered in books were always shallow and speculative. He was not one of the Arys, and accounts of him were sparse, mentioning only that he walked amongst the dead, possibly shepherding away their souls. Sailors burned those that had died at sea, carrying their ashes away by the wind since Veheg would not find them otherwise. If there were deeper or lengthier accounts about him, Casselle had not read them.

But the grim shadow described in those accounts did not seem to match the gentle body language of the being in front of her. His eyes were bright blue and flickered with an inner light much like the flame that had danced across his fingertips. The pale skin of his forehead crinkled as he considered her.

"It was on fire," she offered.

"Oh yes! I do remember that," he said, appearing both surprised and pleased to recall Casselle and those memories.

"You found the Wolfmother there, and took her away with you."

"Wolfmother?" he questioned. "Hah! Oh yes, what a clever name that is. I shall have to tell her that when I see her next. Though I will confess my memory is not what it used to be. I hope I do not forget."

"Is it hard to remember because of the Ehronfall?" Casselle asked. "Because you remain when the Young Gods died?" It was an incredible assumption, but with so many unanswered questions hanging over their heads, she wanted to wrest any information she could from him before he left.

"No, it doesn't have anything to do with that. I remember that well enough. As with most things, I'm sure I can blame this on Her," he said, a thin pale finger tapping what must have been his chin, though everything below the bridge of his nose was obscured by layers of cloth, much like the Khaliil had worn in the desert.

"Emeranth Kell?"

"Who? No. That's not the right name. Not unless she's changed it, which is entirely possible, just look at what happened to me, I used to be someone else, and now I'm… What's my name again?"

"Veheg," Casselle offered.

"That doesn't feel right, but since I can't remember anything better, I'll use that one," he said. His words were sharp, but his mind seemed to twist, reminding her again of her grandmother. In her old age, she would often get confused and call Casselle by her mother's name, especially after her mother had died. Had Veheg lived so long that his own memories had become twisted?

No, he said someone did this, she thought, *press him on what he does know.*

"If not Emeranth, who took your name?"

"Maughrin, of course," he stated as if she should have known it all along. Just hearing it made her blood run cold for a moment. "Or did she change her name to that other one you said?"

"No, I don't think so. Emeranth is no dragon," Casselle confirmed, "but I do think she may serve Maughrin."

"Then you should definitely be careful. You're likely to get hurt if you get in their way," Veheg said, as if he had already forgotten that he found her broken and dying just a few moments ago. Casselle winced. Though her body felt better than ever, she recalled the all too recent pain.

"I mean she did eat me alive, after all."

"What?!"

"Well, for a time, I mean," Veheg clarified. "I had to leave my body there to escape, most likely some of my memories, too. I mean, if you don't have all of your memories, it only goes to reason that you must have left them somewhere, right?"

She caught him looking at his own hands, as if they were suddenly strange things to him.

"Well, best I be off," he interrupted abruptly, as if he'd just remembered a pressing engagement elsewhere. He stood up, dusting off his robes. "You'd do best to leave here, too. If this is a nest of Her's, you're likely to run into trouble."

"Wait, isn't there something you can do to help?" Casselle asked. Even if Veheg wasn't one of the Arys, It wasn't likely she was going to run into a god again anytime soon, if ever. She scrambled to her feet after him.

"Help? No, no, I certainly don't want to get mixed up in that again. It didn't go very well the first time around," he said. "I did mention that she tried to eat me, didn't I? I'm pretty sure I did."

He was only about a foot taller than she was, even though he seemed as if he should be much larger. As he looked around, his eyes lingered on the dead forms of Passal Cooper and the Thundering Lance soldier. They hadn't been taken away since her fight with Emeranth, which must have been some time ago, given the suns were much lower in the sky. The Long Evening had begun.

"You and you I have already collected from." He turned away from Passal and the unknown soldier, patting down his robes, where he had tucked the flame earlier. "Okay, everything's in place."

"What? What did you take from them? Are you ushering them into the Dark? Did you take their souls?" Casselle felt entirely foolish, rattling her mouth off just to keep his attention.

"I took... Souls? The Dark? Where did you come up with such things? I don't do any of that," he said, sounding somewhat flummoxed by the accusations. "No, I just take the life-ember that remains. When you die your inner fire is extinguished, but if one is skillful, they can capture it at the right moment, right before it flickers out. That life-ember can persist beyond you. You should be thankful, that's what I used to re-kindle your dying fire."

"As to their... soul? I don't do anything with that. I don't even know what that is."

"But what happens when you die?" she asked with exasperation. What kind of God of Death was this?

"How should I know? I'm not dead," he said defensively, before adding as an aside, "though in this body, most days I feel like it."

"In that body? What does that mean? What do you take the embers for? Can they be used as a weapon?" Casselle asked.

"You ask very odd questions," Veheg said, picking a direction seemingly out of random and beginning to walk. Casselle felt foolish. She was not normally the one to rattle on and on, but without Temos here…

She caught herself, remembering for the first time that she didn't know what had happened to her friends. She didn't even know if they'd made it back safely.

No time for that now. She had almost lost track of Veheg. Casselle ran to catch up to him. Though he didn't appear to have a long stride, he moved quickly enough. Apparently, he had not noticed her lagging behind and was in the middle of answering some of her questions.

"I mean to even get the life-ember, you would have to kill yourself. Dying seems like a long way to go to have a weapon you can no longer use, don't you think?

"It's getting darker," Veheg said, abruptly shifting the conversation, "I should really be off."

"Off to where? To meet with the Wolfmother? How are you and she related?"

"Related? There's a notion. How would I describe our connection? How would she, for that matter? She's been gone for so long that it's become difficult for us to communicate," he confessed.

"Where has she been? We saw a picture of her falling into the dragon's mouth. You said you were eaten but escaped. Is that what happened to her? To the others in the picture?" Veheg came to an abrupt stop.

"The others?" he whispered. "I… others… yes… we were all…" He made a pained noise and one of his thin hands came up to touch his forehead, fingers fluttering for a moment, as if there was something they were supposed to do. His vacant stare made it clear his thoughts were far away.

Casselle heard the sand shifting behind her. She turned, her hand reflexively moving to grip the hilt of her sword. When it found only empty air, she remembered the weapon had been lost when she disabled Emeranth's hand. Her eyes locked on the shadow detaching itself from the side of the building just a few feet away.

The H'Kaan leapt straight at them. Instinctively, Casselle attempted to shove Veheg aside. When she pressed up against him, she found him hard and unyielding, as if she might have a better chance to move one of the crumbling buildings around her than whatever was under those robes. She practically rebounded off him, a pebble thrown against a mountain.

Off balance, Casselle's mind raced for a solution as the creature finished its arc through the air. It was on them.

Or rather... it was held by the throat at arm's length by Veheg. It clawed furiously against his thin arm, though it had as much success in wounding him as Casselle had in attempting to move him. Black tatters of his robe fell away, but not even a scratch registered on the pale skin. The beast's frantic energy was silenced as Veheg's grip tightened. There was the sound of something breaking, like twigs snapping, before the H'Kaan just simply disintegrated. The remains fell to the ground in a heap, almost as if it had been composed of black sand the whole time and had just now remembered.

"I'm so very sorry," he said, his voice surprisingly mournful. "She took your fire, leaving you nothing but Darkness and dust."

"You... knew that H'Kaan?" Casselle asked as Veheg shook his hand clean.

"Not personally, no. What did you call it? H'Kaan? They used to be something else, like me," he said.

"Were they also eaten? Are they one of the others?" Casselle watched as the dry wind began to scatter the ashen remains of the H'Kaan. Why hadn't that happened to her when he touched her back in Flinderlass?

"Please stop. My head already hurts enough," Veheg replied. Casselle was worried. He sounded exasperated. Her grandmother would get like that from time to time when you challenged what she thought, when the world didn't match up to what she expected. Casselle needed answers, but feared what may happen if she pushed him further.

"No, no, I'm done talking about such things. Certainly there must be something better... Do you like clouds? I'm quite fond of them," he said.

"I... I don't really have any opinions about clouds," Casselle admitted.

"I like that you can look at them and sometimes see things," Veheg confessed. "Sometimes like you're remembering something from a dream."

"Do Gods dream?"

"Why wouldn't we? Don't you dream?"

"Yes. But not often," Casselle confessed.

"You should put more effort into it. Dreams connect us with one another... the past and future and every living thing," he said wistfully.

"We must have very different sorts of dreams, then."

Veheg stopped for a moment, looking down the lane he had been walking along.

"Probably best not to go that way. There's a lot of dying going on over there, which would typically be the kind of place I would go to, but there is too much Darkness there as well," he said.

"You mean H'Kaan?" Casselle asked.

"If that's what you call them, then yes. Do not go there," he warned.

"I must. My friends are there and I will help them, just as you came to help the Wolfmother," Casselle said sternly. His eyes seemed full of conflicting thoughts. Casselle thought he was trying to fight back tears.

"She devours all. You will die and your friends will die alongside you. The only option is to run." She was taken aback by his admission.

"You were the only one to escape," Casselle reasoned. "Until the Wolfmother found a way, you were alone."

"Yes," he confessed, his eyes full of heartbreak, his voice sounding deep and focused now, like he was speaking clearly for the first time since she had awoken. There was a quiet power in it she had not heard before. He held up his hands to look at them. "And I hid here."

"What does that..." Casselle's question was interrupted by a thunderous roar from the direction Veheg refused to go. She looked that way, but only the empty city sat ahead of her, the echoes reaching her from somewhere beyond her sight.

"I must go to them," she said, turning back to Veheg.

But he was gone.

"Thank you," she said aloud. "I forgot to thank you." She stood still for a moment, hoping some response would come back to her.

When none came, she considered her options. She was alone, her armor was damaged, and she had only a dagger to stand against a horde of H'Kaan and whatever Emeranth Kell was. As she reached back to draw her remaining blade, she realized there might be another option.

She pulled out the journal, haste making her fingers clumsy as she extracted the needle from its place in the spine of the book. She flipped through it, trying to find the correct page.

She quickly found what she was looking for. The woman on the page had blonde hair, but something in her face made the truth perfectly clear. The angry woman holding the sword and spear was Emeranth Kell, or a very close relation. She was surprised she hadn't made the connection before now.

So why didn't you have these weapons? The rough iron sword she'd been using was certainly not the one pictured in the book, and she hadn't been using a spear at all. Did it have something to do with Maughrin's influence?

It didn't matter. If Emeranth didn't have them, Casselle now had an opportunity to arm herself. She pricked her thumb with the needle, setting it on the page. She tried to hold it open and steady as the needle spun wildly for a moment before finally snapping to a direction.

She closed the book on the needle, using it as a place marker while she hurried in the direction it had indicated. She stopped frequently, using the needle to confirm the path. The third stop sent her in a different direction, and by the fifth stop, she barely had to slow down at all.

She squatted next to a building, her back to the wall, the book open in her lap, the needle just touching the tip of her thumb, ready to be pressed in. She could feel where it was bruising up already. She hesitated, taking a deep breath.

As she started to push, there was another thunderous roar, strong enough to shake the ground beneath her feet, sudden enough to throw her off balance. The book fell to the ground and the needle stabbed much deeper than she expected. It had pierced through her thumb, coming out the fleshy pad just past where her nail ended. There was pressure there, like her thumb had been pinched, but it didn't hurt for the moment. She knew that feeling would change the minute she pulled it free.

As she gripped it by the end so she could remove it, something drew her attention to the fallen book. She snatched it up, surprised to see the crawling text that had previously been revealed only by spilling blood. But she'd been careful to only bloody the needle. This wasn't even Emeranth's page.

How odd, she thought. She reflexively flipped the pages with her thumb, realizing she hadn't yet removed the needle. Laying the book in her lap again, she used the other hand to turn to the correct place, ready to put the needle on the page once free. She was surprised to see the text fill each page as she flipped them. Curious, but under pressure to hurry, she took another quick breath to steady herself and then pulled the needle out.

She watched the text vanish instantly. She held the needle in her hand, ready to place it, but now perplexed by this new mystery. Unable to leave it be, she grit her teeth and set the tip of the needle back at the entrance of the puncture.

Knowing to think on it any longer would simply make things worse, she inserted the needle back in. She thought that having just died might have numbed her slightly to the pain, but it still hurt, albeit not as much as having her chest caved in. As she opened her watering eyes, she saw the text again, filling the previously blank spaces around the picture. Then she pulled it out cleanly, inhaling sharply as she did so. She watched the words vanish once more, as quickly as they had appeared.

Ok, so that's something, she thought, sucking on her sore thumb. She certainly couldn't keep it stuck there, but it was clear that just bleeding onto the page or the needle every few minutes wasn't a workable long-term solution. She looked up at the sky now darkening from rust to black. Time wasn't her ally.

She held the book open with one hand, the other rolling the needle between her thumb and forefinger. She couldn't believe what she was considering, but was it any more outlandish than anything else she'd seen in the short time since taking on the oath and responsibilities of a Laegis Templar? The Wolfmother? H'Kaan? Veheg?

No, this seemed well reasoned and thoroughly rational compared to that.

She set the needle between her teeth for a minute, unbuckling the straps of the gauntlet on her left arm. She wrestled with the sleeve, finally rolling up enough to expose the underside of her forearm. Her fist clenched with nervous energy as she took the needle from her mouth and pressed it to her arm about halfway between her wrist and elbow.

She paused again, wondering where the doubt had suddenly sprung from.

"Just do it," she told herself sternly, setting the needle against her skin. With a quick exhale, she slid it in at a shallow angle, as if it were just a splinter.

It certainly hurt much worse. She put pressure on it, gritting her teeth as the sharp pain turned hot. She was getting tired of feeling as if she was burning up from inside, and the sensation did not die as quickly as the life-ember had. It subsided, but did not vanish altogether. As she released her grip on her own arm, she watched the red marks from her fingers slowly fade.

What now? She didn't feel any different. She picked up the book. The results were clear and immediate.

Page after page, the letters were there. The whole book was open to her. As she turned to the page with Emeranth and her eyes fell upon the drawing, she felt a strange sensation. The needle in her arm was warm, and it felt like it was moving, like someone was gently pushing on it. As she lifted her arm and moved it in the direction she had been travelling, she felt the needle respond, a light pressure guiding her.

More to the left. More...

Stop.

A bit to the right...

Stop.

Forward. Somewhere there.

She could feel the direction.

She rolled her sleeve back down and fixed her gauntlet back into position. She was worried that the tight fit of the bracer would be a problem, but it felt good having her arm bound and protected. She looked back at the book once the armor was in place, her eyes starting to strain as the light overhead faded.

Even though she could not make out the picture and text as clearly, concentrating on the thought of it seemed just as effective.

She closed the book as she stood, putting it back into her pouch, keeping her focus on the picture of a very different Emeranth and the sword and spear raised in the air. She felt the needle nudge her in the right direction.

She moved carefully. The feeling of the needle was subtle, delicate. When she moved too quickly, her concentration faltered and her connection with the needle seemed to dull, so she kept herself moving at a light jog.

The thought of running into a clutch of H'Kaan worried her, but she found distracting thoughts also disrupted her ability to sense the direction the needle was urging her towards. Nevertheless, she pulled her dagger from its sheath at her back, holding it in a reversed grip against her right forearm. At least it enforced the illusion of protection.

She was well into the Long Evening now, the shadows deep along the length of the avenue, the sky a warm red and the promise of darkness lurking just beyond. She didn't have a source of light and that was a building pressure in the back of her mind.

She stopped, feeling the needle tugging back the way she'd come. She retraced her steps back to an opening that most certainly had never been a shop or home.

A flight of stairs led downward into a narrow space between the buildings.

Where did it lead? Was she certain this was correct? She concentrated on the image in her mind and felt the needle nudge her. It was directing her down the stairs.

Her heart was in her throat. She thought of the H'Kaan, how they navigated the shadows like they were born to them. Down there she would be completely helpless.

She didn't have any other real options, though. The Long Evening was almost over and soon it would be almost as dark above as it would be below. Even if she could see, she was totally lost inside the city, the only familiar street that might have led her back to the others now long behind her. Staying put would only waste time, a commodity she could not count on lasting even until morning.

She felt trapped and the stairs were most likely the quickest way to secure her death a second time. Her face was hot, her blood thumping in her ears. She clenched her fists and as she thought of the picture of the sword and spear, the needle urged her forward.

She took a deep breath.

She thought of Temos and Greffin and the squad that might not survive without her help. She thought of Strossen and Jaksen and his wife, who planned for a family together. She thought of her father and his wife and her step-brothers, now so far away from her. Her thoughts finally settled on her mother, who most certainly would not have suggested this life for her.

With her chestplate gone, she could feel her mother's ring underneath her armorjack. She pressed on it, and it pushed against her skin, just below where her collarbones met.

"To hold the Dark at bay," she whispered to herself, "we lift high the torch."

The words of the Laegis oath afforded her some amount of reassurance. That is why she was here, wasn't it? To be in service of others? To fight when others could not?

She tightened the grip on her dagger until her hand hurt. She calmed her breathing.

Focus.

Casselle walked forward, taking her hand off her chest and placing it against the wall on her left as she moved down the stairs. At first, the stone was still warm to the touch, bleeding off the heat it had absorbed over the long day. She felt it slide underneath her fingertips as she slowly descended. It had only the faintest texture to it, worn smooth by the sand and sun.

She concentrated on those details, pushing her feelings aside and keeping the image from the book in her mind.

The needle urged her down until the Darkness swallowed her once again.

- 19 -

Breaking the Hold

Ten and Seven, Vehnya, the fourteenth day of the Expedition, 37th since Landfall

Ostenvaard is burning.

Deep in a ravine - our view is limited, but can smell smoke and see haze wherever a lone shaft of sunlight finds its way through the trees. Danor ordered a halt to rest and am using the opportunity to record recent events while I still can. So much has transpired since the cun've'dictuus just a few days ago.

Where do I begin? Have to record Danor's story about Ossien's imprisonment and escape - wanted to after dinner, but there was just no time! When the alarm bells sounded, we -

Several lines were illegible, the rushed scrawl of Triistan's handwriting all but wiped out by a large, dark-brown smear. He slammed the journal shut and cleared his throat to dislodge the lump there while trying to organize his thoughts, simultaneously wanting and dreading to take up his story again.

His voice had failed him for the second time not long after moonset the night before, just a few short hours after giving the command to ungag and feed Lankham Voth while the rest of the survivors tended to the launch's and their own personal needs. He knew the others would have preferred not to waste any of their food or dwindling water supplies on the bitter old purser, but Triistan thought it was important to maintain some modicum of order and discipline to what was left of their world. It was a risk, he knew; not just to his own authority but also because there was little doubt that Voth would do everything he could to discredit Triistan and the others if they were rescued.

They had committed mutiny. It was a capital offense regardless of the circumstances, according to Seeker doctrine. They would have an easier time explaining themselves to Fleet Command without Voth there to testify against them, but Triistan could not bring himself to murder the man. Nor would he allow someone else to do it for him. His thoughts kept returning to Rantham's story about being shipwrecked and what he and a fellow castaway had done to survive. He did not know what his own shipmates were capable of, but his time on Aarden had taught him that the path to savagery was a downhill slope made even steeper when it was already slick with blood.

"Breakfast is ready, Cap'n!" Wil called from below.

Triistan waved from the crow's nest, then made one final scan of the sea around them. He'd been up here since just before dawn, when he'd awoken from a fitful sleep littered with fragmented dreams, his hair and clothes damp with sweat, the air as thick and cloying as seaweed. He'd climbed aloft, hoping for a bit of breeze and perhaps the shadow of distant land. He found neither, and now the Maiden had dragged her full bulk above the horizon, casting the world in a hazy orange glow that promised a hot and humid day ahead. The only good news was that there was no sign of the storms he had predicted the night before. As far as Triistan could see, the ocean stretched out in all directions; an empty plane of hammered copper beneath an arc of endless blue.

Maybe tomorrow.

He climbed over the edge of the crow's nest onto one of the futtock shrouds. As he clambered down, he reviewed where he had left off the night before, knowing that he would need to begin his story again while the crew shared their morning meal.

He had recited most of his story from memory so far, reliving the experience as if he were there again. The process was painful, but it was also cathartic in its own way, just as Dreysha had said it would be. The merciless weight of his experience and knowledge was too much to bear alone, and the oath of secrecy he'd sworn to Captain Vaelysia seemed pointless now. She had been doing her duty, protecting The Sea Kings' rightful claim to the discoveries they had made, worried that spies might somehow steal away with the information during the *Peregrine's* voyage home. But she had gone down to the Deep Dark with nearly all hands, and his oath - once a thing he had clung to the way a drowning man clings to a piece of flotsam - had followed it not long after.

The others were already eating, but Triistan wasn't quite ready to meet their expectant gazes. In a last effort to stall, he brought a bowl of pan-seared fish and fresh water to their prisoner. He was pleased to see that Dreysha had not tied Voth's gag back in place after removing it the night before, but surprised to find the man still fast asleep; once the crew was roused and going about their first-light duties, the launch was a fairly noisy place. Triistan could not recall a morning where he had not caught Voth sitting with his back to the mainmast, watching them with that ever-present, contemptuous sneer on his face. Yet here he was, snoring softly, beady eyes closed beneath red and swollen lids, a thin line of drool running down his slack jaw.

Triistan kicked the bottom of Voth's foot lightly. "Mister Voth," he said, but the older man did not stir.

"Mister Voth." After trying again with no effect, he crouched beside his prisoner and put a hand to the purser's cheek, then his forehead. Voth did not seem to be running a fever, so the young captain shook him by his shoulder, wincing as he felt the man's hard, knobby bones shift under his fingers. Voth brushed his hand away and rolled over, muttering something that sounded like "...moldy hardtack, three jars of herring, six jenga melons..."

Triistan tried once more to rouse him, but without success, so he shrugged and returned to the others.

"What's wrong with Lanky?" Dreysha asked around a mouthful of food.

Triistan shrugged again as he sat down. "Must have had trouble sleeping last night and is making up for it now."

"Too bad, I could have used some good news for a change," she grinned and winked at him.

He frowned but did not reply, preoccupied with the feelings of guilt and remorse that his journal entry had reawakened. Wil tried to fill the awkward silence.

"Anything topside, sir? Maybe today's the day - surely we must be getting close to the southernmost shipping lanes."

Rantham snorted. "That might not sound so idiotic if you hadn't wasted those fucking dreamroot seeds, Mung. Then we might have some hope of a patrol finding us before the Kingsbane do."

"There's still hope that a merchant vessel will see us first," Wil shot back.

This time Rantham laughed outright. "Merchy's don't chase strange sails, you fool. They run from them. You'd be better off hoping the ridgeback returns so that we can harpoon it and ride that black-eyed bitch back to Thunder Bay. Gods, man, I think that bloody monkey has more sense than-"

"Alright Seeker, that's enough," Triistan said, feeling awkward for pulling rank over the more experienced sailor. To his surprise, Rantham glowered back but closed his mouth with an audible click of his teeth.

Triistan ignored the look. "No, Wil, I didn't see anything, but the weather's clear and that's better than I'd hoped for last night. Maybe tomorrow."

After they finished eating, they spent another hour or so putting the fishing nets back out, and cleaning and trimming the launch. Triistan was able to find some peace in the work - mostly because he felt closer to Scow while doing it - but it did not take very long, and all too soon he found himself back with the others, forcing himself to find the thread of his tale again.

***

"I remember the day we launched... can still smell the mixture of sea, sweat and steel," Danor was saying. There was a wistful gleam in his eye. "One thousand strong: twenty fists of our very best. Volunteers, all, ready to set aside our lives, our families, lovers - all for the greater good. Many Laegis came to see us off.

"'L'Viviit Muurum... L'Viviit Muurum!' they shouted at us, over and over as we marched onto magnificent ships fashioned by Derant the Builder, Ogund the Craftsman and Cartis the Navigator... great leviathans upon whose backs we should be carried to our doom."

Triistan felt the hair on his arms and the back of his neck rise as Danor spoke his next words; the same ones from that ancient book he had found in doyen Rathmiin's study so many years ago.

"Where this wind ends, our Oath begins..."

"What about the gods?" Captain Vaelysia asked from her oversized chair nearby. Her long legs were stretched out before her, the supple leather breeches and high black boots she favored gleaming dully in the amber glow cast by the fire. "Did any of them go with you?"

Danor grunted. "Many were still here, on Aarden, finishing their work and preparing for our arrival. Still others, including Thunor and Shan, made the journey with us to ensure The Worm did not escape either by his wiles or a treacherous sea." He chuckled quietly. "Never has anyone made such a long voyage with such favorable winds and weather, I can promise you that. Even Sigel checked his fury, making the Burning Sea little more than a warm bath."

"How did you transport him?"

"With great care, Captain. Great care and ingenuity. Ganar, Sylveth and Veda devised a... vault I suppose you could call it - or cocoon, maybe. The outside was jhetstone bound in bluesteel, the core of solid xhemium. Don't know how they did it, but somehow they encased him in it, like a fly trapped in amber. We just called it the "containment vessel", and eventually just "the box". There were chains of bluesteel affixed to large rings at each end, and they were careful to carry the box by those rather than coming into direct contact with it. Binding wards were placed on the box, you see - make your hair stand straight up if you got too close to it - so I imagine touching it directly might be a bit uncomfortable. I never got close enough to find out until it was placed in The Hold, and once that was done no one could get within thirty feet of it."

The big Vanha leaned forward and tossed another log onto the fire, then shoved some of the hot coals against it with the iron poker. His expression was bitter in the ruddy glow.

"Kept him wrapped up nicely for nearly a thousand years, while the rest of you moved on without us." He finished stoking the fire and leaned back, lacing his thick fingers behind his head. His chair creaked in tired protest.

"Well, not completely without us I suppose. For the first seven hundred years or so, there was regular traffic between Aarden and the mainland. It was all tightly controlled by Obed and the other Arys, of course, but we had regular visits from merchants and family, and even the Young Gods went back and forth quite a bit in those first few centuries."

"Were there children?" Triistan had keyed in on the word 'family'.

Danor stared into the fire in silence for so long Triistan didn't think he'd heard him.

"Su'ul? Were there -"

"Heard you the first time, Salty. There you go again with that surgeon's knife, cutting to the bone right quick. No, there were no children - not here, and never anywhere by us. It was forbidden to us, forbidden by the Oath. Too much potential for distraction, conflicting loyalties..." he paused, chewing on the inside of his lip bitterly. "The Worm was our child and the only charge we need concern ourselves with."

"I'm sorry, I -" Triistan faltered, but Danor held up his hand. "Not your fault. Nobody's fault. It was the right call - the only call. As incredible as this citadel is, it - and Aarden - are no place for children, so they would have had to remain at home on Niyah, anyway. And the stronger our connections to home, the harder it was to do our duty, a duty that grew progressively worse as time wore on. You'll remember that The Worm was not alone - he had his followers, and they persisted even after he was taken. Despite our best efforts, those that weren't killed or captured during the purge of Talmoreth were forced into hiding, but somehow being forced underground only made them stronger, more pervasive." He grunted. "Underground's where they're most comfortable... where they belong. So there was always the threat of an attempt to free The Worm; always the need to remain vigilant. And it never got easier. Quite the opposite, really."

"How?" the young Seeker asked.

"Our share of the burden grew over time, as the Divide between Auruim and Dauthir grew, eroding their attention here, the way the stream gradually wears away even the rock canyon it passes through. Eventually they left, but arranged to visit at regular intervals to check on the binding wards, bring news and supplies, or the occasional replacement Guard should one of us suffer some mishap. They came twice a year at first. Merchants were no longer allowed to travel to Aarden because of the threat from The Worm's growing faction of followers. Somehow they'd managed to smuggle themselves over here already, though. Not many, mind you, but enough to harass us with acts of sabotage and the occasional murder. Once they've got a foothold, it's like trying to catch smoke; the harder you try, the more it spreads.

So the reinforcement ships became our only form of contact with the outside world. Family and loved ones were still allowed to visit, but there were fewer and fewer of these, as the reality of living in two separate worlds took its toll. By the time Markos murdered Lyrin the Judicator, we were down to one visit every two years, manned by Laegis only - no Arys even bothered to make the last two trips."

Captain Vaelysia's voice was skeptical. "Forgive me, Su'ul, but how could the gods have become so complacent? They knew better than anyone how dangerous he was."

Danor nodded. "You would think so, wouldn't you? That's why I don't think it was complacency. I think it was calculated."

"Calculated?" repeated the Captain. "Why? What do you mean?"

"We think Obed prevented them from coming. He was given complete authority over The Worm's imprisonment, and although the other gods could have challenged him, we think they were... distracted at the time. The Guardian is far-sighted, and we believe he saw what was coming and did his best to prevent it. Unfortunately, he was only able to delay it a few years."

Danor sighed. "Of course, much of this is guesswork on our part. You have to remember that by this time, we were isolated from events on the mainland. The Godswar erupted, what - three years after Markos murdered Lyrin? No, more like five. Regardless, the rift between the Auruim and Dauthir had spread to the Templars long before then, so the Laegis on Niyah were split down the middle. The Oathguard remained neutral, but that didn't stop our visitors from trying to sway our opinions in one direction or the other. At first, the conversations were your standard political debates among friends, with both sides fairly passionate about their views but respectful of their opponents'. Whatever the differences were, they were "their problem", not ours, you see? But on the last visit before the Godswar started, something changed."

"How do you mean?" Triistan asked.

Danor shook his head slowly, sadly. "The Templars who came on that voyage were angry, resentful... desperate. Many of them asked us for asylum. An entire fist - fifty sworn Laegis - deserted, joining the Worm's underground network here. Some were angry with the Templar leadership, feeling we'd lost our way; others were angry at the gods. A few were openly fearful that the Divide would eventually lead to open war between the factions..."

"You turned them away," the Captain said softly. It wasn't a question.

"Of course we did. The Oath is absolute. There were nearly three hundred men aboard that ship; too many to just absorb without having been properly vetted. We were so afraid of being betrayed that we missed the one opportunity that might have prevented it, or at least could have helped us prevail in spite of it."

Triistan shook his head. "I don't understand. Did they attack you when you told them they couldn't stay?"

"No, they left. Sailed back to Niyah and their doom... taking two hundred and forty-five strong sword-arms with them. We will never know for sure, but it might have been enough."

"Enough for what?"

"Within a year of their departure, we knew the Godswar had begun. Don't know how or why, but each of us could feel it somehow, and our more gifted seers - Eso and Crixus, among them - confirmed it. For ten years we waited, every day watching the horizon for sail or sign, but none came."

"Why didn't you sail your own ships back to Niyah?" Tarq asked.

"No blue-water vessels were ever allowed to moor here for security reasons. Incoming vessels were required to drop anchor outside the bay and transport supplies and personnel via launches - ketches like the one you arrived on - and none are ever left behind. So after ten years of silence had elapsed, we began building our own. But without a proper yard or deepwater harbor, that was a lengthy process. The addition of the Laegis deserters to the Worm's underground force didn't make things any easier, either. Made them bolder, stronger, forcing us to fight a guerilla war at the same time. The delegation arrived before the ship was finished."

"Delegation?" Triistan echoed. Danor smiled his not-smile.

"Yiin, Salty. Three fuundaris gods and a crew of one hundred and eighty-five stalwart loyalists."

"Loyal to whom?" Captain Vaelysia asked in a grim voice.

"Themselves, mostly. The Auruim, officially. Heketh the Ravager, Taisha the Seductress, and my dear father, Theckan. The Rogue Himself." He smirked again. "Quite the impressive delegation, eh? A rat, a whore, and a conniving thief."

"Did they attack outright?" Commander Tchicatta growled. He knew what was coming; by now, they all did.

"No, Theckan's far too cunning for that. Had they, I think I'd have a different tale to tell you. Standard protocol was to view all incoming ships as hostile until proven otherwise, so Lord Marshal Haagen had two hundred and fifty of us drawn up in the mouth of the valley. We would have paid a heavy price, but we would have had the high ground, defenses to fall back on, and reinforcements." He clenched his thick fist and pounded it on the arm of his chair for emphasis. "At least we would have had a chance to fight, and I think we could have held."

"So what happened?" asked Triistan.

"They talked their way in. Convinced the Lord Marshal that they had grave news; news that must be heard, counsel that must be asked for and given. They claimed to be acting with Obed's blessing, and even produced papers bearing his seal. Haagen bought it, and ordered the scaling ladders lowered. I'd like to hate him for it, but any one of us probably would have made the same mistake. Heketh will make your skin want to crawl off your bones, but even the immortal Arys would have a hard time resisting the combined charm of Taisha and Theckan."

"So Haagen left one fist to keep an eye on the boat and the few crewmen left aboard, while the rest of us escorted the delegation back to Ostenvaard. Or followed them would be more appropriate. You've been up that miserable fuundaris river, so you know what it's like. Just imagine trying to move a force of almost four hundred men that way. We maintained it back then - a series of locks to help with the traverse points, for example - but it was still slow going for a large group, so the Lord Marshal took a small honor guard with him, and he and our Arys 'diplomats' went on ahead."

"I take it that's how Tau Regis became the Lord Marshal?" the Captain asked.

"No, Theckan and the others did not kill Haagen there, when they had the opportunity. They still needed to gain access to the city, and Tau would not have allowed it without hearing directly from Haagen. Besides, I think they were hoping to pull off their mission with a minimal amount of bloodshed, perhaps even convincing many of us to return with them."

"So they really intended to free Oss-" Triistan caught himself just in time. "They really wanted to set him free? By all the dead gods, why?"

Danor laughed darkly. "Because of all the dead gods, boy. Things were going badly - for both sides I guess. Lyrin was the first, but she soon had plenty of company. According to the delegation, Sigel and Ganar struck first, combining their powers to encase Minet in molten rock and making a living - well, a dying statue of her. Thunor flew into a terrible rage and slew them both before being driven from the field by the combined might of Shan and Niht - though Theckan told us Thunor left of his own accord, so he did not have to fight Shan or do harm to the Stormfather's wife. They were all family, but the Conqueror and the Stormfather were most like brothers.

"By the Godswar's ninth year, things had become desperate, they told us. Most of the Arys had fallen, and those that were left were fighting not just on Niyah, but in Ehronhaal as well - jeopardizing the internal machinations that somehow kept the thing in flight. Both factions had committed grievous sins, they said, but the Dauthir had gone too far and were actively seeking to bring the fabled Auruim city down."

Several of the Expedition members expressed their surprise and disbelief.

"Aye, Salties, I speak both truth and madness, but neither diminishes the other. Needless to say, we were... skeptical. It would have been suicidal and besides, it seemed clear to us that Theckan and his two co-conspirators were overstating things in order to win our support. It was perfume for the poxy whore they were really trying to sell us: Obed had been slain by a member of his own family and with him, the last voice of moderation amongst the High Houses. Thunor would most certainly seek the means to finally ground Ehronhaal, assuming the Auruim couldn't find a way to break the resolve of the Dauthir first. They wanted to bargain with the Worm, trading his freedom for loyalty in the hope that he would tip the scales in their favor and put an end to the war."

"You've got to be joking," Jaspins breathed. A few of the others voiced their disbelief as well.

"I wish I was. But I was there, with over two hundred other Oathguard who'd gathered in the High Hall to hear news of the War, and of home. No amount of honey - whether on Theckan's tongue or Taisha's quim - could temper our response. We were outraged, and the hall erupted with angry protests, so we all missed the warning signs in the commotion.

"Looking back, I can see them now, plain as the nose on your face: Theckan trading pointed looks with Taisha and Heketh, as those two stepped back from where they'd been standing behind the Rogue, spreading out; Hecketh unfastening a sack he'd been carrying over one shoulder; and the Rogue's hands dropping out of sight beneath the table he and the Lord Marshal were seated at. The gods did not receive the answer they had hoped for and were preparing to execute Plan B, but we were too busy yelling and shaking our fists in righteous indignation to notice."

Danor shifted uncomfortably in his chair. "Not that it's worth a fart in a hurricane, but I think Theckan genuinely hoped to avoid bloodshed. I could see it in the set of his shoulders and the way he dropped his head... " he paused and his lips twisted bitterly, "just before they began butchering us."

"Lord Marshal Haagen was the first to die. He stood and held up his hands for calm, and as we quieted, he spoke his last words to the delegation: 'Your request is denied', he said. 'Only Obed may release us from our Oath, and he must do so in person'.

"With a look of savage triumph I still see in my nightmares, Heketh shouted 'I was hoping you would say that!' and upended the contents of his sack. By the time Obed's head struck the table, Haagen was slumping back into his chair, his throat ripped open - his own head nearly severed. I didn't see it happen, but I saw Theckan kill scores of us the same way in the slaughter that followed. Tekagii - Jharrl Claws."

"Jharrl Claws?"

The Firstblade answered for Danor. "Leather bands or half-gloves that encircle the hands and wrists, with curved dagger blades sewn into the palms and knuckles. Favored by thieves and assassins because they are easy to conceal."

Danor nodded. "Against heavy armor, they are virtually useless unless you take your opponent unawares, but against light or none and in the hands of a strong, skilled assassin, they can be brutally effective. In the hands of a god who happens to favor the weapon... they are devastating.

"Few of us were armed; fewer still wore any battle dress: Theckan cut through us like an enraged jharrl loosed in a sheep's pen. He was a dark blur, a shadow moving almost faster than I could follow. A score of men - seasoned veterans, all - fell in the first few seconds, throats torn out, guts spilling onto the floor, and so much blood it made a mist in the air around him. Apparently he'd reconciled whatever misgivings he might have had."

Danor shook his head slowly, eyes wide, gaze fixed squarely on the past. "Twenty dead in half as many heartbeats," he said. His voice was half-growl, half-whisper. "Over a hundred in the next few minutes, as the Ravager joined in. Hecketh began vomiting swarms of black wasps, thick as your thumb. Their stings left festering welts behind and any that survived the battle in the High Hall died writhing in agony a few hours later, the venom turning their skin a sickly purple, but not before swelling to the point of splitting. The lucky ones" - he practically spat the word out at them - "fell right there in the Hall, either suffocating at the center of the swarm as the wasps filled their mouths and noses, or being torn to pieces by Theckan on its outskirts."

He reached for the pitcher of sref, muttered a curse when he discovered it was empty, and stood to retrieve more from wherever he kept it. Triistan and the others exchanged looks but said nothing.

The giant settled into his chair again but did not offer them any of the sref this time, leading Triistan to suspect he had drawn it straight from the keg at full strength. After a deep draught, Danor continued his tale.

"About fifty of us - led by Crixus - withdrew from the High Hall and tried to seal the doors, hoping to mount a defense in the hallway outside. It's a semi-circular chamber and the corridor hugs the one curved wall, with three sets of double doors. They aren't meant to be sealed from the outside, but they're thick and heavy, and at least they provided us with choke points and a temporary reprieve from the fuundaris wasps. We sent runners for reinforcements, but no one noticed - minuerto, no one even knew she was capable of it! - but apparently Taisha had shape-changed, taking on the form of one of our own. She ran right by me on her way to the gatehouse, to 'welcome' whatever remained of the escort force moving up the river.

"They were half a day behind us, so by the time they reached Ahbaingeata, we'd already started Low Tide."

"Low Tide?" echoed the Captain. Danor nodded.

"Low Tide - the catchy name some overzealous officer gave to the strategy upon which all of Ostenvaard is based: a fighting withdrawal from one bulwark to the next. Select fists surge forward to bloody the enemy - like waves on a beach, you see? - while our main force gradually falls back, tightening our lines around one central point, the reason we're all stuck on this fuundaris rock in the first place."

"The Hold."

"Yiin, the fuundaris Hold and its precious crystal box, and in that fuundaris box the sleeping pool of rat minuerto someone fashioned into a god. Anyway, by the time the escort force reached the river gate, we'd lost almost four hundred men and withdrawn all the way to the Weir - twin citadels guarding the approach to the pass leading up to the Hold, on the opposite side of the city. Taisha was in control of the Rivergate, probably having fucked the guard force there to death for all I know. The poor brokuuros coming upriver were caught between hammer and anvil and slaughtered. Two hundred men cut to pieces, led by a good friend of mine named Stypos."

He paused and offered a silent toast to the fallen before taking another long pull of his mug.

"They gave a good accounting of themselves, though: only one fist of the traitorous pukes survived to engage us at the Weir, and most of them - including The Whore herself - were badly wounded."

The others were surprised at this revelation. "Do the Arys bleed... like we do?" Triistan asked.

"Yiin, they bleed, Salty. Though stubbornly. Hacking at them is like chopping at the trunk of an old tree; you'll eventually do them harm, but it takes a great deal of effort and time, and they're not likely to stand around waiting for you to cut them down."

"Why engage with you at all?" asked Commander Tchicatta. "Why didn't they just fly past you?"

This time Danor's smile was full of fierce pride. He stood and left the room for a moment. When he returned, he was holding something metallic, about three feet long, that gleamed dully in the firelight. He held it out to the Firstblade, and Triistan could see it was some type of grappling hook, although there was no rope attached to it and the prongs were folded back, nearly touching the steel shaft like retracted wings. The end of the shaft was pointed and wickedly barbed, like a large hunting arrow. Tchicatta took it from the Vanha and examined it, frowning thoughtfully as he manipulated the prongs. There were five, and when the Firstblade lifted one away from the center shaft of the device, all of them moved simultaneously, extending outward, like evenly spaced branches around a tree trunk. They only extended so far before there was a loud, metallic 'click' and the arms fixed in place. The barbed ends of each prong looked deadly - and all too familiar. He shivered at the memory of the nagayuun's tail.

"Impressive," said the Firstblade, handing it to the Captain. "Fired from ballistae?" Danor's lips twisted crookedly.

"From your perspective, yes: we use them in our crossbows. The eyelet you see at the base of the center shaft is a tie-off point for an ultra-light cordage we call strathus - 'webrope'. We make the line from cocoon webbing harvested from grelos nests in the jungle."

"What's a grelo?" asked Triistan.

"Grelos. Large, predatory moths native to Aarden. Their cocoon silk is stronger than any spider's webbing, even the dog-sized ones that haunt The Worm's lair." Triistan was only partially successful at suppressing another shudder. It seemed that everything on Aarden was gigantic, hostile, or both.

"Anyway," Danor continued, "the flesh of the Arys is difficult to break, but the wings are something else, at least their undersides. Not easy to get to - damn near impossible when they're retracted - but when in flight, they can be pierced with enough force."

"If the head pierces the wing, anything the target or the bowman do is certain to engage the arms, locking them into place and making the bolt a grappling hook. It generally takes two or three solid hits to bring one down, unless you're good enough to hit one of the major bones or ligaments.

"Only one in a thousand can make that shot, and when Theckan and Hecketh broke free of the High Hall, into the open air, my loving wife made two." He smiled wistfully. "Always overachieving, that one."

Triistan remembered the fierce-looking Vanha with the multi-colored cloak of feathers - Syr, daughter of Sylveth - and wondered how many of those feathers were from their Arys betrayers.

Danor held out one long, heavily-muscled arm and pointed to a place just below his elbow. "She took both of them here, breaking both ulna and radius bones. Even gods cannot fly with a broken wing." He shook his head, frowning. "It was a glorious moment, and we rallied around it. We made our first stand right then and there, and actually mounted a counter-attack, pushing them back inside for a short time. But their rage would not be contained for long.

"Hecketh... Hecketh was a terrible thing to behold, growing stronger and fouler with each man he killed. In retrospect, some of us think we might have been better off had they flown past us, believing we could have come at them as an organized force when they reached the Hold."

"What do you believe, Su'ul?" the Captain prompted quietly.

"'What if' is a game for cowards and fools. She helped us regain our composure and remember our training. The counter-attack bought us a few crucial moments, enough time for Tau Regis to arrive with reinforcements and commence Low Tide."

He snorted derisively. "Giving... meaning to our deaths didn't matter. Staying alive didn't matter. The only thing that mattered was making them bleed - for every step, every single yard; bleed them out before they reached the Hold and freed the Worm... and bleed them out before we did."

Triistan could hear the tremor in the giant's voice.

"So with Long Tau guarding our rear, we began our withdrawal through the city. He used the rooftops and alleyways to constantly come at them from different angles, pressuring and stinging them before pulling away. He was brilliant, several times getting them completely turned around, pursuing his feints in the opposite direction they really wanted to go; leading them away from the approach to the Hold, chasing shadows while our main force melted away completely so that we could regroup at the Weir. It was costly - he lost nearly a hundred men in the process - but far less so than a direct engagement would have been, and it bought the rest of us nearly half a day to rest, regroup, and treat our wounded.

"By the time they finally reached us, we numbered four hundred and fifty-seven, thirty-one of which were too badly wounded to fight." He drew a deep, slow breath. "Twenty-five of those - every man that was still conscious - took up sword, spear and bow to help in the defense anyway."

Danor's description of the ensuing battle was riveting. Tau and two others - Linessa and Braxus, the only other Oathguard to survive the rearguard action - broke out of the lengthening shadows of the buildings crouched along the outermost edge of Ostenvaard and began loping across the hundred or so yards of open ground between the edge of the city and The Weir. Two were actually astride their jharrls, while Tau sprinted after them, his long bladestaff flashing in the late evening light.

The plaza was tiled with large slabs of stone, creating a wide open space that ran the entire length of the walls guarding the approach to the Hold, deliberately designed to rob an attacking force of any cover as they approached the redoubt. When Tau and his men had crossed only about a third of the space, the buildings to either side of the lane they had just exited collapsed in a torrent of stone and dust. The new Lord Marshal and his two mounted comrades spun around at the commotion just as a dark, winged shape appeared out of the billowing cloud of debris. It was Taisha, although she had shapeshifted again. She was much larger, with a wingspan approaching at least forty feet, and thick, powerful legs covered in black scales and ending in wickedly-hooked talons that looked large enough to hold a warhorse. In one hand she held a long spear. In the other was a whip with multiple barbed lashes that sparked in the suns' light - flaying knives that had been woven into the braided leather, according to Danor. Her flight was erratic as she tried to gain altitude, and the Vanha healer described ragged holes in her wings, as well as several wounds on the rest of her body that oozed the unmistakable blue of godsblood. But there was still plenty of fight left in her.

"Yin, plenty of rage in all three. They were blinded by it by then, making them reckless. When The Whore spotted Long Tau and the others, she let out such a piercing wail that many of us fell to the ground trying to cover our ears. When she cracked that fuundaris whip, it sounded like thunder echoing across the plaza."

An answering roar rose up from the city as the surviving warriors that had fought for her at Ahbaingeata charged into view. Tau signaled Linessa and Braxus to retreat and they and their jharrls sprinted for the safety of the Weir. But Taisha was not about to lose her prey. Oblivious of her wounds, she hurtled after them, gaining quickly on the unmounted Lord Marshal. As she swooped down, talons outstretched and spear cocked back, ready for the killing thrust, Tau suddenly tripped and went tumbling head over heels across the stones."

Danor paused, shaking his head. Triistan could see the gleam of his teeth in the firelight and realized their host was grinning with real amusement.

"Clever brokuuro, our Lord Marshal. Up he suddenly pops at the end of his 'fall', in a crouch and facing her. From where we're standing on the wall, we see a flash between them, just before The Whore smashes into him at full speed, and the two of them go rolling across the stones in a mass of feathers, scales and steel. When they come to rest, her body and wings completely obscure him... but not the four feet of his bladestaff sticking out of the fuundaris bitch's back where he'd impaled her!" He slammed his mug on the arm of his chair.

"But she was still moving - her back hunching up and down in some obscene parody of her favorite pastime. Every last man and woman - on the walls and across the plaza in the enemy ranks - was holding their breath. Except for Linessa and Braxus: they'd already dismounted to run back and roll The Whore's body aside - I distinctly remember hearing their footfalls echoing in the otherwise silent plaza - and as sure as you're all sitting there with your jaws wagging, old Long Tau stood up, placed his foot on The Whore's chest, and ripped his bladestaff free. Never have I heard such noise! Four hundred and fifty throats opened in a roar that shook the walls under our feet.

Swords and spears slammed against shields, gauntlets pounded on the parapets... would not have surprised me at all if the Weir and the walls had just crumbled into dust right there. Tau and the others dragged the scaly bitch back to the gates while the lickspittles following her just stood there staring."

"Glorious," rumbled Tchicatta. "I can see why the Oathguard would follow such a man."

"Indeed... just as the sky is glorious right before the suns set," Danor answered cryptically. "Perhaps it is made thus by the knowledge that darkness must follow."

"For Darkness did follow, Salties," he continued. "Out of the dust and smoke... through and around the stunned ranks of the poor dumb brokuuros arrayed against us, slithering and sliding across the paved flagstones of the plaza, there came a dark fog the color of night. Except that it moved not like fog, but rather like a reaching, grasping thing, stretching out tendrils of writhing black smoke and then seeming to drag itself forward. There were scores of these appendages, and wherever they touched one of our foes, the smoke crawled up and over them the way vines will crawl up the trunk of a tree - though in seconds rather than months."

Danor shook his head slowly back and forth. "I've seen a lot of things in my long life, Salties, but I've never seen anything quite like this. The smoke-thing began to rise, slowly taking the form of some giant, man-shaped thing that was picking itself up off the ground. The Vanha in the plaza were first engulfed by the smoke and then absorbed into it - we could see them rising off the ground even as the thing pulled itself erect, as if they'd become part of its body - though it had no body, not really. Just the shape of one, made of roiling black smoke shot with occasional flashes of blue lightning. It was like a storm in the shape of a towering colossus. When it stood completely erect, it must have been two hundred feet tall, each leg as thick as one of the Weir towers. The rough shape of its head bent back and a hole full of blue fire opened - its mouth as far as we could tell - and it roared, or howled... its voice was like the combined screams of those poor brokuuros it had absorbed, but magnified tenfold."

"Gods," Triistan breathed.

"Just one, actually," Danor answered. "As the smoke-thing lumbered across the plaza, we could see Hecketh striding out from between the ruined buildings. Whatever movements he made, the smoke-thing mimicked, as if it were his shadow - if shadows were two hundred feet tall and contained the suspended bodies of fifty-some misguided Templar warriors, that is."

"You could still see them?" Captain Vaelysia asked.

"Not once the thing stood and began to move, no... at least, not until it began to attack the walls. Then, wherever it struck a solid surface, it left one or two of their smashed bodies behind, the way a man might leave smears of blood or skin on the surface of a wall he struck. Still, that was preferable to when it made contact with one of us."

"What happened then?" asked Tarq.

"The same thing that happened to our enemies in the plaza - it absorbed us, becoming stronger and larger as it did so. The harder we fought it, the bigger it became. It was taller than the barbican between the spires when I finally realized that it wasn't actually doing any real harm to the towers or the walls. Most of it was just noise and terror from watching this monstrous thing threatening to breach the Weir, while out in the plaza - out of bowshot, of course - The Ravager pantomimed the assault. The clamor was deafening - bodies slamming against the walls like a hail of trebuchet-thrown boulders, and the thing howling away in its voices-of-the-damned scream - but it was all a sham. Besides the loss of those absorbed by the smoke and subsequently smeared across the walls, we were not in any real danger of a breach. Sadly, it took us too long to figure that out."

"A feint," the Captain offered.

"Yin, meant to draw our attention to the center while the real threat slipped past our flank. I still don't know how he scaled the wall, but somehow Theckan made it past The Weir. I suppose I should be thankful that he didn't set on us from the rear while that thing was attacking, or we might have been wiped out completely.

"As soon as they realized the nature of the smoke-thing, Tau ordered his men to pull back out of reach. Shortly after that, someone discovered the bodies of the six men the Rogue had killed on his way through, and they understood the full scope of the gods' ruse. Tau left his own skeletal force to stall The Ravager as long as possible - forty-three men, most of whom were walking wounded, with orders to appear wherever they could along the walls to make it look as if the Weir was still defended. He took the rest of them - seventy-nine Oathguard including me - and set out in pursuit of Theckan.

"By the time we reached The Hold, it was too late. Looked like a fuundaris cyclone had hit it. The Wyvhard - wardstones in your tongue, huge blocks of jhetstone carved with binding runes - had been toppled, and the air stunk of arxhemestry... and something else. Something foul and rotten, like the bottom of a bog." His mouth drew down in a sneer as if he could smell it now.

"We found Theckan lying slumped across the shattered remains of the box, alive, but only just. What was left of his clothing was smoking, his skin black with soot and blood. Whatever ritual or tools he'd used had cost him dearly, though that price paled in comparison to what he was about to pay...

"Ossien was free."

Once again the cold, slimy thing in Triistan's gut moved. Whether it was just his overactive imagination, Danor's use of The Worm's forbidden name, or the note of real dread in the giant's voice - perhaps a mixture of all these things - the young Seeker could feel fear settling over the room like a heavy, cold fog crawling across the lowlands.

Just then, somewhere above them in the vast fortress-city, alarm bells began to ring.

- 20 -

Breach

Danor jumped to his feet, knocking his mug of sref off the arm of his chair to shatter on the floor. He sprinted into an adjoining room and re-emerged seconds later with a huge polearm. The bladed hammer's shaft was easily as long as Triistan and as thick as his wrist, made of the same gleaming black wood used in other Oathguard weapons.

"Stay here!" The clamoring alarm bells coming from multiple directions suddenly stopped.

"What is it? Can we help?" Triistan asked, his voice overloud in the sudden silence. The Captain and Firstblade exchanged a look that seemed strangely guilt-ridden, but Danor's back was to them as he swung the door open.

"Atuu, coh'me!" he called down the hall as he stepped out of the room, then glanced back in their direction. "If we need you, Salty, then the worst has happened. Your weapons are in a storage room at the back of this apartment. Arm yourselves, but wait here until we send word for you."

The old jharrl with the broken tooth bounded past him just before he slammed the door shut. As it crashed closed, the crew was up and moving through the apartment, searching for the storeroom.

"Get Thinman up, now!" the Captain ordered as she passed by the prostrate sailor. There were only a handful of rooms and it did not take long for them to find their belongings.

"Triis!" Jaspins tossed Taelyia's kilij to him. He snatched the curved scabbard out of the air, then belted the baldric around his waist as he turned back to Thinman. The beefy Seeker had managed to get himself into a sitting position, but still had only one eye open and was in mid-yawn when the Captain grabbed the pitcher of sref and hurled its contents into his face. Thinman coughed and sputtered and staggered to his feet, but she did not wait for him to regain enough breath to protest.

"This is probably our mess, lads. While we were wined and dined, Myles and Miikha went topside, looking for an escape route."

They waited expectantly for her to explain, their patient silence a testament to their trust in her command. She pointed to the large, grated opening above Danor's central hearth.

"There is another opening like this one in the room where Mister Halliard was treated. They are designed to allow fresh air and sunlight into the underkeep. Although they are fortified against intruders by heavy metal grates inside the shafts, they lead all the way to the surface. Biiko mixed some sort of paste from his bag of tricks that should eat through the mortar, and if it worked, Myles and Miikha were to scale the shaft and determine whether we could escape or not. They may have tripped an alarm or been caught in the process."

"Oh shit," Thinman burped, but it wasn't clear whether he was commenting on the Captain's news or how he felt.

"Orders, sir?" Lieutenant Jaspins asked crisply.

The Captain hesitated. It was one of the few times Triistan had seen her appear even the least bit indecisive, and it was unnerving. "Danor told us to stay put..."

"But if they've caught Miikha and Myles trying to escape," First Mate Tarq finished for her, "they'll be killed before anyone bothers to come and fetch us."

"Maybe, but I don't like betraying Danor's trust, or wandering around here blindly. We have no idea what we're walking into."

"With all due respect, Captain, we have no idea what we're waiting for by sitting here, either. For all we know, they might have been successful, and this is our best chance to escape."

Triistan felt an enormous sense of relief when she finally nodded in agreement.

"Alright, let's move. Commander, you're up front with me. Lieutenant, you and the Whip will take the rear." She glanced at the hilt of Triistan's kilij. "Looks like we're about to find out how much you've learned, Mister Halliard. Let's hope you're a quick study."

They ran down the curved stairs leading to the suite where the rest of the crew was quartered, slowing when they reached the last few steps. They expected to find some kind of commotion, but instead were met with an eerie silence. Eventually they heard muffled conversation from further down the hall, towards the large common room. The Captain jerked her head that way and they proceeded quietly down the corridor, weapons drawn.

They passed Triistan's room first. It was empty except for the faintest haze of blue smoke and a pungent, sour smell. The Captain led them past without stopping, so he wasn't able to see into the grated sun-shaft from this angle, but someone had shoved one of the room's tables underneath it. Triistan assumed Myles and Miikha had used it to reach the shaft. He wondered if Biiko had gone with them and his insides went cold.

They found the rest of the crew members gathered in the common room, speaking in hushed voices. They rose as their Captain entered, several of them talking at once. Triistan did not see Biiko anywhere.

"Stand down!" Tarq shouted. They fell silent and the Captain stepped forward.

"How much do you know? Did Danor come through here?"

Creugar shrugged his huge shoulders. "Not much, Captain. The big man came through right after the alarms stopped, but he told us little - little we could understand, anyway. He was in a fit, that one - Creugar thinks he stopped in Titch's room first and discovered our little reconnaissance project. He ordered us to stay put or we would be killed on sight, then left, heading down the passage we took earlier to the Low Hall."

"Did Myles and Miikha get out then?"

"Aye, Captain. Old Blackblades went with them too, but we've not heard anything since."

Triistan suddenly felt vulnerable without the Unbound's constant presence. That realization made him somewhat angry with himself.

"How long?"

"Half a watch, Sir," answered Brehnl. "We was just talking that they should be back any time when the bells started ringin'."

She locked eyes with her First Mate. He shrugged. "Who knows what these bastards would have decided tomorrow. It was the right call."

She nodded sharply before turning to the others. "Gear up, we're getting out of here right now. Halliard's room as soon as you're ready."

Triistan ran back down the hall to gather up his own pitiful pack of belongings. As he snatched them up and stuffed them into his pack, he heard a loud scraping and scrabbling noise behind him, followed by a heavy thud. He spun around, but the room was empty. His gaze drifted up to the shaft on the other side of the room.

Bits of stone and dust trickled down to land on the table below, then something let out a long, low hiss. He was suddenly very cold, his legs and arms leaden, as if they were made of mud. His fingers found the hilt of Taelyia's sword and he drew it, the weapon heavy and awkward in his hands. He longed for that spark of familiarity he'd felt when first drawing the blade a few days before, when for an instant everything had felt exactly right, like he'd wielded a sword all his life. But he might as well have been holding a spar.

The shadows in the opposite corner of the opening gave birth to a dark, wet shape. His breath caught in his throat when he saw its mottled coloration - the same as the skin of the nagayuun in the tunnel - and his stomach cramped in remembered pain. He wanted to call out but couldn't seem to draw enough breath to do so. He was trapped, paralyzed by fear, and it was all he could do just to hold his sword out in front of him.

The thing's head and shoulders emerged a little further, enough to tell that it was different from the creature that had attacked him in the tunnel. Its head, though triangular like the nest guardian's, was much longer and narrower, and rather than looking like some mad combination of a reptile and a giant scorpion, this one was more like a huge salamander. It was powerfully built, greasy skin stretched tautly over a thick neck and wide shoulders. But despite its bulk, it moved with the sinuous grace of a snake as it extended its two forelegs, each ending in broad, six-fingered 'hands', and sidled out a bit more.

It hissed again, ending with a drawn-out, staccato clicking noise emanating from the back of its throat.

It hung there for another moment, slowly rotating only its head as it took in the large room. He could see one of its eyes, a large oval of glistening midnight with no visible pupil, and then suddenly it swung its head in his direction and froze. He wanted desperately to sprint for the door, but could not even slide his foot sideways.

He squeezed the hilt of the kilij, convinced the sword was going to slip right out of his sweating palms, his heart hammering against the inside of his chest as he tried to recall the few short lessons Biiko had given him before he'd become too sick to practice them. But it was no use - his mind was as leaden as his limbs. The creature shifted its forelegs closer to the opening and its muscles tensed, as if it were preparing to spring.

He was going to die.

Just then he heard voices coming down the hall. The beast's head twitched towards the noise, and then it began to withdraw back into the opening. Too late.

There was a loud crash from somewhere inside the sun-shaft. The creature came plummeting down onto the table beneath the opening, a huge warrior on its back. The table collapsed, shards of wood and other items flying in all directions. The giant wore ornate armor and wielded a bladestaff that was easily twice Triistan's height, part of which now impaled the monster and pinned it to the splintered remains of the table. It writhed violently, screaming and hissing as the warrior leaned on his weapon, so loud Triistan had to cover his ears. Then, so swiftly that the Seeker's eyes could barely follow, the warrior stomped an armored boot down on the thing's chest, yanked the blade free, and spun the weapon in an arc that raked across the creature's neck, severing its head completely.

Just as quickly, he brought the blade up to a guard position as Captain Vaelysia burst into the room with the Firstblade, Tarq and several others close on her heels, weapons drawn. They nearly collided with one another as they skidded to a halt, but it only took them an instant to assess the situation. The Captain held her hands up, palms out, to show that she meant no harm.

Triistan finally took a breath - his first since the creature had appeared - and lowered his own blade, suddenly feeling self-conscious about trying to use it.

"Thank you," he croaked.

The giant warrior stepped down off the tangled heap of mottled flesh and splintered wood, green eyes flashing. Triistan assumed he was another Oathguard, but didn't recognize him; he had not been at the cun've'dictuus. He was tall, even for a Vanha - taller than any of the others they had seen so far, except perhaps for the one called Vendros. His long, silver-colored hair was bound back in a braided ponytail, revealing a sharp face with snow white, arching eyebrows and a close-cropped beard of the same color. A jagged gash along the right side of his brow bled freely, but he seemed oblivious to it.

"Move back," was all he said as he turned to face the sun-shaft, his bladestaff held out crosswise in front of him. His hands were protected by ornately-wrought silver guards fitted close to the center of the weapon's black shaft and covered in curved spikes that looked like talons.

They could hear more sounds coming from somewhere up inside the shaft. The Captain motioned some of her men to back out into the hall, but she, First Mate Tarq, and Commander Tchicatta fanned out to the Oathguard's left, also facing the opening. Feeling conspicuous, but not knowing what else to do, Triistan stepped up on the giant's right side, eyeing him warily and still holding Taelyia's kilij in his shaking hands. The giant looked down at them, glowering.

"Brave fools," he growled, but did not send them away.

From where he stood, Triistan could now see the slain creature in clear detail, and was suddenly aware of how small he was compared to it. From the underside of its chin - at least an arm's length above the stump of its throat - to the end of its thick tail, it must have been eight or nine feet long and half again as wide. Its legs, gathered in against its belly in death's final embrace, looked to be four or five feet long, and he could see now that its feet were huge - large enough to grasp his entire head easily and covered in suction cups that looked to be ringed by tiny jagged teeth.

And it stunk. A rancid, bottom-of-the-bog smell that made his eyes water. He choked back a gag.

"What in the Deep Dark is it?" he breathed.

The Oathguard regarded him curiously for a moment before uttering a single, guttural word. "H'Kaan."

The noise from the shaft grew decidedly louder, but it sounded like a man intermittently grunting in effort and pain rather than another creature. The Oathguard muttered a curse in his own language and stepped towards the opening, pointing the end of his bladestaff at the nearest edge. Then he cocked his head to one side and stepped completely under the opening, holding his arms up.

"Give him to me, Patroniis."

A pair of booted feet appeared, followed immediately by the rest of a man's body in battered Seeker clothing as someone was lowered through the opening. The Oathguard gathered the limp form into his arms easily and carried him over to Triistan's bed. Whomever it was cried out in pain as he was laid down, but the giant's body was blocking Triistan's view and prevented him from seeing their face.

"Salt and stone, its Myles," Tarq rasped.

"Do you have the other one, Patroniis?" the Vanha shot over his shoulder as he began cutting away Myles' pants leg. Triistan glimpsed a confusing mass of blood and blackened, torn flesh before a deep voice spun him around.

"No. They took him." It was Biiko, and he was covered in blood.

The Unbound stepped down from the pile of rubble, placing one hand on Triistan's shoulder and nodding briefly to him as he slipped past. He moved with his typical fluid grace, and it appeared that most of the blood wasn't his own. That didn't stop Triistan from asking though, and once the questions started, he couldn't stop.

"Are you alright? What happened up there? Where's Miikha? What do you mean someone took him? Who -"

Myles screamed in pain, cutting him off.

"Minuerto," the Vanha muttered. "He's going to lose his leg, if he lives that long. Still, a better fate than his friend." He stood, turning to face Biiko.

"Were you followed?"

Biiko shook his head, but to Triistan's surprise, he did not retain his customary silence. In fact, not only did he speak, but his tone seemed oddly quiet and respectful.

"No, Su'ul. Not yet. I slew two of them while protecting him," he jerked his chin towards the bed, "but the others fled after capturing the Reaver. Syr pursues them." The Captain and the others spun towards him.

"Captured? You mean he's still alive?"

Biiko nodded and shrugged. "The last I saw him."

"We have to go after him!" she blurted out.

"You cannot. There will be more," the Vanha warrior answered. "Your little stunt has seen to that. I should slaughter you all for the harm you've caused." He was staring directly at the Captain. To her credit, she bit back a retort, squared her shoulders and faced him openly.

"There are too many," he continued. "If you try to follow your friend now the H'Kaan will do the same to you. But I may have use for you before this is over. We need to leave though, right now."

He glanced at Myles' torn body on the bed. Triistan could see the scout more clearly now, and was sorry for it. Myles' left leg was twisted, with most of the flesh of his thigh hanging in torn shreds. Bone was visible, but it was strangely black, as if it were burned. His clothing was blackened and full of holes, through which Triistan could see large, puckered burn marks. Half of his face was similarly burned, so badly that a crescent of blackened cheekbone peeked through. His chest moved up and down rapidly in quick, ragged gasps.

"You would be doing him a mercy by killing him and leaving him here," the Vanha said.

"No!" Myles' hand shot out and grabbed Tarq's, who was standing closest. "Don't you fucking leave me here, sir! Don't you let those f-fucking… things get me like they got Miikha!" He struggled to rise, then fell back, gasping and moaning.

The giant fixed Captain Vaelysia with those brilliant green eyes. "Do what you will, but I am leaving now. If you cannot keep up, you will all die." He spun on his heel and stalked out of the room, the rest of the *Peregrine's* crew falling back to get out of his way.

The Captain addressed her First Mate.

"Use the sheets to make a litter and bring him with us."

Tarq was moving before she finished her sentence. Triistan went to the foot of the bed to help as the Captain addressed Biiko.

"Is there anything you can do to help with the pain?"

He shook his head. "Not quickly, no. But he will not be conscious long."

She began to turn away but stopped. "What in the bloody dead gods happened out there?"

The Unbound just looked at her, one eyebrow raised.

"Not all of them are dead."

By the time they caught up to the Vanha warrior, Captain Vaelysia was able to coax most of what had happened out of Biiko. Apparently, Kuthan, Linessa and Danor's wife, Syr, were dispatched to scout for the Lord Marshal and find out why he had been delayed. Triistan recalled seeing Crixus speaking with them as they had filed out of the Low Hall after the cun've'dictuus, then he suddenly realized who the Oathguard warrior was who had rescued him.

"Tau Regis," he blurted out as they were jogging down the wide hallway that led back towards the Low Hall. He knew he shouldn't be surprised - besides the Vanha's impressive appearance, there was an aura of power and charisma to him that went well beyond what they had felt from the other godkin. This was someone other men followed instinctively, no matter how strong or powerful they were in their own right. It wasn't hard to see why the Oathguard had chosen him as their captain.

"And they say Reavers are slow," Jaspins quipped and winked. She was jogging next to him, as they each had a corner of Myles' litter, with Wrael and Izenya trailing and supporting the other end. Mercifully, Myles was unconscious, just as Biiko had predicted, but he had not gone quietly: he screamed for several seconds when they lifted him off the bed, so that when he did pass out, Triistan's first thoughts were of relief that the noise had stopped rather than wondering whether he might have died. He was also grateful to be at the head of the litter; there was a foul, rotting smell coming from the man's wounds that turned his stomach.

Commander Tchicatta led the way, with the Captain and First Mate Tarq directly behind him. Biiko followed them, then the litter bearers, then Chelson, Anthon, Brehnl, Jaegus the Younger, Thinman, and finally Creugar guarding their rear.

As they ran, the Captain questioned Biiko. Triistan was struggling with the normally reticent warrior's sudden willingness to talk. He had not heard Biiko speak more than a single sentence since joining the expedition, and hearing him carry on a conversation - even the clipped, awkward one he was currently having with the Captain - was surreal.

"The vents were as you said - they led to the surface. There were several turns, but only one more grate. At the top."

"Where did you come out?"

"Rooftops."

"Really?" Tarq interjected. "That's clever. Keeps them hidden, at least from the ground."

"It was a low building though, not good for scouting."

It had been impossible to tell where they were within the fortress-city, so they set off to scale a tower they could see just a few blocks away and ran headlong into a pitched battle between the four Oathguard - Tau, Kuthan, Linessa and Syr - and a writhing, seething mass of shadow.

Triistan's thoughts went immediately to Danor's story of Heketh and his giant smoke-creature.

Judging from the look he received from Jaspins, she was thinking the same thing.

According to Biiko, however, the shadow was actually a horde of H'Kaan. Like the nagayuun beneath the Rivergate and the creature that had crawled through the sun-shaft, there was something unusual about their skin. Somehow it changed colors, adapting to its surroundings.

"The perfect camouflage," the Firstblade growled.

"But it is more than that. When they are together, they draw the darkness to them."

"What do you mean?" asked the Captain.

Just then they rounded a corner of the wide hall they were jogging down and nearly ran into a huge mass of hair and teeth. Triistan recognized the jagged silver stripes and sable fur of the Apex, the massive monarch jharrl they had encountered just before being captured by the Oathguard. It growled and curled its upper lip, showing a row of curved teeth - each as long as Triistan's dakra - but it stalked aside as if to let them pass. Down this new corridor perhaps fifty yards, Triistan could see why: several of the Vanha were gathered there, including Tau Regis and Crixus. Keeping a wary eye on the huge cat, the Captain led her party past and strode up to the assembled Oathguard as if she herself were one.

He saw the twins, Rhea and Rhiisa in the group, as well as Eso, Fyruun the Fair, Brekha, Ariis (his severed arm covered by a strangely curved shield), Val and Vendros, and finally Protaeus with his sharp beard and cunning eyes. Several others were missing, though, including Danor. Some of the warriors glanced in their direction, but most were listening closely as the Lord Marshall issued orders.

As Captain Vaelysia and the others drew close, the Oathguard snapped off smart salutes and left, leaving Crixus, the twins, and the Lord Marshal. A few of the departing Vanha whistled and shouted as they disappeared down a connecting hallway. They were met with answering roars, and seconds later four more jharrls loped out of a side passage and followed after. The Apex remained where he was, guarding the corridor that led back the way they'd come.

"What can we do to help?" the Captain asked.

Crixus lifted a silver-colored eyebrow but remained silent. He was dressed for war, as he had been when they'd first seen him in the sewers. It suddenly occurred to Triistan that the exotic-looking black armor they all wore must be made from the boiled hides of the H'Kaan. Somehow the Oathguard had preserved its strange coloration, for even standing this close to them, Triistan still had a difficult time focusing on the High Master - whenever the Vanha moved, his shape seemed to blur slightly. Except for his unadorned head and the silver filigree on the hand guards of his massive trident, everything about the High Master was shadow.

Rhea and Rhiisa were similarly clad, but along with the pole arms they had borne in the Low Hall, they now wore matching black helmets that hid their blonde braids. Twin sets of blue eyes glittered fiercely from the "Y" slits cut into the fronts, but his gaze was drawn to the objects draped over their shoulders, which Crixus also carried. He had mistaken it for a cape when he'd first seen the High Master in the sewers, but now realized they were actually weighted nets woven of bluesteel and barbed in the same fashion as the much larger one that had been used to capture the expedition. He wondered how effective they were in combat, then realized with a sudden chill that he was likely to find out all too soon.

"Listen carefully, and do exactly as we tell you. You have not faced anything like this before." Tau swept his gaze over them and it was all Triistan could do not to duck his head. "A large force of H'Kaan Respis - 'Respawn' is the name Danor has given to Ossien's pets in the Low Speech - has infiltrated the edge of the city. The creature that came through the sun-shaft was an advance scout.

"The fact that it found its way down here is ruinous."

"But you killed it," Triistan blurted.

"It matters little. The Respis are of one mind; what one sees, the Swarm sees. We are found, and we must flee to higher ground before Ostenvaard is overrun."

"But as you say, Su'ul, the river no longer holds them," one of the twins said. "Where will we go?"

Captain Vaelysia shook her head in confusion and frustration. "What do you mean? What about the river?"

"There's no time to explain the past two and a half centuries, Captain-"

Just then they heard a low growl that Triistan felt in his feet. They all turned towards the Apex, which was still watching the corridor leading back to their suite. Its huge tail - as thick as Triistan's arm - twitched back and forth in agitation.

"They come. We will explain more later, if there's a chance. For now, we will protect you - do not engage them directly. As you've already guessed, this- " he pounded a gloved fist against his black cuirass, which Triistan could see was scarred and pitted in multiple places, "is made from their hide. It protects us from the dracosa spit, which will eat through your armor, flesh and bones. Come!"

He led them at a run down the same wide corridor that Eso and the others had taken a few moments before, with Crixus at their rear and Rhea and Rhiisa to either side. The floor sloped gradually upwards.

"Vuuthor! Coh'me!" Crixus shouted over his shoulder. The huge saber-tooth roared and fell in behind the High Master, giant black paws thumping softly on the stone floor and mighty lungs huffing echoes off the walls.

As if in answer, a high-pitched, screaming howl rose from somewhere down the twisting labyrinth of passages behind them.

Ostenvaard was breached.

- 21 -

Fight or Flight

All was gray, roiling smoke. It stung Triistan's eyes and mouth, set his lungs on fire. There was a familiar smell and taste to it and after a moment he realized it was a more intense version of the stench coming from the H'Kaan Tau Regis had slain in his room. The rest of the expedition began coughing and cursing as they streamed out of the postern door and into the chaos.

They had taken a wide stone ramp that wound its way back and forth, up through the underkeep, until it eventually deposited them in a cavernous room ringed with massive marble columns stretching up into the shadows like great white tree trunks lurking in the gloom. They did not have torches, and those that lit the hallways below had not followed the ramp as it climbed. What little light there was in this hall bled in through several tall and narrow windows set along two walls: a faint, flickering orange glow that had the look of a distant fire.

Tau led them across a grime-caked floor strewn with rubble. The sprawling chamber must once have been some kind of formal reception area or entry hall, likely intended to impress visitors with its bold splendor. Huge copper braziers hung suspended from chains throughout the room, but it must have been decades since they had last been lit. Long banners dripped from the walls and columns like monstrous curtains of moss, now torn and so badly faded it was impossible to guess their hue in the feeble light. It must have been a spectacular sight in its day; now it seemed a sad and haunted place.

All this he took in at a sprint, for as soon as they reached the level floor of the chamber, Tau ordered Rhea and Rhiisa to take Myles' litter before he started to run. He led them away from a massive set of doors that could have been the main gate on some of the palaces Triistan had seen, towards a hallway off to the side. The corridor apparently flanked the main entrance, ending in the heavy steel door they had just exited.

"Ware the spitters!" the Lord Marshal shouted as they left the building. Rhea lifted Myles and carried him over her left shoulder as easily as Triistan might have hefted a sack of grain, hurrying to join the other Oathguard as they fanned out into a protective arc around the smaller members of the expedition. A temperamental wind gusted hotly across the wide plaza, pushing the smoke in every direction but only rarely tearing gaps in it sufficient to see through. The same flickering orange light Triistan had glimpsed through the windows pulsed through the smoke, though it seemed to be tinged with green, making him wonder what kind of ghastly fire raged just beyond its oily coils.

They heard the clash and grunt of combat off to their left, punctuated by the powerful roars of jharrls. Vuuthor threw his huge head back and answered. As the shattering noise echoed off the surrounding walls, the beast rocked back on its powerful haunches and sprang, vaulting over the Oathguard's picket line and disappearing into the noxious clouds. Something else in that direction screamed - the same piercing howl they had heard below - but the cry was abruptly cut short. Vuuthor's unmistakable voice thundered again and his pack-mates replied.

Tau barked out a command in his own tongue, and while Triistan could not understand him, his meaning became clear as Rhiisa raised a war horn to her lips and blew three blasts, two short followed by one long. She paused, then repeated the pattern.

A moment later, towering dark shapes rose up in the smoke. Triistan's heart stopped when he saw how large they were, dwarfing the Vanha they had seen thusfar.

"Doesn't anything ever get smaller in this fucking place?" someone muttered from behind him. *Thinman*, he thought.

"Steady lads," the Captain growled.

But they were just the shadows cast by more Oathguard making their way through the smoke; the uncertain light behind them was enlarging their shadows in the shifting haze. Ariis appeared first, helping Brekha, who looked to have sustained a nasty wound to her right thigh. Somewhere beyond the smoke the terrible sounds of combat continued: snarls, roars and the teeth-grinding howls of the H'Kaan. He heard a much more human voice roaring in the Vanha tongue as well.

Linessa saluted the Lord Marshal and addressed him in that same language, but switched abruptly to what they called "Low Speech" when she noticed the expedition behind him.

"Did you find Danor's group?" Tau was asking.

She shook her head. "No, Su'ul. We were attacked just beyond the parade grounds. It was all we could do to hold there."

"How many?"

She frowned through the "Y" cut in her glistening black helmet, shrugging her broad shoulders.

"Only three score. Mostly hounds, but two dracosa as well. Well - one now," she added, flicking black slime off of the long blade of her greatsword. It bubbled and smoked on the flagstone where it struck, although the bluish-black steel of her blade seemed unaffected. Triistan thought of the pitted scars he had seen in the watchtower they had scaled on that first night here.

" 'Thor's timing was fortuitous, as always," she continued. "Kuthan and the pack can handle the leftovers now that he's there. But the main force that followed you is massing to our east. At least ten fists, Su'ul."

Five hundred, Triistan thought with dread. *Salt and stone.*

"Trying to cut us off."

"Likely. You know one of the L'suu is with them, yes? Hammerhand. And he's mounted."

Several of the surrounding Oathguard swore vehemently.

"Yiin," Tau answered clearly, cutting through the murmurs. "It is Sithis. I tried to draw him out, away from Ostenvaard, but he ignored me and led his force straight here."

Linessa cocked her head. "Doing his master's bidding then. A probe to test his new hounds?"

"Possibly, but we've no time to figure it out now. We need to get everyone out. If we can get through the Weir, we can hold them back and decide what to do from there."

"Interesting..." Linessa paused. She seemed about to say something else, but then shook her head sharply. "Never mind. Avoid the Causeway, Su'ul - he'll place his main strength there as a blocking force if he indeed means to cut us off. Flank him to the east, around the academy campus." She looked at the other Oathguard.

"Give me Fyruun, Val and Vendros. With Kuthan and the pack we'll hit his lines from the west, then meet you at the Weir."

They gripped each other's forearms.

"They are beneath us in the underkeep as well, so watch your back. Find Danor and the others - and Syr if you can," Tau said.

She nodded confidently. "Khazar is with the pack. I planned to send him after Atuu before we were attacked. He will find his sire, and Danor. If Syr isn't with them by now..." she trailed off with a slow shrug. Tau nodded, and she saluted him before jogging back out into the smoke, shouting for Kuthan. Triistan heard the fight still going on, though it had grown decidedly quieter. He was relieved when Kuthan's booming voice called back. He almost sounded like he was enjoying himself.

"Let's go."

Tau led them away from the commotion. They drifted through the smoke, slipping down an alley that was wide enough for three of the Oathguard to walk abreast. Tau and Crixus led, followed by the expedition bunched in a loose group. Ariis and Eso followed next with Brekha limping between them, then Protaeus, and finally the twins providing the vanguard. Despite Brekha's injured leg, the Vanha kept up a swift walk, which meant Triistan and his comrades were forced to jog to keep pace. At least they were leaving the noxious fumes behind; the back of his throat felt like he'd swallowed a mouthful of nettles.

They moved quietly, slipping through the back alleys and side streets that wound their way through the sprawling city. Triistan thought of a desiccated network of veins that once pumped life through what was now just a vast corpse.

He had no idea what time it was, other than it was night and there was no moon. There were no clouds either, so the stars shone hot and white against an endless black void. The buildings rose on either side of them, all different shapes and sizes, white marble and other exotic stone glowing ghostly in the starlight. Delicate footbridges arched overhead, some with the familiar hanging gardens slung from their undersides like the ones they had seen during their first foray into this strange place. Triistan remembered the huge, spider-like thing he had glimpsed then, wondering if it had been one of the creatures that hunted them now.

The acrid stench of the fire was still on the air, though none of the oily smoke was actually visible. Occasionally they heard the chilling howls of the H'Kaan coming from different directions; sometimes very close, but most fairly distant. Each time they heard the cries, Tau turned them down another side-street to lead them further away. Triistan had become disoriented in the process, but had the sense they were drifting consistently southward and wondered how far away the Weir was.

Another chorus of howls rose from somewhere close ahead. They always seemed to be just in front of the group, but they still had not seen...

He stopped abruptly. "Something's wr-"

Creugar collided with him, nearly knocking him to the ground.

"Aiii, monkey-man!" he whispered. "Warn Creugar first before you stop so, lest my axe carve a deeper crack in your buttocks!"

Tau had also stopped at almost the same instant, hand up, motioning for silence. Next to him, Crixus was eyeing the rooftops warily. He whispered something to the Lord Marshal as he reached for the steel net draped over one shoulder, unfastening a strap that held it there like a cape. Triistan heard the soft hiss of oiled chain links behind him and knew the twins were doing the same. He felt a chill race up his spine. They must have noticed the same thing.

The Lord Marshal motioned towards the rooftops, mouthing the word "trap". He held his bladestaff out for emphasis, his message clear: ready your weapons.

Jaspins stepped close. "How did you know?" she breathed into Triistan's ear. He turned his face towards her to answer.

"No screams from the south," he answered softly. He was momentarily distracted by how close she was, especially her lips, which curled ever so slightly when he made eye contact with her.

"We are being herded," she breathed. He nodded while swallowing the lump in his throat. He wasn't sure if it was fear because of their situation or something else; he only knew he suddenly felt an odd mixture of relief and disappointment when she stepped away.

Tau motioned them forward again, moving with slow caution. Heads swung back and forth, scanning the eaves and bridges overhead, as well as the shuttered windows and doors to either side. The light had not changed - the stars still glittered obliviously overhead - but all seemed darker, the shadows deeper.

They proceeded in this fashion for close to an hour. Triistan felt only the smallest relief as they passed from a narrow alley into a sprawling octagonal courtyard ringed with taller buildings, each one set at an angle facing the center and separated by lanes that emanated from the courtyard like the spokes of a great wheel. The center was dominated by a huge stonewood tree, its grey-green trunk as wide as a tower and reaching up at least a hundred feet before the first massive branches split off to form the canopy, which stretched out in all directions over the courtyard and several surrounding blocks. The branches were widely-spaced and the foliage hung in tight bunches, no doubt allowing plenty of sunlight through in the daytime. Now, though Triistan caught glimpses of stars here and there, the gloom grew deeper still, and the shadows seemed to close in around them.

His forearms and shoulders ached from the tension and from gripping the hilt of his kilij so tightly. Sweat trickled down his back, stuck his hair to his face and neck. Whatever wind had swirled the smoke earlier had died off, leaving in its wake a thick, humid stillness.

Tau led them to the left, skirting the outer edge of the courtyard. He stopped at the entrance to each bisecting alley between houses, motioned them to wait, then drifted a few yards down the lane by himself. There he would pause for several excruciating moments, waiting and listening while Triistan strained to hear over the thunder of his own heart. Then he would return and quickly motion them on to the next intersection. They had crossed three streets in this fashion when Triistan noticed that the foliage above them was moving. He lifted his face expectantly, hoping the breeze would reach them on the street, just as Tau signaled them to halt at the corner of the next lane.

A few leaves drifted down towards him, as large as his whole head, twirling in lazy spirals on their way to the ground. Strange that the wind did not seem to catch them and send them skittering sideways, especially as strong as it seemed to be blowing in the limbs above them, setting the shadows there jumping -

"ABOVE US!" Crixus suddenly hissed. "They're in the tree!!"

"They draw the darkness to them", Biiko had said. Now Triistan understood what the Unbound had meant. The *shadows* were moving, not the branches or the foliage.

"This way! MOVE!!" Tau shouted and led them down the street he had just been about to clear.

As the others leapt forward to follow him, the shadows detached themselves from the canopy, scores of them flowing like smoke down the trunk of the tree, while dozens more simply let go and dropped, as if the night sky had shattered and now rained pieces of itself down upon them. The worst part was that they did so in near silence: there were none of the howling screams they had heard previously - just the rustle of movement, like the soft sigh of rain cascading down through the jungle, or the final gasp of a dying man.

They ran.

There was no more caution, no more hope of slipping past Ossien's forces. Somehow, they had wandered right into the main body. All this time Triistan had been picturing mindless beasts, but the thing leading them - "Sithis", Tau had called it - was smart enough to divide his forces and trap them. Their only option now was to make a dash for The Weir before they were overrun.

What happens then? How could a wall or a gate stop these things, when they could suspend themselves upside down from bare stone, or flow through and over the limbs and trunk of a tree like black water?

Somewhere behind them rose an eerie clicking, hissing noise, growing louder as they fled. He risked a glance back over his shoulder and saw the first surge of their pursuers enter the alley, climbing over each other as they advanced en masse, like a writhing river of shadows. It was difficult to make anything specific out in the roiling swarm of beasts, just vague glimpses of legs, tails and claws - and teeth.

He ran harder, heart rattling against the inside of his chest, blood pounding in his temples, breath ragged. The wound on his calf burned. The flesh around it was tight, affecting his gait and making him work harder. But the pain galvanized him as well, reminding him of the horrors that awaited if these things caught up to him. He gritted his teeth and pushed himself harder.

They skidded around the curved corner of some kind of amphitheater, only to find another group of H'Kaan waiting for them, perhaps twenty yards down the street. There were roughly a dozen, very similar to the thing that had entered Triistan's room through the sunshaft. A "hound" they had called it. Perhaps it was one of the groups that had helped drive them into the ambush.

Tau and Crixus never slowed. They moved with the fluid grace of a river, and fell upon their enemies with all the fury of the sea.

No more than five paces from the H'Kaan, both warriors leapt high into the air. Crixus hurled his chain net at three that made the mistake of jumping to meet them. The beasts crashed down in a tangle of dark, slimy limbs, snapping and spinning to escape but only succeeding in cutting themselves to ribbons on the cruel barbs woven into the net's mesh. Ignoring them, the High Master brought his huge trident to bear on three more, gutting one and forcing the other two to fall back.

Tau spun his whole body as he came down, one end of his bladestaff tucked under his bicep, braced against his armored back, leveraging the other six feet of staff and deadly bluesteel as an extension of his own arm. He cut two of the monsters in half as he landed, still spinning. With a flick of his wrist the bladestaff rotated in the opposite direction so he could slip his hands into the silver-guarded grips. He was a blur, slashing and stabbing left and right as he waded through the H'Kaan within reach. All four were dead in the few seconds it took the rest of the party to get there.

Barely slowing, Triistan and the others followed the warriors through the carnage. The remaining Oathguard never broke formation, holding the company's rear and demonstrating their discipline while Crixus dispatched one of the last two, almost casually catching it in mid-leap on the end of his trident and using the creature's momentum to lift it high into the air before smashing it head-first into the flagstones. Too casual, perhaps, as the move left an opening for the last attacker.

It came at them impossibly fast, thrashing its body from side to side as it charged into their midst. The expedition members had stayed clustered in a tight ball, trusting the larger Oathguard to defend them, and now they could not get out of each other's way. It battered them aside, sending the First Mate, Anthon and Lieutenant Jaspins sprawling. The Captain and Commander Tchicatta were on the wrong side of Tarq, trying to get around him, and with Jaspins down, Triistan and Chelson found themselves staring eye to soulless eye with the beast. It lunged at Chelson, almost too quick to see. He raised his arm reflexively and the H'Kaan's jaws snapped shut on it. With a rapid twist of its head it tore his arm and most of his shoulder completely off. Chelson went down, screaming, while it whipped back around and came at Triistan, jaws gaped wide to reveal two nested rows of curved teeth now slick with Chelson's blood. His brought his sword up in one of the defensive positions Biiko had taught him, but it was too slow and his legs weren't in the right position. For the second time that day, Triistan thought he was going to die.

The H'Kaan crashed into him, knocking him over backwards and landing with all of its weight on top of him. The impact drove the breath from his lungs and sent stars exploding across his vision. He tried desperately to take a breath, but his entire body was pinned, his arms and sword trapped uselessly against his chest. He knew in the next instant that the monster's teeth were going to snap shut over his head...

But they didn't. Instead, he felt the terrible pressure of its weight lift. Opening his eyes, he found Creugar and Biiko looking down at him. Biiko's face was inscrutable as always, but in his eyes, Triistan thought he saw the glimmer of something that might have been pride.

They hauled him to his feet. His head swam and something was wrong with his hearing. A few steps away, Captain Vaelysia and First Mate Tarq were bent over Chelson. His eyes stared emptily at the night sky, until Tarq reached out and gently brushed them closed.

Sound came rushing back, as if he had just surfaced from being underwater, and he realized Creugar was talking to him.

"... clumsy a kill as I've ever seen, monkey-man," the huge Reaver was saying, "but Creugar is glad to find the beast did not slay you as well."

"Kill?" he mumbled, still staring at Chelson's ravaged body. It could just as easily have been him. How was he still alive? He looked down at his hands, but they were empty.

"My sword!" he coughed, still trying to catch his breath as they pulled him into a stumbling run. Jaspins fell in beside him, carrying two of the curved kilij. One was covered in black gore, which she passed to him with a slight smirk.

"You'll want to clean that off when you get a chance. No telling what that spawn-juice will do to it over the long term."

"I... I killed it?" he managed. The stance he tried was designed to impale a charging opponent, but his feet and legs were all wrong and he didn't think he'd gotten his weapon up in time.

"You're welcome," was all she said as Tau urged them to run faster. But Triistan hardly heard her; his mind was still stuck on Chelson's dead stare.

The Lord Marshal led them diagonally across the street, aiming for an alleyway off to their left, hoping to make the turn and get out of sight before their pursuers entered the avenue behind them. They turned right at another intersection a moment later, down a narrow lane, forcing the Oathguard to move in single file. Triistan felt a strange sensation in his head, a warm rush from his brow back down to the base of his neck, as if someone had just poured warm water on his scalp. Eso's voice suddenly hissed in his mind.

"Ware the roofs! They're coming down the -"

But her warning ended in a terrible scream of pain that threatened to split his skull open and made him claw at his ears. Like her voice, the scream was somehow inside his head. Others around him were clutching their own heads as he spun around.

Although he and his fellow Seekers were small enough to maneuver around each other, the larger Vanha were much more constricted by the alley. Eso and Brekha had been following just behind the Expedition members and he could see them towering over Creugar's head. Eso's back was turned and she was clawing frantically at something on her face and hair. Still screaming, she spun back around, mad with pain, while a pair of dark shapes dropped from the walls to land on either side behind her.

Triistan barely noticed them: his eyes were glued to the horrific wreckage of Eso's head and hands. Like the other Vanha, she was also wearing the strange armor wrought from the dead H'Kaan hides, but she wore no helmet, and her arms were bare below the elbow. Wherever there should have been flesh was now a ruined, boiling mess of blood, muscle and bones.

"Su'ul! Recuun a'namonaas!" another, deeper voice interjected in Triistan's mind, smothering the scream. It was Crixus, and somehow Triistan understood his meaning, if not the words themselves: *Su'ul, remember who you are!*

The screaming stopped, leaving a burning sensation behind his eyes, as if he'd been staring at one of the suns. More shouts and screams sounded from further back down the alley. Eso fell to her knees, giving him a better view of what was going on as Creugar tried to get around her, brandishing his axe. Whatever had come down the walls was tearing Brekha apart, while Protaeus and Ariis tried to fend them off. They were dark, muscular beasts, roughly man-sized but with long, thick tails that whipped from side to side, and they moved as quickly as the hounds. Unlike the hounds, however, these appeared to be fighting on two legs. Ariis dropped to a knee with one on his back, its tail wrapped around his midsection and long, reptilian jaws closing on his shoulder. He went down in a confusion of snapping teeth, spit, blood and shadow.

Tau and Crixus were shouting something from behind Triistan, and someone was grabbing him by the shoulder, pulling. He felt the warm rush slide over his scalp again, but this time it was much weaker, Eso's voice in his mind just a ragged sob.

"Flee..."

The grip on his shoulder tightened painfully and he was spun around. It was Biiko.

"This is not your Path," the warrior said simply. More screams and shouts.

Triistan tried to twist out of his grasp. "Let me go! We have to help them!" He clutched the Unbound's fist, struggling to wrench it away, but it was like trying to rip out a tree root with his bare hand.

Biiko hauled him away from the chaos, towards Crixus and the Lord Marshal.

"Captain!" Tau roared. "There is nothing your people can do! Get them out of the way!"

They squeezed against either side of the alley as he waded through their midst, bladestaff flashing. Suddenly he stopped and shouted. "Eso, NO!"

A brilliant flash left Triistan momentarily blinded. When his vision cleared, he saw one of the strangest scenes he had ever witnessed.

Eso was still on her knees where she had slumped a moment ago. But now her back was ramrod straight, her shoulders square, her head bowed as if in prayer. Her arms were held out before her, ruined hands clenched into fists. Strips of bloody, smoking flesh hung in tatters from both arms and hands and he could see the white gleam of bone in several places. But that was not what held his attention.

The Oathguard was burning.

Blue fire danced around each fist and writhed in her hair. The tendons and muscles of her forearms tightened as she clenched them harder, until her hands and arms began to tremble from the effort. The fire dripped as if she were squeezing blue incandescent blood from her wounds. It spattered onto the cobblestone street where it flared briefly before vanishing, like sparks thrown from a blacksmith's wheel.

She staggered to her feet, the fire still burning around her hands, cerulean power dripping from her fists. She lifted her face and Triistan took an involuntary step back.

She was a terrible sight to behold. The injured side of her head burned brightly, and while her undamaged right eye was fixed on Tau, her left was an empty socket spitting the same eerie blaze. Vaguely familiar glyphs appeared all over her armor, their bluish glow faint at first but brightening quickly. Triistan recognized several arxhemical symbols, but most of the markings were foreign to him.

"A've necuuto fiero," Eso's voice whispered again in Triistan's head. *To the last ash of my fire...*

The beasts behind her suddenly howled and leapt at her just as Tau spun back around, arms outstretched.

"GET DOWN!" He tackled four of the confused Seekers, shielding them with his body. Biiko shoved Triistan to the ground.

There was a sizzling, crackling noise as the howls turned to high-pitched wails of pain and terror. An instant later, the air was rent by a deafening clap of thunder. The ground trembled beneath him for several seconds, as a cloud of dust and small debris clattered down around them.

When the rumbling subsided, they stumbled to their feet, coughing and calling out for Eso and the others. Triistan could barely hear his own voice for the ringing in his ears, so he had no idea if anyone was answering.

Two charred husks lay smoldering where Eso had stood just moments ago. Judging from their vaguely familiar shapes, they were the remains of the two dracosa "spitters" that had wounded her and savaged Brekha. The flagstones of the street were cracked and white, the way stone will react after being exposed to intense heat, although Triistan had felt none during the blast. Immediately to either side, the walls of the buildings lining the alley were pitted where sizable pieces of stone had spalled off, and just beyond the damaged area and H'Kaan remains he could see Brekha's torn body, partially buried in rubble. To Triistan's surprise and great relief, Protaeus and Rhea appeared in the haze, the latter still carrying the unconscious Myles over her shoulder. Rhiisa and Ariis appeared a moment later just behind them, the one-armed Vanha looking remarkably hale given that the last Triistan had seen of him was just before he disappeared in a frenzied attack by one of the dracosa.

Of Eso, however, there was no trace.

The Lord Marshal dropped to one knee and reached out to touch the damaged area of the street, head bowed.

Crixus spoke, his voice sounding cruel and harsh in the aftermath of what they had just witnessed. "Su'ul, we have to leave. The swarm will be on us any moment. Our only chance is to reach The Weir and make our stand there."

As if in answer, another chorus of screaming howls rose from somewhere close by.

Tau stood and scanned the faces of Triistan and his comrades.

"And what of them, my pragmatic friend?" he asked with a sad smile. "We might win that race, but they certainly won't."

Crixus shrugged his broad shoulders. "Perhaps the H'Kaan will follow us. Either way, they chose this path; they came where it is death to trespass."

Tau's glance strayed to Biiko.

"Perhaps..."

Suddenly a deep, familiar voice growled down to them from somewhere above.

"I suggest you minuertos take up this little chat sometime in the future. Unless you fancy being torn apart, eaten and eventually shat out by four hundred or so H'Kaan." Triistan could just make out a bulky silhouette on the roof above them, but he would know that gravelly rasp anywhere: Danor. He felt rather than heard a low rumble as another shape appeared beside the healer, this one the unmistakable head of one of the jharrls. Triistan assumed it must be Atuu.

"Where are they?" Tau called up to him. Danor chuckled.

"Oh not far, but your rear is clear for the nonce, Su'ul. Look out below."

He clambered over the side of the low parapet wall he was leaning on, lowered himself until his arms were fully extended, then dropped the remaining fifteen feet or so to the ground. He landed awkwardly, cursing, but managed not to go sprawling on his backside.

"You're no sapling anymore you fuundaris idiomata," he growled to himself, straightening and working at a kink in his back with one hand. The other held the huge lucerne hammer he had left his apartment with, its head now covered in black gore. He caught Triistan's eye and winked before addressing the Lord Marshal.

"Helix and Arthos are leading them on a merry chase, but that isn't likely to last long. I broke off when I saw and heard the Necuuto, and I'd bet my left bullock they'll work back this way as well. Who..." he trailed off and looked around at the others.

"Eso," Tau answered gravely. Danor's face dropped.

"Ah," he said quietly. "Of course. That much punch, it'd have to be either her or Crixy. She was that bad off?"

"Yiin. Two dracosa ambushed us, and she took the worst of it trying to protect Brekha. We lost her as well. What of Syr?"

A brief smile flitted across Danor's lips, but it did not remain. "Found her. She's with the other two. Braxus is gone though."

Several of the other Oathguard cursed, but Triistan was thinking of something else.

"What about Miikha? Did she find him?"

"I'm afraid not, Salty. Your friend will be halfway back to the Worm's lair by now, wishing he'd shown more appreciation for our generous hospitality."

Crixus snorted bitterly. "It won't be long before he'll be wishing he were dead."

Captain Vaelysia grabbed his arm. "What do you mean? Why did they take him in the first place?"

Lord Marshal Tau shook his head. "There's no time. If we make the Weir, perhaps there will be then. You'll have to bear your own wounded now; we can't leave Brekha's body here. Rhea, Rhiisa, will you carry her?"

They answered together, and Rhea passed Myles' limp body over to Creugar. The injured Seeker moaned in pain as Creugar hoisted him over his shoulder.

"Ah, still some fight left in you, eh? Good, good. Creugar does not carry dead men - they smell even worse than you do." Myles muttered a colorful expletive and the big Reaver chuckled. "Of course, the live ones be complaining a lot more."

They set off at a fast jog, with Danor leading them. Every so often, Triistan would catch a glimpse of Atuu above them, stalking along one of the roofs or leaping across an alley or street from one building to the next; a silent shadow against the star-filled sky. As they moved through a maze of side streets, the healer explained that Syr and the others would pull the H'Kaan as far west as they could before turning southward and making for the Plaza, the large span of open ground between the edge of the city and its southern entrance.

"How do they plan to break away?" Tau asked.

Danor pulled up in the shadow of a taller building on the edge of an intersection of larger streets. Triistan saw the glint of his teeth as he smiled his not-smile. "Wormy's not the only one who can lay an ambush. Justice and his group are waiting for them."

"Linessa found you then," the Lord Marshal said.

"Aye. All in a lather, too. Said she was supposed to create a diversion for you but couldn't find the fuundaris swarm, ha! Sent us off to find them, while she, Justice and the others rigged a little surprise party. Was only dumb luck that we were close by when they came after you."

Tau gestured out at the intersection. "She thought they'd be waiting for us on the Causeway."

The street running perpendicular to the one they had just traversed was considerably broader, and paved with large flagstones rather than the smaller cobblestones they had seen in most of the alleys and side streets. To their left, the vague outline of towers and a high wall loomed behind the streetscape like a strangely-shaped storm front drifting in from the south. The broad avenue was empty as far as they could see in both directions, but in the darkness that was not very far.

"Oh, no doubt they are, Su'ul," Danor finally whispered and pointed diagonally across the intersection.

Triistan strained to see what he was pointing at, but saw nothing except ornate stone and wood structures festooned with vines and other undergrowth. The other side of the street was darker, so it was more difficult to discern details, but he certainly did not see an army of H'Kaan gathered there.

He was about to ask what Danor was pointing at when Crixus growled, "Sithis. On a longstrider."

"Minuerto!" more than one of the other Vanha breathed behind him.

"Shit is right, brodiirs," answered Danor. "We're about to find ourselves in a mountain of it."

"Danor, lead them back one street, then up to the Crossroads." Tau's voice was quiet, but heavy with authority. He scanned the group. "Take Ariis, the twins and Protaeus with you."

Danor frowned, nodding slowly. But it was Protaeus who voiced the question they were all thinking.

"And where will you be, Su'ul? We will need all hands on the defenses."

The Lord Marshal locked eyes with Crixus, who nodded once, his eyes flashing brightly.

"We will not yield Ostenvaard without a price."

"Then do not send us away, Su'ul," answered Ariis passionately. "Let us all stand together!" The other Oathguard growled their agreement.

Tau shook his head. "This is not our last stand, brodiirs, not yet. You have to get to the Weir before the swarm does. If you succeed, we stand a good chance of wiping them out. But Sithis cannot be allowed to reach it. He knows our tactics, our defenses. Protaeus will need all of you, and you may yet have to fight your way through. This is the only way."

Danor made a whistling noise. "Yiin, it's going to be a big mountain."

Tau turned to the grizzled healer. "How many do you think he kept with him?"

"No more than two fists, if your initial estimates were right. They'll only be a distraction for the two of you - but you're going to have your hands full with the Worm's warling, not to mention there's no telling when the rest of the Respiis will show up..."

"Then we'll just have to be quick."

"That is a longstrider, Su'ul." Protaeus countered. "There's nothing quick about killing one of them. At least let us deal with the swarm so you can focus on Sithis and his mount."

Tau shook his head again. "I don't intend to kill it."

"You don't? Then what -" Protaeus stopped short. "No, Su'ul, that's just a theory, I -"

"But it's your theory. And it's based on a real application that worked brilliantly. It's sound and I trust it."

"But that was completely different! The Worm's vault and its environment were static. This is all kinetic - I wanted to experiment with some of the Respiis first, get a chance to observe -"

Tau smiled. "Then you'd better take good notes, brodiir. Danor, take them to the Crossroads and wait there until we're able to draw out his reserves. Once they've committed, take the Causeway."

"Why not just stick to the back alleys?" asked Rhiisa.

Danor was scratching the stubble on his considerable chin and nodding slowly. "'Long Tau thinks he'll be waiting for us there as well, and I'd guess he's probably right. Sith's grown much smarter since we last saw him. Our best chance will be straight up the middle; by the time they realize where we are, it'll be too late." He shrugged and slapped the Lord Marshal on the back.

"Or we'll be dead. Either way, we'll be clear of the shit."

Tau gripped him on the shoulder. "Take care of them, old friend."

Danor grunted. "Who's going to take care of me, and who are you calling old?"

Triistan hesitated as the groups began to separate, wanting to say something to the two Vanha commanders but feeling foolish and unsure of what was appropriate. Before he could sort out the right words, Biiko interrupted by stepping up to Tau and Crixus.

"I will stay," he said bluntly.

Crixus bristled. "We did not ask for your help, Patroniis. We do not need it."

"I have walked that path. If you do not accept it, you will fail, as will the rest of us."

Crixus snorted in disgust.

"So if you stay, we win?"

"If I stay, our Path continues to the next Divergence."

"Well, that's comforting," quipped Danor.

"We cannot give what we do not possess. Comfort was the cold, certain decline towards entropy, taken from us when the Forge of Stars was sundered."

Triistan felt a chill ripple along his spine.

"In Ahmet's name, we bring hope and vengeance, though not in equal measures."

"We welcome your aid, Patroniis," Lord Marshal Tau said with a meaningful glance to silence Crixus. "Now let's go pick a fight with the enemy, brodiir.'"

They turned to step out onto the main street, ignoring Triistan. He reached out and grabbed Biiko's arm.

"Biiko, I -" There was so much he wanted to say, to ask, but all he could think to do was mumble "Be careful."

The warrior fixed Triistan with his strange golden eyes. "That is not my purpose but... thank you."

Then he left, slipping after the two Oathguard as they stepped out from behind the cover of the building. Before Triistan could follow, he heard Danor's voice.

"Wrong way, Salty. You'll have a fine view where we're going, so long as we hurry."

Heart racing, Triistan followed the giant onto a connecting side street, where the others waited. Danor pushed his way to the front and led them at a brisk pace, not slowing until he reached an intersection several moments later. He turned left on another broad avenue, keeping as close to the front of the buildings as possible. This area was badly damaged, so the remains of broken columns and other debris made the footing treacherous, but the overgrowth swallowing the ruins gave them excellent cover.

Danor slowed as they approached the end of the last building on the street, beyond which sprawled a circular plaza with a huge statue occupying the center. It was covered in vines, but Triistan could make out four vaguely-shaped pillars with some kind of large, rectangular dais between them. The flagstones of the street they were on ended at the intersection, where they transitioned to mosaic tiles, joined with such craftsmanship that not a single weed had found its way through. The colors of the tiles were muted in the starlight, but he presumed they depicted some kind of huge mural.

A sweeping second-floor balcony followed the curved facade of the building they now stood before, dripping vines, moss and other overgrowth around them like a green waterfall. Triistan felt a surge of relief as they ducked into its deep shadows. They made their way along the structure as it traced the outer edge of the circular plaza on their right. When they reached the end, they found that the last ten feet or so of the balcony overhead had collapsed long ago, its remains now lying in a heap of overgrown rubble. They climbed it easily and soon found themselves with an excellent vantage point looking back down the wide road the Oathguard called The Causeway.

It also afforded Triistan a decent view of the mosaic covering the plaza, which depicted several scenes laid out around the perimeter. The one adjacent to them showed figures in elaborate dress evaluating something in a barred wagon. He recognized Shan the Stormfather among the figures and assumed the others were probably Young Gods as well, wondering why their expressions seemed so horrified. He looked more closely at the cage. The thing inside was a pregnant woman with wings and it dawned on him: this must be the story Danor had told them about Ossien's "Ternion". The section he was looking at showed the moment just before the other gods captured him and exiled him here, to Ostenvaard. He wondered briefly what became of the abominations after Ossien's capture. *And what of the child..?*

"There they are," Captain Vaelysia whispered.

She pointed down the Causeway, back in the direction they had come from originally, where the two Vanha commanders were striding out to the center of the avenue. Biiko followed just behind them, looking almost like a child from here.

They stopped at the center of the intersection, and for a moment Triistan wondered if they had been mistaken; that there was no

H'Kaan commander waiting in ambush and this was all just a waste of time.

Then the overgrown remains of the building on the opposite side of the intersection began to move...

- 22 -

The Dust Settles

Temos watched as the world fell apart.

The rubble began to fall gently down while the dust rushed up and past them all. The thundering noise that Theander Kross had used to collapse the buildings still rang in his ears and echoed off the structures that had escaped his power. The calculated failure of that many buildings had crushed the H'Kaan caught beneath them and managed to stem the seemingly endless tide that had been pouring in from that direction.

It hadn't been more than a heartbeat or two before the scene changed again, the dust condensing and curving back towards the surface. Sand shifted and blocks began to roll or deform into new shapes, like some unseen giant hand was quickly sculpting the remains into new forms: walls and buttresses replaced the buildings and passages alike. Some distance away, shielded behind the lines of Thundering Lance soldiers and Laegis Templar lancers, one of the arxhemists that Richard Lockewood had brought with him was hard at work.

Jem Nevai was a slip of a woman, tucked inside the bulky, wide-sleeved robe that the rest of her order wore. Her face was hidden in the shadows of the hood drawn over her head, but even at a distance Temos could see the wisps of smoke curling away from her exposed arms as she directed the bricks and blocks from the remains of Theander's explosions to fill the roads and corridors that led into the northern reaches of the city. Through the power of her arxhemestry, she was literally building walls in minutes that would have normally taken months. The question now was whether her life would give out before her work was complete.

Temos watched Jem collapse, as one of her fellow arxhemists caught her and lowered her softly to the ground. He knew that grand feats of their magic could kill them, and what he'd just seen certainly qualified. It was the second such wall she had erected, covering both the north and south approaches, sealing off the square save for the eastern path they'd come in on and the dominating bulk of the Temple to the west that the Lockewoods were so intent to secure.

Captain Ardell was next to Temos, urging him to help reposition a series of hastily erected spiked barriers to the front, to fortify the only accessible entrance left. As he worked, the painful protests of his body grew louder, finally overcoming the pain and urgency of the moment that he'd been living in ever since...

We abandoned Casselle.

Somewhere in his head, he knew it had been him all along, but dragging the wounded back to the square already under heavy siege by the H'Kaan had eaten up every measure of his attention and energy until this moment. How many hours had they lost since then? The Long Evening was upon them, which meant too many had passed. He was bruised and bloodied, his limbs aching and sore from running and fighting. How many feints, counterattacks and rallies had they performed, until a desperate act of magic was used to give them even a moment's respite? As much as he hoped Jem Nevai would survive, the weight of what they had done back in that street now felt every bit as sharp and painful as a knife to the chest.

No, he thought. *Captain Ardell had done the right thing, he'd minimized the casualties to the Laegis under his command. It wasn't his fault or any of the other Templar.* Temos let the fault rest fully on his shoulders.

I abandoned her.

It didn't matter that he was the only one who had spoken up at the time, he had deferred to the Captain's judgement, as he had been trained to do. He remembered a promise that they would return in strength once they had reunited with the main force in the square. Part of him knew that even a great commander like Greffin Ardell was in no real position to promise anything of the sort.

When they arrived at the outskirts of the square, they faced the grim truth. Their fortified position was not safe; it was a killing field. The Thundering Lance were an experienced cavalry force, but less effective when not on horseback. Beset on all sides by H'Kaan, they were suffering heavy casualties, pulling into tighter formations closer to the base of the temple.

At the time Temos was surprised he and his squad had even managed to cut through the line of H'Kaan in front of them to rejoin those in the middle. It was nothing short of years of superior training wrapped inside a small miracle.

They had barely caught their breath and handed off Passal Cooper to one of the field surgeons when Commander Zan Cohl had appeared out of the crowd, bright armor stained by black blood, ordering them to shore up a position that was threatening to collapse. The afternoon was filled with the roars of men and women fighting bravely, punctuated by the terrified screams of those who died around them.

He'd caught glimpses of familiar faces during the fighting, other Laegis, though he had no sense of who was accounted for or missing. When the H'Kaan pulled back, the defenders seized the opportunity to drag their wounded behind the lines and take a break, if just for water. Gunnar, in bad shape but still fighting better than most of them, said that he'd seen Duran Holst's knot return, missing only one. Unfortunately, John Kettle's four Templars hadn't been seen since they'd left that morning. He'd also heard that the Templar Lancers had suffered worse, having been deployed to a weak position where their polearms proved less effective against the H'Kaan than expected. Those that survived had been used to reinforce another section of the constantly shrinking square.

Between larger waves, Finn Archer had questioned why they hadn't attempted to break free of the city, to return to the base camp outside of Lex Vellos. Ardell shut those questions down quickly. There'd be time for discussion later, the implication being that questions were reserved for those that survived.

At that point, Temos had swallowed a suggestion for a second push to save Casselle, and perhaps any other living Templars. Given that the day was waning, he knew it was likely to be shot down as well, but during that slight lull, he almost worked up enough courage to suggest it.

At that moment, the largest group of H'Kaan yet descended upon them. They spilled out of the northern and southern avenues like a river bursting through a cracked dam.

The soldiers scrambled back to the lines, exhausted but defiant. Temos wasn't sure what was driving the others, but he was working off of a desperate desire to make amends with someone who was most likely already dead.

With no warning, the arxhemists had picked that moment to begin their work. Theander Kross leveled the buildings first. Temos almost fell over as the air buckled and the ground heaved from the thunderous roar. On unsteady feet, he and the others watched as Jem Nevai took the remains and rebuilt them, making the square into a fortress.

He knew that had only been moments ago, moments in a day that seemed to gain time rather than lose it. Now Temos was wringing the last bit of use from his stiff muscles, moving the spiked wooden barricades from where they had been used on the northern and southern approaches to the eastern side. With the walls Jem had erected, it was the only entrance left, ending at the temple on the western side of the square.

Unless they climb over the wall, he mused. They seemed pretty adept at climbing. He tried not to think about it anymore as he wrestled with the fortification. He was grateful when Jhet showed up beside him and helped drag it into place. His squadmate looked like hell, which could only mean that he looked no better, probably worse.

After they placed the barricade, the two of them moved back towards the middle, to meet up with Captain Ardell and check on Passal. The rows of the dead and dying had greatly increased. It smelled horrible. There were precious few with training in the healing arts. Many more had been temporarily drafted just to tie bandages and deliver water.

He saw the arxhemists there, one of them tending to the injured, hood drawn back, his face pale and sweaty. It looked as if he was trying to use conventional techniques where he could, but it was clear he'd been using his magic as well, and it was taking a toll.

Certainly not as bad as it had been for Jem Nevai. Temos saw Theander Kross attempting to calm her, to relieve her pain. The tiny woman was missing the lower part of her leg, and he could see burns across half of her face, presumably more hidden by her hood. The one arm that seemed to work clawed at her throat and chest, as if she struggled to breathe. Theander clumsily attempted to give her water, his motions made awkward by the thick bandages wrapped around his own hands and wrists. Temos had a hard time looking away from the two of them. The power of the Ashen was said to be the power of the Young Gods, but he could not imagine the gods being so fragile.

We were never meant to handle such power, Temos thought. *But what chance do we stand without it?*

Overhead, the Long Evening crawled towards night. For the first time since childhood, Temos feared what lurked in it.

"C'mon, Pelt, time for a meeting," Captain Ardell was saying as Temos was nudged awake by a gently prodding boot. He'd fallen asleep with his back against a barricade, and his neck was criticizing him for it. Grumbling, he got to his feet and stumbled after his captain.

"What's going on?" he asked behind a yawn.

"Commander Cohl called for us. He's speaking with the Lockewoods," Greffin said, leading them towards the front of the Temple. The Long Evening was just ending; he hadn't slept long and his body complained about it with a hundred tiny aches.

"Any other news?" Temos asked hopefully.

"No," Greffin replied, clearly chewing on some other words that he wanted to say, but didn't.

"Alright then," Temos said, keeping quiet as well, looking around at the makeshift fires and other necessities they had been trying to erect since the last attack. His mind wandered to the actual camp they'd set up some distance outside of Lex Vellos. Were they safe? Had that mad woman sent the H'Kaan to destroy them already? If they did get through this, would they be able to survive any journey out of the Wasting without provisions? These were questions that Temos craved answers to, but was terrified that his heart already knew the truth.

The sand crunched beneath their feet: everything was unnaturally quiet.

Captain Ardell and Temos walked on, past the wounded and dying, where comfort was offered but rarely achieved. For most, being unconscious was probably the best they could hope for. It was hard to tell the difference between the injured and the caregivers who sat among them, heads slumped in a light sleep, trying to take advantage of the quiet.

Greffin led him down to the waiting temple, which loomed over the enclosed square, the faceless statues offering no reassurance of safety or salvation. They climbed the steps, finally stopping at the top before a set of massive metal doors, similar to those they'd seen in the mansion on the south side of the city, save that these were much larger and stood wide open.

On the inside, Temos saw a few fires, lamps and torches that gave the interior of the building a warm glow, more comforting than seemed appropriate given the circumstances. He also saw several people he knew, though was not necessarily glad to see.

Richard Lockewood and his son Arren were the most prominent, standing tall amongst the others. Theander Kross was there, the Arxhemist looking pale, but at least steady on his feet. Indalia Nox, the Lance's scoutmaster was there as well, as was another woman wearing the robes of the Order, marking her as an Arxhemist like Theander. The man with the scar across his face was Jedgar Parse, the First Captain of the Thundering Lance, someone Temos only recognized because he had been there to greet the Templars when the two groups first combined ranks. The Laegis commander, Zan Cohl, was the final member.

Greffin held back a moment until Cohl motioned them forward.

The inside of the Temple was just as impressive as the outside, and slightly less worse for wear. This floor was mostly open space. Corridors snaked away into the darkness, coiling around the building or up and down dimly lit stairwells. Given the size of the Temple, Temos wondered how much they weren't seeing. Aside from the leadership in the middle, there were others on the periphery, clearing rubble, making notes and generally moving quickly from one task to the next.

"Reporting as ordered, Commander," the Captain said as he and Temos stopped and presented a couple of exhausted salutes to Commander Cohl.

"Thank you, Captain," Zan replied. "We're trying to make sense of a few things and would welcome your input."

"Tell us about the woman," Richard Lockewood said. Temos noted again how his short cape seemed out of place, a bit of flair adorning his otherwise utilitarian armor. It was draped to cover up the loss of the limb he'd volunteered as punishment for his crimes, but Temos found it incredibly distracting. He tried hard not to stare at it, and was mostly successful.

Greffin gave a shortened account of the past several hours, which felt like it had been much longer than a single day - more like an entire week compressed into one frantic afternoon. No one interrupted the Captain, waiting until he had finished before they began to ask him any questions.

"This is highly disturbing," Theander said. "I have not heard of the H'Kaan taking on our appearance. It is something that has never been recorded before."

"I don't think they took on the appearance," Temos said. They all looked at him. "I mean, they spoke. Both the girl and Emeranth Kell spoke to us. Emeranth even said, 'I was'... I as in me, as in she recognized something about herself that was more than H'Kaan."

"I agree with him," Nox spoke up. "H'Kaan were not known to name themselves. This is something new."

"Emeranth Kell is not a made up name," Richard said. "It belonged to someone before the Ehronfall."

"Looks like it still does," Temos replied.

"Or the memory of it," offered the female Arxhemist, who almost seemed surprised with herself after speaking.

"Go on, Asai," Theander prodded.

"I mean, if this body was once this Emeranth person but it was taken over by the same force that creates and animates the H'Kaan, maybe it is both these things, a creature born of the Dark, but climbing in and stealing the memories and the body of one who has fallen."

"The same force that animates the H'Kaan? You're talking about Maughrin, right? I mean, unless there's something other than the Dragon with the ability to spawn H'Kaan?" Temos asked.

"Y... Yes," Asai said hesitantly.

"But you're saying She could restore someone to life from long ago? How? This is power she's never displayed before," Richard pressed.

"I don't know for sure," Asai quickly defended. "I can only speak on what we have witnessed here. We only have vague stories to go on, testimonies in books at best, no firsthand accounts. There is so much about them we don't know, so much knowledge lost to us. I'm conjecturing based on the best information I'm aware of."

"This Kell person did tell us from her own lips that she was 'Her Wrath,'" Greffin recalled. "I think we all felt very clearly what she meant when she said it."

"So then, this is something new?" Arren asked. "Not just another member of the swarm, but a champion? A leader?"

"They did seem to follow her command," Temos remarked.

"Does this feel like your other experience?" Arren Lockewood asked Temos, "In Flinderlass?"

"No... I mean, I don't think so. This looks all different," Temos replied.

"Unfortunate," Richard Lockewood said, "I was hoping that there might be a common thread. We may not understand it, but at least it might have sprung from the same source."

"I don't think they tie together like that," Temos said. "Not directly."

"Something we'll have to explore at another time. For now, we need to find what we came for," Richard emphasized.

"We are trying, Lord Lockewood," Asai replied, "but the tower is large and deep. It was meant to be a last line of defense for the Laegis. There are many doors, many locks and even more secrets. We expected to have much more time."

"Time is no longer a luxury," declared Jedgar Parse, who Temos had never heard speak before, but had the immediate impression of a man always one moment away from barking orders loudly.

"We are aware, Captain," Theander said authoritatively, yet respectfully. "Master Oolen is doing her best. To push her, or any of us too hard, would sacrifice our lives and your chances at finding anything useful. Sister Nevai has already lost a leg, and suffered some severe internal damage. We were lucky the exertion didn't kill her outright."

"None of you are looking particularly good at the moment, Master Kross. I trust you to take care of yourselves. Need I remind you of the stakes of this operation?" Richard said, sounding more like a threat than a statement of concern. Theander nodded. Temos was about done with Richard Lockewood's near constant reminder of: 'only I can save the world'.

"We are aware," Theander replied. "The Order of Veda does not require us to sacrifice ourselves foolishly, but all of us feel a duty to help those in need."

"Temper that feeling," Lockewood instructed. "This may be our greatest obstacle right now, but it is merely a fragment of a much larger conflict. There are greater stakes - and players - that we haven't even seen yet."

"I understand, and will encourage the others to keep that in mind," Theander replied, perhaps a bit too forcefully given the look on Richard's face. Temos could tell Lord Lockewood was not overly fond of people who reminded him that they were under no direct obligation to follow his orders.

"Master Oolen, do you feel like you have uncovered anything that might be leading you in the right direction?" Lockewood asked.

"No, sir," she replied, casting her eyes down to the floor, more out of shame than fear.

"Well, that's disappointing," Richard said. He turned to Commander Cohl next. "Any chance you or yours might have an idea where the Laegis of Lex Vellos would have hidden something?"

"I wish I could tell you 'yes'. Before the Godswar the Laegis were a sprawling organization under the direction of the High Houses. Each of these was as unique and individual as the temples of the Young Gods around them," Zan said.

Temos thought of Casselle. Her book might have been able to give them some clues. Both of them had been hesitant to reveal its unique magic to the Commander or Lockewood, but he wondered if they would have seen things differently now. He cast a sideways glance at Captain Ardell, one of the few people Casselle had trusted with the knowledge of the book, wondering if the old Templar had been thinking similar thoughts.

But the Captain was intently watching Lockewood and Cohl with his good eye. He did not seem the type to get lost in thoughts of what couldn't be. If they were going to survive, Temos concluded, it would have to be by their own hands, however improbable that seemed at the moment.

"Let's figure out the best way to maximize our search," Lockewood said, before looking to Nox. "Do you think any of the information you recovered from the Vale could help us here?" Temos knit his brow in confusion.

"Trying to locate anything worthwhile was difficult to begin with," the Scoutmaster said, "especially since I had to dodge Unbound as well, something you failed to mention."

"I knew they had plans in motion, I didn't expect them to be in the Vale, though. That's not our concern right now."

"Right," Nox replied, noting the look on Richard's face which seemed to put an end to that sidebar. "Anyway, I've only been able to translate a fraction of it with the help of Masters Oolen and Kross. So far it speaks mostly in vagaries with outdated references. There is certainly no clearly marked maps amongst the documents I procured. In time it will yield some value, but I don't think it will be of use under these circumstances."

She'd stolen documents from the Ghostvale? Temos hadn't seen much of her during their time there, but he assumed that was because the Laegis had been kept in a separate location from Richard's trio. It must have been part of Lockewood's plan all along, which grated on Temos' nerves all the more. He'd treated Casselle like a failure for doing her best during his trial there, but he'd been betraying the hospitality of the Khaliil the entire time, by stealing from them while their attention was elsewhere. Temos had a few dozen angry words come to mind, but he chewed on them and swallowed his pride rather than speak up.

As much as it pained him to admit, they needed as many swords as they could get right now. Divisions inside their own camp would not help any of them. It was the right call, but it tasted of bitter swill.

"Let's still put you and a couple of your scouts here with Master Oolen to add some extra eyes and helpful hands," Richard told Nox.

"I'll personally help with the efforts," she replied.

"Do you think we could use this like the Laegis did?" Lockewood asked Asai.

"The structure is intact, if that is what you are asking," the Arxhemist replied. "But not all the passages are clear and I'm not familiar with all the access points. If you are asking me if the building is tactically sound, I'm not sure what to tell you."

"Captain, do a quick assessment and report back to me," Richard told Jedgar Parse. "If it is a solid chokepoint, I want to make sure we can fall back to here."

"Don't you think that puts an unreasonable expectation on our forces? Defending against an opponent of unknown strength while holding out for an unverified advantage?" Zan Cohl challenged as politely as possible.

"Are you looking to leave, Commander?"

"Not looking to, just raising a question that impacts our remaining troops," Zan replied calmly. Temos noticed that he had said "remaining troops." Was he saying that Richard killed them? Or was he just pointing out that any further loss of life, regardless of who might be responsible, could be mitigated, if not avoided altogether?

"We do not have the option of waiting for help," Richard said. "Even if we could deliver a message instantly, it would still take time for reinforcements to arrive. Leaving is as much of a gamble as staying. At least here we might have a defensible fortification. The open Wasting will afford us no such luxury. I trust we are in agreement on this, Commander?"

"We are. I just wanted to make sure we considered all options, even ones that might seem uncomfortable."

"I can respect that, but let's focus on what we can do. Captain Parse will confirm the Temple's security. Master Oolen and Indalia will be working on trying to safely access areas of the Temple still undiscovered or unopened. Master Kross, if you would help find a place for the wounded and work with Brother Shields to move them safely in here, recruit whomever you need to see to their relocation. Arren and I will work with Commander Cohl's men to refortify as the lines are tightened." Richard looked around at them to confirm they had all received proper instructions. "Are there any questions?"

The group collectively confirmed there were none and Richard told them to begin. Temos fell in line behind Captain Ardell, just a few steps behind Zan Cohl, Arren Lockewood and Richard. He did not like these circumstances and he most certainly did not like the idea of being packed into a box, surrounded by angry shadows with teeth and then slowly slaughtered.

He hung his head a bit as he walked. It felt like a march to the gallows. The oppressive darkness of the sky overhead and the soft sounds of the dead and dying did little to bolster his spirits. Outside of Jaksen, there would be no one to mourn him, now that Casselle was gone.

He'd only ever known his family to be his father, a proud man who'd hidden his own sickness in order to ensure Temos had no misgivings in leaving once he found that he'd been accepted as a Laegis Initiate. Temos found a family amongst the Templars, especially with those bright souls in his squad. He mourned those that died and held closer in his heart those that had survived.

All the others had people they could return home to, but not him. Temos had no home left, certainly not the small trapper's shack that had fallen into disrepair since his father had seen him out the door, promising he'd be better soon and come to visit his son in Strossen. A visit that never came...

He found out later that his father died before Temos even received his sword. The young man tried to live bravely, to honor the memory of the father that had sacrificed everything for him. He poured his heart, wit and skill into proving that he was something more than just a strange boy from the edge of the forests.

Now it wouldn't matter.

He clenched his jaw and gripped the hilt of his sword. He felt his eyes watering and fought the tightness at the back of his throat. He never wanted to be a hero, he just wanted to protect those close to him. But now he wanted something more, something that he hadn't wanted before.

His father had always taught him to be a good man. In the face of everything he'd suffered, he always kept that close to his heart. He tried hard to live up to those expectations, but now in the face of these overwhelming odds, all he wanted was to hurt someone. He didn't want to kill, he wanted to inflict pain. He wanted to gather up all the hurt from all the things that had been taken from him and from his friends and hone them all to deadly sharpness...

... so he could drive them like nails into the skull of Emeranth Kell.

***

The first sun teased its appearance over the eastern horizon as the last of the wounded were moved inside the Temple. Space had been secured above the main floor for them, leaving the doors and steps clear for defense.

Jedgar Parse didn't have a great plan, but he had managed to convince Jem Nevai to perform one last bit of Arxhemestry, creating a hardened barrier at the bottom of the steps to act as a sort of breaking point behind which the Templar Lancers and the Skirmishers of Richard's army would provide a formidable wall of shield and spear. Further up the stairs, archers could fire down into the crowd, and should that fail, the Shield Templars and what remained of Lockewood's Thundering Lance would try to hold the doors.

Jem did her best, propped up by her fellow arxhemists at the top of the stairs. Temos watched as the hardened walls became like sand, shifting and flowing by some unseen hand into a new shape before hardening into a chokepoint that would funnel anything coming at them into a tight corridor. It was fine work, but the effort of it burned her up, turning her fingers to ash even as the last wall settled. The other members of her Order tried to comfort her, to save her, but she could not hold on.

It seemed as if they had just draped a cloak over her still cooling corpse when the H'Kaan attacked. They showed up in small packs at first, harassing the edges of the fortifications strung across the square. They returned without warning as the morning was wrestling to overcome night, making it all the more difficult for them to be seen.

With the defenses at the tower now established, Captains Parse, Ardell and Boen sounded the retreat for troops that had been left holding the square. As they fell back to their final positions, packs of H'Kaan broke into the open, dogging their heels.

From the edge of the door, it looked to Temos as if they were merely toying with the soldiers attempting to withdraw. He wondered if the H'Kaan felt such things as joy, because it seemed as if they were excited to have all their prey corralled in one convenient container. A few attempted to breach the line, but were swiftly dispatched by the reinforced rows of deadly spears behind hardened defenses. The rest pulled back, jogging idly towards the far end of the enclosed square before disappearing altogether.

Temos was assembled with the surviving members of the Shield Templars. With Passal Cooper out of commission for the moment, they were down to half strength: only ten of the twenty that had marched from Strossen.

"What I wouldn't give for a well to climb down right now," Vincen von Darren joked with Temos. The green Templar had managed to survive, probably mostly because of luck, Temos assumed, but was still attempting to put up a weak show of bravado. Nevertheless, it was clear that the joke had a strong element of truth in it.

"If you find one, let me know," Temos said with a wink, faking the casual ease he usually displayed to bolster Vincen's spirits. In truth, he wouldn't have left even if a magical escape was discovered. He had too much hate invested in breaking Emeranth Kell to leave now.

"Don't pick at that, or it won't heal," Lennard Torks was telling Gunnar Hawken. Nearby, the large Vanha scratched at the scabbed over wounds he'd received over the course of the previous day. His ability to heal from injury bordered on the unreal.

"It itches," Gunnar grumbled, clearly annoyed by his wounds and the mounting pressure of their predicament. He wasn't alone. On the other side of the doors, Duran Holst stood with his three remaining squad members, who appeared as tired and anxious as the rest of them. Temos had learned their names, but hadn't pressed for further details. After all, there was little use getting to know the dead.

Near the bottom of the steps, Captain Boen and Commander Cohl were working with Captain Parse on how best to arrange the spearmen and the order of rotation they would take as the battle commenced. Above them, archers checked bowstrings for fraying while others tried to redistribute arrows, knowing that they would never be able to completely fill their hip quivers without the supplies from the encampment outside the city.

The sky continued to lighten and Temos wondered if any of them would see a sunrise beyond this one. The first sun had climbed high enough into the eastern sky to light the scene ahead of them. In the glory days of Lex Vellos, it was probably inspiring to stand at the front of the Temple and greet the morning, but here it worked against them, lighting the scene from behind to cast dark shadows towards them while stinging their eyes with bright morning light.

The captains readied their men and moved into command positions.

A hush fell as something stirred at the far end of the square. A black shadow began to spread slowly, moving methodically forward, absent of the madcap energy they had seen up to now. Temos heard the rustle of armored bodies, the subtle shifting of leather on leather, and somewhere underneath it all he heard a rhythmic tapping, if but for a moment.

The shadow continued to grow, pulling itself forward on hundreds of clawed feet. Temos hated this about the H'Kaan, the way that darkness seemed to stick to them, like the way mist clings to a river on a cool morning. He wished he had his bow, but knew it would be a foolishly redundant gesture at this moment: the longbows of the Templar Archers below him were more than capable of inflicting more damage at greater range.

The H'Kaan drew up short of where the shadows gave way to morning light. It was clear they did not prefer it, but something urged them forward, over or through the temporary wooden barriers that had been left in place from their previous defensive stand.

Commander Cohl and Captain Parse had joined them at the top of the stairs, pausing at the open door. Captain Boen remained with his Archers, at the front of their group so he could relay commands to the Lancers just below them.

The H'Kaan moved far enough to be mockingly outside of the archers' range before they stopped altogether. They churned and pawed at the ground, looking like they wanted to dash forward, but were being restrained, as if they'd run into some sort of boundary or barrier that they could not cross. Temos saw a few of Richard's archers anxiously pull at their bowstrings, not drawing them, but clearly eager to do so.

"Hold steady," Captain Boen instructed them calmly.

In the following stillness, Temos heard the tapping again. It was coming from somewhere behind them, in the Temple itself. He could only reason that it must be Master Oolen or someone helping her, attempting to unlock the unexplored doors. He was about to mention it to Captain Ardell when he saw Vincen point a finger towards the middle of the black mess in front of the temple.

"Look there!" The Templar pointed to a section along the line, which was slowly parting like curtains before a show. Emeranth Kell emerged from the shadowy cloud, towering over the others following just behind her. Temos recognized the small girl that Finn had chased, the long black barbed tongue that had scarred him still lolling from her mouth, twitching and twisting at lazy intervals. She also still bore the stem of the arrow he'd shot into her, a black stain on her clothes where the broken shaft protruded from her chest.

The child was not the only one with her, though. Temos saw several others in a similar state. One wore the tabard of Lockewood's Thundering Lance, but his head flopped to the side, at such an angle there was no doubt it was broken. Another barely had a head at all, most of it replaced by a swirling mass of blackness, fringes of it waving like hair in a strong breeze, even when no such wind existed.

"That's John Kettel," Captain Ardell growled. Temos saw the Veteran, one of the Captain's squad leaders, and longtime friend. The former Templar's lower left leg was replaced by a tightly knit cluster of writhing black snakes. Temos thought he saw another in Templar armor behind Kettel and prayed to all the Dead Gods that it wasn't Casselle. His anger was finely honed, but fragile. Seeing her might be more than he could handle, so he refused to look further, putting all his attention on Emeranth Kell instead and letting the details of those that walked with her to remain unfocused.

The giant warrior moved forward with an overconfident swagger. She was already in range of the bows, but kept advancing. Her entourage had stopped, however, standing in front of the black mass of H'Kaan blocking up the square, while Emeranth continued on her own. The sun shone through the holes in her tattered cloak, the light also appearing to perforate the shadow she cast on the ground ahead of her.

"You're not welcome in my city!" Emeranth yelled. "There is part of me that wishes to allow you to surrender and in doing so, grant you safe passage out of Lex Vellos. But every step forward I take is one step further away from that voice. I left it behind me on the ground, slowly dying. Perhaps it still has the strength to convince me of mercy, but I fear this will be the last time it is able to speak on your behalf."

"You were part of something greater than yourself once, Emeranth Kell, but you have forsaken that to embrace the Great Darkness." Richard Lockewood's voice was clear and powerful. Temos felt him pass through the door and watched him walk down several steps.

"It sings a seductive song, little man. Perhaps after I break your jaw, I'll pour some of that down your throat so that you may taste how sweet it can be," she responded, running a black tongue across her lips.

"You're supposed to hold up a torch to that Darkness. You swore an oath to keep it at bay. Now you are so bold as to serve it openly?" Richard asked. "We're fortunate that not all Templar are so weak willed as you."

"She's a Templar?" Vincen asked, his voice wavering with fear.

"Sounds like she used to be," Temos replied. "But I thought..." He swallowed the rest of his questions. Assuming they survived, there would be time later to beat answers out of Lord Lockewood.

"I have plenty of conviction, little man," Emeranth replied. "I have come to realize, though, that it had merely been applied to the wrong cause."

"Then show it to us, little girl," Richard challenged, "and don't waste your remaining time with words." Before she could reply, Lord Lockewood turned away and marched back up the stairs. Emeranth stood there, her face going through several angry contortions.

"There goes any chance we had at negotiating a truce," Finn groaned.

"There was never a chance," Captain Ardell said grimly. "The only way out of this city is through them."

Temos winced as Emeranth Kell turned her head to the sky and screamed, the spine crawling howl that they had all too recently come to fear.

The H'Kaan charged, an angry tide let loose to break the defenses and the will of those defending the Temple. They filled the lane, flowing with ease around Emeranth Kell without breaking stride.

"Loose!" came the command of Captain Boen, his only word chopped off by the chorus of bowstrings from the assembled archers.

Temos saw ripples in the shadows, undoubtedly bodies falling, but the darkness continued forward, the H'Kaan rushing over the slain.

Not enough, Temos thought as the arrows began to fly in a less coordinated fashion, sticks thrown in desperation at a tidal wave.

The H'Kaan were already at the steps, crashing into the locked shields of the soldiers below, Templar and Thundering Lance alike. They had never trained together, but they were united in desperate determination and defiance. From the steps above the front line, polearms stabbed over the shields, biting deep into the shadows.

Critical minutes passed as the front lines held back the heavy press of H'Kaan bodies, claws and spines. Captain Boen shouted a command and the front rank slipped back past the second rank, whose shields locked in after their retreat. The fresh troops continued to hold as flights of arrows poured over their heads into the surging shadows at their feet.

If they didn't suffer heavy losses, the lines could fight and refresh themselves all the way up the stairs, but eventually they would be at the top, and there would be no place left for them on the outside of the Temple. Temos wrestled with the desire to leap down into the thick of it, but knew without a spear, he'd be more hindrance than help.

Emeranth and her bizarre entourage were lost in the wake of it all, somewhere in the rolling black cloud behind the front lines. Even the rising suns could not fully pierce the miasma, a river of shadows crashing against the shield wall below them and surging at the sides of the enclosure ahead.

Temos was afraid, but he pushed it aside. In the time he had left, he would not allow it to council him. There was still work to be done, even if there was no hope left.

- 23 -

The Weir

At the opposite end of the Causeway, the shadows shifted, and a portion of Ostenvaard's ruins came to life.

A long, mottled limb unfolded into the street. It was segmented and encased in a hard shell, like a crab's, ending in a serrated spike half as long as a man. The sharp tip touched the stone-paved street with a strange delicacy just as a second jointed leg swung down beside it.

"Salt and stone," Izenya d'Gara breathed from behind Triistan. "What in Shan's munghole is that thing?"

Tau and Crixus, with Biiko between them, fanned out in the center of the street. Both Vanha stood over twelve feet tall and they were still looking up into the moving shadows.

"That, my briny friends, is a mantiisa - a longstrider - shat out of the Worm's ass, not the Stormfather's."

The monstrous thing came fully into view, lowering itself from where it had been perched in the overgrown ruins. If ever a nightmare could crawl out of someone's head, this is what it would look like.

It reminded Triistan of one of the priest bugs he used to catch as a boy, but altered in some ways and grown to an impossible scale. It had a lower abdomen roughly the shape and size of a skiff supported by four of its six legs; a mid-section that was only slightly smaller; and a wedge-shaped head that pivoted back and forth. Its whole body was covered in elongated overlapping plates that flexed as it moved.

It drew itself up, lifting its torso vertically and brandishing its two forelimbs. Like the priest bug, its front appendages had three jointed segments, with the last two serrated sections able to fold back on themselves like grasping claws - claws that ended in three-foot long spikes.

And something else rode upon its back.

"Sithis," Danor spat.

At first glance the rider appeared to be another Oathguard, although his armor and weapons seemed crude and mismatched. Parts of it seemed too large, while other pieces seemed to be missing or broken. His helmet only seemed to protect half of his head and part of his face. How it stayed on, Triistan could not begin to guess.

The thing called Sithis sat astride the beast's torso, near the base, in some type of elaborate harness that fitted the mantiisa much like a backpack. He held a massive maul in his left hand, though there was something wrong about his grip on the weapon's shaft: the angle seemed strange and he was holding it very close to the head. A massive lance was couched under his right arm, which he thrust in the direction of Tau and Crixus as he spoke. His voice was loud and unnaturally deep, echoing harshly off the surrounding buildings.

Danor translated for them, explaining that they were trading insults, with the Lord Marshal and High Master giving Ossien's lieutenant an opportunity to withdraw before being slain. The grizzled old Vanha laughed humorlessly.

"Still has his honor, the Lord Marshal. Even as despicable a creature as Sithis has become - mark me, salties, he's as dangerous to us as anything that swims, walks, crawls or flies on Aarden - old Long Tau's got to offer him a chance to withdraw from the field." He turned his head and spat. "We should have killed him at the outset."

"Who is he, Su'ul?" Triistan asked, trying to keep his voice steady.

"Not who," answered the old healer quietly. "Not anymore."

"Another creation then, like the ones you told us about? A Warling?"

Danor shook his head, while in the intersection Tau, Biiko and Crixus slowly circled, seeking an advantage as they exchanged words with Sithis. The longstrider matched their movements, skittering sideways like a giant crab.

"Yes and no - more like a reviiso - a 'mimic' you would call it I think. That... thing out there used to be one of us."

The others murmured in surprise. Triistan was about to ask him what he meant when Crixus shouted and attacked.

The High Master tried spearing the mantiisa with his trident, coming at it from the left flank, between its legs. It danced away, turning so that Sithis could counter-attack with his lance, but Crixus was only probing and parried the blow easily before stepping back out of reach. Tau moved to his left, increasing the distance between them to force Sithis to divide his attention between the two Oathguard, who were now nearly on opposite sides. Sithis backed his mount up to avoid being flanked.

Up until now he appeared to have been ignoring Biiko, who was about thirty yards away with both swords drawn, between and somewhat behind the two Vanha. But suddenly the longstrider threw its head back and let out a hissing scream. At the same time, the layered plates on the back of its lower body sprang open like a huge fan, revealing brilliant red and black wings. It leapt directly at Biiko, clearing the ninety feet with ease, the wings helping it to glide the way Triistan had seen some grasshoppers do.

From their vantage point down the street, it looked as if it landed directly on top of the Unbound, causing Triistan to cry out in alarm, but an instant later he saw Biiko rolling sideways in the street. He came up out of the roll on one knee, between the thing's back legs, sweeping his black blades to either side. Even from where they were they heard the ring of steel clashing against something hard and unyielding. The beast spun quickly, punching out with one of its foreleg spikes, trying to pin Biiko to the ground. But the Unbound was quicker and the spike smashed into the paved street, sending shards of stone flying. He counterattacked, striking the leg twice before leaping back out of the way, but it sounded as if he'd struck the side of a building and the longstrider appeared unharmed.

Tau and Crixus were only a step behind, attacking simultaneously from either flank as Biiko leapt clear. The Lord Marshal vaulted onto the creature's back, where its wings had partially retracted. He raised his bladestaff high and brought it down like a spear, hoping to strike softer tissue between the armored plates covering its wings.

The mantiisa screamed in pain, rotating its upper body and swinging one of its forearms wildly, trying to dislodge its assailant. Tau evaded the blow, but his movement brought Sithis close enough to strike with his maul, catching Tau just below his shoulder. It was a glancing blow, but solid enough so that he lost his footing and toppled sideways. Somehow the Lord Marshal was able to retain his grip on the bladestaff, wrenching it free as he fell. He hit the street and rolled to absorb the impact, but when he came up, rather than attack again, he struck the street with his weapon, hard. There was a brilliant blue flash at the point of impact, lasting only an instant before Tau was moving laterally again, circling while Crixus and Biiko pushed from the other side. Triistan tried to blink away the afterimage, but then realized it wasn't just his vision: the ground still glowed blue where Tau had struck it.

"What was that?" he asked, but Danor ignored him.

The longstrider crabbed sideways, trying to avoid Crixus, who had slid underneath it seeking a weak point with his trident. They caught glimpses of him dodging and thrusting, but Triistan couldn't tell whether he had succeeded or not. Judging from the creature's movements, even if he did wound it, it didn't appear to have any more effect than Tau's earlier strike had. As Biiko pressed his attack, Crixus rolled clear, sprang to his feet and raised his trident above his head. He was shouting something, but he was too far away to hear as he swung his weapon at the ground with such force Triistan was surprised it didn't break. There was another flash, and two blue spots now glowed hotly in the street, perhaps thirty yards apart.

"Su'ul, what in the Dark are they doing?"

The grizzled Vanha healer grunted. "Playing with fire. But they'd better hurry."

As if to illustrate his point, the sky had grown paler; daylight was creeping back into the world.

The three warriors stepped up the intensity of their deadly dance, with two of them drawing their opponent in one direction while the third tried to find a vulnerable spot. Whenever Tau or Crixus succeeded, they immediately withdrew and struck the ground, leaving behind another blue brand. Very soon there were seven or eight ghostly fires shimmering, in no particular pattern that Triistan could discern. He was about to ask Danor again when Sithis caught Tau full in the chest with his lance, knocking the Lord Marshal backwards several feet. His bladestaff went spinning out of reach and he landed hard on his back, just outside the ragged arc of blue fires. The mantiisa hissed and sprang after him, flicking open its wings and knocking Crixus aside in the process.

But then something strange happened: in mid-leap, the longstrider lurched to the ground, as if it had been yanked down by a leash. It landed awkwardly, legs splaying out in all directions, only a short distance from where the Lord Marshal lay.

There was a murmur from the other Oathguard. Protaeus put his hand on Danor's shoulder, smiling.

"Obed's armored bullocks, it worked," Danor muttered.

"What?" Triistan blurted. "What worked?"

"A binding ward, boy. A bloody fuundaris binding! Looks like you were right, Protaeus."

The smaller Vanha shook his head slightly. "With all of the alterations he's made to them, I wasn't sure... but now..."

"Now comes the tricky part," Danor finished for him.

"Indeed. They must secure the second line before Sithis and his mount realize they can still go the other way..."

Sithis had kept his seat and was shouting something in his guttural voice, urging his mount ahead. It lunged at the Lord Marshal again, but appeared to be struggling mightily, leaning forward, as if it were dragging some huge, unseen weight.

Tau still lay on his back and was just beginning to struggle upright. Only a few yards away, the longstrider strained to reach him. Then suddenly it reached out one of its forelegs and swung the deadly spiked end downward, striking the street just inches from Tau's leg, showering him with chips of stone. The beast screamed and lifted both forelegs, lunging forward again.

"Oh shit," someone whispered.

The pincers swung down, but stopped abruptly just a few feet off the ground. Biiko appeared from nowhere, standing in front of Tau, black blades crossed high to catch the mantiisa's blow. It screamed in rage and frustration and struck again, even harder. But the strength behind its attack worked against it this time, and both spikes sheared off as they struck the black steel. The Unbound shuddered under the impact, but kept his feet.

Crixus leapt onto the thing's back, lunging at Sithis with his trident. The mantiisa whipped around, allowing Sithis to knock the blow aside with his maul. Between the growing daylight and the blue glare from the strange fires, Triistan could now see why the hammer hadn't looked right to him before: it was part of his arm. A thick steel rod emerged from a badly misshapen elbow, with the business end of a maul mounted to it, cast in a sick parody of a massive clenched fist.

Hammerhand.

The longstrider took a step back and pivoted, forcing Crixus to one knee as he struggled to keep his balance on its back. Sithis thrust with his lance, but he was badly positioned, so he roared another command to his mount. This time the creature threw itself sideways, finding it could move easily in that direction, back across the pattern of blue fires and away from Tau. Biiko was helping the Lord Marshal stagger to his feet.

"Has it broken free?" Captain Vaelysia asked.

Danor smiled his not-smile. "No. It just hasn't found the end of its leash yet. Protaeus? This is your brainchild..."

Protaeus continued watching the fight as he explained, eyes smoldering with excitement. "The mantiisa is not free, no. Not yet at least. You saw the energy released as they struck the ground, yes? Think of each of those blows as anchor points... like driving pitons into the side of a cliff, like so." He brought his two fists together in a hammering motion. "Only these are being driven into something far stronger."

Biiko had left Tau's side and was now attacking the longstrider again, concentrating his efforts on its rear legs. Crixus was on the thing's back, but on his hands and knees clinging to one of the armored plates as it tried to shake him off.

"Anchors for what?"

"They bleed him, using his own essence - and that of his creator's - to hold him to this place, in much the same way that The Worm was first bound in The Hold. Unfortunately, we do not have nearly as much power as our fathers had at their disposal, nor do we have their mastery of the Wyvha - the Wards - so this is only a crude version of a Binding. Still, it should restrain the mantiisa if we are able to create enough anchor points."

Tau had rejoined the fight and even now was striking the ground, producing another blue flash. Sithis hesitated, rotating his huge, misshapen head from one crude line of flames to this newly created one.

Triistan asked if it would also hold the warling, but before Protaeus could answer, Sithis tipped his head back and roared. There was such power and brutality in his cry that for a moment Triistan expected one of the jharrls to answer in challenge. Instead, the howling screams of the H'Kaan rose up from the side streets all around them.

"Show time," Danor growled.

A dark tide rushed around the corner behind them, flowing into the wide intersection, around the statue in its center, and towards the fight.

"They're not ready," Protaeus groaned. "We have to give them more time!"

Danor stood from where he'd been crouched, watching the fight. He hefted his huge hammer in one hand, even though the shaft alone was half again as long as Triistan.

"Somehow I knew you were going to say that. Get them to the Weir, brodiir. I'll catch up when I can.

"Atuu! Coh'me!!" he cried and leapt off the balcony, landing atop the last few H'Kaan running past. A dark shadow detached itself from the rooftop above their heads, and the old jharrl landed beside his friend and master, roaring as he hit the ground. The two of them struck the rear of the H'Kaan ranks like the ram of a man-o-war smashing through the hull of a ship, sending bodies - or in some cases just parts of them - flying in all directions. Atuu's attack was particularly devastating - Triistan had never seen anything fight with such ferocity before. The jharrls seemed to have a special hatred for Ossien's 'respawn'.

Behind him he heard Protaeus ordering the others back down the rubble pile, but it was hard to tear his eyes away from the battle below. While Danor and Atuu tore through their rear flank, the front ranks of the H'Kaan swarm seemed oblivious to the threat as they sprinted at full speed towards Biiko and the others. He saw Tau gesturing at the Unbound, directing him to intercept the approaching horde, no doubt looking for more time to finish their ritual. A strong hand gripped his shoulder, tugging him.

"Come on, Triis, we have to go." It was Jaspins. "Captain's orders. They know what they're doing."

Did they? He tried to swallow the doubt and fear he felt, but it refused to go down. The last thing he saw before turning away to follow her was Biiko in a fighter's stance, both blades gleaming in the odd half-light, while a dark, writhing mass of oblivion hurtled towards him.

Protaeus led them at a dead run past the overgrown statue in the center of the intersection and up the wide avenue they called 'The Causeway'. A few straggling H'Kaan came at them from side streets but the group dispatched them with ease. Ariis ran alongside Protaeus, while the twins Rhiisa and Rhea brought up the group's rear, still carrying Brekha's body. The Seekers followed in a loose column, Myles still slung over Creugar's shoulder. The wounded man had not uttered so much as a moan in so long Triistan feared he might be dead.

The road began to slope upward almost immediately. It was gradual at first, but even that gentle grade was hard on the crew's shorter legs. They had been up all night and on the run for the past few hours, and it was taking its toll on all of them. Thinman was the worst off, gasping and sputtering even with Izenya and Anthon helping him along. They started to lag, forcing Creugar and the Twins to hang back and stretching the group out.

"Su'ul, we need to stop and rest!" the Captain called out.

Protaeus slowed, but did not stop. He glanced back over his shoulder. "That was only two fists back there, Captain. We have no idea where the main force is or what's become of Linessa and the others. We must reach the Weir before they do."

Captain Vaelysia stopped. "And if they hit us in force before we get there, we'll be too exhausted to fight."

Triistan bent over and put his hands on his knees, grateful for the break. Behind him Thinman fell to the ground, groaning. Izenya grumbled something about him being more ship than man.

"For you've the tonnage t'prove it, mate." Thinman was too winded to respond.

The Vanha also came to a stop around them, as Protaeus shoved his way back through their ranks, glaring at the Captain.

"You have yet to grasp the full scope of what is at stake here, huunan," he spat as he strode up to Thinman. The heavyset Seeker was on his hands and knees, one hand massaging his chest. Anthon and Izenya stood to either side, trying to help him stand, but took a step back as the Vanha dropped to a knee beside Thinman and roughly grabbed him by his curly hair, lifting his head. The Seeker's face, typically a healthy, ruddy brown, looked pale and gaunt beneath his sparse black beard. His eyes were squeezed shut and Triistan saw that he wasn't just massaging his chest; he was clawing at it.

Protaeus sighed, muttering something in his own language. Then, so quickly it was over before Triistan realized what he was seeing, the Vanha whipped out a long, narrow dagger from a sheath on his arm and slipped it into Thinman's neck at the base of his skull. The big Seeker slumped over, dead, while the rest of the Expedition erupted in outrage and confusion.

They all surged towards Protaeus, and Izenya actually swung his broadsword at the Oathguard. Protaeus caught Izzy's wrist and twisted his arm, forcing him easily to his knees. With his other hand, the Oathguard held his long dagger poised at d'Gara's throat.

"Step back, or he dies too. It will only make our lives easier to be rid of you all, so I suggest you hear what I have to say."

Izenya spat at his feet. "Fuck you and what you have to say!!" he hissed through clenched teeth. Protaeus squeezed his eyes shut, searching for patience.

"Now I remember why I signed up for this duty," he muttered.

He opened his eyes and found the Captain standing directly in front of him, her cutlass held at her side.

"I'm listening," she said coldly.

"Let's hope so, because I will only say this once. We've already wasted too much time here." He released Izenya's arm and straightened, while the Seeker rubbed and flexed his wrist. Izzy was a burly man, well over six feet tall, but still he looked like a child compared to even the smallest Vanha.

"This is bullocks, Cap we should -"

"His heart seized," Protaeus said, nodding at Thinman's body. "He was already as good as dead. I simply spared him the agony of dying and us the time and effort trying to stop it."

"How can you possibly know that?" the Captain shot back. Several of the others muttered angrily in agreement.

Protaeus raised his eyebrows and shrugged. "A simple enough deduction if you know what to look for. The heart is just another muscle, and every muscle has its limits, Captain. His girth had likely already weakened his considerably, long before you made landfall here. He asked too much of it, and it failed him."

She shook her head. "You murdered him!"

"Call it what you wish. As I said, his death was inevitable, and he was a liability."

She took a step towards him, but both Commander Tchicatta and Lieutenant Jaspins interposed themselves. "Captain, he's probably right," the Reaver medic said quietly. "I have seen this before - sometimes men will recover under the right conditions, but..." she shook her head.

Captain Vaelysia studied her for a moment, then looked at the Firstblade. He acknowledged her with a barely-perceptible nod. "Should have left him with a blade and a chance, but he's right: it was his time."

Her lips twisted bitterly but she turned away from Tchicatta and raised her sword arm, pointing at Protaeus with it. "Your

Cun've'dictuus is over. Our fate is our own and you are not gods. You do not get to decide when we live, or when we die."

Protaeus smirked and sheathed his dagger. "As you wish, Captain." He sketched a mock bow. "Then your decision is simple: stay with us, and live, or fall behind... and die." He signaled to the other Vanha and they began their ascent up the causeway again.

"Cap we can't just leave'im here," Jaegus the Younger pleaded. "Those things will -"

"Those things will do worse to all of us if we linger!" she snapped. But she relented and glanced around. Although the buildings to either side of the causeway rose along with it, the slope of their grade was not as steep, so the road was now elevated a full story above the ground.

"Toss his body over the side; at least he won't be directly in the path of any pursuers, and with luck the jungle will claim him before anything else does."

Izenya and Anthon bent to pick him up, shaking their heads and muttering under their breath. Triistan and Jaegus had to help them, and Triistan was shocked at how heavy the body was. It ultimately took six of them to lift it over the low parapet wall. Fortunately, the undergrowth below them was thick enough to swallow Thinman's corpse whole.

As Triistan and the rest of the Expedition ran to catch back up to the Vanha, he felt sick to his stomach. From the looks on the faces of those around him, he wasn't the only one; they all realized that Protaeus was right. Despite the Captain's assertion, they were still little more than prisoners, held fast by circumstances now rather than walls or bars, with their survival dependent upon the will and strength of these strange, unforgiving warriors.

The causeway leveled out for a stretch as it passed through a sturdy wall between two squat towers. The vague shapes of nearby structures began to take on more detail in the growing light, including the twisted remains of steel gates partially visible in the encroaching undergrowth to either side. Like the much larger ones at The Rivergate, these looked to have been blown outward, which Triistan now assumed must have been from Ossien's escape. He was almost thankful when the ground began to rise again, forcing him to concentrate on simple things like pumping his legs and moving forward, while distracting him from imagining how much strength and power the renegade god must have possessed then - and how much stronger he must be now.

They passed through two more such gates before the road finally leveled out for good. Since breaking free of The Crossroads, they had not seen or heard any sign of pursuers, so Protaeus called a brief halt. The expedition members either flopped on the ground or doubled over, hands on their knees, gasping for breath. The Vanha stood in a loose ring around them, facing outward, looking relaxed but alert. None of the Oathguard were even breathing hard.

Creugar groaned as he set Myles gently on the ground, then straightened and began massaging his lower back with two meaty fists.

"Better be checking on him, Jasp. He gone awfully quiet."

Lieutenant Jaspins knelt beside Myles' body, while the other members cast wary glances at Protaeus. He watched them, but otherwise said nothing. The Captain crouched down next to the Reaver medic, while the latter talked quietly to Myles and inspected his bandages. His eyes fluttered open and he seemed haggard, but Triistan told himself the scout still looked better than Thinman had in his last moments.

Jaspins uncorked the same wineskin she had given him when he had been infected with the nagayuun spawn and squeezed a few drops of spiced rum onto Myles' cracked lips. He licked them and smiled weakly, then opened his mouth. She allowed him a small drink, which he swallowed without mishap, so she offered him a second. He licked his lips again and whispered something. She chuckled and patted him lightly on the chest, then stood. The others were watching them intently, waiting for her prognosis.

"He's in a lot of pain, but his wounds are not bleeding. Whatever these... dracosii? Whatever venom these things spit, it actually cauterizes the flesh the way fire does. If he can withstand the pain, he will live."

"We have salves for it," Protaeus answered, "but all of that was left behind. Once we cross the Weir - if we cross it - we should be able to find the appropriate materials to mix some. It will not alleviate all of the pain, but it will make it bearable."

"Biiko might have something as well," Triistan added hopefully. "Shouldn't they be here by now?"

"Should?" Protaeus shrugged. "There are too many variables to accept your premise, huunan. Could they have been here by now?

Yes, certainly. But the only relevant fact is that they are not." He walked a short distance away and began speaking in a low voice with Ariis, using the Vanha tongue.

"What is the point of changing languages - Creugar could not understand him when he was speaking ours anyway." The big Reaver clapped Triistan on the back, nearly knocking the wind out of him. "Do not fear, monkey-man. They will return. Your Blackblades will see to it."

Triistan was about to respond when they heard a distant horn blast, followed by a powerful roar. There could be no mistaking Vuuthor's voice, nor the howling screams of their enemies rising in answer from several locations. A few sounded as if they were only a street or two away from where they had stopped, so Protaeus motioned them all in close.

There were more jharrl cries answering as well, most of them from the direction of the apex's call, and when they heard the blast of a second horn from back the way they'd come, the Vanha all grinned fiercely.

"Well, there's your answer, child. That second call was Danor's. The first was Linessa's -" A third horn interrupted him.

"- and Syr answers her husband! We may yet live to see the Long Evening this day, brodiirs. Gather yourselves. We are a few blocks from the edge of The Plaza. Once we get there, we will have no cover until we reach the Weir. Six hundred yards of open ground, with the Darkspawn at our heels - history's great wheel come round again for another turn." Several of the other Oathguard thumped their chests in a silent salute. With a chill, Triistan realized he was referring to the story Danor had told them about Tau defeating the god Taisha as she pursued him across The Plaza.

Protaeus, the only known son of Cartis the Navigator, raked them with his gaze, eyes blazing fiercely. Any trace of his former disdain was gone.

"Come. Now we will see what the Children of Tarsus are truly made of."

So began the longest race of Triistan's relatively short life.

The Oathguard led them at a jog, holding to a pace they could keep fairly easily at first. Still, Triistan's heart hammered in his chest in anticipation of the moment when they would break cover and have to run in earnest. He tried to control his breathing, to will himself to calm down, but it was useless; the harder he tried, the more difficult it became. He did manage to sheath the curved kilij though - no small accomplishment while on the move - and that at least made running less awkward.

A low thrumming began to build in the air around them, which he took for distant thunder. The sky was overcast, but behind the heavy clouds the first of Ruine's two suns had crested the horizon. There was just enough light to see a widening gap in the buildings ahead, with a clearing behind that must be the edge of The Plaza. A bone-chilling chorus of howls rose up behind and to their right, very close, and suddenly a torrent of dark shapes poured over the rooftops and ruins not fifty yards from their flank.

"Now - RUN!!"

The beleaguered survivors of the Aarden Expedition - only thirteen of the original twenty who'd set out just a few weeks earlier - ran for their lives. It didn't take long to confirm that Protaeus' uncompromising brutality in dealing with Thinman had saved them all from almost certain death. The Vanha loped along with them effortlessly, allowing their mortal charges to set the pace this time, but it took everything Triistan had to keep up with his fellow Seekers, and he knew that they were all in far better condition than Thinman had been. Even if he hadn't been dying as the Vanha claimed, he would not have been able to match this pace, they would have stayed with him rather than leave him to his fate, and they all would have been overcome by the dark tide rushing after them.

Even so, the H'Kaan horde still closed the distance with alarming speed. Triistan risked a glance over his shoulder and stumbled at the shock of seeing so many. They were everywhere, flowing down the faces of the buildings lining the causeway and rushing towards them along the street like a rogue wave. Only this wave was full of teeth and claws. He was certain they would be overtaken before they ever reached The Plaza.

The rumble of thunder was louder out here, away from the other buildings. 'Thrum' would have been a better word to describe it, for he fancied he could feel it as a dull, continuous vibration as they ran. He wondered if it was part of some impending attack - Ossien or one of his lieutenants preparing to level them with a blast of lightning or some other arcane calamity.

As they sprinted between the last two buildings, a shadow fell across them. Triistan looked up to see a large winged shape hurtling down from one of the rooftops like some giant bird of prey. He cried out in panic, thinking that somehow the goddess Taisha had returned to exact her vengeance. His comrades slowed, looking up in alarm as he fumbled for the hilt of his kilij...

... then realized with a start that it was actually another Oathguard. What he had mistook for wings was a billowing cloak made of dazzling feathers he had seen before, in the Low Hall. It was Syr.

She glided over their heads to land behind them, rolling to absorb the impact and coming up in a crouch with both arms out wide. In each hand she held a strange-looking crossbow. Both were smallish for a man, but for one of the godkin, they were ideally sized to operate one-handed. Remarkably, each weapon had three bolts loaded, and as she squeezed the triggers, she was able to fire them all in rapid succession. She dropped the six closest H'Kaan an instant after coming out of her roll and was back on her feet and urging them on only a heartbeat after that.

"Keep moving!" Protaeus shouted as Syr fell in between Rhiisa and Rhea.

"Nice entrance," one of them said.

"Danor?" came her clipped response as she began reloading each crossbow on the run. Her hands moved with swift skill and precision.

"With the Lord Marshal and Crixus. Buying them time to complete a Binding on Sithis."

Syr glanced sideways at Rhea. "Did it work?"

"Seemed to be when we left them. No one knows how long it will hold, though. Danor told us about Braxus, but what of Helix and Arthos?"

She turned and fired without breaking stride, taking down three more H'Kaan, just as Protaeus and Ariis entered The Plaza. The swarm flowed over and around the fallen respawn, no more than fifty feet behind them.

"Exactly where they're supposed to be," Syr answered.

As the three reunited Vanha burst from between the buildings out onto the open parade ground, Triistan heard a shout from the rooftops. Protaeus and Ariis stopped and turned to look. The others followed their example, and saw Helix and Arthos standing atop the closest corner of each building. A huge wheel stood before each warrior, mounted vertically to the side of a wedge-shaped metal trough. Triistan later learned that the wheels were attached to a long axle that ran the length of each building, and that the troughs were anchored to the axle. A thick handle jutted out perpendicularly from the outer rim of each wheel: as Helix and Arthos shouted, they leaned into the levers, straining hard to tip the troughs. Suddenly they lurched forward and the sluice crashed against the low parapet wall, sending torrents of dark liquid cascading over the side and into the street below, just as the first wave of H'Kaan passed between them. The two warriors stooped, momentarily lost from view behind the wall, then reappeared again, blazing torches held in each hand.

"Deuth paas a-mani Ostenvaard, brokuuros," Syr said grimly: Welcome to Ostenvaard, bastards. Then she added over her shoulder, "You should duck, huunan."

Helix and Arthos flung their torches into the void between the two buildings and immediately dove away. Triistan was too mesmerized to heed Syr's warning, watching the flaming brands tumble through the air towards the seething mass of shadow pouring through the gap. Well before the torches hit the ground, the entire area erupted in light and flame, and a heartbeat later a clap of thunder echoed across The Plaza, so loud he could feel it. The next instant a rush of hot wind singed his eyebrows and hair and knocked him staggering backwards.

Several of the Seekers let out surprised cheers, but the Oathguard remained stoic, as did the three Reavers - although Creugar flashed him a grinning wink when their eyes met. As the sound of the explosion subsided, the strange thrumming noise continued, now strong enough to feel through the soles of his boots.

"Keep moving," Syr ordered. "That won't slow them for long."

"What in the dead gods' names was that?" Captain Vaelysia asked as they started off again. "I've never seen oil go up like that before."

"That is the Liina Fiero," Protaeus answered her, his voice full of pride. "The Fire-Line. There is oil in the mixture to increase its viscosity, but the real agent is a substance we extract through a complicated process not entirely dissimilar to the stills you use to make your rum. Extremely flammable and -"

He was interrupted by another explosion off to their right, a few hundred yards away. A huge gout of flame shot out from between two more buildings perched on the outer rim of the The Plaza.

"- volatile," Protaeus finished with satisfaction. "It looks as though at least one of the other scouting parties got through. Mind your footing."

A shallow gutter cut through the huge stone slabs that paved the Plaza, bisecting their path, but it was only two feet wide so they all crossed it in stride. Triistan was surprised to see water running along the center of the gutter as he crossed over, trying to remember the last time it had rained. Though less than a foot deep, the bottom was in shadow and he could see the distinctive blue luminescence they had seen in the Glowater and throughout Ostenvaard's underkeep.

Syr said something to Rhiisa, who lifted her horn to her lips and blew a single blast. A moment later they heard the answering call from the direction of the last explosion. Triistan could make out another group of Oathguard and jharrls loping across the open ground, more or less on a line that would intersect with theirs right about...

"Salt and stone," someone gasped. The Weir rose before them.

It was all Triistan could do to keep running and not stop and gape stupidly. He had been so distracted by the pursuing H'Kaan and the two explosions that he had yet to look ahead in the direction they were running.

Everything they had seen thus far - the colossal statue in the bay, the massive wall rising out of the jungle and the Rivergate that pierced it, even the grand fortress-city behind them - all of it seemed but a pale mockery, a child's attempt to copy a master sculptor's art with clumps of wet sand.

The large flags of the Plaza ran out before them for several hundred more yards, broken at regular intervals by gutters like the one they had just crossed; they hopped across another only twenty or so paces later, and as before, a steady stream of glowing water ran down its center. The gutters created a sort of grid pattern which ultimately converged on two points at the far edge of the plaza, where two massive towers rose into the sky - seeming almost to scrape the swollen bellies of the clouds hanging fat and heavy above. A misting rain had begun to fall, but Triistan hardly noticed: his eyes were drawn to the towers, and the giant shadow looming behind them in the haze.

The spires backed against the exposed face of an escarpment bisecting Aarden, connecting its northern and southern coasts with a natural wall that was all but impassable. Here at the Weir, a shallow steephead valley cut into the cliff, several hundred yards wide and bracketed by the towers. As far as Triistan could see in either direction outside of that opening, the upper edge of the cliff bristled with ramparts and smaller spires, many of which seemed to be suspended out over the bluff's edge. Between the towers, blocking the entrance to the valley, a high wall had been built from huge blocks of lightly-colored stone, unadorned save for the battlements along its crown and the tall, arched shadow of a gate at its center. The right hand spire was noticeably shorter than the left one and looked to have been broken off somewhere near the top.

Behind this redoubt, rising several hundred feet into the murky sky, a giant stood with his arms outstretched, immense hands lost in the battlements atop either side of the valley's edge. The figure was vague and distorted by the mist, but after having seen the gigantic statue in Haagen's Bay, Triistan knew it was something similar, though on a scale he had heretofore been unable to imagine. This statue was hundreds of feet taller, easily four to five times the size of the one in the bay.

The source of the deep, thrumming vibration, which had continued to grow louder and stronger as they continued across the open ground, soon became clear: water cascaded over the statue's heavily-muscled shoulders, falling in a great curtain in front of its body like a shimmering tabard, before disappearing somewhere behind the massive wall in a dull roar. What he thought had been rain was more likely just mist caused by the huge cataract.

Above this thundering cascade, the statue seemed to be missing a significant portion of its head. Enough remained that he could tell it had originally been carved to look as if the head were lowered, either brooding or laboring under some great effort. Long, wavy hair draped wetly across both shoulders, but something had sheared the head nearly in half, cutting a diagonal line from above its right ear to just below what remained of its left jaw. More water tumbled over the jagged edge from the place where the hollow of the figure's cheek would have been.

Triistan's reverie was rudely broken when a nightmare chorus of howling screams rose up behind them as the remaining H'Kaan entered the Plaza and caught sight of their prey.

"MOVE!" Syr urged them from the rear.

The Fire Line had bought them some time - they were about halfway across the clearing - but the dark tide of their pursuers was devouring the gap quickly. To their right, the other group of Oathguard and Vanha had changed their angle somewhat so that their paths would converge sooner. That would still only bring their number to ten Oathguard and thirteen Seekers, however, against who knew how many hundred H'Kaan - or how many of that number were the much more dangerous dracosii 'spitters'. Triistan ran harder.

They came to the edge of a much wider channel running diagonally from the base of the rightmost tower to a point where it converged with a second channel emanating from the left-hand one. The two became one wide river that cut through the Plaza, sweeping away to their left and disappearing out of site along the edge of the city's outer perimeter. Framed by the two smaller channels and this confluence, a large island of paved stones formed the only approach to the mighty gates looming ahead of them, now only a hundred or so yards away.

They ran along the paved embankment of the right channel, passing abandoned footings of several narrow bridges that had once spanned it. They leapt over another shallow gutter, which he could now see was a means of controlling potential flooding if the water level in the channels rose too high, as it was now, causing the running water he had observed earlier.

"Well met, brodiirs!" Linessa called as her group fell in with them. Val, Vendros, Kuthan, and the five jharrls accompanying them - including the Apex, Vuuthor - fanned out behind the party.

Even though they were still vastly outnumbered, Triistan felt a sudden surge of hope. They were close to safety and they were going to make it. Cramps lanced his side, and his lungs and injured calf were on fire, but somehow he ran faster, found the energy even to gasp out words of encouragement to Jaegus when the young Seeker stumbled.

It was a near thing all the same. They followed the edge of the channel until it ran through three heavy steel grates layered across a wide opening at the base of the tower. The noise of the rushing water here was almost loud enough to drown out the H'Kaan: it was churning madly inside the tower, a cacophonous roar echoing within the stone chamber before tumbling out through the grates like the rapids of a river. From here they also had a fairly good view of the main gate, two monstrous, arching wings of glimmering black metal that could only be blacksteel. He had never seen so much of the precious material in one place, could not even conceive how it would have been forged and shaped on such a scale. Despite the imminent danger, this new architectural wonder captured his imagination and his head felt like the tumultuous water: it was filled with too many questions and theories all trying to force their way out through the choke point of his mouth and tongue. He clamped his jaw shut and forced the tide back, and not for the first time since discovering Aarden, he felt a sharp twinge of sadness at what the world had lost with the gods' demise.

As they made their way along the base of the tower, he cast one more glance upwards at the walls and gates and caught a faint shimmering: water was running down their steel faces and over the huge blocks of the wall as well, in much larger quantities than he would have expected just from this misty rain. It was as if the entire structure were weeping...

Before he had time to pursue that thought, however, Protaeus hurried them around the curving base of the tower to where it joined with the cliff face. There was a narrow alcove there, just wide enough and tall enough for the Vanha to pass through. As Protaeus and the others disappeared into it ahead of him, he discovered it was actually a passage that ran about thirty feet into the base of the tower. The wall on their right was rough stone, likely the natural face of the escarpment itself, and everything here was wet; like the gates, both walls were slick with running water, the ceiling dripped in countless places, and a steady stream of it ran along the floor of the passage, deep enough to splash through as the company followed it to the solid metal door at its end. More blacksteel, of course.

There was a sudden commotion at their rear as the jharrls engaged the first wave of H'Kaan outside the entrance to the tunnel. For an instant Triistan feared they were trapped, until the door suddenly swung open to reveal Fyruun, whom Danor had warned the Seekers about - the one the others called 'Justice'. His mother had been Lyrin the Judicator, whose murder by human hands had touched off the Godswar. He saluted his Oathguard brethren as they passed, but had only a hard stare for the Seekers.

They entered a large room, unremarkable save for a domed ceiling and the steady roar of rushing water, which seemed to come from everywhere. Empty weapons racks lined the walls and an arched opening in the corner opposite the door they had just passed through showed the hint of a wide, curved stair leading upwards into shadow. Every surface was wet and gave off the familiar ghostly blue glow. At least it allowed them to see without the need for torches.

It was hard to hear above the din, but he could make out the sound of shouts and snarls as the jharrls slowly gave ground in the passageway. Fyruun took up a position next to the opening, opposite the door, a huge two-handed sword held before him. Elaborate runes ran down the center of the wide blade, which Triistan half-expected to burst into flame like some of the old stories he had read as a child.

Ariis and Protaeus moved behind the blacksteel door. It was nearly a foot thick, with three fat bars nested inside channels in the main slab of the door itself. Triistan had seen this in several portals in the underkeep - the bars were attached to an ingenious mechanism on the back of the door which allowed the Oathguard to slide the bars into adjacent keyways in the jamb. If these bars were anything like the ones he'd seen, they would penetrate at least three feet into the adjoining wall, sealing the portal shut and making it very difficult to breach.

Syr backed in, both crossbows pointed down the passageway but unable to get a clear shot, so she gave way to Val, Vendros, Kuthan and Linessa. They must have lost one of the jharrls, as only three came through the door. Vuuthor was guarding their rear now on his own, but between his rage and the narrow passageway, the H'Kaan were keeping their distance. At the last second, they charged, but the Oathguard had no trouble slamming the portal shut and throwing home the locking mechanism. The door thudded dully from the assault on the other side, but it did not seem to be in any danger of failing.

"Justice, close the passage," Protaeus ordered.

Fyruun hesitated. Several of the other Vanha looked at Protaeus.

"My husband is still out there," Syr said coldly.

And Biiko, Triistan thought with a sharp pang of despair.

Rhiisa was nodding. "As are Tau and Crixus - the postern doors have never been breached. Give them more time."

Protaeus shook his head. "The towers have never taken this much load before. Not to mention those dracosii were different - stronger and faster. The Worm's been busy and we don't know what other modifications he's made, what else might be out there. We can't take the chance. They can still use the other tower." As if for emphasis, something struck the door, hard. Bits of mortar and a thin stream of water trickled down from the ceiling near the doorway.

Syr ignored it and stepped close to Protaeus. She was slightly taller, which she used to her advantage, looming over him.

"There's a fifty-fifty chance they'll choose the wrong one and come here, where they'll be trapped. This isn't the best time to make a power play, son of Cartis." Her voice was all ice and sharp steel.

Protaeus did not seem impressed, though. He tilted his head to the side, smirking.

"You don't give them much credit, Syr." His behavior was almost boyish, as though he were enjoying being the center of attention, even if it was negative. He nodded his head in the direction of the door, which thudded under another impact. More dust drifted down, and the trickle became a small but steady stream.

"They'll see our horde of friends out there, and I daresay even your lover is smart enough to choose door number two."

Syr's jaw muscle twitched, and she spoke through clenched teeth. "If you close the passage, the surviving H'Kaan will disperse, and there will be no indication of which way we've come. They will probably come out on the same side of the channel as we did and will therefore be-"

"If they are not in sight of the Weir by now," Protaeus cut her off, his voice rising in frustration, before finishing more gently, "then they are already lost." Syr blinked.

The door boomed again, louder than any of the previous strikes.

Val spoke for the first time. Her voice was surprisingly soft and in marked contrast to the huge double-bladed axe she was fingering.

"Whatever's hitting that door, it's bigger and stronger than any of the Respiis we've faced so far."

"There's something else," Linessa added, nodding. "Their movements are too well coordinated, and there are more of them than our - than my - initial estimate of ten fists. Far more. There has to be another L'suu here - perhaps all three."

Several of the other Vanha swore, and Syr closed her eyes for a moment, her lips compressed in a tight, thin line. Triistan had been staring at her and Protaeus and was surprised to see the arrogant smirk on his face soften. He actually touched her elbow hesitantly, as if trying to give some comfort, before turning away to address Fyruun again.

"Drop it," he said softly. Justice nodded, sheathed his huge sword and strode over to a large lever set in the wall, to the left of the postern door. He reached up to grasp it with both hands, then pulled down hard. He kept ahold of the lever, straining to keep it in position.

There was a brief pause before several loud clicks could be heard inside the wall and above their heads, followed by a terrible grating noise and the sound of chains moving over metal, not unlike the sound of a portcullis being raised or lowered. Everyone's eyes followed the sound across the ceiling. Then the noise stopped, except for the din of the water and thumping impacts on the outside of the postern door as the H'Kaan continued trying to batter a way in.

Fyruun looked across at Protaeus, who gave a single nod, and the son of Lyrin practically jumped back from the handle, releasing it. The lever slammed upwards and a tremendous crash shook the walls and floor, the echoes trembling along the stone surfaces for several seconds after, until only the sound of rushing water remained.

***

The climb up the curving tower stairs was a difficult struggle for Triistan and the other members of the Aarden Expedition. The steps had been cut for Vanha strides, so Triistan found himself leaning forward, using his hands for extra support and leverage. Syr had left before the vibrations from the collapsing passage had ceased, presumably heading for the postern door in the other tower. Linessa, Val, Vendros and Kuthan had followed her, taking the jharrls with them. Protaeus urged the Seekers to hurry, but did not bother to wait, and he and Ariis soon disappeared out of sight above them. That left Fyruun, Rhea and Rhiisa, who no longer carried Brekha's body. The twins had laid her gently against the wall of the first room and arranged her as if for burial, with her arms crossed over her sword. They took the rear, while the sullen son of Lyrin led, keeping his own brisk pace until he came to a landing, where he would wait until they caught up and then continue on without a word.

They passed several doors on their way up, most of which accessed small rooms with arrow ports through the outer face of the tower, but occasionally they would pass wide archways on the opposite side of the stairwell. These opened up onto huge, circular chambers dominated by a massive round column in the center. As they climbed, the din of rushing water gave way to a deep, steady hum that he could feel with his whole body. While the stairwell itself was dry, the column, ceiling and floor immediately adjacent to it were wet in every one of these central rooms. Water flowed down the surface of the column as well, leading Triistan to surmise that it was seepage from vast quantities of it being transported through a central core and out through the churning rapids they had seen at the tower's base. Why, he could not begin to fathom. He yearned to stop and investigate one of these rooms, which also contained innumerable gears, rods, chains, pipes, beams and other devices he could not name.

By the time they reached the top, however, he was too exhausted to wonder about anything but his next breath. His legs and back ached, and his wounded calf felt as if it had been flayed. Even the Reavers were winded, and for a moment the only thing he was aware of was the collective panting of he and his comrades, most of whom were doubled over, hands on knees, sucking in what air they could. Above that he heard the roar of falling water, which had returned with a vengeance. After a moment, he stood.

They were on an expansive, round platform with a stone floor and low ramparts all the way around. Massive columns made of polished black stone rose up around the perimeter, nine in all, evenly spaced, all of which were broken off only a few feet up from the floor. The stairs they had been climbing continued up six or seven steps before stopping in a broken line, suggesting they had once spanned this open area and reached up into the missing portion of the tower. The cliff face that had formed one wall of the passage leading to the postern door far below continued upwards along one side, eventually disappearing into the rainy gloom above. Several paces away, a wide fissure split the rock face of the cliff, but Triistan could not see inside it; the clouds had settled in lower and the rain had quickened, reducing visibility.

"By the dead gods," Captain Vaelysia whispered. "Lift your eyes, lads. This is what we signed up for all those long leagues ago."

One by one the rest of the party straightened and stared upwards, mouths agape.

The gargantuan statue they had viewed from the plaza now loomed directly overhead. Its broad, muscular chest and torso took up most of their field of view in one direction, and above them, Triistan could see its massive left arm, stretching out to where it connected with the battlements wreathed in mist at the top of the cliff. Like the statue in the harbor, this had been wrought from the same smooth, black stone that looked like marble but which held the barest hint of transparency. Most of the head was gone, making it impossible to judge its likeness, but what they could see now had been carved with incredible skill. The figure was naked, with every muscle, tendon, and strand of hair meticulously etched to depict a being of flawless strength and vigor. The statue in the bay had depicted an Oathguard and two jharrls: to Triistan's eye, this looked like a god.

A great torrent of water cascaded over the broken remains of the statue's jaw, but it was barely a creek compared to the roaring falls behind it. The barbican with its two anchoring towers closed the mouth to a narrow valley. Adjacent to each column, the walls of the escarpment bent inward to frame the valley, converging at a large outcropping of stone that stuck out like the prow of some world-breaking ship thrusting through a wave of rock and earth. The giant stood with his back against this natural spire, arms outstretched to either side, as if he were holding it back, or as if he were ripping the valley open with his bare hands. Cataracts spilled over both sides of the outcropping, thundering down in great jets over the stone god's broad shoulders. Now that half of its head was gone, some of the water was also finding its way into and over the remains, creating the smaller falls they had first noticed from the plaza. It appeared that the valley was flooded, but from where he stood Triistan could not quite see past the parapet. As he drank in the magnificent sight, the words of the Seeker Vow whispered in his mind.

To sail beyond the Wind, to find that which has been Lost, and to drive back the Darkness with the torch of Discovery.

Most of the crew had grown jaded towards the Vow: life aboard a Seeker vessel was hard, life aboard a Mapper even harder. The romantic whimsy with which most of them had first heard the words had long since been bleached out by sun, wind, rain, and the strict regulations of Seeker Protocol. But in that moment, Triistan and the others were transported, feeling nothing but a joyful sense of awe and wonder. It was the last peaceful moment most of them would ever know.

Fyruun did not allow them to linger, nor did he offer up any information about the statue or their surroundings. Instead, he ordered them to follow and led them around a large heap of blackened rubble occupying the center of the platform. Triistan decided it must have once been some kind of siege weaponry, like a trebuchet, though much larger than anything he had ever seen. As they circled it, the other tower with its undamaged spire was faintly visible through the rain, but barely noticeable next to the unobstructed view of the stone giant, and the fact that it stood waist-deep in a large lake. Much of the great water mystery that had dogged Triistan since they first approached this incredible structure suddenly became clear.

The Weir wasn't just a fortified gate; it was a dam.

On the far side of the circular floor, overlooking Ostenvaard, a gap in the battlements gave way to a wide terrace and another set of stairs curving downward around the outside of the spire. Fortunately, it was for accessing the top of the wall, so it was a relatively short descent and they weren't exposed to the dizzying view of how far up they had climbed for very long. Even with the rain and the limited visibility, Triistan - who loved the continuously shifting heights of a ship's rigging - had felt the sly pull only the ground seemed to have when viewed from a treacherous height like this.

Since the stairs followed the curve of the tower's outer wall, they were afforded an excellent view of the valley as they descended. The stone god stood nearly twice as tall as the barbican, rising up from the center of the lake, which reached his midriff.

As they neared the bottom of the steps, Triistan dodged around those in front of him and ran to the edge of the wall to confirm his suspicions. When he did, he was shocked to see a face gazing back up at him.

The water of the lake was clear, allowing them to see not just the submerged floor of the valley but also the inside surface of the great gates and the massive bars that held them fast.

At the foot of the gates, large eyes stared up at them from beneath a thunderhead brow, past an aquiline nose the size of a ship's rudder. They belonged to a face they all knew from countless illustrations, books, paintings, statues and works of art that featured his image. A face he could still recognize despite the leprous scabs of algae that now covered it.

"Tarsus," Triistan breathed.

- 24 -

The Calm

"They're withdrawing!" Tarq shouted from the opposite side of the wall. Triistan tore his gaze away from the drowned face of Tarsus, last of the Old Gods, and ran to join the others.

Rhea and Rhiisa were with his shipmates, pointing towards the city and talking excitedly to Fyruun in the Vanha tongue, but Protaeus, Ariis, and the group led by Syr were nowhere to be seen. Triistan assumed they had gone to the other tower to defend its postern door in the hopes that Danor, Tau, Crixus and Biiko would make a dash for it. He looked down the length of the rampart in that direction, but a large, semi-circular structure at the center of the Weir blocked his view. Fyruun sprinted towards it just as Triistan joined the others.

"I'll be drowned, its Danor and the others - there!"

The First Mate pointed across the open plaza to another broad street spilling into it a few blocks to the right of the Causeway. A storm of shadow was pouring forth from the gap, swirling around a tight knot of frenzied activity at its center. Triistan could make out four large figures at the eye of this strange vortex; three man-shaped and one jharrl, and even though they were too far away to recognize clearly, it had to be Danor, Tau, Crixus and Atuu. He felt his chest tighten when he did not see Biiko. He didn't see the mantiisa creature or its rider, either, and he feared his friend and protector had been captured or killed.

"They'll never make it," Brehnl Highdock muttered. "There's too fuckin' many."

"Stow that shite, Docks," Izenya growled under his breath, looking at the nearby twins warily. "Not sure our hosts will take too kindly to it. Besides, I think you're wrong. Sure as that cock you call a nose I ain't bettin' against'em."

Triistan agreed with d'Gara despite the numbers. From their elevated position, it was easy to see how effective the Oathguard were, as their tiny group carved a swath through the sea of dark bodies. The three Vanha fought with that same fluid precision he'd already witnessed with Tau and Crixus, moving around each other in a complex dance, while Atuu leapt in and out of the surrounding ranks, tearing the H'Kaan apart with teeth and claws wherever the jharrl landed. There were no blue flashes in this battle, just a boiling tide of indistinct black shapes and the occasional wink of the day's meager light sparking off steel. Yet the Oathguard drove steadily forward across the Plaza towards the other tower despite the swelling ranks of H'Kaan surrounding them. Several of those watching began to urge them on, quietly at first, but with growing intensity.

Triistan was still searching for Biiko when suddenly a heavy hand clapped down painfully on his shoulder. "Ha! Creugar told you your Blackblades would see them through! The stink-lizards are no match for him!"

At that moment the Pathfinder's much smaller figure appeared from behind the trio of Vanha. From this distance Triistan could not make out his twin black blades, but there was no mistaking the way he moved, or the fate of the H'Kaan he left in his wake. He couldn't contain a small cheer as the others began to call out more loudly.

A moment later, Fyruun and Ariis emerged from the semi-circular building, which Triistan assumed must be some form of gatehouse. They approached swiftly, but kept their eyes fixed on the battle below.

Captain Vaelysia gestured at the swarm of H'Kaan. "That's a lot more than five hundred, Su'ul. Where are they all coming from?"

Ariis frowned and spat over the wall. His partial right arm was fitted with a large buckler shaped like an elongated tear drop, with the broad end near his shoulder. The narrow end had been cleverly cut and fashioned to create two nasty looking blades, making the shield a weapon as well as an aegis. A broadsword with an elaborate ivory hilt was sheathed at his hip.

"The Worm's been busy, and has built himself quite a nest. Now it seems he wants ours."

"Now?" she echoed. "Haven't they attacked you before?"

"Not like this. Not in strength."

The Captain glanced sidelong at First Mate Tarq and several of the Seekers exchanged worried looks.

- 389 -

"Do you have any idea why?" But for answer, Ariis only spit over the wall again. Fyruun muttered something in the Vanha tongue, his tone dark and his expression bitter.

Protaeus appeared from around the back side of the gatehouse just then and joined them at the battlements.

"Now we shall see how far they've come," he said cryptically as he watched the drama unfolding below. Danor and the others had made it about two-thirds of the way across the Plaza and were wading into the river being fed by the two towers, a few hundred yards downstream from the confluence in front of the Weir. The group had almost fought their way clear of their attackers, so that the majority of the H'Kaan were swarmed at their backs; as yet there were none on the opposite bank. The H'Kaan that had abandoned their assault on this side of the Weir had not crossed the river yet either, but they were alarmingly close to the point where Lord Marshal Tau was leading his beleaguered group into the water. When this second pack reached the bank, they dove into the channel without slowing.

A few quiet cheers burst forth from the Oathguard on the battlements, startling Triistan and his shipmates. Only Protaeus was silent, standing a little bit apart from them and shaking his head. When the H'Kaan surfaced a moment later and began moving towards Danor's group, the cheers became gasps of dismay.

"No!" one of the twins cried, whirling to face Protaeus. "Why do they not drown as before?" It was obvious from their expressions that the other Vanha had expected the same.

Protaeus shook his head, muttering to himself. "The paradigm shifts again..." He suddenly realized the others were staring at him, waiting for an explanation. "It's rather obvious, isn't it? They have adapted."

"What of our defenses then?"

"We must do the same," Protaeus shrugged.

"What do you mean, 'adapted'?" Captain Vaelysia asked. "What were you expecting to happen, Su'ul?"

The H'Kaan were heading downstream fast, aided by the swift current and an apparent affinity for the water. Their sleek reptilian bodies cut through it with a serpentine motion, propelled forward by thick tails.

"There are two fundamental sources of power in this world, huunan," Protaeus replied, and made a sweeping gesture with his hand. "The first you know. Ostenvaard. The Young Gods. Us. We use a power infused within us, born of logic and manipulated through precise formulae, the mathematics of reality, revealed to us by the Young Gods, who acquired this knowledge from Tarsus.

"But there is another power. Most know nothing of it, for good reason. Those few that do call it The Forbidden Arts, a practice left over from the time of the Old Gods. This power cannot be measured or controlled, not by any means we know. So the Laegis and the Ashen and a few others sought to eradicate it, or at the very least to bury it.

"And while knowledge of it is all but lost, the power itself is... resilient. Evidence of its use continues to pool in dark places. Dragonsblood we call it now, for its present-day spring is Maughrin, seeping from her prison through the shadows and into this world. It is endless, like the H'Kaan that are spawned from it."

Protaeus made a dismissive gesture. "A misguided characterization though, in my opinion, for She is a beneficiary of the power, a vessel, but not its true source. Just as the Vanha are vessels for arxhemestry, depending on a catalyst to tap into the innate powers of our immortal sires."

"Xhemium," Triistan said, remembering Danor's use of it to rid him of the nagayuun parasites.

Protaeus gave him an appraising look. "Yes... xhemium. When Tarsus rebuilt the world, he made it part of every living thing. Every plant, stone and animal - yes, even huunan and Vanha alike - have xhemium to some degree. Even moreso in Ostenvaard. It is an essential ingredient to everything we have constructed here, and an invaluable part of our defenses." He nodded toward the struggle below. "The Worm has turned to Dragonsblood for his creations. And the two powers, as you may have noted, do not get along."

The channel was fairly shallow where Tau had decided to lead his men across, the water coming up to just above waist-level for the taller Vanha, but Biiko and Atuu were forced to swim. The jharrl was large enough to touch the bottom, but must have found it easier to simply paddle across, with the Unbound clinging to its fur. While the main body of H'Kaan was still milling along the edge of the canal, the group in the water was closing fast. They would likely catch their prey before they'd made it halfway across.

"Left over from the time of the Old Gods?" the Captain asked. "But the Old Gods made Ruine. Why would they allow..."

Protaeus laughed, quietly and cruelly, cutting her off. Before the conversation could continue, however, the battle was joined below.

As the H'Kaan converged on Tau and the others, Biiko pulled himself onto Atuu's back and sat astride the jharrl like a horse, using both blades to fend off the creatures to either side. In response, many of them dove beneath the surface to attack Atuu's vulnerable legs. He screamed in rage and pain, bucking and lunging like some wild stallion being broken for the saddle.

Meanwhile the larger horde of H'Kaan respawn, still perched on the edge of the channel, seemed to take their cue from the first group and suddenly surged into the canal. The water churned and frothed with black and grey bodies, while the Oathguard fought desperately to protect themselves and continue moving forward. Tau and Crixus fought on opposite sides of the group, their long polearms sweeping and thrusting dozens of H'Kaan bodies aside while Danor drove his way to Atuu's flank. There he was abruptly dragged under, re-emerging seconds later with a roar and an explosion of water, holding one of the H'Kaan aloft by the back of its head. The beast writhed, tail whipping back and forth for an instant before the big Vanha crushed its skull and hurled it away from him. Another scrambled up his broad back, but Atuu seized it in his jaws and snapped its spine with one powerful bite.

The group fought valiantly, but for every H'Kaan they killed, two more took its place. Even though they were more than three-quarters of the way across the canal, their progress had slowed noticeably, and now some of the H'Kaan had reached the opposite side and were clambering up the bank to cut them off.

"We have to do something to help them!" Triistan cried out in desperation.

Protaeus looked at him with disdain. "Do you think we have stood this watch for centuries because we are weak? Or that we have outlived the gods by being fools? Watch, Child of Tarsus."

Most of the swarm was in the water now, when suddenly Tau, Danor and Crixus came together, raising their weapons high in a sort of pyramid. When bladestaff, trident and lucerne touched, something changed in the air, suppressing sound and making the inside of Triistan's ears ache. He saw Tau shout something over his shoulder at Biiko, while a myriad of tiny blue sparks flared to life in the air above the plaza, no larger than fireflies but glowing with ferocious intensity. Biiko vaulted from Atuu's back, clearing the heads of the H'Kaan climbing out of the water and landing on his feet just as the sparks simultaneously converged on the three Vanha, as if sucked in by one giant breath. The heads of the weapons disappeared in a brilliant flash, and the Oathguard swung them out away from one another, striking the surface of the canal. The water flashed - not just that flowing through the channel but the entire grid of gutters carved into the floor of the Plaza as well - blazing so brightly the onlookers had to shield their eyes. For just an instant, Triistan thought he saw something familiar in the pattern of spillways.

It isn't a grid... But before the idea could fully form an unpleasant itching sensation coursed through his body. There was a muffled groaning noise which he felt more than heard and an instant later a clap of thunder broke across the plaza.

Sound rushed back in with a roar as the water in the canal leaped upwards in a wide ring around the beleaguered Vanha, catapulting the bodies of their attackers backwards. Fine veins of blue lightning crackled through the water, snaking over the bodies of the H'Kaan and jumping between the airborne ones in vicious blue arcs, like giant sparks. They plummeted back to the ground, burning. Black smoke curled from lifeless husks on either side of the canal, or became hissing steam as water flooded back into the channel.

Triistan and his fellow Seekers gaped. It had lasted only a few seconds, but when it was over, hundreds of H'Kaan corpses littered the Plaza in a large circle centered on the Lord Marshal's party. Still dozens more floated down the canal. Other than Tau's group, who had reached the near bank unharmed and were climbing out, nothing moved on this side of the water. On the opposite bank, a few score still crawled about aimlessly, but they seemed too badly injured to pose a threat any longer.

Out beyond the blast radius, however, roughly half the swarm had survived. They withdrew quietly, ebbing from the Plaza like a dark tide receding from a stony shore. A strange stillness descended in their wake, heavy with disquiet, and rather than a sense of victory or relief, Triistan felt only foreboding, wondering what would come next. It was a sensation he and his fellow Seekers were all too familiar with: the moment when the wind dies before a big storm.

He jumped when Ariis cursed quietly.

"Something is wrong with Atuu."

The jharrl was stretched out on the bank of the canal, his back end and rear legs still in the water. It looked as if he'd given up while trying to climb out, an act which should have been as easy as a simple bound for the great cat. Danor knelt beside him, bent over with his head close to the jharrl's ear, while Tau was still in the water, examining the cat's hind quarters. When he and Danor tried coaxing Atuu farther up onto the shore, the jharrl suddenly roared and snapped at Danor, actually striking the big healer in the chest with his broad muzzle and knocking him sprawling. It might have been comical had Danor not simply sat where he landed, head lowered like a despondent child.

Vuuthor appeared, loping towards them from the base of the far tower. A moment later, the other three surviving jharrls came into view as well, followed by Syr, a long black bow in one hand and her cloak of feathers billowing out behind her as she ran. Vuuthor and the other jharrls trotted up to stand over Atuu, while Syr stopped beside her husband.

The Apex lowered his huge head and sniffed at the old jharrl, then nudged him with his muzzle. The injured beast gathered his forelegs and, trembling from the effort, pushed himself upright, dragging his hind quarters from the water as he did so. Tau and Crixus took a step back, and several of the Vanha atop the Weir groaned. Danor buried his face in his huge hands.

Atuu swayed, barely supporting himself on three legs, as the fourth had been torn off at mid-thigh. The old jharrl bowed his proud head, gently nuzzling the underside of the much larger Apex's jaw. Vuuthor allowed it for a moment before pulling back and emitting a short, barking roar, at which point the other three jharrls approached. As the giant Apex looked on, they gathered around Atuu, nuzzling and licking him about his ears, face and neck.

After a few moments, Atuu lifted his silver-gray head and roared, drawing the sound out until his pack-mates joined him, their song blending in one long, mournful note. Vuuthor did not join in, but moved closer to stand beside Atuu.

"Agriivo ventiisi me," murmured Fyruun, "a'cretu paasi et fieto l'vhard. Ultiimo, me'fiero paasa sutu." Later, Danor translated the exchange for Triistan: "My friend goes before me, to clear the way and warm the hearth. Until then, my fire burns here."

The other Vanha responded quietly, in rough unison: "A've necuuto." To the last ash.

The jharrls broke off their cry, and the Apex lunged forward and crushed Atuu's neck with one swift bite, killing him instantly.

Taking advantage of the temporary lull, most of the survivors regrouped atop the Weir.

Danor came out of the eastern tower first, followed by Lord Marshal Tau, carrying Atuu's body slung between them like hunters returning with a kill. Biiko exited the tower next, and had it not been such a solemn occasion, Triistan would have embraced him. Last came Kuthan and Crixus, the High Master with his head bowed and massaging the bridge of his nose. Syr and Linessa had been dispatched to scout out the enemy, along with Vuuthor and his surviving pack, leaving Arthos, Val and Vendros to guard the remaining postern door at the base of the eastern tower.

Danor and the Lord Marshal found a sheltered corner where a low wall intersected with the western tower, and there they gently laid Atuu's body on the ground. It was badly mauled in addition to the missing leg, and Triistan was amazed that the old jharrl had been able to stand at the end, let alone fight as long as he had.

Danor knelt and lowered his head until it touched the jharrl's brow. There he remained as each member of the Oathguard left to gather a piece of rubble from the broken western spire and returned to place it around and over Atuu's body in a crude cairn. Triistan and several other members of the Aarden Expedition silently followed suit, wanting to honor Danor and these strange warriors in whatever meager way they could. When they were finished, Danor rose and set the final piece of rubble, covering the great beast's head.

A few moments later, Tau gathered them together.

"It is clear that we badly underestimated the scope of this attack. We need to assess just how badly before we can determine our next move. The essential question before us is whether or not we can still hold the Weir when they come with all of their strength. Given this latest adaptation, our defensive strategy has been compromised and we are in danger of being overrun." He turned to look directly at Captain Vaelysia. "But first, we must safeguard the future by revealing the past."

"Danor," the Lord Marshal spoke over his shoulder without looking away from the Captain, "how much have you already told them?"

"Up to when we found Theckan, Su'ul," the healer said flatly. If there was any hint of inflection when Danor spoke his traitorous father's name, Triistan did not hear it.

Tau nodded. "A good start, but it is time you and your people learned the whole story, Captain.

"When we arrived at The Hold, it was badly damaged. Most of the Wyvhard - warding stones - were broken, the containment vessel was shattered, and the blacksteel chains that had held it in place lay broken on the floor. Some terrible energy had been unleashed to break The Hold, and dozens of our comrades who had arrived in time to see it lay dead, most of them burned beyond recognition. Theckan was still alive, though barely. And Ossien - yes, I speak his name freely, for we are past the need for that precaution now I think - he whom we called the Dark Son, had awoken."

The fitful but insistent breeze that had tugged at their hair and clothing since gaining the top of the Weir died. The Lord Marshal's voice was quiet, but there was a reassuring strength to it; the fortitude of a man who only spoke the truth, no matter how hard it was.

"He... finished Theckan, then fled The Hold. We let him, for we were few, many of us were badly wounded... and all of us were lost in shock and despair."

"And shame," Fyruun interjected. Tau nodded, as did many of the other Oathguard.

"Aye, perhaps the worst of our wounds was to our pride. 'L'Viviit Muurum' had been broken."

The Living Wall, Triistan translated in his mind.

"Not completely," the Captain protested gently. "If my math is right, you've kept him contained here for over two hundred and fifty years since then."

Protaeus chuckled ironically. "Your math is right, child," he said, "but your scale of measurement is useless. To an immortal a quarter of a millennium is only a few moments, especially after having been imprisoned for so long. He's just catching his breath."

"Where?" Triistan asked.

"Where all worms go," Kuthan rumbled. "Underground."

Tau continued. "When we finally did give chase, his path was easy to follow - at first. Some of the scars are still visible today."

"The Rivergate," Triistan whispered, remembering the shattered remains of the huge gates they had found in the river.

"Yiin, he broke Ahbaingeata, among other things" the Lord Marshal nodded, glancing over his shoulder at the broken statue of Tarsus looming in the mist. "Much of what he destroyed on his way out was needless and purely for spite.

"But it was also for power. Among the many black secrets Ossien acquired in his research, stealing a life - literally taking the life from someone and adding it to his own - is the darkest. He used it first to finish off Theckan - ripping his sibling's heart from his smoldering chest and consuming it right before our eyes. It gave him the strength to flee us. After that, he slew anything that crossed his path, leaving a trail of savaged corpses for us to follow. It didn't matter which side they were on - the misguided Templars who had tried to free him or our own - he consumed them all."

"What about The Ravager?" asked Captain Vaelysia.

Tau nodded. "There at least he did us a favor. Heketh the Ravager was spent from his assault on the gates, so he did not recognize the madness and rage that practically dripped from his brother's body. They embraced, and a moment later Ossien dropped Heketh's lifeless body and fled.

"But if he... consumed two gods and all of those men..." she probed.

"Why did he flee?" Tau finished for her. She nodded.

"We don't know, exactly," he shrugged. "We have our theories - whatever strength he gains is temporary and perhaps easily spent being the current favorite."

"It was enough to kill two gods."

"That is true, but both were badly weakened, and neither put up a struggle. Theckan was nearly dead, as I mentioned, and the Rogue's remaining essence gave Ossien his initial strength, perhaps allowing him to chain from one victim to the next." He shrugged again. "For all we know, it may be easier for him to use it on another Arys - something about their physiological make-up perhaps.

"In any event, as we gave chase, we gained strength as well, picking up stragglers and organizing. Many of the survivors had regrouped into smaller squads, to harass the invaders. As we moved down through the city, they joined up with us, so that by the time the Worm reached Ahbaingeata, we had nearly three fists - one hundred and thirty-three men, to be precise.

"I believe we could have brought him down, and I think he knew it."

"What about the attackers - the other Templars?" asked Triistan.

Tau's eyes flashed. "They threw down their arms and begged our forgiveness. We slew them on the spot."

"Even the wounded?"

"The Oath does not allow for mercy."

Triistan and the others stared at the floor.

Viviito et Maugh: Live or die?

After a moment, the Oathguard commander continued. "We lost his trail in the jungle, and when night fell, I called off the hunt. Even broken, Ostenvaard was still our strongest position. We gathered our dead, treated the wounded, and began to fortify. Over the next few weeks, we sent out search teams - never fewer than fifty men - while the rest of us labored on our defenses. They found his trail easily enough. Too easily, in fact. On the fifth day after his escape, he lured the search party into a trap and slew or captured nine of us."

"Captured?" the Captain echoed.

"You have seen one of them."

The hair on the back of Triistan's neck stood up. "Sithis."

"The same. There are two others. We call them L'suu. It means 'The Defiled.'"

"After that, we pursued him more cautiously. There were no more traps - he had acquired what he'd wanted, both time and resources - and not long afterwards the trail finally grew cold. We focused all of our energies on strengthening our position here. There were too few of us to defend the entire city, so we fortified the underkeep first, then gradually worked our way out from there. We knew it was just a matter of time before Ossien was strong enough to attack us, but we did not know how much time it would take him to recover."

Tarq looked puzzled. "Why didn't he just leave Aarden and go somewhere else? Back to Niyah where few could have stood against him?"

Captain Vaelysia was nodding. "Aye, after Ehronfall most of the world was reduced to raw survival for decades."

The Lord Marshal gave her a knowing look. "We are the Oathguard. We are the Living Wall; the First Line…

"These are the first words of our Oath. They are not idle boasts, they are truth. All of Aarden is his prison; each facet, from its unscalable shores, to Ostenvaard's ramparts, to the Hold… to us. It is all linked, interwoven in a Binding only the gods could forge. As long as we still live and breathe - as long as we hold the line here - he is still Bound."

"Then you can't leave either," Triistan whispered. Tau shook his head.

"Only in death."

"And I will hold my post until Ruine's Ending," Fyruun rasped, staring hard at the boy.

Triistan looked down at his feet, feeling selfish and small in the face of such sacrifice. An entire continent continued to live out their tiny, self-absorbed lives completely oblivious to what these men and women had been through on their behalf. Most of them had forgotten the Oathguard ever existed, and the world was only what they saw immediately in front of them.

The Captain seemed to be thinking the same thing. "Thank you, Su'ul. Your honor and sacrifice are... humbling, to say the least." She bowed her head in a gesture of respect.

"But there is still much we do not understand. What happened down there, when the H'Kaan entered the water? What were you expecting?"

"What didn't happen is the problem, Captain," Tau answered. "Protaeus, perhaps you should explain."

"As you wish, Su'ul. We can continue our earlier lesson, huunan, when you stated that the Old Gods made Ruine." A few of the other Vanha smirked at this, and Kuthan snorted from behind his great black tangle of beard.

"The Old Gods found Ruine," Protaeus went on, sounding very much like a school master lecturing his young students. "They were not of Ruine. A common misconception, but in truth they came from somewhere else - no, we do not know where. Our parents did not see fit to share that little detail with us, assuming even they themselves knew in the first place, but it is irrelevant anyway. What matters is that Maughrin, the Living Darkness, was here first."

The Seekers gasped in surprise and muttered to one another. That statement shook the keystones of most of the histories any of them had ever heard. Protaeus smirked.

"It is not unlike your voyage here; I imagine your first assumption was that you'd discovered a large, uninhabited island.

"Surprise," he added smugly.

"The Dragon was the first predator, and the Old Gods looked like easy prey. But they came with Arxhemestry, which burned in bright opposition to her Dark-born power," Protaeus continued. "Xhemium was poison to the Living Darkness and her endless spawn. So the gods forged their weapons from it and etched its power into the very bones of their citadels to make them stronger. They passed the art on to their children, and the Young Gods passed it onto us, though with each transition, some of the potency was lost.

"So try to imagine," he said, sweeping an arm out wide to indicate their surroundings, "how truly wondrous the world must have been back then, if this place is a wanting step-child."

"You do the Young Gods and yourself a disservice, Protaeus," Tau chided. "Ostenvaard is no unworthy bastard: there is still considerable power here, and beauty."

Kuthan grunted and thumped the butt of his huge axe on the stone floor. Triistan took that to mean he shared the Lord Marshal's opinion. Some of the other Vanha murmured their assent as well.

Protaeus shrugged. "I will grant that this was their best work - a testimony to what the Arys could accomplish through their combined efforts, when Auruim and Dauthir put aside their petty differences and remembered they were gods. Though I have always found it deliciously ironic."

"What do you mean?" Captain Vaelysia asked.

He laughed bitterly and massaged his temples. "Ostenvaard is a monument to guilt - the High Houses offering their penance to the rest of the world. The Worm was one of them, remember. He was their brother, and so he was a glimpse of what they could be, the side of themselves none of them wished to acknowledge, but all of them knew was only a shadow away."

Kuthan leaned forward and spat on the ground between his feet. He was chewing on some type of dark root. "He isn't going to wait all year for you to finish your story, builder."

Instead of responding, Protaeus simply held a hand out, and Kuthan gave him the root. Protaeus took a bite before passing what remained to Crixus, sucking on it like a piece of hard candy as he continued.

"Danor told you the story of Ossien's rise, and what ultimately led to his banishment, yes?"

The Expedition members nodded.

"As the Lord Marshal indicated, his... research... was focused on the power I mentioned earlier, which we call Dragonsblood - a power that pre-exists the Old Gods' arrival."

The mist from the cataract behind them had become a steady rain, and the air seemed to have grown heavier.

"He delved deeply into the Dark, mining power from it that the other gods did not understand. His creations were distorted, twisted things, but even so it was not difficult to see their progression and guess his aims. It badly frightened his siblings, so they built this, using every scrap of arcane lore in their possession, all of it based on the Old Gods' ways, dependent on xhemium. No doubt you have seen their symbols and formulas inscribed everywhere throughout the city, and, as the Lord Marshal told you, all of it - from Haagan's Bay to here, every rock, lintel, timber and tile, everything - was meant to work in conjunction, all components to a master binding formula."

He ran his hand along a huge block of stone that formed the base of one of the battlements. It was almost a caress. Triistan gasped; the area immediately behind his trailing fingers flared briefly with dozens of tiny runes etched in soft blue light. It was like wiping his hand across the surface of a still pool; the symbols rippled there for a moment and then faded to nothing.

"Some of the components served obvious, practical purposes, though this one has since been... repurposed. When it was originally created, this wall was intended to hold things out. Now, it holds the waters of the Aniiene in."

"Why?" Triistan interjected.

Protaeus' eyes found Triistan's. "For power, child."

First Mate Tarq leaned forward, nodding. "I thought as much. The Khaliil use the power of water as well. When harnessed, it can do great things."

Protaeus smirked. "Indeed. Laha'na'li and its wonders - shaped by Minet, Ganar and Udgard - were the seedlings of many of the ideas we crafted here. But I am not just talking about using the volume and speed of water to move things. I refer to the single largest source of xhemium in all of Ruine."

"The river?" Triistan said, thinking of its phosphorescence in the tunnel of Ahbaingeata and within the underkeep. Even the flooded lake they had camped beside had glowed when struck by the rain.

"Yiin. The Aniiene's source is close to the Hold - indeed, it was the reason the Young Gods selected that site. Beneath the mountain's thick skin are great caves, the walls and ceilings of which are encrusted with xhemium deposits, planted and cultivated there by Ganar and Udgard. It grows in glittering, solid curtains, like the webs we harvest from the grelos to make our rope."

Triistan saw Captain Vaelysia and Tarq exchange a look he had seen before, whenever they'd caught the scent of a new discovery. Or treasure. He rubbed his eyes, trying to relieve the dull, throbbing ache that had settled in behind them.

Lieutenant Jaspins looked skeptical. "It grows there?"

Lord Marshal Tau nodded. "We call it L'Hortuus. It means 'The Garden'. It is the most sacred place on Ruine."

"And up until now," Protaeus continued, "the principal reason Ruine still exists. The Worm picked up almost where he'd left off in Talmoreth, experimenting on the wildlife indigenous to Aarden. Danor has a better grasp of the biology, but these new beasts served to accelerate his research, despite the fact that he did not have the resources he had enjoyed previously. Somehow he is able to exploit the variations between each species. In any event, barely five decades had passed before we began to see evidence of his machinations. Strange mutations started to appear within the wildlife we hunted - too many eyes, the wrong number of appendages, extraordinary aggressiveness, flightless creatures with misshapen wings... all of them failed experiments, but clear stepping stones in a path we knew was intended to lead to our destruction. Ten years after the first abominations were sighted, he left his calling card right on our doorstep." He looked directly at Triistan. "Or should I say, under it."

The young Seeker winced at the memory of his encounter with the nagayuun.

"The winged beasts you call kongamatu arrived first. Their appetite and aggressiveness caught us by surprise, and we lost three men on a routine patrol. They are remarkably intelligent, although not to the point where they can shed the yoke of their animal instincts. Using this against them, we were able to capture several, and Danor studied them at length. In a fine bit of irony from The Worm, it appears that they have been engineered to crave xhemium as a food source; the very substance the old gods - and us - relied on to combat the H'Kaan hordes. They are... impressive. His first 'success', at least as far as we know, and probably his most natural creation. Danor believes it's why they have thrived - they are close enough to their origin species to coexist with their environment. Over the years, they have even adapted - mutated themselves, if you will, the way all creatures do, though they seem to be doing so at an accelerated pace."

Triistan shivered. "What about the nagayuun? They're like something out of a nightmare. Surely they aren't something that lives here naturally?"

"No," Protaeus answered. "They are an abomination, and a clear warning for us. Even as ferocious as they are, the kongamatu actually gave us a small amount of hope, insofar as they were evidence of a... rational intelligence, even a recognizable level of creative genius. We considered the possibility he could be reasoned with... but when the nagayuun arrived, we realized our naivety -"

"Syr found them," Danor interrupted. While Protaeus was speaking, he, Fyruun and the Twins had moved over to the battlements, looking out over The Plaza.

As the group stood and looked towards the city, they saw a bright green flash arching high into the air. It looked to Triistan like a burning brand, only its flame was a brilliant jade color. Some type of signal arrow, he reasoned, shot from the huge black longbow he had seen her carrying earlier.

"Green means the enemy has been sighted. If they are moving towards us, she will send up a red-"

A blue flare shot into the rain-smeared sky. It was difficult to tell, but Triistan thought the flares were coming from the general direction of the Causeway, where the Lord Marshal and the others had fought the L'suu.

"- and blue means they are encamped," Tau finished. "She will assess their strength now and return, or send up a red if they begin to march." He nodded to Protaeus, signaling him to continue, then went to speak quietly to Ariis. The one-armed warrior jogged off in the direction of the other tower. Triistan returned to his seat, rubbing his temples. His headache was growing worse.

"Why do you allow the nagayuun to live so close to you? Haven't they infested the city as well?" Captain Vaelysia asked.

"An intelligent question, Captain," Protaeus answered. Triistan couldn't tell if he was being sarcastic, until he continued.

"There are very few of them - less than two dozen the last time we surveyed the nest - about twice their original population. Their methods of reproduction are rather nefarious, as you've discovered, requiring hosts. Since learning this, we have not obliged, and, oddly, the kongamatu seem to be immune to the nagayuun stings."

"What about other beasts, like the jharrls?" asked Lieutenant Jaspins. Protaeus shook his head.

"The jharrls patrol the underkeep, but they stay clear of the nest, and something prevents the nagayuun from ranging. Again, despite whatever enhancements have been made to them, and despite their heightened intelligence, they do not seem to be able to overcome their basic animal instincts. This has clearly frustrated Ossien's efforts to infiltrate the city… "

Triistan did not hear the rest of the Vanha's sentence, because the pain in his head had suddenly magnified. He squeezed his eyes shut and ducked his head momentarily. After a moment, the pain receded, though it did not go away completely, and there was a faint ringing in his ears.

"I'll never get used to these fuundaris headaches," Kuthan grunted quietly beside him and broke off a small piece of the strange root the big warrior had been chewing. He passed it to Triistan.

"You have one too?" the young man whispered. But Kuthan ignored his question.

"Suck on that like your favorite tit, boy, but don't swallow it."

"What will happen?" Triistan said as he took the root and looked at it skeptically. The huge Oathguard grunted again.

"If you suck on it, you might lose some of that pain. If you swallow it," he winked conspiratorially, "you might lose your mind."

Triistan gulped and considered giving it back to the giant, but his headache was getting steadily worse. He tucked the root carefully into his cheek, alongside his gum, and clamped his teeth together tightly to make sure it stayed there. Almost immediately he felt a sense of warmth, faint but pleasant, that spread from his cheek, up the side of his face and down his neck. A few seconds later, his headache began to dull so that he was able to focus on Protaeus again.

"… besides," the Vanha architect was saying, "they make a fairly effective deterrent to unwelcome visitors. But that isn't the point. As I mentioned earlier, the Worm's creatures were engineered to crave xhemium - they hunger for it the way some mortal men have an unquenchable thirst for wine. This addiction was as strong as we'd seen it yet in our new tenants, but not strong enough to overpower their own instincts. There is a peculiar struggle going on between whatever vestiges remain of the original model species and the Worm's mutated versions, and although they attacked us relentlessly whenever we ventured near the nests, they would not pursue us into Ostenvaard. We adapted to their presence, further frustrating the Worm's efforts to weaken our position.

"Several years passed. We continued to search for his whereabouts while fortifying here. Eventually, we narrowed it down to two likely locations and dispatched a scouting party to search the site we felt most confident about, a large network of caves carved into a plateau at the east end of the continent. It had once been considered as an alternate site for Ostenvaard, so we were relatively familiar with it. Atop the plateau is a huge lake, which spills over the mesa's outer edge in multiple locations, flooding the lands below and creating a vast marsh around its base. Some of the marshes actually penetrate into the caves, creating a bizarre underground swamp -"

"The closest thing to a shithole you'll find on this rock," Kuthan interjected. "Perfect for a worm to burrow into."

"Yes, thank you for the colorful similitude, Kuthan.

"It was the perfect environment for him; different in every possible way from the lofty perches he and his siblings - particularly his fellow Auruim - had descended from. And as likely a place to find Dragonsblood as any on Aarden."

The pain in Triistan's head was still there, but it had dulled considerably, and was no longer constant. Instead, it came intermittently, a slow tightening that began at the base of his skull and migrated through the rest of his head, moving from back to front. It lasted only a few seconds, but returned in a regular rhythm, like the slow drum beat of heavy footsteps.

"Were you right? Did you find him?" he asked Protaeus, hoping to distract himself from the discomfort. But Danor answered instead, his gravelly bass surprising the young Seeker.

"Yiin, Salty, we were right." He was still leaning against the battlements, watching for his wife's signal.

"But his new pets found us first."

Protaeus looked mildly annoyed at being interrupted. "The Worm had followed his stratagem to its ultimate conclusion, resulting in a new breed of mutations that were remarkably close to his original inspiration, the H'Kaan. Frustrated by earlier prototypes that were still slave to their instincts, he stripped them of all self-awareness and self-determination. These new monstrosities were single-minded, lacking even the most basic intuition for survival. Their only driving force was an insatiable appetite for xhemium.

"I must make this point clear, because Maughrin's spawn were killers, but never hunters; they never consumed their kills. The Respiis were another matter altogether. Their hunger was astonishing - like nothing any of us had ever witnessed before - and for the first time, we were overmatched. Not only had their blind aggression made them much more formidable, but The Worm had introduced variations as well - the dracosa 'spitters' and the hounds, which you've seen - as well as other even more dangerous variations. One was in the postern access tunnel when we collapsed it.

"Perhaps most significantly, this also marked the first time he began breeding them in large numbers. Our scouting party was... ill-equipped -"

"Speak plainly, brodiir," Danor growled. "A horde of nearly two thousand of the fuundaris things caught us in the marshes and tore us to pieces."

Protaeus pressed his lips together in a thin line. "Yes, as I was about to say, our scouting party was ill-equipped and outnumbered. Danor, Ariis and two others were the only survivors."

The Seekers all looked at Danor with astonishment.

"Two thousand?" Triistan asked. "How did you escape, Su'ul?"

The giant looked over his shoulder and the boy could see the sadness in his eyes.

"We fought our way clear and the jharrls bore us away while the Respiis feasted on the fallen. Was like watching a school of long-jaws swarm over a wounded fish - they even attacked each other and ate their own dead. It's like Protaeus says: their minds are black, and they exist for one purpose only - to devour."

He turned back to watch for Syr, still speaking over his shoulder. "Anyway, we fled. I think we could have reached the East Gate, but we had no intention of leading that horde back to the city. They nearly caught us at the edge of the Aniiene Valley, but there are a handful of hidden defiles that cut down through the canyon's flanks, barely wide enough for one of the jharrls to pass. The tight quarters slowed them down enough for us to gain the river, which we crossed, hoping to keep it between us at least as a defensive barrier or, if we could get to cover, maybe it would throw them off our trail."

Realization dawned on Triistan. "The Glowater..." he said aloud.

"Sharp as ever, Salty. Turns out we didn't even need to hide. Stupid Respiis drowned themselves. Tried to drink the whole fuundaris river."

Protaeus smirked. "Despite our good healer's penchant for hyperbole, he is not too far from the truth. His desperate gambit proved to be a moment of serendipity that gave us an invaluable defensive tool. Unlike earlier versions like the nagayuun, the Worm's latest mutations were incapable of distinguishing between different sources of xhemium; they were effectively blinded by the water, unable to see past the Aniiene to locate their quarry. Many of them did in fact drown, while scores of others set upon each other. We have relied on this effect ever since, rerouting the Aniiene throughout the city, cutting channels for it wherever we could. We made improvements to The Weir so that we could better control the River's flow and distribution, laying out defensive lines much as you would when preparing for a siege."

"What happened to the H'Kaan?" the Captain asked.

"The Lord Marshal led a brilliant counter-attack and destroyed them."

Tau barked out a short laugh and shook his head. "There was nothing brilliant about it. They were disoriented, distracted. Most seemed unaware we were upon them until they felt the bite of our steel. It was butcher's work, nothing more. We should be lauding Danor's decision to lead them to the valley rather than the East Gate."

"Best-timed bout of dumb luck I've ever had the pleasure of experiencing," Danor grunted in response.

"Seems our luck's about run out," Kuthan said and stood, pointing towards the city. Not one, but three red flares were arching across the sky.

Tau was on his feet as well, giving orders in the Vanha tongue. Although Triistan could not understand the words, he was still comforted by the tone of quiet confidence the Lord Marshal used. When the boy found himself standing next to Danor, who was still leaning against the breastwork and watching the Plaza intently, he tried to find something comforting to say. But all that he could come up with was to state the obvious.

"I guess they're coming."

Danor laughed, but without a trace of humor.

"Yiin, they're coming, Salty. And he's coming with them."

- 25 -

Trapped

The soldiers on the steps of the Laegis Temple of Lex Vellos rattled and shook like shutters trying in earnest to turn away the howling wind of the storm that was the H'Kaan.

The shield wall was determined and strong. The soldiers listened to Captain Boen, following his orders precisely as he rotated the wounded or exhausted from front to back, if only for a moment. The initial push forced them back one step, then another, but they yielded no more ground, using their height and the reach of their spears to hold the shadowy horde back.

Arrows rained into the black mass surging at the foot of the Temple's stairs. Temos knew not every one of them was a killing shot, but still many must have found their mark, somewhere under the obscuring darkness that cloaked the H'Kaan. They were called the Endless Spawn, but surely that was hyperbole. Everything must have a limit.

Everything, Temos tried to reassure himself.

At that moment, a dark shape flew up over the shield wall, landing between them and the archers. It was one of Emeranth's entourage, one of those that had taken the form of the fallen. Another came directly after, as if it were thrown crudely and without concern for how it would land.

In a Shield Templar wall, there were specialists positioned to deal with such occurrences. Although this was a combined force of Templar and Lockewood's Thundering Lance, the Templar commanders had arranged the final formations, which meant that Jhet Anlase had been positioned near Captain Boen, his twin swords flashing in the early morning light as he closed on one of them.

Captain Boen drew steel on the other, but was distracted as a third was thrown over the shield wall, nearly landing directly on top of him. Caught between two of these more capable combatants,

Captain Boen died almost instantly, even as a fourth creature arced over the heads and shields of the Lancers in the front ranks.

Many of the archers began to panic, attempting to scramble back up towards the doors, composure and weapons lost in the shuffle. A few had dared to fire point blank, but their arrows seemed to be ineffective, hitting flesh, but even chest or head wounds were all but ignored.

Jhet seemed capable of handling one, but even he would be hard pressed to fight four of them by himself, and if they started attacking the shield wall from behind...

"Laegis! Clear the path!" Ardell commanded, sword drawn and pushing past the retreating archers. The rest of the units under his command followed him, rushing down the stairs, waving the survivors to move on. Temos heard the Captain calling to the soldiers of the shield wall, a few of whom had finally turned to see the danger just behind them.

Ardell was giving them the command for a controlled withdrawal, hoping that those in back and the Templar coming down the steps would be enough. Temos couldn't help but notice how the front line of lancers were also pressed by a new wave of activity.

He almost stumbled over the corpse of an archer as he found the back of his enemy, naked pale flesh save for a pair of well worn pants. He drove the point of his sword into the thing's side, just above its hips. It staggered from the impact, and Temos repeated his thrust, spilling the same inky black blood as the H'Kaan from its ragged wounds.

It spun around, flailing its arms. It had no lower jaw, just a mass of those black feelers; a foul beard of dark worms. No fingers, either, just more writhing tentacles trying to grip at the edges of his shield. These things were strong, but they didn't move very well.

"If you're planning to go to war, perhaps you should dress appropriately!" Temos mocked as he gave the creature the edge of the shield it wanted so badly, shattering one of its unarmored kneecaps with a swift drive downward.

If the thing could feel pain, it certainly didn't register, but it did stagger down a few steps before regaining its footing.

Captain Ardell buried his sword into the skull of one that had killed his fellow captain, but despite the steel lodged in its head, it was still trying to grab at the Templar instead. Jhet was holding his own, waiting for his opponent to overextend itself before selectively chopping off limbs and bits of blackened flesh.

Gunnar suddenly blocked Temos' view. The large Vanha charged down the stairs, his black warclub already in motion as he approached the third H'Kaan. Temos caught a flash of blue as the weapon connected with its chest and pitched it backwards through the air, a leaf thrown by a hurricane.

The shield wall fell back in response to Ardell's commands. Lancers in the back rows turned to engage the three remaining beasts from behind.

Vincen appeared beside Temos, ready to assist in taking down the one with the shattered kneecap, which now seemed unnecessary as it was currently on the receiving end of several spears.

Surprisingly, Theander Kross was just behind Vincen, along with their healer, Brother Shields, each of them cradling what looked to be roughly finished round clay jars. Arren Lockewood had also joined them, carrying a few more. A small array of remaining Templar and Thundering Lance were trying to help clear the steps behind the three of them.

"You there! Take these!" the leader of the Ashen yelled at Gunnar. Temos joined in, trying to catch his attention. Gunnar met Theander a few stairs up.

"Throw these into the H'Kaan! But spread them out - some deep and some shallow!" Without hesitation, Gunnar took one and hefted it for weight before turning to the crowd at the bottom of the steps and casting it deep into the back ranks of H'Kaan. He continued to throw the jars, one after another, flinging them near and far until they were all gone.

One of the creatures on the steps appeared to have finally been killed, pinned to the stairs by several spears and no longer moving. Greffin had moved to help Jhet effectively cut the other one into a dozen or so mismatched parts, still twitching, but unable to act. The one Temos had engaged was also driven to the stairs, but kept straining against the lances that skewered it. *What was it that kept them alive?*

"Let me help, Theander," Temos heard behind him.

"No. Save your strength. I'll need you to patch me up, old friend," Master Kross told Brother Shields as the leader of the Ashen reached out his arms towards the square, catching Temos' eye at the last second. "Tell your Captain to withdraw right now!"

"But..." Temos began, as Theander Kross closed his eyes, whispering to himself in unrecognizable tones - the Language of the Old Gods few could master.

Temos made his way down a few steps to Captain Ardell, who was encouraging the rear lance to keep the monsters pinned and slowly ordering the shield wall back up the steps to meet them all.

"We're about to have an opening to retreat!" Temos warned him.

"What kind of..." Captain Ardell's words were cut short by the explosions of blue flame that ripped apart the darkness ahead of them. Pillars of cerulean fire shot upwards, in many places blasting flailing H'Kaan bodies up into the air.

Captain Ardell called for the lancers to rapidly withdraw. They moved as quickly as they could up the steps in an organized formation, nearly trampling Temos, who was momentarily transfixed.

There, at the center of the darkness being ripped apart by the bright blue flames, Temos caught sight of Emeranth Kell. She stood calmly in the midst of the H'Kaan, her eyes wide, but unafraid. She was waiting. She had all the time in the world to make her next move and judging from the smile on her face, she planned to enjoy it.

Theander Kross staggered and threatened to fall down the steps, the left side of his face blackened and smoking.

"Carry him!" Greffin yelled to Gunnar. The large Templar caught Kross before he fell over, scooping him up with one massive arm and throwing him over his shoulder like a sack of flour. Temos, having lost sight of Emeranth, followed them.

A few steps up, Brother Shields was engaged in his own ritual, unseen extensions of his arms pulling arcs of blue fire from those Theander had started to the now empty space at the bottom of the stairs, adding an additional temporary barrier to discourage pursuit. None of them had time to be impressed: the H'Kaan would not afford them that luxury.

"Shut the Godsdamned doors!" someone was yelling.

The large metal hinges groaned in protest as several soldiers worked to close off the entrance. Temos looked around for Captain Ardell, hoping for something he could do. His heart was beating madly - part of him wanted a H'Kaan to make a mad dash and come through the doors before they closed, so that he could vent his frustration. He wanted to spill more of their blood.

The doors came together with a mighty boom. Gears clicked and thunked as locks tumbled into place.

With the lamps and torches lit, the inside was as bright as a temple could be, but with the doors now closed, it was as quiet as a tomb.

***

"The doors won't keep them out forever," Indalia Nox said, eyeing the massive portal that had remained mostly quiet while the survivors had tended to the wounded and allowed the others to rest.

"I'm more concerned with other doors at the moment," Richard told her dismissively, moving past her to the preoccupied Asai Oolen. The Arxhemist was supposed to be updating him on the exploration of the Temple, but her gaze was fixed on Brother Shields while he wrapped treated bandages around the charred remains of Theander Kross's left hand. The leader of the Ashen was moaning: the strain of his last feat had rendered him mostly incoherent, taken some of his fingers, and left him with severe burns on his face.

"Master Oolen, I need you here with us," Richard barked.

"Yes, yes," she said, trying to refocus. "I... there is... a problem with the excavation."

"Speak plainly, woman!!" Captain Parse barked, voicing the anxiety they all felt.

"Please, Jedgar," Arren Lockewood said, trying to calm the captain so the conversation could continue. Temos didn't approve of Parse's tone, but he couldn't deny that there were plenty of reasons to be anxious.

The main doors had been closed for some time now, but the quiet they had brought with them faded quickly. At first you had to stand close to the doors in order to hear the faint sound of clawing and scraping from the other side. But the more time passed, the louder it became. The H'Kaan, as they expected, never intended to leave them alone.

"You're going to need to see this anyway," Nox said, pointing towards one of the side passages off of the massive chamber dominating the main floor.

"Yes... let us show you," Asai said, still looking distracted. She moved behind Nox, casting one last worried look towards Theander. As important as he was, he was just another in a growing list of wounded threatening to outnumber those hale enough to fight. Those that remained capable enough to swing a blade were busy formulating strategies on how best to stop the H'Kaan once they broke through. Commander Cohl had taken charge of that effort.

The edge of Temos' hate hadn't blunted, but he felt more frustrated than angry at the moment. He remembered how calm Emeranth Kell looked, even amidst the flaming explosions. He'd almost convinced himself he'd be able to take her, challenge her as he had Gunnar, assuming he didn't have to cut through the horde of H'Kaan to get to her.

If he hadn't left Casselle alone on the streets, there'd be no need for such foolhardy plans. The thought of that made his heart grow heavier.

Temos trailed after Nox and the others, following Captain Ardell primarily because he'd never been told not to. They hurried out of the main hall, down a side passage and finally a twisting spiral of stairs at the end of it. Temporary lamps cast enough light for them to make out some details. The stairs emptied into another small room, which ended abruptly at an arch that seemed to lead nowhere.

"It's clear that something was supposed to be here, but it has been blocked off," Asai said. "For what reason, we're unsure, but we... assume... I mean speculate... that it leads to sections of interest, including... possibly, the armories."

Temos saw their faces as he heard the noise. It was not the scratching and clawing they heard at the front door, it was the tapping they'd heard earlier, but it was louder, stronger... closer. Something was coming up from that blocked passage.

"It was a trap the whole time," Jedgar said. "They meant to corner us in here!"

"How much time do we have?" Richard asked sharply.

"I... I don't..." Asai stammered.

"Not much," Nox said. "The problem is that if we try to seal this off more, assuming we even can..."

"We lose access to what we came for," Arren said. Nox nodded.

"More than that," Richard said. "We lose our lives and any chance we had to stop Maughrin."

Tap... rap... crumble. Somewhere beyond the floor they heard more stone give way.

"It seems like losing our lives might be inevitable at this point," Greffin said calmly to Richard. "If you and Commander Cohl approve, I can have my Templars ready to meet what's on the other side. If it's something we can handle, we'll push down until we can't push anymore."

"What if it's something you can't handle?" Lockewood asked.

"Pray you'll have better luck," Greffin replied calmly.

"Or we seal this off and prepare for a push out the front against a known enemy," Jedgar said.

"We might be able to yet find a way out through one of the other passages," Nox offered. "It looks as if there's a large network of tunnels underground."

"Assuming it's not already filled with H'Kaan," Jedgar rebuffed.

"You two keep working on the other passages," Richard said to Nox and Asai. He didn't sound as if he put much faith in that plan, but not to give it any effort might be too demoralizing to those that remained.

As they turned to leave, Richard pulled Nox away for a quick word.

"At the very least I need you to survive and get word out..."

"d'Yano?" Nox whispered, though not soft enough that Temos didn't catch it. He watched Richard nod before letting the Scoutmaster go.

Who or what is a d'Yano? Temos wondered.

"I trust I can leave the rest of this to you now, Captain?" Richard asked in his more typical dismissive tone.

"Yes, sir," Greffin replied. "If you would inform Commander Cohl, Templar Pelt and I will remain here.""Yes, sir," Greffin replied. "If you would inform Commander Cohl, Templar Pelt and I will remain here."

"I will," Richard said. He left with the others in tow, leaving the two Templar alone in the empty passage.

Rap... crack... crumble.

That one was even closer, Temos thought. Like Greffin, he was attempting to determine which way they would enter from. Below was the most obvious, but perhaps from the side...

Temos pulled his blade free, moving next to his Captain to help block the passageway that led back up to the floor above them. This part of the passage was just wider than the two of them. He cast a look behind him, wondering how long it would take reinforcements to reach them.

Tap... crack... crack...

Temos felt the floor shudder. He exchanged a look with Captain Ardell, who motioned them to step back. It was happening now, much sooner than either of them had expected.

Crack... crack... crash.

It was just ahead of them, under the stones that Master Oolen had indicated. He tightened the grip on his sword, waiting for the next blows.

The first strike was much louder than he expected, making him clench his teeth as the floor shuddered in resistance. Almost at the same time, he heard Finn's voice from the stairwell.

"Hurry!" Temos cried.

The stones ahead of them heaved again, jagged cracks forming as the rock fractured under the pressure. Whatever it was must be incredibly strong. Finn and Vincen were just behind them, but they weren't able to square up the formation before the next blow struck.

Something just beyond the floor screamed, the sound of inhuman resolve, making it look like the stone itself blasted apart from the sheer determination of whatever lurked beneath it. Temos and the others threw up their shields to block the spray of fragments exploding up from the floor.

As the dust and debris settled, that section of the tunnel revealed a yawning hole into the darkness below. In the center of it, a torch burned, a cerulean flame flickering softly. Temos tried to peer beyond it.

"Are you going to just stand there or you going to offer me a hand up?" came a quiet voice from the darkness.

Temos' heart skipped a beat.

"Casselle!"

He started forward, but Captain Ardell blocked him with his shield.

"Pardon me for asking, Milner, but any particular reason we should assume you're not one of them now?" the Captain asked.

"The H'Kaan can't abide the touch of Bluesteel, right?" Without an answer, the flickering blue torch gently arced up out of the hole, clattering to the intact floor in front of the Templars. Temos was able to see that it was no torch, but rather an elaborate war hammer, a bit larger than most. Its head was now a misshapen lump of bluesteel, deep holes in several places, sparks and sputters of blue flame dancing and dying along the surface of the head.

"I think that one's about done, but I've got a few more where that one came from," Casselle said, stepping just under the hole in the floor and squinting at the light from above. Captain Ardell lowered his shield and sheathed his sword.

"You look like you've been rolling around in H'Kaan mung," Greffin said, trying to keep a smile hidden.

"I probably smell equally pleasant. It's quite foul down here," Casselle replied, her eyes wet, her voice cracking slightly.

"Well, don't just stand there," the Captain barked at his men. "Someone offer the lady a hand."

***

Richard Lockewood seemed more excited to see the Bluesteel weapons than the missing Templar that had returned bearing them. The Laegis, however, had been ecstatic. Before she had even been allowed to eat or clean up, the rest of the Shield Templars had enthusiastically welcomed her back. Temos was afraid that Gunnar's hug might actually break Casselle in half, but she weathered it well, with equal measures of humility and gratitude.

A blanket wrapped around her shoulders, she slurped at a bowl of the broth they had managed to cobble together for the wounded from supplies Brother Shields kept with him. Temos sat with her, too excited to say anything, the knot of hatred in his chest finally loosening its grip on his heart. He still wanted Emeranth Kell dead, but now he felt the responsibility was no longer solely on his shoulders.

Nearby, Asai Oolen was examining the cache of weapons Casselle had returned with, speaking directly with Richard Lockewood and his son, Arren. It was a good load for a single person, but far too few to arm even a single finger of Templars, much less for the Thundering Lance's larger numbers. Two swords, one longer than the other, a large shield, the worn hammer she'd used to dig her way out of wherever she'd been, and two mismatched daggers. The only thing she'd kept with her, now laying across her lap, was an odd looking, long hilted sword, with a short, leaf like blade. It looked as if you could put power behind it with a double handed grip, but it was too short to take any real advantage of.

Richard had started to protest, but Commander Cohl was quick to point out they had been recovered by the Laegis and there was an expectation the weapons, assuming any of them survived, would be divided in some fashion.

Casselle looked in surprisingly good shape, if not filthy, covered in dust, dirt and some sort of clinging black slime - thinner, but not altogether unlike the blood of the H'Kaan. Temos had not asked what had happened, and as of yet, she had not volunteered anything. The leaders of both factions had not pressed either, since the scraping at the Temple door remained the most urgent matter at hand.

"How bad was it?" Casselle asked. She had taken assessment of the numbers around them. There was no way to hide the fact that they had suffered heavy losses.

"What we saw in the street was nothing. It's like there's no end to them," Temos confessed. "You didn't run across anymore when... okay, I must ask... How did you get down there? And how did you find your way back?"

"Mostly the same answer for both," Casselle said, subtly miming the motion of opening a book. Temos nodded slightly. That made sense. At the very least he knew she could find her way back to Gunnar's warclub.

"But how..." Temos began, before stopping short as the Lockewoods and Captain Ardell walked over, with a couple more behind them.

"Welcome back, Templar Milner," Lord Lockewood said to her directly. She nodded in acknowledgement. "I must say your return was more timely than you might have ever expected. While certain questions must remain unanswered if we hope to take advantage of this, there are things I must know."

"I'll do my best," Casselle replied.

"You found these below the Temple, but what else did you find down there? Specifically, did you find a well, or a fountain that seemed to leak the black blood of the H'Kaan?" Richard asked.

"I could not see very far," she replied, "but when I found the weapons, I was knee deep in what you describe. It was very cold. I thought I might freeze until I found the war hammer, almost by accident. Once I gripped that, I felt warmer."

"How did you manage to find your way out, almost directly back to us?"

"Luck?" Temos heard Casselle lie. "I felt like the hammer just knew where to go."

"I don't believe that," Richard said.

"There is no other answer," Casselle said flatly. Richard was staring at her, but Temos looked to Captain Ardell, the only other person who knew the truth. He said nothing, glancing over to the double doors.

"We are not graced with the time to get to the root of this, so I'll take your arrival as a well timed blessing," Lockewood said with a judicious amount of venom. "Don't think that this is the end of our conversation, though."

"Maybe we can all chat later over a nice cup of khava," Temos shot back defensively. "I know a great place in Strossen, assuming enough of us survive to get back there."

"Lock that up, Templar," Greffin growled. He may be on their side, but he still wouldn't brook insubordination.

"We certainly don't have enough to arm as many of us as I'd like, but we'll use what we can to take the fight to them," Richard said. "I trust you'll be ready for that?"

"We're always ready," Temos responded sharply before adding a much more subdued, "sir."

Casselle nodded.

"Very good. I'm going to allow you to distribute a few of these weapons to your men as Commander Cohl and you see fit," Richard told Captain Ardell. "It won't be long before they get through those doors. Hopefully it will be long enough."

"For what, sir?" Greffin asked.

"For us to help level the field," Lockewood said. "If Milner's account is accurate, we might be able to burn out the H'Kaan nest while they think we are trapped in here. While it won't immediately kill the bastards, it will keep them from reinforcing themselves. If we get lucky it may also weaken their morale."

"If not?" Greffin followed up.

"If not, Captain, we're in no worse position than we are currently, just a few steps short of dead," Richard replied, taking a moment to straighten the small cape over his left shoulder.

"I trust we're planning to avoid that fate if at all possible?" Indalia Nox asked from just behind him.

"With as much resistance as we can bring to bear," Lockewood answered. "Now that we have these weapons, our next strategy has a much greater chance of success."

"Is that a strategy you can fill us in on?" Captain Ardell asked.

"You'll learn enough when it's time," Richard answered. Turning to Arren, he ordered: "Let's move ahead with what we planned." Without even acknowledging the Templars, Richard marched back towards Asai Oolen, his other advisors in tow.

"That will never not be a bit insulting," Temos griped.

"I'll let Commander Cohl know he's up to something," Greffin said. It was hard to tell when the Captain was legitimately frustrated because he sounded somewhat put out at all times. As he walked away, it left Temos alone with Casselle again. Even though they were inside the Temple, surrounded by Laegis and Thundering Lance alike, this tiny moment together somehow felt private.

Casselle set her unfinished broth aside. She stared at the giant metal doors, her hands in her lap, the one on the bottom loosely clutching the weapon resting there.

"I thought..." Temos bit back his words.

"You thought I left you," Casselle confirmed. "Like your dad left you. Like my mom left me. Like Raabel and Odegar left us."

"They didn't leave, you know," Temos said, "You don't have to say it like I'm a small child and my dog just died."

"You don't think they're all chasing rabbits in a warm, sunny field somewhere far away from here?" Casselle asked with a grin. Temos smiled.

"You heard that story, too?"

"From a childhood friend. We had a cat," she confessed, "Dad told me he'd run into the woods to hunt big, fat mice."

"Ha! Imagine that big idiot Raabel chasing rabbits," Temos laughed, thinking of their former teammate running hunched over to grab at a fleeing hare. Casselle must have had a similar image in her head as the two of them shared a laugh.

"I'm sorry," Casselle said.

"Just don't go trying to get yourself killed again without me," Temos said. "I'd rather go chase rabbits or mice than have to deal with these jerks all by myself." Casselle smiled and nodded.

"Ok. Next time we'll do it together," she said.

Temos looked around, struggling to keep the silence from settling between them again.

"Why keep that one?" he asked.

"It feels right," she said. "It used to be hers... It's like the books back in the Ghostvale. I can feel some of her in it. It's like walking into a room and smelling something familiar cooking. It's nothing you can touch, but it leaves you with the impression of it. A memory that can make your mouth water. It's... a poor comparison."

"No, no," Temos said. "I understand. Like returning someplace familiar. Sometimes it triggers a memory, sometimes just a feeling, like happiness or pain. It's not the thing, but the attachment to the thing."

"Yes," Casselle replied. "Part of her is still with this."

"She used to be a Templar. One of us. Laegis," Temos confirmed. Her brow knit slightly.

"But I thought I..." Casselle paused, her hand tightening around the weapon. "No. You're right. That feels right. Something about the way she fought."

"Why didn't they tell us? Why make such a big deal about you being a Templar, if there had been women in the Laegis before? It's like they were trying to hide it. I never even read about..."

"We'll find out," Casselle said, softly at first, but then more confidently. "We'll get out of here and find out for ourselves."

"We're going to have to get through her first," Temos said.

"Then we will. I'll make her face the truth that's locked in here," Casselle said, her knuckles turning white on the hilt of her weapon, her face hard and determined.

"Then I'll make her choke on it."

- 26 -

The Storm

"Creugar thinks today is a good day to die, little Monkey-man." The huge Reaver looked down at Triistan and grinned, white teeth gleaming brightly against skin the color of dark rum. "But tomorrow is always better."

Even as tired as he was, Triistan couldn't help returning the warrior's infectious smile. Their relationship had changed a great deal since he'd first stolen aboard the *Peregrine*. The Reavers were usually hard, sullen folk, the product of a harsh punishment for criminals that wiped out all memory of their former selves and then trained them to be soldiers, fighting in service of the Sea King fleets. It was heralded by its supporters as the ultimate form of rehabilitation; a true chance at a clean start. It was also the subject of contentious and sometimes violent debate among the Isles' citizens. Up until the Expedition, Triistan had avoided the Reavers out of fear and prejudice, unable to accept that who they were now had little to do with who they had been, or what they might have done. Now, after all they had faced and overcome together, he not only respected and admired them, he felt a genuine kinship with them - especially Creugar.

They were standing at the battlements atop the fortified dam the Oathguard called The Weir, just a few dozen yards from the West Tower, looking north across the Plaza. Nothing moved in the stone-tiled killing field below, save for the dark coils of smoke that still rose from the hundreds of H'Kaan corpses, the hissing rain, and the water of the Aniiene rolling through its canals.

His head throbbed with a steady, pulsing pain, but the piece of root Kuthan had given him was still tucked into his cheek, making it bearable. Captain Vaelysia and a few of the other Expedition members had complained of headaches as well, but Creugar and the rest seemed unaffected. Kuthan had given those in pain the same root he'd given Triistan, admonishing them not to chew.

"But what's causing them?" the Captain asked as she accepted her piece. "And why aren't we all affected?"

Kuthan ignored her, but Danor answered from nearby.

"Can't say why you're not all affected. Probably the same reason some of us feel it more than others. As for the cause, you'll have to ask the Worm. Happens when you get near him, and the nearer you get, the stronger the effects. We've a theory, but that's all it is."

"What's your theory?" Triistan asked.

"You recall that the will of the Arys can be palpable - a physical thing you can feel?

"I think something in him changed during his imprisonment. I think it's some kind of... projection. Haven't figured out yet if it's involuntary or a skill or tool that he uses deliberately, but not much doubt he learned and developed it during his time in the Hold. Since he couldn't get out, I can't help but wonder if he went in. His research into The Between before he was exiled could have planted the seeds, and two hundred-odd years is a long time for them to germinate."

Triistan blinked in astonishment. "You mean he was awake for all of those years?"

"Oh, yiin, Salty. Couldn't move a fuundaris eyelash, but he was awake - and completely aware."

"No wonder he's fuckin' pissed," Wrael muttered.

Triistan shivered, thinking back on the conversation. Over two centuries locked in what amounted to a coffin, unable to move, but aware the whole time. The reality of their situation was gradually settling in, like the clammy chill soaking through his skin as the rain continued to fall. There would be no diplomacy - no peace terms negotiated or quarter offered. Somewhere out there beyond the shimmering veil of rain, a god was coming, bent on vengeance and likely insane.

Shortly after that discussion, Tau had begun positioning them for Ossien's assault. He sent Ariis to help bolster the squad holding the base of the East Tower, then divided the remaining Oathguard evenly on both sides of the gatehouse. He'd kept all of the *Peregrine's* crew together, just west of the gatehouse where Triistan was standing right now. Lord Marshal Tau took command of the eastern half, bringing only Fyruun with him, since Ariis, Arthos, Val and Vendros would be counted on to hold that side as well, once they abandoned the East Tower. On the western side, High Master Crixus would command Protaeus, Kuthan, Danor, Rhea and Rhiisa.

Just how that defense was going to be fought hadn't been explained yet. The Vanha seemed to have a plan, but they were a few hundred feet in the air and Triistan didn't see what they could do except wait for the attackers to scale close enough to engage with their weapons. Other than Syr, Commander Tchicatta and Lieutenant Jaspins, he hadn't seen anyone else with a bow, so aside from the one intact trebuchet on top of the East Tower, he could not imagine how they were going to fend off an all out attack. It was expressing this worry aloud that had elicited Creugar's boast.

Struck by some intuition, he drew his kilij and saluted his friend, pressing the weapon's crossguard to his forehead.

"I am honored to fight by your side, Reaver. My... blood for yours," he concluded awkwardly, feeling foolish. He was thinking of the exchange between First Mate Tarq and Danor while he was recovering from his wounds, which had struck him as noble and heroic, but now he just felt like a foolish child play-acting. Creugar's response didn't help any.

He threw his head back and laughed, long and hard, then clapped Triistan on the back, nearly knocking the young man over.

"Save that for the First Mate and his sand ghosts, Monkey-man! Creugar doesn't want your blood! Just your promise that you won't draw his when you start swinging that pointy stick around, eh?"

The young Seeker's face wrinkled in a wincing half-smile, wondering if he would be able to swing the blade at all. He was exhausted, both physically and mentally. Although they had all gained nearly a week's worth of invaluable rest while he was recovering from the nagayuun sting, they had been on the run and in constant danger for the last several hours. He couldn't speak for the Vanha, but looking around at his companions he wondered how any of them could possibly fight a pitched battle. He tried telling himself that if the H'Kaan were encamped, then perhaps this would be a true siege, and they might have at least a few days respite before any serious fighting began. He was about to mention this to Creugar when a shout went up from the other side of the gatehouse.

"There!" Rhiisa echoed the call from closer by. She was pointing at the far edge of the Plaza where Vuuthor and his three remaining packmates had suddenly appeared, racing along the eastern edge of the canal.

Triistan cut off a groan when he realized there was something wrong. "But where are Syr and Linessa?"

She laughed. "You've dull eyes for a seafarer, boy. They ride!"

Two of them did indeed have riders on their powerful backs, bent low so that he hadn't noticed them initially. He was astounded at the jharls' speed. Unlike the rhythmic gait of a horse, they bounded forward, each leap covering fifty to sixty feet at a time. In just a few seconds they were halfway across the Plaza.

Behind them, several dozen smaller black shapes issued forth from between the buildings, but they were well behind Syr and her scouting party and broke off their pursuit a short distance into the open ground. The rain was falling more heavily, so as they returned to the alleys, they simply melted away.

"Picketers?" Lieutenant Jaspins wondered aloud. She and Commander Tchicatta had been conversing quietly, while he ran a whetstone along the blade of his sword.

The Firstblade shrugged. "We'll know shortly."

***

It wasn't long before Syr arrived to confirm Jaspins' assumption. Ossien's army had established a perimeter line of sentries on top of the buildings that ringed the outer edge of the Plaza. The scouting party had slipped through it easily enough on the way in, but had eschewed stealth for speed on their return. After outdistancing their pursuers, she and Linessa had left the jharrls defending the East Tower entrance and rushed up here to report their findings to Tau and the rest of the defenders.

The two Vanha women were a study in contrast; Syr was almost petite (for a Vanha), while Linessa was tall and thick-limbed, with a warrior's broad shoulders and uncompromising posture.

"He's been busy," Syr was saying. "They number in the thousands, plus however many are picketed." Some of the Seekers muttered quietly to themselves, but the Oathguard did not even blink.

Linessa was nodding. "Plus two mounted L'Suu, and Sithis has abandoned his bound mantiisa and joined them on foot. They've split into three armies, most likely to attack the gates and towers simultaneously. By now they must suspect how few of us there really are, and will seek to spread us as thinly as possible."

Tau nodded. "With the tunnel collapsed, we can defend the West Tower from here, but for now I agree we should keep the East tunnel open for a possible counter-attack, at least until we see what they throw against it."

"Remember, Su'ul, that the longer we wait, particularly under a direct attack, the riskier it becomes to close the tunnel," Protaeus interjected. "If the Tower becomes structurally compromised, we lose the floodgates, and I can't control the main gates. We could lose the whole Weir."

"That is a chance we'll have to take," Tau answered. "Our options are limited, and we've seen what the dracosii can do to even our best stone if given enough time. We're just as likely to lose the entire structure in that scenario as well."

He turned back to Linessa and Syr.

"Ossien?"

They looked at one another before Syr answered. "Yiin, Su'ul. The Worm is here. He is... changed, however."

"Changed? How so?"

But before she could answer, a crippling sensation of pain and pressure washed over them. Triistan dropped to his knees, covering his head with his hands, crying out. He heard several other agonized cries around him. A rapid series of images forced their way into his mind: a great procession of robed and hooded figures through a gleaming city; the flash of a huge sword followed by pain and humiliation; tall figures wearing elaborate ceremonial armor, standing in a ring and performing some kind of ritual with blue fire; then a darkness so complete Triistan thought he'd been struck blind. He was lost in a black abyss of nothingness, but he was not alone: there was something or someone else out there in the Darkness... something vaguely familiar.

Suddenly a black wave of loathing crashed into him. He felt it as a physical weight, forcing him to put his hands out to keep from being driven from his knees to his belly. For a fleeting instant, he was struck with an impulse to kick away from his body, like a drowning man struggling out of his clothes. Gasping in fear and desperation, he wanted to beg someone to help him but was too terrified of being discovered by whatever it was that could feel so much contempt. It was the terrible paralyzing fear of a nightmare, only he knew he was wide awake.

Then, just as abruptly, the intense pressure relented and the intrusion was gone. His vision cleared as he slowly climbed to his feet, body trembling, heart racing. He had to fight an absurd urge to cry, so he drove his knuckles into his eyes until it passed. When he lowered his hands, he saw several of his crewmates doing the same thing, many of them looking dazed or embarrassed. It was the same five who had been experiencing the pulsing headaches.

"He grows stronger," Crixus said, watching those affected collect themselves.

Danor grunted. "Or he's losing control."

"Can you include them in your ward?" Tau asked Crixus.

The High Master shrugged. "Perhaps. I will try, but their sensitivity surprises me."

"It just has to be long enough to get them out of here."

"We're not going anywhere, Su'ul," Captain Vaelysia said. "You're going to need all the help you can get."

"Aw, fuck m-" Wrael began in protest, but stopped short when Izenya grabbed him by the back of his neck.

"Don't tempt me," the big bosun's mate growled quietly.

Tau ignored them and addressed the Captain. "We appreciate your noble gesture, Captain, but this isn't your fight y-"

She took a step towards him, eyes flashing, craning her head back to look up at him even though she was close to seven feet tall herself. "It is our fight - it's always been our fight, but you arrogant bastards keep hiding us from it, treating us like children! Let us help you!"

Crixus snorted derisively. "You've helped us enough already, huunan."

She spun to face him. "What's that supposed to mean?"

"It means, ignorant Child, that we're here because of you. This place is necessary because of you. The gods slaughtered each other because of you. You came where it is death to trespass. Your men led them to the underkeep. And rather than mount a counter-attack, we had to get you out! We could have easily over-powered the initial invasion before the main force arrived, pushed them back and held the defenses we've held for two centuries, but instead we lost our own so that you could escape! We should have killed you all when we had the chance," he finished with a snarl.

Tau put a hand on his shoulder. "Peace, brodiir. That was the will of Tarsus then, and you know why they must survive now. If we don't get them back to their ship everything we've stood for -"

Crixus knocked the Lord Marshal's hand away. "Yes I know, Su'ul," he spat, the honorific dripping with venom. "That's the point! Everything we've stood for is about to be annihilated. It will be left to these mewling babes to pick up our arms, to defend all we've fought to preserve with little understanding of it and even less appreciation for what has come before them! We have given our lives to this cause, and for what?! Speak not to me of peace, brodiir. For it, like us, shall never be known in this world again." He stalked off towards the West tower.

Lord Marshal Tau watched him walk away before turning back to the others. "His fire has always burned the hottest, and I believe it will still burn long after ours have been extinguished."

Captain Vaelysia had mastered her own temper, but she still spoke with unabashed intensity. "Let us fight alongside you, Su'ul. He's right, we do not fully understand your sacrifices, and we know little of the world before our time or the debt the rest of the world owes you. But we are here now, and we would do our part to begin repaying it."

Tau allowed the hint of smile. "And what of your men, Captain? Would you resign them all to certain death - or worse? By some grace the Worm has not yet discovered your camp, but he has one of your crew now and it will not be long. Remember that he has even less information than we do. He has had no contact with the rest of the world for centuries..."

"Salt and stone he doesn't know," Triistan blurted out. The others looked at him, some curiously, others with mild annoyance.

"Doesn't know what, Halliard?"

"Of course not," he muttered to himself. "The last Ossien saw of Niyah would have been... "

He recalled the images from a few moments ago: a great procession through a gleaming city, his wings being cut off, tall figures wearing elaborate ceremonial armor, standing in a ring and performing some kind of ritual -

"He doesn't know the other gods are dead," he said aloud before he could remember the terrible void of darkness and hate that had accompanied those visions.

Tau glanced at Danor, who simply shrugged his massive shoulders as if to say "I told you so". The Lord Marshal nodded at the young man.

"Yiin, Triistan Halliard. As far as he knows, this is the safest place for him, at least right now. His focus is on us - to destroy or capture us, to seize Ostenvaard and Aarden for himself. Once he accomplishes that, many more paths will be open to him. He will be curious about why and how your comrade came to be in Aarden. If Ossien defeats us here, he will look to satisfy that curiosity: your man's mind will be flayed open, and everything he knows will be consumed by the Worm. He will realize that the rest of the world is his for the taking, and that is exactly what he will do. So you see, you must flee - not just to warn the rest of Niyah, but to keep him here - in the dark if you will - for as long as possible."

Captain Vaelysia was shaking her head. "I understand, but we can't just leave you here. I can send my First Mate back to the *Peregrine* -"

"Captain, no," Tarq began, but Tau spoke over both of them.

"Thank you, but I will not allow it - no, hear me, Captain. Let it not be said that the Children of Tarsus lack courage or nobility. But as I said, this is not your fight - yet. We have discussed this already, and you know what is at stake. Your people must return to Niyah, to share all that you have learned here. Help them prepare for what is coming. Sing our song so that our lives were not lived in vain. It was no simple voyage here, and the return will likely be harder. You will need your best to ensure the knowledge you carry - knowledge that is vital to the rest of the world - reaches those that can make the best use of it."

He paused, fixing her with a hard stare. "You know your role and what must be done should we fall."

She shook her head in exasperation. "But -"

"Enough!" the Lord Marshal cut her off. He did not need to raise his voice; its quiet steel brooked no resistance. "You will get your chance to repay the debt, Captain, just not now. Danor, you and Syr will take them."

Both Vanha reacted in surprise and outrage. "Absolutely not, Su'ul!" Syr's higher voice cut through her husband's gravelly baritone. "You need us here!"

He smiled wistfully. "Indeed I do, and had I fifty more Odenvaard of your ilk, we would meet The Worm on open ground. Then there would be a reckoning such as this world has only witnessed but once before." He shook his head. "But that song shall never be sung. The *Peregrine* must sail before he discovers it, and it must be given every chance to reach Niyah. Therefore you must see the Captain and her crew safely back to their encampment. Even if they remained, they would be of little use to us here. It will be nearly impossible for them to fight from these battlements until we are overrun, and by then it will be too late."

Syr opened her mouth to protest, but Danor gently laid his hand on her arm and she bit off whatever she had been about to say.

"When?" the healer rumbled.

Tau seemed almost grateful and let out a sigh, as if he'd been holding his breath. "After the Spirare Sigelo. If we time it right, we should be able to handle what's left of them."

"And The Worm? How will you stop him?"

The Lord Marshal smiled grimly. "We're going to find out if he can swim."

He turned and addressed Captain Vaelysia again.

"The Tears are a difficult climb even when rested, so you should take what time we have to regain your strength." He strode away without another word, leaving them staring dumbly at each other, wondering whether they should feel relieved or ashamed. Most of them felt both.

***

It was several hours before Ossien's army finally attacked. During that time, Triistan and his companions ate what meager rations they had carried with them and dozed fitfully. The strange pulses continued at odd intervals, but their ferocity was blunted, something Triistan attributed to the "ward" Tau had asked Crixus to protect them with. Whatever it was, he was grateful for it, as he did not think he could have endured if they continued to be as severe as the first one.

Even so, the images and emotions forced upon them were disturbing. Several were of dark, twisting caves festooned with roots and other strange vegetation, the floors moving with all manner of slimy, crawling things that made him want to scratch his skin to stop the sensation that they were climbing over him. Many more were just raw feelings - primarily hatred, but also confusion, despair, and a deep sadness and sense of loss so powerful that it made him and some of his comrades weep. In between these were brief glimpses of Ostenvaard itself, viewed from someplace high, like a rooftop perhaps, the ruins, streets and alleys teeming with H'Kaan. Once or twice he glimpsed one of the L'Suu from up close, and he eventually realized with horror that in these glimpses they were seeing exactly what Ossien was seeing. It was unnerving, far worse than any of the other images.

And there was always pain. The worst of it was in his back - two searing lines of it running down each side from his shoulder blades to the base of his spine - but at one point every part of him ached, burned or throbbed. By the time the assault finally began, he and his comrades were almost relieved for the distraction.

Rhiisa's warning shout drew them to the parapets atop the West wall. From there they watched a black stain flow into the Plaza, as if the rain were somehow draining the sullen storm clouds of their dark bruises and depositing them into the ruined city.

"So many," Triistan breathed.

It was difficult to see them individually, in part because of the distance and the rain, but also because of some other effect, some shadow that seemed to darken the air around them. If he hadn't known how high above the coast Ostenvaard had been built, he would have sworn the sea were rushing in to swallow it.

As the horde spread across the Plaza, Triistan heard Crixus grunt in pain. The High Master staggered, then put a hand out to steady himself against the battlements. An instant later, another pulse rolled over them, and this time, the vision that accompanied it was of The Weir, as seen from the Plaza below.

"He comes," Crixus hissed through clenched teeth.

Even now, standing on the emergency launch relaying this story to his fellow shipwrecks, Triistan still had difficulty describing Ossien's appearance.

"If I've understood Danor correctly, we perceived him more than we saw him," he told his fellow castaways. "On one level, my eyes beheld a figure, taller than any of the buildings that ringed the Plaza. It was man-like, in that it walked on two legs and had two arms. But I cannot describe his features or what he was wearing - sometimes the figure was there, but just as often what I saw was his absence - as if his shape had been cut out of the scene leaving a void, filled with a twinkling darkness like the night sky in winter."

When there was a visible figure, its appearance shifted rapidly. Triistan and several of the others gasped when Shan the Stormfather strode into the Plaza, veins of crackling energy rippling along his arms and legs, snaking across the stone tiles with every footfall; three giant strides later, the figure unfurled great black wings and brandished a mighty sword. Danor told them it was intended to look like Shan's brother and eventual nemesis, Thunor. He explained that they were perceiving what Ossien wanted them to perceive, that he was projecting his appearance, choosing one of his siblings' likenesses and then quickly discarding it for another. There was no pattern to it, no rhythm: sometimes the likeness appeared and disappeared in the blink of an eye, while others remained in place for long moments.

But it was in between these transient images that the defenders glimpsed the real Ossien. Their eyes saw the void-shape, but on a much more basic level, they knew that the real substance of this thing was far more terrible. It was huge, man-shaped but only just, with too many appendages; in addition to its arms and legs, something that might have been thick tentacles writhed behind it, rising up from its back to form the scaffolding upon which the god strung the illusion of Thunor's great wings. It had the hairless, mottled skin of a Rotter, covered in a thick slime of pus and blood and Tarsus-knew-what else; in place of clothing, it was draped with random swatches of dripping grey-green moss and twisting vines; and it stunk of rot and fetid marsh pools and feculent latrine trenches. It was horror incarnate.

"Behold, Salties," Danor growled. "Where Maughrin is the Darkness of the night, The Worm is the beast you fear beneath your bed."

The rogue god halted a few hundred feet in from the Plaza's edge, apparently content to command from the rear for the moment. As the H'Kaan horde filled the plaza, it split into three forces, each commanded by one of the L'Suu. Sithis marched on foot as Linessa had reported, but the other two sat astride their own mantiisas. The H'Kaan gave these a wide birth, and after a few minutes the defenders saw why: when a small group of them strayed too close to one of the huge beasts, it suddenly reached out with a serrated forelimb and speared one with the long spike at its tip. It brought the writhing H'Kaan up to its wedge-shaped head and began feeding on it with four scimitar-sized mandibles, while the L'Suu on its back patted its neck as if it were a grazing horse. Triistan felt his stomach turn over at the sight and looked away. To distract himself, he asked Danor why Ossien wasn't attacking them himself.

"For the same reason he's never come against us in force before. Doesn't know our true strength, our true numbers. We've been careful to disguise ourselves, always attacking from ambush, never engaging him directly."

"And," Protaeus added, "what he does know is that we haven't been idle here. Besides the obvious danger of assaulting a dam of this size, he also fears a more subtle trap. So after centuries in prison, he is content to spend a few more hours or days to ensure he does not return there."

Kuthan spat over the wall. "And a few thousand Respiis lives as well. Here they come."

Like some massive, crawling thing made of smoke and shadow, the horde surged forward. The L'Suu led them, and apparently now that battle was joined, Ossien's creations no longer need fear the mantiisas' grazing habits: they swarmed around and under the spider-like creatures as they poured across the canals to the base of both towers.

Triistan had never witnessed a major engagement before, and had certainly never been in a siege, so the detached, nearly-silent experience of those first few moments was disorienting. He knew they were in terrible danger, that the thousands of creatures below were bent on his destruction, and that the thing that drove them was possessed of unknown power and malevolence. And yet at that moment the enemy seemed so far away and so small, while the defenders around him seemed as tall and stolid as trees, immutable and resolute.

These are Vanha, he told himself, *the first-born children of the gods!* They were larger-than-life heroes from a forgotten age, standing ready atop this massive structure of timber, stone, and steel, a marvel of engineering and construction infused with arcane power that even now he felt stirring beneath his feet.

He'd become accustomed to the roar of the falls behind them, and the deeper throb of water moving down through the center of the anchoring towers, but now there was something else. It was not just in the stone rampart he stood on, but in the air around him as well.

Nearby, the Oathguard on this side of The Weir spaced themselves out and set aside their weapons. They stood with heads bowed and arms outstretched, fingertips touching the battlements. Farther down the huge barbican, past the central gatehouse, he saw Fyruun and Linessa in the same stance.

The fine copper-colored hairs on his arms stood straight up.

Danor was nearest to him, and where the big healer's fingers touched the stone, the same intricate pattern of runes Protaeus had awakened previously began to appear, their soft blue luminescence radiating outward, spreading across the surface of the parapet, like water soaking into linen. Danor was chanting or singing in a low voice, though Triistan could not distinguish the words above the ever-present roar of the falls. He was about to ask the giant what he was doing when First Mate Tarq spared him the trouble.

"Ehnita-ka, my grandmother called it," he murmured to his shipmates. "'Moon on water on stone' is the best translation I can come up with. She saw the Templar do this during the siege of Deranthaal, Column of the Suns."

"What does it do?" Triistan asked as he watched the soft glow crawling across the face of the battlements. "Make the walls stronger somehow?"

Tarq shrugged. "I think that's up to them - Ehnita-ka is more of a preparatory step, more or less their version of the arxhemists' calcination. If I had to guess, I'd say old Long Tau named it earlier - Spirare Sigelo, whatever that means." He clapped the young Seeker on the shoulder. "Wait and see, Halliard. I'm sure whatever it is, it won't be pleasant for our new friends down there."

The front wave of attackers surged across the canals like a wildfire of shadow, racing towards The Weir while the Oathguard continued their ritual. The battlements projected out past the face of the wall, so in order to watch, Triistan threw back a trap door to peer down through the nearest murder hole. It was a dizzying perspective, despite the fact that he spent most of his time at sea aloft, and he had to get down on all fours to steady himself. The stone was surprisingly warm, like it had been sitting in bright sunlight all day, even though it had been raining off and on and they hadn't seen the suns since the day before.

The face of the great wall shimmered wetly, just as he'd seen earlier in his glimpse of the main gates: the entire Weir seemed to be seeping water. Beneath the glistening sheen, the soft blue glow of the Ehnita-ka was now visible on the outside of the wall as well, an incandescent stain spreading slowly from the battlements, creeping inexorably towards the attackers.

He let his eyes follow the wall down to where, far below, an opposing stain had begun spreading upwards: the H'Kaan horde had reached the base of the wall and started to climb. It was still difficult to make them out individually, but the roiling mass seemed to be climbing over one another, boiling upwards in a thick wall of shadow that had to have been four to five creatures thick. Like some huge hand of smoke clawing its way out of the ground, it reached upward with thin, dark fingers, stretching towards him with alarming speed. Soon he saw why: this first wave of H'Kaan was different than any of the creatures he'd seen thus far. Their bodies were narrow, elongated things like tree limbs, and they had spindly, insect-like legs similar to the mantiisa's. They appeared to be working cooperatively, chaining together in a ladder of sorts.

"Fuckin' things are scaffolding, like warrior ants," Izzy growled from where he squatted next to Triistan. He had never seen warrior ants, but he had heard stories about how thousands of them could work together to take down a large animal.

More of the dark fingers surged up the wall, while the first few ladders swelled as dozens of other H'Kaan began scaling them. Meanwhile, the two mounted L'Suu stood several paces back, oddly shaped stones thrusting up from a river of black water. Triistan assumed Sithis was attacking the postern door at the base of the eastern tower. He was wondering if the Oathguard there were aiding in the Ehnita-ka or preparing to launch a counter attack when an excited murmur pulled him upright.

The other Seekers were standing at the outer parapet wall, away from Danor and the other Vanha, peering out through the crenellations. Triistan hurried to join them, gasping as he looked out across the Plaza. On the opposite side, Ossien had taken the form of a towering figure of billowing smoke and fire. He faced away from the Weir, waving two massive arms and the strange appendages on his back, weaving them in slow, graceful arcs, almost as if he were dancing, though his feet and legs remained still. He was at the head of the street Tau had led them through in their flight here, where Helix and Arthos had triggered the fire trap. Smoke still drifted up from the alleyway, and Triistan could see the tiny flicker of flames licking the blackened husks of the dead H'Kaan that littered the street.

Suddenly Ossien raised his arms dramatically, then swept them sideways, the six tentacles on his back following the same abrupt motion. Eight dark shapes trailing flame hurtled through the air to hit the side of one of the buildings, where they exploded in green and orange splashes of fire. At least two of the objects appeared to break through the wall to disappear inside the stone building. Then the god stooped, the tentacles reaching out so that he looked for a moment like some giant deformed spider. He lurched upright again, holding several of the burning bodies of the H'Kaan, and waved them around in the air. It was like watching a manic child playing with toys, finding unrestrained joy in their destruction.

There was more than mania to his actions, however. As the flames began to lick the wooden eaves of the first building, he lurched to his left, hurling eight more fiery missiles at the structure on the opposite side. They exploded in green and orange fire. One of them crashed through a set of decorative wooden doors opening onto a balcony and struck something volatile inside: an instant later the top half of the building exploded upwards, sending a geyser of flaming debris into the sky. He began to move faster, picking up more burning bodies and hurling them into the city beyond. They shot through the air like catapult missiles and exploded into flame wherever they landed.

"Whatever these things are made of," Jaspins said to no one in particular, "they burn like a flask full of seal oil."

Triistan nodded. "I think it's something in their blood reacting with whatever's in that fire-oil mixture the Oathguard used."

Wrael snorted. "You two are thinking too hard. Seems pretty fucking clear to me - he's a fucking god and he's using his godly-fucking powers to smoke us out of here."

"Maybe... but I think you have it backwards."

"Yeah, Titch? Got it all figured out, do you?"

Jaspins was nodding. "Yes, I think he does. Ossien used his godly powers to modify these things, like we saw with the dracosii - the spitters. If their spit can be some kind of corrosive acid, who knows what their internal organs might be like?"

"Exactly," Triistan finished, "and Protaeus and the rest of the Oathguard would know. We've already seen how they've used the H'Kaan's hunger for xhemium against them."

Wrael looked at each of them as if they were speaking another language, then just shook his head. "Well whatever it is, it's going to get pretty fucking hot around here."

Across the plaza, Ostenvaard began to burn, and Triistan thought he now understood why the Weir had been designed to constantly weep water. He was wrong.

The air began to take on a thick, charged feeling around them. The Oathguard's voices swelled so that they were now loud enough to be heard above the din of the falls and the pulse of the water moving through the Weir. He could not understand their words, but he could hear the strain in their voices. The cords on Danor's huge neck stood out and sweat dripped from his face. His powerful shoulders bunched and twitched as if he were trying to topple the wall he touched, though his fingers still made the barest contact with it. The other Vanha in Triistan's line of sight seemed to be struggling as well, especially High Master Crixus, leading Triistan to wonder how long

- 435 -

he could continue this new ritual while still shielding them from Ossien's mental onslaught.

"INCOMING FIRE, GET DOWN!" Captain Vaelysia shouted.

They crouched against the parapet wall as a ball of flame shot by over their heads. It landed several yards beyond them with the sickening sound of breaking bones and ruptured flesh, followed immediately by the *whump* of fire igniting. The mangled remains of a large H'Kaan tumbled several feet across the wall-walk, trailing viscera and green and orange fire behind it. Two more of the grisly missiles struck in rapid succession, and a third actually hit the parapet wall they were hiding behind, close enough that Triistan felt a wave of heat roll over him.

In a panic he looked to see if any of the Oathguard had been hit, but they were kneeling now so that they had cover, at least on this side of the gatehouse. He risked a quick glance through a crenellation above his head, but couldn't see Ossien from this angle. He did glimpse several more fiery missiles arcing through the air towards the Weir, but most fell short, striking the wall somewhere below. The handful that hit the ramparts overshot the defenders and burned harmlessly in gruesome patches here and there behind them, but with no ready fuel other than the bodies themselves, they were little more than distractions as long as everyone remained in cover.

That is, until one of the missiles hit the side of the gatehouse, sending pieces of flaming H'Kaan corpse reigning down on Kuthan. Remarkably, he did not move from his kneeling position, nor break contact with the wall in front of him. He kept chanting with his comrades despite a streak of fire burning from the back of his right shoulder to his left hip, and two smaller flames smoldering where some of the gore had splattered on the backs of his greaves.

Jaspins and the Firstblade sprinted over and quickly smothered the fire with their tattered cloaks, but not before it had singed away some of the Vanha's hair, leaving a patch of angry red skin on the back of his head and neck. Yet somehow he continued chanting.

"Shan's salty balls, whatever they're doing, they'd better do it fast," Izzy called from beside the murder hole. Triistan's heart lurched as he hurried back to its edge: the black tide of H'Kaan had risen past the halfway point, close enough to distinguish one beast from another despite the shadows that clung to them.

He was surprised to see so many different types of creatures within the H'Kaan horde. There were plenty of the wolf-sized, lizard-like hounds, but they were just one of nearly a dozen different types. The elongated, stick-like creatures that used their bodies as scaffolding were the largest, easily as big as the mantiisas though they were much slighter. There were also bulky, powerfully-built beasts that were nearly as large, with six legs and short, wide jaws full of gleaming teeth. Marveling at their mountainous shoulders, Triistan wondered if one of them had been trying to break down the postern door earlier. He saw plenty of the man-sized dracosii too, who were aiding the scaffold-things by spitting their acid on the stone and carving out handholds of sorts. There were a handful of other variations as well, each more twisted than the last. It was a menagerie of madness.

Triistan had to avert his eyes as one of Ossien's flaming missiles suddenly exploded directly below him. He felt the heat from it waft up through the murder hole, and when he leaned forward to look again, he saw with grim satisfaction that much of the debris had cascaded down onto one of the scaffolders. It was rearing back, its first two legs pulling away from the wall as its elongated body ignited in multiple places. Several H'Kaan that had been scaling its back were now hanging on for dear life while it struggled to pull itself back flush with the wall, but the added weight proved too much for it. It slowly fell backwards, peeling away at least two dozen more H'Kaan fighting and scrambling over each other as they tried to get to safety. Ultimately, nearly thirty of the creatures plummeted to their deaths far below, eliciting a ragged cheer from the Seekers looking on.

Their triumph was short-lived, however, for barely a minute later, another scaffolder had moved into the vacant spot, almost completely covered with swarming Respiis. It was a bleak reminder that there were far too few defenders to have a real impact, and unless the Vanha were planning to destroy the entire dam, Triistan could not see a way out.

The horde crawled closer while the Oathguard continued their chanting. They reached the two-thirds mark unopposed, close enough for the defenders to see their black eyes and sharp teeth, and the slaver that foamed and ran from their muzzles like a vast pack of rabid dogs. When they were three-quarters up the wall, the missile onslaught from Ossien ceased. Whether the rogue god had run out of bodies or had decided he no longer wanted to risk hitting his own troops, Triistan had no way of knowing. Perhaps he was about to join the attack himself, a thought that sent a jolt of fear coursing down Triistan's spine.

The Vanha abruptly stopped chanting, and stood.

As one, they lifted their right hands to the sky, fists clenched. Brilliant blue flame flashed from each upraised hand. As it had with Eso in the alley, the flames behaved more like liquid than fire, running down their upraised arms and dripping around them like burning rain. Triistan heard it hiss as it struck the stones at their feet, where it sent up tiny puffs of steam. The luminescent etchings that snaked through the parapet pulsed brighter, and more steam rose from where each Oathguard's left hand still rested on the wall.

A deafening howl erupted from the direction of the city, while at the same time another wave of pain rolled over them, so strong the Seekers felt it even through Crixus' protective aegis. It was a tidal wave of rage and hate crashing down upon them, threatening to crush them and sweep them off of The Weir's battlements into the lake behind.

Surely no force on Ruine could stand against such terrible hate, such pure Darkness, Triistan thought. Despair welled up within him like blood from a wound.

"En'vaar et Odenvaard!" a clear, powerful voice rang out across The Weir, cutting through the din of water and war like a herald's trumpet.

A chorus of other voices answered, repeating the refrain. "EN'VAAR ET ODENVAARD!"

Triistan felt the black rage falter. He knew those words, and he knew those voices.

Across the length of The Weir, the last of the Vanha Oathguard stood with right hands upraised and wreathed in blue flame, as if each had torn a star from the heavens. As one, they shouted their sacred oath, hurling the words at their enemies like arcane ballistae bolts. At the same time, some of their voices rang out in his mind as well, and he knew their meaning even without speaking their tongue.

"We are the Oathguard!" they cried.

"We are the Living Wall; the First Line..."

As they spoke, it seemed their voices gained power, beating back the oppressive sense of rage and despair, resonating with the deep, thrumming strength of the water moving through The Weir. Triistan and his fellow Seekers felt hope stir in their hearts.

"I will hold that Line…

"To the last drop of my blood..."

Screams rose from the horde below as they came rushing on.

"The last dust from my bones..."

Strands of his hair lifted away, though there was no breeze. The air felt charged, prickling his skin.

"The final ash of my fire to ride upon the Wind..."

Triistan's eyes flooded with tears, so fierce was the determination that surged within him, to stand and fight, no matter the odds. He had never felt something so poignantly in all his life.

"I -" and as each said their own name in unison, their chorus did not falter, but thundered with the chest-rattling strength of the falls behind them -

"I AM THE END OF THAT LINE..."

The blue bolts in their upraised hands pulsed, sending more sparks of hot luminescence cascading down around them -

"AND I WILL HOLD MY POST...

"UNTIL... RUINE'S... ENDING!!"

As one, they brought their right fists down, smashing them on the top of the parapet wall. Blue fire flashed at each point of impact, burning so hotly Triistan and the others had to look away. A great crack like thunder rent the air, followed immediately by a booming roar from beneath them. He fell to his knees at the edge of the murder hole, trying to make sense of what he saw.

All along the wall, veins of crackling blue energy as thick as a ship's mast lanced downward from each Oathguard, like bolts of lightning that had been somehow trapped inside the stone itself. Along the path of each vein, steam exploded, huge branches of white vapor bursting outward, boiling the H'Kaan climbers and hurling them from The Weir. As the main branches reached the ground, hundreds of smaller veins split off in every direction, crackling across the face of the barbican. Wherever they connected with one of the main trunks, the lateral branches flared hotly, tracing another path of blasting steam and sending more H'Kaan to their deaths. It reminded Triistan of when the *Peregrine* had sailed within sight of Sigel's Wrath. The sea had literally boiled around it, fed by dozens of molten rivers and streams that bled down the volcano's flanks. Between the action of the tide and the lava flows, steam was constantly exploding upwards in great, elongated geysers, rivers of mist suspended just above the ground to create an aerial mimicry of what lay below. The Weir looked something like that now, except that in place of the red and orange magma, blue fire crackled beneath the streaming clouds. Triistan wondered briefly if a thunderstorm might look like this from above.

And then it was over. The tableau dissolved slowly as the steam dissipated. The blue fire faded along with it, though it still flickered in small pockets here and there. Atop the battlements, the Oathguard slumped where they were, either leaning against the parapet wall or sitting on the ground with their backs to it, while Triistan and his comrades looked down through the murder holes in stunned silence.

The wall was clear.

- 27 -

Prodigal Son

The heavy fog of steam slowly dissipated to reveal a great swath of H'Kaan corpses covering the Plaza floor, filling the wide semi-circular area between the Weir and the canals arcing out from the base of the anchor towers. One of the mantiisa lay on its back, its long twisted limbs sticking up in the air like some huge dead spider. Stunned, Triistan wondered how many they had slain. Hundreds? Thousands? He wasn't accustomed to judging such numbers and let the question go. Besides, the more important question was how many were left.

He lifted his gaze to look across the canal, but between the falling rain and tattered clouds of vapor still hanging in the air, he could only make out a dim mass of darker grey shadow close to the ground. He assumed it was the rest of Ossien's horde. Unfortunately, it was still moving.

Atop the battlements, the Oathguard were slowly coming to their feet, looking weary but resolute.

"Minuerto, lost a finger," Rhiisa spat as she shook her hand. To Triistan's horror, the top half of her ring finger disappeared in a cloud of ash. The rest of the Vanha barely registered her comment, and overall they seemed unimpressed with the whole affair. After exacting such a heavy price from their enemies, he could not find a trace of triumph in any of their expressions. Instead, they seemed to be waiting for something.

In sharp contrast, many of the *Peregrine's* crew members were thumping each other on the back and paying loud compliments to the Vanha, oblivious to their muted reaction. They quieted as Lord Marshal Tau appeared from the other side of the gatehouse a moment later, striding up to them with Fyruun in tow.

"How long?" he asked Protaeus quietly. The Master Architect shook his head. His expression was grim, with none of the arrogance they'd become accustomed to.

"Not long, Su'ul. More than a day… less than three."

"Can you accelerate the process?"

Protaeus reached out and brushed the stone of the nearby wall. "Perhaps..."

Captain Vaelysia glanced questioningly at Tarq, but the First Mate only gave a slight shrug and a subtle shake of his head.

"That was brilliantly done, Su'ul," she said to the Lord Marshal. "Clearly you can manage the defenses without us. What happens next?"

As if in answer, a deep, tortured groan ending in a heavy thump sounded from somewhere below them. It was loud enough to startle them all and solid enough to feel through the soles of their boots.

"What in Shan's beard was that?" Wrael exclaimed.

"The beginning of the end, Child of Tarsus," Protaeus answered before tilting his head, listening. "In more practical terms, one of the floodgates failing - number four, if I'm not mistaken."

Wrael and the other crewmen looked at one another nervously. The Vanha remained impassive, their expressions impossible to read. Rather than answer Captain Vaelysia's question, Tau began issuing orders.

"Protaeus, get to the floodgate controls and see what you can do. Justice, instruct Arthos and the others to begin a tactical withdrawal. Collapse the eastern tunnel - we won't be making a counter-attack after all. High Master, find Linessa and prepare to defend the ramparts."

Crixus, Fyruun and the Master Builder thumped their chests in salute and hurried away, at which point the Lord Marshal finally acknowledged the Captain.

"What happens next, Captain, is that you and your crew will take your leave, as agreed."

"I don't understand," she said, gesturing towards the battlements. "After what we just witnessed -"

"You'll pardon my lack of manners, Captain, but we don't have time for a polite discussion. What you just witnessed cannot be repeated before The Weir fails."

He nodded towards Rhiisa. "It exacts a heavy price, even from us. What's more, it requires an enormous amount of energy - power that must be built up and stored before it can be released. It is a process that takes several days, which we do not have. Remember, this structure was not built for its current purpose. We've done the best we could to fortify it - Protaeus has a mind for this sort of thing like none I've seen since Derant built The Columns - but he warned us that the strain of the Spirare Sigelo might still prove too much. He was right."

"So you're scuttling it to take them all down."

The Lord Marshal nodded. As he did, Triistan felt the stone beneath them vibrate ever so slightly. There was no noise to accompany it this time, although he thought the ever-present roar of the water had changed somewhat; its pitch seemed deeper.

"Come with us then," the Captain urged. "Can't you just... " but she trailed off as Tau slowly shook his head.

"Our work here is not done, Captain. Ossien will come again, and the next battle will be one of flesh and steel, fought here. We have to hold this line - to hold him here - until The Weir fails. It is your only chance of escape, and our only hope of vindication."

"It's suicide."

The Oathguard commander bristled. "It is our duty, Captain. I would expect you to know the difference. Now, please prepare your men to depart." He beckoned Danor and Syr over and spoke quietly in the Vanha tongue; Triistan assumed they were discussing the route the two Oathguard should follow in their escape.

The expedition members were gathering up their few belongings when a furious roar echoed from the doorway in the top of the East Tower. The voice was unmistakable: Vuuthor, the apex jharrl. Before the echoes had died away, Fyruun burst from the opening.

"Su'ul! Ve tu'selaas! Ve tu'selaas!" He had his huge greatsword drawn and was using it to beckon them towards him before vanishing back into the tower.

The other Oathguard leapt into motion, sprinting towards him and drawing their weapons. Tau followed, pausing only long enough to clasp Danor on the shoulder.

"Get them out of here, brodiir. A've necuuto!"

As the Lord Marshal and the others sprinted away, Danor let out a stream of words in his own language that could only have been obscenities. He swung his huge hammer at the parapet wall, sending sparks and tiny shards of the dark stone scattering. As he drew his arm back for another blow, Syr took hold of his wrist and said something low in his ear.

He sagged, all of the rigid fury in his posture bleeding out of him. He gave one last, tortured look at the departing backs of his comrades, and then strode in the opposite direction, towards the Western Tower where they had first come out atop The Weir.

"Stay close, Salties," he growled. "I'm in no mood for stragglers."

Captain Vaelysia ordered four of the crew members to take up Myles' litter. Triistan was closest so he bent to grasp one of the stretcher's handles.

"No. He stays." Syr's husband stopped and turned at the sound of her voice and she spoke rapidly to him in the Vanha tongue. Triistan spared a glance at the Eastern Tower entrance but Tau and the other Oathguard had already disappeared through the doorway.

"You are right, of course Syrinya." He shrugged at the Captain and her crew. "We've a hard climb ahead of us and can't spare the time to rig a lift. You'll have to leave him here. Long Tau will look after him."

The crew burst into outraged protests. Wrael was the loudest of them all, stepping in front of Danor and brandishing his upraised fist, which barely reached the huge Vanha's breastbone. Danor showed remarkable restraint under the circumstances: he merely stood there listening for a long moment, until the Captain laid a restraining hand on Wrael's shoulder.

"You can't be serious!" she said as she pulled Wrael back a step. "We're not leaving anyone, especially not somebody in his condition, and especially not on top of a bloody dam that's about to collapse!"

Danor fixed her with a cold flat stare. Triistan saw the muscles on his huge forearm flex as he tightened his grip on the handle of his hammer. Next to him, Syr shifted her weight, leaning forward ever so slightly.

"I have never been more serious, Captain. The Tears are going to be more than some of you can handle whole and hale. It is simply not possible to haul him up, so you have two choices: either you leave him here alive and hope for the best, or I kill him now. Either way, he stays."

"This is madness!" she shot back. "There has to be another way!"

The Oathguard shook his head. "There isn't. He's a man overboard in a storm, Captain. Would you throw other men in to save him?"

There was another loud crack somewhere below them and the entire causeway shuddered. Triistan was sure the sound of rushing water was louder this time. Captain Vaelysia stared balefully at

Danor, hating the choice she had to make and perhaps hating herself more because she knew he was right.

If she answered, Triistan never heard it: pain suddenly blossomed in his skull as another one of Ossien's pulses rolled over them - not as bad as it had been before Crixus began shielding them, but much stronger than the last few attacks. Triistan wondered if the High Master's defense was weakening, or if Ossien was closer.

The pain was accompanied by a confusing vision of H'Kaan, caught up in a swirling melee inside a dark tunnel. Water cascaded down the walls and covered the floor. Orange and blue light flickered and flashed ahead. Scores of H'Kaan surged towards it, only to be thrown back. They drove forward again, swarming over broken blocks of stone. The carnage cleared momentarily, affording a glimpse of two Oathguard flanking one of the jharrls several dozen yards ahead. Triistan recognized Val and Vendros, standing on a huge pile of rubble and fighting desperately to hold back the tide of nightmare creatures encircling their position. Behind them, a third Vanha was being dragged upwards through a gaping hole above, but before Triistan could make sense of what he was seeing, the pulse faded and the vision was gone. He cried out in fear and frustration, hearing it echoed from several of his comrades.

"Where was that?" Tarq gasped, blinking hard and shaking his head. "It looked like they were inside the tower!"

"Sappers," Danor spat. "Looks like The Worm has found a way in ahead of schedule. We are leaving - now, Captain."

She cursed bitterly and jerked her head at her First Mate. "Get them out of here. I'll catch up in a minute." Without waiting for his reply, she knelt beside Myles where he lay. The Whip pushed and shoved the men forward, urging them to follow Danor and Syr. Triistan had never felt so helpless, but he didn't know what else to do: they couldn't even bid Myles goodbye since he was still unconscious. He and Wrael were the last two to fall in, with Tarq between them, firmly gripping their arms and propelling them forward.

"Lets go, lads," he was saying. "Cap'll do the right th-"

"Oh, fuck this!" Wrael shouted and twisted free. He ran back and knelt beside the Captain, and Triistan was shocked to see she had drawn her knife, though she wasn't brandishing it at her disgruntled crewman. With cold horror, he realized what he was seeing, what Wrael had already surmised.

- 445 -

"You can't do it, Cap. Not while there's still a chance. It ain't fucking right, sir!"

"You'd rather he were left here for those things?" she countered. "You heard what they said, what Ossien will do to his captives!"

"I know - fuck me, I know! Gods and Darkness be buggered... It should be me - I'll stay with him."

"I'll not waste two lives, and to what end?"

Wrael gave her a weak smile. "More like gambling one to save another, Sir. And you've always had the luck, so maybe it ain't even much of a gamble. If the Oathguard hold the Tower and return, or decide to retreat, I'll make sure they take him with us."

She shook her head slowly.

"And if the H'Kaan make it past them? You understand what needs to be done..."

Wrael straightened then and saluted as crisply as Triistan had ever seen the laconic sailor perform one. "Aye, Sir. I expect I do."

She returned the salute and clasped him by the shoulder, leaning in close to tell him something only he could hear. Triistan missed the rest of their exchange as Tarq took hold of his arm and propelled him after Danor and the others.

Rather than take them back into the Western Tower, the Oathguard bypassed it and led them into a large cleft in the face of the adjacent cliff. The Captain caught up to them just as they plunged into the dark cut, and as she brushed past, Triistan cast one final glance back over his shoulder. Wrael had removed all of the arrows from his quiver and leaned them against the parapet wall within easy reach, and now sat cross-legged beside Myles, waiting. Syr fell in behind Triistan, blocking his view, and he never saw the two Seekers again.

The passage was actually a slot canyon barely wide enough for their two Vanha escorts to fit through, with walls of broken granite or some equally unforgiving rock. Moss and lichen grew in abundance, clinging to tiny shelves of striated stone. In some cases larger plants had gained a foothold, creating tiny, succulent gardens no larger than his head. As with the Weir, water was everywhere, trickling down the face of the canyon walls or cascading over some exposed lip of stone, casting everything in the soft, incandescent blue that was so familiar now. It was beautiful, and under other circumstances, Triistan would have liked to just stop and stare. But Danor was moving as fast as he could maneuver through the narrow passage, and Syr was so close behind Triistan he could hear her breathing.

They followed the narrow canyon for over an hour, winding their way in a serpentine pattern, though Triistan had the sense they were maintaining a fairly consistent direction. Soon the floor began sloping upwards, gradually at first but before long the climb was steep enough that the crew members were all gasping for breath. When the party finally halted, most bent over, hands on their knees, sucking in air and grateful for the reprieve. He thought of trying to muscle a litter through here, begrudgingly acknowledging that as harsh as the decision to leave Myles had been, Danor was right. An image of Protaeus and Thinman rose unbidden to his mind, but he shoved it away quickly, refusing to allow his thoughts to get lost in that moral labyrinth.

After a brief rest, Danor had them moving again. The floor ran level for several minutes, until it reached a flight of steep, rough-cut stairs leading upwards. They had been hewn for the Vanha's much longer strides, forcing the Seekers to literally climb each step as if it were a waist-high shelf of rock. It was tiring and time-consuming, slowing them to a crawling pace and making them all painfully aware of the battle going on somewhere below them. Triistan struggled to hear over the sound of their labored breathing, dreading the howling cries that would signify a H'Kaan pursuit.

Water flowed down the steps, making them slick. He clutched at the stone and climbed as carefully as he could, but by the time they had traversed a dozen stairs, his shins were bruised and bleeding; by the time they reached the top, some three dozen steps later, his shoulders and back ached so much he forgot about the pain in his shins.

At the top of the stairs, they exited the slot canyon onto a wide, flat shelf, with a sheer cliff wall soaring up and out of sight to their right and left; they had passed through the face of this cliff out into a wider valley that ran more or less perpendicular to the stairs. The sound of rushing water echoed from the stone walls, filling the valley with a gentle roar. At the far edge of the promontory, some twenty feet away, a stone bridge arched gracefully across the ravine. It was easily wide enough for two of the Vanha to walk abreast, and stretched nearly a hundred feet before joining a similar outcropping of rock on the far side. A matching cliff face lay just beyond the outcropping, forming the opposite wall of the valley.

A flock of bright orange birds rose noisily into the air, chirping and squawking in alarm at their approach.

"So much for sneaking away quietly," Izenya muttered.

The noise of rushing water came from the Aniiene, churning and frothing its way along the floor of the ravine, some thirty or forty feet below the bridge. To their left it fell out of sight over a series of huge boulders and around a bend, presumably on its way to the cascades above the broken statue of Tarsus. To their right, however, it climbed erratically in a series of pools, cataracts, and waterfalls, all glowing ethereally in the dim light. It was a striking scene: this ravine was much wider than the slot canyon, with walls distorted by a multitude of jagged ledges where twisted trees and hardy shrubs clung tenaciously, their exposed roots snaking across the rock like grey and brown vines, or hanging down like wet hair wherever some of the soil and stone had broken away from erosion. Further up the valley, Triistan could see another narrow bridge, but beyond that the view was blocked by the irregular canyon walls.

Danor picked up his pace as he led them across the closest bridge, forcing the smaller crew members to jog to keep up. Just as they reached the other side, Triistan's entire body was engulfed in intense pain. He stumbled and lurched sideways, and had Biiko not been close behind him to grab his arm, he would have pitched over the low wall that ran along the bridge's edge. He dropped to his knees, dimly aware that several of his comrades were collapsing as well, as another one of Ossien's projections washed over them.

There had always been pain of some sort in these attacks, but not like this. This was agony, and rather than being focused to one part of his body as before, like along his back, it was everywhere, as if he'd suddenly caught fire. He felt Ossien scream in rage and pain, and was unable to keep from echoing the cry.

His head was full of blue, pulsing light. There were dim shapes ahead, but his vision was blurry and distorted: he was looking through Ossien's eyes again, and this time the renegade god seemed to be under water. H'Kaan bodies swarmed around him, but rather than commanding them, he was tearing them apart, clawing his way through them with his hands and the tentacles grafted to his back. He surfaced, propelling himself up through the press of creatures, erupting from the water into a circular stone room. Lightning cracked and snapped hotly from body to body, arcing through the water and even smashing into the surrounding walls. It tore over and through him as well, and an answering storm of emotions boiled inside him: hate, frustration, rage -

And then suddenly the vision was gone, leaving Triistan weak and trembling, clinging to Biiko's arm to keep from collapsing. He drew a deep, shuddering breath, his mind reeling.

"He's afraid," he gasped at Syr as he staggered to his feet. "Ossien's afraid of you."

Her eyes flashed with fierce pride. "As he should be, child. The Lord Marshal and High Master are formidable opponents, and they will bleed him dearly for every yard he advances."

"That room looked familiar," Captain Vaelysia said, trying to make sense of what she'd seen.

"The East Armory," Danor grunted as he and Syr herded them all away from the edge of the bridge. "The base of the tower - a mirror to the room you would have entered in the West Tower, adjacent to the floodgate. Stand back."

The Vanha hefted his huge war hammer and strode quickly back to the bridge, where two square, man-sized columns of stone flanked the juncture of the span and the edge of the promontory, serving as anchor points. Heavy wooden timbers as thick around as Triistan's waist were set horizontally in each column at regular intervals, their exposed ends protruding a good foot from all four sides. The wood was dark, almost black, with a smooth, polished look that gleamed wetly.

When Danor reached the right-hand column, he braced his legs and swung his hammer sideways with both hands. He struck the highest timber hard, and it shot out the other side with a hollow-sounding knock. Without pausing, he drew his hammer back and swung it at the next lowest one, driving it clear from the column as well. He repeated this a third and fourth time, and as the fourth timber was knocked out, they heard a heavy grinding noise, as of stone scraping against stone. There were two more beams, but Danor ignored these and moved to the other column. Triistan and his shipmates looked on with a certain amount of dazed detachment; most of them were still trying to re-order their jumbled thoughts and come to grips with their situation.

"Anchoring pins. Clever," Tarq murmured aloud. Danor repeated his actions at the other column. As he struck the fourth timber loose, the entire bridge shuddered. "But why does he leave those last pins in place? Why not cut it loose completely?"

"It will twist and bind," Triistan blurted out, grasping the design intuitively. Syr nodded.

"Yes. Normally this would be done with two men, knocking the locking pins loose simultaneously. It can be done this way, but it is risky. If one anchor collapses first, the mechanisms will twist and the bridge may lodge in place indefinitely. We actually want it to hold for a short time yet, so it is a delicate operation."

Danor was working at the fifth pin now, but rather than knocking it clear with one powerful blow as he'd done previously, he was tapping it free carefully.

Triistan thought he understood. "To give the others a chance to get across if they escape."

Syr gave him a curious look. "No, child." The matter-of-fact tone she used made her words that much more chilling. "There will be no escape. The Respiis will come, and while they do not need these bridges to cross the ravine, it will be much faster for them to use them. It is our hope that in their rush across, many of them will fall when the bridge collapses under their weight, and they will be more cautious at the other crossings. It is crude, but we have few options."

Danor finished his work, leaving the lowest timber in place on each column. The bridge held, and soon they were on the move again.

The path on this side was really a ledge formed by a shallow alcove cut into the canyon wall, wide enough for two men - or one Oathguard - to walk abreast. It rose steadily, and Danor led them on at a brisk pace until they came to an abrupt halt where a wide section of the ledge had collapsed, leaving a gap perhaps six feet across. He hopped over the opening with little effort, then waited on the other side and gestured for them to follow. Six feet was a fairly easy jump for all of them, but because the ledge was rising, they also had to leap upwards, which made it more difficult. They all crossed the gap without incident, however, and Danor squeezed past them to take the lead again. There was no railing or guide-rope along the exposed side of the ledge - nothing but empty air and a fall of a few dozen feet into the ravine - but the giant stepped around the others as nimbly as a mountain goat.

They followed the ledge for about an hour, climbing steadily until they reached the next bridge, but not before encountering two more collapsed sections. One was only slightly wider than the first gap and they barely slowed crossing it, but the second was a long span where less than two feet of the ledge remained. They were forced to turn sideways, and once again Triistan was surprised at how easily the much larger Vanha traversed the narrow space. Heights were no trouble for the young Seeker - he was more comfortable clambering around in the rigging of a ship than with his feet on the hard deck - but the roughly two minutes it took to cross the broken section were harrowing. He was absolutely convinced they would be overcome by another one of Ossien's projections while they were working their way across, and there would be nothing to prevent those afflicted by the mental assaults from toppling over the edge.

Nothing happened, though, and they reached the wider section of ledge safely. In fact, they made it all the way to the next bridge before they were overcome again, this time by a vision of one of the Oathguard being torn apart by Ossien himself. It was impossible to say who it was, but the armor was unmistakable.

Danor quickened their pace, despite the grueling nature of the climb. Wherever something had to be traversed or scaled, he allowed them to do so at their own pace, but whenever the trail grew easier because of a flat stretch or gentle incline, he pushed them harder. When they came to a bridge, he had Syr lead them on while he dislodged the locking pins, then caught up to them. As a result, Triistan soon had little energy for any thought except where to place his hands and feet. This went on for several hours, across several more bridges, and through several more projections from Ossien.

They became harder to interpret. They were much more primal and instinctive; raw emotions and sensations interspersed with the occasional images of what was transpiring around the god. Typically that meant a chaotic jumble of blood and bodies lit by the distinctive blue fire wielded by the Vanha. Triistan had never even seen a battlefield, let alone fought in any kind of melee, so he was ill-equipped to gauge how the battle was going. It seemed to him that countless H'Kaan were being slain - once or twice he had seen a glimpse of the apex jharrl tearing through dozens of them on its own - but he also knew there were hundreds of attackers for every defender. Even to his untrained eyes, it seemed inevitable that the Weir would fall. And when it did...

He concentrated on climbing over the ledge in front of him, onto the next step.

At some point, the rain that had been drenching them all through the morning slackened and stopped. The narrow gap of sky they could see above the ravine brightened considerably, and here and there torn strips of blue sky began to appear through the clouds. Danor seemed to take this as a sign to call a halt, which he did on a relatively flat area where the river had climbed to the same elevation as the path. They drank deeply from the icy water and many dunked their heads to refresh themselves, then sat and doled out rations.

The air was hazy, and what sunlight reached them did so in bright shafts filled with swirling dust motes and something larger than dust that Triistan at first took to be flying insects.

"Don't like the look o'that," Izenya growled around a mouthful of hardtack.

Triistan and the others followed his gaze, back the way they had come. This was the first time the young Seeker had looked back and he was shocked to see how high they had climbed. The land and the river fell away steeply, and although the ravine's walls still reached high above them where they were, behind them they could see a large expanse of open sky. It was stained by several columns of greasy black smoke.

"Ostenvaard is burning," Syr said woodenly.

Danor muttered something in the Vanha tongue and then told them they had two hours to rest, eat and refill their water skins. After a few quiet words with Syr, she left at a brisk jog back down the way they'd come.

Triistan tried to take advantage of the brief halt to update his journal; he hadn't had a chance since before the attack on his room what now seemed like days ago. It was hard to believe it had only been several hours.

"*Ten and Seven, Vehnya, The fourteenth day of the expedition, 37 since Landfall... Ostenvaard is burning...*" he began. He wrote quickly and mechanically, focusing on getting as much information down as possible. He had no energy for any form of narrative, and much of what had transpired was too painful to explore in depth right now anyway.

Several scribbled and smeared pages later, Syr returned to report that the trail behind them was still clear. Commander Tchicatta raised a dark eyebrow at this.

"You are expecting pursuit? From where?" Triistan was thinking the same thing: this ravine ended at the Weir, so anything coming after them would have to have gotten past Tau and the other defenders.

She ignored him and went to fill her own waterskin in the river. Tchicatta just looked at the Captain. She nodded.

"The Firstblade makes a fair point, Su'ul," she said to Danor. "What are you not telling us?"

Danor considered the question for a moment, and then smiled his not-smile. "That's a pretty long fuundaris list, Salty." Then he waved dismissively as she started to protest. "Save your breath, Captain. Just a precaution. If they could tunnel under the east tower, they could have just as easily done so to the west..."

"Which would put them behind Tau's defensive line," she filled in.

"Exactly. He'll be cut off."

"But why would they come after us? Why wouldn't they just attack him?" First Mate Tarq asked.

"Don't know, Salty. Maybe The Worm wants to be sure none of us misses his party, or maybe because they want to cut off his escape and seal him in - or maybe just to admire the fuundaris view. Doesn't matter why they might follow us. Only that they can."

He ordered them to pack up their things and soon had them moving again.

They climbed. The rest had done them all some good, and they were now more familiar with the terrain, so they made excellent progress. Before long, Triistan noticed that Ossien's mental attacks were losing some of their frenetic quality and becoming more measured, almost deliberate. He said something about it out loud and Syr answered from behind him.

"He grows stronger. It won't be long now."

Her meaning soon became clear, based on what he saw in the projections. The Oathguard were falling back, and beginning to suffer casualties. In addition to the unidentified warrior the rogue god had ripped apart, Triistan also saw Val and Vendros die. The two were surrounded by a waist-high wall of dead foes when the hulking, six-legged beasts he'd seen scaling the Weir stampeded through it. Val buried her axe in the lead one's skull, but its momentum carried it through her strike and crushed her against the wall behind her. Vendros went mad with grief and rage, hacking wildly at the other two, but in his recklessness he left his guard open for half a heartbeat, long enough for one of the creatures to seize his arm in its wide mouth and tear it off with a vicious shake of its head. Mercifully, the vision faded as he was overrun.

They climbed faster. A sense of urgency was building in all of them, helping them push through their weariness.

Danor led them on relentlessly, as one by one, the Weir's staunch defenders fell.

Ossien seemed to be learning how to control his projections. Or perhaps he'd always known how but hadn't previously bothered to do so. Regardless, Triistan and the others witnessed every death.

They saw Kuthan fighting like a crazed bear. His shaggy black mane and braided beard were soaked in gore and smoldered here and there from where some of the dracosii's spit must have landed on him. He swung a huge spiked flail around his head, and whenever he brought it down upon one of the H'Kaan, it collapsed in a spray of blood and shattered bone. Two jharrls fought savagely nearby, guarding his back, but there were simply too many attackers to account for. When they went down under a swarm of H'Kaan, Kuthan was doomed.

The party clambered up another set of stairs and across another bridge. Danor left it intact and kept going.

Ariis was next. He was slowly retreating up a set of curved stairs, slaughtering H'Kaan with his heavy broadsword and the bladed buckler strapped to his partial right arm. The relatively narrow stairwell helped control the number of attackers, and with each one he slew it became more restricted as the bodies piled up. For a moment it looked as though he could hold them back on his own, until Ossien himself charged. Ariis managed to lop off two of the renegade god's grotesque tentacles before he went down. Unable to shut out the images, Triistan and his comrades were forced to watch as Ossien shoved one of his remaining appendages into the Oathguard's mouth and down his throat. It took him a long time to die.

Rhea and Rhiisa charged down that same stairwell as Ossien was finishing Ariis, and the fury of their attack actually drove him back. They fought with the fluid coordination Triistan had seen the other Oathguard exhibit when attacking as a group, forcing Ossien to give ground. When he backed through an open archway into an adjacent room, the twins held back, preferring the more defensible stairwell. Just as the Seekers sensed Ossien's frustration at the apparent stalemate, there was a tremendous crash and portions of the ceiling inside the stairwell and part of the room collapsed in a shower of dust and rubble. Maddeningly, the projection ended.

Still Danor drove them on.

Up countless steps, across ledges both wide and narrow, sloped and level, and in many cases, crumbling under their feet. The gap from one damaged section was so wide the Oathguard had previously rigged a rope bridge with wooden planking across it. After crossing it, Danor allowed them a brief rest while he and Syr sawed through the rope anchors at both ends, leaving just enough to keep the bridge suspended. They ate a quick meal, washed it down with a few swallows of water, and were soon moving again.

When the next projection came, however, even the indomitable giant was forced to stop.

This one was different. The pain had receded to a dull unpleasantness in the background, and all of Triistan's senses were engaged, even intensified, as if he was actually there and it was all happening to him.

He ducks under the archway and steps out into the late afternoon sunlight, vaguely aware of the two heavy objects dangling from his right hand as they knock against the frame. He straightens to his full height, flexing his shoulders and shaking out the additional limbs grafted to his back. The two that had been cut off burn, but underneath the pain of the injury he can already feel the very different heat that accompanies their regrowth. It is unfortunate that they are both on the same side, but that will only be a problem for the next few hours.

He splays the remaining four out, arcing them up and over his shoulders, making a show of clasping and unclasping the three-fingered talons at each end. Their dexterity had initially surprised him, but now he does it simply because he enjoys the boney clicking noises they make when he snaps them together. Let his rotting siblings keep their wings; these are much more useful for the bloody work he has planned.

He sweeps his gaze across the top of the battlements, pausing momentarily on the huge statue of Tarsus with its deformed head. His lips twist in a sneer and he makes a mental note of finishing the job he'd started when this current task is done. The statue is far too pretty with all of the water cascading over it into the lake below. Besides, he cannot comprehend why his brothers and sisters honored their father in this way. Tarsus was a wastrel and a fool who had left them all here to rot. And that was after he had nearly destroyed the world.

"Fear not, Father," he hisses in a hoarse, wet voice that has seen little use for the past several hundred years. "I will make it right."

His pets scurry out onto the rampart, keeping clear of him but snapping at one another in their frustration as he prevents them from rushing headlong at his enemies. They were extremely useful, requiring only a small degree of concentration to control now that he was regaining his strength - his true strength, not just the mundane ability to ambulate this pile of meat and bone. He holds them back partly because he wants to savor this moment, but primarily because he wants these last few Vanha mongrels for himself.

Some fifty paces away, the last of them are arrayed against him. Wordlessly, he tosses the twins' severed heads in their direction, sending Rhea and Rhiisa bouncing and rattling randomly along as if they were children again.

He knows them all, of course. For in addition to keeping him locked away in this infernal prison, they are his illegitimate nieces and nephews after all, misspent godseed sprayed thoughtlessly into the unworthy loins of his father's pet mortals.

And he remembers everything: every blow, every shove, every kick, every word, and every insult carelessly discarded in his presence, thinking him imprisoned forever.

Arthos, spawn of Derant, with his pretty braids and dark skin.

Linessa, the bitch littered by that fucking arrogant dung heap Obed. Tall and broad, like her treacherous father, and beautiful in her own severe way. She would make a good mate, if he were inclined to such things.

And speaking of arrogant dung heaps, there struts Fyruun, Lyrin's brat. He will enjoy the irony of butchering 'Justice' with that oversized sword.

He smiles. They have drawn up in a shallow, well-spaced arc across the wall, with the two remaining jharrls at either end. At the center of the arc, in front, are the two whelps he has longed to face for so long, though for very different reasons.

Tau Regis Xarius, dribbled from Thunor's surprisingly underwhelming brand into some mortal bitch in heat. He is dangerous, but not nearly as much as he thinks...

... and last, but certainly not least: Bryn Cazius Crixus. The upstart, self-righteous, whining cur responsible for the past centuries of misery. It was Crixus who staged the raid on Talmoreth and then ran tattling to the others about his research. Centuries of work wasted followed by still centuries more wasting away inside a coffin.

His smile widens and he spreads his arms as if to embrace the High Master.

"Greetings, my son," he whispers wetly. "I have missed you so."

Boney claws clicking, he strides forward to make them pay.

- 28 -

The Doors Come Down

They were terrified. Everyone on this side was frightened to some degree or another, but Richard Lockewood's Thundering Lance were the worst. They'd fought brigands and outlaws, but nothing like the nameless, numberless horror that had barely been held in check by the giant metal doors at the front of the Temple.

And now they had been asked to open those doors. Lockewood's men were visibly upset and agitated.

Only a couple of the remaining Laegis Templar had fought the H'Kaan previously, but even they had struggled since entering the city. The extensive training in the Akist, the Laegis' centuries old fighting regimen, had prepared the Templar for the worst of conditions, but unfortunately this situation was an unhappy mixture of several of those worst scenarios.

Despite all that preparation, Casselle was scared as well. Temos had described them as an endless flood of darkness. She was afraid they would be a tide that even the Laegis could not stem. For some reason she thought of Veheg at that moment, perhaps still wandering outside around the city. She considered praying to the only god she knew was still alive, wondering if it would do any good.

She glanced left and right, seeing the stout, heavily armored Templars on either side of her. She looked over her shoulder at the equally well armored Thundering Lance heavy soldiers. They were most certainly praying: some for victory, others for a miracle, and a few just for a clean, brave death. It was likely they would see none of those things, but Casselle couldn't fault them: this was more than any of them had ever signed up for.

She shifted slightly in her stance. Her own chest plate had been crushed, so a replacement had been found from the fallen, and it did not fit her as well. The helmet fit better, though it lacked a strap to keep it in place. She knew that would most likely be a problem at the worst possible time. She'd also gained a new sword to replace the

Templar blade she'd lost in her last fight. It was a well-crafted weapon offered to her by Arren Lockewood. His father had insisted that he receive one of the bluesteel blades she'd scavenged from the ruins below the Temple. She was grateful, but she was more concerned that the sword they'd given him would be better served in the hands of a skilled swordsman. She'd never seen him fight.

Casselle had kept Arren's sword at her hip. She was still carrying the weapon she'd refused to hand over: a leaf-shaped blade attached to an overlong hilt. She felt a tingle in her fingers, the power of the weapon ready to be released.

"You know, I hear the Sea Kings have men that fight like wild beasts in their employ. They call them Reavers," Vincen von Darren whispered. "What I'd give to have a few hundred of them with us now."

Captain Ardell gave him a punishing stare.

"If they whine less, one of them is welcome to take your place," the Captain growled. Vincen looked appropriately cowed.

Ahead of them, a few of the Thundering Lance soldiers were preparing to open the locks on the doors, exposing them to whatever lurked on the outside. Captain Parse was trying to keep them coordinated. They would throw the latches and back quickly out of the way. Even though they were probably in the safest locations, they looked the most nervous.

Neither of the Lockewoods were here to meet the H'Kaan. They had left some time ago, with a squad of hand-picked soldiers and the remaining Ashen. They were bound for the nest beneath the city, hoping that they had enough Arxhemical fire to burn out whatever remained below. It wasn't even a solution, it was a desperate gamble intent to cut the force remaining in the Temple, or at least prevent any further reinforcements. It would most likely have no direct effect on Emeranth and her seemingly unstoppable army.

The truth was, both groups had about an equal chance of success, which was to say, not much at all. Regardless, they'd stacked as many odds in their favor as they could. Jhet Anlase, easily the most skilled swordsman the Templar had with them, had been given the other bluesteel sword. Normally he fought with two, but for this operation, he'd taken a place amongst the shieldwall.

Finn Archer, probably second only to Gunnar Hawken in size, had donated his shield to Jhet because he had been bestowed the Bluesteel shield. It was an impressively engraved thing and despite its size, Finn swore it was lighter than the shield he'd given up. He was at the point of the V formation they had adopted in front of the doors, and was therefore the anchor position. Casselle hoped the shield would be enough to help him keep the line unbroken.

The two daggers went to Indalia Nox, Richard's Spymaster, who had accompanied them below. Casselle would rather have had them on the line, but they seemed less practical than the traditional swords they normally used for these formations. If Nox ever had to draw them below, they'd be facing overwhelming odds, especially for such a small group, but Casselle pushed that thought aside.

This was her fight. All others mattered little if this one failed.

Captain Parse looked to Commander Cohl of the Laegis. The two of them nodded to each other. They were ready.

"Thundering Lance," called Jedgar Parse, "prepare yourselves for glory!" Casselle rolled her eyes at the Captain's cry.

"That sounds much more confident than 'might as well go down swinging,'" Temos whispered. "Does glory come before or after they shit themselves?"

Casselle shushed him while trying not to laugh.

A cry rose up from the Lance's ranks, but it was just short of inspiring. Casselle thought she heard Captain Ardell grumble "Pitiful."

"Templar!" Cohl cried out, silencing the Lance before it had the chance to fade out. "WE are the sword! WE are the shield!"

Every Templar struck sword against shield in response, two strong thumps that made the air around them hum.

"And when those monstrous bastards come through that door, ever so eager to die... how will we introduce ourselves?" the Commander demanded.

"En'vaar et LAEGIS!" every single Templar replied, in one thunderous voice. The sound of it rattled around the Temple hall. In its wake, the world went still. Captain Parse looked as if even he was somewhat frightened by the intensity of the Laegis.

He should be, Casselle confirmed to herself.

Cohl called for the locks to be opened. The soldiers strained against the heavy latches until they clanged, banged, twisted and finally gave way, unlocking the heavy metal doors.

They picked up speed as they hinged inward, pushed by a frothing, agitated black mass just beyond. H'Kaan boiled through immediately, dashing directly ahead towards Finn Archer. The opening widened as the distance between the H'Kaan and the Laegis shield wall shortened.

The doors halted abruptly, before they had the chance to swing fully open. As part of their plan, Asai Oolen had used her arxhemestry to shape the stone of the floor to raise up in such a way as to block the door from moving past a certain point. They opened, but only enough for one or two beasts to fit through. The rest struggled to get past one another and through the tight opening. It was around this small gap that the defenders had constructed their wedge.

It turned the flood into a trickle, even more efficiently than they had been able to do outside. The first H'Kaan that threw itself at Finn's shield immediately recoiled, reacting to the polished surface as if it were on fire. It was dispatched quickly after that. Others that broke through met similar fates, one or two H'Kaan meeting their impenetrable wall and being answered with a litany of edged steel.

They tried crawling over one another through the gap, but the remaining archers focused a volume of arrows into anything above head height, discouraging them for the moment.

Casselle knew that as tight as their defenses were, this was still, at best, prolonging the inevitable. At some point, someone would make a mistake, or become fatigued, or otherwise open up a gap in the line. Even the incredibly focused and conditioned Templar were still merely mortal, with all of those accompanying faults.

Until then, she contributed her best, stabbing and slashing with her bluesteel blade, feeling it grow warm every time it cut away H'Kaan flesh. Monstrous bodies started to stack up, requiring the new creatures to claw their way over the top of the dead and dying. The battle grew more pitched.

Commander Cohl and Captain Parse called for the next maneuver. With a surprising amount of precision, the Templar composing the front ranks marched back two steps, moving them away from the bodies, but also opening up their line. Members of the Thundering Lance were already there, filling in the open positions of the new, larger shield wall. It also gave them fresh ground.

They had enough soldiers to pull back once more, but any further and they would have gaps whether they wanted them or not. It was time to make the most of the ground they'd been given and Casselle pushed aside her doubts and refocused on the H'Kaan coming through. The Lance soldiers on either side of her had gained some courage seeing the Templar work, but as they fought the clawing, furious beasts, she could see that resolve weakening.

She wanted to shout words of encouragement, but none crossed her tongue. Instead she yelled, bellowing back at the H'Kaan with her own fierce roar. She heard others join in, a surge of angry defiance coursing through them, giving them back a tiny fraction of hope that the day was not yet lost.

She wished it to be true, if for no other reason than to validate that her life had not been restored in vain.

The enthusiastic response put some strength back into her limbs. She blocked and cut and stabbed as the H'Kaan continued to flow into the room, crashing into her shield with wild abandon. They didn't need finesse. The real power of the H'Kaan seemed to be they were as reported: a nightmare, endlessly renewed.

Above the screams and shouts, she heard something unique, something that she sacrificed a fraction of her attention to recognize, the sound of metal straining.

The door on the right side was beginning to move, but neither inward nor outward. It seemed to be warping, the nearest top corner shifting farther than it had been allowed to open. But the door itself wasn't buckling, it had lost its mooring on the bottom corner, the massive metal slab now only held in place by its thick top hinge and the hastily made stone stop on the ground. At one point in the past, it must have had a functioning middle hinge, but that appeared to have been lost or broken some time ago.

"Captain!" Casselle yelled, trying to get Ardell's attention. "The door!"

She wasn't the only one to notice: panic was beginning to ripple through the defensive line, many of them losing focus on the fight to watch the door shiver against the strain of remaining in place. With the amount of pressure being applied to it, it wasn't going to hold for much longer, and if they didn't clear out the soldiers underneath it, all of them would be crushed when it fell.

Either her warning, or the subsequent alarm raised by others, was enough to get the respective officers to act. They shouted out orders to prepare for withdrawal. Casselle flushed with anger. It was the right call, but it would split up their force, moving them back to smaller rooms in the tower that had been identified previously by Nox's scouts. These rooms had already been partially filled by the wounded and dying. Groups retreating to these areas would have no place left to go. Those confined spaces would most likely become their tombs.

The separate groups would adopt a similar tactic there as they had used here, hoping to use tight corridors and restricted access to the rooms as an advantage against the H'Kaan. Optimistically, Casselle thought it only seemed like a way to extend their suffering. She had voiced that objection in a more tactful fashion when the plan was being formed, but few people wanted to give up the option to prolong the fight, holding out that Lord Lockewood might come back at the last minute with a way to save them.

Unfortunately, that door was coming down, and the flood of H'Kaan behind it would care little for any of their plans or disagreements. The officers called for them to move. The reinforcements behind the shield wall were the first, breaking into their groups and moving towards the halls and rooms they had been assigned to. Next they would call for the withdrawal of the shield wall.

The door collapsed before that.

It sounded as if the sky was being torn in half, a rending screech that blocked out cries of surprise or distress. It took only seconds, but it felt like time itself was stretched to the breaking point as Casselle attempted to move herself and those next to her out of the way.

She was facing away and didn't see the door hit the ground, but she knew it had landed because the world flipped head over heels. She was knocked down, or away, it was hard to determine because the moment was lost in thunder and motion.

She coughed up dirt. It was in her mouth and nose. Her mismatched helmet was lost and broken ground and bits of rubble dug into her hands. She struggled to rise, which was incredibly difficult while in full armor. She tried to see who was near her, who was next to her, but she couldn't quite focus, and the constant ringing in her ears was painful and distracting.

She felt the weapon in her hand. She hadn't dropped it. Her eyes were finally able to focus on the edge of a shield. It was not hers, but the bluesteel one that had been given to Finn. She coughed again. The air was thick with dust and debris. She couldn't hear herself cough, but she felt the burning in her chest, the grit in her mouth, the water at the corner of her irritated eyes, the trickle of snot running from her nose.

There were shapes moving around her, towards her, away from her. She fought to make them out as she forced her body into motion. One foot planted firmly, one leg attempted to lift her up. The second scrambled for a moment before she found the footing and the strength to make it work as well.

Something dark was charging at her from her right side. She lurched forward, feeling it brush against her back at the last moment. If she hadn't moved, she had no doubt it would have taken her back to the ground.

She ran her free hand across her face, hoping the rough leather would scrape away enough of the distractions for her to at least see properly.

The ringing in her ears began to have shades of distinction. There were low tones underneath the general tumult and loud peaks trying to distinguish themselves.

She saw Finn ahead of her, underneath an angry H'Kaan, who was trying to claw its way through his plate armor, the sharp talons rending the softer leather that the plate could not cover. She gripped her blade with both hands and drove it into the back of the beast, where the neck met the body. She felt the creature go slack almost instantly and wrenched the blade free, trying to take in everything else.

Something else was there, lunging at her. Akist be damned, she punched the beast in the face, putting all her weight behind the move. She felt the shock along her arm, as it lurched sharply downward from where she connected with it, just above one of its furious red eyes. The padded knuckles of her glove undoubtedly saved her from a broken bone or two, but watching it stagger felt damn good, and the pain helped sharpen her focus.

The first thing she did was finish the monster off, driving the blade into the side of its neck and spilling its inky black blood onto the ground. Then she looked up.

The door was down now, having crushed an unknown number of soldiers. There would be no time to take a definitive count; the H'Kaan wouldn't allow it. She saw Temos beyond Vincen, both of them struggling to right themselves. Finn was cut and bleeding, but still alive, scrambling on hands and knees for the shield just out of arm's reach. Gunner Hawken was single-handedly guarding the middle, putting himself between the open door and the soldiers behind, his bluesteel warclub scything back and forth, battering aside H'Kaan with seemingly effortless ease.

Ardell was there, having kept his own legs under him - or he was miraculously quick to return to them, she wasn't sure which. He was motioning and yelling for everyone to fall back, but his words were lost in the ringing that hadn't yet left her hearing.

Some of them had already been moving to their fallback positions as the door fell. They were probably deafened as well, but they had managed to remain on their feet.

The H'Kaan that could not charge through Gunnar split up and tried to hug the walls to either side, eager to get past the fallen line to those retreating. She turned to see Finn struggling to rise, and offered him a hand. He took it and she pulled him to his feet. He tapped the side of his helmet, where his ears would be. Casselle nodded in agreement. She pointed to some others that needed help up.

Finn must have been in pain, but it didn't slow him down as he moved to help defend those who didn't recover as quickly. He was weaponless, so Casselle flanked his right side and made herself the blade behind his shield. Fortunately for them, the H'Kaan reeled and retreated whenever he struck them with that polished blunt edge, no less so than if she scored only a graze against their hide. The bluesteel was poison to them, no matter the shape.

It was all chaos and fury at this point. Any sense of organization had collapsed just as surely as the door had, sending many of them into disarray. Soldiers, shocked and deafened, clawed their way up and towards the passages they had been assigned, only to be pounced on by H'Kaan from behind. The Laegis fared slightly better, but Casselle watched as Ardell failed to reach Lennard Torks quickly enough, the Sergeant valiantly making his last moments count as he fell stabbing one H'Kaan while another savaged his back.

There were shouts to fall back, which Casselle could now hear clearly. She tugged at Finn's arm and the two of them began a strategic retreat as Temos and Vincen passed them. Gunnar took small steps back, continuing his heroic defense, batting away a H'Kaan that had tried to latch onto one of his legs. Captain Ardell was helping Jhet, who was cradling one of his arms.

When they were about halfway back, Casselle noticed how much the wind had picked up, swirling the sand around them, like a storm was building in the air between them and the front door.

It wasn't a coincidence.

Theander Kross stood in the middle of the retreating Laegis, halfway between the door and the corridors leading deeper into the Temple. His arms were outstretched, his bandaged face contorted in pain and it was clear that he struggled to remain standing.

Casselle broke away from Finn, eyes now stinging from the wind, to move towards the Arxhemist. He stumbled, but she caught him, coming up on his right to prop him up. She couldn't look him in the eyes and he couldn't stop his chanting, but she felt his muscles relax, confirming that he knew her intent. She tucked her bluesteel weapon in her belt and used that hand to hold him upright.

She could hear the pain in his voice, even though she couldn't understand the words. Arxhemestry was spoken in the language of the Old Gods, Tarsus' brethren that had been slain by Maughrin before the world was remade. Those that mastered the power could perform miracles, but as she felt Theander's body heat up next to her, she was reminded of the cost of such power.

The wind howled loudly, whipping the sand around the chamber, but it started to accumulate into large clouds at the front, above the fallen door. The H'Kaan were wary. They hunched closer to the ground, not stopping, but slowing as the dust scraped at their skin.

Certainly this couldn't be what he had planned, she thought. The already wounded Arxhemist wouldn't expend so much of himself just to give them a wind rash.

As they hesitated, Gunnar moved past Theander, his warclub in one hand, the limp form of an armored soldier tucked under his other arm. The sand made it difficult to see if they were Templar or not. Now Theander was the line between them, his body increasingly hot to the touch, only remaining upright because Casselle endured.

The first flash caught her off guard. The subsequent strikes lit up the inside of the Temple in sharp, bright flashes, accompanied by booming thunder. A cluster of lightning strikes arced between the ground and swirling clouds, an argument of raw, natural fury. It was over in just a second, a mad rush of air howling to escape as soon as Theander's control of it had been relinquished.

Casselle felt his body surrender. Her hands were hot underneath the thick leather, but in her attempt to keep him from falling, she gripped him tight and felt that his body was different... changed... lighter. This was not like when Odegar had been overcome in Flinderlass. When she drew back to look at him, the transformation was already complete, his body thoroughly consumed, leaving only a husk of ash wiped of individual features inside the thick robes of his Order.

She stumbled as his body crumbled, reflexively acting as if she needed to lay down the remains gently, even though there was nothing left to save. The quickly cooling cinders came apart under the pressure of her grip. The soft fabric slackened, Theander's sooty remains collapsing to the ground.

She let the empty robes fall to the ground as she reached back for her weapon, her eyes trying to assess what Theander's sacrifice had gained them.

A mess of blistered and smoldering H'Kaan was an excellent start. All those in the doorway were dead, as well as many that had crawled forward. Some of them still twitched slightly, but the space ahead had been cleared, if but for the moment.

The dust swirled and retreated, thinning as it spread out of the area Theander had confined it to.

The last of the soldiers ducked out of sight down the halls, a hollow escape that would only lead them to further imprisonment.

"Milner," Captain Ardell choked out, his voice now raw from trying to issue commands over the din of combat. He looked healthy enough, but his helmet and eyepatch were both missing. She couldn't tell if he'd taken a fresh cut on top of it, or it were the blood of someone else splattered on his face.

She found herself in the middle. The last of the Shield Templars had lingered, either to wait for her, to witness the Arxhemic spectacle, or both. Temos stood next to Vincen, whose eyes were still wide from it all. Jhet had found a way to tuck his broken arm into his armorjack, keeping it out of the way and relatively immobile. Despite the pain he must have been in, he still held the bluesteel sword in his good hand, the length of it stained with black H'Kaan blood.

Finn had found a sword in the dirt, his bluesteel shield still shining, even in the obscured light. Gunnar stood behind them all, having handed off the wounded soldier to those retreating. For the first time since she'd met the massive Vanha, she noticed that he looked tired, a weariness that was more than just simple exhaustion.

What remained of the Templar Lancers were there as well, their squads similarly depleted. Commander Cohl had been leading them directly since Boen's death, with the help of one of his remaining sergeants. Including the two of them, there were eight of their original twenty left.

The few H'Kaan that had slipped around and evaded the lightning were now being dealt with, shocked and temporarily outnumbered by Cohl's Lancers.

Casselle turned back to the door. Shadows moved through the thinning dust, but the horde that emerged was not the one she expected...

...it was the one she feared most.

Emeranth Kell walked with casual ease into the Temple, flanked by the things that had once been mothers and fathers, sisters and brothers, but now were little more than monsters wearing their skins. They outnumbered the Templar, but not like the H'Kaan had. They were fearsome, but they were not limitless.

"Captain?" Temos prompted. Casselle noted there was no fear in his voice. He wasn't asking to retreat. None of them were. Captain Ardell stood up straight, looking over at his Commander. Zan Cohl flicked his sword to clear it of H'Kaan blood as he walked back to join his fellow Templar in the middle.

"I don't care to die in a hole," Greffin growled.

"Well said, Captain," Cohl replied. Turning to Emeranth Kell, the young officer spoke up in a clear voice.

"When I return to Strossen, my report will say that we offered you the chance to surrender," Cohl said, "but I think we'd all just rather kill you instead."

Casselle knew it hadn't been prompted, but she heard the sharp rap of sword on shield. Tired and wounded, bloody and battered, every single one of them repeated it.

Thump. Thump.

"I see," Emeranth said, her lips turning to a scowl. Her eyes narrowed as she focused on Casselle. "Surely you know how this will end. I've already killed you once."

"Try harder this time," Casselle replied coldly. The weapon in her hand grew cool to the touch. She held it out before her and wrapped her second fist next to her first. Then she pulled them apart slowly, feeling the hilt shift and grow, elongating until it was at its full length: a spear with a leaf shaped blade at the tip.

Casselle took a deep breath and exhaled slowly as she felt her feet slide into the proper position, the spear held out before her.

The scowl curled into an angry sneer.

"How did... that was... *you*. You're just full of little surprises aren't you?" Emeranth hissed. "I'll have to make sure I rip you open and pull them out one by one." She emphasized her threat by illustrating the motion with her large hands. Both were now the smoky black flesh of the H'Kaan, the fingers ending in the same shining obsidian claws as the lesser beasts under her command.

A wild howl ripped from the throat of one of the possessed bodies that flanked her on either side. The creatures charged forward, rushing towards the Laegis, who fell into their defensive positions. They were easily outnumbered two to one, or worse in some cases. Gunnar squared off with at least five. Out of the corner of her eye, it looked like Jhet was actually running to meet them head on, part of his scarf ripped open and the corner of a manic smile barely hidden as he charged.

Emeranth moved as well, but the self-possessed warrior that Casselle had fought previously was only barely represented here. She still had all the speed and strength of the woman she'd fought before, but there was a ferocity that could no longer be masked. In the last fight, she had the reach and the skill to quickly break the Templar.

But that was a different fight. The spear afforded Casselle an equal reach and the bluesteel blade would not be turned aside so easily. She broke Emeranth's charge with several short jabs at her face. None of them hit, but it caused her to pull up in order to avoid being stabbed. She reached out to grab at it, but it was as elusive as a snake's head, slipping away only to zip back and bite her on an outstretched hand.

She coiled back, clutching at the wound. Casselle knew it burned. She had seen it cut through H'Kaan flesh like a hot knife. She imagined Emeranth must be experiencing something similar.

The former Templar was now in the same position that Casselle had been in when they first clashed. She sought to close the gap, to move past the spear in order to bring her talons to bear. She used her forearm to bat the haft of the spear away as she drove forward.

But Casselle felt the move before she saw it and the spear reacted to her desires, the shaft retracting, like a serpent drawing back for another strike, slipping back into the shape of the long handled short sword. The nimble blade turned aside the blow from Emeranth's right hand, liberating two of her fingers in the process.

Casselle stepped back, ducking as the other hand raked at her exposed face. Her footing wasn't entirely true and she slid back, going down to one knee in order to recover.

Emeranth lurched forward, both hands closing in for a grab.

Casselle yelled in defiance. The spear grew warm in her hands and it exploded into action. The back of it slammed into the ground just behind Casselle as it expanded, the spiked butt of the spear biting into the sand. The front of it struck faster than an arrow in flight, rending through the front of Emeranth's armor cleanly. It did not punch through the back, because it lifted her to her full height, impaling her, the force of her forward momentum having been rebuffed by the spear's expanse.

She was unable to move forward, her pain and rage driving her mad as she struggled to reach Casselle. The blade was buried in her chest and blue flames flickered around the edges of where the spear had punctured the armored plate.

In the Ghostvale, Theander Kross had explained to her that the histories of the Khaliil were crafted of more than simple words. There were thoughts and emotions transcribed along with the descriptions of the Khaliil's life.

"Part of the teller is bound to the story," was what Theander had said.

She was reminded of his words, because she felt something. It was the hint of a memory, a mere whisper of a feeling. There was a story bound to this spear. But the stories were bound by the tellers.

If that held true, who was bound in the spear? Was it one of the weapon's creators? The smith who forged the blade? The craftsman who had wrapped the hilt in leather? The Arxhemist that had carved the symbols on the surface? Casselle suspected it was none of those.

The fury in Emeranth's eyes seemed tempered as she pulled back. Casselle withdrew the spear and reclaimed her footing. The weapon shrank slightly as she flicked the tip toward the sand, bits of flesh and blood splattering on the ground, the remains still sizzling with heat. The woman towered over her, but hunched slightly, one hand held up over the wound in her chest, which was slowly leaking the same black blood she'd seen from the H'Kaan. Out of the corner of her eye, she saw the battlefield around them was active, the exhausted but determined Templar giving better than they got, valiant but outnumbered.

"You're in this," Casselle declared, pointing the spear towards Emeranth. "Part of you is, at least. Before you became whatever you are now."

"I am Her Wrath," Emeranth replied sharply. "This body... these memories... when I woke up, I thought they were mine, but I see now that they never were. They were but empty seats left behind in an abandoned temple." She made a show of flexing the freshly regrown fingers on her hand.

"You defile that temple," Casselle said.

"It's not the only one we'll defile. This time I'll make sure you're dead, and then I'll seed you like I did them," Emeranth threatened, motioning to the infested bodies currently fighting the Laegis. Casselle didn't bother to speak back. There was something in the spear that radiated anger. She didn't understand how, but she knew she couldn't ignore it; there was no use in talking any longer.

She led with the weapon, testing Emeranth's range once more, a few quick jabs to the rent in her armor, seeing how she would react. She stepped back, slipping away with the same speed Casselle had seen in their last fight. The Templar was breathing hard, but the self-proclaimed Wrath didn't appear winded at all.

Casselle let a bit of frustration propel a clumsy strike. Surprisingly she hit, striking Emeranth through the palm. But even as the larger woman howled in pain, the fingers unraveled into smaller fibers, wrapping around the blade where it met the haft. Casselle tried to set her feet, but it was too late. Even with her hand burning with blue fire, the monster ripped the weapon from Casselle's grasp, sending it flying away to the left.

She rushed forward, her other hand outstretched, each grotesque finger tipped with black talons. It was meant to panic Casselle, but the Templar saw the same opening Emeranth had presented her in their last fight. She responded the way the Akist had trained her, moving in, not away, quickly grappling her by the wrist and pivoting her weight. Plated armor was usually quite good at deflecting blade and arrow, but it was heavy, and many battles came down to who could make their opponent fall over first. It would take time to get up, time that someone standing above you could use to great advantage.

Emeranth was overbalanced and crashed to the ground. Casselle almost joined her, but was able to stagger away and retain her footing. She immediately sprinted for the spear, eager to recover it and finish this fight. As she passed close to Temos, she shoved the malformed thing he was fighting, staggering it and opening an opportunity for him to bash it in the face with his shield and topple it backwards. She didn't stop to see how he followed that up.

She almost fell over on her own, coming to a sudden awkward halt, her fingers scrabbling for a moment in the dust until they closed down on the haft of the spear. She righted herself, spinning to face Emeranth.

She was surprised to see her opponent so close, moving too fast to counter. Casselle's grip tightened around the haft of the spear that she didn't have time to bring to bear and she flung herself to the side of Emeranth's mangled hand. She managed not to be trampled, but was buffeted aside, landing roughly a few feet away.

Her body was screaming in protest, but she was equal parts panic and determination, willing herself up despite the pain. She gritted her teeth and strained against the weight of her own armor as she got to her feet.

A short distance away, Emeranth was also getting up again, the silver eyes of the former Templar burning out from underneath her dark matted hair, a wild monster in the shape of a giant-sized woman. Casselle felt like a small child confronting a nightmare.

Undaunted, she started forward. Emeranth had found a rock, a jagged looking thing that she cocked back in her arm to throw.

Casselle pushed harder, but she wasn't going to make it. She wasn't going to be able to close the gap in time. Even if the spear…

Emeranth lurched to the side, her left leg sprouting a bloody sword point from the side of her knee. She held on to the rock, diverting her attack to this new assailant.

Casselle kept running, her chest heaving, wanting to scream out her rage but not having enough breath to do so. Temos suddenly staggered out from behind the giant, his shield flung away wildly from the impact of the stone. He flailed and tripped over backwards.

Casselle felt the spear lower her aim at the last moment. Emeranth Kell turned around just in time for the weapon that had once been her own to slip between the plates covering her upper chest and her lower torso, driven upward and out through the armor covering her back.

Emeranth's eyes grew wide. Her hand went slack, the rock falling to the ground with a thud.

She lurched forward, driving more of the spear through her own chest, threatening to topple over entirely, but instead merely falling to her knees, halting abruptly less than a foot away from the Templar.

Those large silver eyes became unfocused and distant.

In a voice that Casselle almost did not recognize, Emeranth Kell strained forward to whisper:

"Thank you."

- 29 -

Tears

"Crixus is his *son*?" First Mate Tarq gasped.

The projected vision from Ossien had stopped abruptly, leaving Triistan and the other members of the Aarden Expedition reeling. Triistan wasn't sure which was worse: the shock of discovering that Crixus was the rogue god's offspring or not being able to see how the battle between Ossien and the last of the Oathguard defenders was unfolding.

"And what of it, huunan?" Syr snapped. "Do you question his honor? His fidelity to the Oath? The High Master was the Worm's son when he exposed his depravity at Talmoreth, as he was when he rallied us to defend against Theckan's raid. The gods do not suckle their bastards, nor bounce them on their knees. We are all orphans, loyal only to the Oath and each other. You would do well to remember that."

Captain Vaelysia raised her hands and made a placating gesture. "Peace, Su'ul. We meant no offense. Mister Tarq is just surprised, that's all - we all are. Based on the stories your husband told us, we never expected Ossien to have sired any mortal children."

Danor grunted. "Stick around and you'll find he's full of surprises. Hypocrisy's one of his better qualities, actually. Let's go - if he breaks through, you'll discover some of his worst."

They moved forward again, but their pace was noticeably slower. Continuing on with the knowledge that at that moment Tau and the others were facing Ossien was a stone in their hearts that grew heavier with each step. Triistan's overactive mind tied itself in worried knots wondering at the different possibilities. He was also torn between wanting to see events as they unfolded and the horror of being trapped inside Ossien's head again. But the minutes dragged on without so much as a headache. It was clear that the Worm had been in full control of the projections for the past several hours, so it was a mystery why they had stopped now. Did it mean he was losing? That he'd been injured? Or was he just waiting, maliciously keeping them in the dark until it was all over? Even Danor, who knew the consequences of delay better than anyone there, seemed distracted and hesitant.

After nearly two hours had dragged on this way, Syr called a halt from the rear and moved nimbly past them all to pull her husband aside for a quiet word. They were on a narrow ledge that had been sloping upwards for the past hour, leaving the noisy Aniiene some hundred feet below. Triistan's legs were weary and trembling, so he sagged against the cliff wall and slid down to a sitting position, wiping sweat from his forehead. He unstoppered his water skin and took a long pull, then drizzled some over his head.

He was just noting that his whole body was trembling when Biiko appeared beside him and hauled him back to his feet.

"Move, now," was all the Unbound said as he shoved Triistan forward.

The trembling grew worse, causing him to stumble. As he put a hand against the cliff face to steady himself he realized that it wasn't his body at all: the entire stone shelf and adjacent wall were shaking. Others in the party were looking around in confusion while dirt and small rocks tumbled down from above. Brehnl, Anthon, Jaegus the Younger and Izenya were just ahead of Triistan, with the Captain, First Mate, Commander Tchicatta and Jaspins ahead of them; Creugar now brought up the rear behind Triistan and Biiko, as Danor and Syr had moved several yards ahead during their conversation.

The ledge was wide enough for two of them to walk abreast, but with nothing but a sheer drop on one side, it seemed much narrower to all of them. They felt exposed, their fear intensified by exhaustion and the confusion over what was happening, edging the regular crew members toward panic. Anthon and Jaegus shoved at one another as the younger Seeker tried to push his way past. The ledge beneath them was shaking visibly now, making it hard to keep their balance. A low rumbling noise started and grew rapidly louder.

In front of him, Izenya grabbed hold of Jaegus and cuffed him on the back of the head.

"Belay that, lad!" he shouted. "Follow the man in front of ya and keep yer head afore you send us all overboard!"

They moved forward again, keeping close to the wall and stumbling with each shaking step. Larger boulders rained down from above, but because the cliff wall curved slightly overhead, the rocks bounced off of it and sailed harmlessly by. The rumbling noise escalated to a roar and was clearly coming from the direction of Ostenvaard. Triistan glanced back fearfully, expecting some new nightmarish beast to come charging up the ravine to crush them; perhaps even Ossien himself.

Suddenly he felt the iron band of Biiko's grip on his upper arm and he was pulled to a stop. Creugar cursed as he nearly ran into them.

"Why do you stop, Blackbl-"

A wave of rock and dirt crashed down directly in front of Triistan as a whole section of the cliff face broke away and began sliding downwards, taking the ledge along with it. Izenya dropped as the ledge collapsed and Triistan instinctively reached out, grabbing d'Gara's tunic. Izzy was large and solidly built - far too heavy for Triistan to haul back up - but the young topman's own grip was strong from his work in the rigging and he was able to twist d'Gara, allowing the boson's mate to catch himself on a lip of stone. Biiko and Triistan each grabbed an arm and dragged him back from the rockslide.

The tremors continued as rocks, dirt and debris showered down all around them. Triistan, Biiko, d'Gara and Creugar huddled against the cliff face and covered their heads, while the world seemed intent on tearing itself asunder. Finally, after several long moments, the roar subsided to a dull rumble, and the trembling in the ground faded. They eventually staggered to their feet to survey the damage.

Barely a body's length in front of Izenya, the ledge and part of the cliff face were gone, leaving a deep, uneven scar perhaps thirty feet across and four or five feet deep: a huge section of the bluff had broken loose and slid down into the gorge.

"d'Gara, Halliard, report! Are you all right?" The voice belonged to First Mate Tarq. Captain Vaelysia stood beside him, and Triistan could see the Firstblade, Jaspins, Danor and Syr behind them.

"Aye, Sir! I'm well enough, thanks to Titch. He's whole, along with his silent shadow and Creugar, sir..."

"Doxy, Anthon and Jaegus...?" it wasn't really a question, as they all knew the men were lost in the landslide. Across the gap, the First Mate just shook his head.

"Halliard!" the Captain called, deliberately pushing her crew past the tragedy. "Do you still have your climbing gear?"

Triistan stared stupidly at her for a moment, still processing the loss of three fellow crewmembers.

Climbing gear? He stumbled through a rough mental inventory: Taelyia's sword, two waterskins, and a small sack of rations. And his journal, of course. He could not even remember when he'd last had his climbing gear. It was probably -

"Mister Halliard!"

"No, Sir!" he instinctively replied.

She cursed as she turned to confer with Tarq and the others.

"What d'ya think that was, Titch?" Izenya growled.

Triistan shook his head, still staring in shock at the landslide below them. Part of him hoped to see someone digging themselves out, irrationally thinking they may have just been carried down by the slide and landed near the top, but he knew he was being foolish. Three lives - men he knew, had served with, laughed, fought and cried with - had just… stopped, right in front of him. He was numb, not knowing what to think or feel.

"Halliard," Izenya said, more gently this time. He put his rough hands on the young man's shoulders and forced Triistan to look him in the eye. "No time for that, lad. We'll grieve'em proper when we get out of this squall, but right now we need all hands. Are y'with me?"

Triistan swallowed hard and nodded. He forced himself to answer Izzy's earlier question. "The dam - I think they must have collapsed the Weir. I think that's what we heard… or felt."

d'Gara nodded and held his gaze for a moment, then gave him a wink and straightened. "Good lad. Welcome back - we're gon'ta need that head of yours. And your monkey skills." He jutted his stubbled chin in the direction of the gap behind Triistan. "What d'ya think - can you free-climb it?"

Triistan studied the damaged cliff face for a moment, making a conscious effort not to look down. He decided he probably could make it across, and had no doubt that Biiko could, but he didn't see how that would help d'Gara or Creugar. He opened his mouth to say as much when he heard a shout.

"Back away, lads!" the Captain called from the other side.

Syr stood several paces behind her with a coil of sleek rope over one shoulder. Danor held one end, and there was a loose pile of slack on the ground beside him.

Triistan and the others took several steps back as Syr suddenly sprinted towards the ledge. But rather than leap across, she ran along the damaged cliff wall, using her momentum to move across the broken bluff in two or three quick strides. When she had reached the halfway point, she sprang towards them, clearing the remaining distance easily to land lightly on Triistan's side of the gap. He heard d'Gara give a low whistle of appreciation behind him.

Syr moved past them wordlessly and looped her end of the line around the base of a gnarled tree several yards down the path, then returned to where they stood watching (rather dumbly, he thought as he relayed his tale). She played out several more yards of line onto the ground by her feet, still without saying a word to the others, then took three quick steps and repeated her incredible feat to return to the other side.

"What a woman..." Izzy whispered.

There was nothing large enough to tie off to on that side of the gap, however, so Danor had to improvise. After knotting his end of the rope around his calf and ankle, he accepted the other end of the line from Syr, looped it around his broad back, and tied it off around his upper torso. He then took several steps back until the rope was taut and sank to one knee. The result was a crude rope bridge, with one line higher and one lower, allowing Triistan and the others to slowly and carefully cross. It took them nearly a half hour to traverse the landslide, including a frightening moment where Creugar dangled from one hand. His size had worked against him, as the lower line kept wanting to swing out from under him, and when he was about a third of the way across, he lost his footing completely and slipped off. He held onto the guide rope, however, and crossed the remaining distance hand over hand, grinning the whole way.

As Danor untied the line and began hauling it back across, Triistan gasped.

The ravine they'd been following all day was now in shadow as Ruine's twin suns drifted into the Long Evening. But as the group had climbed higher, the horizon had gradually opened up behind and below them. He could not see The Weir, but the vista that greeted him now in that direction was equal parts spectacular and terrifying.

As a topman, Triistan practically lived aloft while at sea. One of his favorite ways to spend his idle time was watching far off storms develop, especially during the early morning or late evening hours. The panorama provided on the open ocean was unparalleled, limited only by his own sight. He had been moved to tears in several instances, but he had never seen anything quite like this. For a moment, he wondered if the world was ending.

The columns of oily black smoke were gone, obliterated by a singular monstrous tower of billowing white cloud, lit sharply on one side in the golden light of dusk, its opposite edge bruised with deep purple shadow. What remained visible of the sky on that side was a much darker blue, as if night had come prematurely to that part of the world. Perhaps it had.

"The Weir has fallen," Danor rumbled next to him. "Ostenvaard drowns, and the Oath is broken."

"May the Worm drown with it," Syr added bitterly.

They all looked on silently for several long moments, until bright flashes of orange in the ravine below caught Triistan's eye. "What are those?" he wondered aloud.

Danor shaded his eyes, then swore softly. "Pa'piits - the flame-colored birds we saw earlier. They flock like that whenever something enters the gorge."

Triistan felt a surge of hope. "Then maybe they survived after all - Tau and the others?"

It was obvious from the look on the giant's face that he did not share that hope. Instead of responding to Triistan, he addressed his wife in the Vanha tongue and they embraced. When she stepped away, he added in the common tongue, "Come back, my beautiful, fierce Syrinya. We will need you at the Tears."

She laid a hand on his cheek. "Depend on it, vetanuu. All is not lost yet: so long as we two live, so does the Oath." Before he could answer, she seemed almost to fly back across the landslide, her strange cloak of feathers billowing out behind her like shimmering wings. In another moment, she vanished around a bend in the path.

***

A few hours later, they climbed out of the gorge into a valley dominated by a narrow, sinuous lake. The water caught the failing light, tracing a wide ribbon of fire through the handful of low hills that made up the valley floor. Nearby, it spilled down into the gorge in a noisy cascade, glimmering wherever it splashed with that familiar blue glow.

Danor had pushed them hard after Syr left. There were no more mental attacks from Ossien, and with each passing moment they felt themselves buoyed by the hope that, somehow, Tau and the others had managed to defeat him. It gave them the energy to scale the last fifty feet almost straight up, climbing from boulder to ledge to outcropping until they finally emerged in the valley, where most of the Expedition members collapsed onto the long, soft grass, too exhausted to do little more than groan.

Danor allowed them to rest for close to an hour, while he prowled along the edge of the gorge, watching for Syr's return.

She did not, nor was there any sign of her as he led them along the lakeshore in the deepening gloom, or when they crested the first low hill and looked back the way they'd come. The ravine was little more than a ragged scar of shadow into which the Aniiene's incandescent water disappeared, but the grassy slopes and lake shore between here and there were still visible, and clearly empty. Danor rumbled something to himself and trudged on.

Triistan had been plodding along for some time, asleep on his feet, when suddenly he felt something that jolted him into wakefulness. He thought he'd stepped into a shallow ditch, landing hard, until he felt it again.

Thump.

It was a heavy, dull thud, as of something solid striking the ground. He hadn't heard it though - it was more like something he felt in the soles of his feet. He looked around at his comrades, and saw Jaspins staring back at him quizzically.

"Did you... " but another heavy thud answered the question. And this time he heard it, too.

"What -"

Danor motioned them to silence, then signaled them to follow.

They were on another gentle rise. As they approached the top, he got down on his hands and knees, bidding them to do the same. The grass was considerably longer here, tall enough to conceal all of the Expedition members as they crawled. Danor had to lower himself to his belly in order to be fully hidden, which he did just as they crested the hillock.

They heard a dragging noise, followed by another heavy thud and a long, low, groan. Danor slowly raised himself, stopping when his head protruded above the grass. Triistan was surprised at the Oathguard's expression: he looked happy.

He motioned the others forward, mouthing the word "slowly".

There were several sharp intakes of breath. A scant two or three hundred paces down the slope from where they crept were five monstrous creatures they immediately recognized. As large as a decent sized galley, these were the same beasts as the one beneath the Rivergate, whose carcass had been half buried decades earlier, and whose hollow shell had provided them passage through the cave-in and flooded tunnel to daylight. Their wide, pan-shaped heads were lowered as they grazed, but the bony plates and four sweeping horns that crowned them were unmistakable. From time to time they emitted the low rumbling groans the party had heard a few moments ago. Triistan found the noise soothing, for they resonated with a deep, peaceful contentment. Although the ground shook every time one of the beasts took a step, he was sorely tempted to walk up and pet one.

Danor allowed them to watch for a few more moments before leading them back down the hill. When they were far enough below the crest, he stood, picking one of the long blades of grass and chewing on it as he spoke.

"Fortune or whatever you favor these days has smiled on us, Salties. This is a happy chance meeting!"

"What are they?" the Captain asked. "We saw one - or its corpse, rather - beneath the Rivergate."

Danor nodded. "Yiin, that would be Bellaya. One of a herd of eight that make their home in this valley now, though normally they prefer the other end, near Ossien's Tears. We call the species 'armaduura' - 'armored giant' - for obvious reasons."

"You named them?" Triistan blurted. "Are they domesticated?"

"No, they're not domesticated, and yes, we named them. Don't look so surprised, Salty. Before the world decided to shit all over us, I spent decades studying them. They are surprisingly intelligent, with a complex series of calls that come as close as any animal I know has ever come to a language."

"Are they dangerous?"

"As dangerous as an avalanche or a falling tree - you wouldn't want to stand under either one - but they're no threat to us unless we were to attack them... which would be pretty fuundaris stupid, even for the likes of you.

"However," he continued as his lips split in a slow grin. "The same can't be said for the Worm and his pets. The armaduura are natural enemies of the H'Kaan - as opposed to the Dark-spawned as water is to fire. And as for Ossien, Bellaya was the herd's matriarch, and they have long memories."

As if they were listening from the other side of the hill, one of the armaduura emitted a slow, rumbling call. It held a note of sad wisdom that reminded Triistan of whale song, though it sounded nothing like it.

"Come." Danor set off along the base of the hill, towards the lakeshore. "We'll be safe here and can make camp for the night. The herd will alert us if anything makes it past Syr, so it's time for a good meal and a full night's rest. When we reach the Tears by mid-day tomorrow, you're going to need it."

They made a crude camp amongst a series of shallow dunes that ran along this side of the lake. Creugar and Jaspins dug a pit and lined it with stones, allowing them to build a small cooking fire that wouldn't be visible from far away, while Commander Tchicatta, Tarq, and Izzy went looking for food. Game was plentiful, and before long they returned with a brace of rabbits and two pudú, a type of small, stocky deer. Danor disappeared on his own for awhile, and Triistan assumed he had backtracked along their trail hoping for some sign of Syr. He returned just as Creugar was carving off the first slice of sizzling venison, looking troubled, but when asked about it would only say that "Morning will tell the tale that mayhap my heart cannot."

Instead, he told them how the armaduura he called Bellaya had found her way into Ahbaingeata. Apparently, the herd used to live in the open steppes outside of Ostenvaard's walls. During the attack to free Ossien, sections of the curtain wall were destroyed and at some point during the battle, the beasts wandered into the fortress. At the time, the Oathguard had thought it was just dumb luck, but Danor now felt otherwise after studying the creatures for the past two hundred and fifty-plus years.

"Like I said, Salties," he rumbled around a mouthful of venison, "the 'duura's abhor the Dark-spawn. And the big brokuuros are smart. When the Worm fled back through the city, it was a near thing - we almost had him! Bellaya and her kin went mad at the sight of him. Blood and bone, that little trembling we felt earlier when the Weir fell was nothing compared to a herd of 'duura in full stampede. Whole buildings - built by the Arys, mind you - shook themselves to rubble. It was glorious and terrible." His eyes took on a far-away look and Triistan caught that same flash of incandescent blue he'd seen back in the Vanha's apartment, so long ago.

"Anyway," he said abruptly, bringing himself back to the present, "old Wormy showed a surprising amount of resourcefulness, cunning and wisdom... and ran for his fuundaris life. Bellaya gave chase along the Aniiene's channel, down into Ahbaingeata, but alas it was not built for giants of her stature. You know the rest, I think."

They finished their meal and settled in for the night. With no tents, bedrolls or even a blanket, they kept as close to the fire as they dared. Commander Tchicatta tried to set a watch rotation with Creugar and Jaspins, but Danor convinced them it was pointless and that they would benefit more from badly needed rest.

Triistan barely heard their discussion. Exhausted and sore, he found a spot relatively free of stones and other lumps and lay down. For the briefest moment he forgot about the trials and terrors of the past few days and just hung there on the velvet-soft brink of sleep. He reveled in the profound beauty of the glittering night sky above until the soft sighing of the grasslands around them and the armaduura's rumbling murmurs pulled him over.

For the first time in many days, and the last time in many more, he slept in peace.

***

He awoke in panic.

He had dreamt of sleeping through the morning, while his comrades ate breakfast and broke camp. While he slumbered on, they simply left, moving around and past him without ever acknowledging his presence, until someone finally asked if they should fetch him. It was Jaspins, but when no one answered her, she shrugged and followed them over the dunes.

He bolted upright, only to find most of the Expedition members either still sleeping or in the act of waking themselves. He looked up at the sound of Danor's voice and saw the Vanha embracing someone, but in his sleep-befuddled state, it took Triistan a moment to realize who it was.

"Syr!" he half-shouted, startling his conscious shipmates and waking the rest.

Danor led her into the campsite, surrounded by a chorus of concerned murmuring. She leaned heavily on him, and there were several ragged tears in the close-fitting leather armor she wore. Most of the rents were caked with dried blood, though more than a few still shimmered wetly. She groaned through clenched teeth as Danor helped her to a sitting position, and Triistan caught the unmistakable scent of burnt flesh.

He handed her a water skin, which she accepted with her right hand and drank deeply from as both Jaspins and Danor began examining her wounds.

"We'll need to get this armor off," Jaspins said in a clipped voice. "It isn't going to be pleasant."

Still using only her right hand, Syr poured some of the water over her sweat-drenched hair and face, then shook her head like a wet dog. "'Pleasant' has no place here anymore, healer. Do your worst, but spare the cloak - if you cut that free I'll do the same for your head."

To her credit, Jaspins was nonplussed. "As you wish, Su'ul. If you'd care to unclasp the broa - "

Holding the Reaver's gaze, Syr held up her left hand, which had previously been hidden under her cloak. This time Jaspins reacted, taking half a step back. Syr's hand was badly mutilated, with only two partial fingers remaining and bone showing through in several spots; what flesh remained was a black and red mess that looked like charred meat.

Behind her, Danor closed his eyes. Triistan could see the muscle of his jaw bunching, but other than that, the Vanha remained still, except to place one hand on his wife's shoulder. She reached up and clasped it with her right, her gaze never leaving Jaspins.

"You will want to move quickly, healer. We don't have much time."

The young Reaver swallowed hard and nodded, then began loosening the brooch that held the cloak clasped around Syr's throat. Danor was struggling with one of the harness buckles, finally putting his hands up and swearing in frustration.

"Can't see a fuundaris thing after keeping watch over you brokuuros all night," he rasped, but the moisture pooling at the corners of his eyes told another story. Biiko silently stepped in to assist. As he and Jaspins carefully began removing her armor, Syr alternated between cursing at them and telling the others what had happened to her.

She had moved rapidly back down the ravine, slowing only when she heard the second bridge collapse. That had been another stroke of good fortune: up until that point, all but two of the bridges Danor had carefully weakened had fallen during the quake. If that last bridge had collapsed before their pursuers had reached it, she would have had no warning and run headlong into a sizable force of H'Kaan.

"Sizable?" Captain Vaelysia repeated.

Biiko was spreading a greasy paste he'd just finished mixing onto Syr's hand. She wrinkled her nose in disgust.

"Rotting gods, that stinks, patroniis. Yes, Captain. I made their numbers close to five fists at the outset - two hundred and fifty Respiis." She looked meaningfully at Danor, who was now pacing in front of her. "Led by Sithis."

He stopped. "Not Ossien?"

Syr shook her head. "No, husband. Of The Worm I neither saw nor felt any sign."

"Curious." Triistan thought Danor was deliberately avoiding looking at his wife.

"Is he dead, then?" Tarq asked.

Danor shrugged his huge shoulders. "Tough to say. Yesterday, I would have dismissed the idea outright... but the longer it stays quiet... "

Syr winced as Jaspins began stitching an ugly gash running along the swell of the Vanha's left breast. Triistan tried hard not to stare. It turned out she wore nothing under her tight-fitting armor, so her upper body was now completely naked. Modesty was apparently a foreign concept to the Vanha, as she did not seem the least bit aware of her nudity. He caught Jaspins glancing at him and blushed furiously as she rolled her eyes.

"Not that it matters," Syr continued. "Sithis and what's left of his hunting party are more than enough to finish the Worm's work."

"What's left... " Commander Tchicatta prompted.

Syr fixed him with her gaze, eyes bright and hard, like chips of grey ice. "I now make his strength closer to three fists. It would have been less if I hadn't grown careless."

Triistan heard d'Gara give another low whistle and knew what the big Seeker was thinking.

What a woman indeed.

"Impressive," the Firstblade said. Syr held up her damaged left hand.

"Costly. But it may have bought us the time we'll need - if we leave shortly."

"With respect, Su'ul," Captain Vaelysia interjected, "if you were able to slay nearly half of them on your own, why not make a stand here?"

"Too many." She shook her head as she watched Biiko bandaging her brutalized limb. "I had the advantage of surprise and the terrain, plus the first bridge took out nearly thirty of them. Here, even with my husband's formidable help, we would be overrun and destroyed."

"What about the armaduura?" Tarq asked.

Danor snorted. "Avalanche, remember? We'd be trampled right along with our enemies. But if we can put the 'duura between them and us, we've got a damn good chance of making The Hold."

"What then?" Captain Vaelysia asked.

Danor smiled his not-smile. "What goes up, must come down, Salty. We'll ford that river when we come to it."

Jaspins and Biiko finished dressing Syr's wounds, then helped her back into her armor and cloak, while the rest of the party collected their few belongings, divvied up what remained of the previous night's meal, and topped off their water skins. Then they were on the move again, though this time Syr took the lead and Danor fell back to guard the rear. She seemed to have regained her strength, which Triistan attributed as much to Jaspins' and Biiko's care as to the indomitable will of the Oathguard.

She gave the armaduura a wide berth and they were soon moving briskly through the rolling grasslands, pausing for a few moments whenever they crested one of the low hills to rest and look behind them for any sign of pursuit.

The valley they were following was really a pass leading deeper into a mountain range Danor had called "Te'Sanginele", a series of jagged, menacing peaks covered in snow and ice that reflected the sunlight so well it hurt their eyes to look at directly for very long. Closer to hand, however, the cool, clear air and mid-morning light picked everything out in crisp detail. When they climbed their fifth hill almost two hours later, they could still easily make out the herd of armaduura where they grazed, and beyond them the dark scar where the lake emptied down into the gorge. They also saw, at the very place they had emerged the evening before, the sudden stain of shadow that began seeping out of it into the valley. Triistan's insides went cold.

"They come," Danor said simply. The shadow moved swiftly, unerringly in their direction.

"How can they know where we are?" Triistan was ashamed of how whiny his voice sounded.

"Sithis can fuundaris see us, that's how," Danor growled. "The Worm's pet projects have been strengthened in more ways than just grafting bits of armor and sharp objects to their bones. But even without a L'Suu to guide them, the Respiis sense us, they are drawn to us, remember? The xhemium in the water used to camouflage us, but this new breed seems to know the difference."

He pointed. "But see, Lena and the others know something's wrong."

One by one, the armaduura's spade-shaped heads lifted until their hooked snouts were pointed straight up at the sky, then began to sway slowly from side to side. As the dark shadow bled across the grasslands towards them, the huge beasts moved up the closest hillside, ponderously drawing into a broad line, like war galleys moving into battle formation.

"How much further?" asked Captain Vaelysia. Danor gestured in the direction they'd been traveling.

"Three leagues to where the valley bends - there. Less than four leagues past that are The Tears. Then we climb." He glanced back at the line of armaduura moving up the hillside. The H'Kaan were no longer visible, lost beyond the hills. "Pity we can't stay and watch, but if they get past the 'duuras and catch us on our way up, we'll be slaughtered."

He gave a single nod to Syr and she started off at a brisk walk. Given the Vanha's size and the length of her stride, that meant Triistan and the others had to jog to keep up. Still, it was an easy, loping pace, across ground that had more or less leveled out. The biggest impediment to their progress besides their own weariness was the long grass, which was waist-high for most of them. As a result they kept in single file, with Syr leading the way, creating a trail that was easier for the smaller Expedition members to follow.

They kept up this way until they reached the curve of the valley wall Danor had pointed out earlier. From time to time they looked back, but they were now somewhat lower than the last hill they had crested and could no longer see either the armaduura or their pursuers.

The valley bent around a great knuckle of bare stone, a few hundred feet high and crested by a thicket of gnarled fir trees. Danor allowed them to rest there while he climbed up the bald stone face to take advantage of the commanding view at its summit. It was an easy climb - a fairly gentle slope with plenty of small cliffs, fissures and other handholds - and he returned to them barely a quarter of an hour later. He looked troubled.

"The herd is still arrayed at the top of the hill. I saw no sign of the Respiis."

Syr arched an eyebrow and frowned. "They should have reached them by now."

"If they remained in the valley."

"Sithis." Syr spat the L'Suu's name out, making it sound like a curse as she lifted her gaze up the rock face her husband had just scaled.

"He's not going to encounter the armaduura is he?" Captain Vaelysia said quietly.

"No, Salties, he's not. Our old friend has figured out where we're headed and intends to get there first. He's climbing out of the valley to cut straight across this elbow."

"But why? Why follow us at all? He's taken Ostenvaard and broken through your defenses. What can they gain?"

"Vengeance, for starters. And freedom, Captain. As Long Tau said, we are part of the binding that holds him on Aarden - L'Viviit Muurum - The Living Wall. If The Worm survived The Weir's fall, he cannot escape Aarden until all of us are destroyed."

"Then you think he's still alive," Triistan said, unable to keep the ache of dread and crushing disappointment out of his voice.

Danor shrugged. "Not necessarily. There are two factors that speak to our favor. One, that we've heard and felt not a whisper from him since The Weir fell. And the second is that he's not pursuing us himself. Either he has been slain or he is still engaged with Tau and the others."

Commander Tchicatta frowned. "If that were the case, Su'ul, wouldn't his captains still be fighting alongside him?"

"You think I'm clinging to false hopes, eh Reaver? Perhaps. But consider this: Sithis may be following his last order - the L'Suu are a single-minded lot. If he came through the West Tower while The Worm was attacking the East, he may not know his master's fate. In that respect, Commander, he's not so different from you and I - doing his duty to the bitter end." He looked them over.

"I'd hoped to maintain the pace we've been setting to conserve your strength for a fight, but making a stand anywhere short of The Tears is folly. And so begins another crucible to test your mettle."

He nodded to his wife and Syr set off at a jog. The others fell in behind her, running at full stride to keep up. Fortunately, the thick grasslands gave way to scrub once they made their way past the stone outcropping, allowing them to spread out in a loose formation. The ground provided better footing as well, as they left the thick grass for a hard packed blend of much shorter turf and lichen-mottled stone.

The lake continued along their left side a few hundred yards away, but Triistan found himself watching the valley wall on their right. The outcropping Danor had climbed gave way to a steep rampart of grey stone several hundred feet high and topped by an indistinct mass of vegetation that was impenetrable from this distance. An entire army could be hiding up there and they wouldn't be able to see it. If Danor was right - and Triistan had little reason to hope he wasn't - their pursuers could come pouring over the face of the canyon wall at any moment. He had seen the H'Kaan flow effortlessly over buildings and trees and knew they would have no trouble moving down the cliff in an attack. He picked up his pace.

Ahead, what at first he had mistook for the end of the valley began to distinguish itself as they drew closer, slowly becoming a strange forest of separate stone columns festooned with vegetation. Vines, shrubs, plants and even trees clung to the edges and sprouted from the tops of these upthrust fingers of granite, completing the illusion of a giant rock forest. They were at least as tall as the valley walls, and as the party passed into their shadow, the temperature dropped considerably. A white dusting of frost was visible in many places.

Triistan estimated that each column was some fifty feet in diameter. The bottoms were mostly bare rock for the first thirty feet or so and covered in deep scratches, the source of which he discovered a few moments later when they passed a heap of thick brown scales, each the size of a ship's wheel.

"L'Fievhard, we call this place," Danor said from behind him. As he had so often done in the past, he seemed to be reading Triistan's thoughts. "The Stonewood, in your tongue. Inspired, I know. Sometimes the 'duuras rub against these to dislodge old or damaged scales. We harvest them to make our armor, among other things." Triistan thought of a half dozen questions he wanted to ask, but did not have the breath to do so.

Soon they began to see more light ahead, as the columns thinned and the gaps between them widened. Danor called a halt while they were still in relative shelter, sending Syr ahead to scout and ordering them to take what rest and nourishment they could.

"Once we clear these columns, we'll be completely exposed until we reach The Tears. If Sithis is already here, he'll try and take us out in the open where he has the advantage. But the clever brokuuro will wait until we're well clear of L'Fievhard before springing his trap, so we can't retreat to cover. So listen, and hear me well, Salties."

The gravity with which he said this last sentence caught all of their attention.

"You all heard what Long Tau said atop The Weir, what young Master Halliard guessed rightly: the Worm has no idea what's transpired - no inkling that the rest of the Young Gods are dead and Ruine is his for the taking. So although he doesn't know it yet, as he's so wrapped up in avenging his imprisonment and exterminating us, he needs you. If he yet lives, he'll need your knowledge, and most of all, your ship. Our orders are to get you back to your boat so you can get off this fuundaris rock and warn the rest of the world. So here's what we're going to do..."

***

They left the shelter of L'Fievhard at a dead run, keeping as close to the lakeshore as they could in order to maximize the distance to the canyon wall, where they expected Sithis to attack from. Syr had returned to tell them that she had found no sign of the L'Suu. Even better, the forests above the valley seemed calm, with none of the typical signs a large force of H'Kaan would cause among the local wildlife. If Sithis was up there lying in ambush, she explained, they would see all manner of creatures in mindless flight - some would even chance the cliffs rather than face the Darkspawn.

"How do you know they haven't already fled?" Triistan had asked her.

"There are no corpses in the valley."

They ran in a strict formation set by Danor, with he and Syr protecting the right flank, the three Reavers spread out across the rear, and the remaining Seekers led by Captain Vaelysia forming two rows in front. The valley floor just beyond L'Fievhard was rocky and dotted with scrub and hardscrabble trees, sloping upwards towards a series of gently overlapping hills. The lake cut into the hills, following another gradual curve of the valley out of sight to their left. When they crested the first hill and could see around the bend, they were greeted with a striking vista that took their breath away.

The lake they'd been traveling alongside ran away from them on their left, forming a mirror image of the sky in its flawless surface, as if it were a window and the world had been inverted. The right-hand shore was formed by a series of overlapping bluffs where wind and time had carved away the edge of the rising hills, leaving an irregular line of jagged stone chimneys, marching along like the ruined towers of an old city.

Where the valley ended, dozens of waterfalls cascaded down the face of a sheer cliff of stone so dark it was almost black. They poured into and out of scores of pools that had formed in the shallow stone shelves and outcroppings marring the face of the cliff, eventually finding their way into the lake below. Later, Triistan would describe it in his journal as a "web of glistening silver strands hung with fat wet pearls cascading down the mountain side".

Exile's Tears, he thought now. *A spectacle worthy of the gods.*

They ran on. The ground rose beneath their feet as they climbed through the hills. All the while the bluffs forced them closer to the opposite canyon wall, until it was within a hundred paces. It was too close for Triistan to watch the cliffs above them any longer, but he fixed his eyes on The Tears and told himself they were going to make it, that they were nearly there. Somehow they would scale the falls and escape this horrible trap, and Danor and Syr would lead them back to their boat and the rest of the *Peregrine's* crew - though how they were going to accomplish this last feat from here, Triistan could not even begin to guess.

They were less than half a league from the valley's end - close enough to hear the hissing roar of the waterfalls ahead - when the bodies began to fall.

Triistan did not even notice the first few impacts, mistaking them for the footfalls of his companions, until a huge black bear crashed to the ground not fifty paces away.

Somewhere in his mind, just ahead of the rising shadow of fear, a thought registered that the animal hadn't cried out on its way down; it had leapt off a cliff hundreds of feet high and fell to its death without so much as a growl.

A great cry did go up then, however, a din of animal screams and the panicked calls of birds as hundreds of beasts fled the forest perched atop the canyon wall. The birds took to the air, but the beasts were not so lucky. Many of them ran along the cliff edge, some better equipped to climb and scrabble down the steep incline, but many more either leaping or falling to their deaths.

"MOVE GODS DAMN YOU!!" Danor bellowed at them, for they had all slowed to take in the horrifying spectacle.

They sprang ahead, fleeing the sickening rain of bodies, each waiting for the inevitable howls as the H'Kaan caught sight of them. Triistan's heart pounded in his chest and his lungs burned, but his fear propelled him forward. Taelyia's sword slapped relentlessly against his leg, driving him on as if in mockery of his earlier oath atop the Weir. "My blood for yours," he had said to Creugar. He did not want to bleed, and he did not want to die. He just wanted to run.

Mercifully the ground leveled out for the last few hundred yards, leading them into a roughly triangular plateau bordered on the left by the bluffs overlooking the lake and on the right by the encroaching canyon wall. The apex of the triangle was formed at the far end where the valley wall intersected the line of bluffs, alongside the rush and roar of Ossien's Tears. There was nowhere left to go.

As they doubled over, gasping for breath, they finally heard the sound they had all been dreading: an otherworldly chorus of high, barking howls that chilled their blood. Triistan straightened and turned to face his fear, while something niggled at the back of his mind, a sense that this idea mattered - that it was somehow *right*.

He tried to capture the elusive thought even as that fear cascaded down upon them.

As the canyon narrowed, it also deepened; the valley's wall now soared out of sight above, blending into the Te'Sanginele Mountains somewhere above the billowing mist thrown off by the cataracts. It created a natural barrier preventing the H'Kaan horde from cutting them off at the top of the Tears, which was crucial to Danor's strategy: he wanted to funnel them into this chokepoint, significantly reducing their advantage.

High above the "base" of the triangular plateau, where the panicked animals had first emerged, the edge of the overhanging forest suddenly exploded, showering the valley with shattered leaves, tree limbs and even whole trunks. The dark tide of H'Kaan erupted from the chaos and charged down the hillside without pausing, led by a phalanx of the gigantic, six-legged beasts that had trampled Val and Vendros in the East Tower. The L'Suu captain was mounted on the largest, brandishing his huge hammer-shaped fist, while the beast's powerful body moved down the incline with surprising grace and agility. They reached the valley floor and sprinted across the rocky tundra straight at their quarry. The ground shook.

"This way, quickly!" Syr called, startling Triistan and the others. She was standing at the foot of the cascades, so close that the water was splashing her. Then she just... disappeared.

Triistan heard Danor chuckle.

"She does have a flair for the dramatic, doesn't she?" The giant strode quickly up to the edge of the cascade while the Seekers followed. The ragged chimney shapes of the bluffs on their left had given way to a sheer cliff overlooking the lake below, and the cascades fell past the intersection of this cliff edge with the end of the valley. A wide ledge ran out from the plateau, across the valley wall and behind the waterfall, only visible once you were immediately adjacent to the falls.

Danor stood aside, gesturing for the others to follow the ledge with his massive hammer. Captain Vaelysia led the way as the roar of the falls enveloped them, drowning out the thunder of the charging H'Kaan.

They hurried along the ledge for about fifty feet before reaching an arched opening framed with the same large stone blocks they had seen in Ostenvaard. It was an entrance to a wide tunnel that ran back into the mountain, and Syr stood just inside it holding a blazing torch.

"Not much farther." She set off at a jog up the tunnel, the others following at a stumbling run, with Danor falling in behind Creugar. The floor sloped upwards at a slight incline.

Syr led them around a sharp bend to the right and through a heavy steel door, which Danor pulled shut behind them before dropping a thick metal bar into place to secure it. Triistan didn't think it would hold back the huge six-legged beast Sithis had been riding, but perhaps it was only meant to buy them a few more precious seconds.

The passage bent sharply to the left again, then ran straight and true for a hundred yards or so, before ending at a smooth block wall pierced by a single archway. Syr stopped beside the opening, where three large wheels and two thick levers stuck out of the block wall immediately to her right. The wheels looked like ship's wheels to Triistan, but were unadorned and made of metal.

She set the torch in a bracket on the wall above the devices, illuminating strange markings engraved in the stone beneath each wheel. She then drew a long, slender sword made of the same dark blue steel the Oathguard seemed to favor in their weapons and jerked her head in the direction of the opening.

"Get in."

They hesitated, until a chorus of howling screams came echoing down the corridor, made faint by the door and the switchback, but growing rapidly louder.

"Now is not the time to question your trust in us - go!" Syr shouted at them.

They filed through the opening as quickly as they could, stepping across a narrow channel of glowing water into a circular room some thirty paces across. The walls were washed with the same blue glow, but what caught Triistan's attention was the footing: the floor was made of wooden planks laid in an intricate pattern and bound with bands of copper... and it was floating.

"Alright, Salties," came Danor's tumbled-boulder voice from the opening. His baritone easily cut through the rising din of the H'Kaan. "I'd be lying if I said I'd enjoyed your little visit, but I have enjoyed your company. Heed me well, now."

Something in the giant's tone and words nagged at Triistan, but he was distracted, trying to figure out why the floor was floating. Dimly, as if in a dream, he heard something slam into the metal door down the corridor. Danor began speaking more quickly.

"Just sit tight and let the lift do the work... "

He grunted with effort as he pulled down on one of the levers. They heard the sound of a heavy object somewhere above them sliding and falling into place.

"When you reach the top, there'll be another lake, much smaller, and dark as night." Something struck the steel door again, the sound reverberating down the stone corridor like a ship's signal bell. The H'Kaan howls rose in pitch.

"It's fed by a narrow channel that passes through a gap in the cliff behind the lake... " He had set his hammer down and had both meaty hands on one of the wheels, trying to turn it, his voice straining with the effort. With a screech of metal on metal, the wheel lurched a few inches, then a few more. As it moved, the sound of rushing water began to fill the room. Above them, lost in the gloom, some heavy piece of machinery moaned in protest.

"Follow it to the Hold - no time to describe it, but you won't have any trouble recognizing it when you get there. At the other end of the Hold is a cave system, accessed through a hole in the ground. Once you're in, there's only one way to go - down."

Another creaking groan echoed through the circular chamber, followed by a metallic rattle. For the first time, Triistan saw there were four - no five - heavily rusted chains running through holes in the perimeter of the room's floor and up into the shadows above them. Each link was the size of his head, impressive but not so large as the *Peregrine's* anchor line. A few kinks snapped into place as the chains came under load, popping loose small explosions of rust and dust. As

Triistan felt the floor shift beneath his feet, he heard Danor give out another grunt of effort.

"Eventually you'll reach the Mordiiene - dark stepsister to the Aniiene. It will take you back to Hagen's Bay, where your ship is moored."

Another loud crash resounded from around the corner, accompanied by the sound of tumbling stone. The howls of the H'Kaan grew sharply louder. Danor looked over his shoulder at the noise, and when he turned back, the expression on his face finally jolted Triistan into understanding. The young Seeker shook his head.

"No… come with us, please… "

Danor smiled his not-smile, but this time its customary irony was replaced by sad resignation.

"No, Salty, that we cannot do. Our duty is here."

Triistan couldn't stop shaking his head. His eyes burned. "But you said… the Living Wall… that as long as you lived, whatever bound Ossien to Aarden would live -"

Syr appeared beside her husband. Her eyes blazed with blue light.

"L'Viviit Muurum needs Vanha blood, and there are those among you within whom it still flows. Your Captain knows her duty, Child of Tarsus. Do yours by aiding her." The sound of rending metal and falling rubble rumbled down the tunnel, followed by a triumphant roar.

Syr put her wounded hand on Danor's shoulder. "Let them go, husband."

Tears spilled from Triistan's eyes and he took a step towards them, but Biiko restrained him.

"NOOO!" he screamed.

"Goodbye, Salties. Remember us - not that we died, but how we lived, and what we died for..."

Danor thumped his fist against his chest. "A've necuuto, brodiirs."

He stepped to the second lever and jerked it down. With a roar of chains and metal, a huge curved gate made of solid black steel slammed into place over the opening, sealing the circular room shut. The sound of rushing water grew louder, then suddenly everything seemed to blossom with phosphorescence: the walls had disappeared behind falling sheets of glowing liquid. Bewildered, the Seekers edged towards the center of the room as the floor lurched beneath them.

Slowly the floor rose. Like the gates of Ahbaingeata, the curved door for this room must have been crafted to create a tight enough seal to contain the water pouring in. The chains around the perimeter were no doubt part of some massive counterweight system, but the water must have been a means of counterbalance and control, allowing the lift to operate independently once it was activated.

The muffled sounds of combat bled through the thick gate. Something crashed against it and they heard Danor's voice roaring out in the Vanha tongue. Screams and howls answered him, until the floor rose past the top of the gate, leaving only the sound of falling water and the mournful creak and clatter of the hoist way.

***

Triistan fought back the tears that blurred his vision. Even now, months later, the pain was just as raw as it had been at that moment.

Dreysha's forehead creased. "What happened to them?"

"I don't..." Triistan began, shaking his head. His voice failed him so he cleared his throat and tried again. "I don't know. We never saw them again."

The other survivors were silent for several long moments. Triistan found comfort in the rush of water sliding along the boat's hull and the occasional snap of canvas overhead. Wil had shown a surprising knack for steering the emergency launch and presently they ran before a sharp, steady wind out of the south.

Rantham finally broke the silence. "How did you escape?" he asked quietly, with none of his usual rancor.

"We rode the lift in silence for what seemed like a very long time. I don't know how long. It's hard to say. I was exhausted and... "

He trailed off, struggling for the right words.

"Of all of the things we saw, all that we went through... the fantastic creatures, lost ruins, legends... the Exile... what I remember most clearly is standing there on that platform, looking up. Water fell all around us, and some of it splashed onto the chains, showering us with drops of liquid light like... like the tears of a god. They gave so much -" his voice broke and he had to stop for a moment to regain control of it.

"Anyway, it was just as Danor had said. The lift finally opened in the center of a large stone platform - sort of an island in the middle of the dark lake he described. I remember just wanting to collapse there, but the Captain kept us moving. There were a number of wide, low skiffs drawn up nearby which we used to cross to the shore."

Triistan flipped open the two-page illustration he had drawn of The Hold during their return voyage along the underground river, unaware that it was the same picture that had piqued Dreysha's curiosity when she had stolen his journal the first time. He held it up to show it to his fellow survivors.

"This is The Hold - where Ossien's "box" was kept. It -"

He froze in mid sentence, suddenly unable to breathe.

Hot tears rose and spilled from his eyes, but this time he made no effort to hold them back. Directly between the confused faces of Dreysha and Wil, a tiny finger of white broke the unending blue curve of the horizon.

For so long he'd dreamt of shouting the words that now came out only in a dry, cracked whisper of disbelief:

"Sail, ho..."

- 30 -

Waking Up

Lex Vellos was quiet.

The dead did not complain and the living were mostly asleep.

Casselle sat in the middle of the Temple, fixated on the body of Emeranth Kell, who appeared to be kneeling in quiet prayer. It seemed fitting, since her last words were stripped of the malice that had brought her here in the first place.

The fight had ended with a whisper.

"Thank you..."

After those words, without her strength, those that had been possessed like Emeranth had been quickly cut down by the Laegis. They expected more H'Kaan to charge through the door, but in the heavy silence that followed, no more ever came.

Hours later, after the grounds were swept and re-secured, Richard Lockewood's group returned from the extensive labyrinth underneath the city. They had been successful in finding and burning out the H'Kaan nest buried at its center. It was only upon their arrival that the survivors of the Temple battle acknowledged the truth of it: the H'Kaan had never fled or regrouped, they were simply gone.

As the suns rose again the next morning, they shed light on the Thundering Lance caravan, now within walking distance. They had repositioned themselves in the dark of night, at Lord Lockewood's request. Previously having been parked outside the city, they had managed the deft logistical feat under the wan light of the single moon. The caravan had been ignored completely over the past days, spying not even a single H'Kaan while the Thundering Lance and the Laegis were decimated.

The fresh supplies were welcomed with cheers and the support staff worked briskly to cook meals for hungry survivors and tend the wounds of injured soldiers. Casselle had eaten enough to make up for several lost meals before finding herself drifting off, almost in mid-bite. She put the food aside and returned to the Temple, moving away from the noise of the caravan.

She found herself swimming in and out of sleep until mid-day, that heavy lidded half-awareness that accompanies an uneasy rest. She cared little because her belly was full and her mind blissfully unburdened for the moment.

It took Casselle a few moments to drift fully awake, her mind catching up with what her other senses were telling her. Alone and in the middle of the ground they had recently fought so hard to defend, she was momentarily awestruck.

A few shafts of light fell in from a hole in the side of the Temple, no doubt created by the powerful forces unleashed during their last battle. Motes of dust swirled gently in the golden rays, drifting peacefully around Emeranth's corpse. For a half second, Casselle found herself wondering if the fallen Templar would feel the warmth on her face and rise once again, now cleansed of Maughrin's taint. She even toyed with the idea of what it would be like to meet the Templar that had known Lex Vellos in its prime.

Footsteps disturbed her reverie. Temos approached her from the side, a tin mug in each hand.

"I brought you some." He offered her one, which she gladly accepted. It gave off a deep, earthy smell of roasted beans and herbs.

"This isn't the normal swill they serve," Casselle noted. "Where did you…?"

"From Lockewood," Temos replied. "Seems like giving us his own personal stash of bakkat was the best thanks he could offer us for the moment." He slumped down beside her, wincing as he rested his other arm in his lap.

"How is that?" she asked before taking a deep sip of the nutty brown brew.

"It's fine," he replied. "Brother Shields said it was merely dislocated. They didn't waste any time putting it back into place. Hurts like hell, but it still works."

"Thank you again for that," she said.

"Yeah, well, I'm pretty sure if the roles were reversed..."

"Well… don't be too sure," Casselle teased. The two of them laughed.

"If you change your mind to dislocate anything on my behalf, you might want to wait a while. The good Brother is almost out of bandages and certainly out of strength for the moment," he added. "At least he's better off than Master Oolen. She's lucky to be alive at all."

Casselle nodded. She'd seen Asai Oolen return unconscious in the arms of Arren Lockewood, her body ruined from the strain that closing the H'Kaan nest had put on it. It was nothing short of a miracle that she was even still alive. Of the small group that had gone down, she had suffered the most, the Lockewoods looking none the worse for wear and Indalia Nox sporting only a few superficial cuts and bruises that she hadn't left with.

"Did Brother Shields get the chance to look at the rest of our squad? Any news?" she asked.

"They are as well as can be expected," he replied after a short sip from his own mug. "Passal's likely to live, but not sure he'll fight again."

"Jhet?"

"Arm's broken, but healing. He'll be ok. I think he was even given a nudge by the good Brother's magics," Temos added. "Vincen, Finn and the Captain are in surprisingly good shape, nothing they can't walk off. The Commander looks better than new, like he's been freshly polished."

Temos chuckled at his own joke before pausing for a moment, clearly unsure how best to continue.

"Did you know that Gunnar is almost as small as I am?"

Casselle cast him a sidelong glance.

"It's true!" he replied defensively. As he continued, he talked even faster, at points almost tripping over his words. "Like your spear, he got smaller... like a whole different person. I think that's how he was when he was younger? I only know because I accidentally walked in on him getting bandaged. He told me he was trying to help them save bandages."

"How...?"

"It's just something that some of the Vanha can do, he said. He showed me some arxhemic formulas tattooed between other designs on his chest. I guess it's how the Young Gods and people like us could..." Temos stammered, blushing slightly, "...I mean even though they can apparently be selective on what they make smaller..."

"Whoa!" Casselle interjected, cutting him off.

"Sorry," he replied, "I may have accidentally just answered several questions you never wanted to ask, let alone know the answer to." He took another big sip of bakkat and cleared his throat before continuing.

"Anyway, most of the remaining Lancer Templars are fine or will be soon enough. All things considered, we should be dead."

"We should be," Casselle said, staring at Emeranth kneeling a short distance away, "but we're not."

In the distance behind the former Templar's corpse, the Thundering Lance's Quartermaster and his subordinates worked like carrion crows, stripping the dead of any equipment that could be salvaged. Bodies were moved respectfully outside, where a building far away from the square had been designated to serve as a resting place. Casselle knew they would be burned later. There were too many to bring back for proper funerals.

Most of the creatures Emeranth claimed to have created were given a similar treatment, though they did not wait to burn them.

"She's not going to be destroyed, though," Temos indicated the corpse with a nod. "I heard Nox instructing them to prepare Emeranth's corpse and one of the others. They're to be wrapped up and prepared for travel."

She disliked the idea, but Lockewood clearly had his mind set on it, which meant Commander Cohl would most likely relent to his demands, if he hadn't already. She knew that the few remaining Laegis were simply too tired to resist them.

For now, however, while the other bodies were being managed, Emeranth's corpse remained alone in the hollow chamber of the Temple's main floor. Casselle couldn't help being moved by the sight: a sole Templar, knelt in serene prayer, a sacred reflection of a lost age.

"I guess this means Lockewood was right," Temos began. "If that one was Her Wrath... I guess that means 'She' is not far behind."

"Maughrin."

"Yeah. I am not looking forward to that," he confessed. "Not at all."

Almost of its own volition, Casselle's hand tightened its grip on the shortened spear lying in her lap.

"He's collected up all the other weapons," Temos said. "I'm surprised he hasn't come for that one."

"I'm not inclined to give it up," she answered, not knowing what she'd do if Lockewood came for it. "Commander Cohl let him take them all?"

"The Commander didn't like it, but Lord Lefty reminded him that the Laegis were under orders to comply. Cohl was angry, but I guess not angry enough to fight about it. Hopefully we don't need them anytime soon."

"I think we're ok... for now anyway." The thought of fighting more H'Kaan, let alone another creature as strong as Emeranth, threatened to crush the small amount of peace she'd managed to reclaim for herself that morning.

They'd all been shaken by the events of the last few days. It was more than any of them had expected, save perhaps for Lord Lockewood, who appeared wholly unfazed by the experience. Then again, the man had fought the H'Kaan before. He'd also killed a Young God, his own grandfather at that. It was more than likely he just considered this a busy week.

"What happens if we don't have enough weapons when the time comes? What happens if we can't win?" Temos asked, his thoughts clearly in a similar place.

"We didn't become Laegis to win," Casselle said.

"Is that so?" Temos asked with a smirk.

"You know it is. We became Laegis to fight. Not blindly, but with purpose."

"You think we're on target here?"

"I'm not sure," Casselle answered. "Standing in opposition to something is always clearly defined. Win or lose, finding order in the void that comes after the battle is more difficult."

"That's from one of our study texts," Temos said. "That whole bit about 'resolve does not ensure a resolution.'"

"That's the one. It always stuck with me. I think I understand it better now," she said. "We can only fight the battles we know. We can make plans for the ones we anticipate, and if we are lucky, we can put ourselves in a position to deter ones arising in the future."

"I don't think I would ever call this lucky," Temos said.

Casselle nodded.

They finished their warm drinks in silence.

Casselle wanted to sleep more, but Temos convinced her to walk with him, out to the edge of the city. Beyond the walled square, everything was quiet once again, though both the Templar found they were a bit jumpy. More than once, they paused, quieting quickened pulses as they realized they had heard nothing out of the ordinary, just the subtly shifting sands beneath their feet.

Buildings grew shorter before they fell away altogether. The twin suns were starting their descent into the west, and their shadows trailed behind them as the two Templar neared the collapsed edge of the city, yet some distance ahead of them.

Temos had spotted a likely vantage point ahead to their right, an elevated platform for a large pillar or statue that had long since crumbled. The two picked out a path through the remains of the city and helped one another up the flight of stairs to the platform.

An altar was set close to the top of the steps, although only a remnant of it remained. There was also a giant foot, barely discernable after hundreds of years of neglect and the unchecked elements. Neither of these, however, compared to the view ahead of them.

They could see where the city stopped, a hundred feet away or less, simply opening onto naked sky.

Ahead of them, and at the bottom of an impossible drop, lay a vast expanse of emerald green water. It stretched out as far as they could see, blemished only occasionally by rough spars of rock, mere pebbles in a pond from this distance.

They knew there was an end to it, somewhere beyond their vision; past the grey horizon, the other edge of the sea was boxed in by another equally impressive drop, where great cascades of seawater were said to tumble in a series of falls to the sea below. That was beyond their sight, but the great break in the world lay just ahead of them.

Casselle had heard that the Ghostvale was like a scar running through Old Cartishaan. If so, then the Fallen Sea was an open wound caused by the Ehronfall, left exposed and untreated.

Though now, from this high place, she thought it looked warm and inviting, a rippling bath touched by golden sunlight.

It is beautiful in its own way.

She was startled by the sight of a small flight of birds cutting through the open space over the water far below them. She was humbled by this sudden, bright affirmation of life.

The planet had shuddered and collapsed, but it had not ended. Even if that great disaster had killed them all, here was steadfast testimony to what would happen next.

"It will outlast us all," she said, breaking the silence between them.

"It always has," Temos replied. "I've seen it even after bad fires in the forest... A year, maybe two later you can even see the sprouts without looking hard. My pa told me there are even trees whose seeds won't open unless they are cooked by the flames.

"We keep on talking about things like the end of the world, but it's a lot more resilient than we are," he finished before falling quiet once again.

She knew he was right. They weren't doing this to "save the world," as Richard had claimed. They were doing this to save themselves, and to save those that would come after them.

This was no grand revelation, she knew. These were things she'd realized long before now, things that had driven her to become a Templar to begin with. The world would survive without them, but she wouldn't leave it without a fight.

***

Temos had kept an eye on the sky, giving them plenty of time to return to the Temple before the day was over.

As they turned into the long, walled corridor that now led to the front of the building, they saw the light from the fires casting warm glows and long shadows onto those walls. The Long Evening was upon them, and the camp had called a halt to the most strenuous of the day's activities. Nothing would be done that night. In the morning they would assess the wounded and determine if they could travel.

Her weary bones did not look forward to another long journey over rough terrain, but the inevitability of it pulled her forward with a strength she knew could not be resisted. She wanted to retreat to a comfortable place, if but for a while, not this dead city clinging to a cliff over the Fallen Sea. She wanted time to train herself against what they had faced, time to understand the words of the book that remained a puzzle to her and time to contemplate the fragments of a greater mystery that she was just beginning to glimpse the entire face of.

Emeranth Kell had been a Laegis Templar here, some time before the Ehronfall. Now she was a fragment of a story that had been kept from them, a character from the chapter of a book they had not been allowed to read. It had been clear from the beginning that Richard Lockewood was intentionally trying to manipulate them for what he considered the greater good. What she hadn't expected was finding out the Templars were similarly guilty.

No, she thought, *not all of the Laegis.* Temos had said Captain Ardell had been equally as surprised. It was a lie they had all been told. But by whom? And for how long?

Inside of this city, one might make the mistake of assuming that the world was changing, crumbling around them, like the ruins of Lex Vellos itself. But she knew that was not the truth.

The world is waking up.

The Wolfmother, Veheg, Maughrin and her Wrath... they lived in the shadows, in memories so distant they had become stories, rumors, myths. But now the myths were coming back to life, crawling out of the past like Emeranth Kell had climbed out of the muck beneath the city.

What happened here in Lex Vellos would not be the last of it. There was more of this to come, probably more of it already in motion than they were aware of.

The thought of it terrified her, struck her cold to the bone.

Temos nudged her with his fist. She turned to look at him, his smile wide even under the layers of dried blood and dust they'd accrued from their previous days of battle.

"You look a bit lost in there. I just wanted to remind you that we beat her," Temos said. "We beat the stuffing right out of her."

Casselle smiled. He was right. They had beaten the odds. For now that was enough. Whatever secrets and challenges still lurked out there in the dark, they would wait for at least another day.

The suns were setting now, but they would rise again tomorrow, bringing with them warmth... and something else...

Hope.

- 31 -

Loose Ends

After months at sea, the hours it took for their rescuers to reach them felt like the longest span of time any of them had ever endured. Triistan was constantly haunted by the fear of another ridgeback attack, while Voth droned on and on about how they would all be court-martialed and hung, until Drey finally replaced his gag.

When the ship drew close enough for them to see her colors, Mung let out a delighted whoop, reflecting the relief they all felt. They knew the stories of the Kingsbane's cruelty, but those fears were laid to rest as the two-master tacked to starboard and the blue banner streaming from the top of the mainmast unfurled in the cross-wind, proudly displaying the seven blazing crowns of gold that comprised the Sea Kings' sigil.

The *SKS Kings' Hound* was a brig class patrol ship out of Sitsii's southernmost harbor, commanded by an old salt named Arusha. Captain Arusha was a no-frills, no-nonsense career officer whose square shoulders and bandy legs mimicked the overall contour of his ship.

Scow would have liked him, Triistan thought with a pang.

Unfortunately, Arusha knew Lankham Voth. They had served together some years ago, and although he did not recognize the bound and bedraggled purser at first, for some inexplicable reason he asked the whereabouts of "Mister Voth". Though Dreysha glowered at Triistan and shook her head, he felt compelled to identify their prisoner. Captain Arusha apparently had no desire to discuss the specifics of their voyage in front of his crew, so after ordering that Voth be unbound, he insisted they be quarantined immediately and subjected to a bath, delousing, and full medical exam before he heard another word.

Although Triistan had longed for one for months, the bath was not a pleasant experience, despite Dreysha being required to strip down and subject herself to the pump, hose and sponge right along with the rest of them. Fresh blisters that hadn't broken open yet soon did, joining the hundreds of other sores and abrasions that covered their sagging skin and made scrubbing torturous. After being rinsed off, their heads and beards were shorn, and then they were subjected to a hail of white powder that both killed lice and treated their open sores. The powder was laced with something that dulled pain, so for the first time in as long as any of them could remember, comfort meant more than just a lesser degree of misery. The ship's physician applied the powder before giving each of them a brief exam, checking for serious infectious diseases that might threaten the rest of the crew. Seeker Protocol, of course.

"Quarantine" consisted of the ship's holding cell, a ten-by-fifteen foot room with three walls formed from iron bars anchored in floor and ceiling, set against the bulkhead at the fore of the cargo hold. The cell door was left open as a formal courtesy, but Captain Arusha had stationed two sentries outside of it as a not-so-subtle reminder that they were not to move about the ship on their own. Fresh clothing and food were brought, and by the time the Captain visited with them they looked and felt nearly human again - provided you ignored their skeletal frames, hollow eyes and the boney white of their powdered skin.

Convinced of his impending redemption, Voth had resumed his pompous demeanor. He wasted no time accosting Arusha, accusing the others of mutiny and demanding quarters and a uniform that befitted his rank.

Arusha stood a few feet beyond the two sentries, holding something out of sight behind his back. Triistan dreaded what he thought was about to unfold, wondering how he was going to convince the taciturn Captain that their actions weren't sedition but instead had been in the best interest of the Kingdom, perhaps all of Niyah. The Captain of the *Kings' Hound* eyed Voth carefully for a moment before responding.

"Sir," Arusha began frostily, "please do not mistake my hospitality for foolishness or naivety. Your command was - despite her size and rigging - essentially a lifeboat." Dreysha snorted out loud and Triistan had to bite his cheek to keep from doing the same.

"Your... ah... ship is now under my command. You and your crew have been deemed Persons of Interest by the High Chancellor himself, and are to be kept under supervised protection until you are safely delivered to his agents. All of your belongings have been confiscated for safekeeping and will be returned to you once we reach port."

He addressed the two sentries. "I need the room, please." The men saluted smartly before climbing to the mess deck through one of several ladders that communicated between the ship's hold and the upper decks. Once the overhead hatch was closed, he brought forth the object he'd been holding behind his back. It was Triistan's journal.

"Now, which of you belongs to this...?"

The young Seeker swallowed nervously. "I do, Sir."

Arusha's lips twitched beneath the snow-white braids of his beard in what might have been a slight smile. "I thought as much, Mister...?"

"Triistan Halliard, Sir. Topman, first class." He snapped to attention out of habit.

Arusha turned the weather beaten book over in his hands. It had been removed from its waterproof case, leading Triistan to wonder if the Captain had also found the sealed letter from Captain Vaelysia hidden inside. Although Triistan hadn't read the letter, he'd been told its contents and thought it might go a long way towards helping him plead his case.

Unfortunately, Seeker protocol dictated a very harsh sentence for tampering with officers' correspondence, so it was unlikely Captain Arusha had dared to open it. Triistan would have to cling to the thin protection of operating under orders to deliver the journal and the letter directly to the Chancellor, and maintain that he'd been forbidden to speak of its contents to anyone else. Of course, he was facing a court martial as soon as one of his fellow castaways revealed the fact that he'd already divulged most of it to them.

"This is some interesting reading, Topman. You're quite the artist."

"Thank you, sir." He held his breath; Arusha's casual tone belied the shrewd look in his eyes.

Voth made a disgusted noise. "The boy is a liar and a mutineer, Sir. You should hear-"

"Thank you, Provisioner."

"But Sir-"

"That will be all, Mister Voth." He fixed the disgruntled purser with a penetrating stare. "You will have a chance to tell the whole story, but in the proper venue. I have very specific orders concerning you lot, issued jointly by both Seeker Command and the Trade

Commission, so I don't need to tell you the level of importance they've placed on whatever information you're carrying - information they don't apparently want me to know. Smells like trouble to me, and I've got a hull full of that already. So until you are brought before Command and Council, you'll settle your differences and not breathe a word of this to me or to anyone else, am I clear?"

Voth looked like a petulant child. "Yes, Sir."

"Good. With favorable weather, we'll make port in less than two weeks. You'll remain confined to quarters until then. I regret the imposition after what you've been through, so I have ordered my officers to make their cabins available to you. At least you'll be comfortable - a far cry better than your recent accommodations I'd imagine. I will see that my men provide for your every need."

He saluted them smartly. "Welcome back, Seekers. I know you'll find this strange to hear under the circumstances, but it is an honor to have you aboard."

He left, taking Triistan's journal with him.

***

There were three officer's cabins containing a total of seven berths. Dreysha quickly seized one of the doubles for herself, which left Biiko, Triistan, Voth, Rantham and Mung to split the remaining two rooms. Biiko took the other double and made it clear that Triistan would be his cabin mate. As usual, no one dared to question him.

Besides the bunks, each cabin also featured a table attached to the wall with hinges, which could be swung up and propped in place with wooden dowels to serve as table legs. Two chairs, a lantern, a few books, and a pair of trunks completed the sparse furnishings. The bunks were too short for most of them, and what passed for a mattress was a sack filled with something soft and lumpy. For the launch survivors, they were the most luxurious beds any of them had ever slept in - which is exactly what Triistan did for the next fourteen hours straight.

He woke to find Biiko sitting at the table, mixing something with his mortar and pestle. A sweet smell permeated the small cabin, reminding Triistan of hot cinnamon cakes his old Doyen used to make. He breathed in the pleasant aroma and stretched.

"Is that breakfast?" he yawned. Biiko glanced at him and shook his head negatively, his expression unreadable.

Triistan shook his own head in mimicry. "No, I didn't think so. Have I missed anything? What are the others doing?"

The Unbound added a shrug to the head shake and continued with his work. He was adding water to the mixture now, thinning it. Suddenly it dawned on Triistan that Biiko had somehow retrieved his belongings - the leather satchel that served as his field kit was lying on the table, along with several assorted vials, small instruments, and other objects of unknown purpose. He looked around the tiny cabin but nothing else was visible - none of their weapons or, regrettably, his journal.

"How did you get that back?"

Biiko briefly touched his fingertips to his mouth and then his chest.

"Medicine? For who? Is someone sick?"

The Unbound just shrugged and made another gesture that meant "not yet". Triistan decided he would have better luck questioning the other castaways, so he slid the cabin door open and stepped into the narrow passage outside. To his right the hallway ran another ten feet or so before ending at a ladder leading up to a closed hatch. To his left the passage ran about fifteen feet until it turned a corner. The two sentries that had been standing outside the brig were now stationed there, and one of them nodded when Triistan made eye contact. He waved in response.

Immediately across the hall was another door, which led into Dreysha's room. His heart beat faster, but he steeled himself and raised a fist to knock on it, then froze as the door slid open before he had the chance.

"Well good morning, Your Laziness," she said with a broad grin. "Nice of you to grace us with your presence." She had fashioned a belt by braiding two or three lengths of thin rope together and now wore it around her waist, cinching the sleeveless Seeker tunic tightly and accentuating her figure in the process. The ship's physician hadn't spared her the indignity of his straight razor either, so her scalp gleamed softly in the lantern light. Somehow, despite this, and despite her badly-chapped lips and blistered, peeling skin, he still found her alluring.

He stammered something about never having slept in a more comfortable bed, and she raised an eyebrow and let her grin slide into something suggestive.

"Really? Maybe I'll have to give it a try then."

He smiled, feeling completely foolish, and tried to think of something witty and charming to say.

"What about the others?" was the only thing that came to mind, though, and he knew it was a mistake as soon as he said it. He could feel his ears getting hot. "No, I mean, how are they? Is everyone OK - have I missed anything?"

"Yes, I should think so, and I'm still trying to figure out if it be caution or cunning that leads you so often astray..?"

Fortunately, another door slid open to Triistan's left and Mung poked his head out. "Ah! I thought I heard voices! Oi, there Triis!"

"Hello, Wil." He lowered his voice. "How's your room?" He meant how Voth and Rantham were as roommates, but as usual subtlety was completely lost on his friend.

"Oh, the room's wonderful - a bit crowded now with the four of us but certainly a delightful improvement over our previous arrangements!"

"Did you say four?"

Mung nodded vigorously and then patted the side of his leg. An instant later, Snitch appeared and scampered up to perch on his shoulder, chattering away and bobbing its head as if in greeting.

"Mr. Voth isn't too keen on him but Rantham's grown quite fond of our little fisherman. Seems to be helping with his... well, you know," he finished awkwardly. "Anyway, glad to see you're up and about... ahh... what do I call you now, Sir?"

"Not anymore, Wil. Just plain old Triistan again."

"You make a fine Captain, Triis," Dreysha said loudly, "and you'll have your own command long a'fore a few others I know." The door to Wil's cabin promptly slammed shut, and she chuckled.

"I knew that miserable bastard was listening. Looks like Snitch could use some breakfast, Mung."

The monkey had begun grooming its master, poking and petting Wil's newly-shaved head as if it were searching for bugs. It was comical watching him duck and wince as Snitch pushed and pulled at his ears, scalp and face, until he finally shooed it away. The monkey squawked in apparent disappointment, jumped to the floor and scampered off down the hall past the guards.

"Speaking of breakfast..."

"A splendid idea, Triis! The Captain was as good as his word - allow me." Wil approached the guards and had a few quiet words with them. One left, returning a short time later with a cabin boy named Mirkos and a basket full of food. They had no desire to spend any time with Voth, so they retired to Dreysha's room to eat and share whatever news they could with Triistan. Her room was along the outer hull so it had something the others didn't: a window.

It was at chest height for Triistan and just large enough for him to lean his head and one shoulder out. He hoped to spy land, but instead was greeted by another surprising sight. He ducked back in.

"We have an escort."

"Aye." Drey began pulling items out of the basket. "A dromond - The *Hound's Teeth*, they call her. She's normally paired up with this tub and must have been laying off just over the horizon when they found us."

A chill passed along his spine when he heard the warship's name, but he couldn't say why. Then the smell of food and the churning in his belly distracted him, and the moment passed.

* * *

They spent the days in relative comfort, eating a great deal and sleeping even more. Voth was an awkward presence they tried to avoid as much as possible, which he aided by keeping primarily to himself in his quarters, scribbling madly on an ever-growing pile of paper he had demanded from the guards. They knew he was documenting everything he could remember (no doubt making up much that he did not) hoping to strengthen his case against them. There was nothing they could do about it, however, except to reinforce their story amongst themselves. They felt strongly that they had acted in the best interests of the Kingdom and all of Niyah, and as their health strengthened, so did their confidence.

They spent most of each day in either Drey's or Triistan's room, carrying Rantham in and setting him up comfortably in one of the beds. Though no explanation was given, Biiko was allowed to venture topside, which he did on a regular basis, leaving the four companions to while away the hours speculating about the mysterious Unbound, playing games, and plying Triistan for more details about the Aarden Expedition.

Of course they were all worried about those they had left behind, so much of the early conversation centered on why the Captain had elected to only send back half of the *Peregrine's* crew.

"What did she mean when Syr said 'The Living Wall needs Vanha blood', Triis?" Wil asked him on that first day.

"Sounds like some kind of sacrifice had to be made," Rantham growled. His mood had improved since befriending Snitch, but not by

- 511 -

much. Even if they weren't executed or scrubbed, his future was bleak.

Triistan nodded. "A sacrifice, yes, but not the kind of ritual you're thinking, Ranth." He heard Scow's voice in the back of his mind: *There is no honor without sacrifice.* The Oathguard understood that better than anyone.

"When the Arys created Aarden and imprisoned Oss- that is, The Worm, they used something Danor called a 'Binding'. I think it's something like I described when they bound the mantiisa - some type of powerful arxhemestry that literally traps a thing, somehow tethering it to a specific location. From what little I know, it requires Vanha blood - in the relatively small case of the longstrider, the Oathguard were shedding their own blood as well as the creature's. If I understand it correctly, a larger Binding - say one large enough to hold a god on Aarden - requires much more. It's like an equation... or a recipe. The Vanha are key ingredients, so without them, the recipe is ruined. The Oathguard were just as imprisoned as The Worm."

"And now the Captain and crew as well, because she's Vanha?" Wil asked.

"Aye."

Rantham made a sour expression. "Doesn't add up. She was one hell of a Captain, and we've always known she's godkin, but she's no Oathguard. If they're all gone..."

Triistan could only shrug. "I only know what they told me. And I'd like to believe some of them survived, that there's a chance, some way for them to hold him there."

"And if there isn't?"

Triistan didn't answer, as if by saying the words it might come true. Instead, he just shook his head and looked out the window.

"Then the Dark-damned bastard comes for us," Dreysha answered for him.

"All of us."

***

It's time. I've put this off long enough.

But first, she had to take care of some unfinished business.

Close the deal.

Captain Arusha's estimate had proven true: with fair weather, they sighted Khiigongo nine days later and were approaching Tikuu Harbor on the neighboring island-kingdom of Siitsii two days after that. Not wanting to brave the tiny chain of barrier reefs that crouched off the southern shore at night, they were anchored just beyond; close enough to catch random snatches of revelry from the shoreline, where tier after tier of the harbor city rose in light-bejeweled splendor.

Dreysha rechecked the small pack she had procured earlier, making sure that she hadn't overlooked anything: coil of rope, money pouch, hooded cape, veil, push dagger, and Longeye's supple boots. She was extremely pleased to have found these last two items locked away in the armory along with the rest of their belongings, as the knife had long been one of her favorite tools, and she had become attached to the boots. She slipped the knife into the rope belt she wore but left the boots where they were for the moment; she wouldn't need them just yet.

Satisfied, she picked up a weather-beaten book and turned it over in her hands for a moment before slipping it into an equally worn pouch with an extra long flap that wrapped around the object several times.

"At least I'll have part of you with me for a bit longer," she whispered. She tied a leather cord around it, dropped it into the pack, and set the pack on the floor under the window. Then she quietly slid her cabin door open and stepped soundlessly into the passageway, easing the door closed behind her.

Finding their supplies had been simple enough, and the ancient padlock protecting the armory had been child's play for her. The window in her cabin gave her access to the entire ship at night, which was of course why she had claimed it immediately, although without one she would have figured out another way. Keeping Tresha l'Sonjaro confined to a single room was like trying to hold a whisper in your hand.

She paused outside the door across from hers and drew the push dagger. The cross-grip settled into her palm with the familiarity of a lover's caress as she drew a deep breath and let it out slowly. Then she carefully slid the door aside and stepped in, crouching defensively. A ship's lantern glowed faintly, its wick turned down as far as it would go.

"Drey...?" she heard Triistan say sleepily. Her eyes scanned the room quickly, expertly, before she allowed herself to relax: Biiko's berth was empty and Triistan was alone. She hadn't really expected the Unbound to be there - he had gone over to the *Hound's Teeth* the day before and she hadn't seen him return - but if she was a whisper, he was the breath that preceded it. She felt certain he knew what she intended - indeed, that he was facilitating it for some reason - but since she couldn't fathom what that reason might be, her natural suspicions led her to believe he intended to betray her.

She closed the door and removed the thin rope belt she wore around her waist, then used it to tie the door closed. It wasn't much, but she had worked it out in her own room and knew the small handle would hold long enough to discourage a casual tug. Just enough for any would-be visitors to pause and probably knock or call out.

"Drey, what are you -"

She placed a finger on his lips.

"What I should have done a long time ago," she whispered.

She set her dagger on a nearby chair, stripped off her clothes, and slid into bed beside him.

For the next several hours, they made love. His part was awkward, fervent and joyous, while hers was desperate and wild, full of passion and something that felt like fury. When they were finally spent, she lay draped across him, waiting. The gentle rise and fall of his chest slowed as he drifted into sleep, and she was grateful he could not feel her tears.

***

Triistan woke to a thunderous pounding on his cabin door.

He stumbled out of bed and was nearly knocked over as Captain Arusha pushed the door open.

"We have a problem, Mr. Halliard," the Captain growled.

Belatedly, the young Seeker realized he was still naked from –

He glanced back at his empty berth. "Drey?"

"She's gone, son," Arusha said. "Which bodes ill for the lot of you."

"Why?" A cold ache tightened in Triistan's chest, because he already knew the answer.

No. Please, no.

"Because your journal's been taken, son, stolen from my personal strongbox" Arusha said, sounding almost sympathetic. "Along with Captain Vaelysia's letter."

Triistan's knees buckled. It was hard to breathe.

Suddenly there were guards. He heard his friends cry out as they were being put in irons.

"I'm sorry, Mr. Halliard; we'll be in port soon, but we can no longer afford to be courteous."

He was on his knees. Hard hands grasped his shoulders and a shirt was pulled roughly over his head.

She's gone. The Captain's words echoed hollowly through him. *My journal, everything we've learned… everything I am…*

"Lost…" he mumbled aloud as the irons went around his wrists.

He didn't struggle. It didn't matter what the guards did, or what the Ministry would do.

We are lost.

Like the Captain's strongbox, Dreysha had broken into his heart, and taken everything. And he'd been the fool that let her do it.

Gods, what have I done?

End of Book Two: Between the Darkness & Dust
Fate's Crucible will continue in Book Three

###

Appendix A

People of Interest

The Aarden Expedition (assembled from the crew of the SKS Peregrine):
Triistan Halliard
Biiko
Captain Vaelysia Be'landre
First Mate Tarq ("Tarq'nilonqua-hi", a Khaliil)
Myles
Wrael
Jaegus the Older - killed in kongamatu attack
Jaegus the Younger
Thinman
Welms - killed in kongamatu attack
Anthon
Chelson
Izenya d'Gara ("Izzy")
Pendal - killed in kongamatu attack
Brehnl Highdock ("Docks")

Reavers assigned to the Aarden Expedition:
Firstblade Tchicatta
Lieutenant Jaspins
Miikha
Cruegar
Taelyia - killed by nagayuun

Other Key Crewmembers of the SKS Peregrine
Dreysha - an alias of Tresha l'Sonjaro
Wiliamund "Mung" Azimuth
Rantham d'yBassi - paralyzed (waist down) from knife attack by Sherpal Icefist
Lahnkam Voth – Provisoner and temporary Captain of the *Peregrine's* emergency launch

Longeye - lookout; died when *Peregrine* capsized
Mordon "the Mattock" Scow - badly wounded by Sherpal Icefist; died a few days later
Pelor Icefist - killed in ridgeback attack
Sherpal Icefist - killed by Biiko during fight with Mordon Scow
Jode Cooper - died of wounds after ridgeback attack
Acting Captain Fjord - committed suicide after ridgeback attack
Breaghan - killed in ridgeback attack

Other People of Note
Marquesso d'Yano - Dreysha's mysterious employer
Keranos Lugger – A Dreamroot Interpreter working for the Sea Kings' Ministry of Trade; of questionable loyalty

The Laegis Templar
Command Structure:
Fist of Templars is 50 soldiers, split into 5 fingers of 10 soldiers each. Each finger of 10 is split into 2 squads (called knots or knuckles) of 5 soldiers each.

Former Notable Laegis:
Captain Odegar Taumber - killed at Flinderlass
Raabel Schuute - killed at Flinderlass
Jaksen Furrow - retired after being crippled at Flinderlass

Laegis Templars assigned to Richard Lockewood's Thundering Lance
Commander Zanith Cohl
Shield Templars (Two fingers/20 soldiers):
 Captain Greffin Ardell - leader of squad 1, leader of the Shield Templars
   Cassell Milner
   Temos Pelt
   Finn Archer
   Jhet Anlase
 Sergeant Lennard Torks - leader of squad 2 - former squad member of Greffin
   Ingst Engmar VII
   Vincen von Darren - met by Casselle's old squad in Flinderlass. Son of the local lord.
   Passal Cooper

Gunnar Hawken

Sergeant Duran Holst - leader of squad 3, Greffin's sergeant and former squad member

Four Templar Subordinates

Veteran John Kettel - leader of squad 4, former squad member of Greffin.

Four Templar Subordinates

Lancer/Archer Templars (Three fingers/30 soldiers):

Captain Jaan Boen - leader of the Lancer/Archer Templars

The Thundering Lance (Lord Lockewood's personal army)

Lord Richard Lockewood

Commander Arren Lockewood

Captain Jedgar Parse - Arren's second-in-command

Indalia Nox - Scoutmaster

Arxhemists of the Order of Veda (Ashen)

Master Theander Kross

Master Asai Oolen

Brother Petr Shields

Sister Jem Nevai

Appendix B

Of Gods and Other Monsters

The Arys and Their High Houses:

The Young Gods were given life by Tarsus. They were divided into two factions, the Auruim and the Dauthir.

The Auruim - "The Winged Ones", "The Sky Gods", who lived in Ehronhaal, the city in the clouds:

The House of Knowledge: For those who seek to master intricate skills or lore. Learning and experience are the foundations here.
Heraldic Symbol: Burning torch
Ekoh the Archivist, God of History and scribe of the High Houses
Flynn the Bard, God of Music and Stories
Lyrin the Judicator, Goddess of Law and Philosophy
Minet the Creator, Goddess of the Arts

The House of War: The frontline against the Endless Spawn of Maughrin, led by Thunor.
Heraldic Symbol: Gauntleted fist
Thunor the Conqueror, God of War
Wicka the Herald, Goddess of Competition, Sport and Glory
Obed the Guardian, God of Vigilance and Ancestry
Heketh the Ravager, God of Vengeance, Famine, Pestilence and wanton Destruction

The House of Pleasure: Celebrates passion, desire, and fulfillment.
Heraldic Symbol: Two cupped hands held together; sometimes holding wine or flower petals.
Eris the Maiden, Goddess of Love, Chastity and Romance
Taisha the Seductress, Goddess of Pleasures
Theckan the Rogue, God of Luck and Fortune

Paola the Matron, Goddess of Hospitality, Food and Comfort

The House of Secrets: Dreamers, schemers, visionaries - all those who covet The Unknown.
Heraldic Symbol: Eyes peering above a veil
Ossien the Dark Son, Master of the Forbidden Arts
Veda the Scholar, Goddess of Math, Magic and Arxhemestry
Estra the Dreamer, Goddess of Insight and Intuition
Sylveth the Silent, Goddess of Cunning, Riddles and Deceit

The Dauthir - "The Shepherds", "Ruinebound", who lived on the ground amongst the Children of Tarsus (whom the gods called "huunan").

The House of Storms: Where the raw power of Ruine itself is both harnessed and worshipped.
Heraldic Symbol: Lightning bolt
Shan the Stormfather, leader of the Dauthir and master of both Storm and Sea
Iemene the Gentle, Goddess of Rain, Nourishing Waters, Mist and Rainbows
Ganar the Unbroken, God of the Undergreen, Patron over Rocks and Metals
Niht, wife of Shan, Goddess of the Night, Lady of the Gentle Breeze and the Trade Winds. It is said her anger (though infrequent) is also the cause of heavy winds and tornadoes.
Sigel the Untamed, lord of Fire and Rage. Unlike any of the other Arys, Sigel has been depicted as both male and female.

The House of Passages: Often directly associated with the construction of things, but also relates to the passage of time, distance, and journeys.
Heraldic Symbol: An astrolabe
Derant the Builder, God of Design, Architecture and Carpentry
Ogund the Crafter, God of Invention, Tinkering and Smithing
Cartis the Navigator, Goddess of Exploration and Mapmaking
Vell the Eternal, Lady of Spring and Summer, Birth and Youth
Fjorvin the Reaper, Lord of Fall and Winter, Maturity and Death

The House of the Wilds: The true caretakers of Ruine, devoted to all manner of wildlife and the wilderness, as well as agriculture and domesticated beasts.

Heraldic Symbol: Jharrl's head, roaring

Arcolen the Verdant, Goddess of the Green, Plants and Wild Places

Udgard the Planter, God of the Harvest, Farming and Animal Husbandry

Feness the Wild, Goddess of Wild Animals and The Hunt

Tauger the Scavenger, God of Vermin and Resourcefulness

Beyond the High Houses

Maughrin - The Living Darkness, the Demon Dragon, Mother of the Endless Swarm and Destroyer of the First World. To some, she is vanquished. To others, imprisoned forever. To most, she is a fairy tale, a terrifying adversary that was ultimately defeated by Tarsus, never to be forgotten, but never again to plague Ruine. Only the H'Kaan carry on her legacy, and even they have been seen infrequently since the Ehronfall.

Khagan - Known by most only as a patron of the Sons of Khagan ("The Unbound"), he is generally regarded as the Forger of Fate.

Veheg - Viewed by the Young Gods and the Children of Tarsus as Death incarnate, it is said he existed before the Old Gods and is believed to harvest the final spark of life from the dying. To what purpose is no longer known.

About the Authors

You made it! Thank you for reading our book. We hope you enjoyed it, and if so, we would be most grateful if you took a moment to leave us a review at your favorite retailer.
Yours Very Truly, TBS and RWH

T.B. Schmid lives in upstate New York, though he yearns for a home by the sea. When not haranguing R. Wade Hodges about their joint venture, Lions of the Empire, he enjoys football, movies, music, gaming, rum, and cheering on his kids.

R. Wade Hodges feels like author summaries sound too much like obituaries. He enjoys giant robot anime, good whisky, gaming and anything involving bacon. He is grateful to be part of Lions of the Empire and the world of Ruine. He has survived by spite and the efforts of his wonderful daughter and his fantastic wife.

Read and Follow the Lions of the Empire

These titles are currently available by the Lions of the Empire:

Fate's Crucible Series by T.B Schmid & R.Wade Hodges:
Beyond the Burning Sea
Between the Darkness & Dust
Untitled Book 3 (in production!)

Books by T.B. Schmid:
Feral

Books by R.Wade Hodges:
It Came From Hyperspace!

Books by d.f. Monk:
Tales of Yhore

Connect with us:
The Lions of the Empire website: http://lionsoftheempire.com
On Twitter: https://twitter.com/@lionsofthempire
On Facebook: https://www.facebook.com/lionsoftheempire
At Smashwords:
https://www.smashwords.com/profile/view/LionsOfTheEmpire

Tim is available on Goodreads:
https://www.goodreads.com/author/show/10163038
Wade is available on Goodreads:
https://www.goodreads.com/author/show/15729930

Free Lions stories can be found on Blogger:
https://lionsoftheempire.blogspot.com/

Made in the USA
Middletown, DE
04 December 2021